TOO LIKE THE LIGHTNING

ALSO BY ADA PALMER

Seven Surrenders

TOO LIKE
THE
LIGHTNING

TERRA IGNOTA,
BOOK I.

by Ada Palmer

TOR

A TOM DOHERTY ASSOCIATES BOOK
NEW YORK

TOO LIKE THE LIGHTNING

Copyright © 2016 by Ada Palmer

All rights reserved.

Edited by Patrick Nielsen Hayden

A Tor Book
Published by Tom Doherty Associates
175 Fifth Avenue
New York, NY 10010

www.tor-forge.com

Tor® is a registered trademark of Macmillan Publishing Group, LLC.

The Library of Congress has cataloged the hardcover edition as follows:

Palmer, Ada, author.
 Too like the lightning / by Ada Palmer.—1st ed.
      p. cm.—(Terra Ignota ; 1)
 "A Tom Doherty Associates Book"
 ISBN 978-0-7653-7800-2 (hardcover)
 ISBN 978-1-4668-5874-9 (e-book)
 1. Prisoners—Fiction. 2. Twenty-fifth century—Fiction. 3. Third millennium—
Fiction. 4. Utopias—Fiction. 5. Prisoners. 6. Third millennium. 7. Twenty-fifth
century. 8. Utopias. I. Title.
 813'.6—dc23

2015298981

ISBN 978-0-7653-7801-9 (trade paperback)

Our books may be purchased in bulk for promotional, educational, or business use.
Please contact your local bookseller or the Macmillan Corporate and Premium Sales
Department at 1-800-221-7945, extension 5442, or by e-mail at
MacmillanSpecialMarkets@macmillan.com.

First Edition: May 2016
First Trade Paperback Edition: January 2017

Printed in the United States of America

0 9 8 7 6 5 4 3 2 1

*This book is dedicated to the first human
who thought to hollow out a log to make a boat,
and his or her successors.*

TOO LIKE THE LIGHTNING

A Narrative of Events of the year 2454
Written by MYCROFT CANNER, at the
Request of Certain Parties.

Published with the permissions of:
The Romanova Seven-Hive Council Stability Committee
The Five-Hive Committee on Dangerous Literature
Ordo Quiritum Imperatorisque Masonicorum
The Cousins' Commission for the Humane Treatment of Servicers
The Mitsubishi Executive Directorate
His Majesty Isabel Carlos II of Spain

And with the consent of all FREE and UNFREE
Living Persons Herein Portrayed.

Qui veritatem desideret, ipse hoc legat. Nihil obstat.

Recommended.—Anonymous.

Certified nonproselytory by the Four-Hive
Commission on Religion in Literature.

Raté D par la Commission Européenne
des Medias Dangereux.

Gordian Exposure Commission Content Ratings:

S3—Explicit but not protracted *sexual scenes*; references to *rape*; *sex* with *violence*; *sexual acts* of real and living persons.

V5—Explicit and protracted scenes of *intentional violence*; explicit but not protracted scenes of *extreme violence*; *violence* praised; historical incidents of global *trauma*; *crimes of violence* committed by real and living persons.

R4—Explicit and protracted treatment of *religious themes* without intent to convert; *religious beliefs* of real and living persons.

O3—Opinions likely to cause *offense* to selected groups and to the sensibilities of many; subject matter likely to cause *distress or offense* to the same.

Ah, my poor Jacques! You are a philosopher. But don't worry: I'll protect you.

—Diderot, *Jacques the Fatalist and His Master*

TOO LIKE THE LIGHTNING

CHAPTER the FIRST

❦❦❦❦❦❦❦❦❦❦❦❦❦❦❦❦❦❦❦❦

A Prayer to the Reader

YOU WILL CRITICIZE ME, READER, FOR WRITING IN A STYLE SIX hundred years removed from the events I describe, but you came to me for explanation of those days of transformation which left your world the world it is, and since it was the philosophy of the Eighteenth Century, heavy with optimism and ambition, whose abrupt revival birthed the recent revolution, so it is only in the language of the Enlightenment, rich with opinion and sentiment, that those days can be described. You must forgive me my 'thee's and 'thou's and 'he's and 'she's, my lack of modern words and modern objectivity. It will be hard at first, but whether you are my contemporary still awed by the new order, or an historian gazing back at my Twenty-Fifth Century as remotely as I gaze back on the Eighteenth, you will find yourself more fluent in the language of the past than you imagined; we all are.

I wondered once why authors of ancient days so often prostrate themselves before their audience, apologize, beg favors, pray to the reader as to an Emperor as they explain their faults and failings; yet, with my work barely begun, I find myself already in need of such obsequies. If I am properly to follow the style I have chosen, I must, at the book's outset, describe myself, my background and qualifications, and tell you by what chance or Providence it is that the answers you seek are in my hands. I beg you, gentle reader, master, tyrant, grant me the privilege of silence on this count. Those of you who know the name of Mycroft Canner may now set this book aside. Those who do not, I beg you, let me make you trust me for a few dozen pages, since the tale will give you time enough to hate me in its own right.

A Boy and His God

WE BEGIN ON THE MORNING OF MARCH THE TWENTY-THIRD IN the year twenty-four fifty-four. Carlyle Foster had risen full of strength that day, for March the twenty-third was the Feast of St. Turibius, a day on which men had honored their Creator in ages past, and still do today. He was not yet thirty, European enough in blood to be almost blond, his hair overgrown down to his shoulders, and his body gaunt as if he was too occupied with life to feed himself. He wore practical shoes and a Cousin's loose but comfortable wrap, gray-green that morning, but the only clothing item given any care was his long sensayer's scarf of age-grayed wool, which he believed had once belonged to the great Sensayers' Conclave reformer Fisher G. Gurai—one of many lies in which Carlyle daily wrapped himself.

Following his parishioner's instructions, Carlyle bade the car touch down, not on the high drawbridgelike walkway which led to the main door of the shimmering glass bash'house, but by the narrow maintenance stairs beside it. These slanted their way down into the little man-made canyon which separated this row of bash'houses from the next, like a deep, dry moat. The bottom was choked with wildflowers and seed-heavy grasses, tousled by the foraging of countless birds, and here, in the shadow of the bridge, lay Thisbe's door, too unimportant even for a bell.

He knocked.

"Who is it?" she called from within.

"Carlyle Foster."

"Who?"

"Carlyle Foster. I'm your new sensayer. We have an appointment."

"Oh, right, I . . ." Thisbe's words limped half-muted through the door. "I called to cancel. We've had a security thing . . . problem . . . breach."

"I didn't get any message."

"Now isn't a good time!"

Carlyle's smile was gentle as a mother's whose child hides behind her knees on the first day of kindergarten. "I knew your previous sensayer very well. We're all saddened by their loss."

"Yes. Very tragic, they . . . Shhhh! Will you hold still?"

"Are you all right in there?"

"Fine! Fine."

Perhaps the sensayer could make out traces of other voices through the door now, soft but fierce, or perhaps he heard nothing, but sensed the lie in her voice.

"Do you need help?" he asked.

"No! No. Come back later. I . . ."

More voices rose now, clearer, voices of men, soft as whispers but urgent as screams.

"Pointer! Stay with me! Stay with me! Breathe!"

"Too late, Major."

"He's dead."

The door could not hope to stifle mourning, a small child's sobs, piercing as a spear. Carlyle sprang to action, no longer a sensayer but a human being ready to help another in distress. He pounded the door with hands unused to forming fists, and tried the lock which he knew would not succumb to his unpracticed strength. Those who deny Providence may blame the dog within, which, in its frenzy, probably passed close enough to activate the door.

I know what Carlyle saw as the door opened. Thisbe first, barefoot and in yesterday's clothes, scribbling madly on a scrap of paper on the haste-cleared tabletop, with the remnants of work and breakfast scattered on the floor. Eleven men stood on that table, battered men, strong, hard-boned and hard-faced as if reared in a harder age, and each five centimeters tall. They wore tiny army uniforms of green or sand brown, not the elegance of old Europe but the utility of the World Wars, all grunge and daily wear. Three of them were bleeding, paint-bright red pooling on the tabletop, as appalling as a pet mouse's wound, when each lost drop would be half a liter to you. One was not merely bleeding.

Have you never watched a death, reader? In slow cases like blood loss it is not so much a moment as a stretch of ambiguity—one breath leaves and you wait uncertain for the next: was that the last? One more? Two more? A final twitch? It takes so long for cheeks to slacken and the stink of relaxing bowels to escape the clothes that you can't be certain Death has visited until the moment is well past. Not so here. Before Carlyle's eyes the last breath left the soldier, and with it softness and color, the red of blood, the peach of skin, all faded to green as the tiny corpse reverted into a plastic toy soldier, complete with stand. Cowering beneath the table, our protagonist sobbed and screamed.

Bridger's is not the name that brought you to me. Just as the most persuasive tongue could never convince the learned crowds of 1700 that the young wordsmith calling himself Voltaire would overshadow all the royal dynasties of Europe, so I shall never convince you, reader, that this boy, not the heads of state whom I shall introduce in time, but Bridger, the thirteen-year-old hugging his knees here beneath Thisbe's table, he made the future in which you now live.

"Ready!" Thisbe rolled her drawing up into a tube and thrust it down for the boy to take. Might she have hesitated, I wonder, had she realized that an intruder watched? "Bridger, it's time. Bridger?"

Imagine another new voice here, at home in crisis, commanding without awe, a grandfather's voice, stronger, a veteran's voice. Carlyle had never heard such a voice before, child of peace and plenty as he was. He had never heard it, nor have his parents, nor his parents' parents in these three centuries of peace. "Act, son, now, or grief will swallow up your chance to help the others."

Bridger reached from beneath the table and touched the paper with his child's fingers, too wide and short, like a clay man not yet perfected by his sculptor. In that instant, without sound or light or any puff of melodrama's smoke, the paper tube transformed to glass, the doodles to a label, and a purple scribble to the pigment of a liquid bubbling within. Thisbe popped the cork, which had been no more than cross-hatching moments before, and poured the potion over the tiny soldiers. As the fluid washed over the injured, their wounds peeled away like old paint, leaving the soldiers clean and healed.

Thou too, Mycroft Canner? you cry, indignant reader. *Thou too maintainest this fantasy, repeated by too many mouths already? As poor a guide as thou art, I had hoped thou wouldst at least present me facts, not lunacy.* How can your servant answer you, good master? I shall not convince you—though you have seen the miracle almost firsthand—I shall never convince you that Bridger's powers were real. Nor shall I try. You demand the truth, and I have no truth to offer but what I believe. You have no obligation to believe with me, and can dismiss your flawed guide, and Bridger with me, at the journey's end. But while I am your guide, indulge me, pray, as you indulge a child who will not rest until you pretend you too believe in the monsters under the bed. Call it a madness—I am easy to call mad.

Carlyle did not have the luxury of disbelief. He saw the transformation, as real as the page before you, impossible and undeniable. Imagine the priests of Pharaoh when Moses's snake swallowed their own, a slave god defeating the beast-headed lords of death and resurrection which had made Egypt the greatest empire in human memory—those priests' expressions in the moment of their pantheon's surrender might have been a match for Carlyle's. I wish I knew what he said, a word, a prayer, a groan, but those who were there—the Major, Thisbe, Bridger—none could tell me, since they drowned his answer with their own instant scream. "Mycroft!"

I took the stairs in seconds, and the sensayer in less time, pinning him to the floor, with my fingers pinching his trachea so he could neither breathe nor speak. "What happened?" I panted.

"That's our new sensayer," Thisbe answered fastest. "We had an appointment, but Bridger . . . and then the door opened and they saw . . . everything. Mycroft, the sensayer saw everything." Now she raised her hand to the tracker at her ear, which beeped with her brother Ockham's call from upstairs. "¡No! ¡Don't come down!" she snapped in Spanish to the microphone. "¿What? Everything's fine . . . No, I just spilled some nasty perfumes all over the rug, you don't want to come down here . . . No, nothing to do with that . . . I'm fine, really . . ."

While Thisbe spun her lies, I leaned low enough over my prisoner to taste his first breath as I eased up on his throat. "I'm not going to hurt you. In a moment your tracker will ask if you're all right. If you signal back that everything is fine then I'll answer your questions, but if you call for help, then the child, the soldiers, and myself will be gone before anyone arrives, and you will never find us. Clear?"

"Don't bother, Mycroft." Thisbe made for her closet. "Just hold them down. I still have some of those memory-erasing pills, remember the blue ones?"

"No!" I cried, feeling my prisoner shudder with the same objection. "Thisbe, this is a sensayer."

She squinted at the scarf fraying about Carlyle's shoulders. "We don't need a can of worms right now. Ockham says there's a polylaw upstairs, a Mason."

"Sensayers live for metaphysics, Thisbe, it's what they are. How would you feel if someone erased your memory of the most important thing that ever happened to you?"

Thisbe did not like my tone, and I would not have braved her anger for a lesser creature than a sensayer. I wonder, reader, which folk etymology you believe. Is 'sensayer' a perversion of the nonexistent Latin verb *senseo*?

Of 'soothsayer,' with 'sooth' turned into 'sense'? Of *sensei*, the honorific Japan grants to teachers, doctors, and the wise? I have researched the question myself, but founder Mertice McKay left posterity no notes when she created the term—she had no time to, working in the rush of the 2140s, as society's wrath swept through after the Church War, banning religious houses, meetings, proselytizing, and, in her eyes, threatening to abolish even the word God. The laws are real still, reader. Just as three unrelated women living in the same house was once, in some places, legally a brothel, three people in a room talking about religion was then, as now, a "Church meeting," and subject to harsh penalties, not in the laws of one or two Hives but even in the codes of Romanova. What terrible silence McKay foresaw: a man afraid to ask his lover whether he too hoped for a hereafter, parents afraid to answer when their children asked, "Who made the world?" With what desperation McKay screamed to those with the power to stop it, "Humanity cannot live without these questions! Let us create a new creature! Not a preacher, but a teacher, who hears a parishioner's questions and presents the answers of all the faiths and sects of history, Christians and pagans, Muslims and atheists, all equal. With this new creature as his guide, let each man pick through the fruits of all theologies and anti-theologies, and make from them his own system, to test, improve, and lean on all the years of his long life. If early opponents of the Christian Reformation feared that Protestants would invent as many Christianities as there were Christians, let this new creature help us create as many religions as there are human beings!" So she cried. You will forgive her, reader, if, in her fervor, she did not pause to diagram the derivation of this new creature's name.

"Mycroft's right." It was the veteran's voice that saved us. From where I held him, Carlyle could probably just see the tiny torso leaning over the table's edge, like a scout over a cliff. "We've been saying it's high time Bridger met more people, and honestly, Thisbe, does anyone on Earth need a sensayer as much as we do?"

Cheers rose from the other soldiers on the tabletop.

"The Major's right!"

"About time we found ourselves some kind of damned priest."

"Past time!"

I leaned closer to my prisoner. "Cancel the help signal, or we do this Thisbe's way."

The police insist that I add a disclaimer, reminding you not to do what Carlyle did. When your tracker earpiece detects a sudden jump in heartbeat or adrenaline it calls help automatically unless you signal all clear, so if there is danger, an assailant, even if you're immobilized, help will still come. Last year there were a hundred and eighteen slayings and nearly a thousand sexual assaults enabled by victims being convinced to cancel the help signal for one reason or another. Carlyle made the right choice canceling his call because God matters more to him than life or chastity, and because I meant him no real harm. The same will likely not be true for you.

"Done," he mouthed.

I released my prisoner and backed away, my hands where he could see them, my posture slack, my eyes subserviently on the floor. I dared not even glance up to examine him for insignia beyond his Cousin's wrap and sensayer's scarf, since, in that moment when he could have called anew for the police, the only thing that mattered was convincing him I posed no threat.

"What's your name, priest?" It was the Major who called down to the sensayer from the tabletop, his tiny voice warm as a grandfather's.

"Carlyle Foster."

"A good name," the soldier answered. "People call me the Major. These men are called Aimer, Looker, Crawler, Medic, Stander Yellow, Stander Green, Croucher, Nogun, Nostand, and back there the late Private Pointer." He nodded over his shoulder at the plastic toy which now lay stiffly on its side.

Carlyle was too sane not to gape. "Plastic."

"Yes. We're plastic toy soldiers. Bridger fished us from the trash and brought us to life, but we had a run-in with a cat today, and at our scale any cat may as well be the Nemean Lion. Pointer fought like a hero, but heroes die."

Now the other nine soldiers gathered around the Major at the table's edge. All but the paranoid Croucher had long since stopped bothering to wear their heavy helmets, but their uniforms remained, fatigues and pouches more intricate than any human hand could sew, with rifles frail as toothpicks slung across their backs.

Doubt had its moment now in Carlyle: "Some kind of U-beast? An A.I.?"

"Wouldn't that be a relief?" The Major laughed at it himself. "No, Bridger's power is not so explicable. One touch makes toy things real. You saw it just now with the Healing Potion vial Thisbe drew."

"Healing potion," Carlyle repeated.

"Mycroft," the Major called, "hand Carlyle the empty tube so they can feel it's real."

I did so, and Carlyle's fingers trembled, as if he expected the glass to pop like a soap bubble. It didn't.

"It works on anything," the Major continued, "any representation: stat-ues, dolls, origami animals. We have paper, if you want to test it you can make a frog, just no cranes—frogs can be full-scale, but cranes weren't meant to be a finger tall, it's too unkind, ends badly."

Carlyle peered under the table, where an interposing chair half-concealed the figure huddled in a child's wrap, once blue and white, now blue and well-loved gray. "You're Bridger?"

Huddled knees huddled tighter.

"And you're Cousin Carlyle Foster?" Thisbe's voice and posture took command as she stepped forward. She had freed the sea of her black hair from the wad which had kept it dry through her morning shower, and donned her boots too, tall, taut Humanist boots patterned with a flowing brush-pen landscape, the kind with winding banks and misty mountains that the eye gets lost in. Any Humanist transforms, grows stronger, prouder, when they don the Hive boots which stamp each Member's signature into the dust of history, but if others change from house cat to regal tiger, Thisbe becomes something more extreme, some lost primordial predator known in our soft present only through its bones. She stared down at the intruder, her posture all power: squared shoulders, her dark neck straight, the indig-nity of her slept-in shirt forgotten. I believe there is some Mestizo blood deep in the Saneer line, but the rest of Thisbe is all India, large eyes larger for their long black lashes, so her harsh glance did not pierce so much as envelop its unhappy target as she repeated the sensayer's name. I was the target of her eyes this time, the too-slow syllables repeated for my sake, "Cousin Carlyle Foster." I gave the subtlest nod I could, confirming that, with hidden motions, I had already entered the name into my search, and that the data flicker on my lenses was me racing through police, employ-ment, and Cousin Member records, my clearances slicing through security like a dissection-knife through flesh. In minutes I would know more about the sensayer than he knew about himself. You would be no less careful guarding Bridger.

"I'm sorry." The sensayer too squirmed before Thisbe. "I didn't mean to barge in, it just sounded . . ."

Her gaze alone was enough to hush him. "Convince me that I should trust you with the most important and dangerous power in the world."

"Dangerous?"

"I could have written 'Deadly Super-Plague' on that vial."

Carlyle's pale cheeks grew paler. "You should because I . . . can . . . offer . . . context? And comparison, and scenarios, and '-ism' names for things!" His pauses convinced me more than his conclusion, pauses in which the sensayer wrestled against the gag order, forbidden by anti-proselytory laws and Conclave vows from letting slip whether his beliefs labeled this encounter Chance, Providence, Fate, or the whimsy of pool ball atoms. But Carlyle was good. He didn't slip, even in extremis.

"Names, scenarios," Thisbe repeated coldly. "And then suggestions? This thing or that thing Bridger should make? Gold? Diamonds? And then introductions, one friend, then another, then the rich and powerful?"

Carlyle's brow knit, his youthful skin forming taut, delicate wrinkles. "Money? Why would . . . This is infinitely more important than money. This is theology!"

I saw Thisbe's face shift from the kind of sternness that hides anger to the kind that hides a laugh.

"You can trust me," Carlyle continued. "The Conclave picked carefully assigning a new sensayer for your bash' of all bash'es, of course they did. If I were going to abuse my position, all I need is the Saneer-Weeksbooth bash's door key to wreck the world."

"Very true." I doubt Carlyle meant the reference to Thisbe's work as flattery, but it won a smile. Thisbe touched the wall to taste anew the vibrations of the computer system hiding in the depths, safeguarded by her bash', their ba'parents, their grandba'parents, back almost four centuries to Gulshan and Orion Saneer and Tungsten Weeksbooth, who made this house in Cielo de Pájaros a pillar of our world.

Carlyle was gaining steam. "If I'm here, it's because the Conclave knows I'd never exploit my position. Ever."

Thisbe raised her chin to make her glare the more commanding. "You'll keep this absolutely secret. Everything you see here. Bridger's whole existence."

"Yes. Absolutely."

"Swear." I interrupted, softly. Thisbe would not have thought to ask.

"I swear."

"By *something*?" I pressed.

"By *something*, yes." A smile warmed Carlyle's cheeks here, pride, I think, in the firmness of his faith in the *Something* he had faith in. "I can help you. I'm trained for this. I'm not afraid of the word 'supernatural.' I'm not afraid to explore this, not by pushing anyone to do anything, but with hypotheticals, thought experiments, listening and talking."

"Are you afraid of the word 'miracle'?" I asked.

"No." He was looking at me now, and I turned my head to hide the chunk that is missing from my right ear, lest he match that to the name 'Mycroft' and realize who I was. He gave no sign of guessing. "In fact it's one of my favorite words."

I raised my eyes and looked directly at the Cousin at last, happy to find few insignia at all beyond his Hive wrap and vocational scarf: he wore a red-brown mystery reader's bracelet, a tea enthusiast's green striped socks, and a cyclist's clip on one shoe, but nothing political, no nation-strat, not even a campus ring. I smiled my approval, and on the table the Major nodded his. Thisbe still held us, a dark stare which forbade any interruption of her silent self-debate. When she did soften into a smile, the whole room seemed to soften with her, the pulse-hot current of threat and force swept away by the easing of her stance, like smoke by a healing breeze.

Thisbe knelt beside the table, summoning her softest voice. "Bridger? Would you like to come out and meet this sensayer, Carlyle Foster?"

The boy beneath the table rocked within the cradle of his knees, voiceless crying making his breaths staccato. "Pointer's dead."

I apologized silently inside, to Pointer, to the boy, the soldiers, for letting the crisis of intrusion disrupt the necessity of mourning. Taking care still to tilt my mangled ear away from Carlyle, I crawled under the table and wrapped as much of my warmth around Bridger as I could. I stroked his hair, gold-blond now, losing the white-blond of childhood. It was hard to believe he had turned thirteen. "You know what a sensayer is, right?" I coaxed. "You remember what I told you?"

"A sensayer is"—sobs punctuated his answer like hiccups—"somebody who—loves the universe so—so much they—spend their whole life—talking about—all the different—ways that it—could be."

I smiled at my own definition parroted in child-speak. "Sensayers help people think about where the world came from, and whether there's a plan or somebody in charge or just chaos, and what happens when people die. Carlyle here is a sensayer. They can help you think about those things. Especially death."

Armored in my arms, Bridger found the strength to raise tear-crusted eyes and face the stranger. "Can I bring Pointer back? Is that okay? I can make a potion that'll bring Pointer back from the dead, but I don't know if that's bad 'cause I don't know where they went now that they're dead, and maybe it's somewhere good, so maybe it's bad to bring them back here, but maybe it's bad where they went, or maybe they didn't go anywhere at all and they're just gone. Do you know?"

Carlyle smiled, a perfect, calm, real smile, and I admired his recovery, bouncing back in less than two minutes from violent chokehold to being the only really calm one in the room. A sensayer indeed. "No, I don't know," he answered, "not for sure. People have made a lot of different suggestions, and there are good arguments for many different versions. We can talk about them, if you want. But what do you think? Do you think Pointer went somewhere?"

Master, do you believe that Chance alone, without Providence behind it, would have sent this child, in this moment, so suitable a guide?

"I don't think Pointer just went away." Bridger wiped his nose on his sleeve, and his sleeve on mine. "It wouldn't be fair if they just went away."

Carlyle's smile was practiced enough to betray nothing. "A lot of people agree with that."

"And it wouldn't be fair if they went somewhere bad."

"A lot of people agree with that, too. There are lots of good places they might have gone. Some people would say Pointer has been reborn as someone else. Some would say they've returned to being one with the whole universe, the way they were before they were born. Some would say they went to an afterlife."

Bridger's fingers dug into my arm. "Like Hades or Heaven. And then you get to see all the dead people you knew, like your mom and dad."

"That's something some people think might happen after death, yes."

"Except Pointer's mom and dad never existed, because they're made up. I made them up. Pointer remembered them like Pointer remembered the country their army was from and the war they fought, but none of it ever happened because it's all made up. Do made-up dead people go to the afterlife?"

Carlyle's five years in training and four in practice could not supply an answer. I was deeper into Carlyle's records now, past honors transcripts, parishioners' endorsements, bios of bash'mates—a safe, unfamous bash', all Cousins, mostly teachers plus a masseur, two mural painters and an oboist. I had even found his orphanage records, expected from the surname Foster. I had not expected the word 'Gag-gene.'

Perhaps in your age, gentle reader, the human race is better, good enough that you no longer need so dark a tool? The universal catalogue of DNA, our greatest guard against disease and crime, also ended anonymity for foundlings, whose parents leave signatures in every cell. Courts called it a triumph at first, the empowering of the abandoned, and it took the Cooper scandal and the Chaucer-King triple suicide to force law to admit that one foundling in a thousand carries in its genes a past too hard to bear. Hence the little race of 'Gag-genes,' which does not mean, as rumor claims, genes whose story is so vile it makes you gag, but 'Gag-order-genome,' a court order which denies the child access to the testimony of its own blood, for its own happiness. Law leaves it to the courts, not parents, to decide what case merits Gag-gene status, though parents may plead (and bribe) if need be. Rape is not enough. Incest-rape is likely in your mind, and it is sometimes incest-rape, but it is usually a longer, stranger tale than that. If Troy's Queen Hecuba, impossibly mother of fifty sons, had borne a fifty-first, not in the topless towers of Ilium, but in the slave tents after the city's fall, where the Trojan women clasped their captors' knees with hands still white with the ashes of their husbands, if in such an hour vindictive Fate, judging the queen's defilement not yet absolute, let rape plant one last seed in the womb which had borne so many unto death, and chose no hero's seed, not Menelaus, or an Ajax, or some other king, but gave her royal body over to the pleasures of bow-legged Thersites, the ugliest and lowest creature who ever came to Troy, a son conceived thus would have been a Gag-gene. I smiled now at the name Carlyle. I had thought at first it was lack of originality which made the orphanage choose what has become Earth's most common baby name now that I plunged Mycroft off the list. But you must admit a Gag-gene, denied any inheritance, even his parents' story (which might at least have offered him that patrimony named revenge), deserves at least a hero's name.

"Problem?" Thisbe crouched closed to me and mouthed it, likely spotting my flinch at the word 'Gag-gene.'

"Maybe," I mouthed back. "Best get Bridger out." I mussed the boy's hair. "You want to go home, Bridger?" I coaxed. "You don't have to talk to Carlyle right now. You can go home, have Mommadoll make cookies, and decide later whether or not to resurrect Pointer."

"But . . ."

I squeezed his shoulder. "Pointer's already dead, nothing will change for now. You can take your time and then make up your mind."

"What if they're in a bad place? Like Hell?"

I squeezed him tighter, choking up myself before that word.

The Major faced it better. "Pointer was a soldier, Bridger. They were ready for death, no matter what death is."

The little dam of courage broke inside the boy now, releasing sobs, half-muffled by his efforts to be strong.

"Come on." I scooped Bridger forward, my arms forgetting he was no longer so easy to lift.

"Shou—udn't I—talk—to the—sensay—er?"

His bravery brought wetness to my eye. "They can come another time to talk," I suggested, "tomorrow, anytime you want. Right, Carlyle?"

Rarely have I heard so passionate a "Yes."

Timid as a hatchling, Bridger crawled out from beneath the table. Beside him came Boo, his bright blue dog, three feet long and whining now in sympathetic worry, just as real dogs do. Even on close inspection Boo can be taken for a U-beast or some other high-end robot or genetically engineered companion, since Bridger's touch erases all hint of seams and stitching. It was Boo who first betrayed Bridger to me ten years ago, but I would never have realized what the toy dog was had Fate not placed him in my path in the moment one of Bridger's miracles ran out, so the living beast reverted to plush and stuffing before my eyes.

Bridger leaned forward and pressed his shoulder against the table's edge. "All a—" One more sob. "All aboard."

Murmuring layered words of kindness, the tiny soldiers climbed the warp of Bridger's wrap like a cargo net, and settled in like sailors into rigging.

"What about Pointer's body?" Bridger asked.

"I'll take care of Pointer," Thisbe volunteered. "You rest up, and eat. I'm sure Mommadoll has a big lunch ready."

Bridger rubbed his eyes, smearing the salty wet across red cheeks. "Okay."

I moved to follow the boy out from under the table, but Thisbe stepped close, caging me beneath the table with the firm bars of her legs. Bridger started to move, but froze as I failed to follow. "Mycroft isn't coming?" he asked.

Thisbe excels at making smiles not feel forced. "Mycroft will follow soon, sweetheart, but they have to stay and help me here a little first, all right?"

"All right," Bridger answered. His face showed it wasn't all right at all, but still, brave boy, he tried.

"Hold a second, Bridger," the Major called as the boy opened the door. "Carlyle Foster."

Awe held the sensayer as Bridger paused before him, offering a first close look at these impossibly perfect human figures shorter than a finger. "Yes?"

"Word of warning: we're small, but we're soldiers. Real soldiers. We're no strangers to handing out death." He paused to give the word its due. "We'll be watching you. If you betray us, if you even start to, if you endanger

Bridger in any way at all, we'll kill you. No second chances. We don't gamble with this power, we will just kill you. Understood?"

"You have my oath. I won't break it."

I couldn't see the Major's expression from across the room, whether he smiled at the passion in the sensayer's conviction, or frowned at his face, so bright, so buoyant, so obviously unable to believe the threat was real. "Then you'll be welcome tomorrow, Carlyle Foster. We do need a priest, or a sensayer, whatever you call yourself, the boy most, but the rest of my men too. We've missed that. We'll be grateful, when you come."

Hush held Carlyle, the Major's spell, that tiny voice too seasoned, that tiny face too care-lined, beyond what can be found in all the faces of our kindly age. Even had the Major stood full-size, I think, Carlyle might still have sensed the stranger in our midst.

"Bye-bye, Major. Bye-bye, Bridger. Bye-bye, men." Thisbe killed the moment with a strategic, shrill singsong which spurred the boy away. Her smile lingered only until the door closed tight. "Now the serious part." She faced Carlyle, her stance still trapping me under the table's cage. "The Major meant it that he'll kill you if you mess this up, so listen carefully. Rule one: you tell no one about Bridger. No one. Not your bash'mates, not your boss, not the police, not your lover—"

"Not your mentor at the Sensayers' Conclave," I added.

"Right," she confirmed, "not your own sensayer, no one."

"I understand," he answered.

"You think so? Keeping secrets is harder than it sounds." Thisbe scooched up to sit on the table, so her landscaped boots dangled before my face.

Carlyle met her dark, enveloping eyes and held them. "I am a sensayer. I keep my vows, and I keep intimate secrets, every day and always."

"Rule two: you don't take samples of things Bridger has created to run tests on them. We're all in favor of exploring this with science, but we have our own access to labs, people we know and trust, who can keep secrets. If you want to run a test you can suggest it, we're eager for new ideas, but we'll run it ourselves."

He nodded. "That makes good sense. I'm glad you're running tests."

"Rule three," she pressed, "you don't bring Bridger new toys or pictures or storybooks or anything like that without running them by us first."

He arched his brows. "May I ask why?"

"Attachment," she answered. "Bridger knows they can't fill the world with living toys, but sometimes they get upset when they get attached to a character they shouldn't bring to life."

He nodded.

She nodded back.

Does it distress you, reader, how I remind you of their sexes in each sentence? 'Hers' and 'his'? Does it make you see them naked in each other's arms, and fill even this plain scene with wanton sensuality? Linguists will tell you the ancients were less sensitive to gendered language than we are, that we react to it because it's rare, but that in ages that heard 'he' and 'she' in every sentence they grew stale, as the glimpse of an ankle holds no sensuality when skirts grow short. I don't believe it. I think gendered language was every bit as sensual to our predecessors as it is to us, but they admitted the place of sex in every thought and gesture, while our prudish era, hiding behind the neutered 'they,' pretends that we do not assume any two people who lock eyes may have fornicated in their minds if not their flesh. You protest: *My mind is not as dirty as thine, Mycroft. My distress is at the strangeness of applying 'he' and 'she' to thy 2450s, where they have no place.* Would that you were right, good reader. Would that 'he' and 'she' and their electric power were unknown in my day. Alas, it is from these very words that the transformation came which I am commanded to describe, so I must use them to describe it. I am sorry, reader. I cannot offer wine without the poison of the alcohol within.

Carlyle smiled now. "Those are good rules, good precautions."

I think he meant the words as praise, but Thisbe gave an irritated kick, nearly catching my nose with her heel under the table. Of course they were good precautions. She was Thisbe Saneer of the Saneer-Weeksbooth bash', custodian since birth of one of the most powerful engines of our civilization. Who was this little Cousin to pronounce judgment—good or bad—on her precautions? "Then follow them."

"I will." Carlyle licked his lips, the thousand questions in his mind struggling to choose a vanguard. "Where did Bridger come from?"

She breathed deep. "We don't know. They were a toddler when they animated the soldiers, we don't know anything before that. We've been raising them here in secret ever since, and it's going to remain secret until Bridger is mature enough to fully understand the implications of their powers, and decide for themself who, if anyone, to show them to."

"You've raised them in this bash'?"

"In the flower trench outside," she corrected. "There are hiding places."

"Does the rest of your bash' know?"

"No."

I spoke up, "Cato."

"Right." Thisbe laughed, possibly at herself, or possibly at having a bash'mate so harmless she could forget. "Cato sort of knows."

"That's Cato Weeksbooth?" I saw the flicker in Carlyle's lenses as he brought up the file. "I don't have an appointment with them yet, but I called to make one."

Thisbe frowned. "Cato doesn't know about Bridger's powers, or the soldiers, or even that Bridger lives here in the trench, but we take Bridger to a kids' science club Cato runs, to meet other children, so Cato knows Bridger as a kid Mycroft and I are mentoring. But nothing more."

"Mycroft . . ." At last Carlyle's scrutiny fell fully on me. On my knees beneath the table, I tried again to look as nonthreatening as a man could who had just tackled Carlyle with bestial speed. Should I describe myself here? What Carlyle saw? I am nothing much, perhaps as tall as Thisbe had I not learned to stoop, my skin a little dark, with dark hair always overgrown, and a thinness to my face which makes some worry that I eat too little. My hands have acquired something of a laborer's roughness, and my Servicer uniform of dappled beige and gray hangs on me loose enough to sleep in. On a street you would not give me a second glance, and, even with old photographs before you, you would not know me now without the telltale ear. Mercifully it was my uniform that caught Carlyle's eye, and I recognized the familiar judgmental half-step back which free men take around the guilty.

Murder for profit is the crime most people think of when they see a Servicer's uniform, a crime the convict has no reason to repeat now that law has stripped him of the right to property. Those with more imagination might envision a grand corporate theft, or a revenge killing, avenging some great evil beyond the reach of law, or a crime of passion, catching a lover in a rival's arms and slaying both in a triumphant but passing madness. At the dawn of the Fifteenth Century, St. Sir Thomas More described a humane, though fictitious, Persian judicial system in which convicts were not chained in the plague-filled dark, but made slaves of the state, let loose to wander, without home or property, to serve at the command of any citizen who needed labor. Knowing what these convicts were, no citizen would give them food or rest except after a day's work, and, with nothing to gain or lose, they served the community in ambitionless, lifelong peace. Tell me, when our Twenty-Second-Century forefathers created the Servicer Program, offering lifelong community service in lieu of prison for criminals judged harmless enough to walk among the free, were they progressive or retrogressive in implementing a seven-hundred-year-old system which had never actually existed?

"You've been helping to raise Bridger too?" Carlyle asked.

Thisbe answered, "Mycroft stumbled on Bridger much like you did. I admit it's a bit of a fudge putting 'cleaning services' instead of 'childcare' when I log Mycroft's hours, but it's no violation of the spirit of the law."

I held my breath for this moment, when Carlyle held my fragile future in his power. He could have reported me: my false work logs, my too-close relationship with this bash', almost familial, all things forbidden to we who forfeited home, bash', and rest when we committed crimes so severe that a lifetime's labor can never balance out what we destroyed. But Carlyle is a kind creature, and smiled even for me. "Nice to meet you, Mycroft. You must have a court-appointed sensayer?"

"Yes, I do."

"Who doesn't know about Bridger?"

"Correct."

"And Thisbe, you've never had a sensayer who knew?"

"No."

"Then neither of you has never been able to talk to a sensayer before about the implications of it?"

Thisbe paused. "I suppose not."

"Would you like to? We do have an appointment, if you're up to it."

She gawked. "You're up to it?"

"Always." I liked Carlyle's 'always,' his firm tone, as if some energy in him were awakened by this whiff of his true calling. "And, Mycroft, if you'd like me to arrange a session for you sometime, I'm sure I could get it cleared."

"I'll consider it," I answered, crawling my way out between the table's legs and Thisbe's at last.

She frowned. "Mycroft, you don't have to leave just because—"

"I have a job." It was no lie: a summons from the Mitsubishi Executive Directorate had been buzzing in my ear for some time. I had lingered, since Bridger took priority, but now I had a reason of my own to visit Tōgenkyō. My searches had sliced deep. There were not many Gag-genes born in precisely 2426, not many parents who would produce a child with eyes that shade of blue, hair edged with that tint of gold, and not many hospitals whose records would not open before the security codes I had the privilege of borrowing. That led me to Tōgenkyō.

Thisbe knows she will not learn about my work by asking. "Will I see you tonight?" She leaned toward me, and touched my back, her palm and slow fingers tasting the contours of my flesh. Instantly, I could read it in his face, Carlyle succumbed to the vision of me naked in Thisbe's arms. That was the great service Thisbe did me. Even without lying outright, the practiced femininity beneath her lazy posture could convince anyone, even the ba'sibs she grew up with, that my constant visits were no more than a mundane, forbidden fling. Carlyle had seen Bridger already, so there was no real need for us to deceive him, but someone who thinks he knows a man's dirty secret will usually stop looking deeper.

I returned Thisbe's stroke with my own across her cheek, just as practiced. "Hopefully."

She leaned close to my ear, trusting our pantomime to make it seem natural. "Is this Cousin trouble?"

"I'll know in a few hours," I whispered back. "Meanwhile, use the session, get to know them, test them."

Thisbe gave a warm, wide smile.

I was full of fears as I left. Not fears of Carlyle, or fears for Carlyle, but fears of what Tōgenkyō might reveal about who sent Carlyle. Skilled as he was, and perfect for our needs, I could not believe this Gag-gene of all the sensayers on Earth would be assigned by chance. And I shall bear you with me to Tōgenkyō, reader, but not yet. First I must show you what was happening upstairs in this same bash'house before I was summoned down by Thisbe's cry. I pray your patience. After all, if you choose not to believe in Bridger, then it is upstairs where begins the half of all this that you will admit reshaped our world.

The Most Important People
in the World

ANOTHER CAR HAD TOUCHED DOWN THAT SAME MORNING, March the twenty-third, before the same bash'house. Cielo de Pájaros blazes like a glacier on such mornings, white sun reflecting off the long rows of glass roofs which descend toward the Pacific in giant steps, like Dante's Purgatory. The city is named for the birds, they say over a million, wild but cultivated, hatched and fed in the flower trenches that separate the tiers, so the flocks constantly splash up out of hiding and fall away again into the trench depths, like the wave crests of a flying sea. Cielo de Pájaros is one of Krepolsky's earliest Spectacle Cities, much criticized for its homogeny, row upon row of homes with no downtown or shopping districts, but it has never lacked for residents. Critics claim that people tolerate living without a downtown in return for Chile's perfect ocean views, or even that residents choose the city largely out of Hive pride, Humanist Members excited to think the great Saneer-Weeksbooth computers are humming away beneath their boots. But Humanists are not the only residents; one finds Cousins here, Mitsubishi, clusters of Gordian. I think Cielo de Pájaros is a success because it was the first city designed for those who don't like city centers, whose perfect evening is spent by a window, watching gulls and black waves crashing down. What need is there for bustle in a city built for bash'es who prefer to be alone?

Martin Guildbreaker alighted from the car and crossed the gleaming footbridge over the flower trench to ring the main door's bell. What could those inside see as he approached? A square-breasted Mason's suit, light marble gray, and crisp with that time-consuming perfection only seen in those who perfect their appearances for another's sake, a butler for his master, a bride for her beloved, or Martin for his Emperor. A darker armband, black-edged Imperial Gray with the Square & Compass on it, declares him a *Familiaris Regni,* an intimate of the Masonic throne, who walks the corridors of power at the price of subjecting himself by law and contract to the absolute dictum of Caesar's will. Martin wears no strat insignia, not even for a hobby, nothing beyond his one white sleeve announcing permanent participation in that most Masonic rite the *Annus Dialogorum*. His hair is black, his skin a healthy, vaguely Persian brown, but I will not bore you with the genetics of a line that has not worn a nation-strat insignia these ten generations. There is no allegiance for a Guildbreaker but the Empire, nor a more unwelcome presence on this doorstep than a Guildbreaker.

"I'm looking for Member Ockham Saneer," Martin called through the intercom.

The watchman of the house stayed inside, so only words met the intruder. "Is the world about to end?"

"No."

"Then go away. I have eight hundred million lives to oversee."

"Not possible." The Mason's tone, if not his words, apologized. "I'm here to investigate last night's security breach." Martin let the computer flash his credentials. "I have a warrant."

"I sent for our own police, not a polylaw."

"I know this is a Humanist bash', and I will absolutely respect your Hive sovereignty, but as a globally essential property you fall under Romanova's jurisdiction. They assigned me."

"You think just because your bash' ponces around the *Sanctum Sanctorum* you can waltz in here and improve on my security?"

I don't believe Martin had ever before heard his bash'mates' positions in the Masonic Hive's most honored Guard used as an insult. He managed not to flinch. "Are you Member Ockham Saneer?"

"I am." Ockham pronounced with relish, as if, with all the lives in history laid out before him, he would have chosen this one.

Martin gave a suitably respectful nod. "This isn't a simple security breach. You've been framed for grand theft. We have your tracker ID logged entering the crime scene in Tokyo late last night, and five million euros appeared in your bank account this morning. I know it's absurd to suggest that anyone in your bash' would commit a theft for profit, but I need your cooperation to find out why someone would set up something so implausible. The fact that there was also a break-in here last night can't be coincidence."

The door relented at last, revealing a man of dark Indian stock to match his sister Thisbe, and a physique beyond common athleticism. His shirt and pants, once plain, were now a labyrinth of doodles: black spirals, cross-hatching, and hypnotic swirls, though he wore them as indifferently as if the cloth had never tasted ink. Only his Humanist boots mattered: veins of knife-bright steel framing a surface of pale, ice-gray leather, real leather which had once guarded the taut flanks of a living deer that Ockham slew himself. Like Martin, Ockham wore no sign of hobby or of nation-strat, nothing but his Hive boots and the overpowering self-confidence of a man who guards something so vital that the law will let him kill for it. Ancient civilizations, East and West, knew the special breath of power granted by the right to kill. That's what made sword and fasces marks of dominion, lord over peasant, male over female, magistrate over petitioner. Our centuries of peace have so perfected nonlethal force that even police serve content without the right to kill. But we are not fools. To those who protect the commonwealth entire, the guards around the Olenek Virus Lab, the *Sanctum Sanctorum*, and to Ockham here we grant 'any means necessary,' a knife, a branch, even that deadly instrument the fist, to guard a million lives. Even if they never exercise this rarest right, still somehow every glance and gesture of such guardians still breathes the ancient force of knighthood. "I am Ockham Saneer. What is it that I'm supposed to have stolen?"

Martin nodded respect. "The unpublished *Black Sakura* Seven-Ten list."

Scorn deepened on Ockham's face. "Who'd pay five million for a vacuous editorial that goes to press in two days?"

"I could give you a nice long list. But I don't know who'd pay five million to frame you. Did you visit the *Black Sakura* office yesterday? Have you ever dealt with them at all?"

Ockham still blocked the doorway, stubborn as a sculpture in its niche. "If I cared about newspapers I'd pick *The Olympian* or *El País*."

"The paper's absence was reported at seven o'clock P.M. Tokyo time, six A.M. your time. Any chance you might have taken your tracker off in the hours shortly before that?"

"Paper?"

"Yes. The stolen list was a handwritten manuscript on paper. *Black Sakura* is antiquarian that way."

Ockham's face grew harder. "That's what my breach was, an intruder left a piece of paper in the house, with Japanese writing on it."

Martin swallowed. "May I see it? I do have jurisdiction." He let the warrant flicker across Ockham's lenses.

The Humanist drew back with a mastiff's reluctance. "Don't touch anything without asking."

"Understood." The Mason crossed the threshold with the tiptoe reverence he usually reserves for his own capitol.

There was little in the entryway apart from an ankle-high security robot, which let itself be seen to remind the visitor of its myriad hidden kin. As loyal Humanists, the Saneer-Weeksbooth bash' did try their best to line the entrance hall with the traditional relics of triumphs, but since most of them do little but their work, and their celebrity member keeps his home a secret, their tiny spattering of diplomas and pictures—Thisbe's trophies, Cato's book cover—drowned on the walls like an unfinished mural. Is that judgment in the eyes of this young Guildbreaker? Smugness as he surveys the poor showing of the Saneer-Weeksbooths, whose name rivals his own in the triumphant annals of the bash' system? I researched which of the two is really older, since so many bash'es form and dissolve with every generation that any famous bash' which lasts more than three will spawn the rumor of antiquity. I found what I must call a noble tie. Regan Makoto Cullen broke with her great teacher Adolf Richter Brill on November fourth, 2191. "Break with" is easy to say, but not so easy to do, to face the man who has been your patron, teacher, foster father for twenty-five years, the man all Earth hails as the great mind of the century, who mapped the psyche in undreamt-of detail, who revolutionized education, linguistics, justice, to face him down and say, "Sir, you are wrong. So wrong that I shall turn the world against you. It's not the numbers, not these rare psyches you're charting that stimulate great progress. It's groups. I've studied the same inventors, authors, leaders that you have, and the thing that most reliably produces many at once—the effect you've worked so hard to replicate—is when people abandon the nuclear family to live in a collective household, four to twenty friends, rearing children and ideas together in a haven of mutual discourse and play. We don't need to revolutionize the kindergartens, we need to revolutionize the family." This heresy, this *bash'*, which Cullen shortened from *i-basho* (a Japanese word, like 'home' but stronger), this challenge to Brill's great system Cullen did not dare present without extensive notes. In those notes—still held as relics in Brill's Institute—you will find the test bash'es Cullen set up in the 2170s, including both Weeksbooth and Guildbreaker.

"Is that sound the computers?" Martin half-whispered, not daring to touch the walls, which hummed as if channeling some distant stampede.

"Generators," Ockham answered. "We can power the system for two weeks even if main and secondary both fail. The processors are farther back."

He led Martin on to the bash'house's central chamber, a high, broad living room ringed with cushy gray sofas, with a glass back wall that looked down over the next tiers of the sloping city to the crashing blue of the

Pacific. The western sunlight through the window cast a halo around the room's famed centerpiece: the pudgy pointed oval silhouette of *Mukta*. You know her from your schooling, duly memorized alongside the *Nina*, the *Pinta*, and *Apollo XI*, but you do not know her as we who walked those halls know her, her shadow across the carpet, her texture as you coax dust from the pockmarks scored in her paint by the bullet-fierce dust of 9,640 km/h.

"Is that the original?" Reverence made Martin's words almost a whisper.

"Of course." Ockham gave *Mukta* a careful caress, as one gives an old dog, not strong enough to leap and wrestle anymore. "Heart of the family business. Coming up on four hundred years it's never left the bash'."

Martin gazed up through the glass wall to the sky, where today's cars, *Mukta*'s swarming children, raced on, invisibly swift until they slowed for landing, so they seemed to appear over the city like eggs laid by the chubby clouds. "And the computers? How deep would an intruder have to get to reach them?"

"Deep," Ockham answered. "Many stories, many tiers."

Thumps through the ceiling made both glance up, the footsteps of a bash'mate upstairs.

"How about to reach an interface?" Martin asked.

"The next room has some interface nets." Ockham nodded to his left. "But they're set-set nets, Cartesian, no one who wasn't trained from birth could get them to respond."

Mason: "Your security is mostly automated?"

Humanist: "I could have fifty guards here in two minutes, three hundred in five, but human power is less than four percent of my security."

Mason: "You think there's no danger this intruder could return and cause a mass crash?"

Humanist: "A mass crash is not possible."

Mason: "You're sure?"

Are you disconcerted by this scriptlike format, reader? It was common in our Eighteenth Century, description lapsing into naked dialogue; to such Enlightened readers all histories were plays, or rather one play, scripted by one distant and divine Playwright.

Humanist: "A mass crash is not the danger. The system will ground all the cars if any tampering's detected, and they can self-land even with the system dead. The problem is shutting down all transit on Earth for however long it took us to recheck the system, could be minutes, hours. The Censor told me a complete shutdown would cost the world economy a billion euros

a minute, not to mention stranding millions, cutting off supplies, ambu-
lances, police. That's your catastrophe."

Mason: "Or at the very least the century's most destructive prank."

Humanist: "Utopians?"

Confess, reader, the name had risen in your mind too, conjured by stereotype, as talk of secret handshakes brings Masons before your eyes, or war
brings priests.

Martin frowned. "Not Utopians necessarily, though such mischief is
not beyond them."

Humanist: "They have a separate system. They're the only ones."

Mason: "Do you think they'd reap a profit if they shut you down and
then let the other Hives rent out their cars?"

Humanist: "They wouldn't."

Mason: "Rent their cars?"

"They don't have the capacity to put that many extra cars in the sky,
they don't have the reserves we do. They'd be overrun."

At Ockham's signal the house summoned its second showpiece: a projection of the Earth in her slow spin, with the paths of the cars' flights traced
across in threads of glowing gold. Hundreds of millions crisscrossed, dense
as pen strokes, drowning out the continents so the regions of the globe were
differentiated only by texture, oceans smooth masses of near-parallel paths,
like fresh-combed hair, while the great cities bristled with so many criss-
crossing journeys that Earth seemed to bleed light. Each car's position en
route was visible like a knot in the thread, crawling forward as the seconds
crawled, so the whole mass scintillated like the dust of broken glass. The
display is functionless, of course, a toy to dazzle houseguests, but a Humanist bash' must make some amends for a shabby trophy wall.

Humanist: "Gold is my system. The Utopian cars are blue, and Romanova's Emergency System cars are red. Can you see them?"

Martin squinted as the end of a baseball game in Cairo made the city
blaze with fresh launches. "Not a trace."

"Exactly. I have eight hundred million passengers in the air at a time.
Making them compete for thirty million Utopian cars would do a lot more
harm than profit. A shutdown helps no one."

More footsteps on the stairs above. "¡Ockham!" a voice called down in
Spanish. "¿Can you come help move Eureka's bed? A mango fell behind it.
Well, most of a mango. ¿Can you bring a sponge?"

"¡Busy!" Ockham called back. "¡Ask Kat or Robin!"

"¡Kay!"

The click of Ockham's boots erased the interruption. "I didn't catch your name, Mason."

"Martin Guildbreaker." His eyes widened as he realized his mistake. "I mean Mycroft, my real name's Mycroft, Mycroft Guildbreaker, but everybody calls me Martin. But I'm not in a cult or anything, it's just one of those nicknames that happens."

Ockham nodded. "And Mycroft isn't an easy name to live with anymore." He was unable to resist glancing at the corner, where I sat on a work stool, picking away at a scrubbing robot whose self-cleaning function was not quite equal to the combination of gum and doll hair.

"Martin is worse, actually, but . . ."

Words died. Martin's eyes had followed Ockham's to me: my uniform, my ear, my face. Martin froze. Ockham froze. Both held their breath in a kind of stalemate, searching each other's faces as the questions flowed: Does he know? Why does he know? Does he know I know? What can I say when he asks me why I know?

I tried to ease it for them, interrupting with motion, though I dared not speak first. I rose and bobbed an awkward half-bow to Martin, reaching by instinct to remove my hat, though it was already on the ledge beside me. Ockham caught the gesture, and his face relaxed into the first expression that morning which one could call a smile. "Have we both been feeding the same stray?"

Martin gave a laugh, a quiet one, politely brief, but enough to make his stance less tightrope-rigid. "So it seems. Good morning, Mycroft."

I renewed my half-bow. "Good morning, *Nepos*."

Ockham frowned at Martin's title, an unwelcome reminder of this Mason's intimacy with his distant Emperor. "Of course, Mycroft was also a *Familiaris*." He nodded at Martin's armband. "You know them from that?"

"Yes and no." Martin had no obligation to be so honest. "I commission Mycroft frequently."

"What for?"

"Mostly languages. Hive-neutral translators aren't easy to come by, and a sensitive case like yours may turn up documents in any Hive language, or all of them."

I fidgeted with the robot in my hands as I stared at Ockham's feet. "*Nepos* Martin is as fastidious about Latin as you are about Spanish," I began, "and . . . I do have some functional knowledge of poly-Hive criminal law."

Ockham gave a snort that verged on laughter. "True enough. And will you have Mycroft working on my case? An unreasonable investigator for an unreasonable crime."

The Mason smiled, "I'd be eager to have Mycroft, if you're comfortable with it."

"If I trust a person with my dirty underwear, I'll trust them with my irritating interruption."

Martin blinked. "You commission Mycroft Canner to do your laundry?"

Ockham paused a moment, weighing, I think, whether this Mason would be easier or harder to get rid of if he told the truth. (Or rather what he believed.) "Mycroft is my sibling Thisbe's lover. They manufacture odd jobs as excuses." He nodded at the robot in my hands.

I feigned appropriate embarrassment.

Martin's lenses flickered with fresh files. "Thisbe Saneer?"

Ockham nodded. "I know there are many ways it could be unhealthy, but I watch the psych profiles of my bash' as strictly as any other aspect of security. A Servicer has nothing to gain by exploitation, unlike most people one of us could date."

"Very true," Martin acknowledged. "Mycroft is most trustworthy, and dangerous to no one. I'm glad they've found another bash' that sees that."

Ockham cocked an eyebrow. "Now you've got me imagining Mycroft wolfing down leftovers in the Guildbreaker kitchen."

"There is not no truth in such speculation," Martin answered, with that awkward precision which infects his speech sometimes, and makes more sense when you remember he's thinking in Latin.

The two men looked me over now, and the surreality of it swept over me like headache, the wrong sides of the Earth together, as in some dream when a long-dead friend and some recent celebrity stand impossibly side by side. But this was no dream. "If I may add something, Members?" I waited for approving nods. "I think it would help, *Nepos* Martin, if you told Member Ockham that your team isn't Masonic, it's—I mean, when you do this work it's for Romanova directly, yes? It wasn't the Emperor who sent you."

"Correct," Martin confirmed. "In fact, I believe Caesar is not aware of this particular errand. I'm here as a personal favor for President Ganymede."

Ockham's face brightened instantly. "The President sent you?"

"Yes and no," ever-honest Martin answered. "Your President is not aware that I'm doing this particular favor at this particular time, but they know me very well, and they've used me often in cases like this. My team and I are not police detectives. Romanova sends us when polylegal tangles require an investigation but the place is sensitive, high-level, a Senator's personal bash'house or the Sensayers' Conclave, situations where all seven Hives need to be satisfied but the affected Hives' privacy must remain inviolate, or the investigation itself might cause more harm than the original problem. We solve things while leaving as many feathers unruffled as we can. When your name came up in the *Black Sakura* tracker log, Commissioner General Papadelias had the warrant sent to me immediately, to make sure your doorbell wasn't rung by someone your President trusts less."

As the Mason finished it was my face, not his, that Ockham studied, and I nodded eager confirmation. Ockham's curious expression made me bold. "If . . . if a little of my own opinion wouldn't be unwelcome?" I waited for him to nod permission. "Now that the hand of law is moving, Member Ockham, I think you're not going to get a gentler touch than *Nepos* Martin's. I've seen their work before; they really do focus on delicate situations like this, turning only the stones that must be turned. You're seeing it already: they have a warrant, they don't have to be this accommodating. You can trust Martin. They're a good person, genuinely good. If you can trust anyone Romanova might ever send, you can trust them. May I show them the paper?"

Ockham paused, and we all heard the scraaaa-thump of failed bed-moving upstairs. "Fine. Through there." He gestured to a side door. "And I do appreciate your courtesy, Mason. But I'll feel better when I've spoken with my President myself."

I led the way from the *Mukta* hall to a warmer room with practical chairs, neglected dishes, and an unfinished game of mahjong. As we left the front rooms' No-Doodling Zone, spirals and zigzags like those on Ockham's clothes flowed over the cushions, the wooden chair backs, even up one wall, like lichen starting to convert a bare island to soil. I think Martin did notice napping Eureka Weeksbooth, visible only as feet protruding from disordered cushions in the corner, but he made no comment, and moved only in Ockham's wake. "Your bash' has nine members, yes?" he asked. "Yourself, your spouse Lesley, Thisbe Saneer, Cato and Eureka Weeksbooth, Sidney Koons, Kat and Robin Typer, and Ojiro Sniper."

"Nine-and-a-half counting Mycroft."

Martin smiled. "Any other frequent guests?"

"Our regular guards and maintenance people, plus Kat or Robin bring a revolving array of dates home, Thisbe sometimes too. I'll send you a list of recents."

We reached the fatal spot. "Here it is, *Nepos*. Untouched, just as ordered." I showed Martin the trash bin beneath a corner cabinet, where the paper marked with kanji protruded like a flag between an ancient manikin hand and most of a plastic horse.

Martin moved carefully around the bin to let his tracker image every angle, then pulled out a pocket scanner to search for fingerprints and DNA. "Is this a household trash bin?"

"The trash mine delivery bin," Ockham answered. "There's ten million tons of dump under the city. Aluminum and plastics mostly, nothing older than turn of the millennium. A lot was hollowed out to make space for the computers, but the city's still mining the rest, and every bash'house has a right to rent a bot to look for particular types of items if we want. Thisbe has a thing for ancient toys."

Martin leaned close. "It's certainly the right kind of paper."

Ockham glared at the crumpled sheet as if it were a spider he would squish if not for poison. "Do they really write their articles in pen on real paper? That must take forever."

"Actually, Members," I ventured, "as I understand, they just do it for the notes for the most important article each week." It felt warm, being among men who knew me well enough that I could safely share my newspaper geekery.

"What for?"

"It's *Black Sakura*'s titular tradition," I answered. "The folklore is that the *sakura* cherry tree blooms pink because its roots drink the blood of the dead, so the premise is that a dedicated reporter is so steeped in ink their veins would stain the blossoms black."

Ockham gave an approving nod.

Martin did not, and I caught his eyes straying from the alien characters on the envelope to me. Martin does not acknowledge Machiavelli. When a wrong action will yield a good result, even so small a wrong as breaking the taboo on translating another Hive's language, he halts like a parent unwilling to admit to a child that its favorite toy is lost. It is not that he fears dirtying his hands, nor even that the wrong itself deters him. Rather, I think he hates admitting that this world contains such shades of gray.

Ockham doesn't mind gray. "Earn your supper, Mycroft. What's it say?"

Reconciled to the practicality, Martin scanned the paper's internal contents and brought the Japanese before my eyes. "Don't translate everything, just enough to verify that it is a Seven-Ten list." He hesitated. "And tell me the last three names. The motive may lie in them."

Ockham cocked his head. "I thought the big money was people betting on the order of the big seven."

"That's the bulk of the money, yes, but the three unpredictable names at the bottom, numbers eight, nine, and ten, are about to skyrocket in celebrity, so if investments can be made, interviews or contracts set up in advance, five million is nothing against the potential profit."

"Yes, Cardie does get a rush of calls whenever their name makes a list." Martin frowned. "Cardie?"

"Sniper," Ockham answered. "Ojiro Cardigan Sniper."

I don't know that I'd ever seen Martin snicker before, but everyone snickers the first time they learn that the legendary Sniper answers to 'Cardigan' at home.

"Read it, Mycroft."

I cannot unlearn the skills of my youth. I may let them rot, as a retired boxer sets aside his gloves, but I cannot unsee the words couched in the strokes of languages I have no right to know. I feel guilt, if that consoles you, reader, when I eavesdrop unwillingly on Masons, or Humanists, or Japanese Mitsubishi chatting in their private tongues. I can at least do some penance by sharing my skills on those occasions when translation is a benefit to all.

"It is a Seven-Ten list," I confirmed. "Just names, no notes. The top seven are the standard seven. The final three are"—I wrestled with the less familiar transliterations—"Darcy Sok, Crown Prince Leonor of Spain, and Deputy Censor Jung Su-Hyeon Ancelet-Kosala."

"Crown Prince Leonor?" Ockham repeated. "Not the king? That'll ruffle feathers."

Martin was still leaning close. "This has been crumpled around something, but there's nothing inside."

His scan was at work, re-creating the paper fiber by fiber on our screens, but whatever beginning of a shape the crumpled paper might have traced was erased for me by the scream, three voices at once, which came through my earpiece at the same moment that it echoed up the stairs from the lower floor. "Mycroft!"

I knew those voices. I would have charged headlong across a battlefield to answer them.

Now comes my confession, reader: in the crisis with Carlyle and Bridger I forgot Martin completely, and did not think to check in with him until I was already in the car soaring my way across the broad Pacific toward Tōgenkyō. My pretend affair with Thisbe was the only thing which saved me from questions I could not have answered. Martin was still at the house, combing the room for every hair and flake of skin that might identify the intruder, but finding nothing. After apologies I asked Martin for fresh orders. I had not felt fear yet, reader, not upstairs, not when I found the suspicious stolen paper, not when Martin came. Now, though, the command he gave made two vaguenesses congeal into one threat, distant, amorphous, but unmistakable, as when, against a background of city dawn and back alley clatter, one click and one clack come together into the telltale click-clack of a ready gun, and echo won't tell you whether the enemy's perch is left, or right, or high, or low, only that it is near. "Go to Tōgenkyō."

A Thing Long Thought Extinct

THE SIMILE OF THE THREE INSECTS WAS ORIGINALLY ABOUT knowledge, not wealth. Our age's founding hero, Gordian Chairman Thomas Carlyle, stole the simile from Sir Francis Bacon, the founding hero of another age five hundred years before. In Bacon's 1620 version the ant was not yet the corporation, stripping land and people to hoard wealth within its vaults, but the encyclopedist, heaping knowledge into useless piles, adding nothing new. The spider was not yet the geographic nation, snaring wealth and helpless citizens within the net of its self-spun borders, but the dogmatist spinning webs of philosophy out of the stuff of his own mind, without examining empirical reality. Bacon's ideal, his scientist, was then the honeybee, which harvests the fruits of nature and, processing them with its inborn powers, produces something good and useful for the world. Our Thomas Carlyle, genius thief, co-opted the simile in 2130 when he named the Hive, our modern union, its members united, not by any accident of birth, but by shared culture, philosophy, and, most of all, by choice. Pundits may whine that Hives were birthed by technology rather than Carlyle, an inevitable change ever since 2073 when *Mukta* circled the globe in four-point-two hours, bringing the whole planet within comfortable commuting range and sounding the death knell of that old spider, the geographic nation. There is some truth to their claims, since it does not take a firebrand leader to make someone who lives in Maui, works in Myanmar, and lunches in Syracuse realize the absurdity of owing allegiance to the patch of dirt where babe first parted from placenta. But there is also a kind of truth the heart knows, and that is why our Age of Hives will not strip Thomas Carlyle of the founder's crown. Nor do I mean him any dishonor by calling him a thief. Hive is a stolen name, born from a stolen simile, but the Three Insects which Carlyle stole from Bacon, Bacon had in turn stolen from Petrarch, Petrarch from Seneca, and Seneca perhaps from some more ancient ancient swallowed since by time. There is no more shame in reusing such a rich inheritance than in knowing other kings' hands held this sword before you drew it from the stone.

Night overtook me on my flight from Chile's coast to Indonesia, or rather I overtook the night, racing in two hours so far around the planet's curve that I half caught up with tomorrow. Tōgenkyō's lights skitter far across the night-locked ocean, boats like sparks schooling among the lines of reflected brightness which calligraph the waves for a kilometer around the island. Here seven perfect lotus blossoms rise against the sea, glowing from within with clean, warm light like happy ghosts and dusting the ground around their roots with shimmer. Only as the car curves down to land does the eye realize each petal is a skyscraper blazing with commerce's neon fire, while the shimmer around their roots is the pulsing streetscape of a metropolis. It is a double compromise, this Mitsubishi capital: a compromise between the twin aesthetic loves of Eastern Asia, towers of glass and steel and tranquil nature; and a compromise among the Hive's three dominant nation-strats, since China, Japan, and Korea all feared to let another host the capital, so the three agreed on neutral Indonesia as the Hive's heart.

The summons gave my car clearance to touch down on the eastmost tower of the westmost blossom, where the Mitsubishi Executive Directorate enjoys the best view of city and sea. My drab Servicer uniform felt drabber in these hallways. As March became ever more a lamb, the Mitsubishi were showing their spring colors, time-sensitive dyes within the fabrics of suits, *haori, cheogori,* and *sherwani* changing, so winter's deep hues brightened to cyans and yellows, while leaves and floral patterns bloomed through simple stripes like morning glories through their trellises. Perhaps you too have felt the itch of rebirth and festivity the Mitsubishi carry to every corner of the earth. Even in islands without seasons, or in Cielo de Pájaros, where March means summer's end, still we all liven with anticipation as the Eastern cherries bloom. And why not? Maybe Earth's oldest living poetic tradition, the Asian cycle of plants and seasons, cannot be truly translated, but the cunning of fashion surpasses even language. It is spring in China, Korea, and Japan, so spring everywhere.

"Not the Executive Chamber, Mycroft. This way."

I followed a soft-footed clerk, feeling fear's prickle on my neck as we passed the meeting rooms and the computer lab where I was sometimes put to work, entering instead a bash'apartment which sat above the chambers like the control room above a factory.

"The Servicer you summoned has arrived, Director."

"Send them in."

I removed my hat as I entered, which fear of recognition forced me to keep on even in the corridor.

「We expect promptness when we call.」 Before the door had closed behind me, Chief Director Hotaka Andō Mitsubishi lashed me with harsh Japanese which made my greeting bow into a cringe.

「Apologies, Chief Director. I should have fought harder to break away.」 I answered him in Japanese, and bowed anew with my apology, but dared raise my eyes enough to count the pairs of legs around me. There were five in the room, but four wore the familiar deep green of Mitsubishi guards, so, for an audience with the Chief Director, we were practically alone.

「*Black Sakura*. You know what's happened?」

「Partly yes, Chief Director. I've been assigned to the case.」

I straightened now, and verified my fears. Directorate Guards wear whatever cuts of Mitsubishi suit jacket match their nation-strats: Chinese closed at the front with braided frogs, Korean tied across the chest like *cheogori*, Indian long and buttoned like *sherwani*, sometimes Western blazers, or the Japanese style, crossing at the front like kimono. Today there was no such variety: all Japanese suits with Japanese faces, several familiar, children of executives who held high office in the Hive through Andō's patronage. This was an inner circle, then, gathered for that special kind of meeting where, if there are bruises afterward, no one will dare ask why. The Chief Director himself stood in the center, Hotaka Andō Mitsubishi, to use the customary English ordering of his names. Today's suit was blue-black with a pattern of plain reeds appearing for spring, fine cloth but no finer than his guards', while his simple shoes and plain short haircut proclaimed the supreme confidence of a ruler so secure he can afford to dress no better than his subjects. He was not always so. In our kind age no face (beside the Major's) is truly battle-hardened, but Chief Director Andō's is at least conflict-hardened, with a handsome severity earned over decades battling to break the Chinese factions' hold on the Chief Director's chair. Even our anti-aging drugs, which keep the strength of thirty alive in him as he approaches sixty, have not kept stress from silvering his temples.

He addressed me in Japanese, but for you, good master, I shall render what I can in common English. 「The thief used the Canner Device.」

My tracker bleeped alarm as my pulse spiked. 「I don't have it!」 I cried. 「I don't have any idea where it is! I don't know anything! It was thirteen years ago! I don't have the remotest connection to anyone who might have ended up with it!」 Only this far into my reflexive protest did I realize

I was cowering, my arms over my head to stave off blows, though no guard moved. 「Please believe me! I don't know anything!」

As Director Andō stared me down, I could read in his face the evidence against me massing, ready to draw into a phalanx: my presence at the house, my fingerprints on the paper. 「Where did you hide it?」 he asked.

「It . . . I don't . . . 」

「Where did you hide the device?」

「Maybe there were two?」 Even I could hear the foolish desperation in my voice.

「There were not two. There was one. Who did you give it to?」

「No one, Chief Director! No one! It . . . it couldn't have been the Canner Device!」 The words were as much for myself as the Director. 「The device could swap tracker signals and make someone else's tracker register as if they were Ockham Saneer, but it couldn't get through the rest of the security. I don't know what security *Black Sakura* has, but there are systems at the Saneer-Weeksbooth bash' that nothing I know of could get through, certainly not the Canner Device. It was only for the tracker system, for swapping two signals, nothing else! It can't have been——」

「Martin sent this to you, too.」 The Chief Director brought an image before my lenses, Martin's scan of the paper I had found in the trash that morning, which I had hardly glanced at among the many messages that had chased me through my ride. The reconstruction was meticulous, rendering the paper fiber by fiber, showing how it had indeed, as Martin said, been crumpled around something. In the next instant the Director filled in that something: the unmistakable, sleek, fishlike tapered body of the infamous device which the hysterical public never should have named for me.

「You had it last,」 Andō accused. 「You know who has it now.」

「I don't know! It was years ago. It'll have been sold on to someone else by now.」

「Sold? Did you sell it to someone?」

「No. Yes! I mean, sort of. I left it . . . 」 Plausible-seeming lies multiplied in my imagination, but as I started to voice one I could see Chief Director Andō's face tighten. It wasn't plausible. None of this was plausible, least of all my innocence, though innocent I was. 「I really don't know what happened to it. Please believe me. I was arrested. I don't know what happened after that. The police say the case for the device was empty when they found it, but anyone could have it: crooked cops, organized crime, kids who stumbled on my hideout, anyone!」

「You can't have been that reckless with it.」

「I was a child!」

Andō did not need to do more than glare.

Genuine faintness made it easy to fall to my knees before him. 「Please believe me, Chief Director. I don't know anything about what's happened. You know I have no way to prove my innocence, but you've trusted me a long time and I've never betrayed that, I never would. Even this morning, I could have told Martin the truth about the Seven-Ten list, but I didn't.」

His glare changed. 「What truth?」

「That Tsuneo Sugiyama didn't write that list.」 I saw the Chief Director flinch, and I clung to the new topic like a lifeline. 「Sugiyama always writes *Black Sakura*'s Seven-Ten list, but they think the pen should be wielded like a sword, especially the most publicized article of the year. Sugiyama would never have produced anything so uncontroversial, and, when they listed the top seven, they would never have referred to you as Hotaka Mitsubishi, they would have included your birth bash' name.」

Hotaka Andō Mitsubishi hissed under his breath, and my tracker finally stopped worrying about my heart rate.

「Masami Mitsubishi wrote this list, didn't they, Director?」 I tested. I waited. 「Masami is still interning with Sugiyama, yes?」

The Chief Director scowled down at me, then turned toward the rear of the room, where a partition, patterned with a calligraphic scene of frogs and goldfish holding congress in a waterfall, separated this outer chamber from an inner one.

A new kind of shiver touched me as the partition opened. I cannot date the beginning of the tradition wherein queens and warlords surround themselves with fawning predators: hounds, lions, serpents on silken cushions, ready to loose their savagery at the master's whim. Chief Director Andō has chosen a more dangerous predator: adopted children, ten in all, fox-cunning and ambitious, just finished with school and ready to carve their names into the world. Six were present in the inner room then, sprawling on the floor like cats, and, as the door yawned wider, they watched me, as cats watch a twitching toy they have not yet made up their minds to chase. They all come from one bash', a batch of ba'siblings who lost the older generation and had been scattered to distant foster bash'es before the childless Andō-Mitsubishi bash' welcomed them all. They were just starting to cross from teens to twenties now, and the three eldest had recently passed the Adulthood Competency Exam, one donning Humanist boots, another a Mitsubishi suit, the third a Hiveless sash, but the rest had not yet chosen, so wore only minors' sashes over soft pajamas, and the sloppy sweaters their adopted mother knitted herself.

Masami Mitsubishi was not among the lounging ba'sibs, not today. Instead a different figure rose to join us, pausing first to set down with loving care the branch of plum blossoms she had been about to trim: Danaë Marie-Anne de la Trémoïlle Mitsubishi, Princesse de la Trémoïlle et de Talmond, sister of Humanist President Ganymede Duc de Thouars, and wife of Chief Director Hotaka Andō Mitsubishi. She wore a kimono here in her husband's capital, not the unisex kimono one sees on Mitsubishi streets but a woman's antique kimono, birds and blossoms in golds, peaches, and blues, the fabric thick with labor like a tapestry, the obi sparkling around her stiff waist like a puzzle box of silk. She approached with the small, shuffling steps which in Japan code feminine, her white hands nested pale against the cloth like doves. So perfectly anachronistic were her dress and poise she might have been the model for an antique woodblock print, except for her hair, which sparkled in its cage of hair pins with all the rebellious wheat-lush gold of Europe. I will not call Princesse Danaë the most beautiful woman in the world, since that title doubtless belongs to some obscure person, living happily indifferent to the doors of fame that might be opened by the blessings of anatomy. But I do know who would win a worldwide vote for the face on Earth most likely to launch a thousand ships.

⌜What good luck, that we have an investigator so perceptive, and so discreet.⌟ Danaë's Japanese is elegant and beautifully accented, but too meticulous, the over-perfect Japanese of one who learned it in adulthood and remains self-conscious, even as the decades mount. ⌜Surely Mycroft will protect our Masami.⌟

Her words opened an aspect of this I had not seen before, the poor young intern, still a minor just whetting his eager pen, swept up in a storm of probing questions, which bitter politics would whip into a hurricane to levy at the whole bash'. Suddenly the wide eyes of the lounging siblings watching from the back room felt like fear. ⌜Do you think this is directed against the Chief Director, Princesse?⌟ I asked.

⌜I don't know.⌟ Danaë came to her husband's side. Do not chide me, reader, for using the gendered 'husband' when she stands so close, sheltering against him as she gazes up into his face with her brilliant, pleading blue eyes edged by maternal fear. Our age's neutral 'partner' rings false when her every touch and gesture makes such intentional display of 'wife.' ⌜Masami was so excited by this job at the paper—their dream job. I hate to think someone would destroy that just to get at us.⌟

「I'll do everything I can to protect Masami, Princesse.」 I said it almost without thinking, or with no thought beyond the desire to drive the sadness from that perfect face.

Princesse Danaë rewarded me with a smile, warm, her right cheek framed by one stray golden curl, and I relaxed enough to slump back on my haunches.

「Poor Masami is quite innocent, but I fear they will seem guilty when the public finds out the truth.」

「Finds out what?」 I asked.

She sighed, brushing back the wayward curl, and the passion rising in my breast split between the impulse to leap between her and the sources of her grief like some white knight, or to freeze that moment like a portrait so I could feast my eye forever on her face. I should add, reader, that I hold no particular lust for Danaë. Rather her arts—mastery of poise and gesture—can inflict these feelings on almost any victim, and when she sighs thus in the council chamber where the Nine Directors meet, one sigh can trump a hundred thousand votes. 「As I understand, Sugiyama pulled out of writing the list just a few days ago, and had Masami finish it, but the editor wanted the famous name, so was going to release Masami's list pretending it was their teacher's. Masami's just a junior intern, they had no way to object.」

「Of course not,」 I answered instantly. 「Don't worry, Princesse. I'm sure we can protect Masami. I'll do everything I can, and Martin, too, Martin will understand. Martin understands better than anyone how important it is to keep press and public from hounding Hive leaders' children. We'll keep Masami out of the limelight, I promise.」

「Thank you, good Mycroft.」 Danaë's smile washed over me like sunlight, and she even reached down with those pure alabaster fingers and stroked my hair, as one might stroke a faithful hound. 「What did you do with the Canner Device?」

You, distant reader, and I now thinking back on this scene with the distance of weeks, we two can see Andō looming behind his wife, watching in calculated silence as this exquisite tool extracts what he desires. But the Mycroft who kneels before her, he sees nothing but those eyes, keen as blue diamond, which slice even as they sparkle. 「I . . . I never had the Canner Device, Princesse.」

She cocked her head like a bird. 「You never had it?」

「No. I've never even seen it. I only ever had the packaging. I bought the empty box from some arms smugglers. I'd heard about the device from the news back when it was stolen from the lab, everyone did. I wanted the police to think I had the device so they'd think that was how I was sneaking around. It was just a trick to keep them from looking any deeper.⌟ It all poured out of me, years of careful silence melted by that coaxing face. I had been close to breaking already, really, the truth brought to my tongue's tip by the fear that being incriminated in this theft might cost me my parole, but if Andō's intimidation was a cudgel, Danaë was that perfect scalpel touch against the artery that makes the blood flow free.

She smiled—what sweet reward, that smile!—and chuckled like a teasing child. ⌜Then why didn't you just say so, you little silly?⌟

⌜I . . . didn't want anyone to think I still . . . I can . . . ⌟

Her smile turned from teasing to forgiveness. ⌜You can still do it, can't you? You can still trick the tracker system, however you did before?⌟

⌜Yes, Princesse. Please don't tell anyone! They'll lock me up again, I know they will. But if I'd told them they would've taken the means away, and I didn't want to lose it, I need it in case . . . in case I need it someday to help . . . somebody . . . ⌟

The mercy here was that she instantly assumed my 'somebody' meant her own bash'. ⌜Of course.⌟ She gave my hair a second stroke. ⌜You did very well to protect that ability. I'm sure it is of great service.⌟

⌜Thank you, Princesse.⌟

Danaë turned back to her husband now, freeing me to look down at the hat in my hands. The sight of it kicked off one of those chains of association which leads in an instant through five links to realization, or, in my case, horror. What had I done? How could I have betrayed so much, so fast? The threat of the device, of being implicated in this theft, it had seemed overwhelming, but I was innocent, and Martin would have believed me. I was not innocent of deceiving the tracker system whenever Bridger or other necessity required. Now, and forever after, Danaë could hold that over me. And so could Andō. I cursed myself inside, although, looking back, I forgive myself now. She was irresistible. Remember, reader, though I use archaic words, I am not from those barbaric centuries when men and women wore their gender like a cockerel's plumes, advertising sex with every suit and skirt. Growing up, I saw gendered costume on the stage, in art, pornography, but to see it in real life is unbearably different: her shallow breaths within constricted ribs, her round French breasts threatening to overflow the low Japanese silks. Here, as Andō wraps his arm around her waist, the costume makes me see them in my mind: the husband wrenching the kimono back to bare the honey-wet vagina. You see now, reader, why, to tell this history, I must say 'he' and 'she.' Danaë is a thing long thought extinct, reviving out of time ancient venoms perfected by a hundred generations of gendered culture. We around her—from my weak self to the gaping guards—grew up with no inoculation against this pox we thought our ancestors had vanquished. Movies and histories gave us just enough exposure to learn these ancient cues, weakness without resistance, and we can no more unlearn them than you could unlearn your alphabet when facing an unwelcome word.

Andō took control now, stepping forward so his shadow fell across me. 「You will write up everything you know about the smugglers you bought the packaging from. Thirteen years ago is not beyond the possibility of reconstruction.」

「Yes, Chief Director.」

「I hold you responsible for this. If you had made it known in the first place that the device was still in dangerous hands, I would have worked to track it down. I expect a prompt solution if you want me to conceal this . . . error . . . from the Commissioner General.」

So fast, the price of my indiscretion. 「I understand, Chief Director. I will take responsibility. Should I report my findings to Martin, or to you?」

He weighed that for a breath. 「Did these smugglers have a nation-strat?」

「Japanese, Chief Director. I suspect the original thieves were Japanese as well.」 I hesitated, but it was better now to say things openly. 「Like its makers.」

His face both darkened and calmed. 「Then bring the report to me first. Martin I trust, but, within the strat, my own inquiries will open more doors than a Mason's.」

「Yes, Chief Director.」

He peered down at me. 「Who do you think had the Canner Device built in the first place?」

「Please don't call it that.」

More firmly, 「Who had the Canner Device built?」

I kept my eyes on the floor. 「I know you are innocent, Chief Director.」

「That isn't what I asked.」

I squeezed my hat. 「I believe the project was ordered by the previous head of the Japanese voting bloc, but your predecessor's guilt doesn't make you guilty.」

「It will in China's eyes,」 he snapped. 「In India's, Korea's. In the other Hives'. The accusation alone would be enough to shatter the strat's hopes, and without a strong Japan the Hive will go back to being brawled over by

Shanghai and Beijing, not just at the next board selection, but for a generation.⌋

⌈You think one of the Chinese blocs planned this?⌋

⌈To scare the world with what the device we made can do.⌋

It was a possibility, now that I mulled it over. The thief must have folded
the stolen paper around the device on purpose, to let us know they had it.
In my selfish panic I had assumed they only meant to target me, not the
greater forces that had created the Gyges Device—that's what I call it in
my mind, after the invisibility ring from Plato's fable, which tempts even
the most virtuous to crime.

⌈Bury this, Mycroft,⌋ Andō ordered. ⌈You have Martin's ear, and the
Commissioner General's. Bury this before it plunges the Hive back into Chinese monopoly for another fifty years.⌋

⌈I'll do my best, Chief Director.⌋

⌈And keep Tai-kun away from the members of the Saneer-Weeksbooth
bash'.⌋

You may not recognize this Mitsubishi nickname, reader, but by
'Tai-kun' Andō means the Head of Martin's team, J.E.D.D. Mason. Since
there are too many reasons for Andō's nervousness to list here, I will say
simply that J.E.D.D. Mason is trusted of Andō, trusted like a son, but still
a bit too close to Martin's Emperor.

⌈I'll do my best, Chief Director, but you know I only serve, I have no
power to decide.⌋

Danaë broke in, ⌈We know you'll always do your best for us, good
Mycroft.⌋ I can't express quite how, since there was no threat in her words,
but something in her tone, her smile, spoke of my parole, how now she
could shatter it any instant with just three words to the Commissioner
General: "Only the packaging."

I shuddered, and the Chief Director seemed contented by my fear. ⌈Then
you may go begin.⌋

⌈Thank you, Chief Director.⌋ I scrambled up and bowed, but felt my
failure as the couple turned away, the new leash around my neck called
blackmail. I could not leave myself, or those who depended on me, so deeply
in their power. There was no resort but French. «Do you know who else
came to the bash'house today, Princesse? Apart from Martin?»

Both turned, and the princess relaxed at the music of her birth bash'
tongue, returning slow French syllables which flowed from her lips like
kisses. «There was someone else?»

I could not guess whether her ignorance was feigned or real. «There was a certain sensayer.» I scanned the back room to confirm that Michi Mitsubishi—the one adopted child interning with Europe and likely to know French—was absent. It was safe to press on. «A foster child. Dark blond. Blue eyes.» I searched Danaë's face, but the illusion of eternal youth which masks the matron's decades masks fear lines also. «A Gag-gene,» I added. «Twenty-eight years old.»

A statue of cream-white marble seemed to stand before me in that instant, so rigid she became. I felt my hands twitch with the impulse to catch her should she faint. «What a marvelous world.» She whispered it, less to me than to the world itself, and her lashes fluttered, fighting back a tear.

«You did not know? I have to ask, Princesse, I'm sorry.»

Danaë stepped toward me, away from her husband, who frowned but backed away, respectful of his bride's right to her separate tongue, and separate sphere. «I have never known him.» She brought her alabaster hands up to her breast, as if cradling an infant, real again in her fingers' memory.

I glanced back to the inner chamber, where her many adopted children sprawled and stared, all so different: Hiroaki Mitsubishi with Thai features, Jun European pale and freckled, Ran with Middle Eastern tints like Martin, but none like their mother. No one had been surprised when Andō—proud of his pure Japanese breeding—and Danaë—just as proudly French— had adopted instead of mixing their blood. But still, to have held a child of her body for a day and never again, even imagining it made me ache.

«You must at least have asked where he was taken to be raised?» I asked. «What Hive he joined?»

Another tear-gilded blink. «No, nothing. It was judged kindest that way.»

«Who took the child away? His Grace your brother? Your honored husband?» I avoided the French for 'Chief Director,' since even Andō could recognize that.

«He was handed to the doctor.» The ghost of a smile softened her sadness. «He didn't cry. Brave little one.»

«I told him nothing. I'm sure he doesn't know.» It was the best comfort I could offer.

«Thank you.»

Her thanks warmed me, made me bold. «I found it hard to believe that he, of all sensayers in the world, would be sent to that bash' by chance. Can you think of anyone who might have traced him? Any reason anyone could have to dredge this up after so long? To embroil him in this mess with the theft and the device?»

Three times she parted her lips, a different syllable shaped each time, but only the third time did she voice it. «Is he happy?»

I lowered my eyes. It was the right question, the only real question a loving heart would ask. And had she had a different upbringing it might have been hard to answer. «The Patriarch wrote that the halfwit is always happier than the philosopher, but the philosopher would not trade knowledge for ignorance, not for all the happiness in the world. Your son seemed to me half a philosopher, but still half happy.»

Do you know the reference, reader? Or does your age, forgetful of its past, no longer know *Le Patriarche* by that worthy epithet? Have you forgotten the first pen stronger than swords? The firebrand who spread Reason's light across the Earth, battled intolerance, religious persecution, torture, forced kings to bow before the Rights of Man, and introduced wit into philosophy again? Is Aristotle not still known by the honorable title of the Philosopher? Shakespeare the Bard? Brill the Cognitivist? How then can you forget the Patriarch? Perhaps you protest, *Thou accusest me unjustly, Mycroft. History has not swallowed this great man, rather he has swallowed history. I do not know who created the first government, or built the first wheel—it is so ubiquitous that I do not need to. Just so, my better era does not teach me who first fought for these good heresies you list, for they are now Truths, and the blind age that doubted them is well forgotten.* Perhaps you are right, reader, it is honor, not dishonor, if you forget the Patriarch. We now doubt Aristotle, understand Shakespeare only with footnotes, poke holes in Brill, but the Patriarch, whom all Earth follows without thinking there could be another way, he has indeed swallowed us up. But he has not so swallowed Danaë, reared, as she was, as if in his own age, when he—her Patriarch—needed defending. Voltaire, reader, the Patriarch of the Eighteenth Century, the era which has just remade your own, it was Voltaire.

A Lady of Danaë's education knows the corpus of the Patriarch by heart. «A good answer, Mycroft.» Heartache's remnants gave her French a somber tint. «Thank you. If he has been drawn into this by some cruel manipulator, I know you will protect him.»

I had meant to trade blackmail for blackmail here, but instead found myself drawn into pity, for Danaë, and for young Carlyle, too. My mind buzzed with measures to protect them, the lady from the enemies of Mitsubishi and Japan, the sensayer from the stern Major, from overcautious Thisbe, from himself, mistakes he might make in the first giddy hours after meeting Bridger. That thought warmed me, the strange, sideways kindness of Providence, which had stripped the Gag-gene of bash' and past and family, only to give him a treasure which was, to any sensayer, a thousand times more precious: a miracle. «Actually, Princesse, I think he has both much knowledge and much happiness, at least where it matters.»

If some brave painter captured her smile on canvas it would draw crowds down the centuries. «Thank you.» Then again in Japanese, for all to hear, ⌈Thank you, Mycroft. And we must thank my dear brother for calling you and Martin in to solve this. I know all feel safer in your hands.⌋

Director Andō nodded my dismissal, and Princesse Danaë passed me my Servicer's reward at last, a round lunch box, tied and too heavy to be anything but sushi. My many masters don't always remember they must feed me, that their toil-earned handouts are the only sustenance permitted to we the unfree. But Danaë—this monster from a more barbaric time— always remembers the protocols of servitude.

CHAPTER THE FIFTH

Aristotle's House

I MUSE SOMETIMES ABOUT WHERE ELSE IN HISTORY I MIGHT have picked to be a slave, if I had had my choice. I could have been a slave in Aristotle's house, when he reared Alexander. I could have midwifed at the birth of Caesar. As a slave-convict I might have added my sweat-drenched kilometer to the railroads that saddled the great continents, my heaven-bound cable to the first Space Elevator, or sweated in the rigging of the *Santa Maria* as she erased the dragons at the world's end and knit the whole sphere closed. If we count apprenticeship as an unfreedom, I might have been the typesetter who forged Newton's *Principia* letter by letter with his own black fingers, or the clerk who brought the coffee to Brill's circle as the master ranted into the wee hours, with silent Cullen in the corner, already dreaming of her bash'es. In any of these servitudes I would probably have cursed the great works I touched, the great men I called masters, nor would knowing they were great have lessened my suffering one toil-smeared jot. Yet somehow the idea warms me, that, out of every thousand lives of suffering my ancient counterparts endured, one slave was building something that his soul, if it could view all from outside of time, might call Great. It cannot wash away humanity's great cruelties, but Fate's cruelties, those, I think, it mitigates a little, and, for me, a little is enough.

I was scrubbing spilled perfume from Thisbe's bedroom floor when Carlyle Foster made his timid way back to the Saneer-Weeksbooth bash'house. I watched him through the security system which, for Bridger's safety, Thisbe let me access. He started toward the little stair to Thisbe's door again, but the main door opened for him, beckoning him across the walkway to the front hall, dark and empty.

<i see you, you salty yellow ball of light. come in.> The words appeared as text in Carlyle's lenses, and the log of them makes it easy for me to reconstruct the scene. <come in, i said, in in in.>

The sensayer tiptoed across the walkway and peered into the spartan trophy hall. "Hello?"

"Mycroft said I'd be back?" Carlyle crept along the empty hall, nervous as a new cat.

<they said to tell you they're downstairs. they didn't say why you'd be back. did you forget something? you don't leave your things very often, 09.02.51 is the last i have.>

Carlyle's breath caught when he reached the central room where *Mukta* hung in her place of honor, looking so like the textbooks. Or perhaps it was the two people sprawled on the floor who made him gasp. Both wore time-scuffed bathrobes over body suits of transparent conducting film, tight as a second skin. Thin, molded helmets covered their scalps and ears, and a strip of plastic taut across the eyes kept the real world's light from interfering with the computer's. The films over their limbs were pocked by the round red spots of tactile feedback discs, positioned far apart on the less discerning surfaces of shoulders and fleshy thighs, but dense as strawberry seeds on the nerve-packed skin of hands and faces where a millimeter's difference is perceptible. One of the two snored softly, but the other waved.

<hello.>

Carlyle smiled. "Hello. You must be Member Eureka Weeksbooth?"

<bingo.> Perhaps Carlyle could see Eureka's subtle wiggles as they texted, or perhaps he thought he could.

"And that's Member Sidney Koons?" Carlyle gestured to the sleeping one before remembering Eureka could not see.

<you've read up on us.>

"I have to if I'm going to be your sensayer. My first appointment with you is next Thursday, I believe."

<yup, 15:00. sit for a minute, i have questions.> Eureka flailed vaguely toward a couch to their left. I will use 'they' for Eureka, for there is nothing female about a creature to whom the body is no more than the mind's imperfect interface, and the sex organ one more convenient place to cluster sensors. Even if Eureka's robe falls so loose that this guest can see the spiral of peeking pubic hair, Carlyle would feel nothing but awkwardness. <why are you back? i have your stat trail here, i know how often you go back to parishioners' places same day, it's practically never.>

"My stat trail?" Carlyle scratched his head, his blond hair shining glossy in the light despite its neglectful overgrowth.

<past car usage. everyone has patterns. i don't just have the system send cars when you call, i have to teach it to anticipate who'll likely call cars

when, so it can preroute them sensibly. why did you come back here same day? way out-of-pattern. so exciting! i see radical pattern breaks sometimes but i never get to ask directly why.>

I saw Carlyle's flinch over the cameras: his first test keeping the secret. "Are you looking at my tracker data?"

<part of it. i only receive tracker data related to when you'll want a car. my system doesn't look at your image or audio feeds, just where you are, who's called you, work people, home people, things to tell the system where you're likely to want to go next. you never return to people's houses same day like this, so why did you?>

"I wanted to talk to Thisbe again, or to that Servicer named Mycroft who apparently comes here a lot?" Carlyle's voice had that slight shrill edge of someone who fears he might be less than plausible. "Yours is a very important bash', and this is a very special situation. When you all have the same sensayer and something happens to them you all need to mourn at once, but you've just lost the one person who could help you do it. I need to help you get comfortable with me as quickly as I can, and sometimes that'll mean repeat sessions."

<yeah, it's a problem all having the same sensayer. are you sitting yet?>

Carlyle had not sat, and paled now catching himself staring at Eureka, at her mouth, the pale edge of the tastepad that filled it like a gag just visible between slack, silenced lips. "Sorry." He settled on the sofa. "A bash' all sharing a sensayer is tough in this one situation, but it's still absolutely what I recommend. We can do so much more when we have the whole bash' in context. You're really wise to ask for it, it speaks well of how carefully you're being custodians of yourselves, as well as of the system."

Eureka twitched, but there was no way to guess whether it was a response to Carlyle or the lunch hour of some distant capital. <it's just easier on ockham, not vetting multiple people through security stuff. but i don't know why you're the new pick. we asked for a humanist, and i specifically asked for a sensayer who'd done cartesian set-sets before.>

"There were a lot of factors in picking someone for your bash', you all have special needs. I know I have a lot to learn, but I'm excited to get started."

<i also said no cousins. that shouldn't've been hard. no brillists and no cousins.>

Carlyle fiddled with his flowing gray-green Cousin's wrap, uncomfortable watching a face that could not watch back. "Just because set-set training is illegal in my Hive doesn't mean I'm personally uncomfortable working with you."

"Fair question," Carlyle answered cheerfully, "but I don't have a firm opinion."

<don't dodge. lesley & ockham have a right to know too. first kid they have'll be sent off for training same as i was. they have a right to know if their sensayer is thinking 'child abuse' every time it comes up, and i have a right to ask for a sensayer who doesn't think i'm a horrible human experiment.>

(At this point I received a message from Eureka's brother Cato Weeksbooth, asking me to get the sensayer out of the living room.)

Carlyle smiled the slow, patient smile of one struggling to swallow something difficult with grace. "Let me clarify. I have an opinion, but my opinion isn't firm. I'm fully aware that I don't really know anything about what it's like being a set-set. I have a gut reaction, that to me it sounds horrific growing up all wired to a computer, never playing with other kids, or seeing the real sun. But I also know there's a lot of propaganda surrounding set-sets, and I don't even know if those clichés are true. I want to have my mind made up by getting to know you. I've met other kinds of set-sets briefly, a flash set-set and an abacus set-set, and they both said they were very happy, and I respect their opinions more than mine, since I know I don't know anything."

<that's acceptably unbigoted. either that or you're being cagy 'cause you don't want to be fired.>

The Cousin's face was hard to read at that moment, sad perhaps. "I could get another assignment, but I was proud to be trusted with one this important, so I would appreciate it if you would give me a chance."

<do you really think you can work with me fairly?>

"I think I can if you help me. You can clear a lot of the propaganda."

<like what?>

"Did you really grow up in a computer, isolated from your ba'siblings? Or is that propaganda?"

<i wasn't in isolation, i always knew cato & cardie & ockham & thisbe & the twins, we texted all the time when we were growing up, it's not like we couldn't be real ba'sibs just cause my meat was in seoul.>

A shade of melancholy protest darkened Carlyle's face. I can guess the sorts of deprivations that trickled through his mind: no horseplay by the beach in this text-only childhood, no irresponsible late nights making fortresses of bunk beds, no hugs changing month by month as ba'sibs grow at different paces. Perhaps he thought of his Cousin-run foster bash', swarming with colors, games, too effervescent for even the pain of lost parents to linger. Hers must have seemed a nightmare. As for Eureka's thoughts during the long pause, I can no more guess than I can imagine the set-sets' all-sensory dreams, or take over their all-important task. "May I ask another—"

<less politeness, more asking.>

Carlyle smiled. "I presume it's also propaganda that you never saw the sun?"

<true, actually. well, training is totally different for different kinds of set-sets, but for a cartesian it's true. i first saw it when i was 17. it was smaller than i thought, and glarier. but now i can go watch a sunset anytime, i just don't want to, it's boring, so slow, monosensory. and before you fuss, i may have grown up never seeing a sunset, but you've never seen a six-dimensional homoskedastic crest up from the data sea, and you never will because you're wasting those nerves on telling you your knee itches.>

Carlyle ran his fingertip across his knee. "Can you tell me what it's like? You were watching my car, you said. Are you watching another one now?"

<now? right now i'm reviewing every car that flew in the last 10 hours, played back at 20x speed, and i can keep them all straight, speed, destination, age of vehicle, i can even tell which ones need the climate control retuned.>

"I've heard it looks like schooling fish?" Carlyle asked.

<that's your abacus set-set talking, totally different training, sight-focused instead of all-sense, optimized to do mass calculations fast, not over extended time. i can keep it up for hours and hours, five days straight if I take anti-sleeps, and I use everything. right now i'm tracking nine variables with sight, ten with hearing, five really complicated ones with taste and smell, nine with tactile, six with temperature, and eighteen with nerves your body would use for pain, but mine are totally reregistered, not unpleasant at all, so none of that crap about torture, it isn't torture, it's a sense, I just cultivated it differently, same as when kids learn music early, or languages, it's all different ways of cultivating brain growth.>

Carlyle winced at 'cultivating,' probably remembering the infamous Ongaro anti-set-set poster, clippers snipping the last rebellious shoot from a tightly trimmed rosebush, superimposed over a brain. "So what does it look like to you? Not fish?"

<not fish. it doesn't *look* like anything, trying to say what looks like

with just sight is like explaining how pumpernickel tastes to someone who can only taste sour. you don't have the right senses. see, here you are, salty little yellow ball of light, but if i zoom select, there, now you're a salty polygon, with gradients, ooh, you're pricky on one end, no, two ends, but you have five ends so that's not very pricky.>

(At this point I received a second, more frantic and incoherent message from Cato Weeksbooth, simultaneously commanding and begging me to get the scary sensayer out of the living room. I started up the stairs.)

Carlyle tugged free a lock of hair caught in his collar. "Are set-sets the only way to run the cars?"

<i don't need this nurturist crap in my own home, cousin. i'm not a bird with its wings clipped—you're a bird stuck in its shell.>

I hope, good reader, that the name of 'Nurturist' has faded by your age, that the zealots are quiet, and that the wound sliced by the violence has finally healed. For me it has been two centuries since the Set-Set Riots rocked our young Alliance, so the wound has scabbed over, but reminders like Eureka still pick it raw.

"Please!" Carlyle answered, "I'm not a Nurturist, and I didn't mean the question adversarially, honestly, I just genuinely want to know. It's such an adversarial topic, I can't ask anything without it being a question someone asked in anger some time."

<fair. it's not the only way to run the system. it launched in 2170 but cartesian set-sets weren't developed for another 40 years. before we took over they had almost 100 car crashes every year instead of 9, and the speeds were lower then too, they couldn't fly safely over 900 km/h. now we fly them over 1000.>

He nodded. "You must be very proud, protecting so many people."

<i'll be proud if i get up to 1100, let everyone on earth spend 90 less hours stuck in a car each year. that would be achievement.>

Carlyle smiled; that sentiment at least transcended the barrier of plastic and sensory rift.

<so why are you really back?>

We are fortunate Eureka could not see the shock on Carlyle's face. "I told you."

<you were lying. you say situations like this take multiple visits like it's a normal thing, but it's not normal, your return probability wouldn't be under 1% if it was normal.>

He floundered. "It's not normal, it's a very unusual situation."

"What?"

<i wouldn't blame you. thisbe's great.> A facial expression might have helped Carlyle tell whether Eureka was joking, but a *Homo sapiens* whose world since birth has been raw data swimming in the void does not learn facial expressions like a "normal" child.

Carlyle leapt to his feet. "Absolutely not! Thisbe's my parishioner!"

<you're one of *those* sensayers.>

"If you mean a sensayer who takes my oath seriously, yes, I am!"

Carlyle on his feet, his Cousin's wrap swishing like storm, is what greeted me as I rounded the landing and reached the living room. The sight of me forced instant calm upon the sensayer, but, for the set-set who sees only cars, I wasn't present in the room until I spoke. "Sorry to interrupt, Member Eureka, but you're being a little cruel." I hadn't intended the words to have a double meaning, but they did in some sense apply to how Eureka was treating Carlyle, as well as how they were taunting Cato.

<if my sib's such a big baby they can't cross a room to use the bathroom with a stranger in the house, they deserve toughening up!>

"Sib?" Carlyle repeated, frowning his confusion.

I smiled apology. "It is in no way your fault, Cousin Foster. Cato Weeksbooth is in that room," I pointed, "and has been sending Eureka messages for several minutes. Cato desperately wants to cross through here to get to the bathroom, but they're phobically afraid of sensayers."

Carlyle followed my gesture, and may have been quick enough to glimpse a sliver of black hair and white cloth through the cracked door before it slammed.

"Sorry!" Carlyle called. "I had no idea!"

I shook my head. "It's not your fault. There's no way you could have known." I moved close enough to Cato's door for my gentle voice to reach him. "I'm taking the sensayer downstairs now, Doctor Weeksbooth, no need to worry. I'll make sure they leave by downstairs, and I'll let you know when they're gone."

I will not repeat the sob-strained mix of thanks and curses which Cato muttered back—no, they were not even curses, just those words that sound like curses which children use who aren't quite brave enough to say a real forbidden word. Better not to meet him here, good reader; Cato Weeksbooth is a beautiful if fragile creature, and I will have you meet him when he is a little more himself. Today you meet Eureka.

I turned to Carlyle, and gestured to the stairs. "Shall we go down?"

Carlyle was frowning hard at Eureka, his pale forehead wrinkled by a consternated mix of guilt and blame. "Why didn't you say something? I would have gotten out of the way."

<i don't help cato be neurotic, it isn't good for them.>

Carlyle opened his mouth to object, but caught himself. He smiled, not a forced smile, but the kind where we smile for ourselves, to force away a darker feeling. "I'm the intruder here so it's your business. I'll look forward to getting to know you all better with time. Unless you still want to request a different, non-Cousin sensayer?"

Eureka twitched. <is your opinion firmer now?>

"My opinion about set-sets? I can't make up my mind from just talking to you for two minutes."

<most people make up their minds talking to me for no minutes. i guess you aren't horrible. if ockham approves it, you can stay.>

"High praise, thank you." Carlyle waited, but a set-set does not smirk. "Shall we?" I invited, returning to the stairs.

"Yes, thank you." Carlyle turned toward Cato's door. "I'm leaving now, Doctor! I'm sorry!"

The sensayer made it almost to the stairwell before text froze him in place. <you never said why you really came back.>

A third time the same question; bash' security may be Ockham's domain, but Eureka is a watchdog too, the keener because they know how to make interrogation feel like playful nosiness. My breath caught. It wasn't just the danger in the question, it was the sight of Carlyle's face, which relaxed into a smooth, angelic tranquility, beautiful and captivating, like a piece of art, the statue-smoothness of his cheeks, the childlike delicacy of his brows, the golden glimmer at the edges of his hanging hair. In that moment he might have been his mother. "Sensayer business," he answered in a light, sweet voice. "I don't think I could describe it if I tried. You don't have the right background or terminology. After all, I've cultivated my mind for something too."

It is hard for me to express what extraordinary praise Eureka's reply carried: <voker.>

Why do we shorten the words most precious to us? Ba'pa from bash'parent, ba'sib from bash'sibling, in old days mom from mother, Prince from *princeps*, Pope from *papa*, and here the hasty 'voker,' never the archaic 'vocateur.' In 2266, when the work week finally shortened to twenty hours, and crowds deserted those few professions which required more, the first Anonymous, Aurel Gallet, rushed to defend 'vocation' with a tract which is still mandatory reading for three Hive-entry programs. Why is a calling passive, he asked? Why is one called helplessly to one's vocation, when surely it is an active thing? I find my calling, take it, seize that delight, that path before me, make it mine. I call it like a summoned magic, it does not call me. His new word 'vocateur' (one who calls) was born to remind us that a person with a strong vocation is not a victim driven helplessly to toil, but a lucky soul whose work is also pleasure, and to whom thirty, forty, fifty hours are welcome ones. Surely the inconvenience of pronouncing one more syllable is a small price to commemorate a term so powerful that here it cuts across the barrier to thrill the hearts of both Cousin and set-set.

Carlyle smiled a true, warm smile at the compliment. "You too."

I led him down to Thisbe's empty room. There was a special feeling of release as I closed the door behind us, like shutting out the swelter of a fearsome August. I could see from Carlyle's easing shoulders that he felt it too.

"How did you know I'd come back?" he asked.

"You're a sane person, Member Foster. After what you saw, how could you not come back?"

He laughed, but only for a moment. "It was real, right? I didn't imagine it."

"It was real," I confirmed, and I watched his face relax, as at the touch of dew.

"I've been telling myself it was real. Thinking about nothing else. I mean, I didn't doubt my memory, I remember clearly, but the more I thought about it the more it felt like it couldn't be real."

"It took me months to stop needing to be reassured. Sit, please, Member Foster."

My gesture had offered Thisbe's velvet-covered water-couch, which took up half of one wall, but Carlyle chose instead my little folding stool, on which one could perch with energy, ready to spring. "No need to be so formal," he answered. "Just 'Carlyle' is fine."

"Carlyle," I repeated. "I will apologize in advance for slipping. Formality is rather a habit for me."

"No problem." He smiled. "And you prefer 'Mycroft'?"

"Yes, if you please." I knelt and took up my scrub and vacuum. "It was real. You'll probably need reassurance often. You shouldn't call me, my tracker's monitored, but I assume you have Thisbe's tracker number already, Thisbe should be willing to answer if you need to hear somebody say it's real."

He nodded. "Do you have . . . I was hoping to see proof again, the little soldiers, or something."

"Of course. I brought this for you." I rose and offered him a tiny paper book, too small to cover the surface of his pinky nail even when opened. No matter how keenly our lenses zoom in on that book they only show more detail: the letters finer than pinpricks, the surface of the paper, thumb-smeared corners and food-stained favorite parts. It is not beyond science to make such an object, but it is beyond technology Thisbe and I might plausibly access.

Carlyle took some moments to explore the tiny proof. "May I . . . is it too much to ask to keep this? To remind myself."

"Nothing leaves here, no physical evidence. Not yet. Not until Bridger decides they're ready."

"I understand." He stroked the tiny spine. "It's a big thing."

"Yes."

He paused. "It's the biggest thing, really. The biggest thing."

I did not have an answer which would not have strained his vows. "Give yourself a scratch with the pages," I suggested. "On your thumbnail. They're so thin that static cling sticks them together into clumps, but if you can separate a good clump you can give yourself a very visible scratch that'll last a long time as the nail grows out. It's not proof, but it's how I used to leave myself a reminder that it was real. It'll help."

He looked from me to the tiny relic on his palm. "Yes. Yes, good idea, thank you. That's just the thing."

I smiled as I watched him struggle to get just the right sized clump, laughing a little inside. This was all so easy for Carlyle, with my ten years' experience at his service. I was glad I could make it gentler for someone. When my world had been force-rewritten in an instant, I had faced only tiny, hostile bayonets and toddler babble.

Carlyle finished and sat back, smiling at his precious proof. "What are you doing?" he asked, nodding at my chemical scrub.

"Destroying evidence. There was a break-in upstairs. The police must not find signs of Bridger." I smiled to make it feel less criminal. "Thisbe's out on a date, and Bridger's gone to bed, but I will answer whatever questions I can for you. If you're like me, you'll have a hundred new questions a day for the next month."

His smile grew sheepish. "I do have a lot of questions. What are . . . what are the limits of this power? What exactly can Bridger do?"

The big one first. "I have no idea what limits if any Bridger's power has, I can only describe what I've seen them do. They can animate representations. Any representation real enough to feel real to them: a mud pie, a doll, a drawing. That may be all they can do, or there may be a thousand other things, but Bridger is a timid kid and understands play, and feels comfortable with toys, so that's the only sort of thing they've done so far."

He nodded. "When they make things real, do they become what Bridger imagines, or what the maker of the thing imagines? You know how sometimes a kid might play with a doll that's supposed to be some movie character, but the kid doesn't know the character and invents a different one."

I nodded. "It seems to become something of a mixture. Bridger found a toy hot air balloon once, and burned themself on the fire inside. They knew what the balloon was but not how it worked, but when they miracled it it had fire anyway. And the soldiers' guns and things have working, moving parts which Bridger couldn't name or recognize. The soldiers speak modern English like a child would expect, but they don't have modern attitudes, they have attitudes of hundreds of years ago when those ancient soldier toys were made. They use 'he' and 'she,' and swear by religious things in public, and remember a darker age."

"Do they . . ." Carlyle frowned. "This is a hard question to phrase, but do they remember real things? Real lives? A toy doll of a fairytale prince is pretend, but toy soldiers are representations of real soldiers who really lived. Has Bridger created pretend soldiers, or re-created real people who really lived and died?"

"If they were real there's no way to look them up, they don't have real historical people's names, they have the childish names Bridger gave them: Pointer, Croucher, Looker. But Bridger did miracle a real person once."

Wide eyes. "They did?"

"A photograph from an old book, a friendly looking person they wanted to play with. Emma Platz was their name, Bridger didn't make that one up. With flat pictures it works as if you were talking to each other through a screen. The person on the other side can see and hear you, but you can't reach them."

Carlyle leaned toward me with such energy he almost toppled the little stool. "Is there a whole world in the image? Can other people show up? Does time pass?"

I frowned. "We've only tried it the once. There's a limit to how much you can experiment with creating life before it becomes too cruel, for Bridger as well as for the subject. You know how kids fall apart when a pet dies and it was their fault. It was much worse with Emma."

"What went wrong?"

I felt myself wince at the memory. "Emma couldn't stay in the portrait chair forever, not without food and drink, and having to go to the bathroom. They went out of the edge of the photo, and never came back. We don't know why. Possibly they ceased to exist when they left the frame, but from their end they said they could see all the other rooms and places in the house just fine. We've considered animating another photograph, but it's too hard on Bridger. When they're grown and ready, then we can try more."

He nodded. "What did Emma remember? Was it their real life or an imaginary one?"

"I couldn't confirm. They remembered a whole lifetime up to death, but not a very traceable life; it was a very early photograph, from when unfamous people left few records, women more so. I found documents pointing to a couple different people who could have been our Emma Platz, but there wasn't much to trace."

"Do you still have the photograph?"

"Of course, but the miracle's worn off. The daylight in the room isn't changing anymore."

"It wears off?"

"Yes, Mem——" I caught myself, "Carlyle. For inanimate objects it's permanent, but it seems life is a special kind of miracle that doesn't last so long. Bridger has to re-miracle the soldiers every month or so, and Boo."

"Life is special kind of miracle," he repeated, half-whispered, like a prayer.

I nodded. "That's why Bridger can't just raise the dead."

Carlyle froze. "Right. Right." He paused. You and I cannot read minds, reader, but we both know the torrent of possibilities which were multiplying in Carlyle from that thought. "Did Emma Platz . . . no, it wouldn't help."

"Did Emma Platz what?"

I caught a tremor in his lips. "Did Emma Platz remember the afterlife?"

I felt my heart thrill at the question too. A sensayer's question. "No, but Pointer may tomorrow, when Bridger brings them back."

Pale skin went paler. "You've decided, then? To bring them back?"

"Not yet, but Bridger will feel sad and guilty every day forever if they don't do it. Could you resist, day in, day out, if you could resurrect a friend?"

"No. No, I couldn't. No one could."

I did not correct him. I waited for more questions, but four breaths passed and Carlyle was still mulling on the afterlife, fidgeting with his hair and watching me hazily as I crawled across the floor. I watched him in return, the curve of his little chin, the fierce blue of his eyes, almost un-natural. Many would say it is unnatural, since his mother's perfection had been handcrafted trait by trait from the finest chromosomes French ances-try offered, but Aristotle—*the* Philosopher—reminds us that man is an animal, a part of nature just as much as fruit and vine, so Danaë's too-blue eyes, too-practiced gestures, even her lotus blossom tower of glass and steel, all are as natural as peacock's plumes, or beaver dams. "Why were you given this assignment?" I asked at last.

Carlyle was still staring more through me than at me. "That is the question . . ."

Nothing could have endeared the Cousin to me more. He thought I meant it metaphysically, that I meant to ask what Fate, what Hand, what meddling spirit or inexorable Clockmaker had placed him in Bridger's path. That's all he thought of. Even after Eureka's questioning, it didn't occur to him that I was suspicious of his assignment, that I smelled a rat behind this green, young Cousin who had been granted access to this most private Humanist bash'. If there was a motive, some enemy of the Humanists, or of Andō and Danaë moving in the dark, this sweet, sincere, true vocateur sensayer didn't know.

"When you started to doubt it was real," I began softly, "was it because you thought it was impossible? Or was it because it's something you've al-ways wanted to be true so badly that, now that it is true, you're worried you just deceived yourself into believing?"

Something in the question made him hide behind his hair. "I've never wished to bring toys to life."

"Miracle. That is what you're thinking, I know it is. You said you weren't afraid of the word 'miracle.'"

"You know I can't discuss too deeply."

"You can. This isn't a session, Member . . . Carlyle. You're not my sen-sayer. I have a court-appointed sensayer."

"If this isn't a session, it's borderline illegal."

I rose; some things should not be said while on one's knees. "It's a law we have to break." I met his gaze, and held it. "We have to. In the name of science, reason, all humanity. Something is happening with Bridger, some-thing real, magical, metaphysical. We have to discuss it, test it. We have to figure out what to do. It could be the most important thing that's ever hap-pened. Or things like this could have happened a hundred thousand times throughout history, but there's some deeper reason history hid them all. This isn't a question of us risking disrupting world peace by spreading some

cult belief. This is a question of uncovering the deep truth about the prov-
able reality humanity lives in, and someday sharing that."

I want to say that Carlyle paused to steel himself, but his movements
were all the signatures of weakness: huddling, hugging himself within the
encircling looseness of his Cousin's wrap, like a child amid the covers. But
I think, in his gentle way, that was his steel. "I could say many cults have
thought the same. But you're right. The potential is too great, the immediate, human applications if we can understand this power. We can't investigate it fully without talking about the theological end as well." He took a
deep breath. "And on that note, I've been thinking, is it really right to wait
and not show Bridger to anyone until they're an adult? What if something
happens in the meantime? What if Bridger falls and breaks their neck? All
that potential gone. And even without that, there's all the good this power
could do that isn't being done in the meantime. Not raising the dead necessarily, that has a lot of other implications we have to look at, but smaller
things. Bridger could cure Stereocox."

"We have."

"What?"

"I had Bridger make a cure eighteen months ago and sent it anonymously
to Pele Chemical. Testing is underway."

"You . . . you did . . ."

"Remember three years ago when they found a treatment for Waldfo-
gel's Vein? That was Bridger too."

He swallowed. "But Bridger can do more than just cure one disease.
That healing potion can make wounds vanish instantly."

"And if something like that turned up anonymously on a lab's doorstep, all the king's horses and all the king's men wouldn't rest until they'd
traced it. We've tried to test it, but the potion transformed the microscope
itself. It's beyond current science, or at least beyond equipment we can get
at without leaving a paper trail. Hopefully science will explain it someday,
even reproduce it, but they won't learn to really understand it without access to the source. For that, Bridger needs to be ready to face becoming the
center of all the hope and envy of the world, and before that can happen
they need to learn to talk to strangers."

Carlyle nodded, but there was still an edge of huddle in his poise. "But
every day . . ."

I stood my ground. "Moral calculus like that will drive you crazy. The
people who die today or tomorrow because they don't have Bridger's potions
aren't on your conscience, any more than the people who died yesterday, or

a thousand years ago. We're doing what we can with Bridger. We're on the edge now of moving from baby steps to real steps. You're the first real step. If you do well, the second may come soon. That's all anyone could ask."

He smiled. "Yes. You're right. And I can do it well, I know I ca—" The growl of his angry stomach cut him off.

I laughed aloud. "You forgot to feed yourself today, didn't you?"

"I guess I did."

"There's a lunch box on the table," I offered, "good and fresh. Eat."

"Thank you." He took it and had started on the dainty knot before he realized. "Wait, this . . . I can't take food from a Servicer. You earned this. I'm supposed to feed you."

I almost snickered. "Bridger can make filet mignon out of cardboard. I'm not going to go hungry."

He returned my smile. "Thank you."

"Of course," I mumbled it, distracted by remembering whose delicate fingers had prepared the plump little lunch that Fate and I had placed in the Gag-gene's hands. "I mean, you're welcome. It's the least I can offer after I tackled you before. Thank you for not reporting me."

Carlyle smile grew richer. "You've offered a lot more than that. You did this very well, very gently. You answered a lot, and pushed me when I needed to be pushed. You're right that we have to talk about this, about what we think it means, that we have to use words like 'miracle,' 'metaphysics,' 'fate,' as well as 'magic' and 'phenomenon.' But you haven't pushed me to actually do it yet."

I knelt once more to my work. "It's easy to tell you're the one who's exhausted."

"True enough." He chuckled at himself. "Were you a sensayer?"

This was an unexpected stroke. Carlyle has absorbed a little of that art of cutting to the quick which the current Conclave teaches, but in him it is usually stifled by natural gentleness. I realize, reader, that I should apologize for my confusing language, since if my 'he' and 'she' mean anything then certainly this sweet and gentle Cousin in her flowing wrap should be 'she.' In this case, alas, I am commanded by an outside power to give Carlyle the masculine, to remind you that this long-lost scion is a prince, not princess, a fact which matters in the eyes of some, and of the law. But I shall do my best to remind you often that a Cousin's maternal heart beats beneath Carlyle's broad chest, and I promise, reader, to be consistent in making other Cousins 'she.'

"No, I was never a sensayer or anything," I answered. "I committed my crimes too young."

Pity touched his kind, too-keen blue eyes, willing to forgive any repentant convict, however great our unknown crimes. "Would you have been one? You have that feel when you talk."

"I don't know. I never thought that far ahead. But if I were a sensayer, and if this were a session, I think I would say now that you've had enough new revelations for one day, and that you should take that lunch box home to rest and digest. All the universe and Bridger will still be here tomorrow, as will I."

This may be the highest compliment Carlyle can pay: "You would have made a good one."

HERE ENDS THE FIRST DAY OF THIS HISTORY.

Rome Was Not Built in a Day . . .

. . . BUT IT WAS BUILT IN A YEAR, AS THE NEW SAYING GOES; Romanova, a sparkling sea of marble and bright bronze, built up from nothing in three hundred days to be the capital of our new world of Hives. In 2198, Emperor Agrippa MASON was tasked to choose a plan for the Alliance capital. Among the endless submissions of grand grids and lavish Spectacle Cities, an unofficial entry surfaced, numbered 40½, containing nothing but a cheap tourist's poster of ancient Rome, which had been slipped into the mix by a bold young secretary named Mycroft Ragbinder (or Frustinexor, to give a Mason's name its rightful Latin). The smart-aleck even labeled the ancient buildings with suggested modern counterparts: the Alliance Senate in the Senate House, the Supreme Polylaw Court in the Basilica Julia, the Sensayers' Conclave in the House of the Vestal Virgins. Agrippa MASON saw genius in the plan, a message to the world that, despite how tattered war had left the continents, this age of honeybees could build, as easily as raise a tent, the capital of capitals whose legend had named every capital to follow. This would not be the simple reconstruction of Rome as she had stood before the Church War, though that too Agrippa MASON undertook. This was greatness ex nihilo, to raise from nothing on some blank corner of the Earth the city of marble as she had stood when she had ruled the first Empire to need no name beyond *the* Empire. The evening the Alliance accepted MASON's plan, the Emperor wrote to his oldest ba'sib that he expected, if he raised this young Mycroft Frustinexor to his full potential, then, as with Phillip and Alexander, Agrippa's name would endure in history only in the tales of his successor. (*Nomen meum sempiternum, si hunc juvenem ad totam potentiam tollo, permanebit, sed, sicut Phillipi Macedonis, tantum in biographis eius qui post me regnabit.* —*Epistolae Agrippae MASONIS*, IV, iii.)

The drizzly morning of the twenty-fourth saw me with my fellow Servicers cleaning up what robots couldn't of a sewer rupture in Marseille. It was perfect work for us, work no one wants to do (especially not on Renunciation Day), the kind of work which makes free people glad that we exist to do it in their stead. And we prefer it too, since the absence of our betters frees us to enjoy the company of equals. Does it surprise you that there is camaraderie among the Servicers? Even pride? We are a strat of sorts, as united in our hearts as fishermen or Greeks or skiers are. We have ideas in common, experiences, we share stories in the dorms at night, folk music, tips about better patrons and bad, much as hoboes and beggars did in by-gone days, though you must not imagine any hidden beggar cities in the sewer tunnels, nor any Beggar King.

A man leapt from a car into the midst of the mess, seized me by the collar, and shook me so violently that my hat flew off into the muck. "How many times, Mycroft?" he shouted in my face. "I've been calling for two hours! You're not allowed to waste yourself like this!"

"Hey!" One of my newer comrades (I am not permitted to include their names) shoved forward, fists raised in my defense. "What do you think you're doing?"

Another Servicer, who knew me better, held out a restraining arm. "Let it be."

"But . . ."

"The Censor's in the right, let it be."

"The Censor?"

Perhaps you share this new Servicer's shocked awe as she recognizes, beneath a gray raincoat, the porphyry blood-purple uniform of the Romano-van Censor. If the Alliance has a face it is Censor Vivien Ancelet, embarrassed now at being caught in an act so easy to misinterpret, but even in embarrassment he was intimidating, not with physicality, but with the weight of intellect behind it. The rain made the deep dye of his uniform almost scab-black, and brought out vividly the sparkle of its gold piping, and of the Olympic stripes which rimmed his shoes, proclaiming his youthful medals in mathematics and debate. There is France in the Censor's birth bash', in his vowels and his Rs, and Africa in his face, his dreadlocks, and the darkness of his skin, but he wears no strat insignia apart from the cuff pins of his math and puzzle clubs, investing all his pride in the Graylaw Hiveless sash about his hips, and the purple uniform across his shoulders. The office of Censor is just as paradoxical in our age as it was in ancient Rome: neither executive nor lawmaker, commander nor judge, yet more potent than any in its own way. As master of the census, charged with tracking changes in membership and wealth, the Censor judges when one of the seven Hives should gain or lose a Senator, and thereby holds the balance of the planet in his hands. Since he makes and unmakes lawmakers, we may call him a grandfather of laws, and, as the most prominent life appointment in the Alliance, he is the only officer in Romanova that the media can turn into a prince.

"You're alive today for a reason, Mycroft, and it isn't shoveling shit. Get in the car."

"Yes, Censor. Just——"

"Now." He seized me by the hair, and I could see from angry faces that some of my fellows read abuse in the gesture, but it was actually a tender grip, the roughness of familiarity, as when a mother lion lifts her cub in gentle, razor jaws. "We have five hours to rerun the entire Seven-Ten list impact. Humanity needs that a lot more than they need ten square feet of pavement anyone could clear."

The truth stung. "Yes, Censor. Sorry."

The Censor's guards fanned out around us, and he gestured to one to retrieve my fallen hat. The rest, strong bodies in bold Alliance blue, pushed back my muck-stained comrades, while tiny flitting robots scanned their faces, masks of wonder and concern.

One face still showed anger. "Just 'cause you're the Censor doesn't mean you can——"

"It's all right." Again the comrade who had seen such scenes before restrained my bold defender with a soft hand. "The Censor knows what they're doing. Mycroft's a little . . . damaged in the head, and it takes some gentle roughness to get them . . . re-anchored in the present sometimes, but it's not the Censor's mind we have to change, it's Mycroft's."

The Censor—who, through long acquaintance, permits me to call him Vivien—smiled to find on hand another who understood the burden of putting up with me. Do not misapprehend, reader: all that is wrong in this scene is indeed my fault. Violence, abuse, even unfreedom is abhorrent to our good Censor, who keeps violence's great adversary, our Patriarch Voltaire, forever with him, as a bust in his private office, and a model in his heart. If you see violence here, it is not Vivien's violence, rather I infect those around me with a shadow of my own.

"I'm sorry." I let myself be hurried to the car, smiling reassurance at my fellows. "I'll be fine. See you later, everyone. Make sure you don't miss the speeches!"

"They won't but we might, thanks to you." The Censor released me to a guard, who helped me strip off my muck smock. "It's not just my time you wasted. I had to call around looking for you, interrupting I don't know how many meetings."

I winced. "I'm sorry you had to take the time to fetch me." I stepped up onto the first step of the waiting car, and paused to let its hoses rinse the refuse from my feet.

"Have you heard what's happened?"

"The *Black Sakura* Seven-Ten list manuscript was stolen, then recovered."

"Exactly." He made the car run its rinse cycle twice for him, to get the last muck off his cuffs. "Now the seventh-most-popular list shoots up to number one in everyone's attention, and all our calculations go out the window." He turned to the system console. "Romanova, Censor's office."

We started on our calculations, even as the car accelerated. Riding in one of *Mukta*'s children, the hop from Marseille to Romanova is so brief that we did not even achieve full acceleration, and Vivien set the screens to window mode, to let us savor the beauties of the capital with which, after sixteen years in office, he is still so much in love. The colored banners of the day's festivities flooded the streets, lively but almost wrong, like paint caught in the cracks of an old statue, once colored but nobler in its naked white. The cheerful gold and blue of the Alliance flag were everywhere, but Renunciation Day also brought out Hive pride, and the festoons and streamers color-coded the populations that clustered on our new Rome's artificial hills: Mitsubishi red, green and white up on the Quirinal, Gordian red, black and gold on the Caelian, European blue and gold mingling with Cousin white and azure in the valleys, Masonic gray and purple on the Esquiline, while across the Tibernov river the bright Olympic rainbow made the Humanist district even more exuberant. On such a day one can really see that Romanova is Earth's most Hive-mixed city, even more than Sydney or Hyderabad, since here the ratio of the seven Hives is fixed, not only in the city's charter, but the Alliance's. When the death of Chairman Carlyle made it no longer possible to put off picking a world capital, three issues faced the committee: the design, the distribution of the real estate which would soon be the most desirable on Earth, and who would pay. Spreading the cost equally would hit the poor Hives hard, especially the Cousins and Olympians, who then sheltered most of Earth's surviving poor, but divvying by wealth would take the lion's share from tiny, patent-rich Utopia, which could then reasonably demand the biggest slice of the land all powers coveted. The project languished ten years in committee before the Masons made their offer: we shall shoulder the whole cost of building the city ourselves, and divvy the property among the Hives by population. All we ask is that you let us choose the city plan. All welcomed the end of deadlock, so, for a mere few hundred billion euros, the Hive of myths and empires made the world capital be their copy of Rome. Has any government ever invested so wisely in propaganda?

"The Six-Hive Transit System welcomes you to Romanova." The car's voice greeted us in its recorded ritual. "Visitors are required to adhere to a minimum of Gray Hiveless Law, and to follow Romanovan special regulations regarding concealed weapons, public gatherings, and graffiti. For a list of local regulations not included in your customary law code, select 'law.'" To most, it is a formula familiar enough to bore, but it still lit the Censor's face as brightly as a mother's welcome.

"Took you long enough!"

We were met at the steps of the Censor's Office by his ba'kid, apprentice, and Chief Deputy, Jung Su-Hyeon Ancelet-Kosala, as the public prefers to order his names. Seeing Su-Hyeon now, his short black ponytail half fallen out, his gray and purple uniform veined with the wrinkles of a night spent sleeping at his desk, it felt even more surreal remembering his name on the stolen Seven-Ten list. It was true that this Deputy Censor walked the corridors of power in his master's wake, but it is as hard to imagine Su-Hyeon as a world-straddling titan as to imagine a snowy wading crane battling eagles. Su-Hyeon is absolutely tiny in that special way that only Asia's women can be tiny, as if childhood refused to leave, and kept the frame so light you fear it might blow away like grass upon a breeze, or snap like porcelain. Indeed, Su-Hyeon's delicacy makes it hard for me to stick to 'he,' and there is just enough flesh on the bone beneath his tightly tailored uniform to confirm those are a woman's hips and chest, but 'he' will be easier for you, reader, since that way apprentice will match master. Su-Hyeon had a smile for Vivien, but a righteous frown for me.

A second frown waited on the other face which welcomed us, the Censor's most promising new analyst, Toshi Mitsubishi. She is another of the adopted brood of Chief Director Andō and Princesse Danaë. Africa and Europe are cofactors in her ancestry, visible in her rich, medium-brown skin and afro-textured hair, which she wears in a thousand little twists like tongues of flame, but Japan dominates her syntax, her posture, her reflexive half-bow as we arrive, and she wears a Japanese nation-strat bracelet. The month before this I had been honored with a slice of cake from the celebrations when Toshi passed her Adulthood Competency Exam, and, at the time, I felt some smugness in having guessed correctly that, despite the honorable Mitsubishi surname, she would exchange her minor's sash for Graylaw Hiveless. She could have worked for the Censor even as a Mitsubishi Member, but the gray sash is almost a uniform in the office, required by superstition more than rule, as if these public servants would somehow make the numbers lie if they chose to bind themselves to any other law.

"Where on Earth was Mycroft?" Toshi asked at once.

"Halfway down a sewer."

I apologized to Su-Hyeon with a wince, to Toshi with a bow.

"How much have you done since I last called?" Vivien charged up the steps, already stripping the tracker from his ear as he passed the sanctum's bronze-faced gates.

"A lot, actually. The last list just came in." Su-Hyeon followed the Censor into the vestibule and tossed his tracker to the guards.

"Excellent. We made some progress in the car as well."

I held still as the Censor deactivated and removed my tracker, while his guards confirmed permissions with the police. Tracker free, and shedding even the Censor's robot escort, we passed the inner doors together, and let the Censor's sanctum seal us in. Perhaps, reader, you have never been off the network for any length of time, except on portions of the long trip to the Moon. There are now few places so secure that they forbid trackers. The unfamiliar cold of having nothing in that ear makes that inner chamber feel more special than other seats of government, as a buried temple reached by slithering down the archaeologist's tunnel feels more pregnant with the past than ruins which stand in sunlight. The extreme sensitivity of the Censor's data excuses the ritual, but it is still a ritual, no more nor less necessary than the bath one took before entering this building's predecessor in the real Rome, where it had marked the cremation spot of the Divine Julius.

"Do we have the Brillist editorial yet?" Vivien asked, plunging into his favorite sofa in the center of the octagonal, screen-walled room.

Toshi shook her head. "Just the list. I talked to the Headmaster themself as well as the editor; they promised it within two hours."

"I'll believe that when I see it. Bring up the full grid."

The walls obeyed. Shall we play a little game here, reader? First you read the Seven-Ten lists, then I shall read your mind and tell you in what order you read them, which you heeded and which you skimmed. You think I can't do it? The Censor would not call on me if I did not have some little skill at prophecy. Try me. Read naturally, skipping what you choose, not forcing yourself to study every name just so you can scoff: *Thou underestimatest me, Mycroft—I am unbiased and skim nothing.* It is not natural to study all with equal keenness, reader. Men only read every line of a contract so they may boast about it later. Read what you will—even the Censor reads only what he will.

The Romanov	Audite Nova	The Anonymous	Rosetta Forum	The Olympian
Cornel MASON	Imperator	Emperor Cornel	Emperor Cornel	The Anonymous
Bryar Kosala	Anonymus	The Anonymous	Chair Kosala	MASON
The Anonymous	Procurator Kosala	Bryar Kosala	President Ganymede	President Ganymede
Casimir Perry	Dictator Mitsubishi	G. de la Trémoïlle	The Anonymous	Bryar Kosala
Ganymede	Dux Ganymedes	Felix Faust	Chief Director Mitsubishi	Hotaka Andō
Hotaka Mitsubishi	Praefector Peregrinus	Hotaka Mitsubishi	Headmaster Faust	Felix Faust
Felix Faust	Magister Faustus	Casimir Perry	Prime Minister Perry	Casimir Perry
Vivien Ancelet	*Censor Ancellus*	*Castel Natekari*	*Speaker Jin Im-Jin*	*Sniper*
Hugo Sputnik	*Senator Carlemagnus Confraterni-domitor*	*King Isabel Carlos II of Spain*	*Tribune J.E.D.D. Mason*	*Ursel Haberdasher*
Bazyli Seiler-Cook	*~In Memoriam~*	*Southern Time Inc.*	*Senator Guildbreaker*	*Sawyer Dongala*

Are you done yet? Then I shall begin. If, reader, you are my near contemporary then you looked first for your own Hive in every list, smiling as you see your fortunes rise, scowling as foreign papers underrate you. Next, you read in full the list of your Hive's native paper, then the omni-Hive opinions of *The Romanov*, and the Anonymous (whether you agree or disagree with the Anonymous, you must know what the weightiest voice in politics believes). After that you reviewed *Black Sakura*, which history's spotlight has turned into the "protagonist" of papers. The others you skimmed,

Le Monde	Black Sakura	El País	Brillist Institute	Shanghai Daily
L'Anonyme	Cornel MASON	Emperor Cornel	Cornel MASON	MASON: Masonic
Empereur Cornel	Hotaka Mitsubishi	The Anonymous	The Anonymous	The Anonymous
Ganymede de la Trémoïlle	The Anonymous	Ganymede de la Trémoïlle	Hotaka Andō Mitsubishi	Perry: European
Hotaka Mitsubishi	Ganymede	Bryar Kosala	Ganymede	Andō: Mitsubishi
Casimir Perry	Casimir Perry	Hotaka Mitsubishi	Bryar Kosala	Ganymede: Humanist
Bryar Kosala	Felix Faust	Casimir Perry	Felix Faust	Kosala: Cousin
Felix Faust	Bryar Kosala	Felix Faust	Casimir Perry	Faust: Gordian
Lune Cassirer	*Darcy Sok*	*King Isabel Carlos II of Spain*	*J.E.D.D. Mason*	*Rongcorp & subsidiaries*
Le Roi Isabel Carlos II of Spain	*Crown Prince Leonor of Spain*	*Charlemagne Guildbreaker*	*Julia Doria-Pamphili*	*Xiao Hei Wang (i.e. J.E.D.D. Mason)*
Ektor Papadelias	*Jung Su-Hyeon Ancelet-Kosala*	*Orland Vives*	*Sniper*	*Ting Ting Foster*

noting only conspicuous changes: those who rate Cousin Chair Kosala above the Anonymous, or who raise Brillist Headmaster Felix Faust above the seventh line. And if you are not yourself a Brillist, then you turned last, and grudgingly, perhaps after you began to read this paragraph, to read the Brillist list, for you cannot in good conscience admit that you trust a stranger above the leading commentator of your own Hive, but neither can you pretend that you do not believe the Brillist Institute think tank is a greater oracle even than myself.

And if I am not thy contemporary, Mycroft? you ask. *If I am posterity instead, gazing back from centuries after these 'days of transformation' thou describest?* Then, reader, the list you rely on is the last. You skimmed the rest, eye catching on celebrities: the Emperor, Hotaka Andō Mitsubishi, those already familiar from my tale, while the rest blurred until the final list, for *Shanghai Daily* is the only paper so courteous to the future as to list the Hive names beside their leaders. If my Hives are to you as antiquated as the feudal system is to me, you must not fear that you will understand less of the story because you are not fluent in the names and ranks of my dead age; comfort yourself that these attempts to name the ten most influential people in our world are, in point of fact, all wrong, and that you see the clearer without the nearsightedness of a contemporary. You know already one name which should be on all these lists, but never could be: Bridger.

"I don't like what I'm seeing with the Mitsubishi." Su-Hyeon flopped beside the Censor on the fur-soft couches at the chamber's center. "It's never happened before that a Hive fell a notch on every other list but rose in their own primary journal. It looks like self-obsession, rating themselves so high when everyone agrees they've slipped, and, with the theft bringing everyone's attention to *Black Sakura,* the effect will be amplified."

Vivien nodded, the sofa's texture ruffling his slim dreadlocks, which fall in a shell around his head just to the shoulders, semi-stiff, like the living surface of a willow tree. "The Anonymous rated the Mitsubishi under Felix Faust this year, and there are no Mitsubishi names in the bottom three on any non-Mitsubishi list."

Su-Hyeon frowned. "It's embarrassing. It'll lower *Sam Neung* in everybody's eyes." Su-Hyeon uses the Korean name for the Mitsubishi. "They fell one notch on the lists this year, but with that it'll be as if they fell three."

No one beats Vivien Ancelet's poker face. "Toshi, what do you think?"

Toshi paused a moment to compose her answer. "I don't think it'll be that grim, not with the theft making *Black Sakura* seem important. One notch down, that's what the public will think."

The Censor stroked the gold piping of his purple sleeve as an old sage strokes his beard. "Mycroft? What are you thinking?"

I had paused to strip off my uniform jacket before the scent of sewage made too much headway in the room. "I think everyone hates Prime Minister Perry," I began. "I think the public knows Europe would be higher on all the lists if they had a more popular leader, that Europe's influence is greater than Perry's is. *Black Sakura* included Crown Prince Leonor in their bottom three instead of King Isabel Carlos to remind everyone that the next generation is coming. I think everyone will read Europe as a notch or two above wherever Perry's name appears, which puts the Masons, Cousins, and Europeans all above the Mitsubishi on most lists, even the Humanists on some. The Mitsubishi will come off as the weakest of the big five this year, by a long shot."

"Probably . . ." The Censor held us in suspense, taking a long, deep breath. "You know, any of the three of you at ten years old could have impersonated Tsuneo Sugiyama better than whoever Hagiwara got to write this Seven-Ten list."

"Impersonate?" Su-Hyeon's eyes went wide. "Who's Hagiwara?"

"*Black Sakura*'s editor." Vivien Ancelet knows every reporter worth his salt. "Whom I wouldn't have called an idiot before today. Didn't want to disappoint the readership, I guess, probably strong-armed some unsuspecting intern into writing it, but step one of faking a star reporter's article is telling said star reporter not to message their entire gaming club to say they're taking the week off."

Toshi Mitsubishi had gone very quiet, and very stiff. It was me she stared at, and I stared back, each of us uncertain what the other had learned from her bash'parents at Tōgenkyō. I did not know Toshi well. I knew her intellect and skill, but not the human side of her, how close she was to Masami among her many ba'sibs. If I had had my tracker, I would have called Chief Director Andō to ask permission to discuss the truth. But Toshi is stern stuff, and spoke first. "It has to come out. Masami wrote the list. My ba'sib."

The Censor released a slow, hissing sigh, like a punctured balloon. "The Chief Director's ba'kid . . . This is going to be a firestorm." A deep breath. "I want to see numbers. Su-Hyeon, run what'll happen if the Mitsubishi fall to the bottom of the big five. Mycroft, do a precedent check, see if there's ever been a confidence shift this abrupt. Look especially at the 2380s, right before the Greenpeace-Mitsubishi merger."

Su-Hyeon's eyes widened. "You think there'll be a Hive merger?"

"No, but some of these numbers feel familiar, and my gut says it's from then. I'll comb older records, see if I can figure out what I'm remembering. Toshi—" He froze mid-order, catching sight of her face, her trembling lip. "I'm sorry. Nothing can stop this being hard on your bash', but at least we've caught it a bit before the public. Do you need a minute?"

She turned to the screens. "No. I'll run the Mitsubishi internal numbers, see which way Wenzhou is likely to swing if the Beijing and Shanghai blocs both try for the Chief Director's seat."

Vivien reached out, as if fighting the urge to offer her a warming hug, but he and Toshi are not quite that familiar. "I don't think your ba'pa will necessarily fall."

Toshi shook herself, the springy twists of her hair dancing like wind-swept grasses. "We won't know without running it."

We each took a wall and made the numbers dance. It is tedious work, even with the computers' aid, a thousand judgment calls as we tried to extrapolate the consequences of this crisis of confidence. We didn't only factor in obvious things, like investment trends or youths choosing their Hives this year, but subtle things too, the ratio of rice to wheat consumption, exports to the Great African Reservation, apartment rental prices, the million strands which weave through the world economy, and which we search for snarls in the weft. There was a reason Chairman Carlyle named his corporation Gordian. It wasn't, as so many think today, a symbol of that yet unconquered mystery, the brain. It was the sword which hacked the knot that Carlyle cared about, a sword he turned on clients' economic snarls. When those prophets men call economists predicted revolution or collapse in some weak corner of the globe where a subscriber had investments, Carlyle's Gordian would fly in *Mukta*'s children and evacuate everything: factories, goods, workers, families, capital in all its forms all snatched to safety in a day, like good fruit from a rotting tree. As the tremors of the Church War grew, Gordian carried out the affluent of every nation, leaving governments and poor to slit each other's throats. But *Mukta* worked as a sword back then only because those snarls were geographic. In our world all powers are global powers, and all snarls global snarls. That is why, while Thomas Carlyle could snip out the shape of a new world like topiary from the overgrowth of nations, today our Censor—with the same data at his disposal—laughs at those who put him on their Seven-Ten lists: Vivien Ancelet, the world's accountant, maker of Senators but slave of numbers, helpless as the astronomer who watches the universe's pool balls act out their predetermined dance.

"Run it again," he ordered the instant we had our answers. "Su-Hyeon, you're blurring the differences between different Hiveless too much; Whitelaws side with Cousins as often as with Graylaws, factor that in. Toshi, you're underestimating the pro-Mitsubishi pull of the Indian ethnic strats in the Humanists and Gordian. Mycroft, quit pretending Europe is mucking about without a government; Casimir Perry may be unpopular with Greeks and Spaniards, but they have plenty of supporters: Poles, Georgians, Filipinos, South Africans, tons of EU strats. Deal with it."

It takes Su-Hyeon or me twelve minutes to run the numbers once. Toshi, whose dark fingers play spreadsheets as fluently as harp-strings, can manage it in eight. The Censor would demand twenty-one revisions before Su-Hyeon couldn't take it anymore. "I did factor in the increase in Humanists visiting the Moon this time! Cells HH26 and HN56, are you blind?"

Vivien stayed stern. "That doesn't account for the possibility of third-time visits. Run it again."

"Third-time visits drop out in the margin of error. I've had the same answer the last five times you had me rerun this. If you don't like my numbers then give me a different starting factor."

Toshi leapt to Su-Hyeon's defense. "I agree. We're all coming up with two-year projections of Mitsubishi population down 0.62 percent, land holdings up 0.88 percent and income down 0.62 percent no matter what we try." Fear not, reader. I do not give these numbers because I expect you to remember them or understand, but only to demystify that cave of mysteries which is the Censor's office. It is not some clandestine shrine where secret judgments determine the fate of men. It is simply the world's most high-security calculator.

"Run it again."

"There's no point. The Mitsubishi are losing another Senator this year and the Masons are gaining two no matter how we cut this up."

"It's a holiday! You don't want to be here all day any more than we do."

The Censor's voice took on that granite timbre he usually reserves for announcing Senatorial evictions. "Run it again factoring in Chief Director Andō being publically accused of personally manipulating the *Black Sakura* Seven-Ten list."

It was better not to make them wait. "I've run those numbers already." I summoned my chart, glad I could at least help Toshi and Su-Hyeon toward the freedom to enjoy the afternoon.

Su-Hyeon released a low whistle.

"That can't be right." Toshi was staring. "Mitsubishi population down 1.89 percent, land holdings up 1.51 percent, income down 2.12 percent? That's too extreme. Rome wasn't built in a day, Mycroft, it's not going to fall apart in a day either."

"It's correct." I scrolled the details past her.

"It can't be . . . that many Graylaw Hiveless becoming Masons?" I watched Toshi's eyes dance as she did the quick math in her head at thrice my speed. "Six . . . eight, eight . . . up by . . ."

"Show me the totals, Mycroft," the Censor ordered. "Where it's going?"

Again, reader, do not wrestle with the numbers. Do not even read the chart unless you are an economic historian reconstructing this precarious time. Think instead of Vivien Ancelet, studying the data as a doctor listens to a child's breath, or views an ultrasound and sees disaster where the others see only blobs. His hands clench, tendons stand erect. If you cannot imagine numbers have such power to move a man, imagine instead one of his historical counterparts: you are the tutor who has sensed something strange about this youth Caligula; you are the native who sees a second set of white sails on the horizon following the first; you are the hound who feels the tremors of the tsunami about to crash on Crete and erase the Minoan people, but you know no one will heed you, even if you bark.

HIVE	POPULATION		LAND HOLDINGS		INCOME	
	current	1 year	current	1 year	current	1 year
Masons	31%	33%	10%	09%	19%	21%
Cousins	19%	19%	06%	05%	12%	12%
Mitsubishi	13%	12%	65%	67%	13%	12%
Europeans	12%	11%	06%	06%	10%	10%
Humanists	11%	11%	04%	04%	10%	10%
Gordian	08%	08%	04%	04%	06%	06%
Utopians	04%	04%	05%	05%	28%	29%
Hiveless	02%	01%	00%	00%	01%	00%

My stomach growled, not a little burble but a roar worthy of my hard morning's shoveling.

"Vivien, have you been forgetting to feed Mycroft again?" Toshi gave me the sort of frown reserved for pets. "How long since you ate, Mycroft?"

I looked to the floor. "I ate yesterday."

"Bad Mycroft. You have to say something when we forget to feed you!"

The Censor forced a smirk. "Toshi, Su-Hyeon, how about you two go get lunch for all four of us?"

"We can send out for—"

"Stretch your legs." He gave Su-Hyeon's shoulder a warm, ba'paternal squeeze. "Walk down to Chiwe's or Trois Piqûres, enjoy the day a bit, and you can check if we have any messages outside. Mycroft and I will run a few variants while you're gone. If we're efficient we can be out of here in an hour or two."

They could not refuse a command so heaped with temptations.

The Censor waited for the door to seal behind them, making the air of the room feel bottled once more. "How'd you learn to fake a stomach growl like that?"

"From the other Servicers. It's a useful trick, sir." The antiquarian address slipped out easily, now that we were alone.

The Censor tolerates my bad habits. «I've seen these numbers before.»

His French made me jump, dark and aggressive. «Yes, you have,» I answered.

«Population 33 percent Masons, 67 percent other Hives; land holdings 67 percent Mitsubishi, 33 percent other Hives; income 29 percent Utopians, 71 percent other Hives. 33-67; 67-33; 29-71. I've seen these numbers before.»

«Yes.»

«Twice, in fact. They were in your letter thirteen years ago, doodled in the margin with no explanation. These precise numbers.»

«I wrote that letter sixteen years ago. You just saw it thirteen years ago.»

My correction made him raise his voice. «They were Kohaku Mardi's last message. Written in Kohaku's own blood, those exact numbers, not the killer's name, not a farewell to their bash' or me, just 33-67; 67-33; 29-71.» He rose, turned toward me. Suddenly his hands seemed large. «You tried to smear it out.»

I felt myself shaking. «I have nothing to do with the *Black Sakura* theft.»

«The police thought it was a security passcode. They never found to what.»

«It might have been. I don't know what Kohaku did with—»

He stood over me, close. «What do the numbers mean, Mycroft?»

«I haven't been pulling any strings, I swear! I can't. You know I can't.»

«What do they mean?»

«It's a coincidence. Honestly, those numbers coming up now, it's chance, not design, I swear by Apoll—»

«Don't say that name!» He seized my collar once again, his eyes glistening wet with something more painful than rage. I wish he had the lawful right to hit me, reader. I do not say this as a masochist. He could, he should, he has the moral right, but the deterrents are there nagging at him: scandal, criticism, censure, law. If the law did let him hit me, reader, then I could tell you with pride that he refrained, not out of fear, but because he is a peaceful man who abhors violence, even when it is so justified. If the law would let him hit me, then it would be by his own virtuous free choice that he did not. «I'm ordering you to tell me, Mycroft, not as the Censor, as myself. You can tell me here or you can tell everyone back at Madame's.»

With that threat I could, in good conscience, surrender. «It's the point of no return, sir. It's the numbers Kohaku and Aeneas calculated were the point of no return. You know they were economic theorists as well as historians. If the Masons get up to 33 percent of the world population, they predicted nothing can stop them from growing to a monopoly, over 50 percent, within twenty years. The Mitsubishi will see it coming and try to fight back by raising rents, and if they have 67 percent of the land they'll wind up crippling the economy trying to get at the Masons. But the Utopians don't pay so many rents, they have their own land, so they alone won't suffer, and if their income is already over 29 percent that will skyrocket when the recession starts, and send the whole global surplus straight into their hands. It would be . . ."

«The worst recession in two hundred years,» he finished for me.

«Yes. Yes, exactly. But that was just Kohaku's calculation. I don't think it holds true. Kohaku didn't have a real grasp of the global power dynamic. You know they didn't. Just like I didn't back then. The ties between the Hives are so much stronger than Kohaku could ever have imagined. Think how much has changed, and what Kohaku didn't know. They didn't know Chief Director Andō's sib-in-law would become the Humanist President, they couldn't know that Caesar and Utopia would stay so close, they didn't know about you and Bryar, the C.F.B., about Spain, Perry, anything about Madame, and back then J.E.D.D. Mason was just a child! Remember the Nurturist revival Kohaku predicted, that was wrong too. Kohaku's math was brilliant, but they were working with the wrong map.»

Perhaps, my distant reader, you are floundering again among the names and details of our forgotten politics. The specifics mean little, it is the fact of these hidden ties that matter. Think of them like the wires hidden in a stage magician's scarf, which make it seem that the rabbit is still hidden underneath, though it has long since been spirited away. Kohaku had thought there was still a rabbit—as, in early days, did I.

«You're saying we can stop it from escalating.»

«You have your emergency powers. You can pull things back. But you may not have to. The strings already working in the world will pull it back themselves. The Hives are closer than Kohaku imagined. That will save us.»

The Censor backed away, passions still warring in his face: fear, anger, grief. Grief most of all, perhaps, for I caught his eye straying to the well-worn sofa spot where Su-Hyeon wasn't—no, where someone else more potently wasn't. Kohaku Mardi, dear, keen, brilliant Kohaku Mardi, a match for Toshi in speed, for Su-Hyeon in excitement. He would have been here with us, in the purple, puzzling out the warp of math beneath the warp of life, if that warp had a kinder Weaver.

«Who else knew about these numbers?»

«No one living that I know of.»

«So whoever's behind this break-in, it can't be intentional, they can't know this prediction.»

«No.» I sighed relief, even as I said it. «I think it's just some enemy of Chief Director Andō.»

«Mitsubishi strat politics, dragging the whole world down.» Vivien caught himself scowling and shrugged. «Makes Europe look almost functional.»

Here we sighed together, he the Frenchman, I the Greek. Neither of us were Members of the European Hive, or even formal members of our nation-strats, but I think having some distance just made us more aware of our emotional complicity in the past messes whipped up by Europe's fractious Parliament, and in the future messes which would rise in turn, like high tides, and seem as absurd to non-Europeans as the feuds of China's factions did to us.

Vivien flexed his shoulders and shook his head, letting the weight of remembered mourning fall away with the resettling of his dreadlocks. « Until we have proof that we're past danger, we will take Kohaku's prediction absolutely seriously. Both of us. We'll draw up a list of countermeasures today, and carry out as many of them as we can, backups upon backups.» He made me meet his gaze. «I know you always have many tasks on hand, but, since this literally impacts everyone on the planet, I expect you to prioritize it.»

«Understood, sir. I'll give it priority, believe me, I'm as scared as you are. But do you intend that we tackle this with the powers of the Censor's office? Or our private means?»

«Both. All. Any.»

I nodded. «What will you tell Su-Hyeon and Toshi? There is a limit to how many emergency measures we can propose before they'll wonder why we're so scared.»

Again he breathed that slow, deflating sigh, his thinking sigh. «Nothing to Toshi about Kohaku's numbers. Toshi will be happy enough to put in extra measures to protect Andō.»

«You don't trust Toshi yet?»

His brows narrowed. «I'd trust Toshi to keep a secret with their life, or under torture, but not under Danaë.»

I hope I managed to conceal my wince.

«Su-Hyeon . . . ,» he continued, «Su-Hyeon I'll tell at home tonight. Filling a dead person's boots is always scary, but if I'm asking Su-Hyeon to do that, they deserve to know. From me.»

The canned air of the sanctum felt warmer as we both returned to work. It was the comfort of having a plan—no, less than that—the comfort of having a plan to have a plan, of facing the looming darkness of the labyrinth but feeling prepared because we had a ball of twine in hand. It was not a map, not light to expose the monster in the dark, not even armor, but it was enough to make the task feel possible. Kohaku Mardi had been a prophet, like any good statistician, but he was not a Cassandra. We were listening, I and the greatest puzzle-solver in the world, braced back to back as the math before our eyes bled warning after warning. But we had a ball of twine.

Our comrades would return soon with baguettes and messages, but before I tell of them we must leave Romanova for a time. While you have sheltered with me in the blind seclusion of the Censor's compound, a monster penetrated Thisbe's sanctuary, so close to Bridger's door. Thus we return, briefly, to Cielo de Pájaros, where you shall see another of the wires hidden in the cloth that conspired to keep much-mourned Kohaku Mardi from realizing the rabbit was long gone.

Canis Domini

"THE SIX-HIVE TRANSIT SYSTEM WELCOMES YOU TO CIELO DE Pájaros. Visitors are required to adhere to a minimum of Humanist Law while in this zone. Since our records indicate that this is considerably more restrictive than your customary law code, it is recommended that you review a list of local regulations not included in your code by selecting 'law.'"

Dominic Seneschal stepped from the car as if dismounting an unworthy horse. He did not ring the bell, but struck the front door with a practiced fist. How will those inside interpret this creature? His suit is neither Mason nor Mitsubishi. He wears no Utopian coat, no Cousin's loose wrap, no Brillist sweater. His boots have no personalized design as a Humanist's would, but are generic, high, and black, as one might find on a museum dummy, the plastic coachman waiting on his plastic queen. His clothes are European, but too European to be the Hive marker, not tidbits of fashion like a cravat or double-breasted vest combined with common clothes, but true period costume: tight hose and britches showing off the thigh and calf, a tricorn hat, silk waistcoat which has squandered countless human hours on hand-embroidery, a coat short at the front to display the curves of hip and pelvis, but with ample skirting hanging in the back, down to the knee, pleated and full enough to drape dramatically the over the horse he should be riding. The outfit is all black, black embroidery on black cuffs and waistcoat, blurring into shadow. His dark brown ponytail is curled too perfectly, like a wig, tied in the back with a crisp black ribbon. This stranger would seem at home at Versailles, or with the Jacobins scheming revolution in their basements, but nothing anchors him to our society except for the tracker at his ear, and the black Hiveless sash which swishes lush around his hips, its warning stark as a poison label: here stands a Blacklaw.

Art thou certain, Mycroft, that thou appliest thine own formula correctly? Here thou describest silks and embroidery, curls and ribbons, pleats and skirting, and appliest 'he'? I know the name Dominic Seneschal, and know too there are breasts beneath that taut waistcoat, that the thigh and pelvis which the coat's high cut displays are very much a woman's. If thou must have thy fetishizing pronouns, shouldst thou not write 'she,' when 'she' is so garishly proclaimed?

Innocent reader, I take comfort in your confusion, for it is a sign of healthy days if you are illiterate in the signal-flags of segregation humanity has worked so hard to leave behind. In certain centuries these high, tight boots, these pleats and ponytail might indeed have coded female, but I warned you, reader, that it was the Eighteenth Century which forced this change upon us, and here it stands before you. You saw already Princesse Danaë, with the costume of Edo period Japan, and its comportment, too: modest, coquettish, fragile, and proficient at making the stronger sex risk death for her. Can you not recognize the male of that species? Though French this time, rather than Japanese. Perhaps you argue that a gentle'man' of that enlightened age is effeminate, his curls and silks, his poetry and dances, and you are right if we apply the standards of a Goth or other proud barbarian. But would you then oblige me to call all such gentlemen 'she'? The Patriarch? George Washington? Rousseau? De Sade? Shall I call the Divine Marquis 'she'? No, good master. To understand what follows, you must anchor yourself in this truth, that, by the standards of the era which sculpted him from childhood, the woman Dominic Seneschal is the boldest and most masculine of men.

Unfortunately, knocking instead of ringing was the signal kids from the science museum used when they came to visit Cato Weeksbooth. He answered eagerly, only to find instead this monster out of time, fierce-eyed, inexplicable, with the Blacklaw sash ominous around his hips, and a black sensayer's scarf draped around his shoulders like a snake's old skin. Poor Cato—who could not face even Cousin Foster, gentlest of sensayers—our Cato screamed and ran.

"Cato, what on Earth?" A woman's voice called down the stairs, accompanied by fast descending feet. "Did you start another fire?"

Cato gave no answer but the slam and lock click of his lab door.

«Quel instinct superbe!» Dominic murmured in French to himself.

"What?"

I confess that some of the dialogue in this chapter is invented, reader, for I did not see this scene, and have only incomplete testimony, but I know both of them well enough to impersonate.

"Your bash'mate is perceptive, if cowardly." Dominic smiled, though on his mask-smooth face all smiles feel cold. "I'll let myself in, shall I?"

It was Lesley who intercepted the intruder in the entrance hall. "What are you supposed to be?"

He swept off his tricorn as he bowed. "I am Dominic Seneschal. I was dispatched by Tribune J.E.D.D. Mason to investigate your break-in. Did Martin Guildbreaker not warn you I would inevitably follow?"

Lesley frowned distress, though anyone would frown distress if a 'Dominic' followed a 'Martin' into your home. "I got a notice someone would be coming." She checked the credentials with her tracker, and the security systems confirmed, robots retreating meekly before Romanova's Tribunary codes. "I would have appreciated knowing when."

"I wonder whose oversight that was." He smiled. "No need to take pains, you may go back to work. I shall sniff about the house first, I can interrogate bash'members later." Dominic has an accent, stronger than any you have likely heard, not a strat marker tinting vowel shape, but genuinely struggling with short *i*'s, initial *h*'s, the *th* on his 'the,' lifelong stumbling blocks for one who did not learn English in his first years. "Of course I recognize the famous Lesley Juniper Sniper Saneer."

Dominic knew Lesley as we all did, from the broadcast seventeen years earlier, a plump-cheeked little angel eleven years of age, with tear-bright eyes, rosy cheeks, and a largely Chinese face but enough African ancestry in the mix to shape her black hair into a halo of corkscrew curls. In the film footage, Lesley stands before a row of solemn adults, with Ockham on her right, as confident at thirteen as at thirty, and, on her left, the elusive Ojiro Cardigan Sniper, half shrouded by a hooded wrap, whom you will not find in any other bash' picture, no matter how hard you hunt. Together they tell the press that the five other members of Lesley's tiny bash'—three ba'pas and two ba'sibs—have been killed simultaneously, as their two independent cars hit one another, at a likelihood of some fourteen trillion to one. As the eldest of the Saneer-Weeksbooth children, Ockham and Ojiro volunteered to break the news to the orphan, and, with that resilient purity only children possess, the three kids have conceived a plan. Lesley will be adopted by the bash' responsible for the tragedy, and together with her new bash'mates she will dedicate herself to running and improving the system whose failures are so few, and yet so fatal. "Maybe it may be the safest way to travel ever," she declares in her childlike ineloquence, "but everything good can get even better if you try." Watching the little power trio side by side, you can see they bonded instantly, and you can see too why, when the Saneer-Weeksbooth elders watched the scene, they understood at once that, when childhood ended, Lesley's choice of which of these two princes of the bash' to take as spouse would break the tie and determine the new master of the house. Lesley, née Juniper, adopted Sniper, wedded Saneer, is today the living image of her childhood self, just as bright, round-cheeked, and energetic, and her clothing just as matted with the doodles which, then as now, flow from her like babble from a man possessed.

"Yes, I'm Lesley Saneer." Lesley planted her feet to block the corridor, her stone-solid aggression exaggerated by her heavy Humanist boots, screen cloth, so she can load a different doodle every day. "You'll—"

She gasped as, quick as a thief, the Blacklaw raised her hand and kissed it. "*Mon plaisir*, Madame Saneer. This way I think?" Grasping her waist like a dancing partner, Dominic vaulted past Lesley with a practiced leap, and trotted on down the corridor. "Martin's scans don't do justice to the tension of the room, the hum. Exhilarating."

"Wait!" She chased him. "I still have to verify your clearance personally."

He flexed his shoulders, basking in the windows' slant of sun. "You're welcome to call His Grace President Ganymede, if you want a personal reference."

Lesley testifies that, given the speed of Dominic's speech and the thickness of his accent, it took her some time to realize he was using 'he' and 'she.' "You know the President?"

"Intimately. Have you any enemies?"

The question made her frown. "Are you a sensayer? Or a polylaw?"

"Both," he pronounced with relish. "I serve at the pleasure of J.E.D.D. Mason." That he pronounced with greater relish, though, for her sake, he contracted it 'Jed Mason,' as so many do. "No enemies? I'll ask again later. Now, is there any part of the house which it would be inconvenient for me to search first?"

She planted herself in front of him. "Slow down, Blacklaw. I'm the officer in charge right now."

"In charge of keeping the lifeblood of the world speeding on its course, I understand." He gave a nod—almost a bow—to *Mukta*.

That eased Lesley's frown a notch. "Indeed."

"And I keep the peace among the gods. I believe we are both officers in charge."

At this point Lesley strongly considered exercising her legal right to kick an obnoxious Blacklaw in the (there were no nuts) stomach. It was a reasonable impulse. The Blacklaw sash around this visitor's waist proclaims his choice to renounce all protections of the Law—Hive laws and Romanova's neutral Gray Laws—and to face the Earth with no protection but his own strength, and the restrictions others' laws may place upon their use of force. A Mitsubishi or strict Cousin may not, by their own chosen laws, indulge in fists and brawling, but Humanist Law accommodates those who sometimes wish to settle things with fists. Lesley was considering her aim when her eye caught the line of the dueling rapier almost hidden in the pleating of the Blacklaw's coat.

Dominic smiled as he saw her dark eyes catch upon the sword, and he caressed its black hilt. "When I catch the perpetrator, you can petition to have them tried under Humanist Law, but *Black Sakura* has already recommended a Romanovan panel. I would go with that, if I were you, their penalties tend to sting much more than yours. Shall I begin downstairs?"

Lesley shook herself to fight off the surreality of it all. "What do you mean you keep the peace among the gods?"

Dominic gave a deeper smile, with a soft sound, almost like a purr, deep in his throat. "I mean that, when the Seven-Ten lists are printed, there will be no name in top seven whose house and office I do not frequent. I mean that your President Ganymede is quick to call me when a crisis needs declawing, and all other Hive leaders do the same. I mean that I am how these sensitive matters are settled, are always settled, and I shall settle this one. Martin is the partner of my labors, but is too gentle to impress on people what it is we really do. We keep the peace among those gods who govern those of you who choose to have a government." Again he grasped her like a dancing partner, caressing the small of her back and using her weight for his own spin as he bounded toward the steps, lithe as a show horse. "I'll start downstairs, shall I? Out of your way?"

Lesley charged after him. "Hold on. I need to know exactly what you'll be doing, step by step."

He paused on the top landing. "The carpet is torn on this stair. You should have that seen to, someone could trip and fall."

"What will you be doing? Imaging? Scanning? Viewing files?"

"Sniffing about, I told you. I'm here for the smell and taste of things. Have you any enemies?"

"No," Lesley answered instantly, then paused. "You asked that before. What do you mean?"

"Anyone who would like to see your lives disrupted for personal reasons, rather than the obvious financial and political ones? A jilted lover? Family of a crash victim who blames you? A hobby competitor, perhaps? Sport? Someone the famous Sniper keeps defeating?"

Sane questions calmed her. "Not that I can think of. No one's been particularly upset by any crashes in the last few years."

He darted back up toward her, testing a vent with his fingertip, and in the same motion trapped her between his body and the wall. "No old rivals? No one wronged in an affair?"

Lesley's eyes went wide, the change exaggerated by their Chinese contours. But something kept her from shoving him back. "No."

Dominic leaned even closer, caressing the grating above Lesley's head, his chest not quite brushing hers. "Your spouse is work-obsessed." He smiled, tasting her breath and letting her taste his. "Have you had affairs?"

Blush bloomed on Lesley's cheeks. Is it a sin in your morality, reader, for a married person to admire the body of a stranger? Is she less entitled to recognize the beauty of firm buttocks, or the motions of a practiced hand? And, if you do consider it a sin, then am I right that this scene—virile Dominic with Lesley's small frame pressed against his, breast to breast— is more exciting for you because it is forbidden? Confess, reader. Something in you hungers for transgression here. *Show me, Mycroft! Strip that antique costume from the flesh beneath. Show me whether this she-man wears a strap-on, and if so have him use it! This woman Lesley, doomed from childhood to be the prize for rivals Ockham and Ojiro, let her revenge herself on them by cuckolding the victor here. Let them do it against the wall, or upstairs, with* Mukta *looking on! And, for contrast, throw in limp Eureka and Sidney lounging in the background, blind in their permanent masturbation with the computer!* It was in your mind, reader, was it not? Complete with my 'he's and 'she's which have infected you by now. But feel no guilt. It was in Lesley's mind as well, placed there by Dominic, who can summon more of the heat of pornography with a single gesture than I could with a thousand words. Like Princesse Danaë, reader, he trains.

I have no time, Mycroft, for these, thine interruptions, thy speculations, thy Patriarch, thy Hobbes. My fantasy is not thy business; give me truth. What did they do?

Lesley pressed herself back against the wall, gaining an inch of breathing room. "As a matter of fact, I haven't."

Dominic's eyes did not believe. "This is an open bash', yes? How many of your unmarried ba'sibs date outside the bash'? Any angry ex-lovers?"

Lesley is herself uncomfortable with the fact that her very sensible impulse to kick this Blacklaw in the nuts did not recur. "Cato's not interested, but Thisbe has some angry exes, yes, and the twins might too. It's hard to track what the twins get up to, but they're always dating at least two people between them, usually more."

"I see." Dominic shifted his stance, just brushing the side of her thigh with his half-hidden scabbard. "And are there rivalries within the Saneer-

Weeksbooth bash'?" he asked. "Everyone's content with who does what work, who takes what shifts, who sleeps with whom?"

"Everyone's content. Ockham and I monitor it all very carefully."

His smile widened as he leaned close enough to savor her shampoo. "All nine of you get along perfectly all the time, like little angels?"

Perhaps one as strong as Lesley did not tremble. "Bash'mates squabble, it's healthy. I said we monitor it carefully."

He retreated a few inches, testing whether her flesh would follow his. "You and Monsieur Sidney Koons are exceptions, but the other seven were all born in this bash', yes? Seven children, and none of them wanted to go form a new bash' with Campus friends like a normal twentysomething? That's very unusual."

Her flesh did follow his, though possibly just to ease away from the wall. "We like our work."

"And who's the weakest link in your bash'?" His fingers brushed the soft underside of her forearm. "If I were a criminal, whom would I want to grab and torture? Who would break first?"

The touch of skin on skin was too much, broke the spell somehow, and Lesley scowled, pressing him away. "I thought you said you were going to look at the house before you asked us questions."

"That I did, Madame. My apologies." Dominic darted back at once, down the steps quick as a dragonfly. "I'll start down here, shall I?" He threw wide the door of Thisbe's room before Lesley could reply. "There's someone in here, Madame, did you know that? Not one of your bash'."

"What?"

Dominic grasped his sword hilt as he filled the doorway. "Explain yourself."

"I'm waiting for Thisbe," came a timid voice from below. "I'm their sensayer." It was Carlyle, reader, mercifully it was Carlyle, back again with a fresh round of questions. But it could as easily have been the child.

"Right!" Lesley cried, "I'd forgotten they were back again."

"Sensayer?" Dominic repeated.

"Yes. Can I help you?" Carlyle approached, his pale face beaming energy, for he had risen full of strength that day, since March the twenty-fourth was the feast of the Norse god Heimdall, a day on which men had honored their Creator in ages past, and still do today.

Dominic read Carlyle's body as a butcher scans the contours of a pig. "You're a sensayer?"

"You too, I see." Carlyle nodded to the scarf on Dominic's shoulders. "Are you a set-set specialist? Eureka Weeksbooth was hoping for one."

Dominic stared, eyes marking the contours of Carlyle's face, the sharp blue of his eyes. "What's your name, Cousin?" He pronounced it like the French feminine *cousine*.

"Carlyle Foster."

"Carlyle Foster?"

"Yes. Is something wrong?"

"How old are you?"

Carlyle is—like Dominic and Lesley—in that medically extended stretch of youth that makes it impossible to distinguish eighteen from thirty-eight. "Twenty-eight. Why do you ask?"

"And . . . you're a sensayer?"

"Yes." The Gag-gene dug his fingers into his wrap, patterned today with abstract elephants in white on blue. "Is something wrong?"

Dominic's laugh is complex. It begins with silence, a stare which drags out for a few seconds before the first breath comes, almost a hiccup, then more silence before the next, the next, staccato gasps closer and closer until finally the voice and bitter smile arrive together as Dominic throws his head back into a climactic thirsty gasp. Carlyle shivered when he described the experience to me, and compared it to how he imagines John Calvin might have laughed as he witnessed some atrocity, smug at finding proof that this fallen world was truly as despicable as his sermons taught. Carlyle tried, he said, to ask what was so funny, whether he had done something wrong, but the horror of the laugh kept killing his words before they could take wing. In the end Dominic answered only with the merciful command, "Get out."

"What?"

"Get out of this room. You're distracting me from my investigation, Carlyle Foster." He laughed again, as if the name revealed some new double entendre on second hearing. "Get out before I change my mind. You can wait for your Thisbe upstairs."

Carlyle was quickly herded out into the stairwell, and almost tumbled into Lesley as Dominic sealed Thisbe's door behind him. To my knowledge, not even Martin has ever witnessed Dominic searching a room, so powerful is his preference for solitude. How does he work? By simple sight and touch? A concealed machine? By scent perhaps, the insanity of his devotion driving his mind to develop that sense which feels most right for such a creature? Can you imagine him, reader, on his knees, boot-leather creaking as he sniffs the carpet centimeter by centimeter? He answers happily enough to *Canis Domini*, Hound of the Lord, the old pun on Domini-cani, the Dominican monks who hunted truth and heresy in Heaven's name and that of their great founder. Whatever Dominic's technique, it misses nothing, not a hair, not a stain, not the handprint of a five-centimeter soldier on the barrel of a marker I forgot to wipe.

"Who was that?" Carlyle asked outside, still staring at the door.

"Dominic S-something." Lesley was still short of breath, but she turned a smile on Carlyle, as the two found themselves united by mutual bewilderment. "Is it just me, or is that the weirdest person you've ever met?"

"I'm something of a specialist, so I meet some odd people, but that was certainly in the top ten for weird."

She chuckled as she offered him a hand. "We haven't met. I'm Lesley Saneer."

He matched her smile. "Nice to meet you, Member Saneer."

"Lesley, please."

"Lesley," Carlyle repeated. "I think . . . I think I remember hearing about a Blacklaw sensayer called Dominic. You don't forget a name like that."

"What did you hear about them?"

"Not much. I think they're well thought of by the Conclave."

She stared. "Why?"

"I could ask."

"Please do."

He started composing a message through his tracker.

Lesley too shot off quick messages, to Ockham, Martin, two security captains, and her President's office, to make sure this improbable creature really was dispatched by Romanova. All would answer yes. "I don't know whether it would feel normal for another Blacklaw, but I don't want someone like that as my sensayer."

"My guess is they're a gadfly specialist. Some sensayers practice a special, aggressive style so you can do a one-time session with them if you really want to be pushed to the core, and then you and your usual sensayer work on the new questions it raises. The Blacklaw mystique would certainly work to enhance the feeling of danger."

Lesley, who had tasted more deeply of Dominic's 'aggressive style,' frowned.

Carlyle mustered his most energetic smile. "Speaking of returning to your usual sensayer, would you like to talk about whether or not there's some kind of divinity or divine force in the universe?"

Lesley laughed, a warm and healthy laugh, healing for both of them.

"Sure, why not. We're supposed to have a session soon anyway, we can get it over with. Good way to pass the time while we wait for that creature to get out of my house." Her feet strayed kitchenward. "Come have some figs. One of the twins was on a crazy fig kick when they programmed the tree last month, so we've got a zillion more than we'll ever eat."

Together, armed with kitchen warmth and metaphysics, the two spent a good hour erasing the after-chill of their encounter. They did not see Dominic again, they said. Nor did the others in the bash'. He might have searched just Thisbe's room, or he might passed through the whole house, silent as a plague. Either way, he vanished without another question.

A Place of Honor

Martin: "MYCROFT, THANKS FOR CALLING BACK. SUPPOSEDLY there was a device you had, that you used to disrupt the trackers and make it seem you were one place when you went another."

I: "I know the one you mean, *Nepos*. The Gyges Device, called Canner Device by many."

We spoke Latin, reader, or rather its gentled grandchild, Masonic neo-Latin, stripped of irregulars, but close enough to its imperial progenitor to invoke grand capitals and ancient marbles. I always cringe when I must translate Hive or strat tongues into common English for you, but it is worse with Martin, knowing that he thinks so differently in the two tongues, and cringes himself when he sees his words, conceived in the Imperial tongue, mangled by the vulgar. I will translate, to help you understand, but I have begged permission to leave in Latin words whose English sense is intolerably wrong. Take for example *Nepos*, this title of honor which marks Martin as the student, servant, intimate, and protégé of his Emperor, trusted even to sign laws and contracts in the Emperor's name. To render *Nepos* as 'Nephew' for you would be one part translation, three parts lie.

Martin: "I believe the device might have been used in this *Black Sakura* theft."

I: "I saw your scan of the folded paper."

Martin: "What can you tell me about the device? Could it have penetrated the Saneer-Weeksbooth bash' defenses?"

I: "Are you asking me on behalf of Romanova and the law? Or privately?"

A pause proved that Martin understood the weight of my question. "Privately."

I: "It was never in my hands, *Nepos*. I only ever had the packaging, I just pretended that I had the device to confuse the police. Please keep it private. The Inspector General doesn't know, but yesterday Princesse Danaë forced it out of me in front of Chief Director Andō. I tried to resist, I swear! They're sure to use it against me. If Papadelias finds out they'll be all over me. It could wreck my parole! Worse! I don't know what to do. I'm sorry, I should have come straight to you!"

Martin: "Calm, Mycroft, calm. The Chief Director is a friend. They don't want you locked up any more than I do."

I: "But the Princesse . . ."

Martin: "Is also a friend. Relax. I'll speak to them both about this, if you like."

I: "You will?" The promise washed the tension from me, like a welcome summer rain.

Martin: "I shall. But what I need now is for you to focus and tell me what you know about this Gyges Device. Do you know who has it? Or who made it? Reports from the original scandal blame organized crime, but when I read the report the Mitsubishi Police sent in to Romanova I found it . . . not without omissions."

The clever insult in his Latin understatement (which my poor translation butchers) cheered me enough to smile. "I investigated at the time. I believe there never was any yakuza-run secret research center, like the report claims. I believe the device was produced in secret but funded and authorized by someone within the Japanese Mitsubishi leadership, and stolen from them by traitors within the same. But I have no proof. And also, *Nepos,* if the Chief Director and the Princesse are friendly now, they will not be friendly long if we start poking at this. If it was the Japanese bloc leadership which authorized research into tricking the tracker system, Andō would not want anyone to know, especially not Caesar."

Martin: "You say powers within the Mitsubishi faction. Not Andō themself?"

I: "Not Andō, *Nepos.* I am certain of that. It was probably Andō's predecessor. But you know the Mitsubishi, that wouldn't lessen the demand that the current Japanese Director 'take responsibility' in the grimmest sense, and there is a pit of vipers waiting for Andō to stumble on the tightrope."

Martin: "You faked having the device. Do you know enough about it to determine with certainty whether it was really used in this theft, or whether this is a hoax like yours?"

I: "No, *Nepos,* I have no idea how the device really worked. Just that it affected trackers, swapping signals to make people hard to trace."

Martin: "I see."

I: "Chief Director Andō ordered me to try to track down the thieves from thirteen years ago, through the contacts I originally bought the packaging from."

Martin: "Yes, good idea. Report what you find to me. But not today. It's Independence Day. Give yourself a day to breathe, and work tomorrow."

I: "I . . . yes, *Nepos.* Thank you. You enjoy it too."

I ended the call and turned with a smile to Su-Hyeon and Toshi, who had waited with me on the steps just outside the main gate of the Censors' office, as deaf to my Latin as I am to dolphin song.

Su-Hyeon whistled in his impatience. "Mycroft, how many more messages do you have?"

"Only one more."

The last was text, in French: «Mycroft, we hear a certain thoughtless soul dragged you away from the Marseilles spill this morning before you received your breakfast. France owes you a meal; attend my party tonight. —La Trémoïlle.»

The Humanist President's order was consonant with Martin's, so I determined to obey.

"Sorry that took so long," I apologized. "Shall we get back to work?"

"No." The Censor himself intercepted us as we tried to remount his steps. He was much changed from an hour before, relaxed and energized by having mastered the data, as a musician is relaxed and energized by having instrument in hand. "The numbers are as good as we're going to get until we know more about how *Black Sakura* is going to go about announcing Masami's involvement."

Toshi winced.

Su-Hyeon frowned. "You just want to make it to the speeches on time, don't you?"

The Censor clapped his deputy on the shoulder. "So do you. Toshi, you coming?"

She hesitated, tilting her face away until her dark frizz, fiery like a corona in the sunlight, hid her expression. "I'll go home to Tōgenkyō if you don't mind. My sibs always play basketball the afternoon before the party, and I'd like to be there for Masami today."

The Censor's smile was all warmth. "Of course. Give them my best. Tell them not to worry too much. It shouldn't be hard to spin things right. I'll make some private calls."

"Thank you."

Vivien nodded in promise, then raced down the steps like a schoolchild at recess. Su-Hyeon and the Censor's Guards followed with no less energy. "Come along, Mycroft!"

Will you join us too, reader? You may object that you know the festival already, but have you ever really seen the speeches live in person? Or do you, like many, prefer your beach retreats and family dinners, and skip the history lecture? Thomas Carlyle and our other luminaries are like old candles, and can still shed new light if you pause to light them. And it will be good to glimpse the lights of our age one last time, before they fade like starlight as the sun glare of an elder era dawns once more.

We walked together along the Via Sacra, past the Rostra and the Senate House, empty for once, then around the Capitoline Hill to the teeming street which separates the Forum from the Pantheon. The stores were all flags, as if Athena had covered the city with her weavings, every strat from the Irish to the Dog Show Society adding its colors to the sea. Vendors' carts, bright balloons, candies, sausages, and paper lanterns lined the thronging street. Even the statues dressed for the holiday, vandals decking them with garlands and bedsheets, stuffing their hands with flowers and empty liquor bottles. Such defacement would have been criminal in old Rome, whose statues represented gods, but Romanova's human heroes have a sense of humor. Everyone we passed had smiles for the Censor, and good wishes, some drunk enough to be almost rude, but nothing could dim his smile, not even the teens who half-drenched him with a splash from one of his own fountains. "Hey, Ancelet! Happy Renunciation Day!"

The Pantheon is as solid as a mountain but airy too after the narrowness of Romanova's streets, as when a narrow, crawling cave opens into a massive cavern which feels vaster somehow than the open sky. Pure sun streams in through the open hole in the center of the dome, wind too, and rain, since not even the elements are denied access to this universal sanctuary. The old Romans built their Pantheon for all the gods, but even in the age of geographic nations a more Earthly passion began to fill it with tombs of founders, saviors, artists, and in Paris's copy even our Patriarch Voltaire. Our version in Romanova is well populated but far from full: our priests Mertice McKay and Fisher G. Gurai; our princes, Antonius MASON, Mycroft MASON, two Kings of Spain, the First Anonymous, the Third; our geniuses, Adolf Richter Brill and Regan Makoto Cullen; Terra the Moon Baby, of course; artists, humanitarians, celebrities, and, always with the most flowers wilting around him, the first Gordian Chairman, Thomas Carlyle.

Apollo Mojave is not with them. You should not have voted him down, reader. I know you could not understand why the Emperor and others wanted a hero's burial for this young Utopian you had not heard of until his death, but you should have trusted them. You should have. You know what the Utopians have given you, yet you grant them only one grave in the temple which honors at least four from every other Hive. Your leaders meant it when they said he was the best of us. He should be there, ungrateful reader. You should at least have granted him Olympus, since he could not join his kin among the stars.

When we arrived, the actor who was to portray Chairman Carlyle today was already at the podium between the tombs, in costume in that signature green suit with its antiquated tapered necktie. Terry Lugli has made a career of playing our world's hero in plays and films, even once playing Carlyle's namesake, the Nineteenth-Century historian Thomas Carlyle, distant great-uncle to our world hero. The historian Carlyle argued that human progress is shaped and triggered primarily by Great Men which Nature sometimes drops into our midst. What would he not have given to be able to peek into the future and use his great descendant as an example?

"Mycroft, you made it!"

"I told you they wouldn't miss it."

"You just guessed, you didn't know."

At once my Servicer fellows were around me, a sea of smiles and beige-gray dappled uniforms. They had colonized four benches in the back left corner, by the bust and ashes of Sofia Kovács, who, inspired by St. Sir Thomas More, founded the Servicer program which keeps these guilty but benign offenders from rotting in prison with the malicious and insane.

"Mycroft, want some caramel crunch? A nice Cousin bought us some."

"We saved you a seat, too."

"Right here."

They had, dead center, and I could sense the aftermath of some squabbling over who would get to sit beside me. Perhaps you cannot imagine life when you can no longer summon cars at will, when you are trapped within the reach of your own feet unless some benefactor calls you elsewhere. A benefactor too is needed to pay admission to a film, a play, a party, five euros to climb the scenic tower, one to ride the Ferris wheel. But public compassion has not left us with nothing. I count it among my few unequivocally good deeds that I petitioned to have the Renunciation Day speeches added to the short list of entertainments any Servicer may, at the kind Cousins' expense, attend.

"No working over your tracker during the speeches, Mycroft," the

Censor warned me, his dark face warm and stern at once. "I want you resting. You need it."

"Yes, Censor."

The rest around me were staring fixedly at the Censor, who tried his best to be nonthreatening, slouching to diminish his physique, but that blood-purple uniform still raises and topples Hives. There was one sure way to heal the mood. "How many of you want ice cream when this is over?"

Four hands shot up, then eleven, then all.

"You got it."

"Hurry, Vivien." Su-Hyeon tugged his arm. "It's beginning."

Together Censor and Deputy raced to their reserved seats at the front, almost in time to avoid a smirk from Terry Lugli, who waited on the podium for Romanova's highest officer to get his butt in his seat.

Those who introduce the speeches always ask you to imagine that it is the year 2131. You are terrified by the ever-climbing mortality figures of the latest attacks, more terrified at the backlash promised by the superpower, and most terrified of all by the means it has chosen to replenish its armies, thinned by long prosperity. You know that Chairman Carlyle has spent the last thirty hours cloistered with Cousins' Program Director Sofia Kovács and Olympic Chairman Jean-Pierre Utarutu, the heads of the three great *Mukta* transit groups, which can evacuate members from continent to continent to evade a draft as easily as to watch a sports match. Now these three have called a press conference, and bring with them onto the dais Europe's hero, King Juan Valentín of Spain. You cannot guess their plan, but you know it will set the shape of this new World War, and that they have most affluent third of the world's population behind them. Fear is what the introducer asks you to imagine, the anxiety of living in a world the Bomb might end at any moment, and hope too, fragile, resting in this man. He speaks:

"'When in the course of human events it becomes necessary for one people to dissolve the political bands that have connected them with another, and to assume among the Powers of the Earth the separate but equal station to which the Laws of Nature entitle them, a decent respect to the opinions of mankind requires that they should declare the causes which impel them to the separation.' These words are as true today as they were three hundred and fifty years ago, when a group of idealists set out to found a new kind of nation freer than any that had come before. The nation they founded became great, and remained great even in our lifetimes, but it is not great today. No nation, whatever its power, can be called great when it imposes tyranny upon its citizens—worse, upon people it claims as its citizens, not because they have enjoyed the fruits of its soil, or benefitted from its protections, but because by chance their grandparents were born within that blotch of color on a map it calls its own. These free people—who have never spent more than an afternoon beneath its skies—these free people proud America now commands to surrender the fruits of their labors. Why? To finance a war—no, a campaign of destruction—waged, not between peoples, but between the members of governments, and justified in the name of two gods—two interpretations of God—in whom most of those who must now pay do not believe. Worse, this so-called nation dares, not merely to ask, but to compel these free people to send their children to fight and die for a group of men they do not call leaders, against a foe they do not call enemy, over a patch of ground they have never called home. Friends, an America who would impose these orders is no longer the champion of liberty its founders set out to create. It cannot command your loyalty."

I must interrupt to ask, reader: did you spot Carlyle's omission? Nature's God. As it flowed from Jefferson's pen it was the Laws of Nature and Nature's God that entitled a people to separate but equal station among the Powers of the Earth, not Nature alone. Chairman Carlyle was no atheist. What you see here is the beginning of the silence. As the first bombs of the Church War rain down, those who consider themselves neutral are now afraid to mention the divinity.

"What is a people?" the speech continues, the actor's voice resonating through the dome. "It is a group of human beings united by a common bond, not of blood or geography, but of friendship and trust. What is a nation? It is a government formed by a people to protect that common bond with common laws, so its members may enjoy life, liberty, happiness, justice, and all those rights we love. Americans, America is no longer your nation. Your nation is the friends who live and work with you, in Africa, Europe, Asia, Australia, all of the Americas, and all the other corners of this Earth. Your nation is those who went to school with you, who cheered beside you at games, who grew up with you, traded intimacies with you over the internet, and still today break bread with you in your own house, on whatever continent it stands. Your nation is the organization which you chose to protect your family and property, in sickness and in health, as you traveled the globe to find your ideal home.

"Friends, I stand here today with the leaders of these organizations, to tell you that, once again, the time has come to found a new kind of nation, freer than any that has come before. We speak today for the Cousins, for the Olympians, and for Gordian, three groups which have the means to allow a human being, or a family, to live in this world without a country, without citizenship, without obligations to any power you have not chosen to join. For more than a generation we have not just been your travel agents but your banks, your lawyers, your hospitals, your schools. Now let us be your nations. I call on all Americans who do not support this war to renounce your citizenship and trust us—any one of us, you have your pick. Let us protect you and your families in this new, free world. I call on the citizens of all other countries of the world to respect our members, and accept the passports we will issue, just as you would the passports printed by a country which can boast a blotch of territory somewhere on the globe. Join us if you like, or remain loyal to those geographic nations which still merit loyalty, but either way acknowledge us, and in acknowledging us acknowledge the right of all human beings to choose a different nation if the nations of their birth betray their trust."

Historically, Sofia Kovács took the podium second after Carlyle. No one remembers her speech, the technicalities of how to apply to join these new nongeographic nations, and how they will handle deeds and taxes, legal suits and health care. She is like the big sister packing our backpacks for the camping trip, who tries to make us pay attention as she goes through the items, but we ignore her, entranced already by the wild's call. Only later, when we find we need our bug spray and our lanterns, then we will discover that they are ready in our bags, between our lunch box and our favorite toy. We don't thank her, but she watches us frolic carefree thanks to her good sense, and asks no more.

Today the part of Sofia Kovács was played, not by any actress, but by her modern counterpart Bryar Kosala, Chair of the Cousins. She was costumed for the occasion in a woman's business suit styled after fashions of the turn of the millennium, complete with tight skirt and high heels she could barely walk in, her lush, black Indian hair woven into a stately bun, but even in the androgyny of her everyday Cousins' wrap she would still seem every inch a woman. I think there is no person, myself aside, so hated by the ambitious of this world as Bryar Kosala, since those who fight viciously to grasp the reins of power cannot forgive the fact that she could rise so high and still be nice. Think of Andō struggling make himself the main head of the Mitsubishi hydra, think of Europe's Parliamentary campaigns, of the glitter and furor of Humanist elections. Bryar Kosala just likes helping people, and is good at running things, and when invited to become the world's Mom she said, "Sure." That is what the Chief Cousin is, the world's Mom, as surely as the Masonic Emperor is Earth's stern

Father. Her Hive runs the charities, the orphanages, the nursing homes, the kind Servicer program. Her law is the most forgiving, her newspaper the most sentimental, and, when disaster strikes, she is first to arrive with nurses, soup, and playgrounds. Little wonder that this friendly matriarch, still smiling as she rules the one-point-six billion Members of Earth's second-largest Hive, is the leader whose position in the Seven-Ten lists—high? or low?—the fewest papers could agree on.

The third speech, Olympic Chairman Jean-Pierre Utarutu's, was delivered by an actor, since the Olympian Hive was long since swallowed by the Humanists, and the Humanist President has more important work on Renunciation Day than assuring a bored audience that there will still be sports teams in this brave new world. Historians insist that Utarutu's contribution was as vital as the others', and I believe it, since there were already almost a billion subscribers who trusted the Olympic Transportation Union to clear their flights as they jaunted from continent to continent for the World Cup, or the Winter Games, or work.

In the final speech, the words of the King of Spain were, naturally, read by the King of Spain.

"Friends, all this is not as sudden as it seems. These three are not rash radicals, or business tycoons drunk with their own power. They are taking an inevitable step. The European Union has long recognized that it is absurd to force someone with a father from one country, a mother from another, raised in a third, and working in a fourth to pledge allegiance to one arbitrary geographic nation. More than sixty years ago we instituted floating citizenship, so children of mixed parents would not be compelled to choose between several equal fatherlands. It was not the end of our countries. Almost everyone still prefers to have a homeland to love and return to, and the legal possibility of life without a homeland does not destroy the bonds of culture, language, and history which make a homeland home. What Chairman Carlyle proposes today is nothing more radical than extending that floating citizenship to the world.

"I stand before you today, both as a representative of the European Union, and as the King of Spain. As a representative of the European Union, I am authorized to announce that we too will be offering floating citizenship to any citizen who wants to leave America or any other geographic nation, whether involved in the war or not. Our floating citizenship will be equivalent in every way to what Chairpersons Carlyle, Kovács, and Utarutu are offering through their nongeographic nations. New floating citizens of the European Union may then apply for citizenship in a specific country if they find one whose laws and ideals match their own, or they may remain citizens of the EU only, the same two options that native-born floating citizens enjoy. Those who are frightened of your current countries may think of us as a fourth option, ready to welcome you as the Olympic Committee, the Cousins, and Gordian are.

"Separately, as the King of Spain, and with no directive from the European Union, I wish to express my personal support for Chairman Carlyle and his ideal that citizenship should be voluntary, not forced. To that end, I hereby call on all Spanish citizens—no, on all people who consider Spanish identity an important part of who they are, to show their support for that ideal by renouncing their citizenship, becoming floating citizens of the EU for twenty-four hours, and then reapplying to become Spanish citizens again, this time by choice. What we choose means more than what is handed to us by chance. I will count every citizen who leaves and rejoins my country a more loyal Spaniard, a more sincere Spaniard, a truer Spaniard, than before, and I will stand proud as the king of a people brave enough to leave our fatherland to show support for those endangered by this war, but loyal enough to return again."

The delivery was perfect. The current king, Isabel Carlos II, has watched the recording of his ancestor so many times that he knows not just the words, but the gestures and the pauses. Later this year Spain will go mad with joy as it celebrates King Isabel Carlos's sixtieth birthday, and his twenty-fifth year on the throne, but I prefer to let you meet him here in this plainer ceremony. He is a calm man, not as moving as the actors, but precise and perfect in his duties, a human man holding himself to the elevated standards of a king. His hair is not quite black, his face mild and subtly Asian due to a Chinese grandmother, and his fine gray suit today is a replica of his ancestor's, those simple suits of the early millennium when opulence was expressed only in the expense of cloth and cut. The king can only attend this ceremony today because of the recent scandal, otherwise he would be at the European Grand Parade, where Europe's second choice, Casimir Perry, has been grudgingly given the seat of honor. But we who could see His Majesty's face knew he was happier here, reciting his ancestor's address, than there delivering a speechwriter's concoction to a hundred thousand voters.

"Ice cream!"

The demand rose from the Servicers around me even before the applause had died. Oh, they discussed the performance, too, the first-timers especially, moved by the event, and by seeing three world leaders dignify it with their attendance. But a person's reflections on the foundations of our world are private, and I will not intrude on yours by offering those of a lowly Servicer.

"Ice cream! Ice cream! Ice cream!"

The chant was powerless to call the Censor away from the dais as he waited for Cousin Chair Bryar Kosala to teeter over to him on her mad high heels and plant a light kiss on his cheek. "You said you couldn't make it!"

"I was wrong." Vivien gave her a practiced squeeze, though they clunked shoulders briefly, since the costume shoes made Chair Kosala eight centimeters taller than the couple was used to. "You were great, again."

"Really great!" Jung Su-Hyeon Ancelet-Kosala demanded her rightful hug in turn.

Vivien stepped back so he could admire spouse and ba'kid together, especially what the gendered period costume did to Bryar's figure. It was striking, the crisp outline hugging breasts and hips which we usually saw only through the contoured drapery of a Cousin's wrap. The deep blue of the suit fabric enhanced the subtle amber underglow of Kosala's deep Indian skin, and the extra height exaggerated her tall, imperious beauty, the long chin, long nose, and high forehead which make her face commanding and otherworldly, almost stylized, like a mask or statue staring down at you from some lofty other-realm. "I hate speaking in this dome, I can never tell if someone else is talking over me or if it's just the echo."

"No one was talking," Vivien assured. "I think most of them were actually listening. Not me, of course."

She gave her spouse a mock shove, then saw the crowd of Servicers approaching. "Oh, hello there, [Name], [Name], [Name] . . ." I cannot list my comrades' names here; Chair Kosala herself, as Servicer Program Director, has censored them. "I won't ask if you liked it since you're bound to say you did, but tell me, was my diction clear on 'tax bracket back taxing'? I always muddle that."

My comrades were staring at the faces, so often seen on newscasts, now abruptly real.

"I don't remember, Chair Kosala." I answered, honestly. "If it had been conspicuous, I would remember."

She did not have a smile for Mycroft Canner. "What is it? You're all staring at Vivien as if something's supposed to happen."

The least timid of them answered, "The Censor promised us ice cream."

"What, only ice cream? No hot fudge, or whipped cream, or strawberries? We can't have that."

Vivien rolled his eyes.

Chair Kosala reached to comb his dreadlocks with her long fingers, not because the locks were actually mussed, but because she still enjoys the feel of them. "Be sparing with the Romanovan budget, dear, not ours. Come on, everyone. Vivien's getting us super-deluxe sundaes!"

Cheers drowned the Censor's joking groan.

"Terry, Kirabo, you come too," she called the actors over. "Your Majesty, would you care to join us?"

The King of Spain smiled across at us from near the podium. "Thank you, Chair Kosala, but no, I have another obligation. Mycroft," for privacy's sake he addressed me in Spanish, "¿did La Trémoïlle summon you to their party tonight?"

I replied in Spanish. "Yes, Your Majesty, they did."

"¿What excuse did they give?"

"A very flimsy one, Your Majesty, not worth repeating."

Spain frowned. "I spoke to J.E.D.D. Mason about this invasion of the Saneer-Weeksbooth bash'." Of course, His Majesty did not say "Jed Mason," but as I approximate Spanish with English, so I substitute the name you recognize for one you would not. "They see more in this than just a prank."

"Then I believe it," I answered. "Thank you for broaching the question; someone had to."

"Yes. Until tonight, Mycroft."

I bobbed my slouching bow. "Until tonight, Your Majesty."

Chair Kosala and the Censor watched as Spain graced me with his words, but they would not intrude. As for my fellow Servicers, most here knew me well enough not to be surprised, and the rest would mistake me for a Spaniard.

An aide came now, and offered the Cousin Chair sane shoes in trade for her costume heels. "To the sundae bar!" she cried, and strode down the aisle like Athena before her armies, bodyguards holding the flanks like victories. She usually has at least four guards, though on this crowded day I spotted ten, glad of their numbers as the convicts schooled around their ward.

I did not follow the happy band of princes and paupers, united here by the magic of sugar and cream. Only Su-Hyeon noticed that I lagged behind. "Mycroft, you coming?"

"I'll catch up. We have only honored four of our heroes today. I should pay my respects to the rest before departing."

Hearing my reason, Su-Hyeon joined me. We visited each tomb around the dome in turn, rereading epitaphs, admiring busts, and contemplating the many different human foundation blocks which formed our world. It was somewhat satisfying, but only somewhat. Jung Su-Hyeon Ancelet-Kosala is a good person, a worthy successor to the Censor and deserving of a place on a legitimate Seven-Ten list someday. But Su-Hyeon, like you, reader, would not have understood if I explained that the grave I most wished to honor was not there in the Pantheon.

CHAPTER THE NINTH

Every Soul That Ever Died

"THISBE, I LOVE YOU!"

"Go away or I'll call the police."

"We have something special here, Thisbe! Something eternal! I know you felt it too, that night on the cliffs. How can you throw that away?"

"*We* don't have anything, *you* have an obsession. Now leave, and if I ever catch you around here again I'll have one of my ba'sibs break both your kneecaps."

"You're torturing me, Thisbe!"

"You brought this on yourself."

"I can't live without you!"

"Then go away and die!"

The witch swept in through the front door of the bash'house with a bounce in her gait and a smile on her lips, as if she had a mouth full of chocolate truffle. Did I forget to tell you Thisbe is a witch? I know you won't believe me, but she is, a real witch, mistress of secret hexes that can warp the soul into whatever parody she wills. Did you not see, on first meeting, how her impulse was to steal Carlyle's memory with her pill-potions? That was a witch's instinct, as is the pride she takes here in a discarded lover's pain. You find it strange that I trusted a witch to guard Bridger? I would not bring any normal child to her, but for Bridger Thisbe was the perfect guardian. To Thisbe every secret, from her brother's security passwords to my name, is another chapter for her spellbook arsenal, and Bridger is the greatest spell of all.

"Hi, Lesley!" Thisbe beamed as she entered the living room and found, slouched in the comfort of the sofa, her dear . . . actually it is difficult to decide whether to call Lesley Thisbe's ba'sib or her bash'mate, since adopted Lesley is not a ba'sib born in Thisbe's bash', but neither is she a bash'mate chosen in adulthood. Either way, Thisbe smiles on her like family. "Oh, and Carlyle, you're here too, good." She nodded to the sensayer, who had made a nest of cushions on the sofa opposite. "Sorry to keep you waiting.

I'm sure you want to get our session done so you can get back to the festivities."

Lesley scooted forward on the sofa, ruining the doodles her fingertip had traced into the plush. "Is Holly stalking you again?"

"No, this is a new one. I'll handle it." Thisbe's fast fingers pulled the pins from her hair, and let its black torrent tumble free from the prison of a professional clip. "Did everything arrive for the barbeque?"

"Yes, though I can't imagine how the nine of us are supposed to eat all that one day. What are the twins growing in the meatmaker, a whole bison?" Lesley rose, and offered Carlyle a hand up from the couch whose down-soft foam threatened to trap him in its comfort. "Thanks for the session. Another the Tuesday after next?"

"Three o'clock," he verified.

Thisbe took the least squished fig from the still-too-full bowl on the side table. "Wait, you two just had a session?"

Carlyle smiled. "Yes, but I don't mind doing another right away."

"You're not too tired?"

He shook his head. "I do it all the time."

Thisbe chuckled. "Quite the voker, aren't you?"

Carlyle beamed. "Shall we?"

Thisbe led Carlyle downstairs to the darkness of her bedroom, which showed no sign of Dominic's intrusion. But she did not stop there, stepping out instead into the wildflower trench.

"Are you taking me to them?" Carlyle felt the need to whisper it. "To Bridger?"

"Yes."

Carlyle tiptoed behind her, savoring the song of insects, the buffeting of grass fluff aglow with slanting sun. To an expert, his delight in the Book of Nature might betray something of Carlyle's own beliefs, which his sensayer's vows forbid him to discuss, but I will not strip him naked yet. Eavesdropping through Thisbe's tracker, I caught the warning whistle of the lookout as the soldiers spotted the approaching pair, but I doubt that a child of peace like Carlyle could differentiate All Clear from birdsong.

"Welcome, Carlyle, Thisbe. Thanks for coming out on a holiday." It was the Major's voice, seasoned and powerful, like an old piano which sounds better than new ones because it's yours.

Thisbe spotted the soldiers, assembled on an upside-down plastic bucket, with chips of wood as benches pulled close around a small block, draped like a banquet table. "No problem, Major. I brought something special today."

"All right!"

"Three cheers for Thisbe!"

"Set it here!"

Thisbe drew a small box from her pocket, and from it unpacked a tiny banquet in colored clay: cheeses, salami, French bread, pea-sized apples and peaches, a tiny roast fowl with the brown and green speckles of stuffing painted around the edge, milk, wine bottles with tiny intricate labels, plates of cookies and croissants, even a three-tiered wedding cake two centimeters tall.

"Look at all that grub!"

"You're a goddess of plenty, Thisbe!"

Thisbe basked in their thanks as she set out the tiny meal. Most of the food was not quite to scale with the soldiers, apples the size of volleyballs in their arms, the wine bottles standing higher than the knees of the men who struggled to stand them upright, but it was close enough.

Lieutenant Aimer smiled up at Carlyle. "We usually eat ordinary food, and sawing hunks off a giant strawberry or eating a gingerbread house from inside out is every bit as fun as you'd imagine, but sometimes one just wants to break bread like a normal person."

Carlyle's eyes were bright with wonder as he leaned low over the bucket. "I can understand that. Where's Bridger?"

"Looking at a nest of baby birds." The Major pointed to some brush nearby, where the boy crouched, half-hidden by the stems.

As when a mountain climber on some cloud-locked peak grows so weary that he forgets the world around him in the pain, and pull, and pain, and pull, aware of nothing but his muscles, fog, and stone, but then suddenly a bright wind sweeps the clouds aside, and there open the boundless blue heavens, the sentinel heads of mountains thrusting through the fog floor, and the climber gasps as he sees, sovereign up above, the terrible, all-giving Sun, so Carlyle gasped at the sight of Bridger. And so he should. So should we all.

"Have they . . . ," he whispered when his breath returned, "did they make their decision yet? Whether to bring back the one who died?"

"They wanted to talk you first."

Carlyle's pale brows arched in wonder at the brave patience of this little boy. "One question for you first."

"Just one?" the Major teased.

"One above all. Can you tell me whether this is Bridger's first taste of death? The first time one of the animated toys has died? Apart from the person in the photograph, I heard about that."

A veteran's sigh is always heavy. "No, but it's the first time since Bridger was old enough to understand. There were men from both sides in the soldier playset. When he first animated us we didn't understand what was going on. There were some casualties in the minutes before we managed to spot the giant three-year-old in the sky and call a truce. Back then Bridger didn't know enough of the world to understand resurrection, and we didn't manage to keep the corpses."

"You fought each other?"

"Green versus Yellow." The Major nodded to Stander-Y, who still wore the desert beige of the opposing force. "The world has seen more causeless wars."

Carlyle's brow furrowed in sympathy.

"We all remember our war," the Major continued, "the rage of it, the cities, families that never quite existed. My men are eager to talk to you too, but they've waited this long and can wait longer. It's the boy that matters most." He turned and shouted toward the brush, "Bridger! Come. It's time."

Bridger rose from the bushes and approached, his clothing studded with chaff and seeds. Did I not describe him properly before? His clothes were almost as loose as a Cousin's: a rough, woven child's wrap with broad blue stripes, oversized enough for his hands to hide in the frayed sleeves, and baggy canvas play-pants, once khaki but grass-stained to a mottled chaos no printed camouflage can match. His face was perfect as an angel's. It's not just a pseudo-parent's love that makes me say so. Even the sloppy clothes could not conceal his fine limbs, slim and lively, like when Cupid is painted as a youth, fragile in Psyche's arms, instead of as a pudgy infant. His skin was light but not too light, and luminous, like wheat soap, his hair not pure blond but a pale brown graced with blond, like an antique bronze whose gilding has not completely worn away. If Bridger had had parents, they must have been of European stock, but he seemed more a painter's fantasy than any mother's son.

"They have a tracker," Carlyle observed as the boy approached, marking the device clipped over his right ear.

"Yes," Thisbe answered. "They have to look like a normal kid in case someone spots them. But it's not on the network, jury-rigged, our own." Thisbe smiled softly at the child, who dragged his feet as he approached, as if each longed to hide behind the other. "Come here, honey," the witch coaxed. "I brought you something too."

Mycroft, I know thou intendest this descriptor 'witch' to make me uncomfortable, but thou succedest too well. Some archaisms are nuanced, others merely gross. Kindly leave out this slur against both Thisbe and those good people in history who really did call themselves witches.

As you command, good reader, I obey.

Bridger grinned. "Is it a pretzel?"

"Way to spoil the surprise." Thisbe took out the 'surprise,' fresh in its packet from the Mennonite Reservation in Pennsylvania.

"Does it have cinnamon-sugar?"

"Maybe it does. Better taste it to make sure."

He dashed close enough to seize the treat, then hid behind Thisbe, eyeing the sensayer as a cat eyes a new footstool intruding in its living room.

Carlyle crouched to face the boy more evenly. "Hello, Bridger. Thank you for agreeing to see me again."

Bridger opened the pretzel, wrinkling his cherub nose at the steam. "We're supposed to talk about if I should bring Pointer back."

Carlyle sat back on his heels. "All right."

"Thisbe said sensayering is supposed to be private, but I wanna have the Major listen, to be safe."

"That's fine, if it's what you want."

"And Thisbe, too, and Mycroft's going to listen on my tracker."

"That's fine. It's not strange for you to be nervous the first time."

"And Lieutenant Aimer too, and Crawler, and Nogun, and Medic, and Nostand, and Stander-Y, and Stander-G, but not Looker, Looker's on look-out, and not Croucher, Croucher's back with Mommadoll."

Carlyle made his chuckle warm. "That's quite an audience."

"Is that against the rules?"

"Not if it's what makes you feel safe. But you and I, we'll be the two that talk, the others will just listen make sure you're okay. All right?"

You too shall join us, reader. You may feel like a voyeur, invading this intimacy which only the most scandalous movie dares depict. I know your fear, that if you find yourself agreeing, two of a kind in the same faith, you will have taken your first step toward a Church, and the bigotry and violence Churches vomit forth. But you must come. This will be the gentlest of sessions, as Carlyle takes a child down the many paths of skepticism, not to conclusions, but to questions. I will show you worse in time, but you will never understand this history if you do not dare read about another's God.

"Croucher says you're going to blab and damn us all, and the Cousins will take me away, and lock Mycroft up, and Thisbe will get put on trial, and Boo will get dissected, and the army men will be locked in an evil lab forever and ever, and they'll torture me, and make me make some horrible thing that'll wipe out the world."

I can't tell with Carlyle whether his easy smiles are trade tricks he learned at the Conclave, or whether he is so sweet by nature. "That won't happen."

"It won't?"

"No. Mycroft and Thisbe and everyone are taking every precaution, and I'm not going to tell any bad people about you, no matter what. I promise."

Bridger's light brows furrowed as he weighed the stranger's promise.

"Bridger, can we have a quick miracle over here?" It was Nogun who called, his voice cracking like an adolescent who should not yet be allowed in uniform.

"Yup!" The child reached between the soldiers and touched the nearest of the plastic dishes. Without sound or pomp, a glistening realness spread across the food, as when a dying man's eyes lose their sparkle, but reversed. Feasting and feast's happy murmur followed.

Bridger settled in the grass facing Carlyle and buried his arms in the folds of his sloppy sleeves. "I've been thinking," he began, "about how I'd bring Pointer back if I decide to. I could make a Frankenstein machine and throw the switch, and it would zap them to life, and that way it would be science that did it, not magic, so I wouldn't break science or anything. But then they might come back as a zombie monster. Or I could make a magic resurrecting thing, like the holy grail, or a unicorn horn, or mermaid blood, or phoenix blood, but things like that might have side effects, not just on Pointer."

Carlyle thought for some moments, which I took as a good sign, patience and digestion before he ventured words. "Then, have you decided definitely to bring them back?"

The child frowned at his pretzel. "I want to, but I feel like I'm not supposed to, like it's not allowed."

"That's a very natural feeling," the sensayer assured. "You don't know what it means to bring them back. You don't know how life and death work, if there are some invisible rules you would be breaking. Anybody would be nervous. I'm nervous too."

Bridger munched on his pretzel. "You're nervous?"

"Mm-hmm. I have to do a good job helping you decide, just like you have to do a good job deciding. So we're both nervous."

"That makes sense." Bridger scratched a small rut in the soil with his shoe. "Are there rules to death?"

Thisbe retreated to the sidelines now, exchanging glances with the Major, like parents hovering on the first day of kindergarten.

"Some people think there are rules to death. Other people think there aren't."

The child's frown disapproved of something, and, by his eager munching, it wasn't the pretzel. "If there are rules, would it be like karma?"

The sensayer nodded at the term. "Yes, karma is a good example of a rule some people think death has. And reincarnation, do you know what reincarnation is?"

"That's when you live again and again."

Carlyle nodded, watching carefully the movements of Bridger's eyes, the fidgeting of his feet, signposts of the subtle border between discussion and discomfort. "People have a lot of different ideas of different ways that reincarnation and karma might work," he continued. "If they do exist then they might have rules, and by bringing Pointer back you might affect those rules in some way. Similarly, if there is an afterlife that dead people go to, then there could be rules about that, and you might affect those rules. And there might also be rules for this world that would be affected. Lots of possibilities."

"Rules for this world?"

"Yes. Some people think there are metaphysical rules for this world, just like people think there could be for an afterlife. For example, do you know what Providence is?"

"That everything happens for a reason."

"Yes, that's right. And specifically that everything happens for a good reason. There are lots of different philosophies that believe in some kind of Providence."

"So Providence is rules for this world, like Heaven and Hades is rules for the afterlife?"

"Yes, possibly," Carlyle confirmed gently. "Remember, these are things some people think, you have to decide for yourself what you think, and you don't have to decide quickly, you can take lots of time to talk and think. If there is Providence, and everything that happens is for a good reason, then that could mean that Pointer died for a good reason, so it's good that Pointer died, and it would be bad to bring them back. Or it might be that

Providence made you have the powers you have partly because Pointer was going to die, and Providence intends you to bring Pointer back, so bringing them back would be good."

The boy frowned. "That's backwards of itself."

"Yes, well put. It's difficult to figure out what to do if you believe in Providence. Even among the people who believe in Providence—which is only some people—there are lots of different ideas about how Providence might work. And Providence is just one of many kinds of rules some people think the world might have. Or it might have none at all, and just be chaos." He leaned forward, toward the boy. "With so many possibilities it's important to be patient and give yourself lots of time to think."

Bridger: "I was thinking that maybe I shouldn't bring Pointer back if there's an afterlife, but if there isn't an afterlife then I really really should."

Carlyle: "Perhaps. But it doesn't have to be binary like that. For example, some people think there is an afterlife, but that it's better to be alive than to be in the afterlife."

Bridger: "A bad afterlife. Like Hell."

Carlyle: "Hell is one famous example, but there are other examples. Some people believe in afterlives that aren't full of torment, but still aren't as good as being alive. And some people don't believe in an afterlife at all, but still believe in karma, or Providence, in rules about life, and think that you shouldn't interfere with those rules."

The boy's brows knitted. "Then . . . then I should bring Pointer back if there's a bad afterlife or no rules, but I shouldn't bring them back if there's a good afterlife or rules? Except how do I know if there's rules?"

"It may or may not be possible to know for sure, but either way it usually takes a long time and a lot of thinking to figure out if you think there are rules or not. But," he added, seeing a flare of fidgeting proclaim the boy's discomfort, "there are some people who don't believe in rules, and don't believe in an afterlife, but would still say death isn't bad."

The last nugget of pretzel vanished now, and Bridger welcomed Boo into his lap, a mass of blue fur and affection. "How could death be not bad if there's no afterlife? I mean, you're dead, no more you. That's bad."

Carlyle stretched, letting his body signal relaxation to the child, if not his words. "Have you heard of the Epicureans? They're an interesting example."

Bridger sniffled. "Croucher called Crawler an Epicurean 'cause he likes food too much."

Carlyle: "That's one way the word is used, but it also refers to a philosophy from ancient Greece."

Bridger: "Didn't Epicureans invent the bash'?"

Carlyle: "Yes, sort of. You sure know a lot." He smiled his praise. "Neo-Epicureans invented the bash'. Neo-Epicureans lived many centuries after the original Epicureans, and they thought some of the things Epicureans thought, but mixed them with other things. When the same philosophy has different versions at different points in history, we put 'neo-' on the beginning when we talk about a later revival, to remind us that it's different from the original."

Bridger: "Like neo-Platonism came after Platonism?"

Carlyle: "You really know a lot. Wow!"

That won a little smile. "Mycroft likes to talk about philosophy."

Carlyle: "Mycroft's a good friend to you, aren't they?"

Bridger: "I like Mycroft."

Carlyle: "I know Mycroft likes you too. Did Mycroft tell you about Epicureanism?"

Bridger: "They said Epicureans think it's important to be happy."

Carlyle: "That's right. Epicureanism is a philosophy from twenty-eight hundred years ago. Epicurus thought there was no afterlife, so the most important thing was to be happy in this life. But Epicureans didn't like quick pleasures like food and alcohol and love affairs, because after you've been drunk you feel awful, or when the love affair ends you usually feel awful too. Epicureans focused on kinds of happiness that last a long time, like friendship, a beautiful garden, or thinking about philosophy."

Bridger: "Not pretzels?"

Carlyle: "Pretzels are good, but they aren't going to make your whole life happy, just the few minutes while you eat the pretzel. They're a temporary good, instead of a permanent good. And if you eat too many pretzels it can make you sick, and then you'll be less happy."

Bridger: "I want to test that scientifically!" He grinned. "Can we do that next time at Science Club? Test how many pretzels it takes to make you sick?" It was Thisbe he looked to for permission. "Can we ask Doctor Weeksbooth?"

Thisbe chuckled darkly. "I don't think so. Doctor Weeksbooth wouldn't want to run an experiment that will make everybody sick. But I bet we could ask them to do a lesson on the digestive system, so you can calculate yourself how many pretzels it could hold."

"And then I can eat one less than that!"

Carlyle smiled as the happy tangent eased the boy's fidgeting. "Science Club sounds fun."

"It is! Last week we learned about syphons, and we made a goop syphon that syphoned with no tube!"

"Impressive." He caught the boy's eyes. "It sounds like you learn great things with Doctor Weeksbooth."

"Yup!"

"Now do you want to learn with me? About how neo-Epicureanism and Epicureanism are different?"

Reframed like science class, this death discussion wasn't quite so scary. "Sure."

"Neo-Epicureanism is an economic philosophy from only three hundred years ago. So how many years newer is that than Epicureanism?"

The boy hummed tunelessly as he wracked his memory. "I forgot how old first one was."

"Twenty-eight hundred years old."

"Then the new one is twenty-five hundred years newer!"

"That's right!"

"That's easy." He looked to Thisbe for an approving nod, and got one.

"Neo-Epicureanism says that, whether there is an afterlife or not, people are healthier, more productive, and live longer if they're happy, so the government—for us the Hive—should try to make sure people live in ways that make them happy. Living in a bash' with a group of friends that you have fun with every day is one of the institutions the neo-Epicureans promoted to help people be happy. The original Epicureans probably would have liked the bash', and their ideas helped it spread, but they didn't come up with it, Regan Makoto Cullen came up with it, based on Brillism, which is another fairly recent philosophy."

I smiled as I watched over Thisbe's tracker feed. Some people talk down to children, as if they assume a small body houses a small intellect. Some people talk past them, bludgeoning them with unfamiliar words until the kids accept what they can't understand. Chance or Providence, whichever you prefer, had sent Bridger a sensayer who treated the child as an equal intelligence, just blessed with newness, ready for difficult things, so long as they were presented honestly.

"And Epicureans think it's good to die?" The child hugged his dog.

Man: "No, but ancient Epicureans thought that it wasn't bad to die."

Child: "Why not?"

Man: "Because they thought death was nothing, and there's no reason to be afraid of nothing, since it won't hurt you, it's just nothing."

Child: "But there's no more you!"

Man: "That's true. Do you think that's bad?"

Child: "Of course it's bad! You can't be happy anymore if there's no you. You can't eat, or have parties, or a dog, or play, or have a pretzel ever again! I don't like that. I don't want Pointer to not get to do that anymore."

Man: "But if you're dead you also can't be sad, or in pain, or hurt, or lonely."

Child: "That doesn't make up for it. I like me, and I like gardens, and my friends. I think everybody likes themselves and their friends. How could they think it's not bad to lose all that? I think they're stupid Epicureans."

Man: "I don't think they're stupid, but I do think you have a very reasonable objection. There are many answers to your question when you ask why they thought death without an afterlife could be good. One possible answer has to do with how different life was back then."

Child: "What do you mean?"

Man: "Epicureans thought of pleasure as the absence of pain. That is, when you aren't hurting or hungry or sad or lonely or anything else bad, that's pleasure. It's what we call a negative definition, defining something by what it isn't, rather than what it is, like 'clean' means something isn't dirty, and 'dark' means there isn't light."

Child: "But pleasure is when you feel happy or good."

Man: "That's a positive definition, saying what it is, not what it isn't. They used a negative definition instead."

Child: "Why?"

Man: "A lot of people think it has to do with the difference between what life was like in ancient Greece and what life is like now. Nowadays life is pretty good, don't you think? You aren't in pain very often, or sick, or hungry, or alone, and you don't have to worry about your home getting smashed or your friends all getting killed by raiders." He frowned in sympathy as the boy hugged his dog tighter. "In ancient Greece life was harder than now: there wasn't enough food, there was war a lot, there were lots of diseases, and they didn't have good medicine so doctors couldn't fix things. A lot of people were in pain and hungry all the time, and afraid of getting conquered or enslaved, and everyone had to see lots of friends die. If you weren't hungry or thirsty, and weren't sick, and no one was hurting you, and you weren't sad from having a friend die, that was very rare and good, so they thought of that as pleasure, a state with no pain. Can you see how that would make sense in their world?"

Bridger half-buried his face in the blue fur, sad at the thought of lives so hard. "I guess. Yeah. That's sad to think, though."

Man: "Yes, it is. But if death also meant that all that stopped, no hunger, pain, or sadness, then by the negative definition death was also pleasure."

Child: "Then why didn't they all just kill themselves?"

Man: "Some people did back then, but the Epicureans said that you should still try to be happy as much as you can in life, in simple ways that are hard to destroy, like conversation, or thinking about philosophy. You can do that even if you're sick, or alone, or lose your home in war."

The boy's jaw set, his serious face, adorable in its effort to imitate his battle-wearied guardians. "The Major and the soldiers and Mycroft told me what war is like. They say it's the second worst thing in the world."

Man: "That's an interesting definition. What did they say is the worst thing?"

Child: "Not having anything worth fighting for in the first place."

The sensayer looked again to the frowning Major and his men, thinking ahead perhaps to their future sessions, as Bridger gave him this first sample of a veteran's mind.

Man: "That's a very powerful thought."

Child: "Yeah. But we don't have to have war anymore. Life is good, good enough to be worth fighting for, but we don't have to fight. No more countries, no more armies, no more war."

Carlyle nodded. "I bet your little soldiers still have a pretty tough life, being tiny and not being able to go out into the world and meet people, and remembering the war and friends that died in it. I bet Pointer had some bad things about their life, as well as good things."

Child: "I guess so."

Man: "So before you do anything, you could think about whether those bad things might be enough to make it better not to bring Pointer back."

Hints of pain made Bridger's voice grow weak. "I don't know."

Carlyle took a deep breath. "Bridger, are you sad now?"

Child: "Yes."

Priest: "Why are you sad?"

"Because Pointer's dead." He buried his face fully in Boo's fur, the dog no longer big enough to shield the growing boy completely as it had the toddler. "It made everybody sad, me and Thisbe and the Major, everybody's sad when their friends are dead, even Mycroft."

To my astonishment Carlyle's eyes too grew wet with mourning for this plastic soldier he had never met, or perhaps the tears were grander, for the countless lost souls of the past, whom Time had taken from us. Something shifted in his posture, marking some new phase of dialogue, now that he had pushed the child this far.

Priest: "What does being sad feel like?"

Child: "It hurts."

Carlyle leaned close. "Bridger, Pointer loved you, didn't they?"

The boy wiped his nose on his sleeve. "Yes."

Priest: "Pointer was a soldier too. They loved the other soldiers, and worked hard for you, and them, did hard things, risked their life. Pointer was willing to endure all kinds of pain to help you and the other soldiers, right?"

The Major smiled a self-satisfied smile here, as if he smelled meat in the argument at last, and saw its end.

Child: "Yes."

Priest: "Did Pointer sometimes give up doing something nice and fun, like resting, to do something hard and not so fun for you?"

Child: "Yeah, lots of times. Like being on watch when it was really cold."

Priest: "So Pointer would choose to give up pleasure and face pain, for you?"

Child: "Yeah."

Priest: "Then even if death is better than being alive, do you think Pointer would be willing to be alive again to help you and the other soldiers?"

Child: "Yes," the child answered. "Yes, Pointer would want to be here to help us. Even if death is nice they'd still want to be here to help us. So . . . so then it can be okay to bring Pointer back, even if death isn't bad?"

Bridger smiled at last, and I felt the warmth of the conclusion spread through myself as well. I am no sensayer. In Carlyle's place I would have just said that death is bad, and that of course he should bring Pointer back. But that would have brought a world of pain upon the child. Do you still not see it, reader? The moral consequences ten steps further along, which Carlyle foresees as clearly as signposts on a road? If Bridger had brought Pointer back on the theory that it's always better to be alive than dead, then what about the other plastic corpses lost somewhere in the trench dust? He should bring them back. What about Emma Platz? Lesley's parents? The recently deceased sensayer Carlyle replaced? What about the stranger who died yesterday in a hospital on the far side of the world? Or every stranger, every death, back to the dawn of time? Soon the nightmare guilt that sometimes kept me up at night would kindle in the boy, and make him feel that every soul that ever died was on his conscience for not resurrecting them. But this way, deciding based on what the soldier personally would want, Bridger could bring Pointer back and still reserve the possibility of death being okay, and not take up the burden (yet) of saving all of us. At this point I sent my silent signal to Thisbe and the Major that I thought this sensayer could be trusted.

"But what if there's a God?" Only a child could ask so bluntly, reader.

I will spare you the next part. You may assume that Carlyle stayed with Bridger in the garden for another hour, leading him through the hypotheticals of Nirvana, Gehenna, Guinee, Mictlan, Hell, of nothingness, of reincarnation, of souls returning, souls merging, souls evaporating, no souls at all, presenting many options and leaving many open doors. Their conclusions were neither solely Bridger's nor solely Carlyle's, but discoveries made striding hand in hand through theology's well-trodden ground. When I returned that evening to find Pointer alive and well among his comrades, with no memory of his dead hours but a sleeplike sense of warmth and darkness, I thanked Carlyle in my heart for Bridger's smiles.

Carlyle is gentle, reader. I am not. As you follow me to President Ganymede's party and the truths beyond, remember that, as your historian, I cannot let kindness restrain me when I choose which doors I open for you, and which doors I close.

The Sun Awaits His Rival

I GIVE YOU THE RENUNCIATION DAY PARTY OF GANYMEDE Jean-Louis de la Trémoïlle, Duc de Thouars, Prince de Talmond, President of the Humanists. Versailles was not so gilded, Paris so chic, Hollywood so glamorous, nor Babylon so infamous as the town of La Trimouille since the Duke's return. The French Nobility was officially disbanded on June the twenty-third 1790, but nostalgia is more powerful than any law. So, when this young stranger bought up a clump of lots unworthy of the name 'estate' and declared himself to be the Duke returning to his ancestral lands, the locals rejoiced at this opportunity for fame and tourism. The line of Dukes de la Trémoïlle officially died out some centuries ago, but there are always bastards and lost cousins waiting for a fortuitous conjunction of wealth and DNA testing to reinstate them. The family home had not survived, so the Duke built a fantasy palace, period in style but too opulent, the gilded woodwork too elaborate, chandeliers too huge, halls too labyrinthine, fields of sculpture and topiary stretching too far beyond what the eye can take. So stunning is the ostentation of the place that Ganymede's fellow Humanists have forgiven him for spurning the Hive capital of Buenos Aires to remain here in what was—until the Duke's arrival—European turf. Photographs taken at La Trimouille are blurred by too much light, recordings ruined by too many happy voices, but to stand there blinded by a world of unbroken gold is worth the fortune one must spend to get there. It always costs a fortune, reader, for if time is money, then the hours spent gaining influence enough to receive an invitation means that every guest has paid a fortune.

Only Ganymede is not drowned out by such a backdrop. No thread of fabric touches the alabaster of his skin that is not silk or finer, and no cut of garment graces his figure that Louis XIV would not have worn. His cuffs drip with lace, his waistcoat swarms with embroidery, a monarch's costume to make Dominic seem the servant that he is. The Duke wears no colors but gold, ivory, or sometimes blue, but even true spun gold seems somehow pale beside his golden mane, which shimmers like the Sun around his shoulders. The blue of his eyes is beyond sky blue, beyond sea blue, beyond amethyst, a ferocious blue like the blue of diamonds and star sapphires, the Hope Diamond, the Star of Asia, gems who leave behind a history of murder. Clothed so, he embodies the age when a peasant, glimpsing such beauty through the window of a passing coach, might think that all his toil is worthwhile if the sweat of his back allows so noble a creature to grace the Earth. Nude he is a god.

«Mycroft, good. Walk with me, I want to talk with you.» The Duke spoke French with me, the leisurely, satisfied French of one tired of pretending he is not bitter at his Hive for preferring Spanish.

«Yes, Your Grace.»

The Duke President led me along one of his long galleries, where masterpieces jostled for space on the damask-paneled walls. The party was young yet, a mere few hundred notables chatting in corners, or listening to echoes from the great hall, where Ting Ting Foster teased the Royal Belgian String Quartet by constantly segueing from one aria into another, forcing the strings to shift course like children behind a fickle kite.

«I spoke with Ockham Saneer today,» the Duke President began, pretending to scratch his cheek so the lace of his cuff veiled his mouth from lip readers. «Apparently you were at the house during Martin's intrusion.»

«Yes, Your Grace.»

«Was Martin cooperative?»

«Very cooperative, Your Grace. Martin is offering every courtesy, and taking every opportunity to avoid establishing any bad precedents.»

«But not so with Seneschal.»

I struggled to keep my voice soft. «Dominic came to the house?»

The Duke paused to smile at a trio of Humanists who had strayed close enough to eavesdrop, but dispersed like startled pigeons at his glance. How magnanimous of the President, they must have thought, to grant a glimpse of heaven to this lowly Servicer.

«Mercifully,» he continued, «the only person the bloodhound saw was Lesley Saneer, but I'm not happy having any of my people exposed to him, especially not the Saneer-Weeksbooth bash'. That's why we're going to settle this ourselves.»

«We, Your Grace?»

«I'm lending you my eyes and ears tonight. You will channel my tracker through yours, see and hear what I see and hear. I need you to tell me whether Sniper is behind this.»

«Sniper?» The thought, obvious now, had never crossed my mind. «It's not impossible.»

The Duke President nodded. «I wouldn't put any stunt past Sniper. If this is just the prank of some enterprising Mafioso, then Ockham and Martin can take care of things, but if Sniper did this I have to know. I'll give you a nice, close look, show you the expressions Sniper won't show the cameras, then you'll know.»

«You place too much stock in my abilities, Your Grace.»

He turned his back, the bright tails of his pleated coat almost brushing my knees. «You know no one listens when you say that, Mycroft. You may rest in the kitchens as you watch. I'll summon you to report when the party's done. You don't have to be absolutely certain, your best guess will be sufficient. Give me a direction to set my own hounds; I shall do the rest myself.»

«Yes, Your Grace.»

«And Mycroft,» he called, «if anyone asks, I called you here to look for cheaters in the betting pool. Tell no one you spied for me tonight, not Ancelet, not Spain, not Andō, not Caesar, no one.»

«Your Grace, if a Certain Person asks . . . »

«Make sure that doesn't happen. We have to bury this, Mycroft.» His eyes flashed their diamond-deadly sparkle. «I don't need to point out that, if the public eye turns on that bash', it will mean the end of your comfortable little arrangement with Thisbe Saneer.»

I squeezed my hat, comforting in my hands like a child's doll. «I know, Your Grace. I'll do my very, very best.»

«Good. Now, off to the kitchens with you. Sniper won't show until I've gathered enough notables in one place to set up a worthy entrance.»

I was well installed on my stool beside the ovens by the time the Duke President reached his first targets, whom he had spotted in the Salon des Conquêtes. There was already a crowd within, but as he entered President Ganymede pressed a finger to his lips to silence all who spotted him. The lesser guests knew what he must want, and left the Duke a clear path toward Cousin Chair Bryar Kosala. She had shed her costume from the Pantheon, and was back in a Cousin's wrap, this one less a robe than a chaos of marbled scarves, a dozen shades of green, whose silk-soft chaos made her, if not the most elegant of the present elite, certainly the most comfortable. Censor Vivien Ancelet stood behind her, back to back, still in his purple uniform, the couple trying not to feel awkward among the evocative masterpieces in the aptly named gallery. In stone, in oil, in chalk, the room was crammed with First Nights: Antony and Cleopatra, Romeo and Juliet, Achilles and Patroclus, Don Juan with a variety of beauties. Jupiter appeared in his many amorous transformations, the bull carrying off Europa, the swan coiled suggestively between Queen Leda's thighs, and the shower of gold descending to impregnate the ancient princess Danaë locked in her father's tower. These were not innocent nudes, nor even half-innocent like a classical Aphrodite pretending to cover herself with an ineffective drape. These were all fully sensual, not yet in the actual act of sex, but so intent upon it one could think of little else.

Silent as a lion (which is as much a cat as any other), Ganymede prowled in between the pair. Reaching gently, he massaged Kosala's shoulder with his right hand, while with his left he stroked the underside of Vivien's palm, as lovers do inviting one another to hold hands. Neither victim glanced back, but both smiled at the touch of gentle fingers, Chair Kosala arching her back, while the Censor grasped the President's fingers, soft as a woman's, and held them warmly. Ganymede pressed his luck, moving closer to Bryar until their flesh shared heat, then craned his neck to let his breath reach between the dreadlocks and tickle Vivien's bare ear. Only then did Chair Kosala turn to see why one of her bodyguards was trying so hard not to laugh. She almost screamed. "Ganymede!"

She and Vivien gaped at the Duke between them, who smiled, looking as smug as the sculpture behind him of naked Hephaestion basking in the hungry gaze of Alexander. In fact, since Duke Ganymede himself had been the model for that particular Hephaestion, the likeness was exact.

"You see," he lectured, "this is why couples should stand together in this room, not apart."

As the pair stood frozen, Ganymede gave each kisses on both cheeks, then pressed them into one another's arms as if arranging dolls. "Like that, see? Better."

They held the pose only a moment before balking back. "Ganymede," Chair Kosala began, "I . . . we were looking for you."

"Then it was mutual. Come, there's something waiting for you on the Ruby Walk." He seized Chair Kosala by the hand, the lace of his cuff mingling with her hanging silks like the leaves and blossoms of wisteria. "Something for your bedroom wall."

Pure Indian ancestry has made Bryar Kosala's hair as rich and dense a black as any on the planet, almost dense enough to hide behind. "I thought you'd forgotten about that."

"Dearest Bryar, I never forget anything. Come along, Vivien." He dragged the Censor by his Graylaw sash. "Bryar's not going use this piece alone."

Ganymede swept out of the salon with the speechless couple helplessly in tow.

The long main gallery they entered now had a sleek, reflective red carpet, which preserved the tracks of Humanist boots, no two alike, whose custom soles stamped the receiving fibers with the sigils of the many athletes, actors, thinkers, and tricksters who played the celebrity game well enough to walk Ganymede's halls. Humanist boots are a custom nearly two hundred years old, created when the Olympian Hive, which lived for sport, merged with World Stage, which lived for concert and spotlight, to form the 'Humanists,' united by the passion to excel, achieve, improve, and constantly surpass the past limits of human perfection. I believe there has never been, nor shall be again, a government as stable as the Humanists. Rome grew mighty under Kings, then stifled as they became tyrants, forcing the bloody revolution which birthed the Republic. When that Republic's conquests outgrew the Senate's power to govern, it took a second bloodbath to return to monarchy. How many bloodbaths has France endured? India? China? Florence and Athens, trapped in their constitutions, unable to switch to monarchy when crisis demanded one voice? The Humanists alone have escaped this cycle, trusting voters to choose not only governors, but governments. Humanist elections have no short list of candidates. All may vote for anyone they please, and everyone who receives even a thousandth part of the voting pool receives in turn that portion of the power. Today universally beloved Ganymede commands sixty-three percent of the vote, and so wields sixty-three percent of the powers of government, and adds 'President' to his list of titles. The other thirty-seven percent of the power is distributed among his rivals: twenty-two and the title of Vice President to the runner-up, six to one Minister of Justice, the final nine to a council of minor celebrities currently dubbed Congress. Fifty years ago, when charisma was less concentrated in one star, the frontrunner had boasted a mere seven percent and the title Speaker, while three percent went to a Vice Speaker, and the remaining ninety to a Senate of more than five hundred names. It was a revolution, reader, a transition from republic to dictatorship in fifty years without a single drop of blood. Detractors call it a cult of charisma, but the Humanists themselves use *aretocracy*, rule by excellence.

«Grand frère!»

Danaë's greeting rang through the halls like fanfare. She rushed to her brother, the sleeves of her kimono rustling like a flightless bird which flaps in its excitement, forgetting for a moment that it is Earth's prisoner. The view through Ganymede's tracker camera was stunning as she threw herself into his arms, rivers of spring blooms flowing across her silks like a florist's window with many more colors than mere rainbow. Danaë rained kisses upon her brother, and the sparkles traded back and forth between their silks made the scene almost blinding. Such scenes are even more powerful in person, seeing the twins' eyes lock, the same gem-deadly blue; their hands intertwine, the same china doll fingers; Danaë's cheek brushing Ganymede's mane, as gold as hers. Danaë's station demanded that her hair be bound modestly back, though the sheer bulk of the coil dared one to imagine what ocean of sunlight would pour down if it were free. Her station also demanded that she not throw herself so enthusiastically upon another man in public, and her husband was not slow to place a firm hand on her shoulder.

"Hello, Ganymede. Thank you for inviting us again." Chief Director Hotaka Andō Mitsubishi's voice was cheerless as old stone. His suit this evening was spectacular itself, a rich blue like deep water, whose winter pattern of fine spirals was halfway through transforming into the ripples of a rain-spattered spring pond, koi and turtles appearing through the blue as if rising to feed.

"The pleasure is ours." The Duke crushed the orchid-fragile knot of Danaë's obi as he held her tight.

Director Andō pulled harder at his wife. "Come, Danaë, let's let your brother breathe."

Smooth as a dancer, Danaë peeled one arm off of her brother and netted her husband in its grasp, forcing the pair to sandwich her in one affectionate embrace. The photographers went mad.

"I saw the ice sculptures out front!" She shouted in her joy. "I can't believe that horse's tiny legs are strong enough to support its whole body, and Lady Godiva on top, and so much hair!"

Ganymede let his head rest on his sister's shoulder as she held him. "That's nothing. Wait until you see out back. The whole hedge maze is iced so you can skate the entire course, and it's lit so the colors change each time you move, like skating on the Northern Lights."

"Oh, we must have a race!" She gave her twin and husband each a fresh kiss before letting go. "Wouldn't that be marvelous? I bet I can make it through the whole maze faster than either of you!"

The gentlemen exchanged a chuckle.

"Come, come, let's race!" Her eyes pleaded with her husband's. "It would be such fun, and we can invite the others! His Majesty, Bryar and Vivien, the Emperor, and Felix—can dear Felix skate?"

Ganymede peeled himself away just enough to tap the front of her obi, which bound her belly as tightly as a corset. "And just how do you propose to skate in that?"

"Easy, I'll see which one of you is faster, then I'll hold your coattails and have you tow me through. Then at the last second I'll distract you and pull ahead to victory!"

"And how will you distract us?"

Smiling Danaë threw both arms around her husband and locked him in a kiss, while at the same time her left foot snagged Ganymede by the ankle and toppled him forward. With both still stunned, she flitted aside quick as a hummingbird, and let her brother fall into her husband's arms.

His Majesty Isabel Carlos II laughed.

Danaë had blinded the others as the King of Spain arrived. There are few people in this world whom Ganymede does not hate, but the Duke reserves a special hatred for the King. Isabel Carlos II is not the offender, nor is any Spanish king, nor any Spaniard. Ganymede's fellow Frenchmen birthed the grudge. No line so noble as his cannot boast royal blood, and with wealth, fame, and his golden presence, Ganymede is worthier than many past pretenders to France's throne. But there is no throne for Ganymede. France killed its king in our very own Eighteenth Century, and what few kings it has tried on since it discarded, like a grown man no longer comfortable in childhood's clothes. If he tried, Ganymede might convince as many to call him 'Your Majesty' as now say 'Your Grace,' but what would it mean when every member of the French nation-strat is more loyal to the Marseillaise than to the memory of Charlemagne? The Duke knows he cannot tame France to monarchy once more. That, I think, is why he lets the world call him by the celebrity nickname 'Duke Ganymede' rather than his preferred title 'Prince de la Trémoïlle'; Prince has enough of Machiavelli's stink to make a free man balk. And even if he could win France, she spread her contagious liberty to Europe, too. King Ganymede I of France would be as voiceless in the European Parliament as the Queens of England and Belgium are, or the Japanese Emperor among the Mitsubishi. Not so Spain. While the French Monarchy lay dead these six centuries, the Kings of Spain have been peacemakers and powerbrokers, kindled democracy from the ashes of tyranny, shared the podium with Thomas Carlyle, and caught the dying words of Mycroft MASON. Isabel Carlos II would have but to offer his name on the ballot for every European strat from Swedes to New Zealanders to rally to make him Prime Minister again, while if Ganymede sought power in Europe he would have to fight for it tooth and nail like a mere Casimir Perry. I cannot say whether President Ganymede actually feels himself entitled to a crown, but it is certainly the presence of the King of Spain which forced the Duke to choose the Humanists, not Europe, as his kingdom, and La Trimouille, not Paris, as his capital. That he will never forgive.

"Your Majesty." Danaë bowed stiffly, as a Mitsubishi ought. "Which of these two do you think would be faster at ice skating?"

Spain smiled his modest smile. "If you mean to win, Princesse, you should ride the coattails of the one who built the maze."

"Of course!" She turned bright eyes on Ganymede. "*Grand frère,* will you introduce me to your gardener?"

He cuffed her gently on the forehead. "Cheater."

All laughed together, and the twins exchanged fast French. In fact, between the English and flirtation, you must imagine French fluttering back and forth between the pair all evening, birdsong sibling chatter too quick for even Spain to catch.

"Oh, good evening, Chair Bryar, I didn't see you there." The King nodded his respects. "And the Honorable Censor. How are you both?"

Chair Kosala had retreated into the crowd to avoid the glitter, but stepped forward now, dragging Vivien with her. "We're very well, Your Majesty."

Ganymede stepped in. "We're about to view a new piece these two might take home with them." He offered the King a smile as sweet as the sugar coating around poison. "Would Your Majesty care to join us?"

There is always a hesitation when His Majesty addresses Ganymede, as if he considers each time which style of address to use. "Why certainly, La Trémoïlle. Lead on."

Lead Ganymede did, each step printing his own graceful signature into the carpet surface, an elaborately framed linear rendition of his coat of arms, three eaglets surrounding a chevron. "Hopefully the bookies didn't swarm any of you too terribly as you arrived. They're out in full force."

"I know, begging for hints about the lists, as if we knew anything." Danaë hung on her husband's shoulder. "The children practically had to beat them off of us. Vivien, I imagine it was worse for you?"

"Oh, unbelievable!" Chair Kosala answered for her spouse. "The way they swarmed, it was as if they thought they could absorb the lists from Vivien by osmosis!"

Danaë hid her reaction behind her sleeve. "I hope they'll flutter off when the official odds are set tonight. *Grand frère,* how long until the announcement?"

"Twenty-one minutes. And here we are. Is that not the most tender thing?"

It was an oil piece, Cupid and Psyche. Most artists choose to depict the moment of their final reunion on Olympus, or the earlier moment of betrayal, when curiosity drives the girl to break her vow not to try to see this mystery lover who comes to her only in darkness. But this artist did not show triumph or betrayal, but an earlier moment, when the lovers were still nestled in each other's trusting arms, with yet no taste of sorrow. Psyche's eyes were gently closed, while Cupid's were covered by what might have been a slim, dark mask, but in context was the blindfold which artists sometimes have Love wear. The painting was also, quite intentionally, hung in the center of the villa's largest open gallery, where hundreds gathered to see and be seen—the perfect hunting ground for Sniper.

The King of Spain was first to recover enough to speak. "A new artist?"

"Fairly new, yes," the Duke answered. "Up-and-coming new Ganymedist, Hooper Abbey."

It is odd to hear Ganymede talk of Ganymedists, but there is no excuse to call the school by any other name. It was thirty-two years ago that Lister Dalal, one of the younger New Aesthetes of the Johannesburg Campus, fell into the spell of this golden-haired exemplar of exquisite youth, then only twelve years old. At first Dalal kept Ganymede to himself, producing portrait after best-selling portrait, but as other artists begged for access to his mystery model, he realized this blossoming Adonis could become the center of his own school, hijacking the Art-for-Pleasure rhetoric of his teachers, but focusing on the idealized figure, Ganymede's idealized figure. The Duke's galleries—like most great galleries now—hold a hundred portraits which strive to capture facets of his maturing body in oil and pigment, chalk and crayon, bronze and stone. How could he fail to become Earth's most successful art dealer when half the art world was already in love with him?

"It's a bit much," was the King's judgment, frowning at the halo the dim light cast on Psyche's rosy nipples, erect in her excitement.

"And a bit dark," Andō added.

Danaë—of whom a few modest, clothed portraits hang among her brother's on the walls—shot each of them a pout. "But it's wonderful! So tactile! You can just feel the texture of those sheets, and the wings, the feathers tickling Psyche's thigh. What do you think, Bryar?"

Chair Kosala had no chance to answer, for the room went suddenly dark, as the shattering of glass and the screams of startled innocents announced the arrival of Ganymede's quarry.

Enter Sniper

FRAGMENTS OF LIGHT BROKE THE DARKNESS SPORADICALLY, like the death throes of a battered strobe lamp. A wolf's howl cut across the startled cries as guests huddled together in the dark. Security tightened around the leaders instantly, Spain's Royal Guard, the Censor's Guard, Mitsubishi forces, Cousins, the Ducal-Presidential Guard in livery of blue and gold. Their flashlights cut the blackness, at first revealing only art and wide-eyed faces, but soon one could catch the motion of machinery and great shapes assembling themselves on the ballroom floor like the arrival of a clockwork beast. Startled cries morphed into titters of anticipation, as guests rushed in from other galleries, forcing their way toward spots they hoped would have good views. Then a sudden spotlight brought the beast to life. The center of the hall, which had been nothing but a crowd of socialites, was now a mad laboratory, burbling beakers and giant electrodes raining sparks on bays of ancient vacuum tubes, while in the center a shrouded body lay on a slab, waiting.

"Throw the switch!" The speaker was a picture-perfect hunchback, looming over the machinery in a grungy laboratory smock. "Quickly, doctor, while they're still distracted! Throw the switch and bring our glorious monster to life!"

The crowd burst into exuberant applause.

"Quickly, Doctor Frankenstein! It's too late to turn back!" The hunchback didn't need to drop the name for everyone to know the character. I spotted the doctor now, cowering by a control panel. He made a magnificent Mad Scientist: his Asian black hair was uncommonly wild and wiry in the right way, his shoulders had the academic hunch under the white lab coat, and his hands, forever stained with inks and dyes, had the right inhuman thinness to let him stand proud on a poster between a Werewolf and a Mummy. Even his Chinese features in this context focused the attention on his eyes, almost as black as his hair, and greenish makeup made their glints feel extra maniacal. Poor Cato Weeksbooth. With the eyes of the world upon him, the recluse seemed about to have a heart attack.

Eager 'Igor' stared expectantly at his Frankenstein, but Cato just gaped, his jaw twitching as if he were on the edge of saying lines, but nothing came.

"Quickly, doctor! I don't know how long we can keep the villagers from invading the laboratory!"

Igor was right. The spectators had recovered from the shock of the reveal, and were beginning to advance and poke the edges of the set.

"I can't do this . . ."

"You must! There's no turning back!"

"Why'd you drag me into this? Leave me alone!"

The hulking assistant gestured with a too-huge prop wrench toward the shrouded figure, lifeless on the table between them. "You must finish, doctor! You will! There's nowhere to turn back to. You've already shattered the laws of man, of king and country, medicine, conscience, humanity. There's no forgiveness now, nothing waiting for you but the gallows or the asylum. You have only one choice! Push on, doctor! Shatter the next laws too, the laws of Nature! Then, with the powers of life and death at your command, and your glorious creation at your side, you will lord it over your enemies like a god! Throw the switch!"

I myself am not sure whether the 'unwilling Frankenstein' act was a plan, or an ad lib to cover Cato's genuine stage terror. Either way, there was a chilling passion in his "Noooo!"

"Junior Scientist Squad Attack!" Suddenly a gaggle of kids, aged eight to fifteen, with matching "Chicago Museum of Science and Industry" caps, assaulted Igor with an arsenal of homemade slingshots, water balloons, rubber band guns, and all manner of ingenious and benign projectiles.

"You leave the doctor alone, you meanie!"

"Don't worry, doc! We'll save you!"

Cato slumped back against the buzzing control panels, pale with joy as if the homemade weapons had been Athena's spear. "You came . . ."

Two girls in the back of the squad, the "big guns," fed baking soda into a vinegar bottle through a funnel and let the ensuing explosion drench the adversary. "Eat real science, phony!"

"Noooo!" Igor staggered as if the drenching were a mortal wound, and, since the vinegar spoiled the makeup, it almost was. "I won't let you stop us!" Wild-eyed, the hunchback charged forward through the hail of rubber bands, lunged past quivering Cato, and threw the switch himself.

The video footage can do the special effects far more justice than I.

There were explosions from the machines, rains of sparks, projections of monstrous faces and equations which chased each other through the smoke as if human ambition and the laws of nature were fighting it out before our eyes, and a soundtrack by Lune Cassirer which would be top seller for four weeks.

The body beneath the shroud twitched, jolts of sudden motion like the spasms of electrocution, real enough to cause some in the audience to wonder whether the equipment had malfunctioned. The body lay still next, not even breathing, letting the suspense and music build as a subtle odor of singed meat diffused through the gallery. Only as the last of the wires ceased their hissing did the body twitch once more, then rise, letting the shroud slide down slowly, like the unveiling of a statue. Makeup had reduced the flawless skin to patchwork, dozens of painted shades from north-European pallor to deep African black, which seemed to be sutured together with a gory roughness which only made the perfection of the face and limbs beneath more beautiful in contrast. It was a light, athletic, nymphlike figure, with a childish face and slender, androgynous limbs, every mark of beauty that Duke Ganymede was losing as a decade in office tainted him with the roughness of a grown-up. The monster faltered as it rose, unbalanced like a fresh-hatched chick, and slumped back against the slab, its eyelids sagging like a sleepwalker's. Desperate Igor (recovering from the assault of vinegar) pressed through the cluster of awe-silenced kids and grasped the monster's face, peering warmly into it. "Welcome to life, Sniper."

Sniper's eyes are huge like a child's, almost black thanks to a Japanese mother, but somehow the genius actor made that blackness seem to transform from dull to lively in this moment, as if it were not the electricity but this first sight of another human face that jump-started true life. "Thank you."

The crowd could not hold back its applause.

"Magnificent!"

"Spectacular! Heart-stopping!" critics raved.

"Even better than last year!"

"And far less destructive," Ganymede added, rolling his eyes in memory of Sniper's rampage in gangster's pinstripes, complete with tommy gun and femme fatale, when the techs had dropped two Model Ts through a ballroom skylight and led the Duke President's security on a fifteen-minute cops-and-robbers car chase through the galleries. The poor carpets.

Sniper, all smiles, descended from the laboratory table arm in arm with his hunchbacked 'creator.' (I confess, reader, there is some arbitrariness in calling Sniper by either pronoun, since these stunts involve female costume as often as male, and Sniper's publicity team has worked so hard to keep the public from learning the androgyne's true sex. But since I have made Sniper's two key rivals, Ockham and Ganymede, both 'he,' I shall use 'he' for Sniper, to make their strengths feel parallel). At Sniper's nod the lights returned, so guests could see and thank the black-hooded techies who had made the spectacle possible.

A mob gathered to admire the painstaking stitch-work makeup which made Sniper's naked chest and back seem to be a quilt of real transplanted skin, each patch different not only in color but in texture and moisture, some old, some young, even with the grain of hairs flowing in different directions. Shirtless Sniper is even more tantalizingly androgynous, since the delicacy of his build and tightness of his muscles makes it impossible to guess whether this torso is naturally male or an Amazon, a common enough practice among female Humanist athletes who aim at mixed sports early in life, so have the doctors prevent breasts from developing, opting out of their varied inconveniences.

"Oh, Sniper, the makeup is incredible!"

"Are you going to sell this one?"

"How much?"

"I want one!"

"I want one in kid-size, six or eight!"

Sniper slung his arms over the shoulders of two fans. "Of course, of course, the Frankenstein Lifedoll and the Classic Monster Costume Series hit stores next week, in doll-size, six, and full."

"Series?"

Sniper made a mock gun of his right hand, his signature gesture, and 'shot' a signal to his techies, who threw open the laboratory set, revealing the dolls within. There was the Frankenstein monster model, so like the living being that, had Sniper held his breath, one could not have guessed which was flesh and which plastic. Beside it sat another Sniper costumed as a werewolf, another as Dracula, another as a mummy, draped in bandages which left many parts enticingly bare. Beside the life-size models sat the small dolls, twenty-five centimeters but like Sniper to the life, and also the life-sized six-year-old models, the adorable werewolf pup with pointed, fuzz-covered ears, and little Dracula with fangs just peeking out between child-round lips.

You have seen Lifedolls before, but have you touched them? Each bone, tendon, and muscle of a human body is reproduced precisely, so a hand squeezed folds just as a friend's hand folds, and ingenious systems even keep it warm. Lifedolls are the pinnacle of man's long quest to craft synthetic love. A child with a Lifedoll cries less when ba'pas head out for an evening; a twentysomething with a life-sized Sniper stashed at home rebounds faster when love turns sour. You may call it sick when grown men and women hold these dolls as dear as bash'mates, or, with the fully anatomical Sniper-XX and Sniper-XY models, lovers. And you may be right to call it sick, but should a sickness be cured if makes its sufferers happier than healthy men? When the Lifedoll labs first decided to mass-produce a version of the vice director's two-year-old, they thought no more of it than that the child was exceptionally cute, good therapy for lonely kids and childless couples, especially because his hybrid face, mixing Asia, Europe, and South America, let small changes in costume make him seem like almost any couple's child. When it proved their best seller ten times over, they marketed the child again at age four, again at six, at eight, and it took only one fan to recognize the original on the street to open the doors to young Sniper, instant celebrity.

With the fans distracted by the new designs, Sniper disentangled himself and came to the front of his portable stage. "I thought this was a party! Let's dance!"

Sniper's techies took up their instruments. It was a parody remix of the year's top love songs with wolf howls and zombie moans for ambiance. Not to be outdone, Ting Ting Foster joined in, improvising countermelodies, and the Royal Belgian String Quartet followed, making the instrumental fabric as rich as Handel. Even we down in the kitchens danced.

Sniper himself joined in just long enough to get the crowd well energized, then descended to pose for the mob of photographers that had gathered, begging for close-ups.

The youngest of the Junior Scientist Squad frowned up at Sniper he descended the stairs. "Are you a good monster or a bad monster?"

Sniper smiled, gentle as an elder ba'sib. "I'm whatever kind of monster my creator wants me to be." He turned to Igor, who followed, her gait athletic now that she no longer faked a hunch. "What am I tonight?"

Igor smiled through the scraggles of her dripping wig. "A mostly good monster."

"Mostly good. That works." With a smile that made the patchwork face feel somehow both cherubic and roguish, Sniper leaned toward Igor for a kiss.

"Ewww." Fleeing the 'kissy-part,' the Junior Scientist cowered toward

Cato Weeksbooth, whom the other club members were escorting down the steps.

Cato was still short of breath from the ordeal. Up close he seemed, not less, but more authentically Frankenstein, his face sun-starved and pallid even without makeup, his motions very accustomed to the white lab coat. "Can I go home now?"

"Home?" Sniper clapped his shivering ba'sib on the shoulder. "The party's just starting."

"Yeah, we want our cake!" one of the little scientists cried.

"Sniper promised cake!"

Cato frowned, but not at the kids. "You shouldn't have dragged me out here, Cardigan." He hid his shaking hands in his lab coat pockets.

Sniper leaned on Cato's shoulder, inviting photos of Frankenstein with his monster, which enjoyed a brief spike among Sniper's top-selling posters. "I don't question your judgments about science, Cato. Don't question mine about panache. Now enjoy yourself. You were asking me to help your kids meet movers and shakers who could fund their projects, and I didn't use all my special passes on them for nothing."

Cato's face brightened. "Oh! Oh, yeah. Yeah, that . . . I . . ."

Sniper gave Cato a second pat. "You're welcome."

Striding forward now, Duke President Ganymede smiled on Sniper, as on a wayward but successful son. "Sniper, welcome. Well performed."

"Good evening, Member President," the little monster greeted. "Sorry I'm late as usual."

Ganymede nodded his graceful welcome. "And whose are you tonight?"

Sniper presented Igor. "Let me introduce Mycroft Isabel Senabe, Mizzie for short, one of the stars of our Blue football team for this summer." With only 124 days until the Games, no Humanist needed to follow 'summer' with 'Olympics.'

The Duke President kissed the hunchback's hand, his alabaster touch deepening the blush beneath her ruined makeup. It couldn't deepen much, though, not while Mizzie had her Sniper in her arms. Golden Ganymede is a particular kind of perfection, glorious but overpowering, unable to be anything but Sun King. Sniper has the more versatile perfection of the all-accommodating toy. Childlike and sexless, you can dress him as a monster, a princess, a Cousin, a Mitsubishi, a good boy, a bad girl, whatever your desire. Think of the nonthreatening fantasy lover every budding teen invents when not quite ready for the first time. Setting out to bring that fantasy to life, Sniper invented his own profession, Earth's first and only professional living doll. Tonight he is Mizzie's living doll, and Mizzie picked monster, but tomorrow Sniper will be remade again by the next fan in his loving queue.

"You remember Doctor Cato Weeksbooth." Sniper shoved the doctor forward. "And let me introduce the brave members of the Junior Scientist Club from the Chicago Museum of Science and Industry. Cato runs the kids' events at the museum, an amazing program, right, Cato?"

Cato could not stop trembling as he shook his President's hand. "He-he-hello."

"It's been too long, Doctor Weeksbooth. We hear excellent things about your work on the system, innovation after innovation. Admirable. We all sleep the safer knowing the Hive has you guarding its interests."

"Ye-es. Tha-ank you, Member President." I think that was the title Cato used, but it was so mumbled it might have been anything.

"If you wish to retire briefly to some private space to recover from your performance, ask any staff for the Cabinet de Colombes."

Cato's voice had real force behind it this time. "Thank you!"

"Poor Cato." Sniper mussed his ba'sib's hair. "You were great! No one could have lived the part better. But the spotlight really isn't your place, is it? Don't worry. I'd never mix you up in any real trouble. Cross my heart." Sniper spoke the last words, and made the gesture, looking not at Cato, but straight at Ganymede, holding his President's eyes with a rare expression of true gravity. Back in the kitchens, I almost laughed. Ganymede would not need my skills to translate this message. If Sniper had wanted to bring the world's attention down on Cato, Ockham, and the others, he would have done something far more ostentatious than stealing a Seven-Ten list.

"And Your Majesty," the living doll bobbed a bow toward Spain, "always a pleasure."

King Isabel Carlos II, already dancing with the twelve-year-old princess of Sweden, paused to nod.

Sniper turned his smile on the couples next. "Honorable Censor, Chair Kosala, Chief Director, Danaë-dono." He threw in the honorific smoothly, an acknowledgment to the Mitsubishi leader that the Japanese strat enjoys half credit for this glorious creature. "And your honorable security, of course." Sniper waved across the room toward the rulers' many bodyguards, who had retreated again, like spiders to the edges of their webs. "Thanks as usual for the accommodations!"

"Our pleasure, Sniper!"

"Now, everyone, deep breath! The press is waiting." The little monster shoved the Powers together. "Group photo with the Junior Science Squad and all the leaders. Everybody say 'Science'!"

"Science!"

How fine a photo, the next generation's best and brightest brandishing their slingshots, with Earth's Powers in their finery behind.

The Duke breathed easier now that Sniper's surprise was over with. "May I borrow my sister for a dance?"

At Danaë's eager nod, Director Andō passed her off to Ganymede, or tried to.

"Too slow!"

Sniper cut in razor-quick, took the Duke President in his arms, and dove into the sea of dancers like a dolphin with its toy, abandoning Igor and sparkling Danaë. The Princesse and the hunchback shrugged and, smiling, took the floor together.

It was in this phase of the party that the most valuable photograph of the night was taken, a clear shot snapped by a well-positioned hovering camerabot, which shows the Duke and Sniper, two generations' heartthrobs, cheek to cheek, and earned the enterprising photographer eleven thousand euros that first night alone. It is an extraordinary photo, angled from above so it shows everything: their eyes locked, the Duke's white-gloved hand on Sniper's bare back, even Sniper's Humanist boots, rimmed with the bronze and silver stripes of his three Olympic medals, and made of gray leather cut from the same coming-of-age stag which young rivals Ockham Saneer and Ojiro Cardigan Sniper were the only children of this generation of the Saneer-Weeksbooth bash' brave enough to help kill.

Sniper leaned close to his President's ear. "Tell me you didn't think I pulled this stunt with the Seven-Ten list." His Spanish was so whisper-light that, even with the Duke's tracker inches from his lips, I could barely make it out. "I like to imagine you think better of me. ¿Do you think I could face Ockham and the others after the siege my fans would set up around the house if the investigation tells the public where I live?"

"I believe you're not involved," the Duke conceded. "¿But then who is?"

"¿How should I know? ¿Aren't we waiting on Martin Guildbreaker to sort that out?"

Ganymede's tone darkened, like a garden when a cloud removes the sun. "That is the other half of the problem."

"I thought you sent the Mason in. ¿Aren't they your hush-up crew? Your office said we should let them handle things."

The Duke let his golden mane shield his expression from the camera-bots. "It was a misunderstanding. I do trust Martin Guildbreaker, far better than I trust Romanova, and the Commissioner General knows it, so they usually call Martin's team as a courtesy to me when sensitive cases arise. The Commissioner General didn't know your case was in a different league of sensitivity."

"I see. ¿So you trust this Mason only within limits?"

"Precisely. And the rest of Martin's team is an even greater problem."

"Yeah, Lesley's description of Dominic Seneschal was bizarre. We're not inviting that one over again."

"¡Don't joke! Mycroft started shaking when I told them Dominic came to the house, and they were right to. When Dominic follows Martin, their master isn't far behind."

"¿Their 'master'?" Sniper repeated.

«Le Prince,» the golden Duke pronounced in French first. "J.E.D.D. Mason. They will come to the bash'house, it's inevitable now. There's nothing Andō or I can say to put them off which won't raise more suspicion. You must do all in your power to keep them from talking to your bash'mates for any length of time."

"Tai-kun?" Sniper's mother taught him J.E.D.D. Mason's Japanese name. "I thought Tai-kun worked for you as well as Romanova. ¿Aren't they attached to your Attorney General?"

"They are."

"¿But you don't trust them?"

"One may trust a thing but still recognize that it is dangerous. If they come to the house, make sure they never so much as set eyes on the more vulnerable bash'mates: Cato, Thisbe, the twins. Yourself and Ockham might endure."

"¿Endure? ¿Endure what? You make Tai-kun sound like a Masonic torturer."

"They are no less dangerous in this situation."

Real fear sparkled in Sniper's eyes. "I can't tell if you're kidding."

"J.E.D.D. Mason seeks truth in an absolute sense, not a partisan one. All truths in all directions, all ends of a mystery, victim as well as culprit. I have no doubt they'll expose the criminal quickly, but your bash' is full of weaknesses right now, as well as secrets. Cato Weeksbooth is not well. Thisbe Saneer, the Typer twins, the set-sets are manipulable in their way, and you yourself have secrets, personal as well as professional."

Androgyne Sniper glanced down at his artistically tattered shorts, which hid the sex he worked so hard to keep the public from discovering.

"The Prince does not know how to investigate only some truths and not others," the Duke President continued. "They are Hive-neutral, that's why the Mitsubishi trust them to handle this fiasco, but it's precisely why you can't trust them with access to someone as fragile as Cato Weeksbooth. Hand Cato over to J.E.D.D. Mason and you might as well hand Cato's psych profile over too. Your bash' and our monopoly on what you do has been the linchpin of the Hive for generations, but the other Hives will swarm on us like jackals if they smell weakness. There are very weak links in your bash' right now."

Sniper frowned across at Cato, who was shaking only slightly as he introduced his kids to the Chair of the Esperanza City Nautical Engineering Consortium. "True."

The Duke's blue diamond eyes caught Sniper's and held them. "I need you to err on the side of caution. Think of Dominic Seneschal as a bloodhound who won't give up the chase until it drops, and think of Prince J.E.D.D. Mason as an all-seeing eye which will share all it sees, either with MASON, or with our allies, which may be worse. The Mitsubishi and Europe are already hungry to take over the system the instant they can claim your bash' isn't strong enough to protect it yourselves. It was a hard fight getting them to agree to leave the system in your bash' this generation, when several of you are clearly weak links. J.E.D.D. Mason—'Tai-kun'— must not see the evidence of that weakness, or Andō will see it too."

The childishness left Sniper's face for one salient instant. "Understood, Member President. Every measure will be taken."

"Good."

The smile returned to golden Ganymede, and the song transitioned to another. Sniper soon let himself be passed from hand to hand among the loyal Lifedoll customers who had paid through the nose for a chance to hold the genuine article in their arms. Ganymede, meanwhile, took turns with Andō enjoying Danaë, at least for some minutes. Then all play stopped short at the intrusion of the breathless Chair Kosala, Censor Ancelet, the King of Spain, and behind them, like a chariot behind its team, the Emperor.

CHAPTER THE TWELFTH

Neither Earth nor Atom, But . . .

CORNEL MASON SEEMS NO LESS AN ICON THAN ANY STATUE IN Romanova. He is sixty-three years old and solid as Atlas, not an athletic body but the strength of a man long reconciled to never letting go. His face is bare, his skin a clean, Mediterranean bronze, his black hair short in the Roman style, which brings your eye always to the tracker which channels the world into his ear. His square-breasted Mason's suit is cut no differently from Martin's, but the Emperor's is a shade of iron gray no other Mason dares wear, with the left sleeve dyed black from the elbow down, subtler than fasces but reminder still that he is the only person left in this world with the legal right to order an execution.

Ganymede Jean-Louis de la Trémoïlle, Duc de Thouars, Prince de Talmond, is accustomed to such company. "Welcome, Caesar. Fashionably late tonight, I see."

In public MASON's voice is constant, never stronger nor weaker, never more tired nor less. "News channel 323."

Spain and Chair Kosala nodded fervently, and Ganymede, Andō and Danaë tuned in at once.

I tuned in too, the newsreader's voice harsh after the soft banter of the notables: ". . . must ask what part was played in the cover-up by the real author of the list, Masami Mitsubishi, adopted bash'child of Mitsubishi Chief Director Hotaka Andō Mitsubishi. Assistant Editor Nakahara said they decided to come forward when it was discovered that the break-in likely involved the infamous Canner Device, a technology for manipulating tracker signals to falsify location data, whose full capacities are still unknown. Nakahara stated, 'I couldn't just keep quiet knowing everybody in the world is in danger. People have a right to know if thieves and murderers can hijack their IDs and . . .'"

That was enough. Watching through Ganymede, I could see Danaë huddle against her husband, while Andō grew pale as if watching a half-built cathedral tumble down. Knowing the Censor so well, I could almost see the numbers cascading in his head. Chill settled on the others, too, Kosala, Spain, while the Emperor's black-sleeved left hand formed its dreaded fist.

MASON led this company of princes to a private room, and their guards made it more private yet, blocking the hall and switching all trackers to secure modes which blocked transmission sharing, except with IDs cleared for top access, like mine.

"How many of you knew?" the Emperor began.

Andō looked to Ganymede. "I knew about the break-in, and the Duke and the Censor knew about the disruption to the lists. We agreed to keep things quiet. Disrupting tonight was obviously the criminal's intent."

"You wanted to keep it from the press?" The Emperor scowled like a bust of grim Poseidon. "Since when are we powerful enough to battle rumor? Truth is water in a sieve. It's not enough to put your hand across the holes and hope."

"I don't see that it's your business, Caesar." Ganymede is too graceful to snap, but his voice did gain a flutelike piercing edge. "Only the Humanist and Mitsubishi Hives are directly involved, unless you think one of your Members is behind it."

MASON's dark eyes darkened. "How are your Humanists involved?"

The Duke President did not flinch. "We were targeted by the same criminals. If the details are unknown to you too, Caesar, then I must commend your Martin Guildbreaker for their discretion."

The Emperor's bronze face softened a hair. "You brought Martin into the investigation?"

"Martin is leading the investigation." Andō took over, frankness in his voice. "*Black Sakura* asked Romanova for a polylaw. Papadelias called Martin. I trusted it to them."

Caesar's gaze held Andō's. "To Martin? Or to my son?"

The Chief Director let his hands sink comfortably into the pond-dark pockets of his suit. "To Martin. It didn't seem important enough to require J.E.D.D. Mason." Like Sniper, Andō used the Japanese nickname 'Tai-kun,' an old one, remnant from when the Child first appeared in the media's eye, riding wide-eyed on Hotaka Andō Mitsubishi's shoulders through the eternal overload of Tokyo. But since each Power here has a different name for J.E.D.D. Mason, I will make them all the same for now, to reduce confusion.

"The Canner Device threatens more than just two Hives."

"Much more," Chair Kosala added, moving to Caesar's side.

"That part is news to us." Ganymede ran his fingers through his golden mane, distracting everyone from the guilty glance Andō traded with Danaë. "Your Martin is methodical. If they've not yet reported to Papadelias and myself about this Canner Device, I presume it is because, unlike this rash informant, Martin wanted to verify before they cried wolf to the wide world."

"But this is perfect!" Chair Kosala's voice was light with hope. "We couldn't have anyone better than J.E.D.D. for this." Kosala does not use J.E.D.D. Mason's Indian nickname Jagmohan, preferring the contraction 'Jed,' like most Cousins. "We can announce that they're already on the case, with Romanova and all seven Hives behind them. No one could calm the public more." She smiled. "What do you say, Cornel?"

It is strange how MASON softens when he hears his name. He was a man once, with a given and surname like any other, but he almost never hears them anymore. Bryar Kosala wields the charm best, dropping 'Cornel' thoughtlessly, like an ex-wife who can never quite shed the casualness learned in long years sorting one another's laundry. She is his wife, in a sense, in the World Order, the gentle but all-powerful Mom caring for the one-point-seven billion members of Earth's second-largest Hive, a share of the household duties surpassed only by the Father's three-point-one billion Masons. How could they not fall into the habit of debating over the others' heads? Or meeting after the others quarrel to gripe in private about 'kids these days.'

"Yes," MASON pronounced, "I'll consent to leave it to my son."

Kosala turned to Ganymede. "Can we announce it from here? You have a press room."

I heard the Duke pause, frustration, I think, at the haste with which all Powers settled on this invasion of his most sensitive bash'. "Of course."

The King of Spain stepped forward, facing the august company with an air of graceful and unambitious authority, to which all but Ganymede could comfortably defer. "The announcement will be most powerful if you can say J.E.D.D. Mason's investigation has been ordered by all Seven Hives, as well as Romanova." His Majesty's English is beautiful, decorated with French and Spanish vowels, as when gilding on leather makes a plain book into an *objet d'art.* "How many Hives can we muster here?"

The Emperor raised his hand, joined by the Cousin Chair, Humanist President, and Mitsubishi Executive Director.

"Four," the King counted. "And Gordian?"

"I'll call Felix Faust," Andō volunteered.

Kosala smiled. "Felix will have Gordian give Jed carte blanche."

MASON nodded as Director Andō stepped aside to make the call. "We also need Europe. Who's willing to call the Outsider?"

"The Outsider?" Danaë's nose wrinkled, as at a piece of rotten fruit. "Surely it's enough that His Majesty consents."

"No." The Emperor is never slow to crush ideas. "The King only speaks for Spain now. Europe's consent requires the new Prime Minister."

Grief made Danaë's eyes sparkle the more. "Bryar, you must agree with me that the King's word is enough."

See how the children turn to Mom when Father seems too strict?

Chair Kosala shook her head. "Rules are rules. Is Perry here, Ganymede?"

A subtle smirk touched the Duke's cheeks. "They're downstairs at the bar."

Kosala nodded. "I'll call them."

Andō finished his call just as the Cousin Chair stepped aside for hers. "Felix is coming down from the tower overlook."

Danaë frowned. "They didn't just consent?"

"They consented but they're coming anyway. They want to see the looks on our faces."

Danaë and Ganymede smirked in unison as if to say, 'Of course.' I can think of no one who so enjoys watching the Powers in a crisis as Gordian's leader, Brillist Institute Headmaster Felix Faust. Headmaster Faust is seventy-eight years old, past the sixty-five which medicine has made the midpoint of our lifespan, so he has the right to smile patronizingly on youngsters in their forties. I imagine Faust's great predecessor, the Cognitivist, Adolf Richter Brill, had the same gaze three hundred years ago, as fluent in reading brains as a programmer is fluent in the code which strikes lay eyes as gibberish. Do you believe in it? This is one of the great divides of our society, between those who follow Brill completely and those who respect him only as a step long passed, like Aristotle, or Freud. Felix Faust can do a full Brillist reading, pinpoint a new acquaintance on all eight developmental scales, in nine minutes, often less. If you are not a Brillist, you must know the discomfort of feeling your inner self exposed by a method you can't completely disbelieve in, as if you knocked the deck from a Tarot reader's hand, and she gave a penetrating look at the fallen cards, and then at you. Felix Faust and other Brillists delight in the daily science-game of their mental taxonomy, spotting a 7-5-13-9-3-9-3-11 by their diction, a 5-3-3-11-11-4-2-10 by their fidgeting, or basking in the presence of a rare 1-3-3-4-13-12-9-1 as Ganymede basks in a Louis XV chair. I do not know what rare number sets manifest in MASON, Andō, Kosala, Vivien, or Ganymede, nor could I understand those sets without years training at the Institute, but Faust knows, and races now, like an astronomer to some new-fallen meteorite, to chart these leaders' blinks and twitches as the world panic begins.

"Gordian makes five," the King counted.

"Masons, Cousins, Mitsubishi, Humanists . . ." Does it make you feel better, reader, that even Chief Director Andō resorts to counting on his fingers to make certain he has all seven? ". . . Europeans, Gordian . . . that just leaves the Utopians."

The leaders of those Hives that have leaders frowned.

"They won't object," Ganymede pointed out.

Andō shook his head. "I know they won't object, but we have to ask them. Which do we call? This is a criminal case, but I don't know how to contact their chief of police if they have one." He looked to his wife. "Which Utopian did we deal with after the Chang embezzlement case?"

Danaë's gold brows sparkled as they knit in concentration. "One with a sort of robotic fish world, I think, or was it the one with the walking trees? *Grand frère,* which would you ask?"

Ganymede gave a sparkling shrug. "I can't keep the constellations straight."

Do not criticize the Duke. Not even I (and I have tried) can track that organized anarchy which is more a unit of measure than a hierarchy: a school of fish, a gaggle of geese, a constellation of Utopians. They did not pick the name for the reason you think. A constellation is a group of distant objects which form a tight whole from our perspective, but may really be light-centuries apart, one a nearby dwarf, a second a giant a thousand times as distant, a third not a star at all but a galaxy, which to our distance-blinded eyes seems just another speck. Just so, when Andō wonders, "Who runs their police?" the answer may include some individuals, a wholly separate bash', and a vast corporation somewhere which may never have met the others, since all is done through casual cooperation. A constellation of Utopians is a group which only seems a group to us because we seek familiar institutions in their government, as we use the shapes of beasts and heroes to make false sense of the sea of stars.

"We could ask one of their Senators," Andō proposed. "They should know who their own police are."

MASON shook his head. "Let my son speak to them. That is enough."

The others consented in silence, eager to forget the issue as Bryar Kosala returned with the Outsider's answer. "Perry says they can't decide over the phone. They want to hear details from Andō, and assurances from either you or me in person, Cornel. They say Ganymede and Felix may join us for the discussion or not, as they prefer."

The Duke scowled. "In other words, Perry wants to make a fuss before agreeing."

MASON took a long breath. "Only a fool signs a document without reading it. I will come."

Ganymede tossed his sun-bright hair. "I won't. I don't want the rumor mill claiming there was a secret meeting of the Big Six, that'll fuel the chaos."

Chair Kosala nodded. "Agreed. If Cornel and Andō meet with Perry, we can go reassure the crowd." A lonely sadness touched the long lines of her face. "Vivien, I imagine you must head back to Romanova?"

The Censor already had the aimless stare of one deep in calculation.

The Duke President smiled pity on the couple. "Géroux," he called to one of his staff. "Take Vivien out the back way, get them safely to a car. And find Su-Hyeon, they should be in the galleries."

A hidden door opened at once, to offer Vivien exodus. The escort had to touch the Censor's arm to wake him from his numbers.

"Can I have Mycroft, too?" he asked abruptly.

The bronze of MASON's face hardened to iron. "Mycroft has much to answer tonight."

Down in the kitchens, I give a little squeal. It is reflex, reader. I cannot see Caesar's black-sleeved fist grow tense without feeling the chill on my shoulders of Death's wings passing close.

The Duke knows when a thing cannot be hidden. "Mycroft is here, but I am finished with them, Vivien may take them. If no one objects."

Any of the Powers could have raised a voice, but all looked to stony MASON. He fingered out a message, and down in the kitchen the Imperial word cut through my other tracker feeds like siren through the noise: <Explain.>

<Caesar, I know nothing of the crime, and little of the Canner Device, but what little I know have I already told to Martin.>

MASON took his time considering, three breaths, four, each making the slightly metallic iron gray of his imperial suit shift in the light, as mountains change their shadows with the crawling of the day. "Yes, Mycroft may serve Vivien tonight."

Chair Kosala—lawful guardian of Servicerkind—nodded her consent. "Right." She clapped her hands. "Vivien will work, you'll meet with Perry, I'll go be calm at people."

"I'll join you, if I may," Spain volunteered.

She smiled. "That would be a great help, thank you."

His Majesty Isabel Carlos II offered his arm to Danaë. "You should come with us, Princesse. Perry doesn't trust you."

Danaë clung more tightly her husband's sleeve. "Must I?"

MASON gave the necessary answer. "You cannot come to the meeting, just as Spain and the Censor cannot come. My son is employed directly by the six Hive leaders. The Prime Minister will expect this meeting not to involve outsiders."

"But Perry is the Outsider," the Princesse pouted. "His Majesty is the rightful head of Europe, everyone knows that."

"Caesar is right, my dear." Andō transferred Danaë to the King's arm, as when one coaxes a hooded hawk from one glove to another. "Do what you can to calm people while we meet. We don't need any rumors."

Danaë nodded her consent, then prepared her smile for the crowd, as a hunter prepares his bow. Like the Empresses and Queens of old, Danaë cannot abide being useless, but will accept exclusion when another duty waits. Imagine Empress Livia, waiting in the palace while Augustus forges treaties in the Senate house, content since her offices too throng with clients who spread her imperious touch from Spain to Syria. "Shall we?"

Kosala lingered to give Vivien's hand a farewell squeeze.

"I'm here! I'm here!" Brillist Institute Headmaster Felix Faust arrived, huffing and wheezing like an old wolf, no longer big nor bad. His usual Gordian sweater was not formal enough to be worn on such a night, but the weave of his green suit coat was textured to mimic its markings, so passing Brillists could still read him as 2-5-5-5-11-11-10-1. Faust's flesh always seems to be decaying, pallid European skin and a wasted, hairless body as if the brain which lurks beneath that bare skull were a parasite, sucking the life and moisture from its host. "You must let me come!" he gasped out. "I saw Perry heading toward the Miniatures Room. Who else is coming?" His eyes shot from face to face, keen as microscopes. "Andō and MASON, fine choices. The Duke and King joining Bryar on crowd duty, good." A deep breath and a smile. "Isn't this whole affair magnificent? I just called J.E.D.D. Mason, do you know what they said? 'Excuse me, Headmaster, something important is happening.' I haven't heard our J.E.D.D. call anything important since Spain here fell from Politics! Isn't it wonderful? No offense, Your Majesty."

How shall I describe these princes' faces as they hear that news? Imagine the ancient Senate hearing word that Caesar has just crossed the

Rubicon; they do not yet know how much destruction this will spell, but it cannot end in nothing.

"Come, come, I'm eager to hear what you tell Perry!" Faust herded MASON and Mitsubishi toward the side door, like a teacher counting students on a field trip. The old Headmaster has a privileged ease in dealing with the other Powers, since he is last among equals, resting content in seventh place on Seven-Ten lists. Many say the only bad choice Thomas Carlyle ever made was his last, decreeing that henceforth the leadership of Gordian would be selected by Brill's Institute. The Institute chose well, unfailingly, but Members who were not Brillists felt uncomfortable under their sway, and, as Gordian and Brillist became synonyms, so Gordian dwindled from the largest Hive to second-smallest. Legend says that Emperor Constantine, converted on his deathbed, willed the Roman Empire to the Christian Church, and in one act both ensured that Church's immortality and doomed Europe to nineteen centuries of wars for God; just so, Carlyle's deathbed embrace of Adolf Richter Brill strengthened and crippled Gordian. Others may call it a mistake, but I call it the wisest move Carlyle ever made, for, if Gordian's growth had not been checked, by now its matchless popularity would have doomed us to that dread death-knell of peace: majority.

"The rest of you enjoy the party!" old Faust called to the others. "Ganymede, Sniper's outside preparing to catapult themself over your East Wing using a motor which I think was part of your drawbridge until a few minutes ago. You may want to go voice an opinion."

The Duke broke into such poetic French profanity that those who understood could not help but gaze in awe.

As the others returned to the grand hall, Headmaster Faust, a human tugboat, shoved the Emperor and Mitsubishi Chief Director out the side door to a quieter gallery, and onward toward the salon where the Outsider waited. Here only quiet souls clustered, pretending to browse the Duke's collection of Busts of Unknown Persons while they watched the news over their trackers. The three Hive leaders might have traversed the hall in safety if not for a tiny, brave impediment, nine years old and child-plump beneath her Junior Scientist Squad uniform, who planted herself in MASON's path like Lancelot upon the bridge. "Are you the Emperor?" she asked.

He crossed his arms, the black sleeve darker as it fell in shadow. "Yes."

"Are you rich?"

"My Empire is."

"Can we have a new atomic oven for our science club? We picked out the one we want. It only costs two million euros and it can split the atom!"

The Emperor sighed down at his tiny petitioner. "Write up a grant proposal and send it to Xiaoliv Guildbreaker."

What stifled pain that sigh! What weight for those of us who have enjoyed the gloomy privilege of hearing MASON voice his thoughts! He will not say it to this child so full of aspirations, but he thinks it when he hears her boast, "It can split the atom!" No, it can't. Cornel MASON is the world's most undeluded man. What are humanity's great dreams? To conquer the world? To split the atom? When Alexander spread his empire from the Mediterranean to India, we say he conquered the world, but he barely touched a quarter of it. We lie. We lie again when we say we split the atom. 'Atom' was supposed to be the smallest piece of matter—all we did is give that name to something we can split, knowing that there are quarks and tensors, other pieces smaller that we cannot touch, and only these deserve the title 'atom.' Man is more ambitious than patient. When we realize we cannot split a true atom, cannot conquer the whole Earth, we redefine the terms to fake our victory, check off our boxes and pretend the deed is done. Alexander conquered Earth, we tell ourselves, Rutherford split the atom, no need to try again. Lies. Cornel MASON is the unquestioned master of more than three billion voluntary subjects, a hundred times the ruler Alexander was, but knows he has not conquered the Earth, and never will. If all humanity were so unwilling to lie to ourselves, we might not have given up on our great dreams. Complacent reader, we no longer aim for Earth nor atom, but ...

. . . Perhaps the Stars

THERE IS ONE RACE IN WHOM AMBITION FLOWS STILL. I DO NOT mean the Humanists' lust for fame, Masons' for power, or the driving need of Europeans and Mitsubishi to prove their nation-strats superior to one another—those ambitions are appetite or envy by finer names. What I speak of is the primordial ambition which brought us from the trees, which launched the first ships across then-infinite oceans, and drove one brave ape to approach the heavenly destroyer 'fire' and make it ours. Reader, we no longer aim for Earth nor atom, but, so long as the Utopians still live and breathe, they will not give up on our last great dream: the stars.

"I said on your knees, bitch! Now!"

"Stay calm, friend. Think. You don't want to do this."

"Oh, I do want to do this. In fact, I think we're all gonna take turns doing this, what do you all think, everyone?"

"¡Si, ya vamos a coger este puto!"

Laughter pregnant with threat followed the words up through a kitchen window behind me. There were five or six drunks by the sound of it, close by the back wall of this low wing of the palace, where the lights of Ganymede's party did not reach.

"That's right, we're all gonna have a turn, though whether we take turns getting a blow or kicking the shit out of you astroturds is your choice."

The chefs around me froze, none wanting to acknowledge the atrocity transpiring below. Such things are supposed to be extinct in our Enlightened age, but if civilization continues another millennium, another ten, drunk people will never become less stupid.

"We're going to walk away now," said a second victim, sober if afraid. "Think where we are and how fast security will jaunt in if something happens. You can walk away too."

"¡Chinga la policía! You try to get away and we'll ditch your trackers in the trash and haul you up them hunting grounds, nobody'll find you out there, not for days. Now down on your knees and suck it, U-bitch, before I go Mycroft Canner on your ass!"

By now you are urging me to intervene. I did, but in return we sacrifice listening to the rest of the party upstairs. All I know is that Perry consented.

I leapt out the open window, and a controlled swing from the scalloped railing landed me in the gravel between the marauders and their prey. My fall was almost silent, and I landed on all fours like an animal, so with my dappled uniform of gray and beige I must have seemed a beast.

"¡Carajo! ¿Qué es esto?" the attackers shrieked, though their panic faded fast.

"It's just a Servicer."

I rose, neither threatening nor shying back, just set to spring. "These two were summoned by the Emperor themself. Shall I call Caesar? Or would you prefer I call Police Commissioner General Ektor Papadelias?"

I could see the aggressors now, five Humanists, their jackets bright with sailors' stripes and sport team patches, reeking from a long day's revels. We watched each other silently, as stags face off across a clearing, debating with eyes alone whether or not to break the woodland peace with war.

"It's not worth it," their leader judged, a sinewy young thing who probably deserved the champion colors on his wrestler's cap. "Come on, let's go get seats for the fireworks."

In my place, reader, would you have offered your silent thanks to Chance or God?

"Are you injured?" I asked as I turned to the pair behind me.

"Untouched, thanks, Mycroft."

In the darkness of the alley, the long contours of their Utopian coats glowed timidly, like ghosts threatening to vanish if I glanced away. Confess, reader, you too rush to the window to see when they walk by, and point them out to eager friends, "Look at the Utopian!" Do I assume too much? Perhaps you have never seen one. You may not be my contemporary, but a distant biographer, culling my faded history for data on one of our Great Men. Utopians are common now, but by history's standards they must be ephemeral, winged ants born to pioneer new colonies, who cannot linger long among the workers. How shall I describe these aliens of the past to one whose world is no longer so colorful? Their coats were more than Hive markers, they were windows to another world. Griffincloth was developed for camouflage, a flexible, fabric-like surface which could display in real time the video feed of objects on the other side, making an object properly equipped with Griffincloth invisible. A tent of Griffincloth need not blemish the landscape, and a cop in Griffincloth need not fear being shot on the approach, but these wondersmiths would not leave it at that. Utopian coats are dream visions, created by covering a long trench coat with Griffincloth and programming the computer to process the real image before projecting it, substituting gold for gray, marble for brick, fish for birds, whatever the Utopian imagines. Of the pair who stood before me in the alley, one's coat showed a City of Tomorrow built in Space, so the palace behind us floated in a star sea, the plants fitted with oxygen collectors and the cars with solar sails like flying fish. The other coat showed the palace as a ruin overgrown by swamp, the same stones aged a thousand years, with fantastic creatures sunning themselves on the wreck, like dragons of the Middle Ages, the oddest pieces of a dozen beasts assembled into one furred, scaled, and feathered alien. The coats are not mere games, nor decoration, like the Mitsubishi cloth which blooms and fades with the aesthetic progress of the seasons. Utopia means 'nowhere,' so all Utopians drape themselves in their most precious nowheres.

"Thank you for letting them go peacefully." I nodded toward the retreating drunks.

The coat of ruins shrugged. "We're used to it."

You may not believe me, but I wept. The Anonymous calls these crimes of stupidity, people drunk on rage, power, or chemicals, who realize when sober just how much their fleeting folly threw away. I think of them more as crimes of the Stifled Predator, for Nature built her greatest ape to hunt as well as gather, and if a zoo lion goes mad eating only vat-grown steak, then so can you. Servicers are common targets—that I can forgive. Even when the victims are young friends, who crawl back to the dorms and spend nights shaking in my arms, I can forgive, for Servicers are guilty. What penance, though, must this tainted world perform to purge this instinct to attack Utopians, whose only crime is thinking too much of tomorrow?

"We heard you were here, Mycroft. Which Alpha called you?" Though the voice was brave, the speaker drew her coat of stars tightly about herself, and even the digital blackness could not hide her shivers. Her name is Aldrin Bester, a fine Utopian name lifted from their canon, as in the olden days Europe took its names from lists of saints.

"The Duc de la Trémoïlle called me," I answered, lapsing in my distraction from Ganymede's public name to his proper one, which few non-Frenchmen use. "The six Hive leaders are all at the party. Which shall I inform of your arrival?"

"We're not here for the Alphas. We're here for you." The second Utopian, in his coat of ruins, was taller than Aldrin, his short hair French brown to her Eastern black. He bears the honorable name Voltaire Seldon. The Patriarch deserves to be honored for a hundred reasons, but he owes his elevation to the Utopian canon to the novella *Micromegas*, which makes him a candidate for the title of world's first science-fiction author. "Martin called us about these break-ins, *Black Sakura* and Saneer-Weeksbooth. We have questions, and I expect you to use none of the glamours you use on centrics."

"No deceptions," I promised, translating their Utopian slang. "Never with you."

Voltaire's face switched for a moment from the sternness of business to a more personal sternness. "Have you been using your days well, Mycroft?"

"I've been trying. Chair Kosala has me drafting a proposal for improving the Servicer Program, and the Emperor had me teach a private seminar for their Lictors on the history of violence."

"Are you writing?"

I looked at my feet. "I haven't had time. I've had a lot of assignments lately, and I'm only allowed anti-sleeps twice a week."

Voltaire frowned. "Those are common excuses. You don't get to use common excuses."

"I know. I'm sorry. I'll do more."

"Do less," Aldrin cut in. "I know you. You're filling your hours with nano-charities and calling it productivity. Do less and you'll output more."

"Yes," I confessed. "You're right. I'll do better."

"Good." The illusion of her eyes seemed sad, but even I cannot trust the expressions on a Utopian's transparent-seeming visor. The lenses the rest of us wear display our tracker data perfectly, so in theory there is no need for the heavy visors Utopians prefer, which cover the face from brows to cheekbones, so their eyes never see true sun. Rumor insists that Utopians only wear the visors to deceive us. The Griffincloth surfaces make them seem transparent, so projected eyes meet ours, and seem to smile and squint as real eyes do, but, if the coats can transform day to night or earth to stars, surely the visors can replace their true expressions with what they want us to see.

"Shall we move inside?" I gestured to the door behind me. "There's an empty storeroom nearby."

I let them enter first, so I, selfish creature, could delight in the coats which filled the hall before me with their fantasies. In Voltaire's nowhere the palace walls teemed with cracks, and the cracks with tiny lizard-ants whose micro-civilization assembled the crumbs of marble into knee-high palaces. In Aldrin's nowhere the floor became a shimmering force field between us and empty space, on whose translucence I could see Voltaire striding beyond her, fitted with a space suit, solar panels folded at his sides like veil-light wings.

Aldrin began the interrogation. "Martin told us what you said about the Traceshifter Artifact."

I sighed my gratitude that one Hive at least did not say 'Canner Device.' "I haven't had a chance yet to start tracking down the people I bought the packaging from. The Censor needed me today."

"Were they Japanese by nation-strat?"

The question made me frown. "I believe so. We spoke Japanese, but these were underground meetings, no one wore insignia."

Aldrin nodded. "We scanned the tracker records from the hours around this theft. The artifact's hex left afterpaths. We are beginning to map its movement. It makes tracker IDs jump from victim to victim as people pass close by each other, so yours might jump to mine, then mine to Voltaire's, Voltaire's to another, bumping signal after signal, sometimes swapping back when people cross paths a second time, folding back on itself to make the threads harder to trace. The wielder can cast the hex kilometers from the target, then wait for the desired signal to drift out on the tide of exchanges. The effect entered the Saneer-Weeksbooth bash'house on a guest of Thisbe Saneer, then swapped the signals of everyone in the bash' several times over, and Ockham's signal traveled out on Cato Weeksbooth. From there it was easy enough for the caster to acquire it. We are still combing the records to see how many trackers were affected. Hundreds."

I nodded. "And anyone affected is a suspect. No, anyone near anyone who was near anyone affected?"

"More," Aldrin corrected. "We found this chain by examining Ockham Saneer, but if the caster also traceshifted themself separately, that will take us much more time to track. The chain we've found is just the mask. Until we trace the effects more completely, no one on Earth has a true alibi, nor anyone in orbit. Cielo de Pájaros is close to the Esmeraldas Elevator."

Voltaire nodded, the visor showing me grim eyes. "Meanwhile we must hunt by motive, Mycroft. What motive do you smell?"

I flinched. "There are too many."

"You told Martin that you believe occult powers within the Japanese Mitsubishi forged this artifact?"

"I . . . I have no proof."

"You have instincts. Voice them."

I took a deep breath. "I think . . . I think it was the Japanese Mitsubishi bloc originally. After news of the theft broke, when I was hunting for the thieves, everything I found, everyone involved, makers, smugglers, whatever the continent, they were always Japanese. It's hard to believe a criminal group wealthy enough to develop something so expensive would be that homogenous. And it didn't seem like something a criminal group would want to put together anyway. Why spend so much on research and development when you have veteran killers who drop their trackers for hits all the time?"

"Not criminals, then," Aldrin confirmed. "But why would the Mitsubishi bloc forge such a superprosthesis?"

I smiled at her U-speak, 'superprosthesis,' so much more precise than 'tool' for describing this thing designed to grant humans a superhuman skill. "I don't know. The effect you describe, it's overkill for breaking into *Black Sakura.* That doesn't require juggling hundreds of trackers, it requires a good crowbar. Whoever did this wants us to be looking for the device, wants the panic and the witch hunt back."

A pawing at the door made me jump, but it was only Aldrin's black unicorn, which had followed us up the hallway. It is strange calling it 'normal' watching this unicorn, as sprightly as a lamb and sleek as shadow, scamper to its partner's side, but, with Utopians among us, such happy wonders are common. It is easy, if you look it up, to learn which types of U-beasts are robots and which biological, but most of us prefer not to research how these fantastic pets are made, so, when we see a Utopian pass by with a miniature pterodactyl on his shoulders, or a gold-plumed griffin trotting at her heels, uncertainty lets us imagine that the wonder might, like Bridger's Boo, be real.

Aldrin offered her U-beast a welcoming stroke, then turned to me. "Why did you seek the Traceshifter Artifact in the first place?"

"Did Martin not tell you?"

"We know what illusion you cast with the packaging, but why? Your work was done. You had no further need for deception."

Lies rose by instinct in my throat. I fought them back. "I didn't want my real methods exposed. I didn't expect to use them again myself, but I didn't want that door closed for others." Shame kept me from glancing up, for fear of the disapproval in their projected eyes. "And also, I figured that, if I had the packaging, whoever was responsible for the device would assume that more investigation might link my crimes to them. They'd have an incentive to hurry the trial along, and my methods would never be fully investigated."

I dared to peek now at the pair. They seemed to gaze on one another through their visors, silenced by the darkness of their thoughts. Visor. Why is visor not spelled with a z, reader? Surely an object so associated with futurism should contain one of the futurist letters, z or x. It feels right to say vizor, not visor, lazer, not laser.

"And did someone block the investigation of your methods?"

"Yes."

"Director Andō?" Voltaire leaned forward, so I could see Aldrin through his coat for a moment, a winged froglike creature whose arteries glowed through its transparent flesh like streams of fireflies.

"Y-es." The word caught in my throat. "But Andō didn't order the creation of the device, I'm sure of that. My impression is that they were furious when they found out it existed. Their involvement has been damage control, trying to conceal the bad choices of predecessors and subordinates. If you placed the device in Andō's hand right now they would destroy it."

As I answered, Aldrin had her unicorn extend a winglike screen, and began skimming through its data. "Do you know the Artifact's original purpose? Was it forged for one specific end?"

"I don't know."

Vizors exchanged digital glances. "Does Andō know?"

"I don't know if Andō knows. And I don't know if whoever is using the device now knows either. I think the thief wants to topple Andō. Whatever the device was for, it's easy to make it seem like it was designed for theft and murder. If the Japanese strat seems to be responsible for my crimes, if they seem to have been plotting to use this device for some kind of espionage, it would drive them out of power in the Mitsubishi for a generation, more. And if Andō and Danaë go down, they'll drag Ganymede with them."

Aldrin flipped through more data on the wing-screen. "Do you know why the thief involved the Saneer-Weeksbooth bash'?"

Bridger's face, white with terror in my imagination, made me freeze. I did not want to lie to them, reader, not to Utopia. I did not want to lie, but, for what hides in that one house, I was prepared to force myself. It took some breaths for me to realize that no lies were needed. "I have no idea. I can't think of anything to connect that bash' to *Black Sakura*, or the Gyges Device, or internal Mitsubishi politics in any way. What I do know is that we need to protect that bash'house, more than anywhere on Earth. Martin I trust, Martin is gentle, but now the public knows one half of what's happened. If they find out the other half, and the public screams for a big, showy investigation of the Saneer-Weeksbooth bash', it will . . . I can't overstate how much it could disrupt." I paused. The numbers in the Censor's sanctum rose blood red in my mind: 33-67; 67-33; 29-71. Should I break confidence? Commit the well-intentioned treason of leaking from that most inviolate of Romanova's offices? Or could I make my fears clear without treason? "There are . . . elements of this which align with predictions made by members of the Mardi bash'."

Digital eyes showed neither warmth nor judgment. "What do you see in that?"

"I don't know," I answered. "Disrupting the cars hurts everyone. I can't even say it hurts the Humanists and Mitsubishi most because the Masons and Cousins have more Members so use the system that much more. The only . . ." I choked. "The only Hive it doesn't hurt is you."

They stared at me, both of them, exchanging silent data behind their vizors, though whether with one another or with distant members of their constellation I could not say. They were the only ones immune. They, aloof in their separate transit system, had no interest in the bash' which pumped the lifeblood of six Hives through Earth's broad skies; six but not seven. I told you, reader, that Utopia does not give up on dreams. When a Utopian dies, of anything, the cause is marked and not forgotten until solved. A fall? They rebuild the site to make it safe. A criminal? They do not rest until he is rendered harmless. An illness? It is researched until cured, regardless of the time, the cost, over generations if need be. A car crash? They create their separate system, slower, less efficient, costing hours, but which has never cost a single life. Even for suicide they track the cause, and so, patiently, blade by blade, disarm Death. Death, of course, has many weapons, and, if they have deprived him of a hundred million, he still has enough at hand to keep them mortal. For now.

"You really thought it was us, didn't you?"

The itch of a tear on my cheek made me realize, for the first time, that, yes, I had. I had thought it was them, feared it was them, deep down inside where thoughts aren't words yet. Relief's catharsis washed over me. It wasn't them. It was some viper from the familiar pit putting its fangs to use. Even if a constellation takes a viper's shape to brave the pit, the starlight holds no venom.

Aldrin had her U-beast stow its screen. "We've set watch over the tracker system. When next the hex is cast, we will know, almost instantly, and we'll send in Romanova. The second strike will be the last."

I laughed inside. Next they will deprive Death of the Canner Device. I was right, thirteen years ago, not to even try to buy the real thing. The packaging could deceive long-term, but, if I had used the device itself, Utopia in anger would have had me on the second day. It isn't only the Utopians who become a little more immortal with every blade they take away. It isn't only they who delight in seeing unicorns and wingrays in the street, who gaze through Griffincloth into enchanting nowheres, and ride the shuttles to the brave, bare Moon, which their efforts make a little less bare every day. We all enjoy these wonders, all of us, all Hives, all Hiveless. Reader, you should not have barred Apollo Mojave from the Pantheon.

CHAPTER THE FOURTEENTH

The Interlude of the Interview with Retired *Black Sakura* Reporter Tsuneo Sugiyama, as Related by Martin Guildbreaker

MYCROFT CANNER ASKED ME TO RELATE THIS INTERVIEW, SINCE they were at President Ganymede's party at the time, and did not witness it. Mycroft is very worried that, after having a different guide for one chapter, the reader will be unwilling to trust a criminal again, so they asked me to state clearly from the start that I will author only this chapter, and afterward Mycroft will carry on.

Mycroft insists that I introduce myself, my bash', and family first, in accordance with period custom, though I note that Mycroft broke that rule themself. My birth name is Mycroft Guildbreaker. I do not know why the *Porphyrogene* J.E.D.D. Mason, during their sixth year, began to call me Martin, but I have now been known by that nickname for fifteen years. I am thirty-two years old, born July 2nd, 2422. The Confraternidomitor bash' (in English Guildbreaker) is an hereditary bash' founded in 2177 and unbroken since. My biological parents are Minister Charlemagne Guildbreaker Jr., and August Guildbreaker, currently Romanovan Praetor for the Masonic Hive and formerly personal secretary to Emperor Aeneas MASON. (Mycroft wanted to use "Empress" for female MASONS, but I find Mycroft's gendered language disruptive, and have restored the customary 'Emperor,' both in this chapter and Mycroft's earlier discussion of Agrippa MASON). Both my parents are descended from previous Emperors or their ba'sibs, one from Tiber MASON and the other from a sibling of Antonine MASON, while the other seven ba'pas in my birth bash' are third-generation Masons at the least. I took the adulthood competency exam in my fourteenth year, immediately became a *Familiaris* of the Emperor, undertook my *Annus Dialogorum*, and, on its completion, became, on the same day, Mason, and Minister to the *Porphyrogene* (child of the Emperor), who was then four years of age. I studied at the August Polylegal College of the Alexandrian Campus, graduating at twenty-five, and have, thus far, held all the offices of the

Cursus Honorum at the expected ages. The new generation of my bash' was formalized when I was twenty, and contains seven members, including four ba'sibs born to the Guildbreaker name, and three friends from the Alexandrian Campus. One of them, from a Chinese Mitsubishi bash', became my spouse, now Xiaoliu Guildbreaker, a *Familiaris,* Council to the Emperor, and proud to be the first person not raised in a Masonic bash' to have joined the Guildbreaker bash' in four generations. We have three children, Aeneas, Lissa, and An, and four other ba'kids born of our four bash'mates, though I confess myself something of a stranger to most of them, since I am a vocateur, and my duties to the young *Porphyrogene* mean that I spend more hours in their bash' than in my own. Though it is illegal to speculate about such things, I know I have been widely discussed as a potential successor to the current Emperor; I place no stock in such rumors.

A dissatisfied Mycroft now insists that I append something more vivid about myself, a scene or anecdote, to enliven this list of flat facts. If there is a keystone event of my fortunes, it was the night late in my fourteenth year when I exchanged my first adult words with my Emperor. I was waiting for my ba'pas in a small courtyard garden in the Imperial Palace. I was not aware at the time, but it was a grim day for Cornel MASON, since *Familiaris* Calavine Acton had just confessed to the Amador Treason, so Caesar was considering the first exercise of their Capital Power. This is also why my ba'pas were at the palace well past midnight. I remember a little fountain which was partly clogged, so that a faint spray shot sideways onto a bench. The damp of the stone felt good as I sat, though I was cold, because it made me very aware of my body. I did not notice the Emperor until they spoke.

"What can a child of your age have to think about that makes you look so much more serious than I myself?"

I remember, looking up, that MASON was at first just an immense dark shape, like a pillar merging the black of the Earth with the black of the sky, but, as I watched, the spraying water made glints of light spread along their suit, as if the stars and city lights of the capital were mingling and multiplying in the new space offered by this living being.

Caesar's words I remember verbatim, but my own stumbling responses I do not. I answered that I was trying to decide when to take the Adulthood Competency Exam and prepare for my *Annus Dialogorum.* I have no doubt that the custom will outlast these words, but to please Mycroft I will explain. When an aspiring Mason has passed the exam, and completed the initial courses in Masonic Law and Government, the initiate is clothed for a year in a suit of pure white, and undertakes the 'Year of Debate,' engaging a different person each day in discussion of what it means to be a Mason. After three hundred and sixty-six debates, if the initiate still wishes to join the Empire, there is no further test.

"If you have doubt about becoming a Mason," MASON answered, "the *Annus Dialogorum* will settle it."

I approximate my answer: "That isn't it, Caesar. There's no doubt I will be a Mason. I can't wait to start speaking Latin, and using and understanding power, and serving you. But I know I'm very young. If I do my *Annus Dialogorum* now I'll understand less than if I wait until I'm older, and learn less from it about what it really means to be a Mason. I want to be a Mason now, but I don't want to waste the *Annus*, since I only get to do it once."

MASON's next words were not to me, but to an aide, commanding that my ba'pas be summoned to witness my investiture as an Imperial *Nepos*. That very night—I will not say 'in my honor'—Cornel MASON created the *Ordo Vitae Dialogorum*, "the Order of the Life of Debate." Membership is open to all Masons, and marked by one white sleeve, a permanent invitation to engage the wearer in debate over the Masonic life, not for a year, but lifelong. I wear it proudly. That night too, the title of *Familiaris* was promised to me upon my passing the Adulthood Competency Exam, since, by Alliance Law, a minor may not subject themself to Caesar's Force.

I had long desired, even expected, these honors, but each in their course as I earned them, not all in one breath. I asked Caesar in some bewilderment why they granted me so much so quickly. This was my true investiture: "I have a use for you. You will be my instrument, my touch, my voice, my proxy while my work keeps me away, the one Masonic influence to counter all the others. You will teach and guide my son."

That night I met the *Porphyrogene*.

* * *

The first stage of my investigation of the *Black Sakura* and Saneer-Weeksbooth double break-in has already been related. At 17:57 UT on 03/24/2454 I requested permission to interview Tsuneo Sugiyama, preferring to conduct the interview in person rather than over the tracker system. I was invited to the Sugiyama residence, outside Kanazawa in the Ishikawa prefecture of Chubu, and arrived at 19:31 UT. The Sugiyama bash'house is a compact town house, three stories, pressed tightly on both sides by similar houses. Tsuneo Sugiyama is eighty-nine years old, female, one hundred and sixty-two centimeters tall, dark brown eyes, short grayish white hair, with distinctly yellowed front teeth, no other distinguishing marks. Sugiyama wore a Japanese-cut Mitsubishi suit, green, with a spring pattern of morning glories climbing bamboo. Eight strat insignia were visible: on the right wrist a Japanese nation-strat bracelet and Lune Cassirer Fan Club bracelet, on the jacket front a Journalists' Guild clip and Gazetteer Gaming Club pin, on the shoes skiers' buckles, on the front pocket a Shiba Inu dog breeder's patch and an Ishikawa Region patch, on the left ring finger a Nagoya Campus ring, and on the right little finger a Great Books Club ring. Sugiyama offered me tea, and I accepted. I commenced formal interview at 19:37 UT. The following is a verbatim transcript, interspersed with my interpretative comments:

*   *   *

Sugiyama seemed unusually relaxed at the beginning of the interview, though not in a joking or jovial way. I did not understand the reason until later on.

Guildbreaker: "Thank you for seeing me, Mitsubishi Sugiyama. You are aware this is being recorded?"

Sugiyama: "Of course, Mason, of course."

Guildbreaker: "This is just an initial interview. There may be more detailed sessions later, once I've had a chance to act on your initial statement."

Sugiyama: "I know how interviews work, youngster."

Guildbreaker: "And you know I represent a poly-Hive investigation? If you report anything here which is pertinent to the security of a non-Mitsubishi, I'm legally obligated to inform the Praetors of the affected Hive, or the Tribunes' Officers in the case of Hiveless."

Sugiyama: "I knew outside police would come. It doesn't make sense for this to be handled among us."

Guildbreaker: "I am not police, I am a polylegal investigator. My team is handling the initial stages of this, since it affects all seven Hives at sensitive levels, so they want it handled delicately. Once we've secured the safety of the essential parties, the police will apprehend the actual offender."

Sugiyama: "You're using Utopians for the grunt work, aren't you? I know how it works. I covered the Mycroft Canner case as well."

Guildbreaker: "First, for the record, is it correct that you are not the author of the Seven-Ten list which was stolen from *Black Sakura* two days ago and subsequently recovered by the police?"

Sugiyama: "That's correct, but no one outside *Black Sakura* knew I wasn't writing it this year. Seven-Ten lists are only popular when they're written by big names, and with *Black Sakura* being only the second-most-important Mitsubishi paper, the Hagiwara-san knew our readership outside the Hive would fizzle if the public found out I wasn't the author. That doesn't excuse them trying to pass off Masami-kun's work as mine, but I understand why they did it."

Guildbreaker: "How long have you worked at *Black Sakura*?"

Sugiyama: "I first worked for them from 2382 to '86, then did graduate school from '86 to '90, worked at *Black Sakura* again until 2411, freelance from '11 to '25, then took nine years off to write my books, started again at *Black Sakura* full time in '34, and retired last week. That last run was nineteen years, nine months, eleven days all told."

Sugiyama answered this question with a speed which indicated that they had prepared their answers ahead of time. My flight to Chubu had taken forty-six minutes, and they had clearly spent that time preparing. Having worked so long as a reporter, Sugiyama was experienced with interviews, so it was safe to assume that, if they chose to lie to me, I would have no way to detect it.

Guildbreaker: "You retired last week?"

Sugiyama: "Unofficially. A lot of people invest in the paper counting on me as a draw, so we decided it was best to wait and announce at the end of the quarter when the contracts expired."

Guildbreaker: "Was this a planned retirement, or . . ."

Sugiyama: "Oh, it was sudden. I know doctors keep telling me I have another fifty years left in me, but after seventy-two years as a journalist voker I decided it was time to pay more attention to family. Knowing me, I probably won't be able to keep myself entirely retired very long, but it's the plan for now."

Guildbreaker: "How far ahead had you planned this?"

Sugiyama: "It wasn't planned at all, totally sudden."

Guildbreaker: "What was the cause?"

Sugiyama: "My grandchild Aki tried to kill themself."

Guildbreaker: "I'm sorry to hear it. Do you know why?"

Sugiyama: "Aki's lover killed themself. You see, Aki is already twenty-one, and had been living in a Campus seven years but hadn't really gotten close enough to anyone to think about forming a bash', except this one lover, a bright young Irish Brillist named Mertice O'Beirne. Had a marvelous voice, that kid, but a bit unstable, into gore photos and Canner-beat, but lots of potential. They were very close. Aki wanted the two of them to come join and continue my bash' rather than forming a new one, since Aki's always been close to me and my bash'mates, but Mertice wanted to stay in the Campus longer to see if they could find some others of their generation to make a new bash'."

Guildbreaker: "How did Mertice die?"

Sugiyama: "Car crash."

Guildbreaker: "A car crash?"

Sugiyama: "Yes, the one over Mexico City, nine days ago. You must have read about it."

Guildbreaker: "Yes."

I do not jump to conclusions, neither do I ignore data when it appears before me. Yes, murder entered my mind as a rational possibility. No, I did not have any special intuition of something sinister beyond the facts. I did note to myself that Sugiyama could not know where the stolen list had been found, so they had no reason to share my suspicions.

Sugiyama: "It was Mertice's own fault, the experts say. There's this kit you can get, apparently, that makes the cars crash, scrambles the system. A Thrill-Ride Suicide Kit it's called. It's illegal in most Hives to sell something like that, but Humanists will insist on these things being art for art's sake, whatever the buyer does with it."

Guildbreaker: "Then you believe the crash was suicide?"

Sugiyama: "Like I said, Mertice was unstable, even attempted suicide once before. Mertice called Aki and talked to them over the tracker in the final minute when the car was flying out of control, horrible morbid stuff about death and eternity."

Guildbreaker: "Did Mertice specifically say it was suicide?"

Sugiyama: "You can get the recording from the cops. I don't want to listen to it. Aki tried to jump off a building themself after that, and made another attempt at home the day after, but they've finally calmed down. I'm past being pissed at poor Mertice, the kid obviously needed help, but almost losing Aki made me think about how little time I'd spent with them, or with my ba'kids and bash'mates, since I've always been a voker."

Guildbreaker: "So you decided to retire?"

Sugiyama: "That's right. Maybe I'll write another book. But for now I've spent all week with Aki and my bash'mates, and some from Aki's birth bash', just relaxing. Feels pretty right. I'm still going to do editorials now and again, but no more vokering for me. You're a voker too, aren't you, youngster?"

Guildbreaker: "Yes."

Sugiyama: "Ever calculate what portion of your time you spend with the people you care most about?"

Guildbreaker: "My bash' are all vokers."

Sugiyama: "Ha. No hope for you then."

I considered the possibility that the tangent might be intentional evasion, and cut it off.

Guildbreaker: "What about the Seven-Ten list? You were supposed to write it."

Sugiyama: "Yes, I was beginning the editorials when all this happened. My assistant offered to finish the editorials for me and publish the original list, but I don't like to do things halfway."

Guildbreaker: "Your assistant, that is Masami Mitsubishi?"

Sugiyama: "Yes. Brilliant kid, memory like an elephant and a razor sense of humor, I can see what Andō saw in them. But I told Masami-kun if they were going to write the list they should do it themself, their own list, start to finish. They're young and it's good to have young ideas out there sometimes. I told Hagiwara-san that Masami-kun's status as a member of the Andō-Mitsubishi bash' would be a draw in itself, but do editors listen?"

Guildbreaker: "Had Masami known who was on your list?"

Sugiyama: "Only the three outsider names. Masami-kun set up the interviews for me. Most of the staff at *Black Sakura* can usually guess who my bottom three will be since they know who I've been interviewing lately, but I never show anyone the order of the Big Seven."

Guildbreaker: "Did you write it down?"

Sugiyama: "Of course. I had a paper copy in shorthand, and half-finished essays on most of the ten started on my computer. I know what you're thinking: Masami could have accessed my computer, and it's true, they could have. So could anyone around the office. Thing is, I've seen a copy of Masami's list now, and there's no way Masami would come up with that after seeing mine. You know how you can tell if an artist has studied another even if they don't copy it directly?"

Guildbreaker: "Do you have the original list here?"

Sugiyama: "I knew you'd ask. I've written a translation for you."

Guildbreaker: "Thank you, but I will also want to examine the original paper
   list for fingerprints and other signs of tampering."

Sugiyama: "Of course, of course, just read my translation first."

I read the list at this time. It was on the same type of paper as that recovered by Mycroft, but written in a very unsteady English hand. I was unable
to keep my hands from shaking as I read. I do not have (nor do I believe in)
powers that can sense import in things beyond what reason and the facts
supply, but I do believe that some minds, appropriately specialized, may get
a true sense of a thing at first glance, even before the conscious mind
translates the details into thoughts. Surely President Ganymede, presented
with a painting, knows its period, school, and quality before becoming
conscious of the brushstrokes, pigment, and stylistic traits which are the
grounds for their deduction. Princesse Danaë Mitsubishi, though not as
fluent in art as the President, is experienced enough at least to recognize
the school. As Princesse Mitsubishi is with art, so I am far from the foremost expert at solving crimes, but even on first reading of the list, I knew
that I held motive in my hands.

> #1: Cornel MASON
> #2: Anonymous
> #3: Sniper
> #4: Ziven Racer
> #5: Bryar Kosala
> #6: Felix Faust
> #7: Hotaka Andō Mitsubishi
> #8: *François Quesnay*
> #9: *Julia Doria-Pamphili*
> #10: *Lorelei "Cookie" Cook*

Guildbreaker: "This . . . this is . . . Sniper instead of the President? And Racer
   instead of Perry?"

Sugiyama: "I wanted to stir things up a bit."

Guildbreaker: "Masami Mitsubishi knew about this?"

Sugiyama: "Masami knew I'd been interviewing Racer, Julia, and Cookie, but
   I'm sure they assumed those three would be eight, nine, and ten. In fact,
   I went so far as to start a fake editorial about Ganymede, so anyone

glancing through my files would think my list was normal. Leaks are rare but they do happen, and I didn't want anything to spoil the surprise. Bookies don't even take bets about outsiders making it into the top Seven."

Guildbreaker: "Did Sniper know?"

Sugiyama: "No. Every paper interviews Sniper twice a week, what's one more?"

Guildbreaker: "Racer I understand, but why, if I may ask . . ."

Sugiyama: "Everybody knows Ganymede only had the margin they did last election because Sniper endorsed them. If Sniper didn't always publicly decline office, they'd be Vice President or even Co-Consul by now."

Guildbreaker: "So you say Sniper is the most important Humanist because they let President Ganymede win?"

Sugiyama: "Not just that. They meet a lot, Ganymede and Sniper, behind closed doors. Sniper's careful never to admit anything, but no one would hand someone the Presidency without a big price tag attached. Why share power as Co-Consuls when you can blackmail Ganymede and not have to go to any boring meetings? I've met Sniper hundreds of times, so I know something of how the kid thinks."

Guildbreaker: "And Hotaka Andō Mitsubishi you ranked below even Felix Faust?"

Sugiyama: "When I have time I'll write summaries of my unfinished editorials for you, unless you have someone on your staff who reads Japanese."

Guildbreaker: "I do."

Sugiyama: "Of course: Tai-kun."

(Note: Sugiyama means J.E.D.D. Mason, whose Japanese nickname I understand has something to do with being a young person crowned or near a crown.)

Guildbreaker: "You realized when you wrote this that it would be quite a blow for Director Mitsubishi to be ranked so low by their native paper."

Sugiyama: "Nothing like a good kick in the balls to get people going. You may not be aware, but I've been watching my Hive eighty years now: things are bad. We've been letting ourselves shrink too long. It isn't good for us, sitting like lumps watching the Masons grow. But it's not only my own Hive I'm kicking, there's wallop enough for the Humanists, and for Europe. All three need it, the Cousins too. My draft editorials will make it clearer. I was sad when I quit that they wouldn't be published, but you've got to hand the reins to the new generation sometime. Masami-kun has some pretty stimulating names on their list too, Darcy Sok and

Crown Prince Leonor especially. Give the kid a year or two and they'll be better than I was. Well, as good, maybe."

(I asked Mycroft what I should read of the pattern of honorifics sometimes present and sometimes absent in Sugiyama's English; Mycroft was unhelpful.)

Guildbreaker: "Would you be willing to let me schedule you for an Enhanced Memory Session to recall in detail the activity at the *Black Sakura* offices in the week before the theft?"

Sugiyama: "I don't like Utopians pumping chemicals into my brain."

Guildbreaker: "It could be vital."

Sugiyama: "I still don't like it."

Guildbreaker: "The alternative is for me to send a professional police interviewer, which would take much longer. I've endured both myself, and I dislike drugs, but I vastly preferred the E.M.S."

Sugiyama: "I'll think about it."

Guildbreaker: "Time is a factor."

Sugiyama: "I'll need at least one minute to think."

Guildbreaker: "Of course. Are you familiar with how an E.M.S. works? Do you want to hear about the side effects?"

Sugiyama: "I've done them before, I just don't like it."

Guildbreaker: "I must also ask you to speculate about who else might have seen your list."

Sugiyama: "You're sure it leaked, aren't you?"

Guildbreaker: "The theft seems to be engineered to bring your list before the public eye."

Sugiyama: "My thought as well, someone at *Black Sakura* who saw my list and couldn't bear not to let the public see it."

Guildbreaker: "Or was bribed by one of the Hives that would benefit."

Sugiyama: "You don't know us at all, do you? *Black Sakura* isn't a normal paper like *Le Monde* or *Shanghai Daily*, it's staffed entirely by vokers, not just vokers but total Japanese Mitsubishi culture-obsessed literary zealots. It's not unusual for us to spend a week in the office without sleeping, most of us hardly see our bash'es, and I don't know a one person there who manages to spend their whole salary, since we don't really do anything but work. Most of them wouldn't know what to do with a bribe if you offered it to them, and a lot of them would probably physically attack anyone who suggested intentionally tampering with the press.

There's always the possibility of an outsider sneaking into the office, but if one of *Black Sakura* did it, it was because they wanted the public to see my last great work, not for money or power."

Guildbreaker: "What about this Assistant Editor who went public about the theft and substitution, Hikaru Nakahara."

Sugiyama: "Journalistic conscience, not bribery. If I know Nakahara-san they probably spent a long night deciding whether to go public or hand in their resignation. Well, there will have been some ambition in it. When Hagiwara-san resigns, Nakahara-san will probably take over, and readership will skyrocket with all this fuss. If scary criminals think we're important enough to burgle—"

Porphyrogene: "Imprimantur." (Translation: "Let them be printed.")

* * *

I held out my hand to silence Sugiyama, who could not hear the new voice over my tracker, but was startled seeing me sit so abruptly straight. Others always tell me they could not bear to live with a tracker connection set on permanent priority, so the person on the other end may hear and see through mine at any time without my knowledge, and speak to me suddenly without any warning beep or me having to select 'Take Call.' After seventeen years of the privilege, never facing any scene alone, nor enduring a second's delay before the *Porphyrogene*'s words reach me, I could not bear to live without it.

Guildbreaker: "Quae?" ("What?")

Porphyrogene: "Indices. Collegis auctoribus, petitum est ut indices perendie cum aliis pervulgare liceat. Nihil obstat. (The lists. At the urging of [Sugiyama's?] colleagues, it has been petitioned that they be allowed to be disseminated with the others the day after tomorrow. Let nothing prevent it.)"

Sugiyama: "What's happening?"

Guildbreaker: "I am to tell you that there is no legal obstruction to prevent *Black Sakura* from publishing the two lists, yours and Masami Mitsubishi's, when the other papers release theirs on the day after tomorrow."

Sugiyama: "I was about to ask that."

Guildbreaker: "Yes, they knew you were."

Sugiyama: "Is that Tai-kun on the line?"

Guildbreaker: "Yes."

Sugiyama: "Tai-kun themself. Quite the honor for my little mystery. Has

Tai-kun met with Director Andō about this yet? Has the Directorate approved the publication of the lists?"

Porphyrogene, in English, repeated verbatim by Guildbreaker: "The Directorate has no right to silence words; only the author does. This theft tells us that some specter wants your list in the world's eye. We know not why. By publishing, you blindly serve that specter, but you also serve Truth, and relieve the curiosity-pain of frightened humanity. You must choose, but if within these two days we can name the specter, you will choose less blindly."

Sugiyama: "You're right. Call your Utopians, let's get this E.M.S. over with."

Guildbreaker: "You'll do it?"

Sugiyama: "If it might help, yes. Your Tai-kun's right, the public needs to see what this is all about, but something's rotten here, and someone's trying to use me and use my paper. The only way to stop them is for you to find out what they're after."

Guildbreaker: "Thank you. We appreciate your help."

Sugiyama: "Good. I wouldn't do an E.M.S. for just anyone."

Porphyrogene, repeated by Guildbreaker: "No, you do it for Truth and Charity. Your choice is kind. I thank you."

HERE ENDS THE SECOND DAY OF THIS HISTORY.

Chapter the FIFTEENTH

If They Catch Me

I SEE MARTIN HAS INTRODUCED THE WORD 'MURDER' INTO OUR tale. Technology has eliminated that middle breed of criminal who thinks that, if they wash their hands and dump the body far from home, they can get away with it. Criminals now are either self-labeled geniuses who, through elaborate preparation, think they can outwit the trackers, DNA, and all the practice and experience of law, or else they are plain men with no delusions of escaping punishment. Of every five killers now, three turn themselves in right away, having acted in the grip of rage, or else in the calm confidence that the deed was worth the price. One out of five escapes by suicide. Only the last of the five attempts to hide, having schemed and toiled for months to form the perfect plan. He fails. There are professionals, of course, for the mob will always need its violence, but they too know that someday they must either flee the Alliance entirely, living out their lives in trackless hiding, or else be caught. Gone are the days when the police would gather evidence, conduct their interviews over a few days, and, in the end, discover the boyfriend, ex-wife, or business rival who had seen the opportunity and seized it. I asked Commissioner General Papadelias once which he preferred, the would-be mastermind who challenges the detective to a game of wits, or the honest criminal who waits red-handed at the scene. The former, he answered, was more stimulating, but usually only the latter commanded his respect. I understand it. The Prince of Murderers, said Papadelias, the Moriarty he waited for, would do both, accepting fully and philosophically his inevitable end, yet still fighting with all his strength and cunning to extend his freedom to the last breath. He needed, I think, to meet a soldier.

"Good morning, Major."

"Mycroft! You look ready to drop."

The stiffness in my shoulders made me wince as I ducked the plastic sheeting which camouflages Bridger's cave. It is a cheerful cave, walled with foam of festive colors, carved out by the robots which mine the trash beneath Cielo de Pájaros. Inside the cave is all clutter, the choicest treasures gathered from the trash of which Bridger has first pick: bright marbles, balls, tricycles, toy cars, chunks of dozens of dollhouses assembled into a hodgepodge palace, and mounds of storybooks stacked dense as bricks. My own more hygienic contributions add to the nest: blankets, cushions, clothes, video players and digital readers, good paints and paper, and a shelf of real food: rice, animal-shaped cookies, instant bacon, anything too difficult for the boy to make from mud and grass.

"I had a long day yesterday," I answered.

The Major stretched back in his rocking chair on the roof of a pink plastic castle, switching off the handheld news screen which dwarfed him like a billboard. "Did you sleep?"

I gave a guilty wince. "I napped on the flight back here from Romanova."

The Major always breathes deeply, as if he enjoys the taste of air itself. "Are ten kinds of trouble coming, or only two?"

"It's bad, sir," I answered, comfortable in company where I could say 'sir' and have no one stare. "I don't know how bad yet."

"Bad far away or bad here?"

"Both. I just spoke with Lesley Saneer. Someone very dangerous came to the house yesterday, a sensayer in historical clothes named Dominic Seneschal."

"I know. They spent hours searching Thisbe's room."

I nodded. "If we're wise we'll assume Dominic found enough evidence to know there have been unregistered strangers in that room." I eased myself into my own scavenged metal chair, between the Major's castle and a white-painted cardboard box, transformed into a functioning refrigerator by Bridger's power. "I did my best to clean up yesterday, but we've been so comfortable in that house lately, we haven't been worrying about tiny bits of evidence like skin flakes. We aren't prepared to evade a professional."

The Major nodded, the relaxed but heavy nod of a patient who has already deduced the worst before the doctor works around to the word 'fatal.' "You've crossed swords with this Dominic before?"

"I know Dominic well, though we haven't literally crossed swords. Dominic does carry a sword, though, and has killed several opponents in duels. Not an enemy we can face. It's time to move on."

The veteran nodded slowly, his sigh heavy and frail at once. "Yes."

"Is Bridger—" I didn't have to finish, for light and smiles burst in through the plastic door.

"Mycroft!"

"Oof!"

Bridger was long since too big for my lap, but had never realized it. "Aimer was just reading more of *Les Misérables* with me!" His elbows jabbed my ribs as he climbed onto me, and his legs spilled out of the chair over mine, like a hermit crab in need of a new shell. "I think Jean Valjean would get along really well with Odysseus, don't you? They could talk about what it's like being on a really long journey with lots of different stages and never knowing if it's almost over, and I bet Odysseus would have lots of clever suggestions for how Valjean could disguise themself and never be caught!"

"Yes, they probably would." Bridger needed new pants, too, I noticed, as more centimeters of sock showed beneath ever-rising cuffs. Thirteen years old; he would begin to shoot up soon, and we would have to guess how tall he would become, and teach him how to shave.

Children rarely notice whether or not you're listening. "I was thinking about what you were telling me before, about how the Greek heroes are beloved of the gods, and how that's sort of good but also bad, because it means big scary divine things always happen to them, and they never get to rest, and everyone around them always dies, like Odysseus's sailors all die. That's what happens to Valjean, too, like they're also beloved of the gods, so I bet they and Odysseus could help each other deal with it, and Odysseus could come up with a clever way to make money and feed all the poor people in Paris!"

He got me. My mind strayed first to imagining what ingenious barricade Odysseus could construct, and then I saw it all, the conversation he imagined, the two wanderers breaking bread together, drawing succor from seeing another pair of eyes as tired as their own. The Major gazed darkly at me, reminding me of his objections when the mining bots had dragged *Les Misérables* from the dump, a real old paper copy, somehow still legible. I had not had the heart to forbid Bridger to read it, but at story time Bridger always used to turn on the waterworks even when the 'bad guy' died. Now we were watching the bookmark crawl millimeter by millimeter through the masterpiece which brings tears to the eyes of disillusioned adults. We all imagine happy endings to such books, pick out the page, the paragraph, in which we would step in and pluck the innocents to safety. Only one among us actually can. All it would take is some store manikins, the costumes, and a miracle.

"I don't know," I forced myself to answer. "I don't know if Odysseus could get used to dealing with armies that have guns, or with people who believe in one God instead of lots of gods. You know it's very hard for people to deal with a world completely different from their own." I rubbed the boy's hair, chewing on the future in my mind. Yes, we would have to guess how tall he'd grow, and teach him how to shave, and make decisions like this for himself, not just to be a good boy and obey when we said 'no.'

Bridger's smile would not dim. "Maybe Achilles couldn't get used to gun armies, but Odysseus could. Odysseus is the cleverest ever. If Odysseus can get along with nymphs and gods and goddesses and ghosts and foreigners then they can handle Frenchmen."

"Probably so, but I can't see it going well. Odysseus managed to get lost for ten years in just the Mediterranean, and up in France there's the whole Atlantic to deal with." I mussed his hair again, its blond perhaps starting to dim. "You know that's a very sad book, right? *Les Misérables.* Famously sad."

Bridger hadn't learned to avoid the eyes of others, but always met them honestly. "I know. Lieutenant Aimer already told me some of what's going to happen. I'll be ready when it comes."

I used to forget sometimes that I was not Bridger's only pseudo-parent.

"Why do people like sad books?" he asked.

"You like this book," I answered.

"I'd like it better if it wasn't sad." He leaned his head against my shoulder. "I get mad at authors for doing that sort of thing to characters."

"Some books have to be sad to get across the ideas the author wants to talk about. Victor Hugo is describing a very sad part of real history. Hugo wants you to understand that moment in time, what was beautiful about it, and what was horrible. Books, even made-up stories, can't all have happy endings because they reflect the real world, and the real world isn't always happy."

The Major nodded, sagely slow. "If history is written by winners, fiction like that is written by bystanders trying to guess what the victims would have said if they'd survived."

"So what?" The heedless boy elbowed me in the gut again as he sat up. "Even if it's real life's fault bad things happen, that doesn't mean they aren't bad. Don't you get mad, Mycroft? Major? Whether it's fiction or real life, don't you get mad?"

I nodded. "That's the sort of thing you can talk to the sensayer Carlyle about."

The Major leaned back, his tiny arms swinging over the chair's sides. "Anger doesn't help. Men write books like that because they want history to remember, mourn, and make sure that sort of tragedy won't happen again." His voice was gentle, like an abdicated king happy that his words are words again and not commands. "Most of the characters in that story were willing to die for what they believed in. It's a good bet that, given the choice, they'd be willing to suffer what they suffered in the book if it would insure that you in the real world don't make the same mistakes."

Bridger nodded, not the acceptance of a man convinced, but of a child willing to accept the answers of his elders until he has time to test things for himself.

"Is Thisbe here?" I asked.

The boy wiped his nose on his sleeve, then pretended he hadn't. "Thisbe went to go meet that sensayer, Carlyle. They're coming again."

"Good. Did you like talking to them before?"

"No. But it was all right after."

I frowned down at him. "Did you not like Carlyle?"

"I like Carlyle." He smiled his cherub's smile. "But I didn't like what we had to talk about. This time I want to talk about something happier."

I held his eyes. "Bridger, Carlyle's job is helping you talk about things that are hard."

"I know." He flopped onto his side, winding me accidentally. "I guess we can talk about hard things. We can talk about sad books that make me mad."

I smoothed his hair. "You should talk to Carlyle about what you said to me before, how sometimes you get mad when bad things happen in real life too, the same way you get mad at the authors of sad books. Carlyle can tell you about philosophers who talked about that too."

"About getting mad?"

"About thinking about the world the same way you think about a book. There were some philosophers called Determinists, who sometimes talked about the creator of the universe as being like the Author of a Great Scroll, where all the events of history are written out—the Author of the world."

"Did the Deternists . . ."

"Determinists," I corrected.

"Determinists, did the Determinists also get mad at God for choosing to make the world a sad book?"

"Some of them did, but others said God had a reason for writing a sad book, just like Victor Hugo did, or that the book only seems sad because we're in the middle of it, but if you read the whole thing start to finish you'd see a happy ending. Carlyle can tell you more."

He smiled. It was good to know that Bridger could smile at the prospect of facing a near-stranger. "I like happy endings better."

I smoothed his hair once more. "Is Mommadoll here?"

"I'm here. Have some cookies."

"Yay!"

The boy picked the finest specimens from her tray of mud pies, which transformed to steaming gingerbread as they passed through his hands to mine. Mommadoll is tenderness itself, thirty centimeters tall, with rosy cheeks, bright glassy eyes, golden curls, and a permanent smile. Her tiny fingers are as adorable as an infant's until you touch them and realize that their childish thickness comes from the calluses of a decade's toil, and her apron is cheery with colorful patches when you do not think about the rips and stains beneath. I have caught her sweating as she fights to hoist a roast chicken twice her weight, or blistered to bleeding as she battles real-world cobwebs with her doll-sized broom. No human being can live without complaining even once, but she is a child's mad ideal, far beyond human.

"Are they yummy?" Mommadoll asked, watching me with her too-bright eyes.

"Yes!"

"I've made some for the Major, too, see them?"

"Mmm!" His mouth already full, the boy grabbed the pill-sized cookies from the plate's edge and passed them down.

The Major accepted. "Thank you."

"I'll have milk for the cookies in a moment, you boys just hold on."

"That'll have to wait. We need you here for this." The Major straightened in his seat.

Mommadoll reached up, and at that signal Bridger lifted her and nestled her between his chest and mine. She is warm under that frilly skirt, precariously warm like an infant whose new heat might wink out like a candle. "What's up?"

The Major's silence forced me to go first. "We don't know for sure yet, but we need to get ready in case we need to leave here soon."

Bridger spat cookie in my eye. "Leave?"

"I'm sorry. It's possible some strangers may search this area soon. We have to be ready to evacuate in case they come."

I could hear the other soldiers' mutters, soft as the skittering of insects, as they gathered in a nearby little turret.

"Strangers like Carlyle?" Bridger asked.

I shook my head. "Dangerous strangers. Bad things are happening in Thisbe's bash'. People are coming there, and may come here. We need to pack up your most important things into just a few bags so you and I can carry them."

"And Thisbe," the boy corrected. "You and me and Thisbe."

The Major shook his head. "No. If there are police and press involved, we won't be able to see Thisbe for a while."

"But—"

"Bridger." Mommadoll stroked his cheek with her doll fingers, "Remember, what's most important is that you stay safe. Nothing else matters. Right, Mycroft?"

Still in Victor Hugo's spell, I choked a moment, thinking of what parents do for children. For how many generations have we had no soldiers anymore, no patriots, no proselytes, no causes to die for? Only our children.

"Absolutely," I answered. "Bridger's safety comes first. I know Thisbe agrees. It won't be long until it's safe again, and we can see Thisbe all we want, but so long as Thisbe's being examined by the police we can't risk it, and so long as there are people searching around the bash'house we have to be ready to run."

Hands almost man-sized clutched my shirt. "But you'll still be here, right, Mycroft? You can come?"

I was so glad to say the words, "Of course." I stroked his hair. "No one can follow me." For that power, still mine, I thanked the distant makers of the Gyges Device.

"Okay, I'll do my best to pack." He gave his strongest smile. "How bad will it be if they catch me?"

Only the Major could face that question with a chuckle. "Not as bad as Croucher says. We have a plan. Our Mycroft Canner knows a lot of powerful people, people who can intervene and protect us if need be. Canner, have you picked one yet? Which would be best to go to? The Censor, Vivien Ancelet? He's got resources enough but no ambition, and he's Hiveless so it would keep Bridger out of the hands of any one Hive."

I closed my eyes, using Bridger's warmth to steel myself. "When that time comes, it will be J.E.D.D. Mason."

"I knew it!" Thisbe's voice burst through the plastic sheeting, and the witch herself an instant after. "You do know J.E.D.D. Mason, I knew you did! You wouldn't admit it, but I could tell, the way you look at your feet whenever you hear that name. Tell me everything you know about them, Mycroft, and I mean everything, right now!"

She was in her house robe, her boots half-unclasped, with a pale and harried Carlyle Foster trembling in her wake.

"What's happened?" the Major asked at once.

Since Thisbe's broken explanation will not satisfy you, reader, I shall loop back now, and give my best account of the encounter of that morning, which, like an eclipse, was always coming, yet still makes us quake inside when we see the cosmic clockwork plunge day into night.

CHAPTER THE SIXTEENTH

Thou Canst Not
Put It Off Forever, Mycroft

I WAS NOT THERE, BUT THOSE WHO WERE TESTIFY THAT IT began as a peaceful morning, sleepy after the holiday. The sky was a vivid overcast, white as a canvas against which the endless flocks of Cielo de Pájaros soared tauntingly: you claim, humans, to have mastered the skies, but you race through them on your busy way, while we, we play.

Cato's voice when he calls from his room is usually too soft even to be called a whisper. "¿Is it safe?" Like good Humanists, they would have spoken Spanish here at home, which I approximate.

Eureka lay, as ever, sprawled on the floor in the shadow of the *Mukta* prototype, ancestress of the lifeblood of our world. <yes, cato, it's safe, no scary sensayers today.>

"¿What about Cardie?"

<upstairs asleep.>

"¿Ockham?"

<ockham and lesley went to bed too. even the twins are out, and sidney's upstairs on the exerciser. it's just me and thisbe here this morning, nobody dangerous.>

"¿Does Thisbe have their boots on?"

<no. they're on the sofa, drinking tea.>

Envision Cato Weeksbooth sticking his toe out first, as if testing the water, then, feeling no burn, he sweeps into the hall. He is majestic in his way, the white lab coat billowing like a cape, his black hair full as a lion's mane, though wild and stiff as if frazzled by electrocution. He is not a Mad Scientist. Heartless reality does not grant humans the lifespan necessary to master every specialty of science, so no one genius in his secret lab can really bring robots, mutants, and clones into the world at his mad whim—it takes a team, masses of funds, and decades. But one man can love all sciences, even if he cannot wield them, and he can inspire children with the model of the mad genius, even if he cannot live it. Doctor Cato Weeksbooth is a Mad Science Teacher, who spends what hours are not required by the *Mukta* system at his dear museum plunged in the ecstasy of Show and Tell. He has just enough of every discipline at his command to answer almost all the children's questions, and what he does not know he urges them to grow up and discover for themselves. "I'm going to the museum."

"You're on duty here in two hours." Thisbe spends her empty mornings on the sofa by the window, staring at the sky over her chamomile.

"Screw that."

"I'm not covering for you. I just had the night shift, I'm going to bed."

"Let Cardie cover it. They owe me after last night."

"Fair enough."

<i saw the video. you looked like you were going to piss your pants.>

"I did piss my pants. ¿Where are my boots?"

"There." Thisbe pointed. "Mycroft cleaned them."

They stood in the corner, Cato's own design, Griffincloth, which, when active, shows in an ever-changing cycle the bones, blood vessels, skeleton, or heat signature of feet, sometimes human, sometimes beast feet, or robotic feet, elastic hinges bending as the tendons would. What schoolbook could be better?

Thisbe claims that Cato smiled, but Eureka, blind within the computer's embrace, cannot corroborate. "¿When was Mycroft here?" he asked.

"They just left. They say they'll be around to help as much as possible until the threat is past."

"¿Then those two crazy sensayers are coming back?"

Thisbe slurped her aromatic tea. "The two aren't connected. Mycroft says Dominic Seneschal is a threat but Carlyle Foster is an ally."

"¿And you believe that?"

"Yes. Carlyle's a good one. Lesley and I were so impressed we invited Carlyle to come back today to meet with whichever of the twins we can catch, or you. You must have a session, Cato, it would do you good."

Cato must be careful latching his boots, to keep the cuffs of his hospital scrubs from catching in their seal. "No thanks."

<we can't fake this for you, cato. you have to see a sensayer, or your shrink will put you back on clinic watch.>

Eureka recalls being startled as their brother stomped the floor in his rage. "¿How can all of you be over Esmerald already? ¡Eighteen years means something to me!"

No one can recall what the women said here; perhaps nothing.

"Anyway, I don't think we should let Mycroft Canner be our judge of sensayers."

Thisbe came to my defense. "¿You want to know what Mycroft really said? They said that, if one believed in Providence, one might believe Carlyle was sent here to help prepare us for the coming dangers."

Cato answered as you would have, reader. "Mycroft shouldn't talk that way. Neither should you."

<thiz, ¿how much danger does mcrft thnk w're in?> Eureka resorts to shorthand when spooked by questions their computer cannot answer.

"A great deal. Mycroft won't admit it, but I think they've met this Dominic Seneschal before. They're the worst kind of secret-sniffer, dangerous as they come, trust me. But Mycroft also doesn't think Dominic's behind this. Dominic's a side effect, not the author. There's no way to tell yet who's targeting us, but whoever it is has significant resources and malevolent intent."

"¿Malevolent intent? That's a good phrase to hear first thing in the morning." See Sniper stumbling down the stairs now, eyes vacant as a zombie's. This time of day he would probably have mustered the baggy shirt and moplike straw brown wig he wore at home to keep visitors and low-ranked guards from recognizing him, but he was not yet awake enough to achieve pants. "Morning, Thisbe. Morning, Eureka. Morning, murderer. ¿Did you enjoy the party last night?"

Cato would not look at him. "I'm not speaking to you."

"It'll be good publicity for the museum, throngs of kids."

Wordless, Cato hurried to the door, the winds of his lab coat brushing Sniper's thighs with chill.

"Ockham approved, you know." Would Sniper here have sounded cold or smug? "It was necessary. We can't afford to have the President not trust us."

"¡Never do anything like that again!"

"¿Or what? ¿What will you do, huh?"

What could Cato do? He hurled the door aside, eager to slam it behind him, but froze on the threshold, confronted with a figure there, about to knock. "Weichun?"

I have not met the security captain who smiled from the doorstep, but she is Cato and Eureka's cousin, so imagine Cato, but in a Humanist uniform, black to make the bright Olympic rings of its embroidered patches brighter. "Good morning, Cato. Everyone. We've had call for a security drill."

"Now?" Cato wriggled with the urge to bolt. "We just had one."

"I think the higher-ups want to triple check, after the break-in."

"Can I just—"

"Good call," Sniper cut in. "We're right at shift change, so I'm not even on duty yet. A disruptive moment is the best time for a test." Likely the living doll apologized with a roguish smile for his lack of pants, and likely the captain did not mind one jot. "07:17 local 11:17 UT, I'll clock in now. Eureka, message Ockham and Lesley upstairs, let them know it's a drill."

<done.>

Thisbe dragged herself up off the couch. "I'll head downstairs."

"Good. I'll start the clock at 07:18 on my mark . . . Cato, you were here when the drill was called so here you stay."

"Fine!" Cato spun and stomped back to his lab in a huff that made even this obedience rebellion. "Test my security, my security is perfect . . ."

Sniper smiled at Cato's murmur, as at the sweet babbling of a toddler. "On my mark, then . . . Mark!"

I have never seen the house spring into action, lights and sirens, bolting doors, the robots pouring forth from walls and corners like the wrathful march of ants. I have once seen from a distance the sudden blackening of the sky as the cars race in, guards upon guards, some in the city's police uniforms of white and gray-blue, some in Humanist colors, a second wave in civvies, rushed in from beds and sofas in the surrounding tiers of bash'houses whose residents are proud to add their names to the roster of *Mukta*'s defenders. Ockham's prophecies were sound: fifty guards in two minutes and three hundred in five, who joined the automated system and the few guards always on duty in the computers' humming depths. Soon every room in the bash'house had a guard, and coordinated squads took up their places, each on its appointed tier of the computers which climbed down and down beneath the city's depths, like the vast, true body of the iceberg, a glimpse of which will make the horror-stricken sailor dream of monsters. Troops filled the trench outside too, chatting, cheerful in their proud routine, but Thisbe had showed us where their perimeter falls, so we dug Bridger's dwelling far beyond.

<¡We're going to break our record!> Cato boasted to the house over their tracker link.

Sniper: <Thisbe, ¿is someone down there with you? I'm getting a stray signal.>

Cato: <It's that sensayer again. ¡I knew it!>

Thisbe: <Yes, our sensayer is back again. Carlyle. I called them.>

Sniper: <¿Again?>

Eureka: <¡smitten! ¡i knew it!>

Thisbe: <I appreciate the vote of confidence, Eureka, but it's really just a session. They're very good.>

Eureka: <i'm sure.>

Thisbe: <Not like that.>

Ockham: <Everyone carry on with the drill like all's normal.>

Sniper: <¿What? ¿Is there a problem?>

Ockham: <The police called. Not our police. Romanova. Polylaws.>

Thisbe: <¿Making a fuss?>

Ockham: <Someone's using the Canner Device.>

Thisbe: <¿The Canner Device?>

Ockham: <They've been watching for it. Someone activated it. Here, right here in the house.>

Eureka: <¿just now?>

Ockham: <Eleven minutes ago.>

Cato: <¿Eleven? ¿Just before the drill?>

Thisbe: <Getting my boots now.>

Sniper: <¿Who ordered this drill?>

Cato: <I . . . can't confirm . . . >

Ockham: <Cato, take over the automated systems. Don't let anyone know we're taking action, just have something aimed at every non bash'member in the house. If anyone tries to leave, move, or access equipment, then slow them down, make doors stick, lights fail, robots seem to malfunction. Don't let anyone realize you're doing anything, but slow them down.>

Cato: <On it.>

Ockham: <Cardie, keep on as officer on duty. Go down with the drill captain and start checking off the levels one by one.>

Sniper: <On it. ¿Whose gray pants are these behind the couch, and can I borrow them?>

Lesley: <Mine, go ahead.>

Ockham: <Eureka, assemble a master list of everyone who's here. See if there have been substitutions. No one should be here who hasn't had a background check a kilometer deep.>

Thisbe: <I didn't see any unfamiliar faces.>

Sniper: <Me neither.>

Eureka: <all ids check out.>

Sniper: <Entering green wing elevator now. Ockham, ¿where are you?>

Ockham: <Still upstairs with Lesley. We won't move until we know what's happening.>

Cato: <I see twelve people out of position, mostly near each other, four groups of three, moving . . . moving fast, upper tiers, just under the house, they look like they're searching.>

Ockham: <ID them.>

Cato: <On it. ¿Should I take them out? I have clear shots on all twelve.>

Ockham: <¿Are they a threat to the system where they are?>

Cato: <No, they're nowhere near controls. Not a vulnerable area. Whatever they want, it isn't the system. They're definitely searching. Systematically.>

Sniper: <¿Who are they?>

Cato: <<ATTACHMENT>>

Thisbe: <Cato, ¿do you see the Canner Device? ¿Do they have it?>

Cato: <If anyone knew what a Canner Device looked like, that question might mean something.>

Thisbe: <They might be searching for the device, if it was used here.>

Cato: <You brought Mycroft here in the first place, Thisbe.>

Lesley: <Bicker later. Cato, ¿do they have any tech you can't identify?>

Cato: <Checking. Nothing extraordinary.>

Eureka: <incoming cars. not our cars, emergency system, police.>

Ockham: <¿Reinforcements?>

Sniper: <¿Whose?>

Eureka: <checking.>

Thisbe: <¿Where are these stray twelve, Cato? Give me a location, I'll flush them out.>

Ockham: <Not yet, Thisbe. I want to watch them. Cato, ¿show me?>

Cato: < Sānlíng.>

Eureka: <¿what?>

Cato: <They're all Sānlíng. The stray twelve. It's our Sānlíng Special Guard.> He means Chinese Mitsubishi, reader. Cato and Eureka use their Chinese parents' name for Mitsubishi. Of course, in one sense, Sānlíng is the Hive's real name, since a majority—slim but constant— of its Members are Chinese, but the remainder of the Earth finds 'Mitsubishi' less intimidating to pronounce than pitch-strict Chinese vowels.

Eureka: <i trust our sanling guard better than the regulars.>

Cato: <Maybe.>

Lesley: <¿What about our Humanist Special Guard? ¿Are they moving?>

Cato: <No, they're in place. ¿Do you want to let them know there's a problem?>

Ockham: <Get me a contact list for them, but no word yet. If our Mitsubishi Special Guard can't be trusted, we don't know about them, either.>

Sniper: <¿Should I call Director Andō? ¿Or the President?>

Eureka: <reinforcements landing.>

Cato: <¿Sānlíng reinforcements?>

Eureka: <no. city police and humanists, plus looks like the local alliance officer.>

Lesley: <¿Herrera?>

Sniper: <Someone's calling me. Yes, it's Herrera. Ockham, ¿you want to take it? ¿Or keep pretending you're off duty?>

Ockham: <Lesley, call Director Andō. Cardie, put me through to Herrera, then call the President.>

Sniper: <Done.>

Lesley: <On it.>

Cato: <¿Should someone call Director Huang?>

Thisbe: <No. Cato, ¿where are these stray Mitsubishi twelve? ¿What level?>

Cato: <B117.>

Eureka: <reinforcements all landed. they're heading down the trench.>

Lesley: <On hold, waiting on Andō.>

Cato: <¿Thisbe? ¿What are you doing? ¿Why are you going toward B-block? Ockham hasn't ordered you to move.>

Ockham: <All right, Herrera confirms the drill was unplanned, ordered after the Canner Device went off. Thisbe, Herrera's forces are going to enter through your door, get ready to guide them straight to B-block.>

Cato: <I can take these twelve down myself.>

Thisbe: <Ditto.>

Eureka: <¿why are we trusting this alliance person more than our sanling special guard?>

Ockham: <I don't trust anyone who doesn't talk to me first. Cato, ¿you're sure the block where the stray twelve are isn't sensitive at all?>

Cato: <¡I know my job, Ockham!>

Ockham: <Good. Thisbe, ¿ready to let Herrera's forces through?>

Thisbe: <¿Why my room? It's not a good time with Carlyle here. I don't see why we can't just handle this ourselves.>

Ockham: <I want to see how the two forces react to each other. We see the confrontation, see what each side does or tries, then if there's any trouble, Thisbe, Cato, take them all down.>

Thisbe: <With pleasure.>

Ockham: <¿How are things elsewhere? ¿Drill going smoothly?>

Cato: <We're not going to break our record.>

Ockham: <¿But do all the forces think everything's normal?>

Cato: <Looks like.>

Sniper: <I'm down to H-level, everything's running like clockwork.>

Eureka: <there's another car coming. utopian system, not ours.>

Cato: <¿Really?>

Thisbe: <¿Working for Romanova?>

Sniper: <I'm through to the President. On a scale of one to pissed I'd rate them pissed.>

Cato: <¿At us?>

Sniper: <No. They're calling Andō. They think we can trust our Humanist Special Guard, even if the Mitsubishi ones are being weird.>

Ockham: <Good. I'll alert our Special Guard.>

Lesley: <Still waiting on Andō.>

Thisbe: <I'm in place. Ockham, ¿should I let Herrera's forces in now?>

Ockham: <Yes. In. Now.>

Thisbe: <Done. Herrera doesn't want Carlyle down here in our way. ¿Where should I send them?>

Ockham: <Up to the *Mukta* hall. Cato & guards can watch them there.>

Thisbe: <Right. Cato, incoming sensayer. ¿Are you going to freak out?>

Cato: <¡I'M FINE!>

Eureka: <new car's landed. ¿can anyone see them? i don't know utopian ids.>

Cato: <Can't see from here. But the sensayer's here now and I'm totally fine. ¿See?>

Thisbe: <Bravo.>

Ockham: <Herrera confirms Utopians are helping Romanova track the device.>

Cato: <Thisbe and Herrera's force will reach the twelve Sānlíng in 50 seconds.>

Thisbe: <¡These guys can really book it! ¡This is fun!>

Cato: <¿Was that the doorbell?>

Lesley: <The Utopians.>

Cato: <¡Oh! ¿Should I get the door?>

Thisbe: <You need to be ready to help me at B117.>

Cato: <I'm ready, flick of a finger. Ockham, ¿may I get the door? I'm the only bash'member up here.>

Ockham: <Wait for me to come down.>

Cato: <If they're tracking the Canner Device it could be urgent.>

Ockham: <Coming. Hold on.>

Cato: <¿What's taking you so long?>

Lesley: <We're not decent up here.>

Thisbe: <Oh, you poor things. ¡Timing!>

Cato: <They've rung the bell again. The guards up here are getting antsy. We shouldn't keep them waiting, not if they're with Romanova. ¿What if they have urgent news?>

Ockham: <Fine, let them in.>

With an eagerness which must have baffled the drill troops in the living room, Cato Weeksbooth rushed to the front door and opened it to find a dark figure. Cato froze. He did not run this time. The sensayer's scarf around Dominic's shoulders had given him something concrete to run from, but this Stranger wore nothing so clear. His clothes were all black, as antique as Dominic's: tight britches buttoned just below the knee, stockings, leather shoes, a swallow-tailed coat over a short waistcoat, a fine cravat. It was not the luxurious costume of Ganymede's Eighteenth Century but simpler, a cut from the century's end, when the Revolution's austerity had stripped fashions of their ornament. The embroidery was gone, frills, lace, trim, brocade, gone, leaving the elegance of the style naked, if one can call clothing naked. Only the cloth itself and the long tails of the coat remained luxuriant, falling behind the figure like folded wings. In our age of peace, we easily forget the Revolution's grim equality, whose Terror prescribed the same uniform to peasant, to noble, and to the citizen who handed death to both. When Robespierre—

Enough delay. Thou canst not put it off forever, Mycroft. Thou must describe the wearer, not just the suit.

And so I must, master. And so I try.

His is forgotten flesh, statue-still except for the bare minimum of breath and necessary motions: walking, reaching. His eyes move only to search, His lips only to speak, never to smile. He does not fidget as He sits or stands, but lets His limbs lie abandoned, dead as a vehicle whose driver leaves it by the roadside. His skin is light enough to prove that Europe had some part in His ancestry, but has color to it too, though whether it is

Mediterranean color or something from farther around the globe's wide sweep cannot be guessed from His face alone. His long hair is tied back, rich waves whose almost-blackness makes it harder yet to guess which races mixed to birth this body for Him. His clean face is beautiful, as a well-proportioned stag is beautiful. I think His eyes are black, with a little touch of Asia in their shape, but when I try to picture them I remember no color, just their distant deepness as they focus, never on, but past the base matter before them. A room feels cold with Him in it, not because He drains it of heat, but because He seems to make none, so the air is as empty as if you were alone. He is now in His twenty-first year upon this Earth, with a minor's sash still about His hips, but had you seen Him at seven years or younger, you would still have counted Him graver than His Imperial father.

"¿How long until the next Mars launch?" He asked Cato in Spanish, His voice soft to the point of weakness, as when one talks to one's self to relieve too long a silence.

"Two days, fifteen hours," Cato answered automatically, like a child caught mid-daydream by the teacher.

"¿For how many generations has the Saneer-Weeksbooth bash' been Humanist?"

"I don't know. Ten, maybe."

"Thank you. I am J.E.D.D. Mason. The safety of your bash' and the incomparable service you provide humanity has been entrusted to Me, by order of all seven Hives and the will of the Alliance. I am looking for My dog. ¿May I come in?"

Cato gaped.

The men and officers murmured, and some saluted. The impulse was natural. No insignia of any kind touched J.E.D.D. Mason's black suit, but patches crowded for space on a cloth band around His right arm: the azure Lady Justice of the Cousins' Chief Council's Office, the gold-trimmed red and green trefoil of the Mitsubishi Executive Directorate, the six Olympic-colored swords of the Humanist Attorney General, the Gordian knot of Brill's Institute, the amphitheater ringed with stars of the European Parliamentary Council, the blue and gold scales of the Polylegal Bench, and Romanova's Earth-blue circle bisected by a belt of gray which marks a Gray-law Hiveless Tribune. All these patches ringed the main symbol on the armband: a Masonic Square & Compass in black against iron Imperial Gray, the mark of a *Familiaris Regni*, an intimate of the Emperor. While Martin Guildbreaker's *Familiaris* armband is plain, this one had borders, stark white bands at the top and bottom, edged with the blood purple piping which marks out the *Porphyrogene,* one 'born the purple,' a MASON's child.

"I . . . guess you'd better come in." Cato backed into the house, leading J.E.D.D. Mason and His two Tribunary bodyguards through the spartan trophy hall to *Mukta's* sanctum. This Guest would not have seemed to glance at the articles and papers framed on the walls He passed, but He would remember every one.

Sniper: <Don't talk to them, Cato.>
Cato: <¡But it's Xiao Hei Wang!> The Chinese have their name for J.E.D.D. Mason too.
Sniper: <Don't talk to them. The President warned me about this.>
Cato: <¿How do I not talk to them? They're a Bailiff. And a Tribune. ¡They're in charge of the case! ¡The President and Chair Kosala were on the news saying Xiao Hei Wang's in charge of the case!>

Cato and our Guest reached the *Mukta* chamber now, where the drill troops crowded in wonder around this most elusive Prince.

"Tribune Mason!" The highest ranked officer hailed the Visitor in English, and by His most neutral name. "What an unexpected honor having you here in person! You could have just called."

Only the subtlest motion of His eyes proved that He turned His attention to the speaker. "These bodies have so few senses. How can you be content with less than all?"

Those around the Guest froze in confusion, since His lack of tone made it impossible to guess whether the question was rhetorical.

<well said!> Eureka trumpeted over the public line.

Without moving, the Visitor lowered His eyes to the set-set. "Oklahoma Turner has a new essay on whether computer interfaces are artificial senses or prostheses to the standard five. You will enjoy disagreeing with it."

Perhaps Eureka smiled here, puckering the film of sensors across their lips like half-shed skin. <that's a good way to put it. i enjoyed disagreeing when turner argued against there being meaningful data in intuitively sensed recurring number patterns. idiot.>

"Do you draw strong meaning from the recurrent patterns of your habitat, as Brillists do from minds and geologists from stone?"

Only Eureka remembered His next question precisely. "Are both this home's set-sets Pythagorean?"

"You mean Cartesian," Cato corrected.

He did not, but would not contradict.

Sniper: <¡Ockham! ¡Get Cato and Eureka out of there! ¡Now! ¡Now! ¡Now!>

Ockham Saneer leapt down the stairwell, as quick as a god appearing at the invocation of his name. He had pajama bottoms and one sock, and had seized his sidearm from the bedside table, but the rest of him was naked, Lesley's doodles fresh on his chest and lithe bronze back.

Fear and obedience warred with curiosity in Cato, but fear won, and he helped Eureka to the lab's locked door.

Now Ockham faced the Visitor, his sock and pajamas against the high insignia of every government, but if Ockham hesitated it was the Visitor's strange gaze that chilled him, not His offices. "I am Ockham Saneer. Whatever your charge from Romanova or any other power, Council Mason, I am in command in my house unless my President orders otherwise."

"Your devotion sows respect," J.E.D.D. Mason answered. "I know something of your present small crisis. Would action or inaction on My part be more helpful?"

Ockham took a breath to consider. Meanwhile:

Thisbe: <¡Victory! Our stray Mitsubishi twelve have surrendered to me and Herrera. They're acting natural, saying they came up here following signs of an intruder. Could be true.>

Sniper: <Fishy. I'll come to you, Thisbe. Cato, ¿any signs of an intruder near B117?>

Cato: <Checking . . . >

(I abridge further texts, as we move our focus to the Guest above. You may trust Sniper with their loyal Humanist Special Guard, and Thisbe with Romanova's honest reinforcements, to secure the safety of all things.)

Ockham breathed deep as he faced the new Arrival. "My small crisis seems to be contained, though you would help me if you shed light on the reason for it."

"I can attempt." J.E.D.D. Mason's eyes rolled slowly across the rapt, excited faces in the room. "I love openness, but trust your judgment whether

I should shed My light in front of all these gathered. Secrecy is one of your bash's armors, is it not?"

Ockham paused, then smiled at the courtesy, and turned to the nearby captain. "Zhu Weichun, isn't it? Clear the room. And pause the drill. Keep everyone in place, exactly where they are, just hold position. Nobody moves without my order, except the Humanist Special Guard, and Herrera's people."

Captain Zhu's face grew bright with questions. "Oh, is Officer Herrera here?"

Ockham raised one dark eyebrow, but the Guest spoke first, His gaze now on the Captain. "You need not wound yourself so."

The Captain shook. "Wha . . . what?"

"Some people find that half-lies and omissions do not wound their consciences as direct lies do, but clearly you are no such person. You wound yourself with this deception. Rest in silence, you will suffer less."

"Uh . . . I . . ."

Ockham's voice grew black as storm. "What do you mean?"

Remember, reader, there is no intonation in J.E.D.D. Mason's words, so these men have no way to guess what side He takes, or why He exposes what He does. "The name Herrera that you spoke, Member Saneer, was no strange news to this person. It must be some very deep love to compel such painful self-injury."

With these words, a transformation seized the Captain. A sob rose in her throat, grief on her lips, while tear glints kindled in her eyes, her whole face flushing with that bloodred passion blush which flares so intensely in some Asian faces.

The Tribunary Guards jumped closer to their Ward as Ockham raised his sidearm, though he aimed away from J.E.D.D. Mason, at the Captain, who gave a second sob.

"Why anger?" J.E.D.D. Mason asked Ockham flatly, as if He genuinely struggled to understand. "Only a great good would move such an exacting conscience to this action." He turned His eyes on the trembling Captain. "Was it Charity? Gain for many? Protection for many? Lessen the sum total of human pain at the cost of increasing yours?"

Ockham cut Him off. "My interrogation, Tribune, not yours. Explain yourself." He took one grim pace toward Zhu Weichun, his bare arm and weapon steady, with the rare phrase 'deadly force' behind both. The other forces here bear no such privilege, not even the Tribunary Guards, expert with the stun guns that Law judges sufficient to guard the highest officers of the Alliance, but not enough to guard the precious cars.

Captain Zhu choked down a sob. "I'm sorry, Member Saneer. It's nothing hostile, I swear! It was the least disruptive way to remove the threat. Or, it should have been." She winced, looking around to her baffled fellows. "Can we . . . clear the room?"

"Use text."

Zhu Weichun hesitated. "You will not want this to leave a record."

Ockham Saneer took a deep breath, then announced his orders over his tracker and aloud: "Cardigan, bring our Humanist Special Guard up here. I want people I can trust. Weichun, surrender your weapons. You two," to the Tribunary Guards, "I appreciate your backup." His eyes did a quick count-sweep and settled on the one warm body unaccounted for. Not the Visitor's. "Cousin Foster . . ."

The young sensayer had tucked himself into the most out-of-the-way sofa, watching all with that fascination which draws crowds to a flaming house. "I can leave if you like, or stay," he offered. "No need to worry about security with me, I'm used to high-security bash'es, that's why I'm here." He gave a strong, calm smile, for our Carlyle had risen full of strength that day, March the twenty-fifth, the first day of the Medieval New Year, a festival of spring, as well as the Feast of the Annunciation, a day on which men had honored their Creator in many ways in ages past, and still do today.

There must have been some little sign from red-faced Zhu Weichun: a breath, a twitch, a glance. Reason insists there must have been, to prompt J.E.D.D. Mason's next words: "Let the sensayer stay, their presence doubles confession's benefit."

Ockham turned, a precise, too-energetic movement, his body beneath the bare skin tense with that rare energy that reminds us humans once were predators. "What?"

"Confession addressed to you will heal the peace and your confusion, and perhaps your trust, but, if a priest attends, confession will also lift weight from this sin-fearing person's wounded conscience." J.E.D.D. Mason's eyes rolled down to Captain Zhu. "Will this sensayer suffice? If you prefer one with some formal ordination My Dominic can serve, if he is found. Or I could call Guiomar Capello." The name made both the Captain and Carlyle twitch, since, in our age of theological anonymity, no sensayer is more widely suspected of being a secret Catholic than the personal sensayer of the King of Spain.

A baffled awe mixed with fear and shock on Zhu Weichun's face, unlocking tears in the catharsis of deception's end. "How . . . how did you know?"

That drove Carlyle to his feet. "You can't!" he cried, then paused, as if he was himself uncertain how to phrase his objection. "You can't just say things like that! In front of people!"

J.E.D.D. Mason did not turn, but his black eyes rolled around to fix on Carlyle, as when a too-lifelike painting seems to track you across a room. "You believe in noninterference. Is that not incompatible with benevolence?"

Carlyle went white, holding his wrap tight about himself, as if some trespassing gale had caught him wet and almost naked to the storm. "No . . ."

Nothing changed in the Visitor, except His words: "But I misunderstand. By 'can't' you did not question the possibility of my words, you meant I should not say such things, under local human law. You are correct. I erred. I thought only to diminish present pain. But I concede and recognize that the laws and master of this house are not wrong to rank duty over pity." His eyes drifted to Ockham. "I apologize, Member Saneer, for this mismatch in the radii of our consequentialisms."

The room fell silent. We are unaccustomed, reader, to words like His, which cut through the surface levels of our interactions to the reality beneath.

Only Ockham had the strength to smile. "No need to apologize. It was a handy and original way to expose a conspiracy."

Still no expression. "Should I repeat the action? Conspirators are, by definition, plural."

Fear touched every face but those of Ockham and the Tribunary Guards.

The master of the house phrased his invitation carefully: "If Weichun has co-conspirators, I want to know it."

One by one the drill troops held their breath as J.E.D.D. Mason's dead eyes rolled across them. On the third—a slender Dutch Greenpeace Mitsubishi football player stationed by Cato's door—they stopped. "Which karma do you want?" He asked.

It is hard to name the expression of abject contact, more shocked and intimate than fear, which seized her face. With slow and careful hands she released the clasp which held her weapons belt, and let the whole fall to the floor. Three others followed suit.

Ockham released a slow whistle, while Carlyle, tiptoeing forward from the sofa, gave a deeply shaken little gasp.

Lesley: <Ockham, I'm finally live with the President and Director Andō. They say this drill was ordered by someone mid-ranked in our Mitsubishi backup, as a stupid plan for going after whoever has the Canner Device. Apologies are flying, and the President's in full-fledged righteous fury mode. ¿Shall I add you to the call?>

Ockham: <¿Is anyone trying to defend or justify this debacle?>

Lesley: <No.>

Ockham: <Then no need yet.>

Sniper entered now with the Humanist Special Guard. These twelve were all Humanists by Hive and birth bash', mostly natives of Cielo de Pájaros, proud of their commissions, excited by the drill, and even more excited now that something real was happening. Their calm faces and Sniper's presence eased Ockham instantly, like sea spray in the heat of August. They also eased the five conspirators in a way, since surrender doesn't feel so real when you outnumber those you're trying to surrender to. Ockham's quick orders sent the regular troops and secondary prisoners off to parts secure, until the room was almost what he wanted: trusted Sniper, trusted troops, the oddly forthright traitor Zhu Weichun, all in Ockham's control, save for the little sensayer, this strange Guest and His Honor Guard. And Thisbe. Her arrival in Sniper's wake did not match Ockham's orders, a fact which earned a twitch of irritation from his black brows. But he would not criticize a bash'member in front of outsiders, nor would Thisbe, in any circumstance, admit why she had more reason than any of them to want to get the measure of this new Intruder.

"Hinc . . ." J.E.D.D. Mason began in Latin but caught Himself. "From this point," He translated, "do you desire help or privacy?"

Ockham smiled appreciation at the great Prince-Tribune's deference. "I understand high politics is your thing. If you can sort out that end, and leave me free to check my own security and deal with this supposed intruder, I'll be grateful. I don't know what the Mitsubishi are thinking right now, but I hear they trust you, and the last thing I need is Hive execs in a tizzy thinking there's something wrong with my security."

"Your security's vindication I shall undertake," He answered, inclining his head in confirmation of the pledge.

Thisbe intruded her voice now, as well as her presence. "The *last* thing we need is a *public* tizzy."

J.E.D.D. Mason's gaze fell now upon Thisbe Saneer. "No one comes to stone the servant when they could watch the execution of the king."

Sniper physically interposed himself between J.E.D.D. Mason and intruding Thisbe, and the distant Duke President would have been glad to know Sniper was so mindful of his warning. "I think we're okay on the public front. No one's here except our people, Mitsubishi people, and Cousin Foster."

"My Dominic may be here," J.E.D.D. Mason warned. "Have you seen him? He is perhaps your height, vicious, in dark costume, with a Black-law Hiveless sash. I seek him. He was last seen here, but has gone stray." Ockham and Thisbe did not remember observing that the Guest used 'he' for Dominic—it was too far from the strangest thing He did.

<¡That's who it is!> Cato Weeksbooth could hear all through the door. <¡In B-block! They're on camera. Not now, almost an hour ago, the system didn't register it as an intruder but there was somebody there. I was having trouble with the ID. ¡It's that scary Blacklaw sensayer!>

"Dominic Seneschal?" Ockham said it aloud. "Dominic Seneschal works for you, Council Mason? Does that mean you work with Martin Guildbreaker?"

"Both Martin and Dominic are Mine, yes. But Martin is well. It is Dominic who strays. His tracker has been off since he entered this house yesterday. When was he last sighted?"

"Tracker off since yesterday?" Here, reader, is your rare chance to see Sniper show fear. "Did anyone see Seneschal leave the house yesterday?" <Lesley, ¿did you?>

Lesley: <No. I last saw them near Thisbe's room.>

Glances flew between Ockham and Sniper. "Who else was here then?"

"I was," Carlyle volunteered, stepping gently forward. "I didn't see them leave either. But they couldn't stay in the house for twenty-four hours with no one noticing, right? Not in this house, with your security."

J.E.D.D. Mason's eyes turned back to Ockham. "While your case is Mine, your gates will open for My Dominic."

Cato: <Xiao Hei Wang is right, Ockham. Our system has the scary sensayer registering with the same super executive access privileges you do. More, they also have the back-end system editing privileges I do, and looks like they used them to clear records of themself. ¿You know the setting we use to make the system not record our secure meetings? They turned that on themself. With this they could wander anywhere, and

the system would just delete the records. They may well have been in here all night.>

Ockham took a deep breath. "This is intolerable. Council Mason, I know you and your team were chosen for your discretion, but this is ten times as disruptive as the *Black Sakura* list turning up in the first place."

"I agree," J.E.D.D. Mason answered. "It is not tolerated. Dominic will be disciplined when found. They know this." Carlyle says that, even with the airy naturalness of J.E.D.D. Mason's tone, the word 'disciplined' had an ominous sense of corporeality to it, invited by the *Familiaris* armband with its reminder of Masonic force, and the Blacklaw sash around Dominic's waist proclaiming his renunciation of all protections of the law. "You have My promise and My apology, as One responsible for whom I send."

The apology eased Ockham's scowl somewhat. "You and Martin Guildbreaker have been reasonably helpful. Yourself very helpful in fact, but—"

"That fact gladdens Me," He interrupted.

"Good. But I don't want you coming here again unannounced. No one comes here unannounced, ever. Understood?"

A pause. "Factually untrue, but as a wish I understand it, and shall endeavor to help it approach truth."

Ockham took a moment to parse that one. "Good. And I want that Blacklaw out of my house, and away from my bash'mates. Forever. Get them out of here, or I will." He tapped his deadly sidearm, still in his hand for lack of the holster which rested upstairs with his other clothes. Sniper joined the threat, tapping his own holster, though with a touch of frown, since what he carried was not deadly, or even elegant like the sport pistols he used for the pentathlon, but a common stun gun, unworthy in his hand like instant noodles on a gourmet's tongue.

"These prayers I shall endeavor to grant. If I fail to prevent an altercation between yourselves and My Dominic, I should be infinitely grateful if you spared his life." I wish J.E.D.D. Mason could have expression in His voice, emotion in His face, for moments like this when I'm sure the deadness of His request kept them from understanding how passionate a plea it was, how literal, how vast His Fear when Dominic was threatened. "I am told My third was near here too?" He continued. "He is shorter, in Servicer uniform, full of guilt, cunning, and languages, and answers to Mycroft. I hoped he might have seen the stray."

Ockham, Sniper, and even Carlyle looked to Thisbe.

"I know who you mean, but Mycroft isn't here now," she answered. "If I see them I'll ask."

J.E.D.D. Mason moved His flesh again now, calm, precise steps back toward the narrow entrance hall. "I thank you for your hospitality."

"You're leaving?"

He did not turn, but His eyes found Sniper. "Your Ockham tasked Me to settle the high political concerns raised by this event. This I undertake. But you yourself do not want Me here. If My Martin and Mycroft are more comfortable to you, then henceforth let all My work within this house be theirs."

Even Sniper stared in puzzlement. "Yes. Yes, that sounds good?" He looked to Ockham.

Ockham: "Agreed. Thank you for coming, Council Mason. Thank you for doing what you can to keep this out of the public eye, and to shield us from high politics and Hive leader idiocy, which seems to be primarily responsible for the day's fiasco. But thank you just as much for leaving us to handle our own ourselves."

J.E.D.D. Mason paused, but did not turn. "It may not help. Secrets pour out like water, even from a single hole."

Now curiosity bested even Sniper. "What do you—"

Ockham shook his head. "Stop, Cardigan." How Sniper hates that name. "Just let them go."

All under Ockham's command watched in rapt but disciplined silence as this strangest of Princes padded away on His nearly lifeless feet.

Carlyle was not under Ockham's command. "How . . . how did you do that?" He gave a little running chase, to catch the Visitor in the barren trophy hall.

J.E.D.D. Mason's slow gaze fell upon the Gag-gene. "You cannot be this bash's sensayer."

The comment struck strangely, but Carlyle managed a smile. "I'm new."

"What befell your predecessor?"

Too uncomfortable. "How did you know?" Carlyle pressed. "Back there? You knew. Confession, karma . . ." Even after all was already exposed, the sensayer would not speak the forbidden names of Faiths. "Did you look at their files? That's a horrible abuse of privacy."

"No files." Even as He spoke, J.E.D.D. Mason neither sped nor slowed, but made for the exit with the steady minimum of motion most practical for human limbs. "He . . . *yappari* . . . *premenda* . . ." His eyes searched Carlyle for nation-strat insignia. "You speak only English?"

This Cousin raised by Cousins nodded.

"Then I cannot sufficiently explain."

"But—"

J.E.D.D. Mason's feet still sought the door. "What name was given you, sensayer?"

"Carlyle Foster."

"What happened to this bash's real sensayer?"

Carlyle blinked. "They passed away. Recently."

"Be careful with this bash', Carlyle Foster. I exit now, because I Love Truth, so I perceive I am a danger to this bash', and it to Me. That is clear, as clear to Me as it was clear which of those loyal soldiers inside feared karma and which sin. You too seem to love Good, and Dialectic at least, if not raw Truth. I advise you to part from this bash' before you harm each other. But I recognize your right to incur risk in service of your vocation"—He lowered His voice—"and your Maker."

Carlyle screamed inside at this last and deepest violation of that special privacy which is the last thing in the world our cautious public still calls 'sacrosanct.' It was no easy thing to distill his objections into words, so he watched in silence as this famous Stranger—as strange as He was famous—made His soft retreat. The Tribunary Guards followed Him closely, and one paused, turning back with a frown and gentle gesture of apology for her Ward's strangeness. Moments later the Utopian car took off, and J.E.D.D. Mason had vanished as abruptly as He had come.

What then? It was too much, His strangeness, much too much. They needed answers, all of them. Once the drill troops were dismissed and the house secure once more, each bash'member turned to his favorite oracle: Ockham and Sniper to their prisoners and their President, Cato and Eureka to their computers and their surveillance tapes, while Carlyle and Thisbe raced down the flower trench, to me.

Tocqueville's Valet

THISBE'S SUMMARY HAD FAR LESS DETAIL THAN MY RECON-struction of the scene, but it was enough. "He can't find Dominic?" I cried.

"'He'?" Thisbe repeated, scowling. "What's up with you and J.E.D.D. Mason, Mycroft? No lies!"

I had not heard myself slip. "Martin and Dominic work for Them."

"That isn't what I asked." I feared Thisbe more as she hid behind the black curtain of her thick Indian hair, leaving me no chance to read her face. "They talked about you very familiarly. You know this person well, you knew the investigation was in their hands, you knew they might come here, but you didn't give us any warning they were . . ." Adjectives failed her. ". . . like that!"

Bridger, still in my lap, winced at Thisbe's harshness. He had heard her summary, the Major too, still seated on the rooftop of the dollhouse beside us, with the fascinated soldiers in the plastic rooms below.

"Are you okay, Mycroft?" Bridger asked, furrowing his smooth, young brow. "You're shaking."

"I'm fine." I mussed his hair, using the gesture to disguise the moment when I whispered in his ear. "Start packing as soon as this is done."

His eyes went wide, but, good boy, he nodded.

I met Thisbe's glare. "I see you've made the unilateral decision that Carlyle Foster is allowed to know where Bridger lives."

That mistake stilled her a moment, and she looked around, as if only now seeing the dollhouses and books and playthings piled in the secret cave. She turned to the veteran beside me. "Sorry, Major. I forgot. But I think we've all decided we can trust Carlyle now."

I let my voice stay dark. "That's not your call, Thisbe."

The Major shifted in his doll chair. "Done is done. You are the bigger question at the moment, Mycroft. What is there between you and this . . . we're talking about a Hiveless Tribune?"

"Among many, many other offices." Thisbe loomed over me. "Including that they're Cornel MASON's child."

"Bash'child or real child?" the Major asked.

Thisbe glared at his un-modern denial that the bond between ba'kid and ba'pa is as 'real' as blood.

I supplied the truth. "Adopted son."

"And heir?" the Major asked.

Thisbe indulged in a chuckle. "No. Can't blame you, Major, it's a modern thing, but Masonic Emperors aren't dynastic. They're never succeeded by their children, it's a rule. A *porphyrogene* is usually a *Familiaris*, but they're the only *Familiaris* who can't become Masonic Emperor."

The Major frowned pensively as he wrapped his head around that one. "So, adopting a child makes them ineligible. Interesting choice. Now I want to know even more about this boy an Emperor would choose to hold so close, but block from the succession."

Thisbe would not give an inch. "It's not just the Masons. I knew vaguely about J.E.D.D. Mason, everybody does, but I read more on the way here. I knew they were Romanova's youngest Tribune but—"

"Second youngest," I corrected. "In 2299 Cahya Rattlewatch was elected Blacklaw Tribune at the age of fifteen. It doesn't even require passing the Adulthood Competency Exam."

Thisbe punished my derailment by firing up the screen that sat beside the Major and loading J.E.D.D. Mason's profile from last year's *Romanov Seven-Ten* list. "They have some kind of insider advisor or legal position in five Hives besides the Masons! Europe, the Cousins, Brill's Institute, the Mitsubishi, and us too."

I avoided her gaze. "All the Hive leaders have known J.E.D.D. Mason since They were a small Child, and all the Hive leaders are impressed by Them, rely on Them, and trust Their council. That's why everybody gives Them offices, and that's why They were trusted with investigating this crime that threatens all six."

"Why? Why does everybody trust them when they act like that? Confession? Karma? And their assistants, Dominic and Martin, how cultish can you get?"

I knew better than to meet her eyes. "Martin's real name is Mycroft Guildbreaker."

"So what, J.E.D.D. Mason changed Mycroft to Martin in order to fit in with these other crazy cult things?"

"Are they bash'mates?" Carlyle interjected gently.

Thisbe turned. "What?"

"Dominic, Martin, and J.E.D.D. Mason, are they bash'mates? Ba'sibs? A bash' interested in theology?" The sensayer tried his best to smile Thisbe's wrath away. "It wouldn't have to be a cult. We see this sometimes, a bash' interested in theology, who like to debate religion in secret, and try their best to do so safely."

"Like Mycroft likes to," Bridger piped up, eager as a bird. "Except I know we're not supposed to."

Carlyle smiled sweet forgiveness. "Yes, like with Mycroft and you. It's okay when it's just two people, though. Sometimes it can turn cultlike with larger groups, which is why the First Law bans unchaperoned discussions with three or more, but it usually starts as innocent exploration like you and Mycroft do. That's all this is, right, Mycroft? Dominic Seneschal is even a sensayer, they may be doing officially sanctioned group sessions."

I looked to the floor. "You may not believe me, but I've had an urgent call. I need to go."

Thisbe summoned a too-sweet, too-false smile, perfect to lure us to her candy house. "Bridger, honey, get up off Mycroft for a minute, will you?"

"Why?"

"So I can pin them to the ground until they answer straight."

"Thisbe!" Bridger settled more squarely in my lap, my brave defender. "Why are you suddenly acting like you don't trust Mycroft? You know we can trust Mycroft. We can trust Mycroft more than anybody in the world! Mycroft's busy all the time with jobs, but they've been working as hard as they can to take care of all of us, for years and years. Harder than you work, Thisbe!"

A new expression surfaced on Thisbe, a smile far more terrifying than her glare.

Mommadoll intruded now, gentle, and irresistible. "Yelly people don't get cookies."

Bridger crossed his arms as if to shield me. "It isn't Mycroft's fault bad things are happening at your bash'house! If Mycroft says we can trust J.E.D.D. Mason, and all the Hive leaders say we can trust J.E.D.D. Mason, and everybody else in the world says we can trust J.E.D.D. Mason, then I'll trust J.E.D.D. Mason. Why won't you?"

The witch crossed her arms too. "You didn't meet them. There's something unnatural about them."

'Witch' again, Mycroft? I told thee I dislike that term.

Apologies, reader; the memories of my thoughts and fears in this scene are rather over-vivid.

"So what if there's something unnatural about them?" the child shot back. "Mycroft is weird. I'm weird. You're weird. The army men are weird. That's not important. I'm willing to go to J.E.D.D. Mason right now if Mycroft says I should."

"Not yet!" I cried at once, surprised by the panic in my own voice. "In the end we'll go to J.E.D.D. Mason, but we need to put that off as long as possible."

"Why put it off, if you trust them?" On Bridger's lips the question was timid; glaring in Thisbe's eyes it was an accusation.

"Because there are dangerous people around J.E.D.D. Mason," I began. "No. No, that's not the reason. It's because if we go to J.E.D.D. Mason it'll be Them who decides what happens to your future, Bridger, not you." I turned to the child, stroked his hair. "It's best if you grow up a little more, have more ideas about what you want to do with your powers. In a few years you'll be strong enough to decide things on your own. Even to contradict J.E.D.D. Mason when you want to. But not yet. Best for now that you stay free."

You may not have thought about it, reader, but 'free' is not a word one hears much anymore, not in its pure denotation. Almost everyone is so free these days, just as everyone is so healthy, happy, sentient, and alive, that one only mentions the quality if it is threatened: unhealthy, unfree.

The Major sighed his heavy, veteran's sigh. "Mycroft, is J.E.D.D. Mason your Tocqueville?"

I swallowed. "Yes."

"I see."

"Tocqueville?" Thisbe repeated, frowning.

A voice rose shrill from a lower floor of the dollhouse. "I knew it! Haha! I knew it! See? I told you so!"

The Major stomped the plastic roof beneath him, shouting down. "Shut up, Croucher!"

"I predicted it, didn't I? You all heard me! We never could trust them!"

A rumble like a lion's surfaced in the Major's voice. "You don't want me to come down there, Croucher!"

Prompt silence proved the Major right.

I'm glad it was Bridger who asked. "What's Tocqueville?"

The Major smiled at the boy's confusion. "It's our nickname for

Mycroft's mysterious other obligation. Do you remember when you first met Mycroft?"

The golden smile on Bridger's face healed me, like sun upon a starving field. "Of course. Mycroft was fixing the trash bots and saw Boo run out of juice, and Mycroft's smart so they knew it wasn't just a U-beast, so they came to investigate. That's when you got them."

I almost laughed. 'You got them.' Such injustice to the army men, their months of strategy, of gathering the tools, grenades as frail as firecrackers, darts of paralyzing chemicals, cannon-sized to them. They had spent months practicing, tackling cats, and squirrels, and dummies. An army of Lilliputians might tackle Gulliver in his sleep, but for eleven plastic army men to be ready at any moment to defend this boy against a full-sized human strained the limits of Earth's greatest military strategist. Strained, but did not exceed. They bested me, me, Mycroft Canner. They spooked me with explosions, snared me with wires, blinded and deafened me with flash and smoke. It was hard, they said. I beat all seven practiced plans and forced the Major to improvise an eighth, and then a ninth, right there, but in the end I fell.

"Then you remember how hard it was deciding what to do with Mycroft afterwards?" the veteran continued.

Bridger's face contorted, furrows unnatural on that angelic brow, not yet spoiled by time. "I remember Mycroft was very big."

The Major chuckled. "You were only five years old then, you can't expect to remember too much."

"Mycroft kept asking you to let them go just for ten minutes. I remember them saying that, over and over: just ten minutes, just ten minutes."

The Major nodded, impressed that the words had stayed in Bridger's mind, but humans remember best what is most intense, no matter how long ago it happened. I myself have few memories from the past decade which seem remotely real compared with the memories of my two weeks, thirteen years ago. It may sound mad, but how do you distinguish between memory and reality if not by choosing the more vivid? The smells and faces of those two weeks are burned into my mind, more colored, more alive than the commonplace sensations of this room, this floor, this half-written page before me. Daily—no, every time I close my eyes and open them again—I am surprised to find myself in this strange present. This is not where I am, back then is where I am. This pressure is a weapon in my hand, this itch enemy skin beneath my nails, this taste blood. Whose? What is this at my back?

A rock? A wall? Surely if I step out, I will step onto my battlefield. I find it hard to make myself believe it is a chair.

"The army men's attack knocked off my tracker," I explained for Carlyle's sake. "The police always check on me when that happens. It would've been a disaster if they'd found me here."

The Major nodded. "Yes, it was lucky Mycroft managed convince us to let them go for those ten minutes. They were barely out of the trench before the cops were on them, full force."

It was not just luck, reader. I recall that day, full color, full intensity, one of few solid features in the long haze since my crimes. I remember the tiny soldiers staring up, piano wires striping my skin with red as they bound me to a scavenged chair. That memory is salient, not because of the pain or the blood, I think, for I have many scars whose stories are forgotten, but for the sensation of the bonds around my arms and ankles as I felt myself a prisoner. You must not think that bondage is one of my perversions—I have many, but not that. Rather it linked that memory to another even more potent. The hours after my first capture thirteen years ago, when I sat helpless as an insect in my plastic cage, were among the most intense I have ever experienced, so, when I found myself captured and bound again, that same helplessness awoke me. That, I am certain, was what cleared my mind so quickly. I suffered no shock, no disbelief seeing the soldiers, tiny and alive before my eyes. I absorbed all in an instant, pure acceptance of the miracle, and found my resolution just as quickly: I am here now to protect and guide this boy. Such salience made me persuasive as I pleaded for the gift of ten minutes.

"We needed help," the Major continued, "a full-sized adult who could move things, and get us things, so I decided to draft Mycroft."

"Draft them?" Astonishment swept Carlyle's face.

The Major laughed. "I don't mix well with civilians. But I'll never forget what Mycroft first said when I said I was going to draft him: 'Have you ever read the *Recollections* of Alexis de Tocqueville?'"

I smiled, remembering the Major's face back then, my tiny captor, sternness brightening to relief, recognition, eventually to delight as I explained myself, my Tocqueville. He wasn't happy because of the revelation itself, but because of how I explained it, my literary roundabout, my subtle, weaving words. That was the moment the Major discovered what I am. I could have lied. I could have given my captor an unreserved "yes" and stayed silent about any division of my loyalty. I did not.

"Tocqueville wrote a memoir of living through a French revolution," the Major explained, just as I had explained it to him eight years ago and fifteen yards away. "Not the main one, the 1848 one. In one section Toc-queville describes his valet. The valet wanted to join the revolution, but was also dutiful, and loyal to his master. Every day the valet would come home from fighting, clean Tocqueville's shoes, brush his suit, prepare the room, then beg his master's leave and head back to the barricades for a few hours to risk his life again." He nodded to me. "For Mycroft, minding Bridger is the barricades. Apparently J.E.D.D. Mason is the master."

Thisbe loomed over me. "Is that right?"

The truth caught in my throat a moment. "Y-es."

"Why?"

I glanced at Carlyle, so innocent of who sits before him, so calm and kind without knowing the surname 'Canner.' "I can't explain."

"Which basically means you're not objective on any question about J.E.D.D. Mason!" Thisbe accused. "You won't even answer a basic ques-tion like why they act like a crazy cultist."

I looked down at my hands. "I believe it is possible to be simultaneously biased and right. I work for . . ." The Major's eyes demanded truer words. "I serve J.E.D.D. Mason. I do. I always will. I also, separately from that, believe that we can trust J.E.D.D. Mason better than anyone who isn't standing here right now. They are a good Person, Good, honest, kind, trustworthy, and keep Their promises more absolutely than anyone I've ever known. And They're unambitious. They have all the wealth and power any-one could want, the trust of every leader on Earth. They have nowhere to rise, no side to help. There is no better Being in the world. Believe me. There isn't. Possibly there never has been. They wouldn't exploit Bridger. They'd move sky and Earth to find the way to best help Bridger use their powers for the good of all humanity. That's why I want to keep Bridger away from Them for now, because They're so good and so kind, They couldn't keep from pressuring Bridger to move too fast, to take on too much." I squeezed the child in my arms. "A kid shouldn't have to face that much pressure. You saw how They tried to help that traitor security cap-tain, They weren't being manipulative, They were being kind. Kind and too much, trying to help, but They pushed too hard, made things uncom-fortable. They're always like that. It takes a lot to learn to handle being near Them. Once Bridger has their own plan of what they want to do first with their powers, once Carlyle"—I pointed—"helps Bridger get ready to change the world, then we should go straight to J.E.D.D. Mason, and They'll make sure Bridger gets the best support the world can give. But J.E.D.D.

Mason is too powerful and clumsy to be endured by anybody fragile. I don't mean powerful politically, but personally. You saw what talking to Them was like. They speak only Truth, and do only Good, and They don't know how to mitigate it the way people do. Someday, Bridger, you'll be ready for that, more than ready." I gave the child a squeeze, and felt stronger addressing him, who trusted me, than Thisbe, whose glare stayed black. "And when you are, you and J.E.D.D. Mason will make the whole world so impossibly much better. But only when you decide it's time."

I was grateful, during my ramble, that they listened patiently, but even when I finished they still waited, quiet, thinking on this Stranger, His presence, the many facets of Him I can only call 'too much.'

Thisbe spoke first. "Tell me where J.E.D.D. Mason came from, Mycroft. Why did Cornel MASON adopt this particular kid? I know it was done in infancy. Whose child were they?" She tried to grasp me by the hair, but I pulled away, so she had to lean far down to force my eyes to meet hers. "Are the rumors true? Is J.E.D.D. Mason really Hotaka Andō Mitsubishi's bastard child?"

"Oh, right!" Carlyle cried. "I'd heard that once. I thought it was just gossip."

Still Thisbe leaned close. "In person they do look a little Japanese. Is this some weird alliance between the Masons and the Japanese Mitsubishi? They even say MASON helped Andō get the Chief Director's chair."

I took a deep breath. I took several. "To say there is an alliance of that kind is not untrue. I can't really say more. I have to go."

"Mycroft." Her eyes turned gentle. "Nothing is more important than—"

Like a squeal of electronic pain, my tracker's emergency siren rang out, making Thisbe jump back and the Major draw his tiny, flashing blade.

"Is this coming through?" Harsh as bad music, the voice of Censor Ancelet burst out of the speaker of my tracker for all to hear. "Look, I don't know who's there, but the Servicer in front of you happens to be the one of the best statistical analysts on the planet, and right now you have them ignoring a priority-one call from the Romanovan Censor's office for an urgent analysis which has to be done yesterday, so unless whatever you're doing is more important than the economic future of the human race, would you kindly call a car and make them get their butt to Romanova and leave the odd jobs to people who can't save the world?"

Thisbe went slack-jawed. You would not think she could know me nearly a decade without learning what work I did, especially since you, who just met me, know already. But to you, demanding reader, I reveal all, while I hide what I can from friends, to keep them safer. As for Carlyle, if your eyes are sharp, reader, you may now catch, in his too-blue eyes, a glint of something darker than surprise.

"Can the Censor hear us?" Bridger mouthed.

"Only me," I mouthed back, then spoke aloud for the tracker, "I'll be along ASAP, Censor. I promise . . . Yes, I really mean it, I promise . . ." I waited for Vivien to disconnect. "There. They're gone."

"Was that really the Romanovan Censor's office?" Thisbe asked, almost agape.

"That was the Censor themself," I clarified. "And before you ask, no, I can't discuss my work in Romanova, just as I can't discuss my work for J.E.D.D. Mason, just as you can't tell me the details of what you and Cato do for your own bash'." I tried to let my features show my honesty. "Don't make me lie to you, Thisbe. I can't tell you the truth about this, so either I say nothing or you force me to lie."

"I understand." The Major answered. I looked down at him, leaned forward to try to read his tiny features, but it is nearly impossible to read the subtleties of brow and cheeks on a face a centimeter high. His voice communicated more: intentionally gentle, restraining that commanding roar which rises like distant thunder behind even his calmest words.

Bridger scooted forward off my lap. "You have to go now."

"No, I don't."

His eyes grew round as spoons. "But . . ."

"Bridger, you *are* more important than the economic future of the human race."

All at once and heedless of his weight, Bridger leapt back upon me with the fiercest hug I can remember. "I trust you, Mycroft. I don't care about Tocqueville or J.E.D.D. Mason. I trust you, and I know you never tell me what to do except when it really, really matters, and if you have to go you have to go, so go. You'll come back." Small fingers squeezed my flesh. "You always come back."

I held him. For breath upon breath I held him, and let him hold me. He trusted me. In this circumstance, when I was powerless to do anything but beg them to believe, I didn't have to beg. It didn't matter that Thisbe's eyes stayed dark. It didn't matter that worry wrinkled Carlyle's brow, that down in the dollhouse Private Croucher's mumbling was starting up again. Bridger trusted me. He trusted me despite my strangeness and my silences, despite the others' doubts. And better yet, he trusted himself, his judgment, over theirs. He was so young, our precious protagonist, and yet already starting to trust himself.

I will not endure this pretense, Mycroft, you object. I have indulged thy many eccentricities, thy 'he's and 'she's, thy titles, Patriarch, Philosophe, thy recurrent madness calling Thisbe 'witch,' I have even let thee honor J.E.D.D. Mason with the divine 'He,' but thou canst not ask me to call this boy, who has barely raised his head here in thy tale, 'protagonist.' In a history it is absurd to call anyone 'protagonist,' but if thou must, it should be one who acts, and understands, who drives the story forward. Bridger is not that.

Must we have this argument, reader?

We must, Mycroft. Thou takest too many liberties, thou who claimst to be my servant and my guide. Thou forcest upon me this opinion, biased by love, or, I suspect, by something baser, for thou, self-described pervert, hast painted this boy, this angel, a bit too sensually at times. Read thine own words and see the cause of my distrust.

I take no offense, my wary reader. I know it is hard to believe that Mycroft Canner would not harbor lust for Bridger, or for Thisbe, Sniper, Danaë, or Ganymede, the many beasts and beauties with whom I have such easy contact. Later the tale will prove my innocence. But I must have a protagonist. I struggle to open history's inner doors to you, to teach you how those who made this new era think and feel. In my age we have come anew to see history as driven not by DNA and economics, but by man. And woman. And so must you.

Then have a protagonist if thou must, but not Bridger, the least active actor in thy drama.

Who would you have, then, master?

Why not this sensayer, Carlyle Foster? He has appeared more, seen more. He is intelligent, respectable, his opinions not too strange, his view an outsider's, like mine.

No, reader. A protagonist must struggle, succeed, fail. His fate must determine whether this is comedy or tragedy. Carlyle would make our history too like the plays of Oedipus, whose audience just waits for the protagonist to learn of sins long past.

J.E.D.D. Mason, then, whom thou holdest in such mad esteem?

You do not yet know enough, reader, to speak His name.

Fine, then. I accuse thee, Mycroft. Thou art the protagonist of thine own history, as all men are, as I am protagonist of the world which I experience. In my mind I have called thee protagonist from the first page, thou who art omnipresent in thy tale, and who walkest the corridors of Power so familiarly. How couldst thou not be thine own protagonist?

I smile at the compliment, generous reader, but you are wrong. I have told you, the protagonist must determine whether this is comedy or tragedy. Surely the boy whose powers can reshape the universe itself will determine that, not this tired slave, a tool for others' use, whose days of independent action are long done. I am the window through which you watch the coming storm. He is the lightning.

There were some mumbled partings as I left for Romanova, reassuring Bridger of my return, the Major of my fidelity, and Carlyle and Thisbe . . . I remember only stiffness, my shame as I slunk past them, unable to make myself look up at the faces which held such well-justified suspicions. I should have said something, met their accusing eyes and begged forgiveness for my necessary silence. J.E.D.D. Mason is not the only clumsy one, reader. I should have said something. Anything. Anything that might have stopped what Thisbe did ten minutes later, back in her room, with Carlyle in tow.

"Eureka, could you help me a minute?" She asked it over her tracker, but spoke aloud in English for the Cousin's sake.

<of course, thiz, what's up?>

"Can you use your transit logs to track J.E.D.D. Mason?"

<sure.>

"Thanks. I'm looking for their most frequently visited addresses, home and such. And cross-reference with Dominic Seneschal and Martin Guild-breaker. I think they may be bash'mates. I just want to make sure there's no security problem, or conflict of interest."

<that's mycroft guildbreaker, right?>

<yes, that's right.>

Imagine Carlyle's wide eyes, his trembling lips. "Should we be doing this?" he whispers.

Thisbe mouths back the unassailable excuse, "For Bridger's safety."

<ooh, trixy xiao hei wang. no car id, no records in my system.>

Thisbe's dark brows arch with intrigue. "What does that mean?"

<they don't use our cars, thiz. seneschal & guildbreaker do, but xiao hei wang never uses our cars, doesn't even have an id. they came today in a u-car, left in a u-car, always u-cars.>

"You have Utopian records too, don't you?"

<not their predictor data, but they do share flightpaths and ids. found them. there they are now, flight to togenkyo. loading past records.>

"Great. What are the most frequent addresses?"

<romanovan forum, togenkyo directors' tower, imperial palace, brussels . . . >

"Those all sound like work addresses. Anything that isn't work?"

<here's one, all three go often, and xiao hei wang has lots of overnights there, at least one a week, could be a residence, could be a lover. [XX], rue

[XXXX], avignon, france.> I censor His address here, reader, though I could not hide it from Thisbe. <that one looks good. let's see if there's another place. oooh!!!!! black hole! black hole! they go to the black hole! wow, they go a lot!>

"Black hole?"

<yes! the black hole! that's what sidney and i call it. it's the most amazing place! we don't know what's there. we've been guessing for years, great game. it's a place, and people go to it, you should see the patterns, thisbe, so many visitors, so fast, so spicy cold. nothing looks like that. and sometimes people go but hide the fact on purpose. they hitch a ride with somebody else so there's only one car id, but we can tell there's extra people from how much the car weighs, and lots of people do it, thisbe, lots all the time. they're trying to hide that they're going to the black hole, but they go, over and over, sometimes for an hour, sometimes for a night, a weekend, but if somebody goes even once they always go again, again and again and again, over and over and over. and some people stay forever!>

"Forever?"

<forever, thisbe! people go there and they never leave, never, they stay and stay and stay. there's people there who have been there for a decade, and never gotten in a car, not once, just stayed in paris for years and years.>

"It's in Paris?" Again Thisbe's brow arches; did yours arch too?

<yeah, [XX] boulevard [XXXX], paris. some people stay forever, and sometimes new people come out of it, people who were never ever in a car before, but they're not babies, they get married, they have to be adults, but they spent years never leaving the black hole!>

"And J.E.D.D. Mason goes there?"

<all the time. are you going to investigate it, thisbe? awesome! oh, i don't know whether to ask you to tell me the secret or not. it's sidney's and my favorite guessing game. we have a bet on who can figure it out first. i guess if you win we both lose? but it's cheating actually going there.>

"It's work," Thisbe answered flatly. "I'll tell you if security requires."

<ok. black hole, so cool. do you need anything else?>

"No, thanks, all set. Thank you!"

<sure.>

Thisbe signed off, to face a pale and staring Carlyle Foster.

"Do you . . ." He whispered it, though no one was around, since whispers are the proper tone for fear, and trespass. "What do you intend to do?"

"Turn up and ring the doorbell."

"But—"

"We need to know about J.E.D.D. Mason, Carlyle. We cannot in good conscience leave Bridger in Mycroft's power while Mycroft is so obviously being controlled by this . . . deeply weird person. You said it's probably a bash' doing weird things with theology. Let's find out."

He swallowed hard. "Is this allowed? I mean, using the car data like this?"

"Of course. I'm authorizing it."

"But just turning up?"

She finished fastening her boots. "I've run the public searches. There's tons of cute photos of J.E.D.D. Mason as a child in famous people's arms, and all the useless gossip you could want, but nothing to tell us what they're actually like, or explain how they behaved upstairs today, or why they have this hold on Mycroft C—" She caught herself. "We need to know."

"We're talking about walking up to a high-ranked politician's private home. There'll be a million security."

"Then I'll flash my million credentials," she proclaimed. "I'm a security officer for the Six Hive Transit System, Carlyle. I am authorized to take whatever measures I see fit to protect this bash' and the welfare of the world. I have all the clearances I need, and, while you're with me, you do too."

"I . . . hadn't thought of that."

She rifled in her closet for a jacket. "I'd hoped you could help me investigate whether this is a cult or a theology bash' like you said, but I'll make do on my own if you're scared to come."

"I'm not saying I . . ." Something inside the Cousin started to feel stronger. "I'll come, definitely. I'll come. I'll help. I agree we should investigate. We should investigate. I just . . ."

"Avignon first, Paris second. The car will be here in a moment. Shall we head up?"

The Cousin clutched his wrap. "Now?"

"Best to strike while we know Mycroft and J.E.D.D. Mason are both elsewhere."

Urgency has a way of stifling caution, and conscience. "Why Avignon first? If the Paris address is so strange, it sounds like the heart of things."

Thisbe smiled her careful, calculating smile. "Because if Eureka Weeksbooth thinks this 'black hole' in Paris is one of the most exciting places in the world, I want to know as much as I can before I ring that bell."

The Tenth Director

I FAILED TO WATCH CARLYLE. THE CAR'S FLIGHT GRANTED ME seventy-one minutes before I was locked once more in the silence of the Censor's Office, watching those numbers return and return which my imagination always writes in Kohaku Mardi's blood: 33-67; 67-33; 29-71. But in the seventy-one minutes of my flight, I did not think of Carlyle. I could not. You may scold, reader, that I should have been more careful, that Bridger and his power—if real—are the most important thing in the world. But there is One Whose call makes this world fall away from me like dream. It was He, quick to keep His promise, Who called over my tracker, and bade me join His call to Tōgenkyō, where the Nine Directors, towering oaks whose umbrella branches shield and dominate the Mitsubishi billion, shuddered in the storm.

"The decision to hide this action from Ockham Saneer in the first place is difficult to understand. This persistence in wanting to continue to hide the details from them now is frankly intolerable, and an insult to one of the most dedicated and worthy officers any of us has the privilege of working with."

Chief Director Hotaka Andō Mitsubishi was the first voice I heard over the tracker. The video feed showed him at the head of the long table where the Directors gathered, their spring suits livening the conference room with waterfalls and new grass, cats and calligraphy, clouds and koi. It was night already in Tōgenkyō, cloudy, and through the windows I could see the capital's skyscraper towers painting their lotus shapes in strokes of light against the black canvas of sea and starless sky.

"They're an officer of another Hive, not ours." The Directors speak English in the conference room, the compromise language which makes no claim about which nation-strat is strongest.

Andō scowled. "Humanist or not, we trust Ockham Saneer every day with the welfare of our Hive and all its Members."

"True." It was Director Huang Enlai who answered, the squat and hardy leader of the Dongbei region sub-nation-strat, not the most powerful of the five Chinese Directors, but the safest in his seat, anchored by six decades' experience and the loyal votes not of his small home region, but of the multitudes of Chinese Members too fed up with the endless tussles between the Beijing and Shanghai blocs to throw a vote to either. "I agree we can trust Ockham Saneer in almost every situation, but there are different kinds of trust. I trust my doctor with my life, but not my dirty laundry."

"And Ockham Saneer doesn't trust the transit system to people who infiltrate their home under false pretenses." Andō's glare swept the faces of the five Chinese Directors. "I spoke with President Ganymede. They have agreed keep this incident a secret to avoid a public scandal, but they are justifiably furious. The Special Guard we provide for the Saneer-Weeksbooth bash' is the oldest and deepest seal of friendship between our Hives, and much more than symbolic. Having them undermine Saneer within their own bash'house jeopardizes generations of carefully cultivated relations."

Old Huang Enlai gave a little sigh. "I'm not saying it was a good idea. I'm saying that revealing the entire back end of how it happened is itself a different bad idea."

"How bad?" Andō looked from face to silent face. "The rift this could create between us and the Humanists is the largest crisis we've faced in years. If airing a small piece of dirty laundry can prevent that, it is more than worth it."

Silent faces stared back.

"I hope you're right." Kim Yeong-Uk spoke up now, Korea's hard-won lone Director. "But if you aren't, if revealing the truth to Saneer and Ganymede would be more dangerous than the rift this is already causing, all the more reason for whoever authorized this action to speak up and let the entire Directorate know what we're really dealing with."

The deep lines of years well spent made Director Huang Enlai's frown fold in on itself. "It should be possible for us to apologize to them without revealing every detail."

"By this point they know enough to ask very specific questions."

"How much?" Huang asked quickly. "What are we sure they know?"

Chief Director Andō raised his eyes to the camera. "Tai-kun?"

All turned bodily toward the projected image which made young J.E.D.D. Mason seem to sit at the table with them. To say they listened intently to Him is too commonplace. This was a different focus, deep. As when Utopia has sent a brave and precious probe to skim the surface of all-swallowing Jupiter, and the silence breaks, and the technicians lean raptly over their screens to piece together meaning from this first fuzzed data stolen from the heavens, so these nine men locked upon the words of their unofficial Tenth Director.

"Ockham Saneer knows with the certainty of perception," J.E.D.D. Mason began, "that those whom I exposed were torn by guilt, but believed themselves to be acting in a good cause, and a peaceful one. They know with the certainty of testimony that the Saneer-Weeksbooth bash' and the transit system itself were not endangered by the action. They know with the certainty of analysis that the Mitsubishi Special Guard and their confederates received orders whose pull was stronger than the triple counter-pull of their loyalty to their fellow troops, their respect for Ockham Saneer, and their concern for the safety of the lives endangered should the transit system suffer from their action. And they know with the certainty of experience that events which are improbable and proximal are likely to have a causal link. Thus they know with the certainty of deduction that one of you ordered the Special Guard to steal the Canner Device."

The frowns birthed by His answer were resigned, not critical. "Do you think they will accuse the Directorate directly?" Kim asked.

"In their heart they must have already. No other author would have made the traitors consider their betrayal both necessary and altruistic. This was clearly moved by no bribe, nor threat, nor small-scale gain for bash' or person. Those who acted believed it was to benefit great bodies, cities, peoples, nations. Thus, yourselves. Or one of you."

All Directors searched their fellows' eyes.

Andō scratched his silvered temples. "And you are sure Ockham Saneer thinks this too?"

"Yes, *Chichi-ue*." The Japanese form of 'Father' which 'Tai-kun' uses to address Andō is peculiarly formal and old-fashioned. "Ockham Saneer must have thought all this already. They have anti-proofs."

Old Huang Enlai smiled at the 'Tenth Director.' "What anti-proofs?"

"Anti-proof the first: You know that Saneer will suspect you, and Saneer knows you realize this. If you had proof of your innocence, or of another's guilt, you would have offered it to them. You have not. Anti-proof the second: Captain Zu Weichun will not lie to Ockham Saneer again. When asked who sent them, they may answer nothing, but they will not state explicitly it was not you. Thus Saneer will know it was."

I did not catch which Director muttered the first few frustrated Chinese syllables, musical like Greek, but, as soon as someone broke the hold of English, more Chinese flooded in. I could not follow the words, but the five Chinese Directors' body language was transparent enough: Beijing's Wang Laojing was sparring with the Shanghai Directors, Lu Yong and Wang Baobao, though which side was accuser and which defender I could not say. Old Huang Enlai, interjecting often, was the net to their verbal tennis match, while Wenzhou's Chen Zhongren added occasional notes of guarded brevity. There is something pure to politics without words, raw human side-taking stripped of its veneer of topics and justifications. I saw sighs of recognition pass among the non-Chinese speakers in the room too. Shanghai and Beijing had done this; we could all see it. One of their vast voting blocs had taken this gamble, scrambling to get the better of the other, money-fatted Shanghai against the proud and stubborn former capital. I know it is as egregious as conflating Paris and London, but, to we linguistic exiles in the room, it hardly mattered which of the two was the culprit— when siblings spar, the true cause is proximity.

"Enough!" Andō broke in. "This action endangers the [a/A]lliance!" His angry spoken English contained an ambiguity I cannot preserve in text. Did he mean the unofficial alliance between the Mitsubishi and the Humanists? Or Romanova's Universal Free Alliance, which, like a watchman at some ancient port, tries with its tiny voice to give some aid and order to the man-made leviathans which crowd and jostle in the bay? At times like this I am reminded just how small a bay Earth is, and how vast these leviathans. "I care less who is at fault than how the ten of us will fix this. I'm prepared to be direct if no one else is. At this point we all know vaguely what the so-called Canner Device is, that responsibility for its development can be linked to our Hive . . ."

The newest Director, Shanghai's young Wang Baobao, was aggressive enough to murmur, "Japan."

Andō's pause was brief. "Yes, it can be linked to my strat specifically. And I think we all realize that makes it easy for someone who wanted to harm our Hive to fire up the public about Mitsubishi culpability in everything the device has ever been associated with." I thanked Andō in my heart for avoiding my name, but still it hung in the air like a pregnant storm cloud: Mycroft Canner. "One of you arranged this 'drill' today to try to seize the device. Perhaps you did it to protect the Hive."

"*Chichi-ue,*" J.E.D.D. Mason broke in, his voice soft, like drizzle if the others' words were rain. "Do you genuinely read such kindness in this act?"

Andō refreshed himself with a deep breath and a dark, judgmental glance at each of his fellows, who actually looked sincerely contrite. J.E.D.D. Mason is a hard Being to disappoint. "I would like to believe it was a kind act, Tai-kun. The alternative is that someone wanted to use the device as leverage against me, since the Japanese strat would suffer most from public outcry. But it sickens me to think that factional self-interest could lead any of you to poison the entire Hive in the eyes of the world." He waited to let that blow sink in. "And to poison our relations with our most important ally."

"The Humanists will get over it." Shanghai's confident Lu Yong stretched back in his seat, with an expression something between smug and testy. "We trust you stay in the saddle where Ganymede is concerned, Andō. I would rather hear more about the theft, and about what you let happen at *Black Sakura.*" I think Lu Yong is more blunt and rude in English than in his strat tongue; I think they all are.

Andō controlled his expression, but could not keep wrath's red from rising in his cheeks. "I have *with difficulty* placated *President* Ganymede." He glared at Lu Yong as he stressed the title. "I have also ensured that the investigation of this double break-in is in hands we trust. That means the issue of the device is also in hands we trust, a fact which may be the only thing which keeps this from exploding in our faces." His eyes softened as he turned to the camera once again. "Tai-kun?"

"Yes, *Chichi-ue?*"

"Do you believe anyone here is responsible for the device, for its creation, its use, or any part of it?"

A long pause while He thinks. "I believe not."

The Chief Director almost smiled. "I believe that the world will suffer greatly and gain nothing by the exposure of the device's origins. Do you agree?"

"Directors," the Strange Prince answered slowly. "Does any of you genuinely know the details of the device's origin? Or is it lost in time?"

All Nine Directors aimed earnest faces at the unofficial Tenth.

"From what I can tell," old Huang Enlai was the one brave enough to answer, "the records were systematically destroyed."

Again the Tenth Director paused to think. "I believe the threat to global tranquility is genuine, that your plan to shelter the world with silence is practical and well considered, and that your desire to protect your people is as humane as selfish. The public fears much and rightly from this new use of the device. That truth must be exposed. But the question of origin is both separate and old. The public feels no active pain from that curiosity, and any answer you give would be painfully partial, aiding far less than it harms. I will facilitate your silence on that count. If my Utopians catch the thief who targeted *Black Sakura* and attain the device, I will seek to destroy it, and I consider Myself to have no obligation to reveal its origin."

Many shoulders relaxed.

"To anyone?" Wang Laojing tested. Would it be easier for you, reader, if I adopt the King of Spain's habit and differentiate these Chinese directors by the regions whose sub-nation-strats they represent? Wang Laojing, then, is confident Beijing.

"I have been tasked with this by many authorities," J.E.D.D. Mason answered, "but all task Me to heal the peace, not harm it, and there is none among them who does not keep secrets in return. If I tell *Patrem Meum* that all threat is ended, and say the same to Censor, Chair, Headmaster, Their Majesty, and Their Grace, then they and theirs will rest content."

Andō smiled. "We will do all in our power to help you ensure the device is found and destroyed"—he paused to let the others nod assent—"whether that means giving you what few records we have of it, acting as you direct, or pledging not to act again, since today's action was so horribly disruptive."

"The billions whose happiness you guard would thank you if they knew, *Chichi-ue*," J.E.D.D. Mason answered. "However, I believe the Canner Device is the prior but not the larger threat."

"The Seven-Ten list?"

"Yes."

"It was none of us," Beijing answered for all.

J.E.D.D. Mason scanned their faces once again. "That I believe."

Beijing: "Do we know the reason for the theft yet?"

Shanghai: "Your bash'child was involved, Andō."

Japan: "Masami is another victim of this, yes. And knows nothing."

Korea: "I understand *Black Sakura* is going to publish both lists now. It's not clear to me who benefits."

Shanghai: "Sugiyama's list does hurt us, but it hurts others even more."

Shanghai the younger: "Ganymede especially."

Dongbei: "Yes, Ganymede and Casimir Perry both come out worse than us in Sugiyama's list."

All reviewed Sugiyama's list, which they had now in an advance copy, distributed to the Hive leaders as tomorrow's publication loomed:

#1: Masonic Emperor Cornel MASON
#2: The Anonymous
#3: Sniper

#4: Ziven Racer
#5: Cousin Chair Bryar Kosala
#6: Brillist Headmaster Felix Faust
#7: Mitsubishi Director Hotaka Andō Mitsubishi
#8: *François Quesnay*
#9: *Julia Doria-Pamphili*
#10: *Lorelei "Cookie" Cook*

Korea: "Spain could also be an intended target. Including Ziven Racer on the list is an insult to the King as much as to Perry."

Beijing: "Everyone knows Spain was not involved when Ziven Racer tried to fix the election for them. Bringing attention to Racer will only remind everyone how honorable Spain was withdrawing from the race after Racer's exposure. Casimir Perry's the one who looks bad for benefiting from Spain's misfortune."

Shanghai: "Sugiyama's far from the first to point out that Ziven Racer is the only reason Perry is Prime Minister, but no one's ever said before that Sniper is the only reason Ganymede is President, at least not so publically. That's a far worse blow."

Japan: "What do you think, Tai-kun?"

Himself: "The worst blow is not to Europe, *Chichi-ue*, but to Asia."

Beijing: "To Asia? Why do you phrase it like that?"

Himself: "François Quesnay."

Dongbei: "The eighth name on the list."

J.E.D.D. Mason fell silent here, breathing slowly, like one sick with fever, struggling to stay awake and speak with visitors. "What is the Source?" He asked at last.

Beijing: "Of what?"

Himself: "If you wrote a poem titled 'The Source,' what would be its subject?"

Of the Directors, Andō is least afraid to answer His strange questions. "Nature," he ventured, "the interconnectedness of life, forests, the ocean, maybe rural life, a farm, a spring of water." Such trust, reader, voicing these personal, almost theological, opinions and trusting Him to make the tangent pertinent.

Himself: "Do all agree?"

Shanghai: "Mine would be about Spring. New growth."

Beijing: "Spring, yes."

Dongbei: "Land, perhaps. Land changing, the parting of the snow."

"The ocean, or a well, or maybe a mountain or a tree." This last came from Kimura Kunie, the second Japanese director, who had done well in the decades since he realized it was more prudent to be Andō's strong right arm than Andō's rival.

"Then you are alone." The dead softness of His voice felt cautious now, as when you comfort a wounded animal, and you know your syllables are meaningless, but, seeing it in pain, you must do something. "Faced with that question, a Cousin might answer the heart, a European the past, a Humanist themself, a Brillist the psyche, a Utopian imagination. All are pieces of the Masonic answer: humanity. Only the Mitsubishi place the Source outside humanity, in Nature." Through the tracker I could see fear spread from eye to eye among the Nine Directors. "In this thought, you are the most alone. This is what Sugiyama thought, which Masami Mitsubishi would not have said, but all Earth will read now."

"Why do you see danger in that?" At last Greenpeace Mitsubishi director Jyothi Bandyopadhyay broke her silence. Her vibrant suit was cut like a sherwani, patterned with the fierce, flame-orange spring blossoms of the Palash tree, with a leaf-green sash across her chest representing the veto reserved in the terms of the Greenpeace-Mitsubishi Hive merger sixty-four years before. Her expressions had been the most guarded throughout this, a sad spectator more than a confederate, and I gender her female for you, reader, as a reminder of how far apart she stands from Andō and his ilk. "Everyone knows caring for the land is our great strength, greater now than ever. Are you expecting some new hue and cry about exorbitant rents?"

"That My servant may speak to."

After a moment's silence I remembered Dominic was missing, so He must mean me. "Y-es, Directors," I began, hearing my voice shake as I feared recognition. "Speaking fo-or the Tribune on behalf of Romanova, yes. We do predict new hostility about rents and property." It is no breech of confidence that I share the Censor's predictions here, reader. J.E.D.D. Mason is a Hiveless Tribune; the Censor's data is at His service while He is at Romanova's.

Beijing: "We've capped rent increases, and we've been acquiring land less rapidly, just as the Censor recommended."

I: "Yes, you have. You've made good efforts, the Censor's data reflects that. But people are already so worried about it, and there are so many hostile counter-campaigns, so many people riled up, most people aren't aware you've slowed down, they just see Mitsubishi landlords on every street and feel like you're eating up more land even if you aren't. Sugiyama's list will make it worse, much worse."

Beijing: "Why? Who is this François Quesnay?"

I: "Was, not is, Director. François Quesnay is a historical figure. Sugiyama was planning one of their clever presence-by-absence pieces." Those in the room seemed to lack enthusiasm for the journalistic art. "François Quesnay was one of the leaders of the physiocrats, a group of European economists influential in the Seventeenth Century, at the very birth of modern economic theory. They believed that wealth and value came from land, shared your idea about the 'source' in a sense." I smiled, thinking how much more clumsily I would have phrased this without His frame to guide me. "When Adam Smith came along, a big part of what they did was disagree with the physiocrats, saying the source of wealth was labor, not land. Everyone since has basically agreed with Smith, even Marx and Morais, though they refined it with ideas about capital and axons. But these days everyone pretty much thinks in terms of human labor as the source, population, work hours, especially with the Hive system, Hives competing for more Members, seeming strong or weak based on how many they gain, or lose. Everyone counts people, Directors. Everyone except you."

"I don't disagree with Marx and Smith," Beijing boasted. "We value our size, our people."

J.E.D.D. Mason cut in softly. "How many voting shares are presently pledged to you, Director?"

"One point two billion."

"Precisely how many?" He pressed.

"One billion, two hundred thirty-two million, four hundred thousand and some."

"How many people? How many Members pledged their voting shares to you to make that bloc?"

"About a hundred and fifty million."

"Precisely how many?"

Beijing frowned at his companions. "Maybe slightly under one hundred fifty?"

He does not nod. "You know much more precisely how much of Nature you represent than how many people."

Again I smiled, seeing how His meandering demonstration made the point more clearly than the straight-seeming path. "Exactly," I confirmed. "These days not even Gordian still clings to the corporate model so closely as to distribute Brillist votes by share instead of by person. Sugiyama's editorial on François Quesnay would have been their manifesto that the Mitsubishi shareholder democracy has failed."

"Shareholder democracy makes us strong," Korea objected fastest. "It's an incentive. Our Members work harder to get property, own their homes, invest, knowing hard work will make their voices stronger, one share-vote at a time."

Young Shanghai nodded. "We own more than half the property on Earth now. That proves our system works."

There was pride in Korea's glance at Bandyopadhyay here, or, I should say, at India, for, back when the Mitsubishi Hive proposed its mighty marriage with Greenpeace, it had lusted after more than Greenpeace's twelve billion acres of nature reserve and five hundred million nature-loving Members. It lusted after India. The lion's share of the Indian nation-strat was always with Greenpeace, and an entrenched cultural tick, something between tradition and self-defense, makes Indian landowners intractably unwilling to sell India's land to outsiders. That made the subcontinent the last delicious corner of the Earth which had few Mitsubishi landlords. What Mitsubishi can't buy, they adopt.

J.E.D.D. Mason's voice was gentle as a chant. "One vote for being a Member, two for owning an apartment, five for a house, twenty for a factory, thirty for a forest, none for an idea."

I: "You're the richest Hive measured in land, but what if we measure by manpower?"

Shanghai: "The Masons win by their standard and we win by ours, I see that. That doesn't make us wrong."

I: "But there aren't only two measures, Directors. There are many. Measure by income: half the human race pays rent to you, but Utopia earns more for its services and inventions. Or measure by output: you say shareholder democracy makes your Members work harder, but every single Utopian is a vocateur."

Younger Shanghai: "The Utopians aren't a competitor. No matter what they earn, they can't grow while they spend it all on their Moon Base and lobbing junk at Mars."

"Terraforming," I corrected. "It is terraforming. In two hundred and fifty years it will be done. Even if you own this world by then, Utopia will own another one."

Is it not miraculous, reader, the power of the mind to believe and not believe at once? We all know the powers of Utopia. We see their living wonders fill the streets, cheer as they conquer syndromes, hire them to make the impossible possible for us job after job. We even trust them with this hunt for the dread Gyges Device. Yet we still think and plan for the world. One world. We never doubt that every individual shipment they send to Mars must be successful, that their science is sound, their effort proceeding, but somehow we do not believe the distant end will ever come. These Nine Directors don't believe Utopians will really live on Mars in 2660. Utopians do.

"If land is not the source," I continued, "then you lose to the Masons. If it is, you lose long-term to the Utopians. Sugiyama's editorial will say this, and, coming from your most prominent journalist, it will shatter the public's faith in your timocracy."

"Shareholder democracy," younger Shanghai corrected.

"Timocracy is what the other Hives are seeing." Director Bandyopadhyay leaned forward until the polished board table glowed with the reflected coral-fire blossoms of her jacket. "Whatever you say about the benefits of having both personal votes and property votes, you know the other Hives look at us, they look at me, they look at how our second-largest nation-strat can only secure one seat at this table, because the lot of you"—her gesture encompassed all of them, but her eye fell most on Andō and Kimura Kunie, whose hundred million Japanese strat-Members boasted two Directors while India's near-billion fought for one—"have had your strats eating up property as hard as you can for generations. They think they see us all racing with each other to eat up more, even if we aren't. Every doubt and bad feeling other Hives have, and every late rent fee they've ever resented, it adds up." She turned back to the camera. "This could be some anti-land-grab group playing extremely dirty. Do we even know this is the real Canner Device? Someone with a vague sense that it could smear us may have created their own tracker hacker to make us look dirty."

The suggestion struck me like a ray of light.

Shanghai killed it with a cloud: "Utopians? Hired Utopians could do it, or the Hive itself."

"Do your predictions think they'll benefit from this? What does the Censor's office say?"

I winced. "You can probably guess. The Masons are predicted to gain most from the Members and investments that leave you. Cousins and Humanists will benefit as well. More details are . . . in flux."

"And the Utopians?" Shanghai pressed. "You just said we're in a long-term, two-planet land race, and here we're trusting them with the investigation. What if it was them?"

I could not lie before J.E.D.D. Mason. "There are probably constellations of Utopians out there who could make such a thing, but, to speak frankly, Directors, manipulating politics and public image this way is not the sort of thing Utopia as a Hive cares much about. And if hired Utopians were to plan such a thing for one of the other Hives, they would succeed, and they would make sure we did not suspect them." I cringe even now repeating this, reader. Do not fear the Utopians. Anyone would call Utopia a fearsome foe, but they do not play these Earthly power games, and, like a nest of hornets, they sting only when provoked.

"Have you seen this Sugiyama editorial, Jagmohan?" Director Bandyopadhyay uses India's nickname for J.E.D.D. Mason, practically a pun. "Which angle is it playing up? Maybe Sugiyama was talking to anti-land-grab people."

Beijing nodded agreement. "If so, the worst part of all this may be that this fuss with the editor and switching lists makes it looks like Masami Mitsubishi was party to trying to hush Sugiyama up. I'm already getting snippets of the hue and cry anti-land-grab groups are raising about that. Perfect ammunition for them. Too perfect."

A few had sympathetic frowns for brooding Andō, but Bandyopadhyay's expectant gaze directed the others to the camera once again. They have a special patience for J.E.D.D. Mason, as for an oracle struggling to condense her oceanic message into the thimble-vessel of a sentence. "*Chichi-ue*, do you have personal enemies outside this room? Have any of you, Directors?"

They reviewed each other over a long silence. "You think this is a personal attack?"

"A shark has many teeth for one reason. Just so, this theft wounds from many sides at once. That speaks of a meticulous author."

Again a careful silence held China, Korea, India, Japan.

"Any who answers Me this in private might do great good," J.E.D.D. Mason told them, slowly. "Until then, Directors, I give you more by giving My minutes and My servants' minutes to My investigation than to you yourselves."

The Chief Director nodded. "Thank you for your time today, Tai-kun."

"I Will you well, Directors." ⌈Father. Give My regards to all My step-siblings and the Princess.⌋

Chief Director Andō smiled at this dash of Japanese. ⌈I will.⌋

"Jagmohan?" Director Bandyopadhyay's call made all freeze. "One more question."

"Yes, Director?"

"I know you're using Mycroft Guildbreaker. How much will you two share with MASON in all this? Does Guildbreaker know that the Canner Device can be tied to the Mitsubishi? Will MASON find out?"

His answer was not slow this time. "A Masonic Emperor does not need blackmail. *Pater* gains more from stability than from your fall. You too are allies in that sense. If Martin and I choose to inform *Patrem*, it will be because the Empire cannot help you bury what it does not know. I see doubt on your faces. But you are already struggling to keep this secret; you would do well to accept aid from *Patre*, one whose secrets have commanded supreme awe and curiosity over the centuries, and yet he keeps them still."

Here once again, reader, we manage to both believe and not believe. We say we are not so gullible as to accept the propaganda that the Masons are as ancient as the cults of Mithras and Orpheus. We say that we do not believe they conspired from the shadows, guiding human progress for millennia before the Church War's chaos brought them into the light. But when you push, our denial weakens. We date the Hive to 2137, the war's height, six years after Carlyle's Great Renunciation shattered the nation-states. Those who did not share the uniting ethic of any early Hive—did not love Europe, Asia, sport, stage, kindness, Nature, profit, Brill—found themselves abandoned, their states dissolving, their Churches (first resort when states failed) swept up in the zealot flames. As war matured into chaos and plague, one false hope lay in the Masonic lodges peppering the towns, which fiction claimed were more than what they seemed. We say that Antoninus MASON just harnessed the myth, organized those who came to the lodges into a global force before people realized there was not one already there. "Power I am," this master storyteller claimed, "the Secret Emperor, more ancient than the Pyramids, more far-reaching than Alexander, more long-lasting than Rome. While Ramses and Ozymandias built monuments that fade, I hid in shadow, and reveal myself only now that the fools I left to sub-govern in my place have failed so much. Come back to me, my people. My Empire has endured ten thousand years, and will not be shaken by this petty war." That fiction birthed this Hive which swallowed up the remnants, as a gleaner picks fallen grain after the harvest. Much grain remained, more than enough to make the myth of Empire real. But something inside us can't believe it's all invention. It feels so ancient: the dread Imperial Guard, the awesome shadow of the *Sanctum Sanctorum* tower, the Imperial Palace with its clustered ziggurats, the laws unrolled on crackling papyrus, the cold, iron-gray throne. The language of myth slips from our tongues: ancient custom, ancient law, *Imperium*, millennium, Empire, Caesar. Perhaps it actually is true and false at once. Great institutions——Hive, strat, nation, kingdom, guild——all are built of consensus, willed into reality by we who love, obey, protect, and fear. If Will alone can make these powers real enough to reshape the globe and burn the heavens, perhaps Will can also make them have been real ten thousand years ago.

"Yes," Andō answered. "You may tell MASON if you think it prudent, Tai-kun. We know you'll only make them see the truth. While we have you with us, we are able to count MASON as a friend. I know the whole Directorate is grateful." Andō stopped there, but the grim pride in his eyes added "to *me*." They did need these reminders sometimes, Beijing, Shanghai, vast and wary India, why they are all best off with Andō in the Chief Director's seat.

"Yes, *Chichi-ue*. I will do My best for you."

Flies to Honey

"BUT THIS . . . THIS IS A CHURCH!" THISBE CRIED.

Carlyle checked the address a second time. "Probably it just used to be a church. See, the cross has been taken off the steeple."

Thisbe found little comfort in that as she faced the stone and arches of [XXX], rue [XXXXX], Avignon, France. It had been a church, a simple one, but ancient enough to have the wet scent of a graveyard. The tangle of plants around it was almost tidy enough to be called a garden, and, as March's lion turned to lamb, some hope-green sprouts were peeking from old branches, like stubborn stars piercing a foggy night. I did not see this. In fact, at my interview I invited Carlyle Foster to write this chapter himself, but he does not trust his skill with written words.

That day he trusted himself. "Let's try the basement door," he was first to suggest. "It looks more used than the big front portals."

Thisbe did not have to be convinced, for her boots had already started down the garden path, threatening to crush the green blades, not yet crocuses, which crowded between the stones. I asked each of them to describe the scent that drifted from the windows. Thisbe called it hypnotic cooking, the kind that makes you crowd around the oven unable to stop watching the timer as it crawls toward done. Carlyle said only that it would have made a statue hungry.

Thisbe knocked twice. She had donned her best for this, a short jacket of tea-green silk which matched the landscapes of her boots. I still prefer her in her home clothes, loose and lazy like the lax wings of a flying squirrel forever ready to cuddle back in bed. It is not that the suit looks bad on her, but people have different faces for work and play. Thisbe's home face may be menacing at times, but it is also a bit less false. "Excuse me?" Thisbe called, sweetly as any rose-cheeked princess. "Is anyone home?"

"Coming!" Rapid feet approached within. "I didn't expect you so ear—oh . . ." The voice had a hint of paternal cheer, which faded as soon as the door opened enough to reveal the strangers. "Sorry, I thought you were the grocery kids. Can I help you?"

With the door open, the smell went from delicious to maddening. "I hope so," Thisbe answered. "We're supposed to follow up with Dominic Seneschal about some urgent work, but we can't seem to find them anywhere. We were hoping you might have seen them around here."

That won a chuckle. "You and all the king's horses and all the king's men. What do you need them for?"

Thisbe's false laugh is beautiful. "It's rather absurd, but I'm supposed to be running a pro forma background check on, of all people, Tribune Mason."

"A background check on T.M.?" The chuckle matured into a hearty belly laugh.

Thisbe joined it. "Yes, I know, but every new system has its paperwork. I'm supposed to interview associates, bash'mates, family's going to be exciting. You may well be someone on my list too, Member . . . ?"

"Hiveless," the housekeeper corrected, turning so they could see the Blacklaw Hiveless sash behind her fresh-stained apron. "Gibraltar Chagatai."

I should describe this figure. Chagatai is not much over fifty, but has let silver grace her ponytail, and her face is creased with lines gained through trials, not age. Those features and her silvered stubble, broad shoulders, and jolly belly laugh grant her a weathered handsomeness which middle-aged widows find irresistible. She has enough Mongolian ancestry to look ambiguously Eastern, but wears no nation-strat insignia, and few insignia at all that mean much to non-Blacklaws. Her hands are too thick and strong, better suited to sport or spears than teacups. That day she was wearing only the comfortable pieces of her uniform of servant's black and white, for there was no need for more when the Master was not expected. Carlyle says he didn't see a weapon, but I cannot believe so wise and wild-spawned a Blacklaw would open a door without some blade or pistol hidden in an off hand. Would you, reader, if you lived in days of banditry and honor duels, as she, by choice, still does?

"And who are you?" Chagatai asked.

"My name is Thisbe Saneer. I do security for the facility where—"

"The Saneer-Weeksbooth bash', of course. I had heard."

"This sensayer is Carlyle Foster."

"Checking up on Dominic for the Conclave?" Chagatai offered friendly, too-firm handshakes. "Who suggested this address? I didn't get any notice that you were coming. Usually I should."

Thisbe had her lie ready before Carlyle could flinch. "Mycroft."

"Mycroft Guildbreaker?"

"No, Mycroft . . ."—she glanced at sweet, oblivious Carlyle—"who is a Servicer."

"Ah, *that* Mycroft. You're being very thorough. Why don't you come in? You can check me off your list, and, if we're lucky, Dominic may turn up within an hour or so. Fingers crossed."

Pride glowed in Thisbe's smile. "Thank you."

"Hold," Chagatai commanded as Thisbe's boot threatened the lintel. "I have to check your credentials first. Could you both send them over?"

Carlyle hesitated before giving the 'send' command, but trusted Thisbe's promise that she had cleared all during their flight.

Chagatai's face softened as the data flickered across their lenses. "Excellent. Come in. You can—oops!"

It was the chirp of a kitchen timer that cut the Blacklaw off, and she rushed back toward an inner doorway and the scent of meat beyond. "Please come through. You're welcome to the bathroom if you need it, and to look at the collection. Just be careful touching anything that looks more than a few hundred years old."

Her invitation left little they could touch. The hall was practically a museum, its walls lined with low bookcases filled with books whose spines of aged leather long predated printed titles. On the waist-high tops of the bookcases crowded a mass of tiny statues: Buddhas, Madonnas, Anubis jackals, Venus figures, a thousand votive figurines in bronze, jade, clay, porcelain, silver, even dream-bright gold. The walls above the shelves were crowded too, even more dazzlingly. Icons. Hundreds of them, saints, angels, brilliant in paint and gold leaf, crowded edge to edge, an endless stream of flat, stylized faces. It is hard to believe the world produced so many, though these were just the tiniest fraction even of what survives. Most of them were ugly, crude at least, too rough to be objects of aesthetics in our modern age, the kind of icon poured out thousand upon thousand in that desperate Middle Age when images were objects of utility more than art. Objects of hope, and desperation, remedies against despair and plague before we had our great salvation, Science. There is judgment in their painted stares, but also something pitiable, these things, almost beings, that had been worshipped, loved, brought offerings, sweet burnt incense, that had been the most precious things in their first owners' world, yet today it was hard to believe anyone cared enough to dust them all.

"This used to be a church, didn't it?" Carlyle called toward the kitchen.

"Yes," Chagatai called back, her deep bass rumble easily drowning the kitchen's sizzle. "It was a ruin ten years ago, but T.M. was sad seeing the state of the place, so Chief Director Andō gave it to them as a birthday present."

"T.M." Carlyle repeated. "You mean Tribune Mason?"

"Sorry, yes. I know they have too many nicknames."

"This collection is magnificent."

"Yes. I think T.M. owns something like sixty former churches now, all fixed up and turned into hospices or Servicers' dorms or other useful things. Can't stand to see old churches rot. But they do insist on cramming them all with this collection."

Thisbe gaped. "You mean they have sixty times this many?"

"What, the icons? They're all President Ganymede's, things they dredged up from collection basements. The Art Situation program is fine at finding homes for Greek pots and Ming vases, but nobody wants a hundred thousand identical Madonnas anymore. Nobody but T.M., anyway."

Tempting as this strange gallery was, the smell was stronger, and lured both to the kitchen like a honey trap. It was a magnificent kitchen, six counters each a different temperature, three fridges, four different ovens from the most modern to real brick with firelight within. The kitchen tree which hugged the greenhouse windows was programmed, not for standard snacking fruits and crepe-edged lettuces, but a chef's array, branches of savory and bay and allspice berries crowded between fiery peppers, currants, young pumpkins, tomatillos, with shallots and radishes bulbous among the tree's fat roots. Carlyle says every burner was going, pots of steel and clay smelling of garlic, biting oregano, onion, salt, and infinite butter.

"I don't think I've smelled anything so tempting in my life." Thisbe could offer no truer compliment. "Are you having a belated party?"

Chagatai had taken from the meatmaker a sheet of rosy flesh two centimeters thick, as wide as a dinner plate and long like an unrolled scroll. She had already massaged in the spices, and now, with her larding needle, was injecting slivers of garlic and pancetta. "No, this is just one dish. My own recipe, Carnivore Roll. It's Dominic Seneschal's favorite food. T.M.'s idea. You know when your dog's missing so you get some of their favorite treats and leave them on the doorstep and hope they'll come back?"

"With an aroma like this you're going to attract every stray dog in the neighborhood."

Chagatai's silvered stubble glistened as she smiled. "I know it's cruel to make you smell this and not offer any, but what you're smelling is just the preparatory sauces. The real thing takes hours. Would you like something else in the meantime? I have pear strudel."

"Sounds fabulous!"

Chagatai picked a fridge and started rustling.

"So, Hiveless Chagatai," Thisbe began, twitching her hands as if taking tracker notes, "are you a cook? Or is this just a job?"

Such a refreshing question. In our cast of leaders and vocateurs one would almost think we had regressed to the olden days when people were their jobs. Mr. Smith is a banker, Mrs. Christian is a nurse, as if those twenty or forty or sixty hours made the other hundred of each week nothing. How do you introduce yourself at parties, reader? Are you a cook? A hiker? A reader? A moviegoer?

"Oh, I'm a cook," she answered. "I've published a couple recipe books, banquet dishes mostly, menus for big parties. Never worked restaurants, though. I used to be a smuggler and general thug."

Carlyle says they suddenly felt an ominousness in Chagatai's shoulders and the thickness of her hands.

"Yes," Thisbe bluffed, "the file I got on you was as confusing as it was incomplete. It's one of the things I'm supposed to check out. How did you transition?"

"I messed up a job, then messed up worse trying to fix it, and before I knew it I owed my enemies more money than my life was worth. It was my own fault, and I'd burned too many bridges, so I wasn't going to get any help unless I ran to the Cousins or turned Graylaw, and that was right out." She set the strudel to heat. "I had my pride."

That she did, reader, and does still when she visits Blacklaw country on her days off, the wildernesses urban and natural which we cede to the bold minority who, on passing the Adulthood Competency Exam, would rather invite their fellows to prey on them like lions than accept a law that deprives them of any freedom, even murder. The Universal Laws still make it criminal for them to prey on children, take trackers away, or jeopardize the world with toxic chemicals, or fire, or religion, but they feel in their hearts that humans are a predator, and predators need the right to tear out each other's throats. You must not think they rape and murder daily. Most rarely more than duel, and it is a strong deterrent knowing you have no armor in this wide world but the goodwill of peers who could kill you where you stand. It is liberty's pride that puts the swagger in Chagatai's steps, not bloodthirst, and had our Master not rescued her from vendetta's execution, Chagatai would have accepted her end with grace—combat, but grace. She has a sister, Cutter Chagatai, who once fell pregnant, and lived with Gibraltar here in Avignon the nine months that the Prenatal Safety Act made her upgrade to Graylaw for the child's sake. A caged eagle is not more desperate to see the key turned in the lock than she was to cut the cord, and drape the black again around her hips.

"So, instead of running to the law, you ran to Tribune Mason?" Thisbe prompted.

"I didn't run. I was in a bar trying to plan my last stand when this twelve-year-old in a strange costume came out of nowhere and offered to pay off my enemies and give me room and board for life if I'd come be their chef and housekeeper."

"You'd already worked as a housekeeper somewhere?"

"Never." Chagatai finished with the larding needle, and gazed with pride over their meaty canvas. "I'd been in a couple cooking contests, nothing else. I didn't recognize the kid, and this was a lot, *a lot*, of money, plus . . . You've met T.M., yes?"

"Yes."

"Then you know how off-putting they are the first time or twenty you meet them. So there I was, thinking: is this a space alien? Is this kid insane? It wasn't until they said they'd call their banker to prepare the money and called the Imperial Treasury that I realized who it was."

Carlyle smiled. "They saved your life."

"Yes. But it was also a business arrangement. The contract specifies that, if I ever quit, I have to pay the money back in full."

"That's exploitation!" the Cousin cried.

The Blacklaw laughed the word away. "Believe me, this is a better, longer life than I expected. I was both ambitious and stupid in my youth, you realize. Not a good combination."

Thisbe smiled. "True. So you've known Tribune Mason . . . nine years?"

"Yes."

"And has this always been the residence?"

"A residence, yes. They rarely manage to stay here more than once a week, with all the late nights in Tōgenkyō and wherever. Plus they're enrolled at the Romanovan Campus and Brill's Institute, and I think they have dorm residences at both. And they often spend nights back at their birth bash', though that's an area where you'll need Dominic or one of the Mycrofts for your background check. I'm not allowed near the birth bash'."

Thisbe raised an eyebrow. "Not allowed?"

"I think I'm T.M.'s separate sphere." She took a bowl of butter, flecked with nuts and spices, and painted it across the meat like plaster. "T.M. works for every Hive, right? So they can't live in any capital, it would be a declaration of allegiance. I'm neutral. Not even in any political strats. They need that break."

"Twelve is a very young age to set up a separate residence. I've heard of it with kids who take on the Adult Competency Exam really early, but Tribune Mason hasn't taken it yet, right?"

"And this will be the place to duck the firestorm when they do. Savvy kid, T.M., even age twelve. Plus here they can have guests stay without worrying about clearing umpteen security."

Thisbe jumped on that one. "What kinds of guests?"

"Worried about the security dodge? It all gets filed, it's just not as draconian here as at the *Domus Masonicus.*"

"What kinds of guests?" she pressed.

"Oh, all sorts. At the moment we have two art history students using the collection, and Mycroft dropped off a pretty battered young thing they said they rescued from somewhere. Servicer Mycroft, not the Mason, Servicer business as I understand, somebody's ba'sib. They're in the back now, watching a movie. Movie . . ." She dropped her knife into the butter, spinning on the pair with the enthusiasm of epiphany. "Thisbe Saneer! Oscar winner, 2451, Best Smelltrack for *Blue like Thursday*! I knew I knew that name. And you won it another year for that one about the three sets of kids in different time periods who all tried to build a boat and sail around the world, what was it called?"

"*The Horizoners,*" Thisbe supplied, beaming. "I didn't think anyone but my ba'sibs sat through that part of the Oscars anymore."

"I never miss them." Chagatai was all smiles now, her warm, narrow-eyed suave. "You've won more than twice, haven't you? How many times?"

"Four."

Carlyle probably gaped. "Thisbe, you do the smelltracks for movies?"

Thisbe smirked. "I do have a life outside the bash', you know. I'm not a voker like Ockham and Lesley, I'm only on duty twenty hours a week."

Certainly you too, reader, like Carlyle, had formed a portrait of Thisbe who existed only in that bedroom, drinking tea and waiting for the active cast to come to her. But let me ask you this: would you have labeled her a stay-at-home so easily had I not been reminding you with every phrase that she is a woman?

Then stop, Mycroft. Drop these insidious pronouns which force me to prejudge in ways

I would not in the natural world. At times I think thou makest a hypocrite of me simply for the pleasure of calling me one. Had thou not saddled Carlyle and Thisbe with 'he' and 'she' I would not remember now which sex each was, and my thoughts would be the clearer for it.

No, reader, I cannot release you from this spell. I am not its source. Until that great witch, greater than Thisbe, the one who cast this hex over the Earth, is overthrown, the truth can be told only in her terms.

Thou hadst best be prepared to prove that claim in time, Mycroft. Meanwhile, since thou insistest on thy 'he's and 'she's, be clear at least. I cannot even tell whether this Chagatai is a deep-voiced woman or a man whom thou mislabelest, obeying that ancient prejudice that housekeepers must be female.

Apologies, reader. And I know it is confusing too that I must call this Cousin Carlyle 'he.' With Chagatai, however, your guess is wrong. It is not her job which makes me give her the feminine pronoun, despite her testicles and chromosomes. I saw her once when someone threatened her little nephew, and the primal savagery with which those thick hands shattered the offender was unmistakably that legendary strength which lionesses, she-wolves, she-bats, she-doves, and all other 'she's obtain when motherhood berserks them. That strength wins her 'she.'

"Of course, Thisbe Saneer," Chagatai repeated. "I should have placed you at once. Big name in smelltracks. You invented something major, what was it? Using some kind of neutral smell that can make a quick transition from a negative emotion smell to a positive emotion smell to make scene changes crisper?"

"That's it exactly. They call it Thisbe's Rinse." The witch glowed here, for such compliments are rare as diamonds for this virtuoso whose art aims for the audience not to notice its existence. The smelltrack is as indispensable as the soundtrack, supporting the emotion of the scene with a vocabulary of scents coded to happy, sad, despairing, aroused, but the music you remember, never the smells, which aim to be too subtle to be named, like the scent which makes you feel at home when you return to the neighborhood where you grew up, even if the house is gone. Smell, science tell us, reaches the brain more directly than any other sense, and if you've ever watched a film with a stuffy nose you have surely found it as emotionless as if on mute.

"Thisbe's Rinse, that's right." Chagatai was glowing. "Orland Vives called it the biggest breakthrough in moviemaking since Griffincam."

"Orland and about four other people. You must be a real movie buff."

"More a movie trivia buff. I can't watch movies. *Modo mundo.*"

There was a conversation stopper. "Oh."

"I didn't kill a Utopian or anything," she added quickly, waving her hands as if to erase her last words. "This is a different sort of *modo mundo*."

They tried their best but couldn't leave it there. "I thought the *modo mundo* sentence only existed for people who kill Utopians. They invented it. That's the point."

"Sorry, this is always hard to explain." I can envision Chagatai clearly here, reaching to scratch her silver-sleeked hair, remembering the butter on her fingers just in time. "I wasn't legally sentenced to *modo mundo*, just, the effect is the same. It's not that I'm not allowed to read or watch fiction, it's that I can't."

"You can't?"

"I can't."

"Why not?"

She tried to hide by returning to her roast, layering a paste of spice and onion on the buttered meat. "Well, five years ago I wanted to impress a date who was into old books, so I took a very valuable old manuscript from T.M.'s library without asking and, through a long series of mishaps, about half of which were my fault, it was ripped apart and eaten by rats."

"What? How?"

"The full story is longer than it is interesting. Anyway, I had no excuse, and I was afraid I'd be thrown out and T.M. would demand their money back. Instead T.M. imposed *modo mundo*."

"They can't do that!" the Cousin cried again. "For losing a book? That's gross manipulation of the law, like making someone a Servicer for breaking a tea set."

"That could happen with a sufficiently valuable tea set. But no, it's not a legal sentence, T.M. just did it." Chagatai tried to snap her fingers, but onion butter made them slick. "Just like that."

"Just like that?" Thisbe repeated. "How?"

The Blacklaw sighed. "Look, I can describe it to you, and it'll bother you when you read or watch fiction for the next week or two, but then it'll wear off, since it's different when I say it from when T.M. said it. Is that okay with you? It will wear off."

Carlyle looked to Thisbe. "Um, sure. Go ahead."

"Next time T.M. came home I explained what happened. We were in the study and they were reading, and I remember they put down their book and turned around and looked at me while I was talking—that's unusual, by the way, actually turning toward me or anybody, it's not their way. They looked at me and said: 'Observe, Chagatai, the protagonist of every work of fiction is Humanity, and the antagonist is God.'"

Carlyle and Thisbe waited raptly. "And?"

"That's it. Just, the way T.M. said it, from then on when I would try to read a book or watch a film, all I could see was humanity struggling in vain against a cold and arbitrary God. Or being unfairly helped by a saccharinely indulgent God. Or being toyed with by an abusive toddler God. I hated it. I can physically read a work of fiction but it's agony, even the lightest comedy. Histories and biographies are nearly as bad. That's why I watch light things like the Oscars. It's hard to read God into the Oscars much."

Even describing this to me Carlyle's fists clenched. "People aren't supposed to talk about religion like that."

Chagatai took the steaming strudel from the oven. "Well, it's sure learned me not to step out of line again. That manuscript was irreplaceable. T.M. would've been within their rights to chuck me out and leave me to die, but they didn't. *Modo mundo* makes sense too, once you think about it a long time."

Can you imagine Carlyle scowling here? "Not to me, it doesn't."

"I said once you think about it a long time. The Utopians' idea with *modo mundo* is that, if you killed a Utopian, you destroyed their world, their nowhere, their ideas, their fiction, since they all invent stuff even if they don't all publish. You destroyed a potential other world, so you get banished to this one and don't get to go to any other worlds anymore. I think what T.M. was trying to communicate was that destroying a manuscript is effectively the same thing, destroying somebody's creation, the remnant of the world they created, even if they've been dead a thousand years." She took a saucepan from the stove and drizzled a trail of honey-scented glaze over the strudel before pouring the rest across the roast. "I'd never thought so seriously about the manuscripts before, but I sure take good care of them now."

Strudel could not placate Carlyle. "They can't just go around exploiting and manipulating people's views of God like that."

"That's what my sensayer says too, but you know what?"

"What?"

"That one line of T.M.'s has made me think a lot more about theology than my sensayer has. A sensayer is, what, a couple hours a month? This is all day."

"A sensayer doesn't do it against your will!" Carlyle shot back. "A sensayer doesn't do it to hurt you or punish you. A sensayer's trained, a sensayer's careful, and a sensayer would never . . ." He caught himself.

"What?" Chagatai sprinkled a mixture of cornmeal and fine-ground sausage over the honeyed onion butter on the roast, the last step before rolling the whole concoction like a scroll. "A sensayer would never . . . ?"

Carlyle summoned his grimmest tone, still light despite himself. "Does J.E.D.D. Mason proselytize?"

"What?"

"Has J.E.D.D. Mason ever told you what religion they believe in? Have they tried to get you to convert?"

Chagatai's face grew chill.

"They've already crossed a lot of lines," Carlyle pushed. "Exploiting your theology, these names too, Martin, Dominic. This is serious, a First Law question; on behalf of the Conclave I have to know. Has J.E.D.D. Mason tried to convert you to a secret organized religion? Is that what's going on?"

The true medieval iron of a Blacklaw's gaze turned now on Carlyle. "Do you think I would stay in a house with a boss who broke the First Law?"

"Then, they haven't?"

"Of course not." The iron faded now behind a smile. "One of the first conversations I had with T.M. seven years ago was them warning me never to bring up theology in this house, or to speculate about T.M.'s, or their valet would kill me."

"Valet?"

"Dominic."

Thisbe sat up stiff. "They threatened you?"

"No, it was a friendly warning. Dominic's a Blacklaw too, and mad possessive, and already has it in for me for edging in on the privilege of polishing T.M.'s boots and changing their sheets and all that. T.M. says they want Dominic for more important work than housekeeping, but it's an old fight between the pair that'll probably never finish. I try not to get involved, but if I muscled in on sensayery-business with T.M. too, then smart money says I'd wake up dead."

"J.E.D.D. Mason's sensayer . . . is also their valet and . . . Are they . . ." Carlyle took a forkful of strudel, hoping to keep himself from asking something rash. The strudel, he remembers, was exquisite, but sweetness on the tongue cannot drive gall from the mind. "Excuse me, where did you say your bathroom was?"

"Second on the left."

From here I have less detail, for Thisbe and Chagatai do a poor job reconstructing scenes. Thisbe asked Chagatai if J.E.D.D. Mason had any hobbies or interests apart from work and messing with people's theology.

Chagatai answered that J.E.D.D. Mason's most common activities, at least at home, were reading, conducting business over His tracker, sitting perfectly still doing nothing, and, the all-time favorite, lying perfectly still doing nothing.

"Sleeping?" she suggested.

"Sometimes," the Blacklaw answered. "Often not."

Meanwhile, in the bland but tasteful bathroom, Carlyle, in a rare moment of lie becoming truth, filed a quick report to the Sensayer's Conclave of his deep concerns regarding Dominic Seneschal. Then, cleansed by the feeling of good action, he searched the house. He reviewed the hall of icons first, then the sitting room, with its fireplace, sofas, and coffee table, all wood and silk and ornament to thrill an antiquarian, but with a starkness to it, a show room, not a room for living. In the library he caught the two students admiring a spider they had trapped under a cup, and in the back room he heard sweet things about me from the grateful rescued "young thing." (Sometimes we Servicers retain old business from our dark days, reader, and sometimes we help each other solve it.) Chagatai's bedroom was easy to spot by its stacks of cookbooks and tomorrow's suit ready to go, and the guest bedrooms were clear by their suitcases. That left only one door to try.

"There you are!" Thisbe appeared behind Carlyle just as he opened it. "I told Chagatai we needed to head out. I'm on duty soon. Did you have a good snoop?"

Carlyle stood frozen, staring, unable to release the knob. "Their bedroom."

"What?"

"This is J.E.D.D. Mason's bedroom."

Carlyle pulled the door back. A mattress with plain sheets lay on the floor, without blanket, pillow or bed frame. The closet door, ajar, revealed six shirts on hangers, the antique black He always wore. And nothing more.

"That's kind of scary," Thisbe admitted, checking the empty drawers. "Though it's less scary knowing they don't really live here."

Carlyle stared in silence for some moments. "No. The rest of the rooms are comfortable, guest-ready. This . . . this has to be their preference."

They thought on that for some moments, before Thisbe turned dark eyes again on the sensayer. "I could tell you almost lost it over what they said about Dominic."

Carlyle flinched. "Sensayer and valet, and possessive, and probably a bash'mate too, or worse. All the earmarks of unhealthy. It would be scary anywhere, but, so close to major powers, a cult could be the kind of disaster we're most afraid of. J.E.D.D. Mason has access to the Emperor. To Andō. To everything."

Thisbe gave a long frown. "You're right to be worried. And you're right that it's a First Law issue, but the danger of a cult is a lot more . . . long-term than the danger of eight hundred million cars all shutting down tomorrow, and also a lot less important than what threat this might pose to a certain kid. My questions trump yours, and you need to stay calm so I can keep coaxing out the answers we're really here for. You jump on the conversation like that again and I'll send you home and go to Paris on my own. Understood?"

Objections parted his lips, but stopped there. "Yes. You're right."

"Are you ready to go back in there? I'm sure I can coast on this bluff a while longer, but you look like you're struggling."

"I'm fine," Carlyle resolved. "I'll stay. Though this Blacklaw's main feature seems to be knowing as little as possible about J.E.D.D. Mason's family and political life. Should we move on toward Paris before someone catches us here?"

She considered, but shook her head, black hair flowing like oil. "I want to see if this roast really can lure in that Dominic. Plus our chef says there's a step coming up which we can eat, not the final thing but an intermediate thing that involves almonds, and smells incredible."

The growl of Carlyle's tummy decided for him. "Excellent!"

"One thing." She stopped him in the doorway. "After I'm done and satisfied with my investigation, *then* you report this to the Sensayer's Conclave, not before. I don't want people getting poked and clamming up, not with so much at risk."

Carlyle winced as he described this part. "Of course, Thisbe. You have my word."

It is possible to delete reports sent to the Conclave. It is not possible, amid the many lies, to be quite certain who saw it before Carlyle deleted it.

A Monster in the House

GUNFIRE COULD NOT HAVE SPOOKED ME SO COMPLETELY AS Bridger's silence when I called to check on him after my hours in the Censor's office. Night's westward march had advanced from Tōgenkyō as far as Europe, and I had been ordered to get some hours' sleep, but it did not occur to me that I was sacrificing something as I lied my way into a car. Bridger did not answer. The Major did not answer. No one answered for that agonizing hour's flight across the unyielding Atlantic. Fears drowned me so completely I did not even mark when midnight touched Western Europe and set the Seven-Ten lists free into the world. I did not call Thisbe. I almost did, but what if it was something with her bash'? The thief again? Or the opposite, police? Those were my justifications. Really, I think, I was angry at Thisbe forcing out what I had hidden so long, my Tocqueville. It was the kind of anger we create to mask our guilt.

The cave was dark, but I found Bridger in Thisbe's bedroom, huddling as a caged rat huddles in a sterile corner, praying in its tiny mind for some rag or scrap of newspaper to hide beneath. My arms were Bridger's rag, and he hurled himself into their sanctuary hard enough to wind me.

"They were inside! Mycroft, they were inside!"

"Who? Who was inside? Inside what?"

I leaned against Thisbe's bed so the boy's weight would not topple me. He smelled of the sea, salt, and sun, good things to come between these shadows.

"In my cave! They went through and threw everything everywhere, and broke the dollhouse, and knocked Mommadoll's kitchen over, and turned Boo's bed upside down!"

Boo too jumped on me, frantic as dogs get when they sense panic but have nothing to growl at.

"Is anyone hurt? Was anyone seen?" I asked.

"Mommadoll got hurt. Mommadoll got a heavy box thrown on them and was stuck there pretending to be just a doll, for an hour, Mycroft! An hour!"

He opened his arms just enough for me to see her cradled there, her blond curls mussed by crook of his elbow. "I'm fine, honey," she reassured, her smile never dimming. "It just twisted my shoulder a little bit. I'm fine. The important thing is that you weren't there."

"You weren't there?" I repeated as I stroked his hair.

"I went swimming on the beach. Mommadoll was all alone with just a couple soldiers on watch!"

I hugged him as tightly as I could without smothering the doll in his arms. "It's all right now."

"But!"

"I'm here. I'll take care of it. Whatever happens, so long as you're not hurt, I can take care of it, I promise." I wiped his tears with my fingers, and he granted me a smile. "What happened to your tracker?"

"I left it while I went to swim." He saw the silent scolding on my face. "I know. But the Major says I shouldn't turn it on again. The bad guy did something to it, the men on watch saw!"

"The Major's right." I held the child gently, feeling his trembling subside. But I did have to ask. "Was it Dominic Seneschal?"

The Major answered, seated with his men on a set of dice on the bedside table, just the right size to serve as stools. "Blacklaw, late twenties, sensayer's scarf, antique French men's costume, light skin, brown hair tied back, moves like a monster."

"Dominic must have found something in this room when they searched before." I gave Bridger's shoulder a squeeze. "Was anything sitting out in the cave that was obviously miracled? Did Dominic take anything? Anything you'd made?"

"I was packing!" Sobs resurged. "I was packing like you said, just the important things, and they took my backpack! It was full! It had my drawings, and my red shirt, and my Robin Hood book, and the ammunition, all the army men's ammunition, and Mommadoll's best little frying pan, you remember the one you got her that's just the right size?"

"We can get another one, sweetheart," she reassured.

My mind inventoried what else the backpack must contain: hair, fingerprints. "The ammunition, was it already miracled?"

Bridger sniffed. "It wasn't miracled yet, just lots of little paper guns and boxes, and some paper Healing Potion tubes, I made some ahead of time so I'll be ready. I even have some in my pocket, see?" His trembling hand produced the now-crushed paper tube, already labeled.

"What about the resurrection potion you made for Private Pointer?"

"I have that safe in my shoe. But the No-No Box! They took the No-No Box!"

Thisbe's voice rose behind me, as soft and sweet and threatening as I had ever heard it. "What's the No-No Box?"

I turned to find her on the threshold, the click of her boots cold as the clatter of old bones.

Instinct made me clutch the boy more tightly. "That doesn't matter right now."

"More secrets?" She slipped off her fine jacket, and set down the parcel of leftovers I did not yet realize was from Chagatai. "We were hunting Dominic Seneschal ourselves when we got the bleep that Bridger had come in here. I didn't know you were here, though. Slipped our tracker again, have we?"

I cursed, spotting wide-eyed Carlyle behind her. The shadow of my hat would have been enough to conceal the absence of the tracker at my ear, but not now.

"Bridger isn't up to dealing with you in one of your moods right now, Thisbe," I warned. "Take a minute to relax, and take your boots off."

"Why was Bridger packing?" She stepped toward me, enjoying the unease each step instilled. "You weren't going to spirit Bridger off to J.E.D.D. Mason without telling us, were you?"

I helped Bridger sit beside me on the bed, so I could shield him from her glare. "Not to J.E.D.D. Mason, but this area isn't safe anymore, not with this investigation. I have a safe house ready."

"So you run and leave me in the hot seat?"

"No."

"Don't lie to me, Mycroft. You were trying to take Bridger off somewhere and hide them from me."

I found myself wondering why I was so frightened as the witch loomed close. Was it pathological? She seemed a witch to me in all senses then, a good witch, bad witch, weaver of curses, stalker of children, solver of problems, healer, black widow, conjurer, the devil's whore who chews through mortal mates, an old maid too, young but on course to bloom into that unmarried, ungrounded, uncontrolled old crone which drove past societies to purge with fire or bind in nunneries those thorny women wedlock could not hold. I had come to her with Bridger years ago, just as a village girl might have, desperate to conceal a child born out of wedlock, turning to the midwife who is something more than midwife after dark. Now this same protector-friend loomed before me, like the boogeymen kids fear before they learn real dangers. Was it all in my mind? Her threat? Her craft?

Yes, Mycroft, it was. Remember, thou art mad.

Am I?

Indeed, thou art. Thou provest it often, and if thou doubtest now, read over thy descriptions of this woman, from the incipit to here. Hexes and witchcraft, would Reason use these words? Would I?

You are right, reader. Apologies. You corrected me about this once before, but sometimes, in this hazy present, I forget.

Is that apology sincere?

Sincere? Of course, dear master. All these labors are for you. If you are not satisf—

Then act on it.

How?

Stop calling her a witch. Thy common biases are distraction enough without these fever dreams. Say 'she' if thou must, but no more superstitions. Even thy barely enlightened Patriarch was civilized enough to fear no witches. Follow his good example.

I hesitate, reader. I find Thisbe's masks and layers difficult to describe already. It will be much harder without the frame through which I myself understand her, or try to. But I will attempt, reader, I promise you, my fragile, failing best.

"I'll bring Bridger back later," I pledged. "In a week, a month, when this is over. If you don't know where the safe house is then Dominic can't force it out of you."

Thisbe laughed aloud. "Mycroft, you just confessed you place J.E.D.D. Mason above even the Major. They'll have a far easier time forcing it out of *you*."

"Quit being stupid, Thisbe!" Bridger piped up, glaring at her, bold as day, over my shoulder. "Mommadoll's hurt and the scary person might know about me. This isn't the time to be mad at Mycroft!"

Thisbe was all smiles in an instant, and the room filled with the scent of warmth and mothering. "Bridger, honey, Mycroft and I both want what's best for you, but it's hard when Mycroft won't be honest with the rest of us. They're sincere, but they don't always know what's best."

The Major rose from his die-stool. "Bridger's right this time, Thisbe.

There's a shadow over your house. We can't let that fall over Bridger, whatever the cost."

Thisbe flinched, a real flinch as his reprimand reminded her how precariously things were teetering.

"Major," I asked, "you had men on watch when Dominic came, yes? What did Dominic do?"

We all looked to Lieutenant Aimer, who is usually in charge in the Major's absence. "The intruder ransacked the place pretty thoroughly," he answered, his tiny voice a few horrors lighter than the Major's, but still rich with experience. "I'm sure it was clear a child has lived there a long time, and likes dolls. They took a lot: old drawings, books, a hairbrush, and they scanned things, took photographs, samples of dirt, swatches off the sofa, so they must have skin, and Boo's fur."

"My hairs too, I imagine," I added. "I'll be questioned next." I was almost ready to laugh. "You may be right, Thisbe, I have become the weakest link."

"No!" Bridger dug his fingers into my uniform. "Mycroft, you can't go away!"

"I wo—" I stopped myself mid-promise. "I'll always come back, you know that, even when I go away for little patches."

He had no words for me, just wide, desperate eyes.

"Will Dominic tell J.E.D.D. Mason about this?" Thisbe asked.

"Dominic? Not right away, not after seeing the No-No Box."

Another glint of accusation in her eyes. "No more secrets, Mycroft. What is the No-No Box?"

Bridger shrank against me. "It's bad."

"It's a box Bridger kept, with things in it from the trash that should never, ever be miracled. A crucifix, a globe, a Buddha statue, a doomsday device from an old comic book, a devil mask, a toy bomb, some pictures of old paintings that show God or Satan, a black rubber ball."

"Why a ball?" Thisbe asked it, looking from me to Carlyle, who was already lost in terrifying thoughts. Be happy, reader, you have the luxury of not believing in Bridger's power: to you these possibilities are still abstract.

I heard a little squeak from Bridger's throat, and renewed my hug. "Bridger thinks of it as a toy black hole. Bye-bye planet. There's also one of Cato's old Science Museum toys in there that's supposed to be a model of the Big Bang. The No-No Box wasn't my idea and I didn't encourage it, but I do think it's good for Bridger to think about how serious their powers are."

"If you thought it was a fine thing, why did you hide it from me?" Thisbe snapped.

"I didn't want to talk about it!" the child answered, sparing me the necessity. "It's scary and I don't like it."

Carlyle's fingers dug into the battered knit of his sensayer's scarf. "And Dominic has this box now? Complete with icons and crucifix?"

Possible disasters schooled through my mind. "It's not . . . it's not proof of anything, but it will excite Dominic. A lot." I took a deep breath. "But Dominic won't go to J.E.D.D. Mason with something touching on theology, not until Dominic's one hundred percent sure what's going on. That's probably why Dominic's gone missing, actually, to figure it out before facing son Maître again. You won't appreciate the gravity of it, but this is the first time since J.E.D.D. Mason was born that Dominic's gone missing like this. He won't show his face to Them again until he's sure of what he's found."

"He?" Thisbe repeated. "Mycroft, isn't Dominic . . ."

I had not noticed my slip. "What?"

"Never mind. How long have you been involved with these people? Years?"

"This isn't about me, Thisbe," I dodged. "We need to get Bridger out of here."

"Not with you until you answer."

"Are you part of the cult?" In his way, Carlyle tried to ask it gently.

"What?"

Carlyle brushed back his straying hair to bare a gentle, coaxing smile. "There's a secret religious group going on here, yes? Are you part of it?"

"No!" I answered. "Well . . . no."

Thisbe took a grim pace closer. "That's not an answer."

"I can't."

"The truth."

"I can't."

"The truth!"

"By law I can't!" I nodded toward the sensayer. "*My* sensayer is aware of everything, and keeping a careful watch on me. I—"

"Shhh!" The Major's hiss silenced us all, and his fast gesture sent his men under the cover of a chocolate wrapper. "Someone's at the inner door."

"Is someone there?" Thisbe called, her voice musically loud to cover the footsteps as I helped Bridger to the closet.

"It's me, Thiz." It was Ockham's voice, neither hostile nor friendly. He must have been just beyond the door, at the foot of the stairwell to the *Mukta* hall above. "I know you have someone in there with you."

Thisbe was only half-relieved to find it was her brother. "Sorry, should have logged it."

"I haven't been listening in, I just came down. Look, Thiz, I give you every reasonable liberty, but we talked about this, when you bring danger on this bash' it has to stop."

Thisbe shooed Boo toward me, the dog's fast breaths harsh in the hush. "I know, Ockham. This isn't anything dangerous. I'm being careful."

Ockham took a deep breath. "¿True or false? ¿Whatever you're doing is making the investigators of the Seven-Ten list break-in more suspicious of this house?"

Thisbe hid behind the oil-rich cascade of her black hair. "A little true. But I'm taking care of it. I'm—we're discussing changes to keep this from affecting the bash' anymore. In a little while it'll be totally cleared away. Trust me."

"¿True or false?" Ockham asked again. "You've brought our new sensayer here five times in three days, and you've been lying about why."

We within traded guilty glances. I don't think any of us realized we had been quite so clumsy.

"The Conclave checks, Thisbe," he pressed. "A sensayer is not a safe mark for you."

"It's nothing like that."

"I didn't specify a 'that.' Whatever you're doing, I don't care what it is, move it, postpone it, end it. I do not want to see that sensayer back until someone who isn't you has a session scheduled, and I do not want more trackless people in this room."

Carlyle and Thisbe traded frowns, but there was no good answer. "All right."

"Is that Mycroft in there with you?" He switched to English to remind me that I was an outsider.

"Ye-es, it's just me, Member Ockham," I answered, happy at this chance to screen the others. "I'm sorry. I should have—"

"Until this is over, Mycroft, you can't visit anymore, not even for the investigation. Work elsewhere."

"You need me!" I cried. "I know these people. I know what you're facing. I'm your best chance at stability."

"Your advice is welcome, but while so many eyes are on us you're the biggest danger here. We tried our best, but dozens of people from today's drill know enough to leak that something happened here. Normally I let you visit on condition that you're no threat to our work, but if the media catches Mycroft Canner here you'll be a bigger story than Sniper."

"Canner?" Carlyle repeated it, half-voiced. "Mycroft . . . Canner?"

I turned. I turned white. We had tried so hard, reader. 'Mycroft,' 'Mycroft,' never the dreaded surname, not in front of this good innocent. Three days of purloined trust.

"You're . . . Mycroft Canner?" Carlyle burst out. "*The* Mycroft Canner?" He searched the shadow of my hat for the telltale chunk missing from my right ear. I let him find it. I know, reader, when the avalanche can no longer be stopped. *They made Mycroft Canner a Servicer!*

"Shit, is the sensayer in there?" Ockham called through the door.

"Yes." Thisbe groaned. "Stay calm, Carlyle. Mycroft's not dangerous anymore."

He was already shaking. "Not dangerous? Mycroft Canner!"

I gave Bridger my kindest smile through the crack of the closet door, then backed to the far side of the room, keeping my empty hands where Carlyle could see them, and my eyes on the floor.

"A Servicer!" Carlyle repeated. "Servicers are supposed to be . . . not . . . not . . ." He turned on me, more comfortable when he could point a finger. "You! You tortured seventeen people to death! You videoed yourself vivisecting Mercer Mardi! You crucified your foster ba'pa! You dismembered a thirteen-year-old child and left them a limbless torso to freeze to death in the Arctic! Ibis Mardi was in love with you, and you beat them until they begged for death, then raped them, and cooked and ate their arms and legs while they were still alive! Are you smiling?"

"Sorry." I try my best to remain expressionless during such outbursts. "Everyone has one among the seventeen they think was worst. I'd guessed that Ibis would be yours."

"You ripped out their still-beating heart and ate it!"

"It stopped beating," I corrected softly. "I tried it seven times, but I could never get the heart out fast enough. I think that art is lost now, in our peaceful age."

Carlyle's breath sped as the passions of those days surged back. Carlyle would have been, what . . . fifteen back then? Preparing to move from his foster bash' to a Campus, finding his vocation, that impressionable age when we first solidify our morals. I was formative for him, then, the primordial evil of his personal creation myth, my grim two weeks. My rampage. "Mycroft Canner!" He could not repeat the name without a shriek. "You're the worst . . . the most . . ." Words failed but he did not need them; all Earth knows what I am. "You were supposed to be . . . gone! Locked away somewhere safe forever or . . . or . . ."

"Executed?" I finished for him. There was a Mycroft Canner once who would have swelled with pride knowing he made a Cousin call for blood. "When the Hive leaders agreed to let MASON keep my sentence secret so the public could stop obsessing over the matter, you assumed I had been executed. Everybody did. It never occurred to you they would conceal mercy."

Carlyle had no more words, just horror and its siblings: panic, anger, fear.

"Look, Carlyle." Thisbe donned her gentlest smile. "I know it's a shock, but there's no danger. The Servicer Program handles criminals that aren't dangerous anymore, to let them serve the public good. Sometimes that means serious criminals too."

"You knew!" Carlyle turned on her almost as fiercely as he had turned on me. "You knew and you didn't warn me! You let Mycroft Canner into your . . . into . . . And near . . ."

She gave a tired glare. "You were content enough to sit with a Servicer not knowing what they did. You knew they might have been a murderer."

"Mycroft Canner is not just a murderer!"

Ockham opened the door now, but with Boo and Bridger safely in the closet there was no further danger. "Thiz, do you have the gag order file on hand?"

"Oh, yes, I'll pull it up." Her lenses flickered.

The guardian of the house turned to Carlyle. "Cousin Foster," he began, "we are not responsible for Mycroft Canner's sentence, and have no more power to affect it than you do. Chair Kosala personally signed off on Mycroft's admission to the Servicer Program. If you have doubts, Kosala will give you an appointment, just like they gave us when we discovered."

Carlyle's eyes only grew wilder. "Kosala knows? That's right, Kosala oversaw the trial to make sure it was humane." In Carlyle's face, one could see the horrors of those days awakening in phases. Some readers will remember my two weeks, the hush upon the streets, the fear, the dread-zeal with which you watched each morning for the news to bring you some fresh horror. Only the mildest pictures appeared at breakfast time: a stain, a shrouded body, but by lunch or dinner there would be leaked images, real gore, real red, real faces contorted by emotions only torture can awaken.

For two weeks no one on Earth walked home alone. I know you remember. Even in old age, when names and precious faces start to fade, you will pass again a corner where your classmates huddled whispering of me, and you'll remember.

"Kosala always knew . . . ," Carlyle repeated, only half-believing.

"Found it, Ockham," Thisbe confirmed with a last lens flicker. "Sent."

Another flicker as it arrived in Carlyle's lenses. "What . . . Servicer Protection order?"

Ockham planted himself before the sensayer, his right hip tipped away so Carlyle would not be tempted to rip the gun from his holster and take the long-delayed revenge himself. "Mycroft's sentence and identity are confidential. You can understand the high risk of retributive violence if the word got out. This file has details about the offices in charge, and under what circumstances Mycroft's identity can be discussed. We're under the same order, and it is not in my authority to change it."

"They don't let you warn people? A Servicer, they could go anywhere! People need to know!"

Ockham crossed his arms, his bronzed skin striped with Lesley's fresh doodles. "That's for the Servicer Program to judge, not us."

Carlyle backed away, as if the bedpost and nightstand would shield him from my evil. "I won't believe for a second that that monster isn't dangerous!"

I heard (and Ockham may have too) the stir of Bridger in the closet, fighting to keep himself from leaping to my defense. Poor child. The Cousin's rant was nothing new to me, but the thought of Bridger listening, his sweet heart longing to defend me, that stung. I know your thoughts, reader. *Bridger is thirteen, he was an infant or unborn when thy victims appeared day after blood-filled day. He does not understand, so, foolish innocent, he trusts thee.* Unforgiving reader, do you think you know me better than the child I raised?

Carlyle thought he did. "Mycroft Canner is the worst criminal in a hundred years! Two hundred years!" My lost self might have called this flattery.

Ockham stood so calmly through the outburst, watching hysteria drain the color from Carlyle's pale face. It made me think of Alexander, of his force, the human thunder of our Mediterranean sweeping through deserts, through empires, but India, calm, mighty India, fears nothing. "I am not authority over the Servicer Program, but I am authority within this house, and—"

"The cars!" Carlyle cried. "This house! The cars! Can't you see it?

Mycroft Canner near the cars, they're planning it again, mass murder on a grander scale!"

I am not a mass murderer. I faced my victims personally, one by one. But this was not the moment to correct him.

"I am authority within this house," Ockham repeated, "and you will control yourself."

"Mycroft Canner is the most dangerous person in the world!"

Thisbe reached for Carlyle's shoulder. "You're being hysterical."

"Don't touch me!" he jumped back. "You let them into your bash'! It's just the same! That's what they do, Thisbe, they charmed their way into the Mardi bash' and then..."

"It's not the same."

"Seventeen people, Thisbe! They hacked pieces off of Luther Mardigras for five days before they burned them alive in a wicker man! Burned what was left of them!"

It is fascinating which details people get wrong. To be fair, with Luther I had left the least behind for forensics.

"I have to go," I said without raising my eyes. "I have a call I cannot disobey."

"Not that excuse again!" Carlyle cried, then cried again, "The Censor's office! Mycroft Canner was in the Censor's office!"

"Take a deep breath, Carlyle."

"Mycroft Canner forced the last Deputy Censor to disembowel themself with a piece of bamboo!"

Forced? That isn't right, is it, Kohaku? You were grateful for that dignity, that exit, the chance to smear your vital numbers on the wall for Vivien to find and someday understand. Was I a good second to you, in your makeshift seppuku?

I kept my eyes on the floor, my voice soft. "I'm sorry, Cousin Foster. I have to go. I will return at my first liberty, if you request, to answer any questions."

"You shouldn't be going anywhere except a prison with no key!"

"I have a call I cannot disobey."

"Overridden," Ockham ordered. "Mycroft, you're staying put until we calm this down. Carlyle, sit. If you ask questions calmly we will answer them."

"I'm not going to sit in a room with Mycroft Canner!"

"I can have them restrained for this briefing, if that would make you more comfortable. Shall I call the team?"

I steeled myself. "I'm sorry, Member Ockham. I have a call I cannot disobey."

Ockham shook his head. "My house, my orders."

I had no choice. Slowly, so the motion would not further spook the Cousin, I pulled from my pocket the Imperial Gray armband with the Masonic Square & Compass in death black upon it, the mark of we *Familiares* who, by lawful contract, submit ourselves to suffer imprisonment, torture, or death at Caesar's will. "I have a call I cannot disobey."

Even Ockham hushes at Death's presence in a room.

"The Emperor . . ." Carlyle gulped breaths, like a man about to battle for his life. "The Emperor did this!" A target for his blame at last. "You were under MASON's Law! MASON was supposed to be your judge, jury, and . . . We trusted them! We trusted them to . . ."

I waited for him to speak the dreaded word, but he wasn't brave enough. Not like back then, when Earth cried in one voice for the sentence everybody wanted. They wanted it so much, reader, the wide world in a true blood frenzy, begging the gentle Hives to bring back the long-abandoned greatest punishment, just for me. You cheered when Caesar made it easy, Caesar with his one black sleeve, when he announced that Mycroft Canner was already under the *Lex Familiaris,* the last capital punishment left on our enlightened Earth. When Caesar faced the cameras, "Factum est (It is done)," nobody wondered *what.*

"Go." Ockham nodded his permission, and I bowed my gratitude. There are many masters, reader, many authorities I answer to, but only one can kill me with a word.

Carlyle stared as I paced slowly to the door, and leapt out of my path as if sin were contagious. I hadn't expected this pain. I had known Carlyle must learn someday who I was, but I had come to respect this proud and giving vocateur, to care. I wanted to say something as I left, to heal his wounded trust, not in me, but in the powers he had trusted to do justice, to put the mad dog down. Questions are commands in their way, "What . . . ? How could you . . . ? Why . . . ?" and Carlyle was a free man and a good one, so I owed him the obedience of an answer. But what can Mycroft Canner say? I took a deep breath. "Death was judged too swift and light a punishment. I owe more."

Carlyle sobbed, that's what I think the motion was, one quick, hiccupping twitch as the too-much of it overwhelmed his body.

I left him there, reader, hot with his just hate. But I cannot leave you. You can leave me, if you wish, you who have followed me this far, but see now why you should hate me. I chopped pieces off of Luther Mardigras only for two days, reader, the first three days were teeth, and nails, and flaying him alive. If I repel you, you may set this book aside and turn to other histories of this transformation, there must be some. Or did you know already what I was? Perhaps you chose this history less for J.E.D.D. Mason than to taste the mind of Mycroft Canner? Would you rather I had set this thirteen years ago? Earlier? Do you want to hear my childhood trauma, what tragedy created the misguided creature I became? Would you have me tell you what a human heart tastes like? Or which was the most satisfying stage at which to rape Ibis Mardi, when she was beaten, limbless, half-cooked, or already dead? Reader, there is no autobiography of that Mycroft Canner. Nor should there be. This is a history of Bridger and our transformation, not of my lost self. Yes, you will learn more of me. Yes, I will bare details which not even the police have known until I write these words, but facts about me are servants to your understanding of far greater matters. Why did I do it? Is that what you wonder most, reader? I do not know. At seventeen I was so sure of my philosophy that I gave myself content over to my executioners, yet I now find myself alive at thirty-one, and in a universe I understand only enough to know that I am too small, too finite, too tiny a creation to understand why I was made the thing I was, to do the things I did. I have tasted Bridger's mud pies. I, Mycroft Canner, so improbably alive, was the first human to stumble on this miracle. I am sure of only one thing, reader: there is Providence. There is a Plan at work behind this world, and a Mind behind that plan, Whose infinite workings I cannot hope to penetrate. I could tell you what my old self thought was the purpose of my crimes. I could tell you what I think now. But only our Creator truly understands the ends to which He turns His instruments: why He had me kill those seventeen people, not sixteen, not eighteen; why He sent Bridger this bloodstained guardian; or why He chose that night of March the twenty-fifth to reveal to His devoted priest Carlyle Foster that, in His strange Mercy, He had spared, of all men, Mycroft Canner.

That Which Is Caesar's

I AM GRATEFUL, SO GRATEFUL, TOLERANT READER, THAT YOU read on despite learning of my crimes. With your trust so freshly shaken, this may be the worst moment to disappoint you, but, alas, I must. For, as the first black hour of March the twenty-sixth catches me arriving in MASON's capital, what am I to do about the parts in Latin? Martin Guild-breaker, glaring over my shoulder as I write, insists Latin is only for Masons, and must not be translated. Yet what good is that when even Masons can barely understand? J.E.D.D. Mason does not speak Masons' Latin, He speaks something closer to Classical Latin, as strange for Masons as Homer to a modern Greek. I have promised to treat you, reader, as if you were a brother of our Eighteenth Century, so I should assume you read Latin, else I insult you, though I realize that is probably untrue. Martin will not let me make the Latin into English, but I shall at least translate J.E.D.D. Mason's Latin into modern Latin, so Masons may understand what Masons should.

(I have translated the Latin, but since I'm doing so in secret from both Martin and Mycroft, you'll have to bear with my mediocre skills.—9A)

I felt ease as the car set down in the Masonic capital, leaving at last the spectacle cities of Tōgenkyō and Cielo de Pájaros for a real city, organic and irrational. What city would you have chosen for your capital if you were the first MASON? You cannot have the oldest, Ur and Uruk, for most of Mesopotamia is still a Reservation after the Church War, and in the rest Nature's war wounds will take another century or two to heal. In Greece you would have to choose between Athens and Sparta, wisdom and strength, two assets which no Emperor can afford to privilege one over the other. Rome herself has been through too much to head another empire, and, if you used her, your successors could not then make use of her design in Romanova to such great effect. Vienna and Cusco are too fragile, Chang'an and Paris occupied, Istanbul and Kiev overbalanced by their more recent histories. You have only one choice, young Emperor, one city as imperial as you pretend to be.

"The Six-Hive Transit System welcomes you to Alexandria. Visitors are required to adhere to a minimum of the Masonic *Lex Minor* while in this zone. Visitors are reminded that Masonic Laws do not allow the ignorance plea. To review a list of local regulations not included in your customary law code, select 'law.'"

As I climbed the ziggurat steps to Caesar's threshold, the guards saluted at the sight of my *Familiaris* armband. Why do I not wear the armband always visible, as Martin does? It would be too suspicious, reader. There are only so many *Familiares* in the world, and all but Mycroft Canner are accounted for.

Caesar's voice was only half thunder tonight. "Cur omnes agitati sunt? (Why is everyone agitated?)"

I had not expected to encounter MASON right away. He was in the frontmost meeting room, gray marble with heavy chairs around the central table, and the freshly published Seven-Ten lists spread across the screen-walls like maps of active battlefields. There is no room in Alexandria that is not as grim and awe-filled as most throne rooms, no doorway without its heavy marble lintel, no floor without its labyrinth of patterned stone, no window that does not look out over the glittering gardens of absolute wealth, or the glittering city that is its source. But this was not among the grander rooms, a modest space, used usually by aids, *Familiares*, Masonic Senators on business from Romanova, Guildbreakers doing Caesar's will. I know why he chose it. There is an awe that Cornel MASON holds for the *Domus Masonicus*, the same awe Martin holds, the same that young Cornel held before the throne was his. An awe like a priest's for his temple. I think this Caesar does not wish to taint the rooms where his predecessors sat— Aeneas MASON, Marcel MASON—with the presence of Mycroft Canner.

"Septem-Decem indices (Seven-Ten lists)," he grumbled. "Septem-Decem index modo est propagandulum! (A Seven-Ten list is just a little piece of propaganda.) Quid refert si Ganymedes Andōque haerent? (What does it matter if Ganymede and Ando are [in a tough/sticky situation]?) Cur perturbantur? (Why are they worried?) Cur etiam Anonymus perturbatur, et cur te tres illi lassant? (Why is even the Anonymous worried, and why are they exhausting you?)"

The Emperor was calm, strong as a man just risen from a healing bath when all around are battle-weary. His face as he gazed upon the lists had more the air of a philosopher studying some new phenomenon than of a worried king. Indeed, the only tension in him was his left hand, clenched behind him as he stood. I do not think Caesar is conscious of the habit, but he always clenches his black-sleeved hand behind him when I enter a room, as if he could not otherwise restrain it from sealing on my throat.

"Nescio, Caesar (I don't know, Caesar)," I answered.

He gave me a stony glance. "Non nihil scies, Mycroft. (You know more than nothing, Mycroft.)"

I kept a careful distance from the Emperor, standing by the wall where he and his guards could watch my movements. "Apollo dicebat (Apollo Mojave used to say)," I answered, "ut Franciscus Quesnaeus sententiam Mitsubishorum praesentavisse (that François Quesnay previewed Mitsubishi thought). Sugiyama Apollini nunquam incidit, sed aliquem qui similiter Appollini cogitat gravissime considerendum est. (Sugiyama never met Apollo, but anyone who thinks similarly to Apollo should be given the greatest consideration.)"

The Emperor was pacing, like a lion too long in its pen, his limp conspicuous. I have Cornel MASON's permission to disclose that he does not have his original left foot, and the replacement has never sat well with him, for reasons more psychological than medical. It still goes on, the trial by ordeal. In 2239, the autopsy of Mycroft MASON revealed evidence of old tortures on his body, protracted and professional. The public demanded an explanation, and so you learned how hard it is to be the *Imperator Destinatus.* Ordinary Masons face a law code stricter but no more brutal than any other Hive's, but we *Familiares,* in return for trust and power, surrender all protections, subjecting ourselves wholly to Caesar's will. If Caesar demands our imprisonment, our torture, or our death, we have no right even to ask why. Caesar accepts no less from those few he trusts with the welfare of his three billion. Outsiders imagined this was a symbol. If once a century a known traitor was put to death, you assumed this was the only exercise of MASON's Capital Power. How wrong you were. A MASON will not pass the throne to one who has not been tested beyond the limits of sanity and mercy. Only he who comes through Hell still sane and loyal can, they say, resist the corrupting influence of power this close to absolute. I understand that Cornel MASON's original left foot was hacked away in pieces with a heavy, clean-edged cleaver—not the most sophisticated of tortures (a trained eye can spot remnants of those elsewhere upon him) but one of the most psychologically damaging, as the victim watches pieces of his body turn to meat before his eyes. Young Ken Mardi, the prodigy who had fancied himself as sturdy as a samurai, I broke in an hour with such a method, but Cornel MASON endured three weeks at his predecessor's order, and emerged as strong as he is now. That J.E.D.D. Mason has never disappeared for such a period is often taken as proof that He will not be the successor.

MASON's voice was stone. "Indices mutati sunt. (The lists have been changed.)"

My eyes went wide. "Mutati? (Changed?)"

"Sic. Ecce. (Yes. Look.)"

At Caesar's command a wall displayed video from the Romanovan Forum, where reporters besieged the marble podium of the Rostra, and a slouching figure at its microphones.

"Vice President DeLupa!" called the loudest of the pressmen. "Why didn't the Anonymous realize before now that someone had tampered with their list?"

"The Anonymous can't see into the Censor's office," the Vice President answered. "If someone intercepts the list between when the Anonymous sends it and when Censor Ancelet receives it, there's no way the Anonymous can tell."

"Does this mean other communications from the Anonymous are likely to be fake as well?"

"Absolutely not. Remember, when the Anonymous contacts me there are seven levels of security. The Seven-Ten list is an exception, since it's delivered directly to the Censor. All we've learned is that Romanova's security isn't as good as mine."

It was a perfect answer, but Brody DeLupa could not afford less. Rarely has there been a man with so tenuous a hold on office as Humanist Vice President Brody DeLupa. Humanists love the Anonymous, since it is certainly heroic for a faceless, nameless voice to make itself the most influential in the world, just by publishing such intelligent opinions. Even young Sniper, who studied so hard to boost his fame by making himself a joy to interview, had charisma, sex appeal to keep him interesting, while the Anonymous has only the irksome merit of being always reasonable. The Voting Board was strict: however many thousands of Humanists may wish to vote for the Anonymous, one cannot hold office without revealing one's identity. It did not take long for clever men to circumvent the rule by running for office with Earth's simplest platform: I will be a proxy for the Anonymous.

"Does the Anonymous think there's a connection between this tampering and the incident at *Black Sakura*?"

DeLupa scratched the stubble which persisted in the wrinkles of his cheeks, like mildew. They have all been ugly, the last five Proxies, did you notice? Some say the Anonymous does not want a puppet with charisma of its own, but I think they are chosen for the merit that Ganymede would find them too repugnant to seduce. "There's no saying for certain at this point," DeLupa answered, "but I suspect there's a connection, especially considering the recent announcement that there was also an attempt to steal the Gordian list from the Brillist Institute."

"Then there's a conspiracy?"

The Vice President tried to make his nod feel sage. "I don't know if it's a prank or if someone is expecting profit, but when three of the lists are targeted, that's not coincidence. It may be time to rethink the gambling, and what it incentivizes. Even without thefts and substitutions, the pressure on the columnists makes objectivity almost impossible."

Cornel MASON scowled. "Quid facit Anonymus? Modone attentionem a *Sakuram Nigrem* avertit? (What is the Anonymous doing? Just drawing attention away from *Black Sakura*?)"

If so, it was brilliant. With interference in the Anonymous's list and Gordian's, *Black Sakura* would virtually drop out of the public eye, and with it Kohaku Mardi's fatal numbers, 33-67; 67-33; 29-71. Even the Mitsubishi might be saved. I answered, "Fieri potest, Caesar. (It could be, Caesar.) Quotannis discipuli iocosi aliqui Brillem indicem surripere temptant, et nihil refert. (Every year some student prankster tries out stealing the Brillist list and it comes to nothing.) Causa necessest si hoc anno Magister Faustus populum operam dare vult. (There must be a reason if this year Headmaster Faust wants people to care.) Beneficium alicui necessest. (It must benefit someone.)"

MASON nodded. "Causa gravissima necessest si Anonymus mendacios vulgat. (The cause must be serious if the Anonymous is publishing lies). Hos quoque ecce. (Look at this too.)" At Caesar's will the Vice President vanished, replaced by the newest chart:

I took my time in thinking, my toes tracing nervous circles on the stone. It was brilliant. The substitution was so plausible, just what an anti-Mitsubishi conspirator would have altered to make it feel like all the lists were ranking the Mitsubishi low. The "altered" list was the real one, I had no doubt—we had worked with it in the Censor's office. The Anonymous was retro-fibbing, swapping in a list that made the Mitsubishi come out better, and, by crying, "My list was targeted too!" drawing attention away from poor *Black Sakura*. He found a way. The Censor's powers could do nothing, but the Anonymous had found a way.

Anonymous—"altered" list	Anonymous—"real" list
Emperor Cornel	Emperor Cornel
The Anonymous	The Anonymous
Bryar Kosala	Bryar Kosala
G. de la Trémoïlle	**Hotaka Mitsubishi**
Felix Faust	G. de la Trémoïlle
Hotaka Mitsubishi	Felix Faust
Casimir Perry	Casimir Perry
Castel Natekari	*Castel Natekari*
King Isabel Carlos II of Spain	*King Isabel Carlos II of Spain*
Southern Time Inc.	*Southern Time Inc.*

MASON turned again to me. "Non tibi imperio ut prodas aliquod de officio Censoris, sed solum oppinionem tuum: quid possum facere ut curros protegam? (I will not order you to betray anything from the Censor's office, but only your own opinion: what can I do to protect the cars?) Custodesne Saneer-Weeksbooth bash'domi ponere debeo? (Should I send guards to the Saneer-Weeksbooth bash'house?) Discipulosne mittere ut doceant et pro Sicario aliisque substituant? (Should I send students to learn and substitute for Sniper and the others?) Aut ab Utopianis petere debeone, ut parent sustinere ipsi totam systemam mundi si iste bash' cadat? (Or should I seek from the Utopians, that they prepare to sustain the entire global system if that bash' fails?)" The Emperor looked to the window, where we could see the cars landing across the city like a rain of constant meteors. His fists clenched. "Non vacuus sedebo et permittebo hic jocus mundum meum accidere. (I will not sit idly and let this prank wound my world.)"

Jocuvn hunc non arbitror, Caesar (I don't think it's a joke, Caesar),"

I answered, not quite daring to meet his eyes, "sed aliquid sinisterius, et credo ut vos omnes non prius placebimini quam omnes Septem apud Matronam conveneritis (but something more sinister, and I think that all of you will not be calm until all Seven convene at Madame's). Omnes suspectum habetis ut unus ex Septem hanc perfidiam coniuraret. (You all have suspicions that one of the Seven planned this treachery.) Omnibus convocatis, invenire poteris si recte sentis. (When everyone has been called together, you'll be able to discover whether you guess right.)"

It is maddening, is it not, my non-Masonic reader, watching the Latin slip past incomprehensible? It is worst with Latin, too, for it was by chance you were not raised to speak French or Japanese, but no one is raised on Latin. Latin is a choice. Hives are strengthened by having a tongue, so MASON chose the language of Rome, of Empire, of Power, simplified to make it easier. It is no race's language anymore (not even Martin Guildbreaker dared study Latin before his *Annus Dialogorum*), so all Masons, whether new converts or the sons of Emperors, are equal as they sit down in those classrooms, the true *sancta sanctorum* of Masonic mysteries, which teach the tongue of power, as potent for Martin as for Machiavelli and Montaigne. It was your choice, reader, whether or not to heed the myth and study Latin; now you pay the price. (I didn't have the heart to cut this.—9A)

I oversimplify; One living among us was raised on Latin. "Salve, Pater. (Hello, Father)." J.E.D.D. Mason entered from an inner room, announced by the guards saluting their *Porphyrogene*. "Mater salutem dicit. (Mother sends her regards.)"

A common father smiles at the arrival of his son, but MASON's face does something deeper, graver, like a ship's Captain peering at the morning sky to see what weather it might bring. "Salve, Fili (Hello, Son)," the Emperor greeted. "Bene investigatio estne? (Is the investigation going well?)"

No emotion accompanied His almost-whispered words. "Canis abest. (The dog is missing.)"

"Abest? (Missing?) Dominicus? Cur? Quamdiu? (Why? How long?)"

(This is where Mycroft started to supply Masonic Latin translations of the Prince's rather bizarre Latin, but I'll try my best to give you the sense of the Prince's actual words.)

"Nescio (I don't know)," the Son answered. "Ni ampliorem quam cimicem olfaceret non peccaret Dominicus. (Unless he smelled [something] larger than a bedbug, Dominic would not sin.)"[1]

---

[1] Mycroft's translation: *Nisi aliquid grave suspicaretur Dominicus non abesset.*

The Emperor frowned. "Credisne ut in periculum sit? (Do you think they're in danger?)"

"Nullo cursus pacto. (A very strong form of 'No.') Non ciccus est hic nebulo vero fidus canis. (This scoundrel is not [the membrane around a pomegranate seed, i.e., a negligible thing], [but/truly] the dog [is] faithful.) Quod superest, tibitemet non lucubrandum'st. (That aside, you yourself [emphatic] should not burn lamp oil late at night.) Brevi procaciam conivere potes. (For now, you can blink at this mischief.)"[2]

MASON searched his Son's face for some sign of how He truly took Dominic's absence, for it is hard for a father to believe that any child would not feel something at the absence of his most constant companion. His face showed nothing. Have you ever in a museum, reader, seen a case of lizards or small frogs, and you cannot tell in their stillness whether they are alive or models until you press your cheek against the glass and look for breath stirring their sides? Here you would have to do it with a Man.

"Non sufficit. (Not enough.)" The Emperor turned. "You could make a new car system, couldn't you?" Like magic, reader, hear lightness in his English, as when Hector, breaker of horses, after days handing out death to foes around Troy's ramparts, comes home at last to lift his child in his arms. No, it is not to me he speaks. See there, brilliant in the corner, the nowhere children, Aldrin and Voltaire.

The pair glanced at one another. "A new system, Caesar?"

"Everyone is paying too much attention to the Seven-Ten lists, and not enough to the cars. The Seven-Ten lists are nothing, an embarrassment. The cars are the bloodstream of civilization. You have your own system, your own computers. If the Saneer-Weeksbooth bash' goes down, could you take over running transport for the world?"

They looked at each other through their vizors. I will never tire of studying the space station which Aldrin's Utopian coat makes of Alexandria. It is not new and cold like a fresh-launched shuttle, but a patchwork, bits of mismatched hull barely space-tight. An ancient space station, if you can imagine such a thing, used, battered, and remade, like the museum wing of the ISSC, where field trips pause to see the original parts of the station that grew appendage by appendage into the current city. That is Aldrin's Alexandria. Voltaire's I avoid looking at—exquisite as it is, I cannot bear seeing the capital in ruins.

---

[2] Mycroft's translation: *Pro certo non. Non nullius momentis est hic fur, sed fidus est Dominic. Certe, nocte laborare non debes. Etiamnunc situm praeterire potes.*

"What about the backup station, at Salekhard?" Aldrin asked. "Surely they'd take over."

"I want two safety nets when civilization teeters."

Again they traded digital glances. "It's not our constellation, Caesar, but with time and access to the current systems, I imagine we could develop a substitute."

"How long?"

"I don't know, I'll ask. A lot would depend on whether we can have access to the proprietary parts of the Saneer-Weeksbooth system."

"Why do you need their system?"

"We'd need to control their cars. We don't have enough, and ours are slower, plus . . ."

"Plus?"

J.E.D.D. Mason answered more bluntly than Voltaire dared: "The world will not be content handing such power to Utopia. There will be backlash."

MASON scowled. "Then make it for me. Let it be my Masons, not Utopia, who hold it in the world's eyes. I will not watch this halt the bloodstream of my world."

"All right, Caesar, we'll see what we can do."

"Thank you." Even an Emperor does, on occasion, thank. "How's your part of the investigation going? Well, I hope?"

"Yes, Caesar. The Traceshifter Artifact was only on for two point two seconds at its second activation, inside the Saneer-Weeksbooth bash'house, but we learned much more about its initial effects. We are preparing a report to present to all Seven soon."

"Good. And Mycroft has been forthcoming?" Here the iron returned to MASON's voice.

"As forthcoming as they can be when they don't really know anything. The 'Canner Device' is very badly named."

A glance at me. "Have they been forthcoming about Andō and Ganymede?"

Vizors traded confusion. "Caesar? I'm not sure what you mean."

MASON's eyes fixed on me with no less menace than the barrel of Ockham's gun. "Andō summoned you to Tōgenkyō, Mycroft, minutes after the break-in was reported. And Ganymede summoned you to La Trimouille."

"Ye-e-e-e-es, Caesar."

"Are they frightened for the cars? Or for themselves?" There was disgust in the set of his jaw.

"Both, Caesar, I would say."

"Why?"

The word transfixed me, like a needle through a butterfly. It was not just Danaë's blackmail that made me hesitate, her power to reveal that I still have my method to move unseen. The Mitsubishi need no blackmail to command me. I serve the world, all of it, every Hive, every human. What I destroyed robbed all, so it is to all that I owe my great debt. I owe Andō, from whom I took Kohaku Mardi, Jie Mardi, probably young Ken if he had lived to choose a Hive. I owe Ganymede from whom I took Malory Mardi, and the half of Seine that belonged more to the Humanists than to her dear Apollo. I owe Utopia. But by law my life is Caesar's. And I owe Caesar too, for Geneva Mardi, for Aeneas, for Chiasa, Jules, and I owe, owe, owe, owe, owe them for Apollo.

"Their Grace the Duke suspected Sniper," I answered; that much was easy. I could be good witness to Ganymede's innocence, and ignorance. "I helped them confirm it was unfounded. They were upset, worried, largely about protecting the cars, the Saneer-Weeksbooth system, a-and the peace." Trapped in Caesar's gaze I shivered reflexively, feeling that I must have transgressed, sinned, even though, in fact, it was the truth.

"And Andō?"

Panic took me. Caesar could see it, I read it in his face, imperious like Zeus when he gazes on others, but, for me, he becomes Hades.

If there is a limit on how much righteous punishment Cornel MASON will inflict upon me, that Limit stands beside him. "I can answer, *Pater. Chichi-ue* asked Mycroft about the misnamed Canner Device."

Three breaths as MASON's mind turned. "Why did Andō learn the device was involved so long before I did?"

"That question is of interest, *Pater*. Perhaps the Tokyo police reported the break-in to *Chichi-ue* before calling Romanova. Or perhaps *Chichi-ue* had a special vigil already prepared."

"Why?"

"*Chichi-ue* consents that I disclose to you alone, *Pater*, their inherited complicity."

"Inherited?"

"Prior aliquis publicus Mitsubishus auctor fuit. (Some earlier Mitsubishi official planned/designed/authored it, i.e. the device.)" That part had to be in Latin to keep Andō's truth secret from Utopia, but English was enough for the rest. "Its root and cradle are expunged, its conception rued and condemned by *Chichi-ue* and all his peers, but fearsome is the public storm which threatens if exposure links Japan to the blame and name of Canner, so fearsome that the dread of it is wielded by the Mitsubishi splinters one against another even now, imperiling many beyond *Chichi-ue*."

"I see." Thinking in Latin already, Caesar doubtless found his Son's tangled English easier to parse than the frowning Utopians did. "Then I must remind the minor Directors once again that my friendship extends to Andō, not to them, and that my hand is gentle only with those I trust. Is Ganymede aware of this tie between Andō and the Canner Device?"

"Non credo. (I think not.)"

Slinking a pace toward the shelter of the *Porphyrogene* made me bold enough to speak. "I ha-a-ave told everything I know about it, Caesar, to Aldrin and Voltaire, and I am wo-orking to track down the people I knew who were connected with it at the time." *The* time, reader—for me there is only one time, and Caesar knows it. "But I've been busy with the Censor and . . ." I could not name the other things.

"Then you may pursue that further when I finish with you tonight."

"Prior sumus, Pater. Manere debes. (We are prior, Father. You must wait.)"

I froze here, awaiting Caesar's verdict. We all had to. In this Masonic sanctum all were *Familiares,* even these Utopians, the gray armbands dull against their coats like damage on a painting. Theirs, though, were special, edged in white like J.E.D.D. Mason's (though without his purple trim), to show that, while the Emperor trusts them absolutely, the Utopians do not trust their Members to his Capital Power. These Utopians are not Caesar's but loaned to Caesar, and there is a guardian constellation ready to snatch them back to the heavens. Are you surprised, reader, that you have never heard of the *Familiaris Candidus,* White Band *Familiaris*? It is a recent office, created for Apollo Mojave by Cornel MASON when he came to the throne twenty-nine years ago. That J.E.D.D. Mason's armband too is edged in white is often taken as another proof that he is not the successor.

"Esto, Pater," the *Porphyrogene* conceded. "Prior fias. (You may be first.)"

MASON nodded thanks for his Son's concession.

"Quid vis, Caesar? (What do you want?)" I asked.

Why did Caesar answer in English? I think so the Utopians could witness what good use he put me to. "I will have from you what you give the Censor. You will tell me what these new Seven-Ten lists will do to the world, and what the old lists would have done if only *Black Sakura* were violated and not the Anonymous and Brillist lists as well. Andō, Ganymede, and the

Anonymous are giving this part of the affair far more attention than it seems to deserve. You'll show me why. Then you may resume your other work."

In my heart I raised a silent, grateful prayer that he did not want to ask me about my presence at the Saneer-Weeksbooth bash'. As fear eased, I felt at last the touch of after-midnight. "I will do it, Caesar," I answered, "but I don't think I can do both jobs tonight without another dose of anti-sleeps, and I'm over my limit again."

There are a few souls who would have smiled pity at my fatigue, the Major, Bridger, perhaps you, magnanimous reader, who have seen my labors of these past days and counted how rarely I have taken food or rest. In Alexandria not even the Utopians, who love all of creation with a child's love, had smiles for me.

MASON turned to Utopia. "Will your investigation suffer if Mycroft sleeps and serves you tomorrow?"

Digital glances. "That should be all right. We could use some rest ourselves." They turned to J.E.D.D. Mason. "Is that acceptable, Mike?"

His Utopian nickname is not short for Michael, though the invocation of Heinlein's might be intentional. It is short for Micromegas, "Littlebig," the alien visitor from Jupiter who towers over humankind in grandeur and philosophy in Patriarch Voltaire's famous (and possibly Earth's oldest) science-fiction tale.

He raised His eyes to Aldrin, slowly, intentionally, and the hairs on my neck stood stiff as I saw Him actually seem to look at something in the room with Him. "How long until the next Mars launch?" He asked.

"Two days, one hour." Her eyes wanted to ask the reason for the question, but her tongue knew better.

"Do Utopians ever reject an application to join the Hive?" He asked.

Aldrin exchanged nervous glances with Voltaire, or seemed to. "Not that I've heard of. We can check, if you like, Mike."

"Sic fiat. Rapide quam experiatur theoriam Martinus habet. (Let it be so. Martin has a theory quickly to be tested.)" Then, for Utopia, He translated Himself: "Tomorrow suffices."

The Utopians looked to me in their confusion, but, like them, I could not then understand the purpose of His question. I think, knowing more now, that he asked it for Martin, that at that moment Martin's Master had invited him to listen over His tracker to hear our words. More meat for the investigation.

"Caesar?" An aid intruded. "The Reservation Oversight Commission is waiting in the August Room."

"I come." MASON looked to me, his face as grim as those archaic statues carved before Greece learned to sculpt a smile. "Tomorrow will not do for me. You may eat now, Mycroft. You may sleep when I am done with you." At Mason's nod, a guard rolled a prepackaged sandwich across the table, which slid off to plop at my feet within its plastic shroud.

Voltaire's digital eyes followed me as I knelt to take the food, though I cannot guess what expression truly lay beneath the vizor. "Be careful not to exhaust Mycroft, Caesar. They owe us, too."

Mycroft Is Mycroft

BRIDGER CROSSED HIS ARMS, HIS SMALL HANDS SNUGGLING IN the looseness of his play-stained sleeves. "Reading that stuff is only making you more mad."

Anger tears had made Carlyle's eyes red around the lenses, which shimmered with the records of my deeds. He lay in the grass-and-blossom bedding of the flower gully, facing Thisbe's door. "Sometimes it's correct to be mad."

"Why?" The child's chirp matched the singing of the night's insects.

"Because if I don't have the pictures in front of me, I can't believe a human being really did those things. To make a list of all the nastiest ways to kill somebody and to go through systematically, it . . ."

Bridger sniffed. "I know it was the worst thing anybody's ever done. But that was then Mycroft. Now Mycroft is different."

Carlyle let the glitter of the computer leave his eyes. "People have done much worse things in the past, but that sort of thing doesn't happen anymore. We were supposed to be past that."

Bridger settled in the grass beside Carlyle, gazing up into the strip of Chile's stunning stars above the gully. "You remember back then?"

"Everyone remembers."

He fidgeted with a dry stem. "What do you remember especially? The photos Mycroft took of Ibis Mardi? I haven't seen them but I know."

Carlyle shuddered. "I remember the first one most, when they found Senator Aeneas Mardi."

Bridger nodded. "That was the one Mycroft stabbed to death on the Ides of March, like Julius Caesar?"

"And left the body on the Altar of Peace in Romanova. That's how it started." The sensayer hugged himself within his wrap. We refuse to call them dresses, these 'wraps' that flow around the knees and ankles, tempting one to peek at what lies hidden. But if they are not feminine, why do only Cousins wear them? "I was in Romanova then, studying. I walked by the Altar of Peace every day. I didn't see the body, but I saw the blood, I actually saw it, spattered all over inside of the little shrine. It looked like someone painted red holly berries on the flower garlands carved in the stone, and the basin on the altar was full of blood, all the Nobel Peace Prize medals drenched in it like pancakes in strawberry syrup. Two hundred and nineteen. I remember the news said the killer intentionally sloshed the medals around to make sure the blood got on all two hundred and nineteen."

"Two hundred and nineteen?"

"That's how many years it had been since they stopped giving out the Peace Prize. All the remnants of the Church War were dealt with more than two hundred years ago, so nowadays they just put the medals on the Altar of Peace every year to commemorate another year of peace." Carlyle hid behind his hair. "That year they almost shouldn't have."

Boo settled down between the pair, offering warmth and wagging.

"Were you studying at the Gurai Senseminary or the McKay Institute?" Bridger smirked at Carlyle's astonishment. "I've been looking at Campuses. I'm leaning toward Romanova too. There are really good craft and design schools, so I can learn to make toys of things I imagine, plus lots of philosophy and theology. I need that."

"Yes, you do."

"Plus Mycroft is in Romanova all the time for work, so they can keep an eye out for me. I've been studying for it too, learning about normal life, and Mycroft takes me to Cato's Junior Scientists Club, so I can learn how to make friends, and have a bash' someday."

Carlyle's face warmed for a moment, but only a moment. "Mycroft Canner wants you to have a bash'? You know it wasn't strangers Mycroft Canner killed, right? It was their foster-bash'."

"It wasn't their foster-bash'!" Bridger snapped. "Mycroft was fostered by the Terrafirma bash', which was two doors down from the Mardi bash', and you don't know more about Mycroft from seeing a lot of news reports and icky photos than I do from talking to Mycroft every day for years and years."

Carlyle smiled weakly at the ferocity in Bridger's eyes. "That's true, but I know different things."

Now it was Bridger's turn to hug his knees. "Maybe."

"Mycroft Canner charmed everyone in the Mardi bash', spent time there, got everyone to think of them like an unofficial member, just like Thisbe and their bash'mates have here. That's how Mycroft Canner works, they trick people into thinking of them as family."

"It's different. They're safe now. They wouldn't do anything. Plus the police watch Mycroft all the time. Sometimes Mycroft can't come see me for days and days because they're watching too close. You saw they had to slip their tracker just to come tonight."

Carlyle almost laughed, the stage beyond tears. "That just means Mycroft can still slip their tracker. If they can do it to come help you, they can do it for other reasons."

Boo's whine made Bridger peer more closely at the sensayer. "You're shaking."

Carlyle looked at his hands. "I'm sorry, I . . . it was just very important Mycroft Canner being . . . gone. Mycroft Canner was a tragic, horrible thing that happened, but it was over. The world wasn't like that."

"I thought lots of people liked Mycroft. There's the fans, and photo books, and Canner Beat, and there was just another movie. Thisbe said it was pretty good."

Carlyle gagged. "Those people are sick, Bridger. And there are fewer and fewer of them. We're healing. Mycroft Canner was on a Seven-Ten list in 2441, but never after that. The scars were healing. It's different when you know the monster is still here."

"Mycroft's not a monster!" Bridger rose, burying his arms in the folds of his wrap. "I have to pack. You can come inside and help me clean up and talk, or you can sit there and be wrong. It's up to you."

The sensayer could not accept option two. "How can I help?"

"Can you fold clothes?"

"Yes."

"Come in, then."

A quick jog up the flower bed and Carlyle ducked the plastic sheeting to find the cave in ruins, shelves bare, mattress gutted, every possession strewn across the floor.

"You can pick the clothes out and fold them. Put them there." Bridger pointed to a bookcase near the entrance, standing almost straight. "The soldiers are out on patrol, so you don't have to worry about stepping on them."

"Oh. Right." Carlyle dared not admit he had forgotten.

"You shouldn't be mad at Mycroft anyway, not you. You're a Cousin. Cousins are supposed to forgive everybody."

Carlyle's voice grew light, distracted. "That's the stereotype."

"Mycroft said at the trial it was Bryar Kosala who kept bringing up how this was society's fault for not doing more to help a kid who'd been through all that." Bridger paused to huff and puff as he tugged at a blanket wedged between shards of desk. "That's how Cousins are supposed to think."

Cousin: "We all feel better telling ourselves Mycroft Canner was just a trauma victim, that a monster like that can only happen in the incredibly improbable circumstance of a bash' house exploding and killing every member except an eight-year-old kid who has to recover alone from being blown almost limb from limb. Of course Mycroft Canner went nuts, if we just take better care of traumatized orphans from now on this'll never happen again. That way we don't have to admit that a human being actually chose to do . . ." Tears seized Carlyle again, sapping his strength as he struggled with a fallen bookcase. "But it was so premeditated. There's never been a crime so premeditated. Mycroft Canner spent years learning languages just to make it easier to deceive their victims. That's not lashing out at random, that's . . ."

"Mycroft can't anymore."

"Can't what?"

"Can't kill. The Major says Mycroft lost it." Bridger took a chunk of dollhouse in his arms. "The Major can tell. The Major said a skeptic can't be a killer. And they made Mycroft a Servicer, and all the Hive leaders know, do you think they're all wrong too?"

A deep breath. "Mycroft Canner is very good at deceiving people."

"The Major's killed people too, in the war, lots and lots of people. Are you going to say the Major's bad now too?"

"That's different."

"No it's not!" Bridger's wrath set Boo's blue fur bristling. "The army men are people too! Just because they're toys you can't say killing them doesn't count!"

"No, no, I didn't mean that. They're people, I respect that. But war is different. War is for something, at least in people's minds. Mycroft killed for . . . art, for fun, killing for the sake of killing, evil for the sake of evil." A fast sob. "I remember, whenever a new member of the bash' would disappear, people would start to place bets what the killer would do this time, vivisection, immolation. People enjoyed it, thinking like . . . Mycroft's goal was to make the world worse. That's evil."

"Yes."

That caught Carlyle off guard. "Yes what?"

"Yes, it's evil. But you said the world was getting better, people were thinking like that less. So, same for Mycroft. They were caught, they changed, they got better."

The Cousin gave a scornful snort. "So one day they're happily vivisecting Mercer Mardi and the next—boom!—cured? Impossible."

Bridger faced him across the dollhouse wreckage. "Miracles are impossible."

"That's different."

"Why?"

"It's . . ." I give the Gag-gene credit for pausing to try to find a real answer. "You create things, Bridger, you don't make people into different people."

"You should talk to Mycroft, you'll see how different they are."

A shudder. "I don't want to be in a room with Mycroft Canner."

"Call on Mycroft's tracker, dummy!" Bridger was too young for his brow to really furrow in anger, but he did his best. "It's better to try to find stuff out than to sit around and be wrong! Someone needs to drag you with a flashlight."

"What?"

"When I was little I was scared of the noises from the trash mine, I thought there was a monster in there. Eventually I told the Major, and the army men got a flashlight and made me look. I didn't want to but they dragged me over, and it was just the robots there, no monster. Then I wasn't scared anymore. Someone needs to drag you with a flashlight and make you look at Mycroft Canner."

"Knock, knock!" called Thisbe through the plastic sheeting. "Are you kids playing nice?"

Bridger had a smile for Thisbe. "Did you get rid of Ockham?"

"Yes, they're off filing paperwork. And you, Carlyle, have a lot of documentation to read."

"Why didn't you tell me that was Mycroft Canner?" Carlyle asked flatly.

Thisbe summoned her best false smile. "Bridger, sweetheart, it's much too late for you to be up. Mommadoll's made up a nice bed for you in my closet, all cuddly with lots of pillows, and you'll be safer there."

"I want to wait up for Mycroft."

"Absolutely not. It's much, much, much too late for you to be awake."

"But—"

"Mommadoll says straight to bed. You don't want to make her sad, do you?"

No one could resist that. "Okay. But only if you make Carlyle stop being wrong."

Thisbe gave a little laugh. "I'll try. I promise."

"Good!" My brave defender gave Carlyle a last glare, then stomped off through the flowers to the much-needed pillow fort.

Thisbe turned dark eyes on Carlyle. "Come outside. Now."

The Cousin folded one last T-shirt, overmeticulously to prolong the pause. "Why didn't you tell me that was Mycroft Canner?"

"Because you'd react like this. Come back outside."

He followed, haltingly, like a dog that does not really want to come home from play. "You've had your bash' adopt Mycroft Canner. You know what happened to the last bash' that adopted Mycroft Canner."

The witch's—apologies, master—the woman's tone grew richer as she basked in the night air. "Mycroft's an amateur. Ockham and Sniper are experts, trained, they have to be or they wouldn't be trusted with the system. We're in no danger from Mycroft Canner."

Carlyle winced, as though his stomach turned. "Are you a Cannerite?"

She gave a little laugh. "It's so juvenile, Cannerism. A philosophy concocted by a seventeen-year-old."

"It's sick." He almost spat. "Sensayer training tries to present it like a legitimate belief system, but I've had a couple Cannerite parishioners. It wasn't a philosophy, they were just sick people reciting trivia about Mycroft Canner like some dark messiah. Why do you want that near you?"

Thisbe gazed at him, a long, indulgent pause. "Follow me up to the bridge."

In his distraction Carlyle started up the stairway before thinking to ask, "Why?"

The speed of her ascent made Thisbe pant. "Someone's . . . here from . . . Romanova."

"What?"

"Eureka just . . . called me . . . They've . . . touched down."

"At midnight?" This is Chile, reader, and the Americas' night still young.

"I told you there are . . . protocols . . . when someone recognizes . . ."

"Mycroft Canner," a new voice called down from above them, a woman's but almost too deep to be a woman's. "Age thirty-one, born August 2nd, 2423, brownish black hair, many distinctive scars including a round, two-centimeter section missing from right ear."

Thisbe accelerated. "That's no officer I know . . ."

The stranger leaned forward over the side of the bridge, the better to call down at the now-rushing pair. "Captured on March 26th, 2440, sentenced to lifetime service March 28th, 2440. Registered personal possessions, five: one non-uniform hat, one pair of nonregulation shoes, one writing and computation tablet, one photograph of the members of their birth-bash', and one bilingual paper copy of Homer's *Iliad* with a bookmark made from a lock of Seine Mardi's hair and annotation by Apollo Mojave."

Thisbe reached the bridgeway first. "Who are you?"

"Julia Doria-Pamphili." The stranger stepped into a shaft of streetlight, which revealed an elegantly tailored European suit, double-breasted with champagne cording accenting its blue-black silk. Her hair was dark, thick, bound back in a bun which spiraled like a nautilus, and her grave face tempered by the creases of a perpetual smile. "I'm Mycroft Canner's court-appointed sensayer."

Pontifex Maxima

"JULIA!" CARLYLE GAPED. "WHY ARE YOU HERE?"

Julia Doria-Pamphili paced toward Carlyle and Thisbe, her old-fashioned ankle boots clicking on the walkway. "It's five in the morning by your sleep schedule and your tracker registered a heartbeat as if you were being chased by rampant wildebeests. And then I got a ping about Mycroft Canner. You think I'm not going to check that you're all right?"

Thisbe stared at this European, the Conclave pin on her breast, its little band of gold. "The Conclave Head?"

Julia surveyed Thisbe down to the mazelike landscapes of her boots. "You must be Human Thisbe Saneer." Her pronunciation was slow and luxurious, especially on the Humanist Hive title, as if she enjoyed the act of differentiating people. "Do I have you to thank for the timely call?" Julia offered a well-lotioned handshake.

Thisbe accepted the hand. "Nice to meet you, Jul—... is it July or Julia?"

"Julia."

It was a fair question; even newspapers sometimes substitute the socially correct de-gendered 'Jules' or 'July,' but Roman nobility as ancient as the Doria-Pamphili line, who can boast princes, popes, and (thanks to forged medieval genealogies) consuls and senators, scoffs at the modern fashion which would strip the sex from 'Julia.' In person she exudes antiquity: her tailored suit, her hair as black as baking chocolate, with the perfect ancient wave one sees on busts and caryatids. She wears it always bound back in coils, so one cannot guess how much of it there is. Such a busy vocateur has little time for strats or their insignia, so she wears none but the narrow Italian and Roman strat bracelets. The long sensayer's scarf which winds three times around her shoulders is vibrant violet silk, lined with equally violet velvet, and she wears only the most precisely tailored European suits, so every curve shows through. The Doria-Pamphili palace, with its stunning galleries of art treasures, was fully reconstructed after the Church War and belongs to the family still, but Julia gave up Rome for Romanova when she accepted her post as Conclave Head, and with it her office in the *Regia Pontificis* at the heart of the new Forum. Her kin thought her a fool.

"You're Mycroft's sensayer?" Thisbe asked. "Personally? Isn't that a bit cruel?"

The European laughed. "Is my reputation really as bad as all that?"

"Not bad," Thisbe corrected, "just, from what I've heard your specialty is one-time visits where you . . . um . . ."

"Dismember my parishioners?" Laughter sparkled in Julia's eyes. "How'd they put it in that editorial, Carlyle? I slash my clients to the heart, baring their hidden hypocrisies until they leave . . . what was it, a shattered wreck?"

Carlyle had been glaring stubbornly, but this answer at least matched his mood. "A shivering wreck."

"Shivering, yes, that's good. And then they go back to their regular sensayer, who nurses them back to sanity over months of great epiphanies." Julia stretched her neck to pop her shoulders. "I know it sounds dramatic, but, while my specialty is deep-cutting sessions, I can do normal ones too. I took on Mycroft Canner because I didn't want to give the most difficult case I'd ever seen to someone . . . too sensitive." She gave a little sigh. "And don't worry, I'm not stalking Cato Weeksbooth."

Thisbe snorted. "Good."

"Stalking Cato Weeksbooth?" Carlyle repeated.

Julia smile-winced a small apology. "Mmm. You know Cato's phobic of sensayers. We ran into one another once, and the poor thing fell down a flight of stairs trying to run away, broke an arm and a leg."

"That wasn't in the file." Carlyle's brows narrowed. "Neither was the fact that Mycroft Canner frequents this bash'. Did you know when you sent me?"

Julia drew close enough to pick grass seed from Carlyle's fraying scarf. "I did know, and I'm sorry about that. I filed the paperwork to get permission to tell you, but it's still processing. There's enough red tape around Mycroft Canner to wrap up Renunciation Column like a stick of peppermint. But what was it that threw you into such a panic an hour ago? Something to do with Mycroft?"

"They met," Thisbe answered simply.

"No!" Carlyle's voice is too light to thunder, but in this moment he tried. "We didn't just meet, it turned out I'd met Mycroft Canner days ago but no one saw fit to tell me. You knew they frequented this bash'; how could you send me with no warning?"

Julia reached up to brush back the strands of blond which sweat glued to Carlyle's forehead. "I couldn't leave the bash' without a sensayer for the month right after their old one died. I had to send someone. This is exactly your specialty, so I knew if anyone could cope it would be you."

Thisbe crossed her arms, watching the pair. "So it was you who assigned Carlyle? You know we requested a Humanist."

Carlyle winced as if the words were blows. "If you don't think I'm doing a good job—"

"You're doing a great job, Carlyle, I just think it's important for requests to be honored, especially politically sensitive requests."

Julia turned her smile on Thisbe, a deep, self-satisfied smile, as if every person she meets is some new platter at a banquet. "You also requested someone with security precleared, and who could handle Cato Weeksbooth, and the other . . . particularities of your bash'. I didn't have a Humanist with the right skills. Carlyle is my own student, one of the very best, as well as one of my most skilled specialists."

Carlyle gave a bashful smile.

Thisbe will not be deflected. "In what? Getting us over losing our sensayer? That's a pretty short-term issue to trump our actual request."

Kindly Carlyle bit his lip.

Julia is not so gentle. "Bash' loss. Our Carlyle is a bash' loss specialist. You all should have had one five years ago. I understand why you worked so hard to keep the accident from the public. 'World Transit System Left in the Hands of Traumatized Twentysomethings' is a headline sure to bring world panic. But I looked over your files. Cato Weeksbooth, if nothing else, proves you really should have switched to a specialist when it happened."

See a quiver rise in Thisbe's throat now, on her lips, as she glances back at the glassy bash'house, where generations shared the family duty, loving grandba'pas working side by side with the bright new generation, but where now Ockham, not yet thirty-one, is master of the house. There are many empty rooms upstairs. It was a rafting accident that claimed the Saneer-Weeksbooth elders—Humanists and their heroic risks. Ganymede knew, Romanova knew, the powers that be, they were informed at the time, but there was no obituary, no honors for these brave servants of the world, not one, not when all Hives hover hungry for an excuse to take away this all-powerful family business. I think the hardest kind of mourning is when you have to lie.

Thisbe hid her feelings with a laugh. "Makes sense. Cato does need it.

I didn't think of it." Another defensive chuckle. "No insult intended, but a fluffy little Cousin doesn't seem the type for such a grim specialty."

"It was because of Mycroft Canner." Carlyle can sound grim, in his light, icy way.

Thisbe stared. Thisbe sighed. "You wanted to be the one to make sure it never happens again?" She took a deep breath. "Wow. This . . . was handled very badly for you, I'm sorry. I had no idea the Canner Murders were such an important thing for you, more than for most people." Deep breath. "I'm sorry."

With an expression something between a wince and a slight smile, Carlyle nodded. "It's all right. I didn't tell you my specialty. You couldn't have known."

Julia craned her neck to make Carlyle meet her gaze, warm, earnest, condescending. "I'm sorry too that it worked out this way. Hmm?" She fixed a sweet little pout on Carlyle until he offered up a smile. "But, honestly, I didn't expect you to run across Mycroft so soon, they aren't around that much. You may be my most enthusiastic student, but I didn't think you'd be here every single day; you only had two appointments this week. I got a call from your bash' that they've hardly seen you the past three days, they were wondering where you were, and I hear you stood up Jamussa yesterday." She held up a scolding finger. "I shouldn't have better track of your dating life than you do."

In better light one might have seen the pale-skinned Cousin blush.

"Good. Now," Julia continued, "while it's very poetic meeting under the moonlight, I'm sure poor Thisbe—may I call you Thisbe?"

"Whatever."

"Then you must call me Julia. I'm sure poor Thisbe would like to get to bed. I will escort Carlyle home, we'll talk on the way, they'll get a good night's sleep, they'll spend some time at their bash' tomorrow, rest, and stay out of your hair," she smiled at Thisbe.

A smile of relief touched Thisbe's cheeks, then faded. "No. I can't let you go like this. Carlyle still thinks Mycroft is a danger, and they voiced explicit intent to tell people; that's a threat to my bash' and to the system. I'm a security officer, I cannot let you go until I have confidence that Carlyle is not going to take any destructive action."

"Oh?" Julia chirruped, peering up again, her dark eyes into Carlyle's blue. "You haven't noticed Mycroft's nonuniform shoes?"

Carlyle bit his lip in thought. "No . . . ?"

"They're Ahimsa shoes."

Brightness flooded Carlyle's face, as when dark shutters open to the cheer of noon. "Really?"

"Mm-hm."

"Oh, Mycroft's weird brushy-on-the-bottom shoes?" Thisbe asked. "I thought those were a Servicer thing, to scrub when you walk."

Julia chuckled. "Fun guess. No, it's a philosophical thing, extreme pacifists wear them. It's named for an old Buddhist practice, but people do it for all reasons. The soles are soft bristles on the bottom, like a toothbrush, so they don't kill insects if you step on them. Preservation of all life."

"That's . . ." The last shadows left Carlyle's face. "Mycroft said death was too light a punishment for them, that they have to pay more."

"Exactly." Julia pushed back a stray chocolate curl. "Mycroft Canner is doing a very deep and dedicated social penance, and if their parole officers and I keep an extra-strict watch on them, it's mostly because they have a bad habit of skipping meals, and overdoing anti-sleeps, and working themself to exhaustion."

"Ahimsa shoes . . ." Carlyle ran his fingers through his hair, his voice gaining that nervous tenderness that edges upon awe. The earlier arguments had been the wrong ones for him: Bridger's loyalty, Ockham's duty, Thisbe's good sense; what Carlyle needed was a sensayer.

"Mycroft Canner has had a very difficult path," Julia continued, "and has very difficult things to live with, more difficult than anyone in the world. I've been working with them a long time. I'd love to look over the case together with a bash' loss specialist."

Carlyle took a deep breath, smiling at last. "I owe you an apology, Thisbe. I . . . reacted very extremely, and it was unfair to you. This was an unfair situation, and it wasn't your fault."

Thisbe pursed her lips. "Thank you."

"You don't need to worry about me going public."

Again she pursed her lips. "I believe you. Thank you."

Julia made a little victory gesture with her small fists, as when one successfully plays matchmaker, or scores a goal. "And now, since you're satisfied, Thisbe, I prescribe, in the name of sanity, bed."

Their eyes met here, Thisbe and Julia, the Humanist and European, a long, contemplative gaze exchanged between the pair who had both, until now, thought themselves unrivaled as the most important (living) woman in Mycroft Canner's life. Each must have known in the abstract that the other existed, but neither had, I think, expected their first encounter to be quite so symmetrical. "Agreed," Thisbe concluded. "This was very helpful, and I'm glad to see Mycroft and Carlyle both in good hands." She offered a smile. "Europeans really are so sensible." The addendum 'compared to Cousins' passed unsaid.

Julia gave a gratified nod. "I can put you on a waiting list for an appropriate Humanist sensayer if you like."

"Thank you, but Carlyle's excellent. A perfect choice."

Both sensayers smiled.

Thisbe nodded. "Good night, Carlyle. I hope you get good rest."

"Thank you. Good night, Thisbe. And I hope you're not on duty too early tomorrow."

An unhappy groan confessed she was.

The car was ready, and Julia had a thermos of soothing herbal tea. And now, reader, a conversation of a different kind, and a face of things that I myself was unaware of until later days.

Julia: "How's progress?"

Carlyle: "Slow. Having this investigation on top of us is a big problem."

Julia: "They're accepting you?"

Carlyle: "Yes, though it was scary just now when Thisbe called you on the no-Humanists-available thing. But Thisbe seems happy with me."

Julia: "Any access to Sniper yet?"

Carlyle: "No, nor Ockham. I did make inroads with Lesley Saneer, we're starting off well. And I had a tough but productive little talk with one of the set-sets."

Julia: "Have you seen the twins yet?"

Carlyle: "Not hide nor hair. I get the feeling they're actually more unstable than Cato Weeksbooth, but nobody wants to talk about it."

Julia: "They'll be in good hands with you."

Carlyle: "I hope so."

Julia: "I'm afraid I have bad news."

Carlyle: "What?"

Julia: "The C.F.B."

Carlyle: "What about the C.F.B.?"

Julia: "What about the C.F.B.!" She tapped his forehead. "Earth to Carlyle Foster. Hiroaki Mitsubishi's application?"

Carlyle: "That was today?"

Julia: "Carlyle, you've been following nothing else for weeks."

Carlyle: "Sorry. There's been . . . stuff."

Julia: "Stuff? You've never pleaded 'stuff' before."

282 ☒ TOO LIKE THE LIGHTNING

Carlyle: "Irrelevant stuff, nothing to worry about. What was the outcome?"

Julia: "Point for the enemy. Hiroaki Mitsubishi is now training with a C.F.B. Assistant Section Chief."

Carlyle: "Which section?"

Julia: "Education."

Nothing could stab the Cousin deeper. The Cousins Feedback Bureau. All Hives are proud of their unique governments: Europe's nation-strat Parliament, the Masons' nonhereditary absolute monarchy, the Mitsubishi shareholder democracy, the Humanist flexible-constitution democratic aretocracy, the Gordian Brain'bash and corporate Board appointed by Brill's Institute. And if those Hives have an irritant, it is that the Cousins can remain the perennially second-largest, second-strongest Hive with a system the others wish they could deride: suggestion box. The all-embracing Cousins never did update their structure, not since the earliest days of *Mukta*'s children, when they were just a volunteer group for women to help each other while traveling abroad. They had a volunteer committee with a Chair, some rules of conduct, a family-friendly atmosphere, and a suggestion box, no more. No one thought they could stick to it, not as their membership expanded: women, minors, sexual minorities, then kids of Members, friends of Members, friends of friends of friends, finally anyone willing to act like a distant "cousin" and offer smiling airport pickup and a sofa for the night to a stranger in return for knowing that the stranger would reciprocate. With just shy of two billion members, the modern Hive has fitted its "suggestion box" with an analytic Feedback Bureau streamlined to process a hundred million friendly notes a week, group the overlap, and send them on, every one of them, to the right volunteer to consider the suggestion: "This town needs a new school," "This drug needs a sixty-million-dollar research grant," "This intersection would be a great place for a mural." They get it done, this vast, cooperative 'family.' It works. At least if outsiders have not infiltrated, and sunk their fangs into its living heart.

Carlyle: "Hiroaki Mitsubishi with access to the education processing..."

Julia: "That's not the limit of it. The Seven-Ten lists are public now, and C.F.B. Chief Darcy Sok is number eight on Masami Mitsubishi's list. Every reporter in the world is racing to do a piece on the C.F.B. now, and guess who's now the highest ranked person in the C.F.B. who sleeps on Tokyo time and is already up and available for interviews."

Carlyle: "Hiroaki Mitsubishi?"

Julia sent the image to Carlyle's lenses, the Bureau's friendly, off-pink

building studded with balconies, trying its best to hide between its neighbors on one of Casablanca's broad French-style boulevards, but, in what
should have been the quiet of the night, the reporters and gnat-dense camera robots gave it away. Stories in the Cousins' capital always draw more
press than a scandal in Tōgenkyō or Alexandria, perhaps because we worry
more when Mom is threatened than Father or Uncle, or because the austerity of Cousins' Law, which won't permit even a Red Light District, has
doomed the capital to a permanent slow news day. The press had cornered
Hiroaki Mitsubishi outside the entrance, evidently returning from a coffee
run with a tray of cups in hand. Hiroaki is the only one of Andō's adopted
ba'kids who looks Japanese by birth, and, this night at least, she had paired
Danaë's sleeveless hand-knit sweater with a pair of flowy, silky pants which
invoked a Cousin's wrap despite the minor's sash still about her hips.

I'm sure Carlyle's stomach turned. "Masami and Hiroaki Mitsubishi,
voice and face of the C.F.B. I haven't read Masami's editorial, what does it
say?"

Julia sighed into her tea. "In short that the only real power in the Cousins
is the software in the C.F.B. that processes the suggestions, and that all the
rest, the board, Kosala, are basically carrying out robot orders. That there's
no heart to the Hive that's supposed to be all heart."

Carlyle pressed his head against the car's side wall. "I don't know how
we're going to stop this, Julia. The Mitsubishi brood are in the Censor's
office, the European Parliament, the Humanist Praetor's office, now
the C.F.B., and *Black Sakura* isn't *The Romanov* but it's still one of the most
influential papers in the world. Are you sure it's the Saneer-Weeksbooth
bash' I should be concentrating on? I should be helping more directly. Give
me someone inside the C.F.B."

Julia: "No. You're the right kind of specialist for the Saneer-Weeksbooth
bash', you can do a better job with them than anyone in the world. That's
where I need you now. And better safe than sorry. A compromised C.F.B.
could cripple the Cousins, but a compromised Saneer-Weeksbooth bash'
could touch anywhere, anyone. They haven't been a Mitsubishi target
yet, but we don't know that won't change. I want you in there keeping
them safe."

Carlyle: "It is a great case, yes, an important case, I definitely want to
keep working with them. But I want to do more, Julia. The enemy actually
have someone inside the C.F.B.! If we just knew what their goal was . . ."

She stroked his hair. "Let me worry about that."

"If only we could prove this theft was them!"

She shook her head. "I'm sure it wasn't. I think, if anything, it inter-
fered with what they were planning, disrupting what Masami Mitsubishi
would have done inside *Black Sakura*. But things aren't all bad. I've finally
got Darcy Sok to request a session with me."

Brightness at once. "You have!"

"We'll guard the C.F.B. yet." Julia brandished a delicate, enthusiastic
fist. "And another piece of good news: Headmaster Faust sent Jun Mitsubishi packing with a flea in their ear. No toehold for the Mitsubishi brood
inside Brill's Institute. But Jun has applied for a secretary's post with the
Gordian Brain'bash, so they're still trying to worm in."

"Can this fuss with Masami Mitsubishi help us? If they're fired from
Black Sakura, that would be a good setback."

Julia gazed at him a moment, slim lips pursed tight. "Perhaps."

Carlyle: "I could—"

Julia: "No. I want you where your strengths are, and I don't want to ask
anything that will be a strain on your conscience. Do what you're best at.
We have others who can help protect the C.F.B."

Carlyle: "But—"

Julia: "When the Saneer-Weeksbooth Members know you well enough
to trust you, when you can suggest they start coming to me, then I can take
on some of the burden, and you can take on something new. But not before. We need them close and we need them safe."

Carlyle: "It shouldn't be long with Thisbe."

Julia: "Yes, that seemed promising. But don't push too fast. What have
you been doing going there over and over?"

Carlyle: ". . ."

Julia: "Stuff?"

He gave a guilty smile.

"Do you want a consult?"

"No, it's fine."

"The whole bash' is very guarded, from the files. If you push you'll spook
them. Relax and take things naturally. You're a brilliant sensayer, Carlyle.
I have you where you can do the most good. You'll know if anyone tries to
get at them, and you'll stop it."

"Yes."

"I'm so glad to have you to depend on at times like this."

Despite his gloom, he couldn't fight a smile. "Thanks. Oh, Julia?"

"Mm?"

"What do you know about Tribune J.E.D.D. Mason?"

"The Celebrity Youth Act has never had a tougher case. You met?"

"They're doing the investigation, they came to the bash'house."

"J.E.D.D. Mason is not a problem. Believe me, there's nowhere I'm more vigilant than Hive leadership. Yes, they have ties to Andō, but it's the Mitsubishi brood we have to watch out for. J.E.D.D. Mason has nothing whatever to do with them."

"It isn't the ties to Andō, it's . . . you know about 'Dominic' and 'Martin'? Is it a cult?"

"No. Nothing like that. There's nothing dangerous at all with J.E.D.D. Mason, I check up with their sensayer all the time."

"Their sensayer, is that Dominic Seneschal?"

"Yes. Dominic has an odd comportment, I know, but they're immensely skilled, just right for J.E.D.D. Mason's case, a specialist, like you but different. J.E.D.D. Mason is a very strange young person, it was inevitable for someone growing up around so much power, but I watch, and I'm careful, and there's no cult, no danger."

Relief let Carlyle slump. But not complete relief. "And what is J.E.D.D. Mason's relationship with Mycroft Canner?"

"Confidential." The Conclave Head gave her prize student another shoulder squeeze. "Don't worry about J.E.D.D. Mason. No one is less threat to the world order. If anything, they're the pillar of stability that keeps the rest from teetering. Now, would you like a session?" Her perfect nails played through the fraying crochet of the old scarf she had given him. "Anything new with you on the theological front? New questions? Discoveries?"

Carlyle summoned his best smile. "No, nothing new with me. Could we talk through the post-bash'-loss psych reports on Mycroft Canner? I'd love to hear your readings in light of thirteen years of further development, that's an amazing resource."

"Yes. Yes, Mycroft is quite the resource."

HERE AT LONG LAST, IN THE TIRED DARK OF MORNING,
ENDS THE THIRD DAY OF THIS HISTORY.

Chapter the TWENTY-FOURTH

Sometimes Even I Am Very Lonely

I SLEPT THAT NIGHT IN ALEXANDRIA, AND BREAKFASTED WITH Caesar's staff, though Caesar himself will not break bread with Mycroft Canner. I had no time to return to Cielo de Pájaros before reporting to J.E.D.D. Mason's Utopians, but gave myself a half-hour to stop at the nearest Servicers' dorm, where our tainted and all-forgiving brotherhood was still willing to call me 'friend.' I have been adopted many times since the explosion killed my birth bash'. I was adopted by the Terrafirma Cousin bash' next door. I was adopted by the Mardi bash' next to them, and our four other neighbor bash'es, which all let me grow up half-wild like a cat with several homes, whom no one thinks to check on so long as it visits once a week. I was adopted by Thisbe, Bridger, and the Major. But only with the Servicers has my adoption been completely without lies. I was at first just one more Mycroft who slept and shoveled beside them. They soon noticed that I made good conversation (invaluable in a society which has no other entertainment), and by the time the wiser of them added 'Canner' to 'Mycroft' they already felt too much affection to know fear. Apollo Mojave used to frequent a pub in Liverpool, mad as that seems. He was a Utopian, a vocateur, a *Familiaris,* as in demand with the Powers as I am, with his own bash', his lover and her bash', his constellation, his work, his writing, me, all vying for scarce hours, but he still made time for a pub. It was filthy, one of those dives where locals come for talk and dominos. At first none spoke to this alien Utopian, planted at the counter with his vizor and his coat, but beer erases barriers, and he was soon listening to tall tales and filling in at games, as dear as any puppy. Apollo needed that, he told me. Even if he only saw them once a month, it kept him from forgetting what it meant to be a human being—without that how could he claim to be acting for all humanity? Perhaps the Servicers give me the same.

At a crossroads, three blocks from my destination, hands seized me by the throat and dragged me backwards into the alley with a killer's violence. I do not know, reader, if you are so blessed that you have tasted an embrace like this, a universe in itself, so all the outside world could cease and you would smile uncaring. If you have not tasted something like that, it cannot be described. Fierce, dear arms dragged me to the bedding of the alley's trash, pinning my hands more out of habit than need, as his lips tasted my ear.

«Saladin,» I whispered. It is a name I chant sometimes to myself, over and over, as if language had been invented only to form those syllables.

«Mycroft,» he answered in kind. His breath tasted of meat and wild places, the grit of urban underbellies and the clean of mountain stone. My Saladin. No threat, no order, no torture could have made me speak of him to any living soul, but for you, only for you, reader; never again accuse me of keeping secrets.

His voice is a savage, hungry whisper-hiss. «I've found Tully.»

Sobs without tears seized me, as when one who can no longer pretend he is not sick gives way to coughing, but my Saladin absorbed my sobs, his body like warm hands around a shivering chick. «Where?» I asked.

«Luna City. Thirteen years up there, I can't imagine what it cost.»

I had guessed Luna City. There are places within the human sphere beyond my reach; the nearest is the Moon.

«They're coming back, tomorrow. I saw them on the passenger list, Port-Gentil elevator.»

We spoke Greek together, our birth bash' tongue, the language of our intimacy since forever and forever. «Could be a trap. Tully Mardi wouldn't use their real name on a passenger list—no Utopian would raise a child that stupid.»

I can feel when Saladin smiles, the way his collarbones flex when he bares those human fangs, more dangerous than an animal's since they both bite and speak. «True, 'Tully Mardi' on the list would've been stupid. 'Tully Mojave' transcends stupidity and qualifies as painting a bull's-eye on your face.»

«Tully Mojave?» I repeated.

«How's that for throwing down the gauntlet?»

He laughed, and I laughed with him, our bodies as aligned as clapping hands. I could feel him getting hard beneath me, and heat stirred in my member too, eager to awaken after so long a sleep.

«Pup must fancy themself the successor.» His hand reached up my shirt, his nails tracing paths of fire across my chest. «Let's finish it,» he invited. «Seventeen was never a good number.»

It would have been easier to drive a dagger through my heart than answer. «I can't. You finish, please. Finish alone.»

He seized my throat. His calluses had changed again, some new labor or game making them thicker on the edges. «Who did this to you?»

«No.»

«Tell me!» As too-tender Carlyle expresses anger sideways by weeping, so Saladin's sadness manifests sideways in snarls and lust for blood. «Someone did this to you!»

«No.»

«Tell me!»

He was all around me, can you imagine? His lips hot at my ear, his left hand scraping my chest while his right stroked my inner thigh, maddening and gentle as a cat's rough tongue. I wanted him. I wanted nothing but him and me to have existed for the whole of time. «I can't!» I sobbed. «I can't! They'll do it to you, too.»

His hands tried to withdraw, but I grabbed them, held them to me, tighter.

«I can't take revenge if you won't tell me,» he snarled.

«Then don't.»

«We had everything we wanted! They were going to execute you. Even the Cousins were screaming for your blood. The whole world was going to dirty its hands, and you signed yourself away to MASON. Someone made you do it, and left this shell of you behind!»

I pressed my lips against his throat, so I could taste his last days' marauding: street dust, laurel branches, sweat, goats, gunpowder, sunburn, and, underneath, that skin which is almost my own. «Finish it,» I begged. «Kill Tully Mardi. Finish for the old Mycroft who was yours heart and soul. That's the only revenge I need.»

He snarled—the lightning beauty of that snarl!—and let me nip back at his bare ear, where no tracker ever rests. My perfect, secret Saladin.

«Don't let them catch you,» I cautioned. «Tully will be expecting me, they won't be ready for you. I know you can do it.»

I turned fully, to let myself see Saladin now, the most beautiful face in the world: fierce teeth, eyes narrowed so they seemed all black like a lizard's, with no lashes, no eyebrows to interrupt the smooth contrast of eye and skin. His blond wig had slipped back, baring a scalp with no hair to keep my fingers from enjoying the warmth of blood within. His cheeks had once been as impossibly smooth as rose petals, or as new skin when a callus has just fallen away, but they had weathered fast these last years, and there was wrinkling around his eyes: time. Like me he had just passed thirty, but he looked like an adult.

«You've been forgetting your anti-aging meds,» I chided, cupping his dry cheek in my hand. He'd had his gene-splices as an embryo, as we all do, but every long year of his self-neglect made clearer that they only do so much.

«Meds are such a pain to steal.»

«Don't you dare shorten your days, Saladin, not by one hour, not while I'm still stuck here.»

He stared at me, those wild black eyes.

«I need a favor,» I said.

«Oh?» His teeth traced the edges of the chunk that he had bitten from my right ear in our youth, and I, in return, felt through his threadbare shirt for the old scar above his heart, where I had cut from him my first taste of human flesh.

«You know the child I often visit in the trench at Cielo de Pájaros?»

«I've seen 'em. I've seen nasty business circling there too. Even the Mob is scared."

«About what?»

«The *Black Sakura* theft, and you poking around about who had the old Canner Device. No one I've talked to has a clue what's going on, they just don't want trouble from someone else's crime.»

That aligned with what I'd guessed. «The child's name is Bridger.»

Suspicion turned his narrow eyes to slits. «So?»

«I want you to watch Bridger for me. I want you to . . .» The words refused to come. «You're right, there are dark things circling. Another predator.»

«I've seen them. Just a glimpse, dark, European-looking Blacklaw, keeping out of sunlight, careful as a lynx.»

«If it comes to it, if I can't keep Bridger out of their hands, if Dominic is about to . . .» I had to clutch his arms tighter to steel myself. «I need you to be ready to kill Bridger for me. Please? Not now, just if there's no other way. You can do it gently.»

«Do it yourself.»

«I can't.»

«You grip the skull with both hands and twist.»

«I can't! I love Bridger like family. We're almost out of time, Saladin, please!»

Saladin could not anymore ignore the frantic beeping of my tracker as it felt my pulse race.

He turned over so could I lie upon him, chest to chest, and we ravished each other as best we could in those precious seconds, lips tasting lips, hands spreading ecstasy through backs and buttocks, our rising sexes all but touching through the clothes we did not have time to open. He was the first to find the strength to break away.

«I'll think about it.» With that he turned his back, lifted the hood of his Utopian coat, and, between the Griffincloth and shadows, my Saladin was gone.

Thou traitor, Mycroft! All these years thou hast let me think that there was justice in the world, that thine evil had been caught and punished, yet here I find thy fiercer half still free! I would have locked my doors, and bade my children hurry home at night if I had known! Or perhaps, reader, you take the other side: *Thou traitor, Mycroft! Thou hast left me in despair this decade, thinking that we had lost our Noble Savage, that the last human beast still free of the chains of conscience and society had been captured and tamed, while all these years there were two of you, and the nobler (and hope with him) still roamed free!* Reader, the slave I am now lays open his heart at your command, but the free creature I was back when I roamed with Saladin owes you nothing; I had no right to expose his secret until this history required.

«Be careful,» I called to the air where he had been and might still be. «Don't let the child touch you.»

A subtle swish of something told me he had heard.

I rose as soon as I was strong enough, and barely had time to smooth my uniform and hide the traces of Saladin's nails with a smear of dirt before the police cars descended to block the alley before and behind me like barricades. Five armed police came with their commander, all uniformed in Romanova's blue but with different cuts of jacket, a Mason here, a Brillist there, an Indian or Chinese Mitsubishi, like the many exercises of a tailor trying to pick a final form. Why five? Not because they thought that number could take me if I resisted, but because any fewer would be too scared to approach. Even with so many they seemed unhappy with the task, not nervous faces but those too-grim expressions the police adopt to keep you from sensing anything beneath. Only their chief at the center was relaxed, slouching as he drew from his satchel the special manacles the Utopians designed for me. He tossed them to his men as if pitching a baseball.

"Morning, Papa," I greeted in common English.

Do not read too much into the nickname; everyone who knows him, from a Romanovan Praetor to the lowest clerk, uses that name for Universal Free Alliance Police Commissioner General Ektor Carlyle Papadelias.

"Morning, Mycroft," he answered. "What was it this time?"

"Some kids ran by blasting Canner Beat." It was an old excuse, and often true.

"Will this do, Papa?" one of his backup called, tapping a steel beam which braced one of the buildings.

Papa shook his head. "Car's more reliable."

I kept my arms as limp as possible as they shackled my wrists to the squad car's bumper beam behind me. I know the cops feel better if I make no contact, but I could not keep my fingers from brushing one's wrist, and she recoiled as at the touch of burning coal. Sometimes I think Papa brings novices on purpose for these visits, as if facing Mycroft Canner were their baptism as true servants of the law.

"All secure, Papa," they reported.

"Good."

The Commissioner General's nod let the rest fall back to the periphery, while he settled in, leaning against the curved nose of a second car opposite me. Age seems to have given Papadelias more energy, not less, as fat and muscle waste away, leaving nothing to weigh down his skeleton but his ever-burning brain. He marked his hundredth birthday two years ago, but thanks to modern medicine he still has hair on his scalp and pink in his skin, and still sprints like a jackrabbit. In my mind his true title will always be Detective Inspector, for it was the rank he truly wanted, fleeing promotion like the plague for almost seventy years, but no pleading could keep Romanova from promoting the man who captured Mycroft Canner.

«You've been a busy bee this week, Mycroft.» He used Greek now, childhood's tongue for both of us, tender to my ear, though I don't know how it sounds to those who don't associate those tones with home and storybooks, and a mother so faded in my memory now that she is little more than a warm darkness muddled with images of Mommadoll.

«It's been a busy week,» I answered. «And before I forget, Happy Independence Day one day late.»

Would you correct me, reader? It had been two days since Renunciation Day, but to us the true holiday was the Greek Independence Day, March twenty-fifth, when the four-century oppression of the Turks was finally thrown off, just in time for Greece to enjoy brief nationhood before nations became passé. A Servicer may not, but Papadelias wore his strat insignia, the Greek flag armband in vivid blue and white. Nation-strats like Greece or France or Mexico always offer less conspicuous alternatives, a bracelet or narrow ribbon, but it rankles when I see a Greek declare their pride with anything less than the full armband. Do you laugh, reader? Thinking that every nation-strat considers itself the most important in the world? Well, we are right. Rome was built from Greece, Europe from Rome, our modern world from Europe's Union, and however many worlds Utopia may colonize they will all come from this one. So the triremes which defended Greece at Salamis defended Mars, too, reader, and every Hive, and you.

«They're trying to keep me off this *Black Sakura* case,» Papa began.

«I know. Are they succeeding?»

«I'm Commissioner General, you know what that means?»

«You get an office in the Forum?»

«Cute.» His eyes glittered, the brightness of the passenger within his age-thin frame. «It means I trump the law enforcement of all seven Hives. If one, just one, says they want me on the case, no power on this Earth can keep me off.»

I'd learned over our many interviews just how to lean against the car to keep my hands from falling asleep. «You sent Martin in the first place, didn't you?»

«Yes, but I didn't expect it to be an either-or, especially not now that it's getting juicer. I've called all seven. Not just the seven, I've called Senators, strat leaders, secretaries, Tribunes, you-know-who.» He picked at his sleeves, always rolled up as if the rank stripes around the cuffs offended him. «The whole reason they forced me into the Commissioner General's chair was to get someone they could trust there, but, no matter what I try, no change.» His eyes narrowed. «I called Martin Guildbreaker to help me help them, not to banish myself to paperwork mountain. The only reason to keep the police off a case is if you don't want it solved.»

«They don't want it solved,» I confirmed. «They want it fixed.»

«Are they stupid? There wouldn't be this many tremors without something dangerous underneath. Do they even have a plan for if they find something they can't just sweep under the carpet?»

«I don't know, Papa.»

«See, even you don't know. But that isn't what really gets me. What really gets me is knowing the decision to block me was made in about five minutes in Ganymede's parlor—somewhere I could've come if they'd called me!—but they didn't.» He unleashed his frustration in a kick at an unoffending trashbot. «I thought for sure the Utopians would at least have the good sense to worry when all the others agree on something, but I got word back from them this morning: 'It's being handled.' You can't tell me they settled on that answer by themselves, it's not even U-speak! If I had a euro for every time I've heard that sentence in the past two days I could retire on it.»

«Twenty minutes,» I corrected.

«What?»

«It took them twenty minutes in Duke Ganymede's parlor to decide to keep you off the case, and there were reasons for it. You've heard who is handling it?»

«J.E.D.D. Mason.»

I nodded. «You know J.E.D.D. Mason's a good person. And you know Martin Guildbreaker's a good person. If they find something that needs you on it, they'll come to you.»

A slow breath. «Hopefully. But then why block me from the case?»

«I don't know. I really don't.»

Papa shook his tired head. «Since when have they let politics be this openly incestuous, Mycroft? Tsuneo Sugiyama put Sniper instead of Ganymede on a Seven-Ten list and everyone's acting like it's the end of the world. Even thirty years ago you couldn't find two Seven-Ten lists with the same top Seven, but when's the last time you saw one of the Gordian Brain'bash members on there instead of the Headmaster, huh? Or a European other than the Prime Minister?» The guards around us were growing nervous hearing the Commissioner's Greek so heated. «What worries me is that they aren't even being subtle anymore. The Censor married the Cousin Chair and the Mitsubishi Hive leader is the Humanist president's brother-in-law and no one's crying conflict-of-interest? Do people really not care?» A deep breath. «It shouldn't be this easy for them, Mycroft. The Death of Majority doesn't help if the minorities come together and act like a majority again.»

Do you still believe in the Death of Majority, reader? The First Anonymous's first essay, lauding what they saw as the promise of eternal peace. After the Church War there was no majority race, no majority religion, no majority language, no majority nationality. *Mukta* birthed a world so intermixed that no one anymore grew up among people mostly like themselves: the majority of Japanese people did not live in Japan, the majority of Greeks did not live in Greece, so too for every country in the world. Majority died with Church and Nation, the Anonymous proclaimed, and with it war and genocide died too, for they require a majority united, patriots, an 'us' and 'them' in which 'us' is normal, larger, more powerful, capable of overwhelming and defeating 'them.' I could ask any contemporary here, 'Are you a majority?' and I know what he or she would answer: *Of course not,*

Mycroft. I have a Hive, a race, a second language, a vocation and an avocation, hobbies of my own; add up my many strats and you will soon reduce me to a minority of one, and hence my happiness. I am unique, and proud of my uniqueness, and prouder still that, by being no majority, I ensure eternal peace. You lie, reader. There is one majority still entrenched in our commingled world, a great 'us' against a smaller 'them.' You will see it in time. I shall give only one hint—the deadliest majority is not something most of my contemporaries are, reader, it is something they are not.

«Couldn't you ask to investigate on behalf of the Hiveless?» I asked.

Papa shook his head. «Not if no Hiveless have been affected by the crime. So far none are. If the Saneer-Weeksbooth bash' had kids who were minors I could use them as an excuse, but as it is . . . »

«Dominic Seneschal is missing.»

«Dominic Seneschal isn't a missing person yet, they turned their tracker off themself and didn't specify a duration after which they should be sought if they don't check in. Thanks to a certain Mycroft Canner,» Papa nodded his mock gratitude, «we're allowed to start search and rescue after five days without contact no matter what the person said, but that's still a ways off. Besides, I don't want to go in without at least one of the big Seven giving their stamp of approval, or I'll bring them all down on my head. I need a way to make it look like I didn't push for this, like one of them requested it.»

«I see.» I glanced down at my Utopian manacles, their taut, gelatinous surfaces almost comforting after so many meetings. «You could try King Isabel Carlos. These days the others don't have the heart to say 'no' to Their Majesty's requests. If you get the King to support you it'll be hard for the others to object, especially because Andō and Ganymede can never pass up a chance to piss on Casimir Perry.»

«Spain?» Papadelias took a heavy breath. «Yes, Spain would do, though when the Bourbon dynasty is the least incestuous element of your politics, you worry.»

We laughed together, and I feared the sight of Mycroft Canner laughing would drive the ghost-faced policewoman on my left to an early grave, but Papadelias calmed her with an authoritative nod.

«And with that out of the way, shall we look at March nineteenth?» He did not have to specify the year. «There's a discrepancy in your timeline here.»

«I don't have time today, Papa. I have jobs waiting.»

«Just one question.» His lenses were already glittering with reports, though I cannot believe there were any details of my case left which Papa had not memorized. «That was a busy day for you, you grabbed Kohaku, Chiasa, Mercer, and Luther in one day.»

I shrugged. «I had to move fast. The third body was about to be discovered, and two more bash'members were missing, it wouldn't take you long to put the rest in protective custody. If I grabbed them then, I could finish them any time.»

I wondered what topic the others thought we had moved to, these guards who stood deaf to our Greek but could see our body language grow more comfortable, more like family than enemies. No, I am dearer to this vocateur than family. Modern police work was invented by yet another Frenchman, Eugène François Vidocq, a son, not of the Eighteenth Century, but the Nineteenth. Vidocq's exploits, with their disguises, great escapes, false identities, and lifelong rivals, are so spectacular one can hardly believe in them—indeed he seems more like one of Bridger's miracles than real when one reads of the life which provided meat enough for Vidocq's good friend Victor Hugo to base not just Valjean but Javert too on this one man. Between his exploits, Vildocq invented police networks, salaried informants, plainclothes detectives, all the vital tools of Papa's trade, and Papadelias so idolizes this role model that he even forgives him for not being Greek. Deep down I know Papa longs for the Chinese curse of interesting times. To Vidocq Fate granted prison-breaks, fierce nemeses, an escape from galley slavery, and he made the most of tumults, creating false identities, infiltrating the very criminal world he worked to cage, and, after one great prison break, toiling for years disguised as his own successor in order to win a royal pardon for his former self and then unmask dramatically before the throne. But our present is too orderly to offer such adventures to poor Papadelias. By rights, at some point in his eight decades' toil, Providence owed Papa a multidecade sparring match like Javert and Valjean, or at least the few precious years Holmes had with his Moriarty. But, alas, when Papa's longed-for Master Criminal finally came, our battle only lasted two short weeks; you will indulge us if we won't let those two weeks end.

«Here's today's question.» Papa's eyes sparkled, like a poor poker player's unable to disguise a good hand. «If you'd spent the whole previous day doing jug-and-funnel water torture on Makenna Mardi in Bunker 2, and feeding Leigh Mardi to lions in the Great African Reservation, when did you have time to go back to the Alps and refill the tank for Jie Mardi's Chinese water torture? It only held two hundred gallons, that wouldn't have lasted three whole days.»

«I didn't have to refill the tank,» I answered instantly. «It had already been two days, Jie had gotten used to measuring time by how far the water level rose. If the water supply ran out they would pass out as soon as the dripping stopped, and then when I refilled it and the drip started again they'd wake up and not think any time had passed, since the water hadn't risen. If no time has passed psychologically it doesn't break the spell.»

«But the body recovers during sleep, the mind too.»

«Not enough to matter.»

«I see.» He didn't like that answer. He had that itchy look, like he would go back to his notes and brood, then call at four A.M. with some loophole. In fact, he had one now. «How'd you feed your dog, then?»

«What?»

«Your dog, you can't have taken it with you where the lions were. You left it in the Alps?»

I smiled. «I left it gnawing on Laurel's left arm. Plenty of meat for two days. But that was already two questions. Are we done?»

Papa gave me a wary, probing squint. «For now.»

Sometimes I almost wished Papa would find it, the one elusive question I would have no answer for. He smelled something unfinished in my tale, my seamless web of answers. How did I do it? How did I strike so many, so far apart, such complex tasks, so fast? If nothing else, then, twenty, thirty years hence on his deathbed, Papa deserved to hear me whisper: Saladin.

Madame's

"THE SIX-HIVE TRANSIT SYSTEM WELCOMES YOU TO PARIS. Visitors are required to adhere to a minimum of Gray Hiveless Law and to Parisian city regulations. For a list of local regulations not included in your customary law code, select 'law.'"

Where else could the heart of all have been, reader? In the Enlightenment, Paris was the crown and capital of all things, as if Romanova, Alexandria, and La Trimouille were rolled in one. To live there was to live where all that mattered in the universe could be strolled to in a day, and to be banished thence was to be banished to mud and haystacks. Such a power does not lose its grip upon the world in a mere six hundred years.

"Over here!" Thisbe waved Carlyle over to her table at a corner café, where she had drawn him with the simple lure: <Ockham only said we couldn't continue *at the bash'*.>

Despite his late night, Carlyle had risen full of strength that day, for March the twenty-sixth was the birthday of the Great Sage Zoroaster, and the Synaxis of Archangel Gabriel, a day on which men honored their Creator in ages past, today, and honor also those who give us access to Him. "I couldn't find out any more about this 'black hole' than its location," he said. "Eureka was right about it being very secret."

Thisbe beamed pride. "I found a service entrance. Shall we?"

They were already at the steps when I realized I hadn't checked on Carlyle in a while, and found his tracker signal in the worst place in the world. With a hybrid of Papadelias's clearance codes and J.E.D.D. Mason's I hacked into Carlyle's camera feed at once, and saw the stairs before him, period laundry flapping on the lines above. Blame came first. I blamed Ockham for consenting to let Martin's team investigate the Saneer-Weeksbooth bash'. I blamed Papadelias for sending them. I blamed the thief behind the *Black Sakura* affair. I even blamed Julia Doria-Pamphili, as if Carlyle stumbling in on Bridger four days earlier had somehow been her fault for sending him. I blamed myself above all. I did not, oddly enough, blame Carlyle or

Thisbe—Carlyle in my mind was like a child's ball tossed toward a pit, helpless unless another player intervenes. And Thisbe was . . . Thisbe by nature could not resist the scent of secrets. How could I stop them? That was my only question. There had to be a way to stop them.

It was an old town chateau, vast in its way but cramped between its neighbors, as if the wings of a sprawling palace had been picked up and stacked within one crowded lot, like building blocks carefully packed to fit back into the box. Rows of arched or pedimented windows had not been altered since the days when architects worked with sketches of ancient temples on one side of the desk and tracings of flowers on the other. The columns, moldings, and tracery were fluted stone, the doors and windows ornamented with ivy-fine iron. Double and triple staircases waltzed one around another up the façade like the petaled fabric of a wedding dress. Humans have decorated things ever since cave dwellers first learned to weave, or to fire clay to hardness, gracing a pitcher with figures, a shawl with stripes. I think an ancient craftsman considered each creation a capsule of his immortality: so long as future ages see this work and speak its maker's name, I am eternal. Only in the ages when we slogged through labor eager for our play did we degenerate to mass-production and boring houses. The men who crafted Madame's façade made for themselves a respectable immortality.

"Remember," Thisbe coached, "if anyone asks, we got the address from Ockham for my security check, and we don't know where Ockham got it from." She led the way, the sensayer's hand in hers like the leash of a reluctant pup. She chose well, a servants' stairway half-hidden in a minor street behind the house, one of six, for the mansion was fed by many back ways, like an old rose bush with far more roots than blossoms. "If we just tell them we're looking for J.E.D.D. Mason to ask about the investigation, they'll think we have every right to be here."

My mind raced. Threats, would threats stop them? Would lies? I could tell them something happened, that we had to get back to Bridger. I could tell them Thisbe's bash'house was on fire. No, distraction wouldn't work. They had the address. Even if there really was a fire, they'd just come back once the flames were quenched. Cats stay curious, no matter how many die.

"You want to ask for them directly? What if they're actually here?"

"They're in Alexandria; Eureka checked. If we ask for them we'll be offered close associates, or at least vague answers. At a place this big we can't count on the first person who opens the door being useful like that Black-law housekeeper."

"I wonder what they call them here," Carlyle mused.

"Call who?"

"J.E.D.D. Mason. This is a private address. Eureka said Dominic and Martin also come here a lot. It might be a bash'house, or at least the bash' seems to frequent it, and I'm sure they don't call J.E.D.D. Mason by clumsy initials or titles if this is something like a home. What do you think they call them here? Maybe by their real first name?"

I could have Ockham stop Thisbe, I speculated, by calling and telling him she was about to put the bash' at risk. She would obey his order, but that would bring her black wrath down upon me, and danger with it, to myself and, more importantly, to Bridger. Was there another way?

Thisbe chuckled. "J.E.D.D. Mason's full name, now there's a public mystery to rival what's in Cardie's pants." And proof too, reader, that our age has a least one enlightened aspect, for the Celebrity Youth Act, fierce as it is, could not safeguard these children of the spotlight without the help of a protective public, which has learned (from one too many tragedies) to grant its favorite wee ones what privacies they ask for, and will punish with boycotts—far fiercer than Law's teeth—any journalist or paper which would violate the public prince(sse)s that every bash' on Earth loves as our own. Thisbe smirked. "Well, we know the name starts with the letter J. After Martin and Dominic, I bet it's a scandalous old Christian name, like James or John."

"Or Joseph," Carlyle contributed, "Joshua, John-Baptiste . . ."

"No, then it would be J.B.E.D.D. Mason."

"I suppose. That rules out Jean-Jacques, too."

The instant Carlyle's foot touched the first landing, his tracker let out a siren squeal, while a cheerful electric voice rang out: "This is a friendly warning from the Cousins' legal team. Our Member is reminded that Red-Zoned properties and businesses are off-limits. To file for a special exemption for a legal or social-service visit, select 'file.'"

"Red-Zoned?" Thisbe repeated.

"This . . ." Carlyle gaped up at the building's side wall, rows of windows closed with drapes of damask and heavy velvet. "This is a brothel!"

"Huh." Her eyes grew wide. "I guess it is. Does this mean you can't go in?"

"The Emperor's child frequents a brothel?"

"Should I go on without you?"

"The Emperor's child who is still a minor frequents a brothel?"

"Carlyle!" Thisbe had to snap. "It's no problem for a Humanist to go into a Red Zone. Shall I go on without you?"

"No, I'll just turn my tracker off."

She stared as at an idiot. "Won't your police ask questions if you turn your tracker off on the threshold of a Red Zone? If you need to, we can check into a hotel and you can tell your tracker you're taking it off for a shower."

Carlyle shook his head. "It's all right. I can get an exemption if I explain that you were going in and wanted your sensayer with you."

Thisbe frowned. "It's that easy?"

"Well—yes."

Beware, reader, beware of dogs and snakes and witc . . . women . . . when they glare like Thisbe did. "Stupid! That's what it is! You Cousins ban everything under the sun and then make a million loopholes so no one ever has to follow their own rules. What's the point of having the laws if there's no consequence in breaking them?"

Carlyle stared, unbelieving, as her tirade left all stealth behind. "Thisbe, is this the time for—"

"Hypocrites! Always moralizing about how yours is the strictest law. Dominic Seneschal is a maniac, but at least they picked a law they'll follow, while you all go on about being stricter than a Whitelaw and then walk straight into a brothel!"

Her outburst was surreal. A game, that's what it felt like, as if the two had been playing an infiltration game and Thisbe hit pause, expecting the rules and enemies to wait for her rant as they might wait for a bathroom break or a trip to grab more munchies. Gaping Carlyle still believes the danger and mission here are real.

A cough interrupted. "Ahem. Can I help you two fine people?"

The voice came from the window above the back door. Here stood a resident to match the house. She wore an antique gown, the skirts vast with stiff frames underneath, while the tight corset exaggerated her sex, the upper line presenting her breasts like a platter of pudding, while the corset's lower edge came to a central point, directing the eye to the spot in the ocean of skirting where lurked her most forbidden part. One could not guess her age beneath the white face powder, too-pink circular blotches on the cheeks, sharp lipstick, and, of course, the wig, a tower of mounded, stiffened curls with a cluster of feathers sprouting from its peak like a nesting bird. Other faces framed her in the window, and more appeared through the drapes of surrounding windows: painted ladies like the first, youths with curled ponytails like Dominic's, and younger girls with blushing, modest cheeks tittering at the strangers on the steps as if they had been the burlesque and these creatures normal.

"Are you lost?" the first whore invited (in this chapter, reader, I shall call a spade a spade). "You'll get back to the river if you head straight that way."

"No," Thisbe answered, "we're not lost, we're looking for . . . uh . . ."

"Jəəəh Mason," Carlyle ventured, covering the intentional blurring of the first name by reaching to scratch his nose.

French gossip exploded through the spectators.

"MASON? I'm afraid the Emperor just left," the whore replied, hissing hushes at the nearby window-gapers. "Should I get one of his secretaries?"

"No, I don't mean the Emperor, uh . . . Mycroft said they'd be . . ."

"Mycroft?" the whore repeated, her face suddenly light. "Oh! Bless me! You want the Young Master, Jehovah Mason! I'm sorry, I'm not used to hearing Him called by his last name. Sœur Heloïse!» she shouted toward an upper window. «Invitées pour Maître Jéhovah!»

Only Thisbe catching him kept Carlyle from falling backwards down the steps. "Je . . . Jehovah?"

"She'll be right down." The whore smiled. "Sorry about the confusion, it's not often anyone new comes for the Young Master."

Through the windows, one could track Heloïse's approach by the polite bobbed nods of those she flitted past. I was still concocting schemes to stop them. What options had I left? They certainly weren't prepared to listen to my excuses. If I called President Ganymede he could caution Thisbe to back off. She might listen, but not Carlyle, who teetered now on the steps like a tree half-felled in one stroke.

"Jehovah?" he repeated.

"Are you feeling all right, Father?" the whore asked, frowning down at the sensayer through the lipstick which did not so much frame her mouth as mark the twin peaks of her upper lip like two tiny strawberries. "You look pale. Do you need some brandy?"

"They're fine," Thisbe pretended, doing her best to prop Carlyle between her body and the dainty banister. "Carlyle, deep breaths."

The door opened before them now, revealing a tiny creature, fragile but overflowing with energy like a hummingbird. "Oh, heavens! This won't do at all!" She relieved Thisbe at once, tipping Carlyle's full weight onto her shoulders, which, in their tininess, seemed like they should snap. "You must come in at once! I'll send for a nurse. Candide!" she shouted to a gawking youth above. «Cherche-toi l'infirmière!»

"No, it's okay." Carlyle seized the rail with all his strength and tried to stand. "I just had a little faint spell. I'm fine, really."

"Are you certain?" Heloïse asked. Her face was clean and plain with that natural beauty which makes young princes hunger for shepherdesses, and made Carlyle smile in the moment before he saw her clothes. She wore a shapeless cotton smock, straight black down to her ankles, with a white tabard over the top, and a crisp white wimple covering her throat, brows and forehead so not a strand of hair showed through. Though none have walked our streets for nine generations, how many seconds would it take you, reader, to recognize a nun?

"There's nothing wrong with that Cousin that a little food and spirits won't put right," the whore called down. "Heloïse, take them through to the Salon Hogarth, I'll send for something."

"Right away!" the nun confirmed. Though willing to let Carlyle walk, she would not release his arm, leading him firmly like a half-blind great uncle. "This way, Father."

Sister Heloïse (not I) made them cross that threshold (though the panic which froze me in inaction prevented me from stopping it). They entered a service corridor, neither wide nor grand, ornamented with delicate moldings and small wall-mounted chandeliers, which sparkled disdainfully with electric light, not quite as rich as candles. The doors along the walls were strange, all different heights and widths, some low enough to make one stoop, others curved or slanted as if they had been cut into the wall at random. The cause was clear when Heloïse opened the nearest, for on the other side it was a hidden door, carefully cut to fit the gap between a fireplace and bedpost, so none within could deduce quite where the servants passed in and out. The Salon Hogarth was quiet, with leather seats and a hand-carved lady's writing desk, but dominated by a vast canopy bed and a pair of framed prints. "Before" showed a gentleman dragging a reluctant lady toward a bed with no little violence, while "After" had the lady clinging to him in affectionate desperation as he rose to replace his britches. The pair of images would have been distressing anywhere, but were much worse in a room which was itself a precise re-creation of the one shown in the illustrations.

"Please, sit." Heloïse poured brandy from a bright decanter, her tabard swaying about her knees like an apron. "Here, Father, this should give you back some fortitude." She had the same accent as Dominic, French flavoring English as milk flavors cocoa. "Drink it slowly."

"Stop calling me 'Father.'" I was startled as I listened; I had not thought Carlyle had it in him to make his voice so grim. "Is this a period costume brothel?"

Her virgin cheeks blushed at the word. "Parts of the house could be described that way, yes."

"And you're dressed as a nun?"

"I am a nun. I am called Sister Heloïse. And what may I call you if not 'Father'? You are a priest, are you not?"

"A sensayer."

"As I said, a priest." She smiled. "We call things by their real names here. Now, drink this, Father, it will revive your spirits."

Carlyle crossed his arms in refusal.

The nun frowned. "And you, Madame,"—she turned to Thisbe—"or is it Mademoiselle? I see you are one of the subjects of His Grace the Duc de Thouars."

"Mademoiselle," Thisbe answered, "and if you mean President Ganymede, I'm a Humanist, yes." I should have guessed Thisbe would adapt quickly to this new world and its vocabulary. "I'm Thisbe Saneer. Nice to meet you, Sister Heloïse."

Heloïse attempted a seated curtsey, which made the shadows of her tight breasts bounce beneath her habit. It tried its best, the nun's habit, to leave her shapeless, stripping hips and curves from the figure with its clumsy folds, but all it truly did was dare one to search for them, to wonder how pert the buttocks must be to make the fabric hang so, or to mark the shapes of thighs and calves through the slack cloth. "Pleased to meet you. Marie-Thérèse said you came to see Master Jehovah?"

"Yes," Thisbe answered, glaring at Carlyle to keep him silent, since the name made him jolt on every repetition like a fresh electric shock.

"I'm afraid Master Jehovah is elsewhere at the moment, and occupied with high affairs. But I can request that he come see you as soon as He is free."

"That may not be necessary," Thisbe answered. "I'm running a pro forma background check on . . . Tribune Mason, to clear them for access to the Saneer-Weeksbooth bash'house, for their investigation. I'm supposed to interview close associates, routine questions."

"Oh! Why, then I shall answer anything you like."

"Are you two close?"

"Very."

Thisbe had to ask it. "Do you work here?"

"I live here," the little Sister answered, "and I do my work here, caring for the sick, the mending, taking care of Master Jehovah's errands, and, of course, I pray for everyone."

Carlyle's fists clenched.

"Carlyle," Thisbe warned, "relax, just . . . relax." She sighed. "I must apologize for my sensayer, Sister. I asked them to help with my investigation only quite recently, and they were up imprudently late last night. May I?" She reached to take the brandy from Heloïse's fingers.

Heloïse surrendered the glass gladly. "It's quite all right. It's only natural for a priest to be overwhelmed by such a spiritual place. They often wind up in my hospital room at some point on first visits, though hopefully your friend is not so fragile."

Thisbe shoved the glass at Carlyle. "Drink it, you need it."

"A spiritual place?" Carlyle repeated. "A brothel?"

"It's more than that," the nun corrected, beaming pride. "This is a refuge from the barbarities of the modern day. Our members come here to escape for a few hours to a more courteous and enlightened age, and return to the outside world refreshed by a taste of civilized society."

Carlyle twitched. "And sex?"

She pursed her lips in disapproval—you may never have endured it, reader, but the disapproval of a nun is extremely powerful. "Do you have some problem with sex?"

Carlyle: "I do when you claim to be a nun."

Heloïse: "Then you too advocate clerical celibacy?" Her voice grew bright, as if she had just discovered they shared the same home town.

Carlyle: "I do *not* advocate clerical celibacy, but I don't advocate of mocking it, either."

Thisbe: "Carlyle!" Thisbe's anger threatened to bring her boot down sharp upon his toe. "I think what my sensayer is trying to ask, Sister, is, if you don't mind a mildly indelicate question . . ."

Heloïse: "I have scrubbed bile from the floors of sickrooms—what are words to that?"

Thisbe: "Well, are you a prostitute who's dressed as a nun? Or are you actually pursuing a celibate lifestyle while living in a house of prostitution? You can understand my confusion, I mean, don't nuns prefer to live . . . with other nuns?"

Heloïse: "You're thinking of the Tibetan and Vatican Reservations? Those nuns are not my order. And the business of prostitution is limited to certain sections of this house."

Thisbe: "I see. But even if only in parts, isn't that a bit . . . incongruous?"

Heloïse: "I see no incongruity in it."

Thisbe: "No incongruity in a nun being around so much ... erotic activity?"

Heloïse: "On the contrary, what could be more appropriate? Celibacy is the most extreme of sexual perversions, after all."

That one floored even Thisbe. "What?"

Heloïse: "Sexual desire is the purest and most natural of animal drives. To suppress it in favor of an intellectual and theological satisfaction is a perversion of nature in the most extreme sense. Why, even to fornicate alone, or with many people at once, or with a machine, or an ass or hound, is closer to Nature's intent than abstinence. Do you not agree?"

A long pause. Very long.

Carlyle: "Diderot."

Thisbe: "What?"

Carlyle: "You're quoting Diderot, that bit about celibacy as the most unnatural thing."

Heloïse: "Quite correct, Father! Mademoiselle Saneer, has your sensayer not yet told you of *le Philosophe*? Denis Diderot was a great philosopher, the leader of the Encyclopedia project!"

I wish now, reader, that I had myself introduced you to *le Philosophe* in some lighter hour. Grant me, if you will, a moment for his noble side, before you associate him forever with this house. Once upon a time there was a bright young atheist named Denis Diderot. In his Eighteenth Century, atheism was just blossoming, and keen libertine minds hungered for a firebrand to stir and lead them. He could have made himself the Pope of Atheists, but he refused, for Diderot, while denying any afterlife, dreamed of worldly immortality, not for himself, but for the dead, the dreams and achievements of ages past, and for his world. His Philosopher's Stone would be a book. The second half contained technical plates illustrating all the technologies humanity had achieved: weaving silk stockings, annealing metal, baking bricks; so with a single copy even the lowest peasant could reconstruct all the tools of civilization. The first half was the same for thought. Thus, if a new Dark Age should fall upon on the Earth, but a single copy of this book survived, every achievement of the human race—from bronze to Liberty—could be restored. Diderot named this talisman of immortality *Encyclopédie*, and, fearing that his personal beliefs might bring the wrath of the authorities upon the project, he voluntarily suppressed his own work, publishing nothing of the revolutionary atheism which like-minded doubters of his age so hungered for. The public who named Voltaire 'le Patriarche' dubbed Diderot 'le Philosophe,' the Philosopher, guardian and caretaker of all thinkers and all thought. The grand title of 'Arch-Heretic,' which he deserved, he left to others, to Machiavelli, Hobbes, misunderstood Spinoza, or de Sade. Can you imagine a nobler act, reader? Sacrificing his own chance to add his voice to humanity's Great Conversation to safeguard the Conversation itself?

"And he went to jail for writing porn about nuns." Carlyle snapped it, with a cutting glare.

Heloïse sat unfazed. "True, indeed. Rich, beautiful, philosophical pornography about nuns. I have read it several times." Heloïse turned her sincerest smile on the sensayer. "Fear not, Father, I do not mock those whose robe I imitate. Though sex of all sorts occurs here, I am not involved. There is music here too, art, scholarship, and discourse, and if there are also earthly pleasures, then they are pursued only in harmonious consort with the others, and in sections of the house which I do not frequent."

Carlyle gave up on goading her here, sensibly, for it is madness trying to anger Heloïse. Anger, like envy, impatience, greed, and lust all melt from her like frost from flame, and she takes modest pride in crushing such little demons underfoot. One thing, though, he would not give up on: "I told you not to call me 'Father.'"

"I'm sorry, do you prefer Doctor?"

"Neither. I'm a sensayer, not a priest."

Her brows, where the wimple did not cover them, seemed sad. "Have you not dedicated your life to your God?"

Thisbe forced the brandy into Carlyle's hands. "Drink. You need it."

Both women watched, expectant, but Carlyle just stared at his reflection in the amber spirit, as if trying to take refuge in the only thing in the room which was not mad. "Dominic Seneschal spends time here too, don't they?" he asked. "Do they work here?"

Sister Heloïse's face grew light and frantic at the same time, like a mother desperate for rumors of a runaway. "Do you have word from Brother Dominic? We've been so worried!"

"Brother Dominic?"

Thisbe forced a smile. "I'm sorry, Sister Heloïse, we don't know anything about where Dominic Seneschal is, or where they've been the last few days. We've been seeking them too."

"I see," Heloïse answered, unable to stifle a sigh.

"You know Dominic well?"

"We grew up here together."

"You both work for Jed . . . Jehovah . . ."

"Here you may call Him the Prince D'Arouet, if His true name makes you uncomfortable."

"Either way, you and Dominic work for them?"

"Work for *mon Seigneur* Jehovah? Oh, no. We worship Him as a God." Even Thisbe could only feign so much calm. "What?"

"Dominic's path is his own. As for myself I have consecrated my virginity to *mon Seigneur* Jehovah, and dedicate my hours to the contemplation of His divine Mysteries and the exercise of Good Works in His holy Name. It is a vocation which fills and overflows my every thought and deed, waking and sleeping, and since *mon Seigneur* Jehovah himself has accepted my devotion, I count myself the most fortunate of women, though not in the least deserving of such fortune.

"I was in my early days a very wicked child," she continued, "proud, self-involved, and filled with the most perfidious jealousies. I grew up in this house, not among the common children but one of the elect, raised in the strictest discipline and with the care of many wise and generous tutors, whose efforts on my behalf I never appreciated as they deserved. They offered for my education music, geometry, mathematics, natural philosophy, the historians, poets, orators, Latin, Greek, French, all the authors whose works are proper for the eyes of a sensitive young lady, yet I began to spurn all in favor of the flattery of men. Puffed up by vacant words, I vainly thought myself the most beautiful of my peers, a double vanity, both because I judged myself superior, and because I placed value on appearance, as if true Beauty lay in face and flesh. Wretch that I was, I cared nothing for the logic of the Philosopher, the morals of the Orator, or the light of the Theologian (she means here Aristotle, Cicero, and St. Thomas Aquinas) when I had suitors to taunt and rivals to defeat."

Here you object, impatient reader. *Mycroft, thou hast lapsed too much into thy Eighteenth Century. This life story poured out all in one ramble might fit in the fabricated dialogues of thy Patriarch or thy Philosophe, but not in a history. No sane person disgorges her autobiography before perfect strangers, and no listener, even one as stunned as Carlyle and Thisbe, would sit through this in silence.* You do not believe, reader? Then come, I challenge you, come to her offices, ask good Sister Heloïse to tell you of her vocation, and see if you have the strength of will to interrupt a nun.

She continues: "In the course of things I was betrothed to a good and worthy man, and I endeavored to direct the entirety of my affection toward my intended. Yet, as I felt youth begin to flower in me, I found my passions directed, as uncontrollably as water gushing from a spring, not to my fiancé but toward *mon Seigneur* Jehovah. Naturally all in this house, from my sisters and brothers to the lowest scullery maid, hold *mon Seigneur* Jehovah in the highest awe, for He is the Pillar and Scion of our world, the noblest of princes, most infallible of logicians, most compassionate of statesmen, and most penetrating of philosophers, yet I, and others around me, easily saw that my affection far outstripped the common worship of the crowd. There were days when my sole hope in rising from my bed was that I might glimpse Him passing in the hall, and any day His offices did not allow Him to return home left me in the most profound despair. Knowing my duty, I tried to drive this love from my rebellious bosom, and that battle claimed my happiness and health, for I soon succumbed to a wasting sickness which consigned me to my bed, and very nearly to my grave. I was at first unwilling to confess the cause of my illness, but I was not so impious a child as to stay silent before Madame when she pleaded with me with a mother's tears. With her encouragement I revealed the truth to my fiancé, explaining that, while he retained forever a treasured quarter of my heart, my love for him had been transformed now to a daughter's devotion to her father rather than a lady's for her lord. So kind and compassionate is the heart of that great man who was almost my husband that he forgave me, accepting my filial affection in place of wifely love, and to save his new-found daughter from the grip of sickness he agreed to go to *mon Seigneur* Jehovah, whom he was accustomed to approaching with the intimacy of kin, and tell Him of my love.

"The ways of my Lord are mysterious. At first He answered nothing, and neither my newfound father nor Madame nor any in the house could understand His actions as He sequestered Himself in His library, where none but the most trusted of servants were permitted to intrude. I, in my despair, slipped into a sleep so close to death that my nurses thought me a dozen times lost, but I was saved when *mon Seigneur* Jehovah emerged from His isolation and, to the great jealousy of my sisters, who had never enjoyed more than a few syllables from His blessed lips, presented me with a Commonplace Book compiled by His own hand, every page filled with quotations from the wisest ancients and most refined of commentators, interspersed with pieces of His own divine Wisdom, explaining in a hundred voices that happiest and harshest Rule, all but abandoned in this selfish age: the monastic calling. I saw at once my folly, that in the heat of youth I had imagined He could be the inspiration of a base and Earthly love. That fire within myself, which I had mistaken for common passion, was in reality the first dim flickering of the truer flame of spiritual devotion which, if fed with the good fuel of discipline and virtue, might be cultivated into some semblance of that ethereal brightness which marks mankind as the most fortunate of beasts, for we alone of all the creatures of this Earth may aspire to the understanding of the Divine. All rejoiced at my vocation, and my return from death's door, and Madame saw at once to my initiation into monastic life. I have lived so ever since, consecrated to My Lord God Jehovah in a chaste union far more powerful than any Earthly marriage, and I have never strayed nor thought to stray from this severe path, which is to me the greatest happiness."

She fell into a prayerlike silence as she finished, the expression on her face a portrait of delicate, spiritual joy. They had no questions. Or, more likely, they brimmed with questions, but none they thought this madwoman could answer.

"*Sœur* Heloïse, please step away from the intruders."

Carlyle and Thisbe were not the only ones who had been unable to interrupt the nun, but, now that she had finished, both doors, main and hidden, opened, and gentlemen filled the entrances like floodwaters. I cannot remember how many there were, say five or seven as you prefer, all costumed as the house demanded: silk at their throats, trim waistcoats, swallow-tailed jackets, britches, rich fabrics with richer tailoring and swords (half-decorative) at every belt. Their breeches were tight, far more precisely tailored than the sexless fashions of the outside world, and yesteryear's style made the conspicuous lumps of their sexual members catch the eye, even on those who had nothing more to display than a woman's crotchbone. Yes, reader, half these gentlemen were female in body, breasts tucked snugly under the waistcoats, but with such rearing there was no more of the female in them than there is canine loyalty in a pup raised among wolves. The fiercest, though not the largest, led the pack, his coat and breeches black, his waistcoat copper-embroidered green, his skin European pale, with hints of reddish fire in his hair.

"Chevalier," Heloïse greeted him. "Is there a problem?"

"These two have entered under false pretenses," he explained.

"What?" Thisbe cried in false dismay. "Oh, I forgot to share my credentials. How silly of me!" She began to call them from her tracker.

The Chevalier loomed closer, and the others with him, like vultures around carrion. "No one would give you this address."

"I got it from Officer Ockham Saneer, I'm—"

"No. You did not." The Chevalier smiled wide. "You will come with us, please."

"I'm running a background check on——"

"You will graciously consent to come with us."

Heloïse interposed herself between the sensayer and the marauders, like a fence of frail wicker to stop a charging bull. "These two have been consigned to my care, Chevalier. We are waiting together for *mon Seigneur* Jehovah."

"Then allow me to relieve you of that burden, *Sœur* Heloïse." The Chevalier marshalled a smile whose malice impressed even Thisbe. "I would not wish this petty affair to keep you from your sacred duties."

No sculpted angel smiles so serenely. "It is no burden, Chevalier."

"A distraction, then," he corrected, "one unworthy of your time."

The nun's eyes ranged the others, the magic of her gaze driving hands away from sword hilts, and making smirks pregnant with mischief to grow sober. "The priest is sick," she announced. "It is among the foremost of my charitable duties to help the sick."

"Then, good Sister, you must trust me to see that duty performed in due course, but I must also see foremost to my primary duty, to guard this house, which is my charge when Brother Dominic is absent."

Before Heloïse could answer, a shout and fast feet thundered down the hall outside. «Sœur Heloïse! Sœur Heloïse! Dans la salle des duels, Sénateur Chang est gravement blessé! (In the dueling hall, Senator Chang is seriously wounded.)»

She opened the door at once. «Gravement? (Seriously?)»

«Oui!» answered the messenger, a tearful maid of thirteen, «et tous les docteurs sont occupés en bas. Viens vite! (Yes, and all the doctors are busy below. Come quickly!)»

I had no doubt the Chevalier had arranged the convenient timing of the injury, but the same laws of courtesy which would not permit the men to roughhouse in the Sister's presence also would not allow her to ignore a soul in need.

"You must excuse me, Father, Mademoiselle Saneer," she bobbed a curtsey. "I am needed elsewhere urgently. I shall return to check on you when next I'm free." She made the Chevalier meet her eyes, not easy eyes to face. "You will take proper care of these two, as *mon Seigneur* Jehovah's guests?"

The Chevalier raised his gloved hand as if to take an oath. "I shall see to them according to my duty."

The little Sister was no fool. "May I have your word, then, Chevalier, no harm will come to them?"

Her persistence grated on him. "Very well, you have my word. Now, run along, Sister. Blood does not wait."

She offered the stranded pair a reassuring smile. "You may trust the Chevalier to keep his word. Good luck to you. I'll keep you in my prayers."

With that she rushed away, and decorum with her. You have never seen such dark grins on a pack of men.

"Now," the Chevalier began, "where were we? Ah, yes. Unlawful intrusion."

"Hey, look, the priest's a Cousin." Three of the pack pawed at the loose tails of Carlyle's Cousin's wrap, as circling bandits play with the skirts of a maiden they hunger to unwrap. "She's definitely not supposed to be here."

Here again, reader, I must apologize, since I have accustomed you to assigning Carlyle 'he.' Cousins are 'she' by default in that house, and the exception for Carlyle had not yet been ordered.

"Are you enjoying straying out of bounds, Cousin?" One reached as if to stroke Carlyle's hanging hair, but instead snatched the disabled tracker from his ear and dangled it just out of reach.

"Hey!" Thisbe cried, off guard. "That's so not okay!"

The Chevalier carried a cane as well as a sword, and wielded it with expert menace. "I fear it is not your place to make rules in another's house, Mademoiselle Intruder."

Thisbe rose, and with her boots was almost tall enough to face the Chevalier eye to eye. "Red Zone or no, taking a tracker is Blacklaw illegal!"

The Chevalier looked to the others, and all laughed, raucously, as if she had made a brilliant joke. "I don't think you're the one who wants to call the law in here, Mademoiselle Intruder into a Level One Romanovan Alliance Security Compound whose unlawful breach is punishable by . . ." He looked to his compatriots. "What is it for Humanists? Five to ten?"

"Ten to fifteen years or five hundred thousand euros," one supplied.

The answer freshened the roses in the Chevalier's cheeks. "Of course, if you meant no harm by the intrusion, we might overlook it, if appropriately persuaded."

Like Lesley, Thisbe has no practice dodging when one of these creatures swoops in serpent-quick to kiss her hand. Blush erupted, intense enough to show on her dark Indian cheeks, and her poise changed too, standing straighter, as if remembering her own anatomy beneath her silk suit, and her pride in it. She looked to Carlyle, who had pulled his feet up onto his chair, as if it were a life raft with sharks circling round. "What persuasion do you have in mind?" she asked.

The Chevalier leaned close, closing his eyes a moment as he tested the scent of Thisbe's shampoo. "Let us, just you and I, go see if we can't find one of the household polylaws. Surely they can advise us on the situation. And who knows? Perhaps we'll come up with something on our own along the way." He raised his hand to stroke her cheek, while his body leaned close enough for their thighs to share warmth. Thisbe froze, as Mercer Mardi froze once, hoping the killer would not spot her in the shadows.

"Thisbe," Carlyle urged, "call on your tracker. We need help."

If glares could kill, this would have been Carlyle's earthly end. "You doubt my word, sensayer?" The Chevalier turned on him. "I promised Sister Heloïse that you would not be harmed."

"Thisbe!" Carlyle tried again.

"Thisbe," the Chevalier repeated, planting a fresh kiss on her hand and others further up her arm in an inching line. "A superb name, Thisbe. More parents should be brave enough to name their daughters after women men have died for, don't you think?"

Thoughts and adrenaline mixed in Thisbe's mind as the kisses crept so slowly toward her throat. Fly, says Virtue. Knock his hand away. Kick him in that too-conspicuous crotch. Fight. Call, as trackers can, the fierce and instant law whose agents will swoop from the heavens angel-harsh, and whisk you away from this strange man whose blush is rising to match yours. Thisbe smiled. "What about my sensayer?"

The Chevalier's eyes rolled across to Carlyle, as to an unwanted sibling. "The Cousin is sick, is she not? Let her recover here. My compatriots will give her the very best of care."

"Thisbe!" Carlyle cried out as three of them dug their fists into his clothes as if to rip the wrapping from a birthday package. "We have to get out of here!"

"Stop! That sensayer belongs to Julia Doria-Pamphili!" I was so out of breath as I burst in that I could not keep my words from becoming a shout. I made it in time. Barely, but I had made it in time.

"Mycroft?" Thisbe, Carlyle, and the Chevalier called my name in unison, then eyed one another in some surprise.

"Carlyle is Julia's apprentice," I repeated, still panting, "and this Humanist is a privileged courtier of His Grace the Duc de Thouars. They would not want their creatures spoiled."

The Chevalier's confederates were quick to release Carlyle, while the Chevalier himself spun toward me, in the same motion taking Thisbe in his arms. "Why did they not say so themselves?"

"Because, sir, this is their first time in the civilized world, they do not yet know its ways." I lowered from my back a sack heavy with fabric. "I am to take them to Madame."

In the hush, quick-thinking Carlyle managed to snatch back his tracker.

The Chevalier arched perfect eyebrows. "Madame is expecting them?"

"Impatiently, Chevalier."

How crestfallen his sigh. "Alas, dear Thisbe, such a summons one dares not ignore." He would not leave her without at least one proper kiss as prize. He took it slowly, time enough for a succubus to have sucked the soul out of its prey if such was its aim. He smiled when done, but Thisbe smiled deeper. "Perhaps another time."

Nodding to his men to follow, the Chevalier strode through the door. I was wrong to say there was no touch of the feminine in the company, for, male or female, all of them moved with that artful grace we associate with ladies and dancers, and wielded their blades as gracefully as ladies do their fans. On exit, the Chevalier glared at my Servicer's uniform with proper scorn. "You mustn't let clients see you like that in the halls, Mycroft," he warned.

"I won't, Chevalier."

I cannot comment on his final expression, for I am not permitted to raise my eyes to one of his rank. I bowed low as I closed the door behind him.

"What are you doing here, Mycroft?" Thisbe asked—no, the tone was grim, more an order than a question.

I did not look at her. "Patronage is everything here. When in trouble, invoke the highest ranking person you're associated with."

"Did you follow us here? Or were you here already?"

"I'm under orders to take you to Madame. Contemporary clothing is forbidden in the inner halls. You may wear these, since we do not have time for a fitting." I drew from my sack two cloaks of floor-length dark red velvet, hooded, and heavy enough to muffle sound.

"How long have you been involved with these people?" Thisbe pressed. "Mycroft, I asked you a question."

"You can't have weapons when you see Madame," I recited. "You may give them to me, I'll return them when you leave the premises."

Thisbe crossed her arms. "You will answer me, Mycroft. I recommend that you answer voluntarily." She took a menacing step forward.

I sighed. "I noticed when Carlyle arrived in Paris. You two shouldn't be here. This is number one on the list of places in the world you shouldn't be."

"You did know about this place," Carlyle accused.

"Of course." I tossed them each a cloak. "Where J.E.D.D. Mason goes I go."

"*Jehovah* Mason," he corrected. "You knew that, too?"

I hid my face by diving back into the sack for my own costume. "Tell me you didn't use the transit computers to get this address."

Thisbe's silence answered for her.

"Tell them you got it from me." I met her eyes now. "This is important, Thisbe. We don't need the powers that be getting even more worried about the security of your bash'. If anyone asks, you drugged me and I told you this address when half-asleep. I was the weak link, not your bash'. Clear?"

Silence consented.

"We have to move fast," I continued. "The Chevalier will have left one of his gentlemen outside to make sure I really do take you to Madame. Put the cloaks on."

Thisbe held the garment, stubborn. "Who's Madame?"

"The owner. Please take me seriously when I say this: I'll die before I let you see Jehovah. He'd have the truth about Bridger out of you in two minutes. That will not happen while I live."

Their stares believed me.

"Rumor of your coming already reached Madame. I am under orders to bring you, and hopefully meeting her will satisfy your . . ." I took a deep breath. "You shouldn't have come here, you really shouldn't have. But the faster we move the better mood Madame will be in, and right now Madame's good humor is the only protection you have from . . . consequences."

Thisbe donned the cloak, the velvet hiding every inch of her. "In a place like this I'd have expected masks, too, like carnival."

I shook my head. "You're not of the right rank for masks. Carlyle, put your cloak on."

He glared.

Thisbe glared back. "We don't have time for your Mycroft Canner fixation right now, Carlyle! Do you want to trust Mycroft, or do you want to stay here and let them rape you?"

If Carlyle were a man who cursed, he would have done it then. "They would've raped us, wouldn't they? Your friends."

I did not have time to argue the difference between friends and betters.

"No," was on my lips when I realized this might be my chance. I could scare them off, concoct something horrible, a thousand times beyond reality but plausible in the surreality of this place. Then maybe, maybe, they would run. "They'd have raped you every way it's possible to rape someone," I began, my imagination racing, "the group of them taking turns. Then they'd have tied you up and called in whores from downstairs to join in, and put you through every filthy act imaginable. But the Law only counts it as rape if you still say 'no' at the end. They'd make sure you couldn't. They'd use extremes of pain and pleasure until you'd agree to anything. Experts like that, it wouldn't take them an hour to get you to send messages to your bash' and colleagues saying you were taking a vacation, so no one would look for you for weeks. Then they'd drag you to the kennels where the real work would begin. Even before they entered the room they were probably placing bets on who would succeed first getting you to sign yourself over and become a Blacklaw. And once you did, you'd never leave this place again. Now put on your cloak and let me save you."

I waited to see if my fantasy would work. Carlyle paled. He gagged. At last, he chose the cloak.

I sighed relief. "Weapons, Thisbe?" I pressed, offering my empty sack.

Carlyle's eyes turned from hate-narrow to child-wide as he watched Thisbe pull from hidden places a sturdy knife, a second sturdy knife, a stun pistol, a tranquilizer pistol, and three flash grenades. "Thisbe, what—"

"My bash' is vital to the world order, remember? Ockham and Cardie aren't the only ones who study self-defense." She placed her arsenal piece by treasured piece within my sack.

I regretted doing this in front of Carlyle, I really did. "All weapons, Thisbe."

Death hate reared that instant in her glare.

"There are security scanners every ten feet in the halls, Thisbe," I pressed. "They'll know. I'm sorry. I'll give them back to you, I swear by Apollo Mojave."

Even with that it took her three long breaths to face up to the necessity. She knelt.

"Thisbe," Carlyle called, "what are you—"

"Don't ask."

The clasping mechanisms exhaled long hisses as the woman removed her boots.

Carlyle leaned closer. "Thisbe—"

"I said don't ask! Now get your fucking cloak on before you do anything else to get us in deeper shit!" She set her boots in my sack, gently as a mother lays down a child, then spun to vent her wrath upon the sensayer. "I don't want another word out of you, Carlyle, you hear me? Not about Mycroft, or the costume. Mycroft is rescuing your stupid ass and you're going to do everything Mycroft says to the letter until we're out of here!"

"Costume?" Carlyle repeated, but then saw what she meant.

The sack had a costume for me, too, to cover my Servicer's dappling: the rough grayish brown habit of a Franciscan monk. To you, one monk is probably like another, since our schools don't teach their many founders' distinctive madnesses. Francis was a saint among saints and a madman among madmen, who used to talk to birds, to ravage his own body with scourge and ice, to turn down pious hosts, preferring to beg his supper on the street, who refused to be in command in his order, insisting that his own followers rule him so he could practice the virtue of obedience, and who had to be sternly ordered to eat and rest, or he would have destroyed himself by overpunishing his sinful flesh. Franciscans live on charity alone, owning nothing, not their monasteries, not their plates and cups, or the shoes upon their feet. Carlyle knew this, and watched the monkish gray-brown slide over my Servicer dappling, and shuddered.

"Come." I opened the door. "There's no more time."

They followed me in fear-fast silence. We found not one but three of the Chevalier's men lurking in the hall, enjoying a long bench of rose-pink satin, pocked with buttons like navels repeating along an infinite torso. This bench lined the near wall of the corridor from end to end, breaking only for the doors of labeled rooms: Salon Hogarth, Salon Caligula, Salon Rochester, Salon Salome, Salon de Pompadour. The far wall was one great window, looking down over the central hall below, where stairways, landings, and balconies descended like the terraces of Dante's Hell, all covered with flesh. The lovemaking took place in piles, two, three, four lovers at a time throwing themselves into the vastness of skirts with the glee of kids swimming in chocolate. Men and women of both sexes paraded in the most elaborate gowns and wigs and coats and tails, or what remained of them as bodices and breeches opened to bare their ready cargo. Many were not even in the act of sex, but simply lying upon each other, dining and gossiping amid the spectacle. Waiters threaded among them, bussers, jugglers, a contortionist, and the Royal Belgian String Quartet, performing here with far more vigor than they had at Ganymede's party. Never, reader, have you seen so many people in one place and not a single frown.

"They can't see us," I reassured as I led. "This hallway is the middle level, for clients of more importance. That down there is the Hall of Venus, though the Chevalier's men call it the Flesh Pit. It's the lower clients' level. It's all legal, carefully monitored and hygienic, guests and employees subject to strict health inspection and all that, and our doctors claim a weekly visit does as much for mind and body as a sensayer. It's invitation only, word of mouth, but we get all sorts here. Of course, no one of any real consequence stays down in the Flesh Pit level for long." I glanced back. "Are you familiar with the Eighteenth-Century author Voltaire?"

"Not really," Thisbe answered, drowning Carlyle's 'yes.'

"They were the Patriarch of the Enlightenment," I explained, "so influential they not only dominated literature but could virtually force the hand of royalty, the law, even the Church a bit. Voltaire was also a Deist, which means they believed that all religions are different understandings of the same universal God, Who made the world but doesn't really care what name or names He's called by."

"Mycroft," Thisbe interrupted, "why are you telling me this now?"

I did not have time to pause. "Late in life Voltaire built a small church on their estate. They put an inscription over the entrance, *Deo Erexit Voltaire*: built for God by Voltaire. After so many churches built to saints, they said, it was about time someone built one to God. In a sense it's the high temple of Deism, strange as it sounds to say that a religion which combines most all religions could have a high temple."

We had reached the center of the house, where the wall of doors and couches opened on our left to a grand staircase leading up to a level as far above ours as ours was above the Flesh Pit. A purple carpet led up beneath trickling chandeliers to a double door at the top, framed by a marble arch and the inscription: DEO EREXIT SADE.

We did not have time for shock and silence. "Immediately to our left," I whispered, "is a small door leading to a secret stairway which will take you to the street. To our right is a very heavy candelabrum. If you club me over the head and run, you should make it out before anyone can follow."

Thisbe stepped closer to me, and I prayed the blow would come. "The Marquis de Sade was from the Eighteenth Century too, weren't they?"

"You'll also need this," I continued, letting them see a small envelope in my hand. "It's a more powerful memory eraser than the one you use at home, Thisbe, very safe, no side effects, blanks seventy minutes thereabouts. You can't just go now, with what you've seen, but if you both take this in the car on your way away from here then all this will never have happened. I'll take care of the rest."

I waited, counting my breaths and hoping I could count on Thisbe to do just the right amount of damage. I waited. Surely she would strike. Carlyle would not, of course. The sensayer had crossed Jehovah's threshold; Carlyle, like Voltaire, will not trade knowledge for ignorance, not for all the happiness in the world. Thisbe, though . . . the threat of the Marquis might scare off even such a creature as Thisbe. I waited.

"I thought you said we didn't have time to dawdle, Mycroft," she said at last, her voice soft. "Which way to Madame and *her* answers?"

I did not have the heart to look at them. "This way." I led them to a landing halfway up the stairs toward the inscription, then turned to a secondary stairwell on the right. A dainty flight of steps took us to a door paneled with pastoral scenes of courting gentry, and a vestibule beyond, with cherubs flirting in a painted sky. "I don't intend to leave your sides at any time, but just in case I can't avoid it, a few survival rules. Never allow yourself to be taken to a room where there is not at least one fully clothed woman, by which I mean someone dressed in female clothes, regardless of anatomy; the men here have to behave themselves when there are women present. Second, avoid residents wearing black. It is Dominic's privilege to allow them to wear black, so the more black they wear the more Dominic likes them, which is usually a danger signal."

"You forgot 'never turn off your tracker,'" Thisbe added, doubtless shooting a glare at the Cousin, though I did not look to see.

I shook my head, the habit's fabric rough against my neck. "They're masters of this. They'd get you to take it off. If they tried they could even get you, Thisbe, to take it off." I looked to Carlyle. I know when to surrender. "I was lying before about that stuff I said the Chevalier's men would do to you. I was trying to scare you away. This place isn't like that. The Chevalier wouldn't have harmed you, he would never break his word to Sister Heloïse. And you're right that they couldn't rape and kidnap people without getting caught. They wouldn't, either, it's uncivilized. You're standing in a bubble of the Eighteenth Century now; they pride themselves on being more civilized than the Twenty-Fifth."

"What would they have done to me, then?" he asked after a pause.

"They would've kept bullying you a bit, then one would have played protector, stepping in to your rescue. Most Cousins love that. Your rescuer would have taken you aside and been the most tender and charismatic person you'd ever met, playing on your fear and gratitude while the others placed bets on whether or not you'd consent. My money, if I had any, says you would have consented, but if you refused they'd just have sent you packing with a tender warning to be good from now on, and curiosity would have had you back here within the day."

"I wouldn't have consented," he insisted predictably. "I'm not that stupid"—the universal euphemism for 'I'm not that easy'—"and even if I were, I don't like boys."

I shook my head. "That's no impediment to them. Madame raised gentlemen of both sexes."

"What would they have done with me?" Thisbe cut in. There was no fear in her voice, just collegial curiosity, as when a Western fencing master steps into an Eastern dōjō and detachedly admires a kindred art too different to be called competitor.

"Once they determined you were a person of some influence, they would have treated you very well, and done all in their power to tempt you into joining. You might like the club, actually, though it does tend to spoil your appetite for any other kind of sex." I knocked twice on the inner door, painted with garlands almost moist enough to seem real. "It's Mycroft, Madame. I've brought the guests."

"Just a moment!"

In those last breaths I wondered if they would change their minds now, if wise, cold Thisbe would seize a vase from the *pietra dura* sideboard and strike and run at last. I stood just in front of her to make it easy. It was probably impossible for them make it out from here, but hope is always ready to stifle reason, even in me.

Only Carlyle spoke. "Mycroft, you didn't answer before when I asked if you knew J.E.D.D. Mason's full name."

"Jehovah Epicurus Donatien D'Arouet M-Mason." I always stumble somewhere in that name, as if part of me fears what would happen if I recited the full, unbroken invocation.

"Come in!"

Madame D'Arouet

"COME IN."

I know the trick to opening that door without it squeaking; many do. False windows on the four walls of the chamber showed the seasons: spring blossoms, summer peaches drowning in emerald leaves, harvest wheat and grapes, ice-dusted evergreens, all painted, with painted birds and animals playing in the fields. There were painted children, too, life-sized so they seemed to stand with the viewer in the room, leaning out through the false windows, trying to catch birds, pluck fruit, sporting as seasons demanded, snowballs in winter, flirting in spring. The furnishings were delicate to the point of fragility: gilded candelabra fine as twining vines, couches on slender legs which curved like swans' necks, tables with dainty seats ready for card players, and a harpsichord, petite like the runt of a litter of pianos. Did you expect a throne room, reader? Never. Madame is no queen but a hostess, and rules none but the guests in her salon.

"Madame, allow me to present Mademoiselle Thisbe Saneer of the Saneer-Weeksbooth bash', and the Reverend Doctor Carlyle Foster, a Fellow of the Sensayers' Conclave and protégé of Her Holiness Conclave Head Julia Doria-Pamphili."

Madame curtseyed her greeting, no simple gesture but a grand process as the heights of her wig, its white peaks crowned with ruffles and dyed feathers, dipped and rose like the crags around Olympus nodding their respect to passing gods. Her gown today was midnight blue, open in the front over an inner gown of rosy salmon laced with gold, with a wide framework underneath which made the skirts swell to more than thrice the lady's width, as if she waded in her own private ocean. She wore gems on her fingers, her wrists, at her throat, not distracting but serving her body as gems should, their glitter luring one to notice the curve of an arm or the slope of a tender breast. The face that stared back at the new arrivals was a painting, the precise, stylized ideal which stares from every flattering portrait that ever graced a palace wall in the age when men's portraits showed distinct features and character, but ladies were homogenized into one doll-perfect face. It really was all paint, the heavy makeup of the period whose whites and rouges did not let a hint of skin peek through. Her age? She seems more a time-stopped goddess than a woman whom the count of years could touch, and sometimes I wish our anti-aging drugs were less powerful, so one might see what greater transformations maturity had planned for such a beauty. It is not polite to discuss a lady's age, so I shall say only that, were all the Seven leaders of our world assembled in one room, Madame the Eighth, only Headmaster Faust would recall more of history than she.

"Mademoiselle Thisbe, Doctor Carlyle," I continued, "may I present Madame D'Arouet; also His Grace Ganymede Jean-Louis de la Trémoïlle, Duc de Thouars, Prince de Talmond, President of the Humanists, and His Excellency Chief Director Hotaka Andō Mitsubishi."

I assure you, reader, the pair beside me were no less startled by Madame's illustrious company than you are. Golden Ganymede lounged against the summer wall, his diamond sparkle finally in a setting as brilliant as itself. Across the room from him stood Director Andō, dignified but with something of the harried look of a man who has just rushed to replace his pants. Actually, the Director was not wearing pants but pleated *hakama*, whose belts and knots require much more time and skill than trousers, for at Madame's he exercises the option of wearing the Eighteenth-Century period costume of his own country, marking himself a "foreign dignitary" among so many Parisians. Ganymede, of course, always dresses the same, but here it feels normal.

"Pleased to meet you, Madame." Enterprising Thisbe drew the folds of her cloak up into a makeshift curtsey.

"The pleasure is mine, my dear." Madame approached and embraced Thisbe like a sister, the pinkish tint of her forearms set off by the long trailing ruffles of salmon lace which framed her half-length sleeves. "It's high time one of your household came to visit mine. I'm sorry if your initial reception was a bit rough, but the back door is not the best entrance for new guests."

Thisbe accepted Madame's jasmine-scented kisses on both cheeks. "But more interesting!" she offered.

Madame's smile liked that. "I suppose so. And dear Doctor Carlyle, please sit. From what I've heard you've had a very trying few days, encountering Dominic and Mycroft and my Son." Before Carlyle saw it coming, Madame had kissed the Cousin and swept him over to a daybed, where she plopped him down and settled down beside him, her vast skirts filling the space between the sensayer and curving couch arm, as blankets fill a cradle.

"Yes," Carlyle confessed to the warmth of her inviting smile. "It's been awkward."

"Of course it has, of course it has. And for my part in it I'm very sorry. Sit, everyone, sit, sit." She gestured Thisbe to a vacant loveseat opposite. "And thou too Mycroft, thou art the very picture of exhaustion; take the corner stool before thou fallest down."

I bowed. "Thank you, Madame."

"Good, all settled, now, how can we help you, good Doctor Foster?" Madame glanced at the President and Director, who pulled up ibis-slim chairs to flank her and the sensayer, like family gathered around a troubled child. "You're concerned about my Son?" she asked.

"You, uh . . ." Carlyle's tongue faltered beneath the President and Chief Director's stares. Duke and Chief Director, I should say; in this house Ganymede is far more Duke than President.

"Come, speak your mind!" Madame chided. "We're all friends here, whatever we may be outside. You have worries?"

Thisbe spoke up, her smile growing more . . . 'tickled' is the word. "Are you J.E.D.D. Mason's mother?"

"I am Jehovah's mother, yes," Madame answered.

Carlyle managed not to wince this time. "And you run this place?"

"Yes."

"Which is a . . ."

"A brothel?" Madame chuckled at Carlyle's timidity. "You mustn't be scared of the word. I usually call it a Gendered Sex Club. I offer archaic sex, with old-fashioned gender-differentiated men and women. My clients like to seduce or be seduced, and enjoy skirts and breeches, rather than the neutered egalitarian copulation one gets outside nowadays. Whom did you meet on arrival? The Chevalier? Did you like him?"

Carlyle swallowed hard. "So you don't do anything . . . more extreme here?"

Madame's laugh was indulgent as a nanny's. "I hope you don't think that badly of Blacklaws." Though nearly impossible to spot among her skirts' flare, there was a Blacklaw Hiveless sash about her hips. "Our clients get quite enough of the thrill of the forbidden with gender."

The Cousin frowned. "I'm surprised people find gendered costumes that exciting, frankly."

"Oh, my dear," she chuckled at his innocence, "human culture spent, what, ten thousand years working out ways to code exciting gendered sexuality into every shirt and gesture? Our poor three centuries without it simply haven't had the time develop anything to match." Her eye caught on me. "It's like a language. A young invented language with a couple thousand words might manage baby books and street directions, but Voltaire, Shakespeare, the profound peaks and doggerel troughs of literature, those take a million words. Many of my clients find what we offer here quite addictive."

Carlyle's wrinkled nose showed that he found the thought . . . odd. "So this is all just historical reenactment?"

"In a sense, yes," she answered warmly, "although, since you ask about the forbidden, Doctor, in the intimacy of this room I will confess there is one more . . . borderline thing that goes on here"—she caught a sparkle in Thisbe's gaze, and, smiling, sparkled back—"though we make sure it harms no one. You see, my guests enjoy reenactments of Eighteenth-Century intimacy, particularly the forbidden and scandalous sides thereof, not only my gendered ladies and gentlemen, but the Enlightenment art of mixing forbidden sex acts with forbidden things, especially forbidden talk."

Carlyle frowned. "Meaning?"

"Oh, just the sorts of philosophical debates that were scandalous once upon a time: equality, human rights, rational government, cultural relativism, freedom of religion, specific religious views . . ."

The sensayer frowned. "You're saying you discuss theology while having sex."

"For beginners it's before and after mostly, managing it during sex takes skill and concentration. It's our unique service. Since discussing religion is even more taboo today than it was in our dear Eighteenth Century, it makes the most thrilling erotic talk. I'm sure you've run across this sort of thing before, Doctor Carlyle, professionally, I mean."

"Not in so institutionalized a form, but yes." The sensayer smiled almost smugly. "It's what I expected, really."

"Oh?"

"Your inscription: *Deo Erexit Sade,* 'Built for God by de Sade,' it's a bit too literate for someone who would read Sade so narrowly as to think it was all about sadism. You're using the religious half of Sade, attacking the sensayer system."

"I would never attack the sensayer system," Madame contradicted, holding a hand against her bosom as if wounded. "I told you, we are very careful. What happens here is fun and play, not danger. Taboos are thrilling, and my guests enjoy breaking taboos, especially the triple mixture of sex, gender, and religion, stacking forbidden things to build a richer thrill. No need to worry about bringing this to the attention of the Sensayers' Conclave; they know. We have many sensayers on staff here, Dominic among them, tasked with making sure that things stay safe, and the Conclave sends inspectors frequently to watch for proselytizing. Whenever it's a group of three or more, we have a sensayer chaperone to certify the discussion nonproselytory. I believe the consensus in the Conclave is that my establishment is healthy for the world. The urge to break the religious taboo is common enough, and it's better that it be concentrated here, where it's carefully monitored and directed toward harmless play, than to leave people to vent the same impulses in secret meetings, or visiting Reservations where you have no jurisdiction."

Thisbe's smile faded as she found herself on less familiar ground. "What does proselytizing have to do with the Marquis de Sade?"

"Ask your sensayer," Madame encouraged, "Sade is still on the standard syllabus, is he not, Doctor Carlyle?"

Carlyle perked at the invitation to ply his trade. "Their reputation aside, Thisbe, a lot of Sade's writings were moral and philosophical. They did precisely this taboo-breaking thing Madame is describing, mixing sex with philosophy and theology, usually by literally alternating them in the text: sex scene, philosophy, sex scene, philosophy, and so on. Sade equated racy, forbidden sex acts with radical ideas like atheism, or criticizing the king. It was a lot like that Diderot stuff about nuns that Heloïse quoted, encouraging readers to question what's meant by 'natural' when both celibacy and sex can be defined as perversions depending on how you look at it."

Madame's eyes beamed approval. "An admirable summary, Doctor Carlyle, but our Marquis was more experimental even than *le Philosophe*. My favorite example is his Proof from Design." Carlyle smirked recognizing it, but let Madame continue. "Nature, according to the science and theology of the Marquis's day, makes all things to fit where they belong, forest animals with brown fur, arctic animals with white fur, predators with sharp teeth, herbivores with dull teeth, round pegs in round holes on a world scale. With me so far, Thisbe?"

"Yes . . . ," she answered, cautious. "And before Darwin people used that as proof of the existence of God."

"Precisely. Now, the penis is round, and the anus is round, while the vagina's opening is long and narrow; clearly then Nature designed the penis to fit into the anus, not into the vagina."

Thisbe snickered. "That may be the dumbest thing I've ever heard."

"Precisely," Madame confirmed. "The Marquis is parodying Eighteenth-Century scientific logic. If you want to throw away his Proof of the Naturalness of Sodomy, you must also throw away Saint Thomas Aquinas's proof of the Existence of God from Design. Sade took on all sorts of things, gender, religious and moral concepts, all by experimenting with acts, or at least descriptions of acts, which reverse those prejudices. Since, in our modern day, discussing religion has become risky again, just as it was in the Eighteenth Century when anything radical could get you executed, the thrill is back too. And our dear Marquis's questions are still worth asking, even if today we have more rational laws and open-minded leaders."

"I . . . see it," Thisbe conceded. Then brightened. "Yes, I see it. It sounds fun."

Carlyle did not brighten. "Why are the President and Director here?" he asked, looking to the VIPs who flanked them in silent approval.

A nod from Ganymede invited Andō to speak first.

"I'm here at the moment for family business," the Chief Director answered.

Carlyle's light brows furrowed. "Family?"

Sparkling Ganymede glanced at the Cousin, then gave Thisbe a smirk of quick judgmental humor. She smirked back. "Carlyle, really, you haven't heard the rumors?"

He frowned. "What?"

" 'Tai-kun,' that's the nickname the Mitsubishi use for J.E.D.D. Mason, isn't it?"

Chief Director Andō nodded, not really smiling, but his face perhaps a little warmer now.

"Cardie couldn't get across to me the fifteen or so things the nickname means, but they're actually your child, aren't they, Director? That's what Mitsubishi circles say, that, despite being adopted by the Emperor, J.E.D.D. Mason is actually Chief Director Andō's child."

Carlyle blinked, dazzled. "I never believed. Then . . . President Ganymede, you're J.E.D.D. Mason's uncle?"

Duke Ganymede sighed at the sensayer, as at a newcomer at a banquet who lifts the dessert fork first. "Chief Director Andō has been married to my sister for twenty-eight years. You can't expect him to publicly accept responsibility for a bastard child of twenty-one; what an eccentric suggestion."

Andō's face revealed nothing. "Suffice to say Tai-kun is very dear to me, and I was glad to see my friend and colleague Cornel MASON secure a place for the child where they would have access to the very highest circles. MASON, meanwhile, has been happy to have my help raising Tai-kun, since we're both such busy people."

Carlyle's puzzled gaze shifted from Director to Madame to Duke, and fixed at last on Thisbe.

"So, like an unofficial, makeshift bash'," Thisbe suggested, stretching back catlike across the silken seat as she savored the mystery's solution.

"Or a marriage alliance," Madame suggested, "between two royal houses. Who do you think convinces the Masons not to push too hard for a new Census even though their population's grown enough to merit another Senator? Or who do you think gets the Mitsubishi not to raise rents on the rest of us when they own more than half the globe?" Madame's breast within its bodice swelled with mother's pride. "He is a very important Boy, my Son the Prince D'Arouet, a Pillar of friendship between the Masons, Mitsubishi, and Humanists."

"A personal alliance." Thisbe is always happy to be right. "So which one gets to be called Monsieur D'Arouet? The Emperor or you, Director?"

"Voltaire," Carlyle answered softly.

"What?"

"Voltaire's real name was François-Marie Arouet before they changed it to Voltaire. Sticking 'De' on the front just makes it sound aristocratic—it's the sort of thing ambitious women aiming to become kings' mistresses used to do."

Madame concealed her smile behind a fan of deep blue ostrich feathers veined with gold. "If the Patriarch is no longer using the name, why shouldn't I? After all, Voltaire was my inspiration, he and his age."

"Don't you mean Madame de Pompadour and *her* age?" Carlyle challenged. "That's what you're aiming at here, isn't it? The age when kings' mistresses ruled the world?"

"I'm not aiming at anything," she answered, painted lashes fluttering at the suggestion. "I have created a period venue where clients of a particular taste can vent their unorthodox sexual appetites. If, as a side effect, my Son and I have encouraged peace and stability in the world for two decades, I don't expect anyone will complain."

Carlyle tried to slide away from Madame along the sofa, but politeness held him mostly fast. "And what about you, President Ganymede?" he asked. "Why are you here? Paying an avuncular visit?"

The Cousin was not worthy of the Duke's full gaze. "I was born here, but I'm here now to retrieve Thisbe Saneer." He turned the murder-blue diamonds of his eyes on her. "I thought you were more cautious than this, Thisbe. What if you'd been caught using the confidential data your bash' is trusted with to infiltrate a secret stronghold which I didn't happen to frequent?"

"I'm sorry." There was frankly little apology in Thisbe's apology. Her expression was like a child's at that moment, a child clever enough to find the hiding place where Mom and Ba'pa have secreted some stash of candy for her birthday, and she accepts their admonishments, but in the same breath reaches for her chocolate. Thisbe collects us, you see. She was born to her bash's secrets, but she collected me, the Major, Bridger. Now what a triple prize to set beside us in her spellbook: the President, the Chief Director, and this bizarre Madame.

"Thisbe." The Duke President reconquered his Member's attention with a toss of his golden mane. "If you were concerned about how the Prince D'Arouet was handling the case, you should have come to me directly. You know this must be handled delicately." His eyes locked on me for a stabbing instant. My trembling was my apology.

"Excuse me, President Ganymede," Carlyle interrupted, "did you say you were born here?"

"Here we prefer 'Excuse me, *Your Grace*,'" Madame corrected, "and yes, he was, his sister too, part of my dear family, born and raised here, like Dominic and Heloïse and the Chevalier."

"Inside a brothel?"

The Duke's eyes locked on the sensayer, like a hawk about to dive. "We lived upstairs, the pit is downstairs, and if you're calling my sister something vile then there's a dueling arena downstairs where such things are settled."

Carlyle's limbs withdrew into the cloak like a retreating crab. "Cousins' Law doesn't allow dueling."

"You could find a champion."

"Please, Your Grace," Madame intervened, "we must forgive newcomers for being new."

"Of course." It was Director Andō who seconded Madame's forgiveness, and with such force that Ganymede had to let it go.

Madame smiled it all away. "Anyway, it's not uncommon for a bash' house to have a business in part of it—as yours does, Mademoiselle Saneer, your wonderful cars—nor is it uncommon for some of a bash's children to join the family business while others work elsewhere. Speaking of which, Mademoiselle Saneer, I hear you're up for another Oscar. Congratulations."

Thisbe cocked an eyebrow. "Nominees for this year aren't going to be announced for another two weeks."

"I know." Again Madame's fan hid her smile, but she let it sparkle in her eyes, the smug allure of secret knowledge.

Carlyle, less secret-fluent than Thisbe, was still struggling to keep track. "So Director Andō married President Ganymede's sister, who was raised here in the same bash' as the Masonic *porphyrogene*?" The Cousin's face strained just from outlining the web of what could be labeled neither incest nor nepotism, but smelled like both. "Another marriage alliance?"

"Precisely," Madame answered, glowing, "so the Humanists too trust my Jehovah and let Him help maintain the balance between the Hives. That's why He was asked to take care of this *Black Sakura* mess."

"Was it an arranged marriage?" Carlyle accused. "Danaë and Director Andō?"

"*Princesse* Danaë, or *Lady* Danaë," the Duke corrected, "and, no, it was not."

Carlyle's breath grew harsher. "I talked to Heloïse."

The Duke's eyes narrowed. "What about Sister Heloïse?"

"They were going to have an arranged marriage. The 'fiancé' who had been chosen for them? And they weren't acting, were they? They actually live like a nun here. Think like a nun, and worship your son Jehovah like a god." His eyes fixed on Madame. "The gendered boys and girls you raised here aren't just playing. You've raised them to think inside this box. Like Heloïse, you probably got Danaë to believe the marriage was voluntary, but everything was planned. Am I wrong?" Spitfire Carlyle didn't give them time to answer. "Period costume is one thing, but we got rid of gender roles to free people from this kind of mental subjugation. You've undone that. You've 'raised children in such a way as to intentionally limit their potential and cripple their ability to participate and interface naturally and productively with the world at large.'"

A warning bell went off in all our minds. That last sentence wasn't Carlyle's, it was Nurturism, a quote from the infamous bill proposed in 2238, the height of the Anti-Set-Set Riots, when, in the name of kindness and free will, the Nurturist faction tried to add to the short list of Universal Laws that bind even Blacklaws this grim Eighth: a ban on raising children too strangely. The law that was defeated at such cost.

Madame stretched back across her sofa. "I don't feel particularly subjugated."

"Then why is your male child the Tribune, not you?" Carlyle accused. "Why aren't you an Imperial *Familiaris,* or a player in the Humanist elections, or a Senator?"

"I prefer exerting this kind of power. I could have the other, but I don't want to."

"Separate spheres," Carlyle accused. "Out of curiosity, *Madame,*" he pronounced the title with disdain, "did you do sensayer training research on Rousseau as well as Sade?"

Do you know our Jean-Jacques, reader? If there were three lights of the Enlightenment, the third was Jean-Jacques Rousseau: as brilliant as Aristotle, as disruptive as Alexander, as mad as good St. Francis. Whatever grand goal the Enlightenment took up, he managed to somehow support and attack it at the same time. The Age of Reason celebrated the possibility that science would improve the human condition generation by generation; Rousseau agreed, but cried that this would only make us wretched by pushing us further from the Noble Savage's lost tranquility. The Age of Reason speculated that women might be no different from men if they were reared the same; Rousseau agreed, but cried that this would strip women of their rightful thrones, unmaking society's peacemakers, and making men grow harsher without a fair sex to temper their passions. Even bloodfeuding enemies must negotiate civilly in Madame de Pompadour's presence, he would say; not so Bryar Kosala's, since she is free to wage a feud herself. If newspapers and common discourse hailed Voltaire as Patriarch and Diderot as *le Philosophe,* Rousseau was known tenderly as 'Jean-Jacques,' a fragile firebrand always in need of sheltering lest it burn out, and ladies around the world wrote of how they wished to rush to and embrace this dear, romantic advocate of inequality who, they felt, knew their fragile hearts so well. Jean-Jacques became the favored spokesman of those women who, perversely but sincerely, wanted to remain pet-queens within their gendered roles. To temper your confusion, reader, I shall not call Rousseau "she," but I am tempted.

Madame smiled. "Well guessed, Doctor Foster. I did study to be a sensayer, and Rousseau was my first favorite. It was in Rousseau I first discovered that there are forgotten powers only women used to wield, and my own experimentation proved they still work today, extremely well, in fact, since no one's on guard against them anymore."

"Experimentation," Carlyle repeated. "Then tell me, did you lose your sensayer license for sleeping with your parishioners? Or for abusing their personal information?"

The affront to the lady's honor spurred both Duke and Director to rise, but she forced peace with a smile and dainty restraining gesture. "That is a fair question. In fact, I left without qualifying. I discovered early on that I prefer the boudoir to the Conclave; I don't fancy a life in which I couldn't share theology with friends as . . . fully . . . as I prefer."

Thisbe laughed aloud, and Carlyle spun on her, eyes hot. "You think this is funny?" he snapped.

"I think this is awesome."

"Awesome? It's sick!"

"Carlyle, I've seen the Sensayers' Conclave, and this room is frankly a lot more comfortable. Madame here is a competent adult. If they wanted to go into politics they could. Instead they're exercising supreme political influence while getting to enjoy fun clothes and comfy sofas. How is that bad?"

"But—"

"Women's liberation happened, what, four hundred years ago, but there's still residual bias even if no one wants to admit it. There are always more biologically male political and business leaders than female, at least outside you Cousins. Look at the Seven-Ten lists; Bryar Kosala's the only woman on most of them these days. I think it's good to see another woman on top. So what if Madame's taking the back door into politics, it isn't cheating any more than President Ganymede is cheating by being blond and gorgeous. No offense."

The Duke nodded.

"Are you really asking Madame to give up the power they've created for themselves here?" Thisbe pressed.

"What about Heloïse, then?" The Cousin thrust an accusing finger at the door as if imagining the nun caged beyond. "What about the other kids Heloïse said they competed with when young? There must be ladies to go with the Chevalier and company, but we didn't get to see them because ladies sit in their rooms like fragile baby bunnies and embroider all day or whatever. Madame is raising them to live like slaves, and you're okay with that?"

"Like set-sets?" Thisbe shot back, on Eureka and Sidney's behalf.

Fighting words, these, reader, as Cousin and Humanist see themselves on opposite sides of riot lines, protesting for and against a bash's right to (mis)use Brill's arts to make their children into those intricately programmed geniuses which neither side can call anything but happy, productive, and completely mad. Even doe-gentle Carlyle hesitated in the presence of the sleeping dragon of the Set-Set Riots that, two centuries ago, so nearly reintroduced our world to war.

Carlyle took a long breath. "This isn't like set-sets, it's sexual slavery."

Thisbe rolled her eyes. "Now the Cousin shows their colors—throw sex or violence into something and it has to be evil just 'cause you say so."

"That's not it at all!"

"Sex is in everything, Carlyle, and anyone who pretends it isn't it is heading into battle with one fewer weapon in their arsenal. It's as true in the Senate and the Conclave as it is here. If you don't believe that, you need to get laid."

After a moment's shocked pause they laughed together, Madame, the Duke, Director Andō, healthy belly laughs, as when one of Madame's creations, still in childhood, would toddle in upon the adults in their pleasures and ask, "Does that tickle?" as only children can.

"Oh, my dear Thisbe, you must let me kiss you!" Madame did just as she threatened, placing a more-than-sisterly peck on Thisbe's willing cheek. Witch! I apologize, master. I want to obey you, but she's a witch! I can't explain it to you any other way. Look at her! Look at the two of them! Witch and whore, the two black sides of womankind, they recognize each other surely as viper knows scorpion, or assassin knows thief as they brush shoulders while visiting the same unsavory back-alley toolmaker. Look how quickly Thisbe takes to this, how comfortably she sprawls across the well-named loveseat! Would Lesley take to this so easily? Would Aldrin? Toshi Mitsubishi? Mommadoll? See how even the Cousin Carlyle cringes. Yet Thisbe is already trading smiles with Madame, like the electric ripples with which eels signal the boundary between my hunting ground and yours. These gazes are mutual admiration, Madame and Thisbe admiring each other as the sprinter admires the weightlifter against whom she will never vie. Their games do not share the same goals, not even rules, but they do use the same pieces, and the same board, this same fragile blue orb.

Art thou finished now, Mycroft? Venting thy lunacy?

Yes, reader.

Good, then let this outburst be thy last. My patience and forgiveness end here. Henceforth, I warn you, I shall skip any delirious paragraph with 'witch' in it.

But, reader!

No! Wretch, thou art as mad about women as thy Jean-Jacques. I will hear no more of this, and if thou triest test my patience more I may begin to skip other absurdities as well: thy fevered talk of miracles, thy Bridger. This is thy final warning.

"I am going to talk to the Conclave," Carlyle announced, as much to himself, I think, as to the room.

Madame's smile rained adoring condescension down upon the Cousin. "About what, dear? I told you, the Conclave knows."

"About Jehovah Epicurus Donatien whatever whatever. The theology. The illegal part."

The matron blinked. "There's no law against a Blacklaw or Graylaw having a religious name, or are you going to argue it's proselytizing?"

"Setting aside the proselytizing of encouraging Heloïse to worship J.E.D.D. Mason like a god—"

"No one, certainly not my Son, has ever encouraged that. In fact, my Son quite disapproves, and has commanded Heloïse with the most extreme strictness not to recommend the practice to others. But Heloïse is as entitled to freedom of religion as anyone, even if her choice is a very rare one."

Carlyle frowned, but decided to move on for now. "I saw J.E.D.D. Mason in action at the Saneer-Weeksbooth bash'. They talked about religion, other people's religions, *my* religion, in front of groups of people, without anyone's consent. That *is* against the Black Laws."

"No." Hotaka Andō Mitsubishi broke his long silence here, the foreigner whose dark kimono, plain black hair, the stiffness with which he sat upon the corner of his seat, all lent him an air of separation and objectivity which calmed even Carlyle a bit.

"What do you mean, Director?"

"Have you seen Tai-kun use theology in circumstances where something else more dangerous to the world order was not already taking place?"

Carlyle had to admit, "No."

"The First Law bans religious discourse, or proselytizing more specifically, under the rubric of 'action likely to cause extensive or uncontrolled loss of human life or suffering of human beings.' I don't know what comments you heard, but I am confident you will agree they were not proselytory, and they were done in the service of protecting the global transit system, which is a much more immediate threat of uncontrolled loss of life and suffering." Andō took a deep breath. "Theology is Tai-kun's weapon, and Tai-kun is an officer of the law. Would you rather we had licensed them to kill, as we have Ockham Saneer?"

"I . . ." Carlyle took some moments to think. "You mean it's purposeful? They incapacitate an enemy using theology?"

"Instead of violence, yes," Andō confirmed. "Tai-kun sends enemies to sensayers instead of hospitals, and leaves them with insights instead of scars. Imagine how many lives we could save if every police officer in the world were armed so gently."

Carlyle did imagine, and from his pallor I suspect he had Julia Doria-Pamphili in his mind's eye, the razor words with which she slashes to the heart and, like a surgeon, leaves the patient sounder once the wounds are healed.

"Tai-kun's task in this world is to solve things," the Chief Director continued, leaning so he could fix the Cousin in his sights without losing his view of sparkling Ganymede. "They keep the rivalry between Mitsubishi and Masons from becoming harmful to the public good. They will catch this *Black Sakura* thief and protect the cars before real damage is done. If among their tools they employ a few nonproselytizing religious comments, that benefits the world, and often benefits the people who are stimulated to new reflection by the contact." He paused here to let Carlyle disagree, but the sensayer had nothing. "Though Madame D'Arouet does not have any official government office," Andō continued, "their occupation is similar, to solve things, whether that means tempering relations between myself and MASON, or giving those downstairs an outlet for desires which could be disruptive and dangerous if expressed outside. Here the Duke, and Emperor, and I can talk face to face without the whole world watching. You would be surprised how many crises have been averted beneath this roof."

Two quick knocks sounded at the door.

"At last!" Madame cried, smiling again at half-calmed Carlyle. "Your escort's here. Let her in, Mycroft. Let her in."

I opened the door, and watched shock drive all the anger from Carlyle's face.

"Chair Kosala?"

Thisbe released a long, low whistle as she arrived. It was Mom herself, the Cousin Chair Bryar Kosala, her borrowed black cloak hanging open in the front so a sliver of her Cousins' wrap spoiled the scene with its modernity. "Carlyle Foster, right? Are you all right?"

"What are you doing here?" Carlyle rushed to her, glad to have something sane to cling to in this mad new world.

She smiled. "We had an appointment half an hour ago to talk about Mycroft Canner and why you're not allowed to tell the public they've been made a Servicer. Did you not get the message?"

"I . . . sorry, I haven't checked my messages today. But, how did you find me?"

"I got a call. Are you okay?"

Ganymede's sharp eyes guessed the call was mine.

Carlyle gaped. "You know about this place?"

"I'm the outside inspector." She flashed her credentials. "You know all brothels have Cousins inspect to make sure no one's being abused."

"You do that personally?" Carlyle's face was bright already, healed by Bryar's arrival as everything about her promised normalcy: her modern slouch, her guileless smile, even the plain wedding ring on her finger, a silent promise that she had no part in this madness.

"These days this is the only one I still inspect myself," she answered. "I wouldn't trust anyone else to do it here. Neither do they." She nodded to her colleagues. "Hello, Director, Your Grace."

They returned silent nods.

It was Ganymede's duty to introduce his own. "Bryar, may I present Thisbe Saneer, of the Saneer-Weeksbooth bash'."

Kosala was not close enough to offer a handshake. "Pleased to meet you, Member Saneer."

Take this moment, reader, to ask yourself whether you would mistake these two for one another on the street, Thisbe Saneer and Bryar Kosala. They are both women of India, Bryar slightly taller, Thisbe slightly paler, their inky hair long and almost always loose, but Bryar's hair always falls behind her like a cape, while Thisbe's surrounds her throat and shoulders like a shadowed hood.

"Bryar, dear," Madame invited, "kindly explain to poor Doctor Foster why it's perfectly legal for me to raise my girls and boys the way I do?"

Kosala offered Carlyle a sympathetic face. "You know the set-set issue. I personally check on this bash'house regularly, and make sure the kids are given access to standard education and ideas, and allowed to leave and pursue a different lifestyle if they want to."

"But if you raise them so they're incapable of normal life . . ."

"Carlyle," Thisbe interrupted darkly, "when you hear 'set-set issue,' that's your cue to shut up."

Kosala turned sympathetic eyes on Thisbe. "That's right, your bash' has set-sets, doesn't it?"

Thisbe did not soften. "Eureka Weeksbooth and Sidney Koons are the two happiest people I've ever met."

Kosala tried a smile. "Exactly. I respect your concern, Carlyle, I really do, but the law's clear. However you raise your kid, you're pushing them in some direction, shaping them with languages if nothing else; so long as the direction you push is going to make them productive and happy, there's no justification for interference. It's legal to raise a set-set, it's legal to raise an Italian, it's legal to raise a Cousin, and it's legal to raise an Eighteenth-Century lady or gentleman. Right, Thisbe?"

Still no smile from the ice-eyed Humanist. "Yes. My Hive fought hard for that right. And specialist sensayer or no, I will not have a Nurturist inside my bash'."

Here, reader, was the only moment where I longed to raise my voice among my betters. Thisbe's history was plain wrong. Two hundred years ago, when the Eighth Law vote loomed, it was not the Humanists who battled it. Mycroft MASON fought it, certainly, but even more than him it was Utopia, those strangers behind their vizors who see the true Sun less often than Eureka. Utopia knew, when the case went to trial, that if this Eighth Law passed, if it was judged legal for Lindsay Graff to kidnap children from a set-set training bash', that it would be the floodgate. Next, all as one, the mighty, angry Earth would descend upon Utopia, as Catholics used to descend on Protestants and vice versa to 'save' the others' children. Terra the Moon Baby would be the excuse. The Utopians could protest all they liked that they did not anticipate the astronaut's pregnancy, that early complications made the trip back to Earth too dangerous for mother and fetus, but in most minds Terra is still thought of as intentional, a lab rat, happy, indispensable, who taught us more about space adaptation than a thousand simulations, but still a lab rat, short-lived and crippled from gestating on the light and airless Moon. If Utopia was willing to do that to one child, Earth accused, what might they be doing to others beneath those vizors? How long until cyborg U-beasts, made from iguanas and dogs and horses, had human pieces too? Fear forced Utopia to act. They chose a gentle protest. When the Graff trial began they called in sick, "indefinite stasis," as they put it, not one, not hundreds, but all four hundred million at once. The laboratories, factories, think tanks, presses closed. For three weeks the world tasted life without four hundred million vocateurs. Hate rose, and fear, all the arrows of complacent Earth against Utopia, and it was that threat which steeled Mycroft MASON to step onto the Senate floor and stop the Nurturists' Eighth Law at any price. Your hero gave his all for them, reader, for Aldrin, for Voltaire, for Apollo Mojave, not for his Masons, not for Eureka Weeksbooth, not for you.

Then clearly thou art well named for him, Mycroft, thou who verse on verse recitest this litany of Utopia with thy namesake's passion.

Namesake? You flatter, reader, but I am not named for Mycroft MASON. Rather, we both were named for Mycroft Holmes, elder brother of the fictional detective. Mycroft was smarter than Sherlock, almost omniscient, and with his greater wisdom mocked his brother's attempts to champion justice. Mycroft Holmes spent his days gazing out through the windows of the Diogenes club, watching the infinite tapestry of urban life, and doing nothing, save when government commanded.

Carlyle breathed deep. "You're right. You are right. I'm sorry I snapped. I'm not a Nurturist, really, I'm not. I don't object to set-sets. It makes me uncomfortable, but I recognize why it's right that it's allowed. I embrace the principle. And maybe what you're doing here is actually beneficial, I just . . ."

"You've had a hard three days." Bryar Kosala clapped her fellow Cousin on the shoulder like a drinking buddy. "Come on, Carlyle. I'm going to take you to lunch and answer all your questions about Mycroft Canner, and Jed Mason, and all this. Sound good?"

Carlyle relaxed into a slump at last. "Wonderful. I can't thank you enough." He turned eagerly to the door, and hope beyond. But paused. "One more question, Madame?"

"As many as you like, my dear," she invited, that portrait face smiling so perfectly.

Carlyle had to steel himself. "Who named your child? Was it you?"

"Jehovah Epicurus Donatien D'Arouet Mason?" she recited.

Carlyle looked to Thisbe. "Donatien is the given name of the Marquis de Sade."

Madame nodded confirmation. "All the Prince's ba'pas picked out pieces of His name. As a sensayer, I don't think you would want me to reveal to anyone who chose which."

Finally Carlyle had a smile for her. "That's true. Thanks for catching me."

She smiled back. "I still know how to think like a sensayer. I also think Jehovah is a good name for a person who saves lives by wielding theology instead of a gun."

Carlyle took a slow breath. "Heloïse's fiancé was the Emperor, wasn't it? The 'great and worthy man' who could approach Jehovah Mason as a father to a son? The Emperor was supposed to marry Heloïse just like the Director married Danaë. That's a pretty uncomfortable age gap."

"That's two questions," Chair Kosala chided. "Come on, Carlyle, no more politics for you today, you're politics-ed out. I prescribe a good French restaurant." She glanced back over her shoulder. "See you later, Director, President Ganymede."

Carlyle lingered, a stubborn foot in the doorway. "Thisbe, will you be all right here?"

"With my own President?" Thisbe shot back, chuckling. "Mycroft's making you paranoid, Carlyle. I'm thrilled to be here."

"All right. I'll see you . . ."

"Around," she finished for him.

I held the door for the two Cousins as they left. Kosala glanced down at me. "I might call you, Mycroft, if Carlyle has questions later."

"I'll be ready, Chair," I promised as I closed the door behind.

"Mycroft Canner." I heard Carlyle whisper my name like an incantation just before the door closed. Perhaps we smelled alike to him, me and Madame, the same kind of monster, as when a remote village starts finding bodies in the woodland edge mauled by claws and jaws too huge to be common woodland fauna, and it does not matter whether the killer be wolf or bear or dinosaur, the threat is still the same: extinct things rising. Torture, humanity was supposed to be past that. Gender, we were supposed to be past that, too.

With the Cousins gone, Madame stretched back across her sofa, glowing with satisfaction like a cat between two naps. "Well, gentlemen? Did you get a good look?"

"That's the child, no doubt," Andō answered gravely.

Ganymede nodded agreement. "Thisbe, that young sensayer of yours is a Gag-gene, and must be kept away from here at all costs, for his own sake more than anything. Children can leave this house, and he is proof. Will you watch him for me?"

Thisbe's cheeks stayed still, but I saw her eyes sparkle with delight: another secret for the spellbook. "Of course, Member President."

"Good, now come with me. We're getting you back home, and then I'm meeting with your bash' about this whole affair. If you have problems they're the whole Hive's problems. Time we settled them."

I have rarely seen so eager a nod from Thisbe. "Thank you, Member President. We've been hoping for some more direct intervention." She turned to the hostess now. "And thank you for your hospitality, Madame. It's been most enlightening." She laughed at her own joke. "I'd love to come again, if I may."

"Why, I'd be delighted, dear Thisbe. I shall talk to membership about an invitation for you." Madame kissed her goodbye on both cheeks.

Duke Ganymede can slide like a dancer, strut like a cock, or march like a soldier. Here he chose the last, dragging Thisbe toward the door by force of command.

I opened the door for them, and handed him the sack with Thisbe's boots and weapons. «Thisbe's arts, your Grace.»

The Duke does not thank slaves.

Director Andō rose now. "I'll go too, if we're done here."

"Yes, we're done. Thank you, Hotaka. I knew if anyone could recognize the child it would be you and Ganymede. See you tonight?"

The Chief Director kissed her hand before departing. "Until tonight, Madame." ⌜I expect your presence tonight too, Mycroft,⌟ he ordered, raising his eyes to me for the first time since I had entered. ⌜We'll have work for you.⌟

⌜Yes, Chief Director.⌟

I closed the door behind him. Then I faced Madame, alone at last in her salon. «Nicely played, Madame. Very nicely played.»

She appreciates that sort of compliment from me. «Thank thee, Mycroft. Now»—she shooed me like a pigeon—«to thy work.»

The Interlude in Which
Martin Guildbreaker Pursues
the Question of Dr. Cato Weeksbooth

CALL LOGGED 11:11 UT MARCH 26, 2454

Seneschal: "Not often *notre Maître* asks a question like that."

Guildbreaker: "Dominic! Where are you? Are you hurt?"

Seneschal: "And He asked it in front of Caesar no less. 'Do the Utopians ever turn down an application to join the Hive?' He looked straight at Aldrin when He asked it, too, He actually looked! And did you see how pale Mycroft turned when he heard it? I'm surprised the little stray's tracker didn't summon Papadelias."

Guildbreaker: "*Dominus* is really worried about you. The others may not see the difference, but I can tell."

Seneschal: "Well? Do they turn applications down?"

Guildbreaker: "The Utopians? No, never, I had Aldrin check."

Seneschal: "You don't see it, do you?"

Guildbreaker: "I do see it. There's someone *Dominus* thinks would want to be a Utopian but isn't, so they wondered if their application was rejected. I'll act on it. But you need to come back and tell us what's happening. What have you been doing for the last three days?"

Seneschal: "Seconds before that question, He'd asked Aldrin how long until the next Mars launch. Here's your hint: I heard *notre Maître* ask Cato Weeksbooth the same thing earlier that day, how long until the next Mars launch, and He got just as accurate an answer. Then He asked Weeksbooth how long the Saneer-Weeksbooth bash' had been Humanist and the blessed little coward didn't know."

Guildbreaker: "Cato Weeksbooth?"

Seneschal: "I'll leave it to you. I've found richer hunting."

Guildbreaker: "Dominic, what—"

Call ended 11:13 UT 03/26/2454

*   *   *

From the notes of Martin Guildbreaker:

At 14:22 UT on 03/26/2454 I arrived at the Chicago Museum of Science and Industry to interview Dr. Cato Weeksbooth. I did not give prior notice, so that Dr. Weeksbooth would not have time to consult the other members of the Saneer-Weeksbooth bash' before accepting. I was directed to wait for Dr. Weeksbooth in their office, and found it remarkable that a volunteer should have their own office.

The office contained tanks with fish, mice, frogs, crickets, and a very large ant colony, and was decorated with pictures of famous scientists and photographs of Dr. Weeksbooth with children at science fairs and locations of scientific interest. Notable were five framed handwritten paper letters from former students thanking Dr. Weeksbooth for inspiring them to pursue careers in science—three of the five mentioned receiving significant prizes. In each case the letter was framed so as to be partly covered by a photograph of the author as a child. I scanned the letters and determined two peculiarities. First, in all five cases the photographs had been carefully positioned to obscure points in the letter where the author mentioned having joined the Utopian Hive. Second, my scanner confirmed that the stains on all five letters were tears.

Many people value gut instinct, but in my experience gut reactions make it more difficult to objectively pursue an investigation. I could not shake the sense of murder which I had picked up from hearing Tsuneo Sugiyama describe the suicide by car crash of their grandchild's fiancé, and I could feel myself looking for murder as I worked, and reading it into evidence whether it was there or not. To counteract this tendency, I decided to begin with the question least directly related to murder, that is, the question of Dr. Cato Weeksbooth. This may seem a strange starting place, but much of life consists in repeating actions which are consistently effective, even if the mechanism is not clear. The *Porphyrogene* rarely judges it necessary to help me with my work, and, when they do, the aid is often in the form of such a seemingly tangential question, which inevitably leads me to the end I seek.

Cato Weeksbooth is thirty-five years old, one hundred and seventy-three centimeters tall, of recognizable Chinese descent, with dark brown eyes and wild, wiry hair clearly styled after Einstein. Dr. Weeksbooth wore a mad scientist costume, with an archaic white laboratory coat over blue hospital scrubs, and Humanist boots of Griffincloth which showed the internal anatomy of the feet. Only three strat insignia were visible: two pins on the lapel of the lab coat indicating membership in the Friends of the Chicago Museum of Science and Industry and the Ten Plus Moon Club, and a pair of rubber lab gloves tied into a knot at the belt, which is the insignia of the Chicago Museum of Science and Industry Junior Scientist Squad. Dr. Weeksbooth seemed agitated, and spent much of the interview performing maintenance on the tanks of animals around the room, in a clear effort to avoid eye contact. I commenced formal interview at 14:47 UT:

Guildbreaker: "Thank you for seeing me today, Dr. Weeksbooth."

Weeksbooth: "Can this be fast? I have a thing to do. A meeting. I have a meeting to do, to go to, to run. I have to run a meeting, so I can't stay long for whatever this is. Why do you want to talk to me anyway? I never saw the stupid Seven-Ten list, it's nothing to do with me. I'm very busy. Can't you leave me alone?"

Guildbreaker: "This will be quick, Dr. Weeksbooth, I just need to get some information about the habits of the house, so I can tell when the thief is most likely to have entered. How much of your time would you say you spend at home?"

Weeksbooth: "Most of it. I do work there, you know."

Guildbreaker: "How many hours a week are you at home?"

Weeksbooth: "I don't know. Lots. I'm always there, usually, always usually, unless I'm here."

Guildbreaker: "Do you spend a lot of time here at the museum?"

Weeksbooth: "I guess."

Guildbreaker: "How many hours a week?"

Weeksbooth: "It depends. Maybe twenty. No, more than that, thirty. Forty, maybe forty."

Guildbreaker: "How long have you been volunteering here?"

Weeksbooth: "Since I was fifteen."

Guildbreaker: "That's a long time. You must enjoy it."

Weeksbooth: "Yes."

Guildbreaker: "What made you start?"

Weeksbooth: "Kids aren't learning science right these days! The teachers teach it like it's just supposed to be useful, like, here, learn this geometry so you can design a building, here, learn this chemistry so you can make a plastic bag. Of course kids don't like it! No kid comes home from school and says, 'I want to make plastic bags when I grow up!' We already have plastic bags, and comfy chairs, and flying cars, we've had them for centuries, and they aren't getting better because they work already so no one's interested in replacing them, just making them cheaper, or with more games. That isn't science! Science is figuring out where the universe is going! Science is noticing that the ants crawling up the picnic table like your sandwich better than your ba'sib's and asking, 'Why?' Not 'How is this useful?' not 'Can I make this into a plastic bag?' but 'Why?'"

Guildbreaker: "I meant, why did you start volunteering at that age specifically?"

Weeksbooth: "Oh. My doctor made me."

Guildbreaker: "Your doctor?"

Weeksbooth: "Doctor Balin. Ember Balin. My psychiatrist."

Guildbreaker: "Why did Doctor Balin want you to start volunteering?"

Weeksbooth: "Because I tried to kill myself. Look, this has nothing to do with the Seven-Ten list. If you want a list of what hours I've been at the museum you can ask the staff assistant. Can I go now?"

Guildbreaker: "What's your meeting?"

Weeksbooth: "What?"

Guildbreaker: "The meeting you have to go run, what is it?"

Weeksbooth: "It's a Junior Scientist Squad meeting."

Guildbreaker: "What's that?"

Weeksbooth: "A science club for kids."

Guildbreaker: "What sorts of things does the club do?"

Weeksbooth: "We have club meetings twice a week, and I give special tours and demonstrations in the museum, and we have a reading group, and a lab where the kids do lab experiments, I supervise but they pick the projects and do everything themselves, and they also do solo research projects and present them at our annual science fair—it's getting famous now, the Director of Worldlab came last year—and field trips, we do field trips, to labs, and research bases, and geological sites, and nature preserves, whatever the kids request, and up the elevators, and Luna City, that's their favorite, every year, Luna City."

Guildbreaker: "How many times have you been to the Moon?"

Weeksbooth: "Nineteen times now. This year will be my twentieth."

Guildbreaker: "That must be expensive. Don't the Utopians make you pay the full cost of the trip after the second time?"

Weeksbooth: "They subsidize me because I take the kids. We have a special package where we get to stop at the ISSC, too. Do you realize seventy percent of kids today haven't been to the Moon by the time they head off to a Campus? Thirteen percent of people never go at all, even with the subsidies! You know if you still haven't gone by the time you turn sixty they invite you go for free, and thirteen percent still never do!"

Guildbreaker: "It sounds like a great club."

Weeksbooth: "It is. It's popular, too, we have sixty-one members this year, that's a record. Of course, usually only about thirty come to each meeting, but twenty is still a lot! And I get more at the lectures, and they record the lectures now too and distribute them free. The Museum Director told me they're being used in more than a hundred classrooms."

Guildbreaker: "I watched one as a sample before coming."

Weeksbooth: "Which one?"

Guildbreaker: "The history of vaccination. You're a very passionate lecturer. You made me tear up at one point."

Weeksbooth: "It's the material, not me. An achievement like that would move you to tears if it were written in bad verse on the back of a napkin. That is, if you've any scientific passion left in you. Some people don't."

Guildbreaker: "I don't think it was just the material, you're a very good speaker. You've also written some books?"

Weeksbooth: "No one took it seriously. They say I'm trying to teach science like it's poetry, well, science is poetry, and anyone who doesn't see that is dead inside!"

Guildbreaker: "You're referring to your guidebook for science teachers, *Tomorrow and Tomorrow and Tomorrow?*"

Weeksbooth: "Yes. You were thinking of something else?"

Guildbreaker: "*The Horizoners.*"

Weeksbooth: "Oh, that. Everyone made a big deal about that because Thiz got Orland Vives to make it into a movie. It was just a fun little story I wrote for the kids to circulate among their friends. Did you read it?"

Guildbreaker: "No, but I . . ."

Weeksbooth: "You watched the movie?"

Guildbreaker: "Yes."

Weeksbooth: "Everybody watched the movie."

Guildbreaker: "Did you like the movie?"

Weeksbooth: "It was okay."

Guildbreaker: "Only okay?"

Weeksbooth: "They changed too much."

Guildbreaker: "I heard they cut one of the story lines, is that right? Originally there were four groups of kids trying to build ships to go around the world including a Nineteenth-Century group as well as the ancient ones, the ones in 1495, and the contemporary ones?"

Weeksbooth: "Cutting a group was okay, they only had two hours, they couldn't fit all four. The problem was they made Taylor Harrow into a Utopian."

Guildbreaker: "That's the leader of the contemporary set?"

Weeksbooth: "They said it was unrealistic for a kid to think that way and not be a Utopian, but that was the whole point! Anybody can have a sense of scientific curiosity, not just Utopians. The movie version reinforces the stereotype instead of breaking it."

Guildbreaker: "You wanted to break it?"

Weeksbooth: "Of course. They said it was innovative making a movie with a Utopian as a central character instead of having them be some kind of mystical teacher or a techie or a supervillain, they said it would human-ize the Utopians, like that last Canner movie did, what was it called?"

Guildbreaker: "*Apollo's River.*"

Weeksbooth: "Right, but that wasn't what I meant at all."

Guildbreaker: "You were going for an 'If Taylor Harrow can do it why can't I' type of thing?"

Weeksbooth: "Exactly. In the movie the message is that the Utopians have dibs on science the way the Humanists do on sports, and the other Hives all say, 'We don't need to do any exploring, leave it to the Utopi-ans.' Everybody talks about the Mars project as if only Utopians are ever going to set foot there, while the majority is content to sit around with their plastic bags and comfy chairs. Is that the future you want?"

Guildbreaker: "So you're trying to get kids who aren't Utopians to be inter-ested in science and exploration?"

Weeksbooth: "Exactly. That's why my persona is mad scientist, it's a pre-Hive character so anyone can imagine themself as a mad scientist without associating it with Utopians."

Guildbreaker: "Is it working?"

Weeksbooth: "What?"

Guildbreaker: "Your students, do a lot of them pursue careers in science?"

Weeksbooth: "Lots. Forty-three so far have doctorates in the sciences, thirty are working in experimental science, five in space engineering."

Guildbreaker: "And how many of them became Utopians? Dr. Weeks-booth?"

Weeksbooth: "I heard you."

Guildbreaker: "How many?"

Weeksbooth: (recording too faint to be made out)

Guildbreaker: "I'm sorry, I couldn't hear that."

Weeksbooth: "All of them, okay? They all are. What does this have to do with *Black Sakura*, anyway? You can't think the Utopians are behind it. They wouldn't do something like that! The Utopians aren't dirty like the rest of us, they're not involved, they don't even use the cars!"

Guildbreaker: "Did you ever consider becoming a Utopian yourself?"

Weeksbooth: "What?"

Guildbreaker: "Did you ever consider becoming a Utopian?"

Weeksbooth: "I heard you the first time."

Guildbreaker: "Did you?"

Weeksbooth: "No, I . . . no. The bash' is Humanist. My bash', I mean, my bash', they're, we're Humanists. We've been Humanists forever, it's a hereditary bash', it's not . . . it wouldn't have been practical. I couldn't . . . that's what I do, you know?"

Guildbreaker: "Would they have thrown you out of the bash' if you became a Utopian?"

Weeksbooth: "I . . . it's a Humanist bash'. Besides, Utopians don't do mixed bash'es. I mean, they can, but they don't."

Guildbreaker: "Actually they can't."

Weeksbooth: "What?"

Guildbreaker: "Utopians can't mix bash'es. There's a rule against it."

Weeksbooth: "No there isn't."

Guildbreaker: "There isn't? I thought there was."

Weeksbooth: "There absolutely isn't, I checked."

Guildbreaker: "You checked?"

Weeksbooth: "Yes."

Guildbreaker: "Why did you check?"

Weeksbooth: "I . . . I don't know. No reason."

Guildbreaker: "Why did you become a Humanist? Humanists are all supposed to have a great ambition, what's your great ambition? Doctor Weeksbooth?"

Weeksbooth: "I have to go, I'm going to be late."

Guildbreaker: "Just a couple more questions. The museum director said they offered you professional positions here several times. Why did you turn them down?"

Weeksbooth: "I have a job."

Guildbreaker: "Do you like running the cars? Are you happy doing that?"

Weeksbooth: "Look, I've tried to be cooperative, but I'm not stupid, and we're not going to let you keep taking advantage of this investigation to poke at me and my bash'. Masons already control a third of the world, you want to control us, too?"

Guildbreaker: "I assure you—"

Weeksbooth: "Get out. Get out of my office!"

Guildbreaker: "I didn't mean—"

Weeksbooth: "Get out! Get out! Get out! Get out! Get out!"

Interview ended 15:03 UT.

* * *

Selection from interview with Dr. Ember Balin, 16:03 UT 03/26/2454:

Guildbreaker: "So, that first suicide attempt was the reason you were put in charge of Cato's case?"

Balin: "Yes, in March 2440. Cato was fifteen then."

Guildbreaker: "How many attempts have there been since?"

Balin: "Officially, three."

Guildbreaker: "Officially?"

Balin: "The rest of the bash' watches Cato very carefully, so it's hard to say how many others they've prevented. Several."

Guildbreaker: "The second attempt was the following year, yes?

Balin: "2441."

Guildbreaker: "It was two days after Cato officially registered as a Humanist and got their first boots, yes?"

Balin: "Yes."

Guildbreaker: "Do you think there was a connection there?"

Balin: "What, that if you become a Humanist you try to kill yourself?"

Guildbreaker: "No, but do you think Cato might have been pressured into becoming a Humanist? That they really wanted to be something else?"

Balin: "Cato Weeksbooth is a great person, a great scientist, and a great teacher. Doesn't that sound like the model Humanist to you? Picking your Hive is a very emotional moment, it brought a lot of other feelings to the fore."

Guildbreaker: "I'm going to be direct, Doctor, do you think Doctor Weeksbooth wanted to be a Utopian? The Saneer-Weeksbooth bash' has been Humanist for centuries, there must have been great pressure to stay . . ."

Balin: "I understand the question."

Guildbreaker: "And?"

Balin: "Fuck off, Mason."

Guildbreaker: "Excuse me?"

Balin: "The same goes for all these records you've asked to requisition. Medication records? Dates of past sessions with their sensayer? I know that for legally 'indispensable' Humanists like Cato Weeksbooth Romanova can override doctor-patient confidentiality, and believe me we wouldn't be sitting here otherwise, but enough's enough. Cato Weeksbooth has been a bug under a lens since they were fifteen, and I don't like you taking advantage of their lack of privacy rights, especially when you have no explanation for this inquisition. If you come in here with a judge's order then I'll answer, but until that happens I'm not making Cato's most personal records and feelings public just because the Emperor's curious. I also frankly resent the assumption that Cato wouldn't want to be a Humanist if they weren't forced to."

Guildbreaker: "I can assure you, this investigation is very important."

Balin: "Assure all you like, Mason, but until you can tell me the point of all this, or until I see a judge's signature on my screen, I'm not budging. Ask Cato in person if you want to know how they feel about Utopians: if they won't say I won't."

Guildbreaker: "I see. Then the third suicide attempt was when?"

Balin: "July thirteenth, 2449."

Guildbreaker: "Five years ago. And do you know the cause of that one?"

Balin: "If you're going to requisition Cato's sealed files, Mason, you may as well bother to read them."

Guildbreaker: "I'm sorry?"

Balin: "Cato's parents and the entire rest of the parent generation of their bash' died in a rafting accident."

Guildbreaker: "What?"

Balin: "All their ba'pas, the Saneers, the Weeksbooths, the Typers, the Snipers, all of them, drowned on their annual whitewater rafting trip. It was hushed up, coming only nine years after the Canner Murders, everyone would've gone crazy about bash'-loss making people into monsters. Let an expert tell you, Canner was a much more complicated case. And this wasn't as extreme as Canner, since the rafting trip only included the Saneer-Weeksbooth ba'pa generation, none of the kids died, but anything that has to be compared to Mycroft Canner is a bad thing. Cato was institutionalized for two months after that."

Guildbreaker: "Was Cato the only one who was badly affected?"

Balin: "They were all badly affected, all their ba'pas died."

Guildbreaker: "I mean—"

Balin: "I know what you meant. Lesley Juniper Sniper Saneer was also institutionalized for . . . I can't remember how long, not more than a week.
Lesley didn't actually try anything but it was Lesley's second bash'loss
so we wanted to be extra careful. The ba'kids were all watched closely,
they always are, being so indispensable, but Cato and Lesley were the
only two with any history of instability. You really had no idea about
this, did you? So much for the Empire seeing all and knowing all."

Guildbreaker: "What about the last attempt? You said Cato had one more
official suicide attempt?"

Balin: "December eighth, 2450. That one was . . . let's call it a theological
crisis."

Guildbreaker: "Can you be more specific?"

Balin: "I can tell you to fuck off as many times as you like, Mason, it's kind
of fun. Anyway, I wasn't as deeply involved that time. I always handled
Cato jointly with their sensayer, Esmerald Revere, and Esmerald handled that incident."

Guildbreaker: "For the record, this is the sensayer Esmerald Revere who died
by suicide on March sixteenth of this year?"

Balin: "Yes. It's really only been eight days, hasn't it? Feels like longer."

Guildbreaker: "You knew Member Revere a long time?"

Balin: "Since I took on Cato's case. I've never thought it was a good idea for
that bash' all to share one sensayer. Cato for one needs a specialist. Most
of that bash' does, really, Lesley being orphaned twice, the two set-
sets, Sniper being Sniper, the Typer twins are an odd case, and Ockham Saneer really should have a sensayer who specializes in officers
licensed to kill. But they all insist their bash' has shared a sensayer for
umpteen generations, so who are we to say different. Esmerald was the
finest sensayer I ever worked with. I trust Julia Doria-Pamphili, and
I'm sure this new sensayer Julia's chosen must be something special or
they wouldn't send a Cousin in, but there's not another Esmerald Revere out there, there just isn't. Anyway, it's time for my next appointment, if you don't have any more teeth to pull today, Mason."

Guildbreaker: "One more question, if I may. I spoke to Dr. Weeksbooth earlier and they said, and this is a quote, 'The Utopians aren't dirty like
the rest of us.' Do you know what Cato might have meant by that?"

Balin: "How about I make it into a song? (singing) Fuck ooooff! Fuuuuck
off! Fuck off, fuck off, fu-u-uck off!"

Guildbreaker: "Dr. Balin, please!"

Balin: "You talked to Cato?"

Guildbreaker: "Yes."

Balin: "Sid, get Sora Mitsubishi on the phone, would you? I smell juicy harassment charges!"

Guildbreaker: "Excuse me, who?"

Balin: "Sora Mitsubishi, personal secretary to the Humanist Praetor in Romanova. Any more questions, Mason?"

Guildbreaker: "Sora Mitsubishi?"

Balin: "Are you deaf as well as nosy?"

Guildbreaker: "Is that . . . one of Director Andō Mitsubishi's adopted ba'kids?"

Balin: "Didn't expect to piss off two Hives at once, did you?"

Guildbreaker: "I . . . My office will contact you to collect the rest of Cato Weeksbooth's records as soon as I have the judge's signature. Thank you for your time."

Balin: "Don't expect me to thank you for yours."

Interview with Dr. Ember Balin ended 16:20 UT 03/26/2454.

* * *

Mycroft insists that I add a final comment to express my feelings after these interviews, though I would rather leave the data plain. I spent those hours fighting my feelings, trying to free myself from assumptions and face bare facts—why then should I pass these hard-fought feelings on to others? Did I find it strange that so many of Director Andō Mitsubishi's adopted children were cropping up in the course of this case, if only peripherally? Yes, but I made myself ignore that. Did I find it strange that Cato Weeksbooth had been assigned to a doctor with extremist anti-Masonic sentiments? Yes, but I made myself ignore that. I stuck to my method, and spent the rest of the day reading Cato Weeksbooth's records, which I did receive from Dr. Balin after placating the Praetor. Thus it was due to my rejection of sentiment, and my refusal to be distracted by hunches and tangents, that I kept my focus on the *Porphyrogene*'s question and discovered when I did that Cato Weeksbooth had had an emergency session with their sensayer, Esmerald Revere, on March fourteenth, 2454, the day before the suicide of Aki Sugiyama's fiancé Mertice O'Beirne, and two days before the same Esmerald Revere committed suicide as well.

The Enemy

WHEN PARIS WAS FINISHED WITH ME I STOPPED IN BARCELONA, where I hoped to forget myself for an hour and toil with my fellows undisturbed. We had hauled some boxes from an old movie theater to its new location three blocks down, a job which yielded not only fresh hot bocadillos but ticket vouchers, which burned in our pockets more valuable than gold. I had begun to forget the crisis amid the spice of beans and the burn of my tired arms. I needed that, as Apollo needed his pub in Liverpool, as we all need those indispensable minutes after the alarm wakes you from sleep but before you rise to face the day. I almost had it.

<¡come play! ¡come play! ¡ockham banned you from the house but i want you to come play!>

<¿Eureka?> I replied in text over my tracker, so the other Servicers could not hear.

<thisbe's been telling me about location 133-2720-0732.>

<¿Where?>

<the black hole. madame d'arouet's. thisbe was all surprised finding that place, the president, the emperor, the director, the cousin chair, but we knew, sidney and me. we knew it was special. we know everything and everyone and everywhere anyone goes in the whole world, even tricky j.e.d.d. mason who uses utopian cars, but we don't know about this mad nun heloise.>

I tried to hide my sigh, but the others spotted it, seeing my step grow distracted as we strolled through the shopping streets alive with urban buzz. They've learned to watch me now, to spot the moments when the calls come in and tear me from them. They threaten sometimes to defend me, to make a tally of how many hours I work and shove it in Kosala's face and call it cruel. I do not let them.

"You okay, Mycroft?" one asked. (Protective Kosala will not let me print their names.)

"It's not a job," I reassured. "Just questions."

<¿well?>

<I guess you wouldn't know about Heloïse,> I replied, <they never leave the house.>

<¡i know! ¡never! ¡not once in their whole life! ¡and there are others! this chevalier, more. ¿how many, mycroft? you've been there. ¿how many secret people are they hiding? i have to know.>

<I don't know.>

<guess. ¿how many? ¿10? ¿100?>

<Maybe 50.>

<clever invisible little monsters making the numbers off. the numbers are off, mycroft, ¿do you know that? our numbers for predicting location 133-2720-0732, how many people will come, how many go, how long they stay. we can predict it for anywhere on earth, houses, stores, offices, parks. we know everyone, their habits, where they go, how long they stay. we have the cars ready for them every time just right, but not the black hole, there the numbers are always off, not enough cars ready, too many waiting. now i know why. 50 sneaky invisible little monsters changing everybody's patterns. it's not fair.>

I followed my Servicer fellows still, through backstreets of the city, shops and crowds who took no more notice of us as we passed than of the resting gulls.

<this madame d'arouet is almost invisible too, they haven't used a car in years and years. they're on the wish list, though, 27,331 times. that's a lot of unsatisfied customers for one brothel.>

<That is a lot.>

<there are only a handful of people with five digits on the wish list. you have to do a lot to get that many people to wish you dead. but don't worry, you're still the record holder.>

<Yes, I know.>

<¿you know how many you have now? 989,408,013 and counting. that leaves only 110,634,255 humanists who haven't wished you dead yet.>

We had a storyteller with us, my little band with our hard-earned lunches, and, even in my distraction, I enjoyed seeing the light she brought to their faces. I cannot name her, but I can paint her for you at least, a rambunctious young ex-Humanist, built for play-acting, with huge, expressive hands, eyes that changed color more with her stories than the light, and a versatile androgyny, for she was (as Sniper might be) an Amazon, who, aiming early at the Olympic open divisions, chose to grow no breasts. If Servicer life is a banishment from the surrounding world, one might compare it to the natural prison of a snowed-in winter in the olden days, when the villagers forgot their buried farms to gather around the fire where the story-teller is, for six months, king.

<¿Sounds like the Wish List is circulating more widely than ever?> I asked.

<¿want to know how many times you're on the curse list?>

<¿What's the Curse List?>

<¿you don't know?>

<No.>

<¡it's so clever! it's the opposite of the wish list. you put somebody's name on the curse list if you like them and want to protect them, as if a curse on there is supposed to cancel out a wish on the other. someone must have started it because they saw someone they liked on the wish list and wanted to protect them. that means some people think the wish list is real.>

I shook my head, though Eureka was not there to see it. <They don't think the list is real. That many people wouldn't be willing to put names down on it if they really thought of it as endorsing murder.>

<but they also wouldn't bother if they thought it was nothing. that's why it's wonderful. it's like a superstition. at least nine hundred million humanists have put names on that wish list over the years, and they don't really think there's some assassin out there watching who'll kill off the people with the highest scores, but they must vaguely hope something bad might happen if enough death wishes pile on the same person, otherwise they wouldn't do it. it's like knocking wood, the death wish list.>

A dog came by next, with a friendly owner who let it sport with us: bliss.

<you're on the curse list too, you know, mycroft. 9,231 times. you still have fans.>

<You shouldn't encourage the Wish List, Eureka.>

<¿me? i've never put a name down, not once.>

<True, but I know you're the one who starts it up again when it stops circulating. You read it incessantly, and I've seen you lurk around online and mention it to Humanists who haven't heard of it yet. You need to be careful—it may have started as a joke, but in the wrong hands it could make the whole Hive look like murderers.>

My companions debated the next turn now, left toward the park, right toward the steps and fountain, two equal goods like two colors of candy. Do you wish I would omit these details, reader? In a hundred years there will be nothing left of these Servicers, no descendants, no inventions, no laws they passed or records they broke, even their trials will no longer be current as precedent. Their names may be censored, but I will not deprive them of the chance to be remembered at least as those happy Servicers who walked with Mycroft Canner.

<we're working on lists of who goes to madame's, me and sidney. sometimes they try to hide it, riding with somebody else with trackers off, trixy trixy. but now that we know what's there we can look at whose trackers are off, and who has patterns that don't add up. the black hole causes so much, but now we have the missing puzzle piece.>

<¿Was it you who gave Thisbe the location?>

<they asked.>

<Please don't show Thisbe the list of who goes there. Thisbe needs to stay away from that place. You all do, for the bash's safety.>

<¿why bother showing thisbe? ¿what could thisbe see? ¿a list of names? a list is nothing. thisbe can't see how, when you move one ball on the grid, the others move. madame d'arouet is a ball that doesn't move, but the others move around them, the whole structure orbiting the black hole. if you tried to see it with your silly senses it might look like the center of a web. we didn't know there was a spider hiding there—they stayed still so long. ¿do you think they were hiding from us on purpose? ¿mycroft? ¡mycroft! ¿are you there? ¿hello? ¡HELLO! ¡EARTH TO MYCROFT!>

Eureka could not reach me. Earth could not reach me. We had rounded a corner, and there were words there, words plain and hollow in the noisy street, those *words which must not be.* They overwhelmed me like the massed spears of a phalanx. I told you before how hard I fight to make myself believe in this drifting dream you call the present. Now I lost that fight.

"The Death of Majority is a lie!" the words began, floating through . . . no, I was not aware of what they floated through, the crowd, the air, for none were real to me. "There are lots of majorities today, real and dangerous majorities. Who owns the bash'house where you live? The Mitsubishi! Who owns the shop where you do business? The farm that produces the food on your table? The Mitsubishi! They own two thirds of the Earth, and compared to them the majority is camping on a sliver. The majority! You say it doesn't matter, but it makes everyone nervous, knowing the Mitsubishi could raise the world's rent at any time, double, triple, ten times, and no one could stop it. The majority fears the Mitsubishi, wants to stop them, to seize their land and redistribute it, by force if need be. This *Black Sakura* theft is someone lashing out, but everybody wants to. How long until there is a second attack, and a third? How long until they start to defend themselves?"

I remember when I was a young thing, two years orphaned and finally used to my reconstructed limbs. I was sitting in the garden with the Mardi children, talking to Geneva Mardi about sacrifice. The Senator sat us kids on the ground around him, while the grown-up with his stiff back monopolized the bench. He challenged us to come up with things we would do *anything* to save—a grim theme, but these were the sorts of games that Mardi children played.

The gardens at Alba Longa belonged to the Roman Emperor Domitian first, then to the popes, then to the MASONs, as imperial as a spot of Earth can be, but it was Brill's Institute that suggested to Emperor Aeneas MASON to make the Alba Longa site into a Denkergarten. The Emperor built five bash'houses around the grounds, and reviewed the world's great Campuses, inviting the five most promising, unusual, and ambitious new bash'es to share that paradise, to foster children and ideas, with no payment asked beyond the promise of future greatness and corresponding gratitude. The committee picked one bash' of ex-European Masons, one of Cousins who would later take me in, one mixed Brillists and Humanists, one Cousins and Masons, and, that rarest of treasures, the Mardi bash', which boasted six Hives and a Hiveless, while Apollo's constant visits almost granted it the seventh. Much has been written of my house, the fifth house, the service house, the groundskeepers and maintenance staff that served this think tank, and what inferiority complexes I might have picked up even before the accident as I grew up knowing all my playmates were genius children earmarked for greatness while I was not. It is somewhat unfair of me to contradict my biographers at this late point, but, for the record, I and, while they lived, my ba'sibs knew full well that a committee had chosen the other bash'es, while Aeneas MASON himself selected us. If we had to squander some hours on the not-unpleasant task of gardening, it was the only way the Emperor could secure an undebated seat for the one bash' for which he held the highest hopes. He visited me in the hospital after the accident that claimed the others, and from how he wept I might have been the last chapter of a now-lost masterpiece.

"What would you do *anything* to save, children?"

Laurel suggested "Mama!" first. Laurel Mardi was seven then, the prince of the bash', the Cousins' and Masons' golden boy before Jehovah eclipsed him, and famed for having left his toy cars in so many VIPs' offices that a flippant reporter at *The Romanov* started a weekly column, "Laurel Mardi's Road Trip," half an excuse to show world leaders cuddling a cute kid, but also a chronicle of the rise of what would obviously be one of the next generation's greats. "I'd do anything to save Mama!"

Geneva smiled, as if he had been waiting for the boy's reply. Geneva

Mardi was kind-faced but merciless, as only a Mason reared by Cousins can be: "Would you kill your papa to save your mama?" A lesser man would have stopped there, seeing tears already threatening to wet the child's cheeks. "Would you kill your papa and ba'pa Jules to save your mama?" he pressed. "Papa and Jules and me, would you kill me? And Ibis and Ken and Mycroft?" he nodded to the rest of us in the circle.

"The whole bash' then!" Ibis suggested, nine years old, crazy about animals and already loving me like more than family. "We'd do *anything* for the whole bash'!"

"Would you kill a different bash' to save this one?"

"Yes!" Ken answered instantly. He was six years old, a sponge for history, and inseparable from the wooden training sword which dragged behind him like a teddy bear. "I would. I'd also die for it."

Easy to say, Ken Mardi, but not easy to do, was it? I left you your katana and one hand intact with which to wield it, a way to end your pain, and I even promised to end your parents' suffering if you did the deed. Your mother was brave enough, Kohaku Mardi, when he felt the agonies of my poisons setting in, he slit his belly with a calm to make his ancestors proud, and, woman of iron, even wrote the message in his own blood, 33-67; 67-33; 29-71. You, though, who had boasted yourself a modern samurai, you watched the arctic around you turn the scattered pieces of your limbs to ice, and dropped your sword, and cried and suffered to the end. Hypocrite.

Geneva's lesson was not done. "How about two other bash'es?" he pressed. "Would you wipe out two bash'es to save ours?"

"If I had to."

"How about three? Four? Ten bash'es? How many is too many? Or let's count people. Five hundred people? A thousand people? A billion people?"

"A billion is too many," Laurel judged with his air of princely authority. "A thousand is too many too, even a hundred. One more than there are members in the bash' is too many."

Ibis shook her head. "Killing anyone at all is too many. Killing one more than there are in the bash' is when it turns from too many to too too many." Have you ever heard, reader, such a nauseatingly Cousinly sentiment? She would have been one, never doubt that, had I let her live.

"Then the bash' still isn't something you'd do anything to save, is it?" Geneva asked, eager to see what the children would try next. He never lost that calm, even when he hung dying on the cross, when I visited him to hear his last philosophy, which grew purer and more penetrating as sun and thirst helped him toward his God.

It was Laurel, already thinking like a statesman, who thought of, "The World. To save the world, the human race. You'd have to do anything for that, anyone would."

Ken was duty-bound to criticize his rival. "That's stupid. Of course you'd do anything to save the world, the world includes everything and you, so whatever you have to give up to save it would be destroyed anyway if you don't, so there's no real sacrifice. You have to do anything to save the world, there's no choice."

"No choice?" Apollo was with us too, Apollo Mojave, twenty-five, the hood of his Utopian coat thrown back so the sun could lend gold to his hair, though it hardly needed more. I don't know what Seine Mardi was doing that Apollo was with us and not with her, but I remember him stretched out on his back, his coat mimicking the grass beneath, so he seemed like a spirit only half-born out of the Earth, still wrapped in nature. "Would you destroy a better world to save this one?"

We were children, reader. We did not have our answers yet, not even I, but I do not present this memory as a lesson. Rather it is a sample of what the Mardi children went through every day with Geneva and the others, Kohaku, Senator Aeneas, the historians Makenna, Jie, Chiasa, Jules, the Brillist Fellow Mercer, Leigh who could almost out-mother her old ba'sib Bryar Kosala. Tully was not with us, Tully who was then just born, an infant when we were already imbibing harshest ethics. Tully was eight years old when I killed the others, as I was eight when the explosion deprived me of a birth bash' I hardly remember. Tully knows nothing, reader, and what he does know is more a secondhand reconstruction, built from interviews and old notes, than real memory. Still, even if it was just a shell of what the Mardis were, a feeble echo of *the words which must not be* which he poured out now into the streets of Barcelona, phalanx upon phalanx, I would have done *anything* to silence him.

"But that's just one majority!" Tully continued. I could see him, standing literally on a soapbox on the street corner, pleading with the passersby like an ancient doomsday preacher. "There's another. The Masons are growing. You've seen the numbers: three billion Masons, three point one, three point two. If they grow the others shrink. One point seven billion Cousins, one point two billion Europeans, barely a billion Brillists. They're sucking away the population, and everyone worries: how long until my Hive drops below a billion? Below half a billion? When my children grow up, will their Hive be as rare as Utopians? The majority fears the Masons, wants to strike back, to cut their numbers, see them shrink again. You get angry when you see a young person in the white suit of the *Annus Dialogorum,* don't you? When you debate with them, you don't try equitably to help them decide, you work actively to dissuade them. You think the Masons haven't noticed? You think they don't realize that, the larger they grow, the more hostile the majority becomes? How long until they start to defend themselves?"

Tully at least my mind could recognize in this vague haze of the present. Thirteen years hiding on the Moon had left Tully Mardi tall and artificial, muscles cultivated by prescribed routines rather than play, sustained on a diet rationed milligram by milligram. Childhood's departure had left his hair brown and his face lively and academic like his Brillist mother's, but I saw nothing of his father there, nothing of the eternal grin of Luther Mardigras, a true Mardigras born and raised, professional party-thrower who could turn four people locked in an elevator into a festival and tempt even Utopians to stray. As if to mock his forefathers' happy trade, Tully's face was all urgency, lips which had tasted many vitamins but never candy. He was twenty-two now, old enough to imagine himself a man, but not a Utopian. That step he would not take. He wore no coat, no vizor, just a loose blue shirt and gray pants, neither sloppy nor formal, and a Graylaw Hiveless sash, calculated to make him seem as generic as possible. Everyone can listen to an everyman.

"Don't you see it can't last?" He kept on preaching, words pouring out as from a broken dike. "Why did the French Revolution happen? Because a scattering of nobles took up all the land and oppressed the majority!"

"Don't say it," I mouthed, silent, to myself, to God, to no one.

"Why did the Roman Empire fall? It grew too big, too unwieldy, ignoring the strength and hate and envy of its majority neighbors!"

"Don't let them say it."

"It's happening already all around us. The property flows first, blood later. It's going to happen! It is happening!"

"Saladin, don't let them say it!"

"War! I'm talking about war! Revolution! Blood! You think it can't happen, that without nations, without armies there can't be war? We have police! They're forces enough. It can happen, and it will. You think violence has died out of our society? Look at Mycroft Canner! Look at all the followers that still worship Mycroft Canner! You think the world that made them can't make war? It's still in us, the death instinct, the willingness to kill, it's . . . Mycroft Canner!" Shaking, Tully raised his hand to point at me. "That's them! There! In the hat! That's Mycroft Canner!"

The first moment of a crisis is most precious, but I wasted it. I wasted it seeing. I could see now Tully's audience: four Brillists, two Masons, two Humanists, and a Mitsubishi, stopped in their tracks by this peculiar scrawny Hiveless on his high-tech crutches. I think it was the soapbox that attracted them, mad in this world where text and video can reach a billion at once. The live performance was powerful, the realization that he was speaking not to masses, but to them, words with only one chance to persuade, or fail and perish. They listened, not millions skimming the net, but nine live witnesses as Tully raised his hand to point at me.

"Mycroft Canner!" he repeated. "It's them! They've come to finish the job! Get them!"

Nine people would not have been enough to become a mob, but there were ringleaders waiting, four of them, posted around Tully's podium like guards, with metal pipes and baseball bats hungry in their hands. "We knew you'd come! You're dead, Canner! You hear? You're dead!"

"Run." I seized the nearest of my fellow Servicers and shoved them toward the alley behind us. "Run! All of you!"

A few obeyed, but most stayed, massing around me as if their brittle bodies could have done anything to block such rage. It didn't matter. Before they saw me spring I was past them, past my attackers, bounding along the street with a perfect synchrony of arms and legs that transformed the whole of my height to speed. My old self laughed seeing the others' faces as they watched, or tried to watch. Imagine, reader, in primordial days some vicious dinosaur, heavy with nightmare jaws, which chases a shimmering lizard up a slope, and the predator rejoices, already tasting the kill in its blood-starved mind, when, all at once, its slim prey spreads its feathered fins and takes to the air in a world that had not yet realized life could fly.

You dare try to catch me?

"Now! Play it now!"

They knew their enemy, my enemies. They had prepared the basest and best of traps for me: Canner Beat. I don't know where the speakers were, but they blasted it loud enough for the beats to vibrate through my bones. I lost this shadow world and was again in my two weeks, Ibis Mardi writhing beneath me, charred and already half-carcass as a red-hot crowbar punished blow by blow that brazen bitch who dared imagine she might claim the heart which belongs only to Saladin. I had speculated, when I decided to use my pacemaker to leave behind recordings of my heartbeat as I experienced the thrill of every kill, about what uses doctors and Brill's Institute would make of the tapes. But I so underestimated human genius that it never occurred to me that people might make art. Any rhythm can become a song. The accelerations, retards, and crescendos of my heartbeat, backed by fierce harmonics and suitably bloody lyrics, have spawned a genre and a culture of their own. I would like Canner Beat, I suspect, if I could hear it, but the rhythms strip me of all present tense and plunge my senses into replay. I tasted Ibis's meat again, felt hot blood spatter on my skin as she flailed at me with the shreds I had left of the hands which had too often clutched possessively at mine, and I saw Saladin's loving smile as we consummated our revenge. My opponents chose well. I tumbled blinded to the ground, barely awake as my attackers raised their bats around me.

I was rescued in that moment by a kind of U-beast called a Pillarcat. It is feline but long like a snake, with six pairs of legs all in a line, each a full cat's length apart, so it can wrap its purring coils around your ankles three times over, or nap on your belly wound in a spiral which overflows you like a living blanket. This one was green, a lively new-leaf green, with a golden underbelly and a constant purr which almost masked the hum of electronics underneath. It knew me. It climbed my back faster than anyone could block it, and draped itself around my shoulders like a sensayer's long scarf, just as it used to do around Apollo.

"Crap! Halley! Stupid cat! Get it off them!"

"Halley! Come here, kitty! Good kitty!"

Halley rooted its many, many claws into my clothes and released a hiss which would have made an anaconda proud.

"You stupid cat!" The attackers froze around me, bats and fists slack like wilted branches. "What are you doing? Mycroft Canner killed your maker! You were there! Don't you remember?"

Something killed the music now, and memory released me enough to see, if not to run. Hands seized me from behind, not violent but controlling, gloved in an electric tingling which leeched the strength from my muscles, as laughter does. Numbing gloves. I was steered backwards like a puppet and already safely bundled in a blanket before my invisible captors threw back their hoods of Griffincloth to reveal the glares on their vizors.

"This violence is forbidden." The foremost of them stepped forward between me and Tully's warriors, and let his coat switch from invisibility mode to his Utopia, a storm-black sky where lightning cities appeared and disappeared fast as the pouring rain. "Disperse."

"Fucking Utopians! Why are you protecting Mycroft Canner?"

It was one of the audience that shouted it, not the guards, for they instead stood in silent disbelief. I recognized them now, by their betrayed faces,

European shirts and English strat bands, I recognized them as those pub regulars who had adopted Apollo back in Liverpool. I'm sorry; you did deserve revenge.

The rest of the mob was not so shocked. "Astroturds!"

"They've been hiding Mycroft Canner all this time!"

Flying stones and rubbish joined the words.

"Disperse!" The lead Utopian summoned a dragon now, black but lined with lightning, which spread its wings over the lot of us and glared down at the mob with compound eyes, each formed of a dozen bloodred laser sights which locked on clubs and fists. A second dragon joined it, whiskered, Asian style, long like a ribbon and glowing with rainbow flame. It slid in around us like a wall, purring with the force of fifty lions and dusting the mob with warm mist from the hundreds of tiny jets which helped it float. In truth, the two must have been there the whole time, invisible in their Griffincloth scales, but in the heat of almost-battle no one cared how the dragons functioned: there were dragons. The mob backed off. A moat of dead space opened between them and the U-beasts, and the warmonger himself stepped to the fore.

"Mycroft Canner!" Tully had another Utopian stalking behind him, though whether to protect him or restrain him I could not guess. "Why did you come here?"

Halley left me and ran back to Tully, content, I imagine, now that I was in trusted hands. "It was an accident," I answered. "I didn't know you were here."

Tully let the Pillarcat circle his legs. Its touch pulled his pants taut so I could see the contours of braces around his joints, unused to Earth's harsh gravity. "Give me Apollo's *Iliad*."

"It isn't yours," I answered.

A Utopian car descended over us, and my captor-saviors gave me no chance to resist as they bundled me inside.

"Give it to me!" Tully shouted after us. "I'm the one who's going to finish it. Finish everything! Everything we started!"

The Utopian behind him, wrapped in a coat of pale slow-motion birds, placed a restraining hand on Tully's shoulder. "Stop this, Tully. Canner's right, the book's not yours. Now calm the mob."

He who had spent thirteen expensive years in the protection of Luna City could not disobey his benefactors, but he left me a last glare, defiant arrogance which promised to do all in his power to destroy me. "Everyone!" I heard him begin. "The Utopians haven't been hiding Mycroft Canner. They've been hiding me from Mycroft Canner, and what they did here they did to protect you, to keep you from becoming what Mycroft Canner wanted you to become: murderers . . ."

That was all I was allowed to hear, for the car's door closed and sealed me in its capsule as it spirited me to whatever haven the Utopians had chosen.

"We'll hush it up if possible." One of them was with me in the car, hard to spot since their hooded coat (I could not guess the sex) made nothing of the car seat but a car seat. "There weren't too many witnesses."

"You're helping Tully do this?" I asked. "You can't help Tully do this!"

"Apollo asked us to take care of Tully."

My hands shook. "I saw Kohaku Mardi's numbers in the Censor's office, perfectly, as if someone engineered this *Black Sakura* affair to follow the Mardi's plan. Please tell me that wasn't you."

Their answer was sweet as rescue to a drowning man. "We neither help nor hinder, only ward."

"Even so, what Tully's doing isn't just warning people, they're riling them up, making it worse. They could start the avalanche and really make it happen! Millions could die!"

I heard the rustle of a U-beast but could not see where in the car it lurked. "Don't talk like other people, Mycroft."

I shook my head. "That's not what I mean. You can't let people associate Utopia with Tully's message. Tully's a maniac. They'll make it seem like you're encouraging a war! The other six Hives will all ally against you, the worst combination. It won't go like Tully thinks. The Mardis' predictions were wrong. Kohaku's numbers have already happened. We're at the crisis point, past it, but it doesn't matter anymore. You know about Jehovah. War can't break out between the Masons and Mitsubishi while Caesar and Andō are both fathers of the same Son. But if you let Tully keep pushing for it like this, if you let yourselves be seen protecting Tully, then everyone will think you're warmongers too. I don't know if even Caesar can protect you then."

"We will not let ourselves be seen."

Exhaustion took me. I know when not to argue with Utopia. They knew my thoughts, my arguments, better than my shock-shattered breath could make them. We rode in silence, but I used that silence, offering a voiceless prayer to any God who might be listening: please let my Saladin strike in time.

Julia, I've Found God!

«DOMINIC! WHERE HAVE YOU BEEN? YOU'RE WET AND STINKY!»

«Far less stinky now that I'm wet—I hosed myself off at a hydrant just for you. Julia, I've found God!»

«I wasn't aware they were missing.» Julia Doria-Pamphili's voice had traces of concern, and almost humor, but all drowned in a pleasurable croon at Dominic's arrival. «Did their parents know?»

«Not the True God, I mean This Universe's God, the Idiot Who created disease, and entropy, and decided to imprison sentience within these lumps of dirt.» He thumped his chest. «I've found *Him*.»

I could hear them through the wall, and see a sliver of the room if I pressed my cheek to the crack between door and doorframe, but the makeshift prison of Julia's office closet offered me no further liberty as I sat locked within, my sensayer's harsh prescription when the Utopians delivered me into her custody: after such a shock as seeing Tully after thirteen years, I was to take two hours to rest and think, do nothing and serve no one, and if she had to confiscate my tracker and lock me in her closet to enforce that, so be it.

«Did you ask God if there's an afterlife?» Julia asked at once. Perhaps no one on Earth was as prepared as the Conclave Head for this eventuality.

«We aren't on speaking terms yet.» Dominic stood close to her by the sound of it, close enough that his rich French resonated with the weight of their two bodies pressed against each other. Of course they spoke French together, gentle reader; she is European, and he civilized. «We haven't actually spoken face to face, but I've found His avatar, His manifestation on this Earth, pathetic little thing.»

Fear made my pacemaker offer a gentle warning bleep.

«Can I see the avatar too?» Julia asked at once.

Dominic laughed, and Julia released a little gasp, the herald of others coming. It was too soon for either to have removed their clothes, but not for Dominic's expert fingers to have navigated Julia's slacks and found the entrance to her pleasure.

«Not yet,» he answered, zeal turning his voice into a hiss. «Not until I'm done.»

«You're so mean, Dominic, teasing me like this.»

«I'll make it up to you. Here, I smuggled out some leftovers, another of Chagatai's masterpieces.» I heard the rustle of a package.

«That hardly makes up for it.»

«Oh, that's not how I'm going to make up for it.» I heard the hiss of fabric shifting over skin.

«Mmm. You've a lot to make up for, Dominic, being gone so long, making everybody worry. I'm sure you've made Jehovah worry too.»

«I have. I know I have.» The two of them were close outside the door now, and I heard the source of Dominic's voice move lower, as if he sat, or sank to his knees. «I've caused Him pain.»

«Then we'd better get started.»

«Bless me, Mother . . . for I have sinned . . . It's been . . . eight days . . . since my last . . . confession . . .» A wet slurp came between every phrase, eliciting light gasps from Julia, each sharper than the last as her breath grew fast and shallow. «And in this week . . . I've strayed . . . farther than ever . . . from the path . . . of God.»

«Yes!» Julia's voice lost nothing of its strength as it grew heated. «What have you done?»

«I've abandoned Him . . . cut Him off from me . . . sight . . . sound . . . word . . . I left Him blind. . . . He has so few senses . . . in this universe . . . imagine . . . how it must hurt Him . . . losing touch . . . with one of His own.»

«Yes!» she cried, perhaps more loudly than she intended. «You've been cruel.»

«Sometimes . . . I can't stand it, thinking how it must hurt Him.» I heard fierce motion now, Dominic leaping to his feet perhaps, or pulling Julia down to him, or turning her around to take her from the other side. «Can you imagine, Julia? To hurt Him so much? To make Him think about me, and wish for me, and need me, and be powerless. Desperate, Julia, I've made omnipotent Jehovah desperate.» His voice rejoiced. «Do you think He trembled, Julia? Do you think He cried?»

The Conclave Head had barely breath enough to answer as his rhythms shook her body. «I . . . I . . . can't . . . imagine . . . that.»

«I can.» Dominic panted too, the panting of anticipation, like hounds before they're loosed upon the fleeing fox. «But you're right, that's not enough to make Him weep. Not nearly enough. One straying angel won't make God tremble. But I've done more. I've kept secrets from Him too, this week. Secrets I know He wants to hear. He's been searching so long for some hint, some message from another God, and now I've found one and I haven't told Him!» His zeal made her cry out, a little yelp with every thrust, half-breathed, since he gave her no time to fill her lungs. «Now He's still suffering, still wondering if He's the only creature of His kind, afraid, except it's because of me now. I'm doing it to Him; I'm the one keeping Him alone in the dark, and I'm the one with the power to end it!»

«Nnng! Nnng! Will you?»

«Not yet,» Dominic snarled the words. «It's not enough! Just traces of another God won't do it, I need more. I need to know the nature of this stupid God, access, answers, something horrible.»

«Yes.»

«I need to find out enough about this God to make Jehovah sick, to make Him hate this God and this God's universe too much to forgive.»

«Yes, yes!»

«It won't be hard. There are already so many things about this universe Jehovah can't forgive. He's trapped here, and once I prove this universe is ruled by a horrible and callous Being, He'll lose all hope of ever being able to fix it like His own.»

«Yes! Callous! Yes! Oh, God!»

«Then He'll break down! Omniscient, omnipotent Jehovah forced to admit He can never bring those powers here.»

«What heat! Ah! Fuck!»

«He'll break down, and He'll tremble, and He'll cry and come to me, and then I'll take Him in my arms and comfort Him and make Him mine!»

«Ah! Oh, God damn it! God fuck!»

«Scream! Scream, you holy little slut!»

«Ah! Yes! Fuck! Oh, God! Christ! Yes!»

Enough, Mycroft. Some absurdities I can tolerate, but not this. Make up thy mind: dost thou write pornography or not? If this is not pornography, then skip this vacuous and offensive filth; if it is, then at least fulfill thy dirty duty properly: give me some life, some heaving breasts, some color. Describe fully or skip entirely; this obscene transcript satisfies no one.

Ah! Delicate master! Forgive me if I stare in tender wonder for a moment upon discovering that, in your purity, you do not recognize this form, which is to me so chillingly familiar. It is a quotation, this strange sexual script, not my invention but the spawn of that dark author whose phantom can nevermore be exorcised. We have stared together at the Enlightenment's keen sun, reader, and cannot now escape its tendriled afterglow, which lingers in our vision, black and strange: Donatien Alfonse François Marquis de Sade. Since I cannot perfectly recall the grunts and blasphemies with which the hound and high priestess punctuated their climax, what better substitute than the lines which spawned them? Or, rather, spawned him, then, through him, educated her. Sade's *La Philosophie dans le Boudoir* is an educational treatise, intended for young ladies, its author claims, but with models for all genres of libertine, young and old, expert and novitiate. It is not a thrilling read for the unenlightened; indeed, I reproduce it here quite faithfully, pure dialogue, naked of any description beyond the occasional summary of who inserts what where. Sade writes the least erotic sex scenes you might imagine, alternating with long stretches of dialogue on moral philosophy, politics, religion, family life, the origins of the state and patriarchy, much as one might find in Locke or Montesquieu, or spitfire Thomas Paine.

I confess myself stunned, Mycroft, to find Earth's most infamous pornographer so dull. What is the point of such unerotic erotica? Whom does it satisfy?

Why, its dark author, of course, and his libertine contemporaries, whose lust-blushes fired, not at heaving bosoms, but at the silken rustle of ink-wet page proofs, the rhythmic, stallion groan of the printing press, and the spear-thrust climax of a well-proved thesis. Sade's public was unique in history, new radicals who lapped up forbidden pamphlets professing such scandalous suggestions as that, if he wished, a man might choose to examine his religion rationally, refuse taxation without representation, or stick his dick up a cow's arse. Philosophy and pornography were both forbidden fruits, sold by one circuit of underground vendors. Even Diderot, *le Philosophe*, was jailed in younger days for writing porn—how better for our young arch-atheist to earn his daily baguette? But to guard the Encyclopedia, Diderot hid his atheism, and begged his colleagues too to feign tameness until their Great Project was safely launched. Sade wore no masks. He earned France's fear for what he did to lovers, and he earned history's for articulating why one should. Did you laugh, master, when Madame recited Sade's proof from the roundness of the anus that, if there is a God, then He endorses sodomy? Deeper in that dialogue, as you watch Sade's monsters prove with the same wit (and mid-orgasm) that, if all men are created equal, then nothing is more natural than parricide, you will not laugh. Sade warns that he who would use Reason as a key to open one door opens many, and he who would make Reason a scythe to fell injustices must beware what else the blade might cut. We did not know that the threads sustaining the moral warp of our society were so interconnected until we pulled one. Since before man learned to count his summers, we had sown each generation's seeds in tradition's soil. Suddenly the Enlightenment would sow our seeds instead among the furrowed pages of the Encyclopedia, and water them with Reason. If the fruit grows black and strange, it will not matter that we have a *philosophe* willing to taste first and test for us whether we have raised manna or poison; as *liberté* and *égalité* grow universal, we have no other crop left on which to feed. Forge your new world carefully, Patriarch, warns our Marquis, lest it be filled with me. Gentle master, you have watched Nietzsche and Kafka crawl from that primordium; you cannot call Sade wrong.

«Aren't you afraid that Jehovah will cast you down into the fiery pit and all that?» Julia asked it with the wilting but delighted breath of denouement. «They'll know what you've done, and why. You deserve it, now more than ever. This isn't just breaking commandments, this is torturing your own God.»

«Oh, I'll deserve it, a thousand times over, but He can't cast me out. In this despicable universe He needs every angel He can get. Countless millions He has at home but here, what, four?»

«Does Jehovah really hate this universe that much?»

«Oh, yes, He just doesn't realize yet that what He feels is named hate.» Dominic was already sniffing, moving again around Julia as if scouting the next assault. «He tried to explain in our last session how suffering works in His universe. There sentience can elect to participate in straining experiences to increase its own complexity, like a pattern growing more complicated while the object the pattern decorates remains unchanged. Except, time and space don't exist in His universe, so the pattern also exists without the object, in a sense. I don't understand fully what He was trying to say, He broke down halfway through, as always, no vocabulary in my measly languages, but the basics were clear: if He met the callous Bastard who designed *this* universe of suffering, He'd . . . criticize, protest, scream—do you think He's capable of screaming? Perhaps not. Either way, it's time to prove that, if He did scream, if He wore His sacred throat to blisters screaming, this universe's Maker wouldn't care.»

Again, a pleasure moan from Julia. Did you feel something like this coming, reader? That something was off about our Conclave Chief, that night with Thisbe and Carlyle? Her luxuriant hair, her suit a little too form-fitting, her touch, picking at Carlyle's scarf or brushing back his hair with those perfect filed nails. Gender, reader, a hint of it like spice. It all flows from one spring. Imagine young Julia, just a few years into her teaching, as drunk on the idea of God as Carlyle, when into her classroom stalks this devil Dominic, asking to join her priesthood. Imagine the force of him, how utterly training failed her in the face of this this malicious, masculine, sensual, tyrannically honest beast. All her life she studied modern humans, but this is a mastodon, a phoenix, a lost thing come to life. What arts she learned from him, and how they changed her. You say he corrupted her, reader? Perhaps he did, or perhaps this daughter of popes and emperors was waiting for something to breathe new power into the clichés she learned in training. If Julia has transformed hundreds of one-time clients by slicing those healing wounds that leave them better people, she learned her surgeon skills from Dominic, and Dominic from his God.

«You're serious?» Julia asked.

«Always, but about what in particular?»

«You've really found proof of the existence of God?»

«Yes.» He fired the answer like a shot. «Yes I have, and here's the bargain: if you wait and don't start snooping after it yet, I'll show you, soon, as soon as I'm done with what I need it for. But if you start interfering, then I'm going to hide it from you, and I know you could track it eventually, but I can make that take a long time. You'll have it sooner, much sooner, if you let me bring it to you when I'm ready.»

She sighed. «That's a lot to ask of a sensayer.»

«I know. I'll make it up to you.»

«Mmmm.» Such a contented purr. «And what else have you to confess today?»

«Not much. I tortured some thugs, broke into some houses, stole some things, took three prisoners, tormented and traumatized a child, started to seduce a married woman but didn't bother finishing. You know I don't think I've broken my vow of chastity once this week, except just now.»

She sounded worried. «That's not good for your health.»

«I've been busy. Besides»—I heard here the creak of a straining chair or table—«the world is settling down. There aren't many left who are rebellious enough that I need to get on top of them, and not many with the authority to force me underneath.»

They laughed together, though I'm sure the joke was more in how they lay than what he said.

«Julia, I need your help.»

«With what?»

«A few things. First, what can you tell me about a Cousin sensayer called Carlyle Foster?»

«Carlyle? They're one of mine.»

«One of your what? Students? Parishioners? »

«One of *mine* one of mine.»

Knowing Julia as I did, I had suspected so much, but it was good to be certain.

«Oh, that's too bad.» He laid more kisses now, a series of them with a steady rhythm as if progressing inch by inch along some part of Julia like footsteps. «Are you fond of her?»

«One of my best, extremely sweet and loyal, and credulous. I've no other moles that good at seeming benign. Why, has something happened to Carlyle?»

«Not yet, but may I have her?»

«Once? Or in general?»

«I need to break her. Make her mine.»

«Oh, please don't,» Julia crooned.

«I don't see a way around it.» Furniture creaked again as their weight shifted. «It's a small world and we've learned so many techniques from one another. It's inevitable we'll get in one another's way from time to time.»

Julia's voice turned coaxing, like a child's. «Can't you hold off a bit? Carlyle's in the middle of a mission.»

Dominic enjoyed this laugh. «Using her in your chess game with Danaë, are you? Making a move on the Saneer-Weeksbooth bash'? Good target.»

«Mmm. Frustrating target. They've been impregnable with that stubborn Esmerald Revere refusing to let any of them have even one session with anybody else. You remember the one time I tricked Cato Weeksbooth into coming here?»

«Of course.» An even darker laugh. «It was the same when I showed up at the house, ran for his life. Good instincts, the clever little thing.»

«Yes, that's . . . ouuh.» She lost her breath here, as at the touch of a good masseur. «That's—mmh—why I need Carlyle there, no one can fake harmless like Carlyle because Carlyle isn't faking. That bash' is a fortress; only a mosquito can get through.»

«Was it you who got Esmerald Revere to snuff herself?» Dominic asked.

«No, that wasn't me. Pure good luck, or someone else, but not me.»

His voice turned black. «It wasn't luck.»

«Who, then?»

«I don't know.»

Julia sighed. «I think someone threatened to kill Cato Weeksbooth if they ever talked to me.»

«Could be. You know I'd kill most of my minions if they ever talked to you.»

She chuckled. «Flatterer. Is it someone in the bash', do you think? Ockham Saneer?»

«I don't know.»

From my view behind the door's crack I caught a glimpse of one of them, an arm, and maybe Dominic's ponytail as he tilted back in a chair.

«Come on, you spent time there,» Julia coaxed. «I know you can smell a killer.»

«Not when my nose is too full of God. Besides, Ockham Saneer stinks to high heaven of killer legally, it's hard to scent anything under that.»

«What about Sniper? Wouldn't it be great if it were Sniper?»

I heard a smack of skin on skin, and something in their motion shifted, fabric rustling with subtle struggle as their silhouettes passed across my line of sight.

«Which are you after, anyway?» Dominic asked. «The cars or Sniper?»

«Hm?»

«In the Saneer-Weeksbooth bash'.» Kisses slowed his speech again, drier and more breathy than before: an animal nuzzling. «Those two . . . little set-sets . . . could feed you dirt on . . . the whole world . . . second only to . . . the tracker system . . . but on the other hand . . . Sniper is . . . Sniper.»

«I'm after both.»

A skull clunked against wood. «That's avarice, that is,» he snapped. «A sin.»

«I suppose it is. Which are you after?»

«Neither. I need Carlyle for unrelated business. But if you had to pick, or . . . let me put it another way: can I have Carlyle if I give you Sniper?»

«You can have your pick of all my creatures if you give me Sniper!»

I heard a sharp inhalation, the beginning of a word, or of an ecstasy? «I won't cheat you, Julia. Carlyle Foster is more than what she seems. You should know what you're trading away before we seal the bargain.»

«I know what I have, Dominic. That's why I took them as a student in the first place. Carlyle de la Trémoïlle. Even has a dick between their legs to make them a legal heir. Does Ganymede have any other bastards?»

«She's not Ganymede's bastard, she's Danaë's. But no, the Duke has no bastards I know of, so little Carlyle de la Trémoïlle is heir presumptive.»

«Mmm. Must qualify as an Earl or something, have you looked it up?»

«Doesn't matter; theological titles trump.»

«Ganymede's heir . . . ,» Julia crooned. «Is there a father? My best guess was incest, but if you say the child isn't Ganymede's . . . »

«There was a father, but Madame does not tolerate the . . . spoiling of her creatures. I would have burned the corpse myself, but Hotaka Andō Mitsubishi had that privilege.»

«Ah. Strong man, Andō. So what does Dominic want with the little prince . . . de . . . la . . . Tré . . . mo . . . ïlle?» Kisses or little nips punctuated Julia's syllables. «Is Ganymede getting a bit too independent for Madame's tastes? Needs a tighter leash?»

«Actually, my needs are unrelated to the Cousin's birth.»

«What are they related to? This universe's God?»

«Later.»

«Tell me?» Another creaking. «Tell me now.»

There was a long breath's pause and then a sudden . . . I cannot call it a dash or rush since they stayed in the same place, but I heard some fierce and almost violent shift, someone breaking free of a hold perhaps?

«I said later. But my offer stands. Carlyle de la Trémoïlle for Sniper?»

«For Sniper? Anything.»

«Done!» I heard a rush of paper. I doubt, reader, that Mephistopheles has ever plunked a contract on a table with greater zeal. «Here, look at these.»

I heard shuffling through pages. «A child's drawings?»

In my efforts to stay silent I bit down on my hand hard enough to leave a mark.

«I have a kid I have to break. Fast,» Dominic continued. «I figured my dearest teacher could give her floundering student a few pointers.» Whatever motion Dominic made to sweeten the flattery made Julia gasp. «You remember I flunked child sensaying twice; they're just too alien, these neutered little monsters.»

«Mmm. I remember. It's so fun flunking you.»

The sound Dominic made has no better name than 'growl.'

«Interesting.» Papers rustled one by one. «The iconography is like a young child's but the hand-eye coordination is too good. How old's this kid?»

«Older than ten, less than fifteen, I'd say. I don't know when these drawings were done, though.»

«Mmmm. Short blond hair?»

«That's right.»

«Usually draws themself wearing blue, that's reasonably standard. How old's the ba'sib?»

«Ba'sib?»

«Or sister? This one. See, here is the kid's depiction of themself, and they appear over and over with this second kid in red with long curly hair.»

«A sister?» The paper crunched as if he nearly ripped it. «I've heard no mention of a sister.»

«Wait, the attributes are varying. The hair was red there, here it's got blue streaks, and here they have wings. I think you've got yourself an imaginary big sister here.»

«Perfection!» he half-shrieked. «Twenty seconds and you have it, my exquisite Julia! Let me leave fresh offerings at your divine altar!»

The ardor of his thanks would not let her speak for some few moments. «You can use that?» she asked.

«Oh, yes. God's as good as mine.» Another pause before his words grew fast and serious. «I have your word you won't start poking, right? I swear I'll bring you the proof when I'm ready, but if you probe, or if you breathe a word of this to any living soul, I swear by Lord God Jehovah Himself I'll kill you, dearest Julia, even you.»

She took a long, smug breath. «Too late.»

«What do you mean?»

«It's too late not to breathe it to another living soul. I've got a witness hidden in the closet.»

Anger drove the voicing from Dominic's breath, leaving it shallow as a ghost's. «What?»

«You never asked if we were alone in the office, barging in like this. At this close distance I'm quite sure they've heard every syllable.» Her voice played, not laughter but its beginnings peppering her syllables. «You know what I use that closet for.»

«A spy?»

«We've had quite a session today, too: proof of God, Jehovah, Jehovah's universe, Carlyle de la Trémoïlle . . . »

Dominic took one long breath to steel himself, and then a second. «Julia, Julia, you clever stupid bitch.» Furniture crashed across the room, a sound of shattering, a body hitting wall or floor, and I heard the croak of a throat losing all breath at once. «Why now?» Dominic screamed. «If you wanted me to kill you I could've done it any time, why now? The one week that I don't have time to get away with murder!»

She struggled to gain breath enough to whisper. «To see that look on your face.»

Violence shattered another fixture of the office. «Damn it! I really would've shown you, too! You're a week away from seeing God, Julia! What stupid time is that to make me ... damn it! Damn it and damn you!» I heard the hiss of cold steel being drawn.

«Oh, don't I at least get to watch you kill my witness first?» Her voice still teased like a disappointed playmate. «I've always wanted to see you do the deed in person.»

«You think this is funny, bitch? I don't have time for ... Fine. I'll count that as my teacher's last request.»

The sword made a strange, strained singing as it turned from target to target.

«The key's on the bookshelf,» she volunteered, «no sense you wrecking the door.»

A fresh crash must have been some part of him striking some part of her. «You try anything while my back's turned and I'll flay your face off and show it to you.»

«Mmm. You would, too, wouldn't you?»

I backed up as the key clicked in the lock.

«Your spy's lucky I don't have time for anything elaborate, just a ... Mycroft?»

At first Dominic was just a looming blackness with a sword, but my light-starved eyes soon adapted to the glare enough for detail. He had removed his jacket and his gloves, baring the black of shirt and waistcoat, but the rest of him was fully clothed. Rain had undone his ponytail, letting the black-brown tresses fall damp around his brow and neck, framing a face which was a mask of horror and delight. He laughed, Julia with him, uproarious belly laughs, both of them doubling over as laughter's agony wracked their guts.

«Mycroft Canner!» Dominic repeated. Even the sword hung loose in his fingers as the great joke had its day. «Oh, my dear Julia, what a cruel and fabulous thing you are! Come here!» He hefted her from the litter of broken coffee table where he had flung her, and landed a kiss which threatened to maul her face in its enthusiasm.

Julia reveled in her victory kiss, eyes dancing at the tickle as he lapped the blood his wrath had spilled from her lip. «Mmm. You're welcome, though I wish you hadn't smashed the office so.»

«I'll have it fixed.» He flexed his shoulders. «Oh, you brilliant woman, I feel as refreshed as if I'd had a good duel! And thou, Mycroft!" He switched to English here, tucking his sword point under my chin and reeling me toward him like a hooked fish. "I thought I'd have to go on a long hunt for thee, yet here thou art, delivered in the flesh. So much less effort, not that thou couldst have hid from me for long, couldst thee?"

A tap of the blade against my shoulder bade me kneel, and I obeyed, tucking my hands behind me like a prisoner and keeping my eyes on the floor. "No, Brother Dominic."

Julia had fresh eyes for me now that I seemed to matter. "I didn't know you needed Mycroft." I dared a glance up at her, and saw that she still wore her socks, while her jacket and open shirt clung to her arms and shoulders like a cicada's half-discarded skin.

"Everybody in the world needs Mycroft," Dominic gloated, "but they're not getting him anymore. He's coming home like a good slave, and not leaving until I say so." The rapier traced my jaw line. "No more playing around with toys for thee."

I could not afford to let tears fall here. "Yes, Brother Dominic." Trust the Major. The Major is the most experienced tactician to walk this Earth in centuries. Trust the Major: Bridger will be safe.

"You're not still using Mycroft, are you?" Dominic asked Julia, letting the sword hang limply in his hand, as a violinist lets his bow droop when he stops to chat. "I wouldn't want to interfere."

"No, Mycroft's done with confession for today." Julia drew close enough to pet my head, gently, as one does for an old dog no longer strong enough for vigorous scratching. "They've had a hard day today, our Mycroft. You know the last surviving Mardi just came back from the Moon."

Dominic's brow twitched. "Is that so?"

"Mmm. Tully Mardi. Exposed Mycroft in the street in front of a dozen people, with the Servicer uniform in plain sight no less. Mycroft will need our protection even more now than usual, poor thing. And I'd recommend switching them from an outdoor pet to an indoor pet; outside's not safe anymore."

Dominic laughed darkly. "Such a thoughtful protectress thou hast in Julia, Mycroft, when she's so cold to everybody else. It's quite unfair." His light kick showered me with shards of desk. "Clean up this mess. This is thy fault after all, is it not, *stray dog?*" His actual words were '*Chien errant,*' in French, his common title for me.

"Yes, Brother Dominic."

"Apologize to the Pontifex Maxima for ruining her office."

"I apologize, Your Holiness."

He sheathed his blade. "Now, work."

I dared not raise my eyes, but could see Dominic's smile reflected in a fallen cup as he watched me crawl. Dominic has never sodomized me, hard as you may find that to believe. He gets no satisfaction subjugating something which has never shown the faintest hint of fighting back.

But thou must fight back, Mycroft. Would that be your advice here, my brave reader? *Fight for thy freedom. So much hangs upon thee at this moment, not just Bridger but innocent Carlyle, brave Sniper whom these perverts' dark deal threatens. Save them! This is thy moment, when thine oppressor's blade sleeps in its sheath. This Dominic may be a master swordsman, but thou, thou art Mycroft Canner.*

No, reader. Your visit to my era is brief, but I must live through to-morrow, and the next day, and the next of my long penance. Dominic is the seneschal who controls access to that house in Paris which has been my harbor, longer than Cielo de Pájaros. If Bridger were unguarded, for him I would destroy myself, but Bridger has the Major, and the Major defeated even me. As for Carlyle and Sniper, worthy as they are, I will not do them short-term good at the price of sacrificing all my future useful-ness. Perhaps I could overpower Dominic, escape for now, but I would have to return someday, and soon, to face his waiting discipline. I do not fear short-term retribution—pain and degradation I accept to save good men. But rebellion against Dominic would forever forfeit my place as a trusted servant at Madame's. A cell would wait for me the next time I braved her threshold, where forever after I would wait like a tool in its box, ready to be used but impotent to start tasks of my own. I must have the freedom of that house, reader, I must. I can work there, for all the Powers, for Earth—no, not for Earth, for Him, reader, for Him, for Ἄναξ Jehovah. This is the first time that I have shown you my own title for Him, Ἄναξ (*Anax*). It is Greek, of course. Old Greek. 'Lord' is a feeble translation. Think of the trial-weary Trojans, with the smoke of the war fires rising around their walls, year in, year out, and the prophets warn them, soon, soon, soon the day of death and slavery will come to swallow Troy and all her children, yet, in spite of Fate, remaining pious at heart toward that one power that has shown them loyalty and kindness, the grateful Trojans raise their hands in prayer to distant Lord Apollo. Then they use Ἄναξ, and so do I.

Julia stopped me with a soft hand on the back of my neck. "No need to fuss about cleaning up the mess, Dominic, really. If you're in a rush, take Mycroft and go."

"Are you sure? This is partly my fault too. I haven't had a chance to thank you properly yet."

"Go." She handed him my tracker. "I have another regular coming in half an hour, I can have them clean it up."

He thanked her with a last kiss. "I'm going to pay you back for this, I mean it, and for giving me Carlyle Foster. Clear your schedule for . . . how much of tomorrow can you clear?"

"From noon on if I have to."

"Clear it all. I'll send you word where to meet me."

"What for?"

"Your payment." He kicked me in the side, gently for him. "Fetch thy hat, stray. We're leaving."

I crawled to fetch it from the closet, not daring to rise until he took me by the collar and hauled me to my feet. It was Dominic who first taught me the art of hat-wearing, and gave me the round and shapeless cap that has shielded me from recognition so many times. It was thirteen years ago, almost to the day. I had come to petition his aid in trying to understand Ἄναξ Jehovah. He saw me, with my trembling and my suppliant eyes, and threw his head back, laughing. "Mycroft, thou must have a hat so thou mayest remove it in the presence of thy betters!" He was right. It is a comforting symbol, a way to gesture my submission without alarming people with the antiquated titles 'master,' 'madam,' 'sir.' It is a comfort to have something to fidget with as I stand in obedience before free men. A welcome gift. I thank Dominic for it still, from time to time.

Dominic paused on the threshold, throwing his sword arm around my shoulders like a brother, close and ready to grasp my throat. "Oh, Julia, any advice on interrogating a prisoner you can't touch?"

Her eyebrows perked. "Can't touch?"

"I'd squish him." Dominic's eyes danced as he looked to me. "What's a good comparison, Mycroft? Let's say he has one of those bone diseases so he'll shatter if you shake him too hard. Mentally he's a toughie, though. Sleep deprivation's getting me nowhere slowly."

Dominic had my tracker still, playing between his fingers like a toy. How long, my mind raced, how long since I had last counted all eleven tiny soldiers?

"If you want fast results, threaten a loved one," she suggested. "Otherwise theology as usual, or hot wax. Hot wax is almost too gentle."

He frowned. "Not gentle enough for this little one, but I'll think of something. Thank you, Pontifex Maxima." He turned to me. "Come, stray. I've a thousand questions for thee. I look forward to seeing thee struggle to get out of answering."

DEO EREXIT SADE

THINGS CHANGE HERE, READER. OR, MORE APTLY, YOU CHANGE, while this world you visit stays the same. I promised I would show the wires beneath the cloth. Eureka smells them, tastes them, itches with them, whatever name we pick for her computer senses. She knows the flights of cars are wrong, that there is one extra pull of gravity, to make us realize Dark Matter is out there changing things. Now you are ready. Kohaku Mardi was always wrong. 33-67; 67-33; 29-71, it will not tip us into war, no matter what the numbers say. Sometimes the magician wheels a house of cards onto his stage, and he shakes, and blows, and threatens, pulls the tablecloth from under it, and it doesn't fall. Because it never really was a house of cards. It was one long piece of paper, folded and disguised to feign fragility.

"Felix, come away from there," the Anonymous called. "You're making Danaë uncomfortable."

Brillist Institute Headmaster Felix Faust lingered by his favorite feature of the Salon de Sade: a picture window, framed by damask curtains, looking down over the Flesh Pit. "There are two 9-3-3-11-10-4-3-10s topping each other down there," he said. "That's the third time I've seen that combo, I wonder why that set are so attracted to their own."

"Come away," the Anonymous repeated. "You can do research on your own time." Here the Anonymous, like Faust, wore the costume of the period, lace cuffs and styled wig, his coat a rich green-black over a waistcoat of burgundy-violet silk, almost imperial. He wore a mask, not grotesque or fancy, and certainly not enough to keep one who knew him from recognizing him, just a little black strip around the eyes, a symbol. Many imagine that all Madame's clients would wear masks, but that badge of honor belongs to the Anonymous alone.

Faust's eyes, windows of the ever-churning brain which feeds upon his body like a parasite, rolled across to the Anonymous. "Closing the curtain isn't going to get Bryar ready faster. Neither is you venting your impatience on the rest of us."

The Anonymous squeezed his cane, as if to strangle its heavy gilded head. "You're the one who wanted Danaë at this meeting, Felix. The least you can do is be courteous now that they're here."

Faust let the curtain fall and turned back to the salon with its ring of couches, amber velvet on ebony frames, perfect against the ivory-tinted rug. "I apologize, Princesse. It's strange to think you've hardly ever been in this room, since you're always so thoroughly with us in spirit."

"It's all right, Felix," Danaë answered, forcing a smile for the Brillist Institute Headmaster who reigns as teacher, steersman, and lawspeaker over Gordian. But the blush on Danaë's unhappy cheeks showed that it was not all right, in fact, not until I pulled the curtain closed to seal away the spectacle below.

Here the assembled Powers were as alone as Powers can be, no aides, no bodyguards, no secretaries, the constant watching plague of 'personnel' shut out beyond the door beyond the door beyond the door of Madame's innermost sanctum. Only the most completely trusted servants may attend the nobles in the Salon de Sade: today that meant me. In the car en route to Paris I had . . . endured, rather than answered, Dominic's first questions about Bridger. But Dominic knew I would be slow to succumb to either force or guile, so he had dropped me at Madame's with instructions that I be held until he returned. Then he had vanished once again, like a black and heavy condor, content that no common vulture will dare touch its prey. Since I was on hand, they might as well make use of me.

"Were you never brought in here before you married?" Faust asked.

"Never," Danaë answered. "The Salon de Sade was not judged proper for a maiden's eyes. Besides"—she smiled at Andō seated beside her on their sofa—"until I was united with my husband, I had no contact with affairs of state. I still find this room rather overwhelming, which is why I do appreciate your kindness in exercising restraint when I attend."

"No trouble at all, my dear, no trouble at all."

It was a brash lie, of course, here in a room designed to fill the mind with two things of which politics was not the primary. This was not a room built for restraint. The picture window down to the lovemaking of the *hoi polloi* filled one wall with living pornography. Two more walls were covered with museum cases which preserved the relics of Great Men: portraits, busts, quills, locks of hair, manuscripts in the hands of Patriarch and Philosophe, Jean-Jacques and the Divine Marquis, glittering reliquaries of Madame's favorite Catholic saints, and, when they have survived, tools of love from the boudoirs of history's greatest. The last wall held the tools of love for this one.

Faust's eyes laughed as he settled onto the sofa. "Wearing a hole in the rug isn't going to get Bryar ready faster either, Déguisé."

The Anonymous froze, embarrassed now by his own pacing. At Madame's, in case any outside the inner circle might wander within earshot, the Anonymous answers to the slightly subtle title of the Comte Déguisé, the Count Disguised. Trust Europe to have a system of etiquette prepared even for the eventuality of royalty who must stay 'in disguise' amid a company all of whom know the truth.

"Well put, dear Felix." Madame's laugh lit the room, as did the silver embroidery sparkling on her gown of powder blue. "The Headmaster is right. Come, My Lord, sit before you make us all dizzy." Madame was too far from the Anonymous to grab his sleeve, but she steered him toward an empty couch with a gesture.

My Lord the Comte Déguisé obeyed, but sat only on the sofa's edge, ready to spring up, like a loved one lurking outside a surgery, waiting for news.

Madame's smile pitied his tension, but she could do no more, so she stretched back in the embrace of the two gentleman who flanked her on her couch. To her left, his legs lost in the ocean of her skirts, sat His Imperial Majesty Cornel MASON. His costume was an adapted Eighteenth-Century military uniform, cording and rows of bright buttons, fashioned in Masonic Imperial Gray with the left sleeve dyed black. Their bodies as they sat—Madame's and Caesar's—were intertwined, his lips a neck stretch from her ear, her hand in his lap a light squeeze from excitement. Theirs is a comfortable, habitual closeness, enjoying the taste of a cheek or the tease-thrill of crotches brushing under cloth, all in the course of chat, as if they had forgotten one might sit upon a couch in any other way. See, even as Madame chuckles at the Anonymous's impatience, the Emperor chuckles with her, not even noticing the sympathy of flesh and flesh. I had never seen Caesar unstiff, reader, until I saw him with Madame. On the same couch on the Lady's other side, his costume barely more elegant than his everyday European suit, sat the King of Spain.

"I hear the Outsider is calling the European Parliament again," the Emperor remarked as he nuzzled his Lady's ear. "Something about the land crisis."

Spain nodded. "It is also to approve funds for the distribution of that new anti-aging drug."

"I thought they passed that eight months ago."

"This is another new drug. Utopians work fast."

Caesar tickled something among Madame's skirts. "I just found out about the new drug yesterday. The Outsider works fast too."

"They do," Spain granted, "commendably so." English, reader, they spoke English, despite the pull of Paris, for such a universal company can only speak the universal tongue.

"Her Excellency," an usher called now from the doorway, "Cousin Chairwoman Bryar Kosala."

"Sorry to make you wait, everyone!"

Bryar Kosala entered in a rush of ruffles, her black hair mounded as elaborately as a wedding cake, her gold-trimmed gown of poppy-red satin making her deep Indian skin glow like amber.

"Oh! My Lord!" she squealed as the Comte Déguisé pounced like a hunter, lifting her by her corseted waist and drowning her neck with kisses. Kosala laughed, the others too, delighted, even after so many repetitions, at a pair so very much in love.

Why does Kosala not wear a sari? It is a fair question, reader, why this daughter of India does not wear the Eighteenth-Century costume of her own people, as Andō and Danaë do of old Japan. The Comte Déguisé's tastes, conditioned by Madame, are part of the lady's reason, but exoticism is more. Bryar Kosala is here to sample the strange, romantic mysteries of this exotic France; India is her everyday.

"Now who's making the Princesse uncomfortable, Déguisé?" Faust teased.

It was true. Danaë had averted her modest eyes from the lovers' kisses, filling her gaze instead with her husband, who sat beside her on their couch, and her brother, who lay sparkling across the couple's laps, naked as God intended. Golden Ganymede was stretched out on his side, his head nestled against the pillow of his sister's breasts, with his lower parts in Andō's lap, so the Director's idle hands could enjoy the Duke's flawless buttocks. Ganymede's back is his more dangerous side, I think, the golden mane trailing down his spine as soft as sunlight, since that back could be either a man's or woman's, so practically no spectator is immune. There is no incongruity, reader, in bashful Danaë averting her eyes from kisses to feast on her brother's nakedness. Ganymede's nude form is not licentiousness but art, a public service, no stranger than an Aphrodite in a fountain, and certainly nothing unfamiliar to his sister or the rest of this company. Besides, excepting myself, all the people present here have enjoyed the Duke to some degree, whether completely as Andō does, or the single night which the King of Spain will doubtless regret to his grave.

"Our apologies, Princesse." Kosala had to push the Anonymous away, prying his hands from her bodice and holding them in forced and modest friendship.

"It's quite all right," Danaë answered, adjusting the front of her glittering kimono where the weight of her brother's head threatened to bare too much of her chest. "I know how *le Comte* misses you between meetings."

Her Excellency Chair Kosala settled on her own sofa, and the Comte Déguisé squeezed as close beside her as the framework of her dress allowed. The lust in his eyes bordered on starvation, but, to spare Danaë, he confined himself to stroking Kosala's fingers, where the wedding ring drowned amid more dazzling period jewels.

Drop this farce, Mycroft. I know who thy Anonymous is, all the world knows. Save the trouble and call him by his name. Never, reader. The illustrious title of Anonymous has passed from virtuoso to apprentice virtuoso for seven generations, Earth's most influential voice for so long that even Ganymede considers theirs a noble line. Tradition lets each Anonymous reveal the identity of their predecessor's predecessor upon their death, so Earth may decide whether to honor the body in the Pantheon, but to reveal an Anonymous while still alive? Unforgivable. As you know, disaster forced the unmasking of this Anonymous, but I shall not strip the holder of his regal title in my history a moment sooner.

"Well . . ." Madame's delighted eyes counted the company in their circle, like a collector making inventory of her shelves: the Emperor, then Headmaster Felix Faust alone in his armchair, Andō and Danaë enjoying sparkling Ganymede, Chair Kosala and the hungry-eyed Anonymous, and last the somber King of Spain. It is a living Seven-Ten list, this vista, save that His Royal Highness is a more refined presence than Europe's 'Second-Choice Prime Minister' Casimir Perry. "Now that our little company is complete," Madame began, "Headmaster, would you care to begin the meeting? You called it."

"Thank you, Madame, and to the rest of you, thank you for coming, though I've a feeling Caesar would have called a meeting if I hadn't."

MASON nodded. "What's your business, Felix?"

"Something I've been meaning to say to the Director and Princesse for some time, though I suspect it's something some of the rest of you have been wanting get off your chests as well." He paused for a smile, the wrinkles of his almost-eighty years lending him a jovial warmth. "Do you mind, dear Danaë, if I speak frankly?"

"Of course you must speak frankly, Felix. We're all as family here in Madame's salon, we must keep nothing from each other."

"In that case, my dear," he cleared his throat, "what I have to say is this: keep your revolting little monstrosities to yourself, bitch."

"Felix!"

"Ten of the things you've picked up, and now you're sending them out to fix on the rest of us like leeches: Masami at *Black Sakura,* Toshi in the Censor's office, Hiroaki inside the CFB, Sora with the Humanist Praetor at Romanova, Michi with Casimir Perry, another one, Jun, applied to my Institute of all things, and I heard about another—Ran was it?—applying at the Duke's offices. Even your brother had the good sense to send the creature packing."

Ganymede's voice dripped poison. "No one speaks like this to my sister, Felix."

Faust almost laughed. "I note you didn't deny it was good sense sending the creature packing. Even the Duke agrees. If the pair of you," he nodded to Andō, "want to surround yourselves with bizarre, inhuman life-forms that's your business, but don't send them after the rest of us."

Hotaka Andō Mitsubishi's black *haori* and *hakama* already made him grimmer than the rest in their French damasks; now his face did too. "I recommend, Headmaster, that you not speak of the Mitsubishi house's ba'kids in such terms."

Headmaster Faust's eyes traced the room. "The rest of you don't realize, do you? What those kids are? They're set-sets, every one of them! Tank-reared, psycho-engineered, drug-enhanced living computers."

Fresh tears brightened the jewels of Danaë's eyes. "No they aren't!"

"Oh, yes they are, you think I can't trace a pedigree? Not that I need to, you went so far as to knit them all little Brillist code-sweaters so they can flaunt it. 1-2-16-17-2-2-20-20, does that sound like a set that would exist in nature?"

"Felix, please . . ." Cousin Chair Kosala cut in with her most calming voice.

"Don't you start, Bryar, this is entirely your fault!"

"My fault?"

"You and Lorelei Cook, don't think I don't know about that, too. It's admirable, Bryar, trying to sabotage set-set breeders."

"Felix, I don't—"

"Oh, yes you do. You may not have done it yourself, but you're happy enough to leave Lorelei Cook in office, putting Nurturists in every position they can. We're all here, Bryar. One word from you, 'I don't think the head of the Nurturist faction should be Romanova's Minister of Education,' and the lot of us together could oust them in a heartbeat. But you won't ask for that, because you smile just as much as Cookie every time a set-set facility goes under. Don't get me wrong, I smile too, but you have to be responsible about it, you can't break up the nursery bash'es when the creatures are already eight years old and assume your fosterage programs will turn them into human beings."

Kosala had to push aside the Anonymous's attempt at an ill-timed kiss. "Then the ten Mitsubishi ba'kids are . . . ?"

"Unfinished set-sets. Andō and Danaë hunted through your orphanages to reunite the whole batch. You know how Mitsubishi love to snap up set-sets when they see profit in it, but one thing those kids aren't is human beings, and they never will be. No cuddly foster program will fix that, Bryar, not at eight years old. Those are not human brains anymore, they don't grow and develop, and they don't get well. A whale can grow and develop; Mycroft Canner can grow and develop; genetic constructs like His Grace and the Princesse"—Faust nodded to the golden twins—"they can grow and develop, based on the genes Madame picked, but with infinite variety in what they can become; but a set-set can't! I don't know how much more clearly I can say it."

Bryar Kosala tried to make her frown a gentle one. "Felix, I . . ." A pause as one of her lover's touches hit home. "I do share some of your opinions about set-set training, but a bonsai tree is still—"

"I wish people would stop using that comparison." The Headmaster rolled his eyes. "It's nothing like a bonsai tree, bonsai trees grow. It's not even an Artificial Intelligence, those grow too. It's a *set . . .* set," he punctuated the phrase with pauses. "They pick the developmental level they want on each scale of the set and they freeze the set in place, 1-2-16-17-2-2-20-20 lifelong, no growth, no dynamism. It's a corpse with glucose pumping through it. You can make a sculpture of a tree out of metal, or glass, or wood, but using wood doesn't make your sculpture a tree, it makes it a tree-shaped artificial object made out of the hacked-up pieces of a dead tree. Brain tissue is a very convenient material to make a computer out of, it has high information density, it's easy to fuel, and if you grow your brain-tissue computer inside a human body it has lots of ready-made input-output interfaces. But it is not a human being, it's farther than dolphins, farther than chimps, farther than U-beasts, and it is not welcome in my Institute!"

"Felix, please," the Princesse cried weakly, "you're talking about our children!" Tears gilded her alabaster cheeks. Have you seen real alabaster, reader? Translucent and somehow warm and cold at once, like sun through snow. "They lost their bash' because of what Bryar and Cookie did! Bringing them together again was what they wanted!"

Faust's face did not lighten. "And if they happen to be perfect tools to help you against the rest of us, that's just coincidence?"

"Friends, please," Madame intervened at last, hiding her expression behind today's silver fan. "Kindly stay civil in the presence of ladies."

"Of course, Madame." Andō did not show anger in his face or tone, but his hands on Ganymede's buttocks grew firm enough to make the Duke wince. "You are talking about my children, Faust. Are they to be denied careers in the highest levels because of their background?"

Faust crossed his arms. "In my Hive, absolutely. If the rest of you have any sense you'll keep them out of yours, too."

"What type of set-sets are they?" the Emperor asked flatly.

"They aren't!" the Princesse cried, all tears. "Felix himself admitted they're unfinished set-sets, only eight years of training, not enough. They're not any kind of set-set, all their poor powers incomplete, and they were scattered all across the Earth. It's cruel!"

"But what kind would they have been?" Caesar pressed. "Cartesian? Pneumonic? Flash? Don't mistake, Princesse, I support protecting the right of bash'es to raise children as they choose, but I am curious." Through this Caesar was still enjoying the contours of Madame's neck.

"I believe the term would have been 'Accelerated' set-sets," Faust spat as if it were profanity. "It's a new kind. This bash', if you can call it that, was a first attempt. I skimmed the case notes, they would've been something between Pneumonic and Flash. You know how adrenaline and fight-or-flight reactions enhance processing and memory? Grossly oversimplified, this was trying to make that hyperfocus permanent. When finished the children would've experienced the world in slow motion. Imagine how impossible, to watch a movie or enjoy a conversation when it all seems like slow motion. Talk about 'crippling a child's ability to participate in and interface naturally and productively with the world at large.'" These last words, quoted from the Nurturist Eighth Law, made even touch-distracted Ganymede look up.

The Anonymous took a long breath, enjoying Kosala's scent, before he broke his silence. "Minister Lorelei Cook was on Sugiyama's Seven-Ten list. Is this why?"

Mama and Papa Mitsubishi exchanged fast glances. "Quite possibly. Masami knows that Bryar and Minister Cook conspired to break up their birth bash'. I wouldn't be surprised if they mentioned it to Sugiyama-sensei. But Cook wasn't on Masami's own list."

The Anonymous nodded. "No, if Masami themself had published about it I'm sure their background would have come out, but I do imagine an unfinished set-set might hold a grudge. Was Masami trying to manipulate Sugiyama into aiding some kind of revenge?"

Duke Ganymede laughed now, the motion jiggling his sister's chest. "So, it's not just Spain, Andō, and me! Even our Bryar had something to gain from silencing Sugiyama's Seven-Ten list."

The Cousin Chair seemed to wish she too had a fan to hide behind. "What are you suggesting?"

"Just that it's amazing a single Seven-Ten list could have had things on it to embarrass so many of us. If I were a conspiracy theorist, I'd have great difficulty figuring out which of us to accuse."

"Yes, that's something I have wanted to address." Now the Emperor withdrew his eyes and hands from his Lady. "This *Black Sakura* affair has escalated into more than mere distraction. The cars are in danger. That is not tolerable."

Hotaka Andō Mitsubishi frowned across at MASON. "I thought we'd decided to leave this to Tai-kun."

"The solving of the case, yes," Caesar answered, "but the protection of the cars is separate."

"You don't think Tai-kun can settle it in time?"

"Of course Jed will solve it," Kosala interrupted, "but I agree with Cornel, we can't afford the risk of something happening to the cars before they're done." Kosala pushed at a tickling curl at one side of her hair, tempting her lover to nuzzle before tucking it back in place. "Your Grace"—she looked to Ganymede—"what added security have you ordered for the Saneer-Weeksbooth bash'?"

"The bash' is safe, I've seen to it."

That was not enough for the Emperor. "What about preparations in case the system does go down? Is the backup facility ready to go online? Have you trained a backup crew?"

"I presume you intend no insult, Caesar." The Duke President shot MASON a brief, cutting smile. "I have always had a backup crew, I have always had a backup facility, I have even always had backup set-sets." A quick glare at Faust. "The transition won't be seamless—no one is as good as Lesley Saneer or Cato Weeksbooth—but a transition might cost a few minutes' system downtime, risk of an extra crash or two over the first months the new team is in charge, no worse." His murder-blue eyes narrowed. "You've trusted me with the cars for years, I don't appreciate being accused of being irresponsible with my own."

«Temper, temper, your Grace,» Madame chided in French, her voice light as a nanny's. «These were questions out of concern, not disrespect. We're all here trying to help each other.»

For her, reader, for Madame D'Arouet alone, see true deference temper Ganymede's too-blue eyes. «Of course, Madame. Forgive me.»

Spain intervened now, his voice and posture as serene as if he were waiting to be painted into a double portrait with Madame. "We are grateful for your excellent care, la Trémoïlle," he began, squeezing Madame's hand tenderly until she gave smile of agreement. "We know no one could guard the cars better, and we trust that, if trouble did arise, you would call on us at once. Most of us are, I think, more concerned about the *Black Sakura* end of the problem, and the motives of the actors. Déguisé, why did you arrange to fake your own Seven-Ten list being tampered with? That is the first time we've seen you lie to the press."

"Oh, to help the Mitsubishi," the Anonymous answered, investigating the side struts of Kosala's bodice. "Unless something distracted the world from *Black Sakura*, there was going to be big trouble for Andō, anyone could see that."

"Yes," Headmaster Felix Faust confirmed, "Déguisé showed me some calculations when they asked me to make a fuss about my list too. There's always an attempt to steal mine, it's a student tradition, but make a little fuss and it's amazing how fast the public will stop obsessing about one Hive and bask in the fantasy of conspiracy. You're welcome, Andō."

The Director's eyes were not grateful. "You could have consulted me first, or did you not want me to be complicit?"

The Anonymous took a long pensive breath. "Nope, no good, can't concentrate." Rising, he seized Bryar Kosala by the waist and hefted her over his shoulder, no easy feat given her height and smothering skirts, but they have practice. "Back in a moment."

"Oh, My Lord!" the lady cried, laughing as she struggled to balance on him for the few steps it took to reach a side room which waited for such eventualities.

The Anonymous fumbled for the speaker control, so they could continue to hear the discussion in the central room while we without were spared the sounds of the activity within. "Carry on, we'll be listening."

The others mixed smirks with sighs as they watched the door close behind this most eager of couples. The pair did not, I noted, turn on the light in the little side room, preferring their old habit of meeting in the dark. One might imagine Bryar Kosala would be the hardest of the Seven for Madame to lure to her establishment, but she was clever. Bryar came at first as an inspector, just as she told Carlyle. The Cousin found the curls and skirts and gentlemen charming, but not lure enough to compromise her duty, not until Madame dropped hints that her establishment was graced from time to time by the Anonymous. Oh, how Kosala burned at the thought of putting flesh to the voice she had vied with so many times in print, the wisest of her adversaries. Kindly Madame made the arrangements, a rendezvous like Cupid and Psyche's in pitch black, with the promise of no speaking, so the identities of both lovers could remain unknown. All it took to lure the Anonymous into the arrangement was to let him glimpse the Unknown Lady in silhouette through a screen as she donned the many pieces of the costume which drives him joy-mad. Dominic was the biggest winner in the betting pool on how long the pair could keep up their affair before they recognized each other in the outside world—seven months. After that there was nothing for it but for Kosala to join this innermost circle of those privileged to see and know the face of the Anonymous. *And you say she wears her wedding ring through this, Mycroft? That the 'Lady' crowns this farce of an affair by carrying the seal of those vows exchanged with Vivien Ancelet?* Of course she does, reader, for nothing stokes the fires of love like sweet adultery. The Anonymous wears his, too.

"You had more to say, Caesar?" Madame invited, running a soft finger along his jaw.

"Yes." MASON is accustomed to proceeding while some of the company are distracted. "The degree to which this *Black Sakura* affair has succeeded in threatening not just one Hive but all of them suggests to me that it was planned by someone with detailed knowledge of the inner affairs of all our Hives."

Ganymede raised his golden head within his sister's arms. "You suspect one of us?"

"I know I'm not the only one who does. We're all friends here, but we also compete, within limits, when it's in our own Hives' interests. This has exceeded those limits, but I'm willing to believe that whoever planned it originally did not expect it to. If someone here is responsible, and you speak now, I will be willing to overlook it, and cooperate to see things fixed. Do others agree?"

"Agreed," Faust answered first. "My compliments to whoever concocted this much fun. How about the rest of you?"

"We agree," Andō announced, looking to his wife for her silent consent. "Ours is probably the Hive most wronged, but we will overlook it for the sake of a peaceful solution."

Duke Ganymede twitched slightly as Andō's fingers strayed far up his inner thigh. "Very well," he conceded. "I shall need a scapegoat for the break-in, ideally whatever agent actually planted the list in the house, so I can set the Saneer-Weeksbooth bash' at ease, but a scapegoat is enough."

Madame's portrait face signaled her approval with a slight adjustment of her smile. "I'm sure dear Bryar will be happy to see this finished with as little retribution as possible, and the Comte Déguisé is always content with compromise."

All waited, but the closed door beyond which the couple sported gave no sign of contradiction.

"Your Majesty?" Madame invited. "What say you?"

"I think it is a fine solution, Madame," Spain answered, nodding to me to bring his wine, "if the guilty party is indeed among us."

"Good." Madame planted a gentle kiss on Spain's cheek. "Then let the perpetrator step forward, if they are here."

All waited, each searching the others' faces. No one moved.

"If no one will step forward," MASON challenged, "then I want each of us in turn to swear our innocence before Jehovah. Jehovah, please listen and verify there are no liars."

"Yes, *Pater*." Jehovah's place was the corner opposite mine. If I did not mention His presence in the room before, reader, it is because He was distracted, and He can hardly be called present in a place which is little more than storage for His forgotten flesh. He had His chair here in the corner, His little table, and His cabinet of distractions, always on hand to entertain the Child while the parents played. It was crowded now with books, Sartre, Confucius, Augustine, but peeking between the tomes one could still spy the building blocks and colorful rattles which, in lost years, the Toddler Jehovah had not so much played with as manipulated with the impatient patience of a researcher on the fiftieth step out of five thousand, only the last of which will yield the cure. There was nothing in between among the toys, no dress-up dolls or electronic games, just the tools an infant needs to master coordination, then straight to Plato. He had a book in His hand now, but was not reading it, His mind and vacant senses lost instead in the governance of His distant universe.

"Donatien," Faust called, "do you already know which one of us it was?" You are ready now, I think, reader, to hear each Power call Jehovah by their favorite of His many names.

"No, Uncle Felix, I know not."

The Headmaster's eyebrows danced. "Better and better."

"I'll begin then," MASON volunteered, raising his right hand as he faced his Son across the room. "I swear I had neither involvement in nor knowledge of the planning or execution of the theft of the *Black Sakura* Seven-Ten list, or its planting in the Saneer-Weeksbooth bash'."

Jehovah did not move, but His eyes locked on the Emperor's face so keenly one might imagine he was counting the atoms of breath which formed the words. He said nothing.

Faust spoke up next. "I swear too, I had no involvement in nor knowledge of the planning or execution of the *Black Sakura* theft, or planting the list, but I'm going to buy a drink for the clever fellow who did."

The King of Spain swore next, then Andō, Ganymede, his voice as beautiful to hear as he is to see.

"Anything, Epicuro?" Spain asked.

"No lies, *Su Majestad.*"

"And I of course"—Madame spoke gently, as if whispering poetry, one lover to another—"had nothing whatever to do with the planning or execution of the theft or break-in, I swear it by Your Noble Self, my dear Jehovah."

Still He did not move, but let His eyes slide from face to face, like a computer swiveling its camera while the rest stays bolted to the desk. "Mother speaks the truth."

"Same goes for me!" The side chamber opened suddenly and the Anonymous's strong voice broke through. "I swear I had absolutely no involvement of any kind with this *Black Sakura* theft, or the Saneer-Weeksbooth bash' or anything associated, apart from faking the alteration to my own Seven-Ten list to cover things."

The Cousin Chair and Anonymous emerged now, rosy cheeked but both far calmer than they had been before their exercise. They had done an admirable job retouching their costumes after their recreation, but the scarlet layers of Kosala's skirts had suffered creases during their love-plunge, and hints of the real color leaked around the snowy edges of the Anonymous's wig.

"I'm last then, I guess?" Bryar asked brightly. "I too swear, I had nothing whatsoever to do with any of this, at any level. There. That's all of us, Jed. Any liars?"

"No, Aunt Bryar, none." I suspect that half the world feels like calling Chair Kosala 'Aunt,' but this Child, Who once bounced on her lap, is especially entitled.

With that soft pronouncement, Jehovah closed His eyes again, exhaustion in His face, for all the world like a great-grandfather roused in his sickbed by descendants squabbling over inheritance, eager to return to the higher thoughts of one near death. I approached Him with a tray of food, and told Him He should eat, for He had once again lost track of time. He took the food, and thanked me, and asked if His Dominic had seemed well when I saw him. I answered that he had. Next He asked me whether I thought it was cruel to let angelic intelligences mix with human intelligences long enough for each to learn how the other category's consciousnesses experience a different kind of independence from their God. I did not have an answer.

What means this vagueness, Mycroft? 'He asked,' 'I answered'? Can this lazy paraphrase be that same Mycroft who has hitherto stated the precise language of every line with such care? Give me the words! What tongue does the polyglot J.E.D.D. Mason use with thee, Mycroft? And thou with him?

What tongue, curious reader? All of them. This desperate Being uses all His senses, all His words, our French, our English, Latin, Spanish, Greek, all mixed together to weave His nuance, the fire-tongued commixture that is His native speech, which I alone upon this Earth, thanks to my stolen languages, can understand, and which translation cannot possibly approximate.

"If the Prince D'Arouet says there are no liars," Duke Ganymede declared, "there are no liars."

"Good!" Kosala squeezed her Compte Déguisé close as they settled together upon their couch. "I'd hate to have a traitor among us. Thanks for proposing that, Cornel, I feel much better now."

"But who did it, then?" the Duke asked first. "The Utopians?"

"No." The Emperor's response was instant.

A scowl's shadow dimmed Ganymede's perfection. "I'd like to hear those words from someone who wasn't in love with Apollo Mojave." He waited, blue diamonds flicking from face to face around the silent room. "That is, if there is anyone in this room fitting that description, apart from the Prince D'Arouet and myself."

One by one the Emperor, the Anonymous, the King, the Chair, the Headmaster, even the Director failed to meet Ganymede's eyes. He did not even glance at me.

"I think I was considerably less in love with Apollo Mojave than most," Madame volunteered, "and I don't think this is something Utopians would do, not as politics, or as a prank. It isn't . . . ," she groped, "future-oriented enough."

"It's true," Kosala agreed. "They don't care about the Seven-Ten lists, or the next election, they only care what happens two hundred years from now."

Duke Ganymede rolled over onto his back, and all within the room, Jehovah excepted, leaned forward to savor the spectacle. "But have we actually heard them say they didn't do it?" he asked.

"If I may speak, Your Grace?" I petitioned, though I knew the shadow my intrusion would cast over the company.

"What is it, Mycroft?"

I dug my fingers into my habit's rope belt, since here I had no hat with which to fidget in my nervousness. "I talked to a Utopian today, one who would know, and asked that very question. If a Utopian is involved in this, then even the constellation trusted with their most sensitive project doesn't know about it."

Madame stroked MASON's black hair, gently, as one does to calm a snarling hound. It was not I but Ganymede who had dared pronounce Apollo's name, but the hate still burned in MASON, eyes which had endured the Testing of the Successor moved almost to anger-tears. I speculate sometimes how best I might die, when the time comes. There are many with the moral right to take my life, but Caesar has suffered more than anyone, not just Apollo's loss, but the agony of suppressing his rightful rage when he could kill me any hour, any day. If I can gift my death to anyone, it will be Cornel MASON.

Headmaster Faust is an avatar of curiosity. "What project would that be, Mycroft? What constellation?"

"Cultural preparations for Mars," I answered without actually lying.

That they accepted.

"The Outsider, then?" Chair Kosala suggested.

Andō was first to answer. "No."

"Why not?"

"Because the Outsider knows nothing about anything, and Europe gains nothing from doing this."

She leaned against her Anonymous. "We're running out of logical suspects. Either one of us has a subordinate who's betrayed us"—Kosala's eyes strayed to the King of Spain—"or it's the Utopians, or the Outsider, or something else entirely."

"I think," Spain voiced, mildly, "I think it's time we brought the Outsider in."

I asked myself, reading this over, why I describe the King of Spain less vividly than all the others. In truth he is less vivid, always restrained and stately, trained from infancy to do nothing he could not be seen doing on a coin. I think misfortune too has made him quiet, he who alone among the circle joined more out of necessity than choice, for when Her Majesty the Queen was institutionalized, where could our unlucky monarch turn, whose strict office permitted neither divorce nor a common affair, except to this professional King's Mistress, unrivaled in the arts of secrecy? He has a conscience, this King, a fierce one whose gnawing pains him like an illness. Since his Queen's death I have personally witnessed five of his attempts to "set things right" and persuade Madame to become his lawful wife. But Madame always has Caesar holding her other hand, and so the widower must wait.

"Bring the Outsider in?" Danaë cried. "Over this? No, no, your Majesty, this is a petty thing, all this will pass. The Outsider will be nobody again at the next election, we don't want to be saddled with them after that!"

"As you are saddled with me now?" he asked.

Her eyes filled at once with sparkling tears, enough to make both her husband and brother hot to comfort her. "Your Majesty, I didn't mean . . ."

Spain saved her from finishing. "Perry will win the next election."

Only the Anonymous was not stunned too much to ask, "Why do you think that?"

"Because Perry has seduced the Prince of Asturias."

Duke Ganymede actually choked at the news. "You must be kidding, Spain. That upstart has sunk his fangs in Crown Prince Leonor Valentín?" He looked to Madame as if she and she alone had the right to approve such matches.

"I don't know if there is sex involved or merely money and corruption," the King replied, "but Perry's . . . alliance . . . with my heir is quite complete. At the next election, if I do not run, the Prince will campaign in support of Perry. If I do run, Perry will expose the Prince's involvement in certain inappropriate activities, and that, combined with my embarrassment from the last election, will likely end my family's part in politics for the next two generations."

"We shouldn't invite him in, we should crush him!" Danaë seethed, forming fists, her porcelain fingers clutched in balls which seemed too fragile to strike a real blow. "This affront is outrageous! And against such a venerable line! Madame, you must agree, we should ally and crush this offender!"

Madame's fan could not hide her painted brow, which wrinkled around eyes bright with calculations. "Certainly, dear child, we could do as you propose, but if that were what His Majesty wished, he would have asked it. Is that not so?"

The King nodded. "Perry has not done badly as Prime Minister. Europe is doing well. If Perry has chosen this somewhat underhanded method to remain in office, it may simply be because they know they face a rather unfair alliance on my side. I know that you, my friends, could and would crush Perry if I asked, but I have neither the moral right nor any desire to crush a perfectly competent politician, just because we are competing for the same office."

"And if Perry isn't as benign as you imagine?" You will be surprised, reader, to hear that it was Bryar Kosala who suggested the dark option first. The World's Mom may be the most forgiving, but she is also most vicious when family is threatened. "What if Perry was behind fixing the last election too? Planted Ziven Racer on your staff to sabotage you?"

Cornel MASON nodded. "Sugiyama's Seven-Ten list has drawn fresh attention to Ziven Racer, to your embarrassment, Spain. I wouldn't rule Perry out as a suspect for *Black Sakura* just yet."

The King accepted their counterarguments in gracious calm, as when he hears out all his ministers, though his decision is already made. "All the more reason, then, to test them."

"It would be easy to arrange," Madame took over. "Perry has been a midlevel member of this establishment for six years now. No one could advance so far in politics without some help from here."

"Are they addicted?" the Anonymous asked first.

"Oh ho ho," Headmaster Faust laughed like a merry giant. "As addicted to the ladies as you are, Déguisé. No offense." He smirked, but the Anonymous has long since reconciled himself to the power petticoats and coquetry have over him. "Perry's here twice a week at least," the Headmaster continued, "fond of the Salon Cleopatra, and . . ." I omit here, reader, details—both lewd and Brillist—which are not pertinent to this history.

Whatever his other accomplishments, Felix Faust is an unparalleled voyeur, and quick to forget Danaë's presence at this opportunity to demonstrate his knowledge. "I've seen Perry in the sex-free sections of the middle level, too," he continued, "the dueling ring, gambling rooms, the dance hall, wooing the ladies, that little blonde especially, Clara, is that their name, Madame? Wooing as if to wed, not that one can blame the wretch for wanting some way to be satisfied at home, eh, Andō?" The Director did not acknowledge the jibe. "Has Perry made you an offer yet, Madame," Faust asked, "on the bride?"

"Yes, but it was several millions short of acceptable. Clara is a true jewel of this bash', and Perry has little in the way of funds, though they are growing."

Perhaps, reader, your stomach turns at calling this a bash'? Much as it turns at thinking of the ample payment the birth bash' of Sidney Koons received for sending their infant off, first for set-set rearing, then to be Eureka's partner governing the cars. But if you turn Nurturist on us, distant reader, Caesar will fight you through every generation of the Empire.

"That makes things simple," the King continued. "I propose a meeting, all of us with the Outsider, here where such things are untraceable. If Perry is, as I hope, a good person like ourselves, then we can reach a compromise, wherein either Perry or myself will accept a different office, perhaps in Romanova, in return for Perry's admission to our circle and our help securing their desired bride. If, on the other hand, Perry is the villain some of you suspect, then Epicuro will soon unmask them, and we can crush them in good conscience." Spain smiled at Jehovah as he called Him by the name His Majesty himself contributed to the Prince's list.

Bryar Kosala pulled her lover's arms more firmly around her. "Your Majesty, exactly what degree of . . . inclusion do you imagine for Perry? Our little company here is more than political."

The Comte Déguisé seconded with a nod.

"I imagine it as a strictly political gathering at first, and each of us will see in time whether we become comfortable sharing more."

Danaë hugged her brother closer, as if he were her knight in dark days, or her teddy bear. "I don't like admitting someone who would think to threaten His Majesty. What a horrid mind!"

Hotaka Andō Mitsubishi wrapped a comforting arm about his wife's shoulders. "It's all right, Danaë. I've met with Perry many times, they're inelegant but not offensive. I support the idea of their *political* inclusion, and we can make very clear that it comes with no expectation of sharing other things." He reached deep under Ganymede now, and the Duke President's eyes lost focus for a moment as the hidden hand touched home. "Agreed, Ganymede?"

The Duke wriggled away from the distraction. "Acceptable. Shall I do the inviting, as usual?"

The Anonymous pursed his lips. "I don't want to reveal myself until we are sure of Perry, but I'm willing to attend by speaker."

Caesar frowned. "Jehovah, what is your impression of Casimir Perry? Should we invite them to join us?"

Jehovah awoke again from His inner solitude. "Perry fights for power more fiercely than most fight for their lives. You invited danger by leaving the man outside this long."

Now the frown spread to Kosala. "Have you gotten to know Perry during your work at the Senate, Jed?"

"Barely, Aunt Kosala. This man performs in public, always. Here I should hope to see him without his intention mask."

MASON breathed deeply as all digested the words. "Then we're agreed. How soon can we do this?"

Madame shrugged, the tightness of her breath-strained bodice commanding the attention of both her gentlemen. "I'll need a day or two to make arrangements, but since you are all agreed on it, my friends, I shall act as fast as possible."

His Majesty nodded. "Thank you, Madame. I am sincerely grateful."

The Anonymous was last to nod consent. "Be careful not to reveal me to Perry before we're ready, Jehovah. Do you understand? Perry doesn't know."

His nervousness may seem excessive, but the Anonymous has been burned by Jehovah's acumen before. How else do you imagine Madame added this most elusive Prince to her collection? It was before I joined the house, but I have heard the story. The Anonymous frequented the middle level in his everyday persona, socializing in tea rooms and wooing Madame's ladies, when one day the Young Master, only six years old, addressed him across a card table: "I disagree with such-and-such you wrote in the paper, Monsieur l'Anonyme." The startled guest tried in haste to contradict the boy, "That wasn't me!" but children and sages both grow more stubborn when they know they're right. Jehovah presented proof after proof, and a century and a half of perfect secrecy was no match for Him. Madame silenced the lesser card players with bribes, but Caesar, Andō, and Ganymede, who frequented the middle level too for variety's sake, saw at once the value of being able to negotiate in person with the Seventh Power. Thus was born the guise of Déguisé. Madame was overjoyed; she had expected to have to work much longer to capture her Anonymous.

"Excellent, we have a solution," Madame proclaimed. "Now, I'm sure you all have a thousand things to be getting on with, unless there are other concerns."

Only Felix took the invitation. "One last thing, since we've strayed rather far from my original topic. I want to make sure, Director and Princesse, that we're parting on good terms. Whatever my opinion of those things you have adopted, my affection for the pair of you is unchanged."

Andō could not smile here, but what are wives for if not to be forgiving when husbands cannot? "Of course, Felix, of course. We could never be angry with you."

"That said," her husband added, "I do not intend to block my ba'kids from careers in high office just because of your . . . opinion, Felix. I know what they are doing, it is no harm to you. If their presence inside one office or another"—he nodded to Kosala and the Anonymous—"gives me some small insight into your Hives, it is far less than you yourselves already willingly extend. If nothing else, I hope that, as the children mature, they can become liaisons between us, and help advise me about your own Hives' interests."

Bryar Kosala smiled her approval. "That makes sense."

Faust did not. "Will you at least get them to stop applying to my Institute? I don't know how many times I can restrain myself from shouting 'set-set' in public."

A pause for thought. "Yes, Felix. I shall inform Jun that they are unwelcome at Brill's Institute."

"Oh, they're welcome enough as a test subject." Felix rubbed his hands. "For progress and humanity and all that."

A grim frown. "I will think about it."

"Good," Madame proclaimed, "we are all friends again. And now"—a kiss on the cheek for MASON—"I shall contact you all"—a kiss on the cheek for Spain—"when I have made arrangements with the Outsider. Meanwhile, dear friends, please, for your own health, do take some minutes to enjoy yourselves."

Joy followed. The Anonymous attacked laughing Bryar's bodice, which their earlier haste had left intact. It was Spain's turn with Madame, and His shy Majesty prefers a private room, so they departed, while MASON stretched back to watch modest Danaë help her brother get into position for her husband's sport. Faust, meanwhile, invited Jehovah to join him at the crack of the window curtains, the Brillist itching to take notes on His observations of the lives below. Jehovah, Aristotle still in hand, complied.

I knew my office, and offered Caesar wine. His glance at me seemed tired, though it may just have been the richness of the room. He did not have the stomach to use Latin, not today, not with someone with so little right to it as I have. "I hear you were almost killed in the street today, Mycroft."

"Yes, Caesar. The Utopians saved me."

"You were seen, in uniform. Word is already spreading. This may end your days walking the streets."

I swallowed down my sob. "I know, Caesar."

"The attackers were friends of Apollo's. Thirteen years they'd been planning how to get at you. I'll see to it they're acquitted."

"Thank you, Caesar."

"You've been making mistakes lately, Mycroft. You're worried about something. Is it this Seven-Ten list?"

"No, it . . . May I ask a question, Caesar?" I had not intended to whisper, but his face often drives the voicing from my words.

"What?"

"If you had something, something so wonderful that it seemed that it might . . . that, given the chance, it would make a better world, for everyone, forever, so much better, but first there was a danger, a terrible, terrible danger that it could rip everything we have apart . . . would you destroy that better world to save this one?"

The wine fell as both MASON's hands, black-sleeved and gray, seized me by the rough weave of my habit and hurled me to the floor. "Get out of my sight."

"What? Caesar, I—"

"Never speak Apollo's words again. Get out!"

Dominant Predator

"Mᴍʏᴄʀᴏꜰᴛ!" Hᴇᴀʀ ɴᴏᴡ Bʀɪᴅɢᴇʀ's sᴏʙʙɪɴɢ sᴄʀᴇᴀᴍ ʀɪsᴇ through the dawn-streaked flower trench. "Where are you, Mycroft? Mycroft!" He had been reduced to old clothes, a green striped wrap which was almost more holes than fabric, and socks, no shoes, their threadbare toes ripping open as grass and rough dirt scraped his rushing feet.

I freely confess, reader, that this chapter is half imagination, for I was still a prisoner at Madame's.

"Bridger! Slow down there, kiddo. What's wrong?"

It was a stranger's voice, and the boy turned, brandishing a plastic ray-gun. "Keep away!"

"Whoa!" The stranger put his hands up as he stepped from the cover of the trash mine, chuckling, perhaps, at Boo who bristled at Bridger's side, his sweet blue face not designed to bare teeth. "Mycroft sent me."

"Do you know where Mycroft is?" the boy half-shrieked.

"Nope. I'm looking for them too, but their tracker's been off all day."

"Turn around, put your hands up on the wall!" Bridger braced the toy weapon well in both hands—do you think the Major would not have taught him that?

"If I turn around you won't be able to see me."

It was the truth, for a Utopian Coat enveloped the stranger in invisibility. Overlong sleeves swallowed his fingers, a hood his hair, so only his face and hints of legs and torso showed through the coat's open front, a sliver of a person, like an otherworldly voyager halfway out of the rift.

The boy cocked his head. "Are you dressed as Apollo Mojave?"

The smiling stranger pushed the vizor up away from his eyes and onto his gold-blond wig. "Yes, I am. Mycroft showed you pictures of Apollo, didn't they?"

"Mm-hm."

A fanged smile. "I'm a ghost, you see. It's easiest if I look like someone it's not surprising to see a ghost of." The stranger's eyes measured the boy's limbs, how long his stride, how fast one would have to sprint to catch him; even a common housecat toying with a mouse calculates how far it can let its plaything limp and still keep escape impossible.

"Who are you?" Bridger asked.

"I'm Mycroft's oldest and most trusted friend." The stranger slid down into a crouch, offering his hand for Boo to sniff. "Mycroft asked me to take care of you if things got bad."

"What's your name?"

Saladin offered as kind a smile as his snake-smooth face can muster. "Only Mycroft gets to know my name. And you can't tell anybody about me, okay, Bridger? I'm a secret." He held a finger to his lips. "Just like you."

The tension in Bridger's stance began to ease as he saw Boo wag, seduced by my scent on Saladin. "How come you don't have any eyebrows?" he asked.

Saladin laughed. "When I was a kid I was in a terrible accident and all my skin burned off. See, no hair, either." He lifted the corner of his wig above the temple.

"That must've hurt!"

"Yes, yes it did, but Mycroft grew me new skin in the meatmaker and patched me up with that. I think they did a good job." He traced the back of one hand with the other's fingers, following a seam between two patches, now only detectible to we who know that body perfectly.

"Was that the same accident that hurt Mycroft?"

"Yup, almost killed us both. Well, officially it did kill me." Though he still played with the dog, Saladin's eyes were ranging the trench, the light and shadow, the texture of the walls, where best to climb, to hide, to trap. How do I know he did this, reader? My Saladin always surveys his surrounding thus, as wild dogs do, and soldiers learn again to do when civilization's rose-tinted daydream breaks.

Bridger frowned. "Couldn't you get new eyebrows and hair if you want? Doctors can do that."

"I could, but hair has DNA in it that the police can find. I'd rather opt out."

"Yeah, hair's hard." The child's voice was soft after tears. "Mycroft makes me use special clumpy shampoo that's supposed to make my hair not shed except when I comb it."

"And special soap that makes loose skin flakes dissolve, right? I use it too. Smells terrible, doesn't it?" As wild a thing as Saladin has never learned to make his chuckle friendly. "But look, I can have eyebrows if I want, see?"

He lowered the vizor back over his eyes, and the projection filled in brows and lashes faithfully. Not his face. A different face, the cheek bones higher, skin a Northern European pale, the eyes like sky. He lifted it and lowered it again. "See? Eyebrows, no eyebrows, eyebrows, no eyebrows." The game failed to coax a smile from the boy. "What happened, Bridger?" Saladin asked. "Why were you running just now?"

A fast sob made the ray-gun fall slack at last. "They killed Redder."

"Who's Redder?"

"My friend." Bridger hugged to himself the bag, old army green, which hung at his shoulder, and perhaps a strand of perfect doll's hair peeked from the flap. "They pulled Redder's guts out and strung them all around the cave."

"Who did?"

"The person who's been watching me. They broke into my cave before and stole my backpack, and the No-No Box, and dropped a big bookshelf on Mommadoll, and now they came back and killed Redder!"

Bridger's shudder left him vulnerable, and Saladin pounced in an instant, wrapping the boy in a hug, and in that Utopian Coat, as thick and safe as when, in childhood, even the scariest closet monster was thwarted by the magic of the covers. "Hey, it's okay," he soothed. "Relax. No one else can hurt you while I'm here."

Sobs come quickly once it feels okay to cry. "They've ... been ... wa ... tching me. I took my clothes off to take a shower and they stole them while I was inside. Aimer and Pointer and Nostand were in my pockets and they ... they're gone and everybody's ... scared and Mycroft's missing and I can't go to Thisbe be ... because Thisbe's bash' is being scary."

Bridger tried to break free of the hug enough to look up at Saladin, but the hug locked tight. Animals may hunt by speed, by trap, by disguise, by ambush, but name for me another besides mankind that hunts by trust. "Shhh. It's okay." Saladin lifted the boy in his strong arms and started to carry him back along the trampled path to the cave. "Come, show me where your friend is."

"No!" Bridger tried to wiggle free. "I can't go back there!"

Saladin's practiced fingers locked around the child. "They might still be alive, and need help."

"They aren't."

"You'd be amazed how long a body can stay alive, even after the most astounding things are done to it."

Bridger shook his head. "Redder's not alive, they're imaginary."

"Imaginary?"

The child's throat gave a plaintive squeak. "Redder's my imaginary friend, an old imaginary friend from years ago. They're still in there, and there's red guts all coming out and splattered all over the cave. I wanted to miracle it better but then Redder would be all real and then the bad guy could hurt them worse." Bridger sobbed against Saladin's threadbare T-shirt. "That would be worse, right? Do you think it hurts worse if it happens when you're real?"

Saladin held the child awkwardly, inept at holding without hurting. "They killed your imaginary friend?"

"I want Mycroft. I want my friends back. I want all this to go away!"

Faithful Saladin let the child slip back to the ground, but took the boy's head between his hands, gently but firmly, as when one tests a fruit to see if it is ripe enough to pluck. "Do you want me to make it so they can't hurt you anymore? Do you want me to make everything go away?"

Imagine now, reader, that you are Providence. You have already decided that your Intervention, this miracle with which you have trespassed upon the ordered cosmos, will not die here at Saladin's hands, as I had asked. But how will you prevent it? How will you make my supreme predator ignore the tearful wishes of the one person in the world who matters to him? The answer depends on what kind of Providence you are. Are you the deterministic ricochet of pool balls on a table? If so, then you must already have another pool ball on its way: a bird to startle the hunter and make him let go, or a hole to trip him, dug by some rabbit now five generations dead. Perhaps you are instead a chess master, moving pieces on a board? Then you move a new piece into play; my queen threatens your king so you advance one of your own knights, Dominic perhaps, or Thisbe. Perhaps you are instead a master of puppets? The all-commanding author of the Great Scroll who has predestined every act of your creatures from infinity? If so, you can simply make Saladin choose not to kill, as you make every decision for every person, from creation to the end of days. Or are you perhaps that mildest form of Providence, a parent, who has reared your children carefully, teaching them the values you think will guide them best, different for each, in hopes you might thereafter trust them to make their own decisions as they explore your world? This last, hands-off image of Providence appeals to many, especially to those afraid to face a universe without a Father but unwilling to call themselves unfree; contemplate it longer, though, and you will find it no more liberating than the others, for such a universal Parent would make every one of us a set-set.

Providence had its king defend himself: "I wish you really were Apollo Mojave." The child sniffled. "Apollo would be able to figure out what the bad guys want, and make me understand it, and then we could make a plan, and get Utopians to help."

Will you believe me if I claim the predator's breath caught? That his hands shook? Tame humans are easy enough to surprise, but for a creature always on guard, watching his back, as paranoid as nature intended beasts to be, this was the first time in Saladin's life that he had let a person draw so close and only then sensed danger. I told you, reader, man is a beast that hunts by trust. A lion cub may lash out with claws it does not yet know it has, and so may Bridger. "That's right," Saladin answered. "That's exactly what Apollo Mojave would do."

"If I just keep running away, all that'll do is make more places I can't come back to. I have to make the bad guy stop, but I can't figure out how to make them stop until I know why they're doing it. What do they want? I don't understand strangers enough to figure out what they want. Do you?"

"Me?" Saladin shook his head. "I don't have much experience with other people."

"They want me to come meet them, but I don't want to."

"Who? The attacker?"

"They left a note, an address. But I don't want to go. I'm sure they'll do something awful. I know if I go maybe they'll tell me what they want, but there has to be another way. Some people are good at figuring out what people really want, even if they won't say. Apollo was, that's what Mycroft always says. That's what I need."

This smile Saladin should only have for me. "Sorry, I can't turn into Apollo Mojave for you."

"Do you want to?"

"What?"

Bridger dug his fingers into the contours of the coat. "Do you want to turn into Apollo Mojave? You'd be a lot less scary that way."

What now, Providence? You have saved your king, how will you write yourself out of this little predicament? A stick with a rag for costume is a doll, and a human in a costume is one just as much. But if you wanted Apollo on the board you would not have let me take him in the first place.

"No, the last thing I want is for Mycroft to have to kill me, too. Come on." Saladin took Bridger by the arm and started back toward the cave. "Show me the note, and the body. Human beings I can't read so well, but gore, there I'm fluent."

"No!" Bridger tugged hard. "I don't want to go back there!"

What face would my Saladin have now? Disgust, I think, as when the golden prince Laurel Mardi passed out in his arms on the steps of our guillotine, and so napped through his final moments, learning nothing. "That's the thing about gore, Bridger, if you don't let yourself look at it then your imagination twists it in your mind and makes it into a kind of nightmare instead of letting you learn from it. You have to look at it, see what they did exactly, blood for blood, or you'll never understand it."

"No! I want to forget!" The boy tried to break free, but Saladin hoisted him, and slung him kicking over his shoulder.

"What did you feel when you saw it?" Saladin asked. "Did you want revenge?"

"No!"

"You did, didn't you, just a little bit? You want to forget so you can pretend you're incapable of thoughts like that. Well, all human beings are capable of thoughts like that, kid, and you can act on them too if you want. It's up to you whether you do or not, but if you've had those thoughts you can't un-think them just by running away."

"No! I don't want to! I don't want someone with my powers to think like that!"

Saladin paused, sensing again the danger, as birds and hounds stiffen well before the earthquake. "What are you, kid?"

"I don't know. Mycroft says I'm a miracle."

Saladin set Bridger down once more, and peered into their open face. "You're thirteen, aren't you?"

"Yeah."

"How long have you known Mycroft?"

"Years and years, since I was little."

"And Mycroft raised you to be this soft? Mycroft Canner could've raised you to feast on corpses if they'd wanted to."

Bridger's sobs made Saladin's invisible sleeves rustle, like those almost-present tremors in the corner of the eye which make the credulous tell tales of ghosts. "Mycroft says it's important for me to be a kid, because only a kid can grow up to be a human being. I of all people need to not be a monster."

Of all men, reader, Mycroft Canner does not deserve to have been blessed with so wise and trusting a lover as Saladin. "All right," he answered. "There's a logic to that, I'll accept it. I won't make you look, but you have to stay close to me. If this stalker scares Mycroft, I'm not letting you out of arm's reach for an instant: it's not safe. I'll carry you piggyback, and you can keep your eyes closed. Once I see what the stalker's done, I may be able to figure out why they're doing this, and how to end it. Sound good?"

Bridger's nod was more than half sob. "Mm-hm."

"Let's see if the coat likes you." Saladin lifted the hem and draped it over Bridger's arm, which promptly vanished, leaving only grass. "The coat says yes." Saladin fished inside the coat, the Griffincloth wriggling like heat distortion. "Let's see, this thing hooks to that thing and pull this . . . there." He slipped his left arm out of the coat and let it fall halfway off. "See, there are some straps there that you can sit in like a little seat, see them? You can climb on my back and sit your butt in this loop and hold on to this strap, and then I can cover you with the coat and no one can see either of us. Alley-oop!"

Bridger folded himself into the piggyback seat, a bit too lanky to snuggle. "That's really cool."

"Yeah, it's for moving injured people. This is the best coat ever, when it's feeling cooperative." At Saladin's command the back stretched itself enough to cover his wriggling cargo. "Want me to take your bag?"

"No!" Bridger tucked the satchel carefully against his side as the coat fell over him. "No, I got it, and you have to promise to never ever look in it, okay? It's a really, really secret secret. Mycroft wouldn't want you to see."

A chuckle of thinned patience. "All right. If there's anything else you need before we leave here, tell me where it is in your cave, I'll look for it."

"Leave?"

I wonder what kind of tone Saladin would use trying to be comforting. "After I read the gore, I'm going to take you to some friends who have a safe house ready, somewhere far away where I can make sure whoever's after you can't get at you. Once you're safely there, then I'm going to hunt My-croft down and bring them back to us, no matter what. Sound good?"

"What kind of friends?"

"Some old criminal friends of mine and Mycroft's." Saladin stepped carefully, almost tripping over Boo. "They'll take very good care of you, because they know if they don't I'll drag them into an alley, hack chunks off them, and eat them while they're still alive."

"I like that you're honest. Most people wouldn't say stuff like that in front of a kid."

"I like that you like that. You know who Mycroft is and what they did, right?"

"Yeah. Mycroft doesn't keep secrets from me."

"I'm sure they say they don't."

"I'm sorry."

"What? Why?"

"I got snot on your shirt."

A gentle, growling laugh. "Don't worry about it."

Watch my Saladin now as he slides soundless through the grass, his wary eyes ranging the walls, the bridge above, as a fish watches for insects it can strike, and gulls who might strike back. Have you ever been in the true wilds, reader? There are some still, the deep protected Amazon, the arctic fringes, parts of the Great African Reservation, not the retrogressive towns where warlords cling to their thrones and borders, but the dark wastes where the full spectrum of wild beasts roams in herds and packs, including that rarest hunter, man. Out there you are responsible for yourself, no cars, no cops, no restaurants, no good Samaritans. That world does not exist to help you, does not need you, does not care, and will forget you as soon as the brush has grown over your footprints. For scavengers, our cities are such wilds too: for the pigeons who feast or starve by callous chance, for rats, for strays who have never known the ritual of 'feeding time,' and so for Saladin.

"Is this the place, these plastic sheets under the bridge?"

A shudder prefaced the answer. "Yes. Please be fast, I can already smell it."

Saladin released a slow whistle as he stepped through the tattered doorway. Red spattered the walls, and garlands of red crepe paper twined around the wreckage like toilet paper after a tornado. In the center of the cave, a manikin lay sprawled on the wreck in a red child's wrap, with a long curly wig and paper entrails pouring out of a hole cut in her gaping gut. Her face, chest, and arms were striped with painted knife wounds, red trickling from their depths, so the paint-blood coated the books and toys beneath, the plastic food and doll clothes carefully stirred to let bright gore coat every one. "So that's how you kill an imaginary friend."

"It's not less bad because they were imaginary!" Bridger cried out. "They're still dead!"

"I see that." Saladin tiptoed through the red and wreck with awe, like an entomologist through jungle, afraid of disturbing the morning's perfect spiderwebs. "It's perfect. Absolutely perfect, every touch." He leaned close to a twist of plastic entrail and breathed deep, the smell of paint becoming blood salt in his mind. "Who did this, Bridger? I have to find them. You must know something, a name, a description? You said they left a note that you should meet them. Where? When?"

"I don't know. I destroyed it."

"You must remember."

"You can't go, something horrible will happen."

"You're forgetting what I am, kid. If there's another liberated human out there, they're either my disciple or my rival. Either way, this is a challenge."

"No! I don't want Mycroft's best friend to get hurt."

"I'm going to track them down anyway, it's just up to you whether it's going to be fast and easy or whether I'm going to have to comb through this whole cave for hairs they left behind. Not everyone has our special shampoo."

The child whimpered. "Please don't. Let's just hide and be safe."

Saladin took a long breath. "Bridger, did you ever see the photos of the Mardi killings?"

"Some."

"Did what this person did to Redder look familiar?"

The answer did not want to come. "It looked kind of like what Mycroft did to Senator Aeneas Mardi."

"Exactly," Saladin confirmed, "this is exactly what we did to Aeneas Mardi, cut for cut. It's a re-creation. Bridger, how many imaginary friends do you have? Seventeen? Eighteen? This is a declaration of war. After the stabbing of Aeneas Mardi comes the sound and electricity torture of Laurel, then the guillotining, then feeding Leigh to the lions, then Chinese water torture on Jie, European water torture on Makenna, and by this schedule Geneva Mardi would already have been on the cross a few days."

"No! No, they already have the others! Aimer, and Pointer, and Nostand, and Nogun, Nogun's been missing for two days! They're not imaginary, either, they're already real!"

"Then tell me the address. Either one of us turns up there, or your friends die like the Mardi bash'. There are no other options."

"Dominic Seneschal. Paris, the alley behind Chateau d'Arouet, [XX] boulevard [XXXX], 20:00." It was not Bridger's voice. It was the Major's, rising from the coat at Saladin's back, as if from the speakers of Bridger's tracker.

Saladin would have liked the flavor of that voice. "Who are you?"

"Bridger's very short-tempered guardian angel. Can you kill Seneschal?"

"If I can't, no one can. I do like hunting hunters."

"Don't mess around. Take them from behind, a shot to the back, an ambush, anything that will score an instant, certain kill. We can't have that kind of monster around Bridger."

The hunter's eyes narrowed. "I'm a torturer, not an assassin. I don't kill prey until I've given them a proper taste of death's epiphany."

"This time you have to. There's too much at stake. Kill Seneschal and I can find the hostages myself."

"I'll kill them, but I'll kill them my own way." Saladin started to climb the wreckage around the paint-smeared corpse. "I don't take orders from angels."

Bridger whimpered as he felt Saladin's body tilt. "What are you doing?"

"Last rites. You don't want to leave your friend like this." Saladin gathered the paper guts and fed them gently 'back' into the 'wound.'

"We can't burn them here," the Major warned. "The smoke will draw attention."

"I know. But we can do more than nothing." Laying the body gently on the floor, Saladin scraped a handful of dry earth and sprinkled it over the body, muttering a few words of Greek.

Bridger sniffed, trying not to drip again on Saladin's shoulders. "Do you think Redder'll be okay now? Do you think they're off somewhere, okay?"

"No idea." Saladin closed the coat around him now, so his passage through the plastic sheeting seemed like nothing but a breath of wind. "If you want to pray for them, try Hermes. Gotta figure Hermes likes imaginary friends."

It isn't easy to make the Major smile.

CHAPTER THE THIRTY-SECOND

That There Are Two

THIS HISTORY HAS TWO HALVES, READER, STRANGE AS IT IS that seven days should take two books to tell. But they were dense days, not just with events, but with inhabitants, many, different, like these wild-flowers in the trench where all began. Here one stray footstep snaps many different plants, releasing different saps, and smells, and stirring up the insects hidden underneath. The surge is just beginning now, the armies of crawling life which swarm forth, as if born from the broken stems. You do not see their full numbers yet, but I hope I have, at least, shown you enough to realize that these first scouts you do see, like the others that will follow, were not born from the stems. These swarms, these changes, were all waiting in their sleepy tunnels, all with causes that you can now understand. You do not have to believe. You only have to believe that we believe, that I, that Dominic, that Carlyle who stumbled on so much, believe in Bridger, acted on that belief, and that we believe too in the second Thing that Providence placed in Carlyle's path on this, the morning of the twenty-seventh, in that same fitting spot where, four days prior, he first saw Divinity reveal Itself. Perhaps you will not be satisfied. This last change I am about to show you is too subtle. You want politics, apocalypse. I will show you that, too, as an addendum, the scissors that can still beat paper, perhaps even our deceptive, one-piece house of cards. But if, this morning, Carlyle comes to Bridger's trench once more, despite Ockham's command, it is because Ockham, the cars, the Humanists, the theft, the Earth, are on a different scale. Not on the scale of miracles. Bridger is as much more important to Carlyle, as much more real, as your clothes, your friends, your problems, the floor beneath your feet are more real and more important to you than we and our problems of an age now passed. This is the true last chapter of this first half of my history, the last chapter for Carlyle, for me. Here we glimpse the full and concrete shape of the Intervention—still shadowed but a shape in darkness instead of just darkness, a form with edges, definition, so we may say with certainty 'I saw Something'—the Intervention of Our Maker. The rest is merely what that Maker made.

"Bring 'em out! Bring out Mycroft Canner! We know you're hiding them, you filthy shitsack Servicers!"

Sticks and stones were not to be found in the clean glass tiers of Cielo de Pájaros, but trash flew just as hard, raining down on the heads of the Servicers who cowered amid the grass and petals of Bridger's flower trench. Their attackers were on the bridge above, five lamentably sober Humanists, who had pried open a garbage robot, baring yesterday's deposits ready to burst and smear.

"Bring the monster out here or there's a lot worse where this came from!"

I must say this first, reader: I am no Beggar King. My fellow Servicers have never considered me their leader. If some gather around me in the dorms it is because I am resourceful, and there are certain problems one does not take to the Cousins who are our babysitters. Criminals tend to have unfinished business, which often threatens the bash'es left behind. Many of these Servicers would have moved mountains in the past to save friends and family, but cannot anymore. I still can, begging favors from Madame or MASON when I dare, and when the need is great. So, when my need is great, the others are eager to give back.

A shout rallied the Servicers below: "Protect the food!"

Servicers have few things we can call precious, but a good meal justly earned is chief among them, so this picnic laid out on checked blankets on the grass was as worth fighting for as all the gold in Troy. They formed a makeshift wall, sheltering plates and platters with scraps from the dump, empty boxes, their uniforms, themselves, happy to accept a splatter if it would save a sandwich.

The attackers spat. "You're gonna lose a lot more than your lunch if you don't send Canner out! One call's all it'll take to have my whole crew down here, you'll see what damage a rugby team can do!"

A leader stepped forth among the Servicers, bristling with rage, but nameless here thanks to Kosala's censorship. "Look! We don't know anything about Mycroft Canner!"

"Don't give us that shit! The cops may be trying to cover it up, but the pictures are all over! Canner's hiding out as a Servicer!"

What was once chili struck the Servicer's shoulder, spattering rancid juice across her cheeks. "There are a couple hundred thousand Servicers worldwide! What makes you think we'd even know if it was true?"

The rot rain did not stop. "We're not buying that! Canner had a whole pack of Servicers with them when they came back to finish off that Mardi survivor. You're all in it together!"

Carlyle Foster rushed up behind the attackers now, his wrap and long scarf fluttering like silks around a fleeing nymph. His talk with Bryar Kosala the afternoon before had done much to revive his spirits, though he would have risen full of strength that day regardless, for March the twenty-seventh was sacred to Asclepius, Dionysus, Rama, the Bodhisattva Tara, the Egyptian powers Neteret Renenutet and Neter Nepri, and to St. Rupert of Salzburg, a day on which men honored their Creator in many ways in ages past, and still do today. The good Cousin charged in, ready to place a restraining hand on the nearest Humanist, but their last claim froze him. "There's a Mardi survivor?"

The attackers turned, their anger ready to give way to scorn. "Where've you been, Cousin, Mars? It happened yesterday, the video's all over. Tully Mardi's the kid's name, was addressing a crowd when in charges Mycroft Canner with a pack of Servicers. Good thing the kid recognized Canner or who knows what they'd have done!"

"Not that we'd expect you to care," another added. "This is your fault."

Carlyle drew back. "My fault?"

"You Cousins. Don't try to tell me it wasn't Bryar Kosala who kept the Emperor from putting that monster out of everybody's misery. 'Oh, Canner's just a poor traumatized little orphan!'" he whined, mocking Kosala with a squeaky voice which sounded nothing like her, "'We just need to be extra-nice to them and they'll turn into a good boy!'"

Carlyle's smile stayed serene. "Actually, Bryar Kosala doesn't think that," he corrected.

"What?"

"They don't think that. I've talked to Chair Kosala personally about Mycroft Canner and Kosala had nothing to do with the decision not to kill them."

"You talked to Bryar Kosala?" Fresh fire lit the mob's eyes. "Then it's true! Kosala knew! Do all the Cousins know? You've been covering it up, haven't you!"

"No! No! Nobody knows! I know because . . . I'm Mycroft Canner's sensayer." See how ably our Carlyle lies? "I'm not their regular sensayer, though," he backpedaled quickly, "but I get called in sometimes."

"Their sensayer?"

"How long have you known?" the hoodlums asked at once.

"What's your name, Cousin?"

"Who made the decision? Who kept Canner alive?"

"Was it the Utopians? We saw them save Canner in the video."

"How'd they get the Emperor to agree?"

They surrounded Carlyle, the trash in their hands far less menacing than the hands themselves.

Carlyle seemed surprised himself at his answer. "I don't know."

"Bullshit, Cousin!" One of them seized a fistful of Carlyle's hair.

"I mean it. I didn't realize it until now, but the whole time Kosala was telling me how they didn't make the decision to spare Mycroft Canner, they never told me who actually did. I don't know. I should know!"

"Don't give us that crap. You know. You're just trying to . . ."

"Hey up there!" the lead Servicer called from the trench, cupping garbage-spattered hands into a makeshift megaphone. "I thought you might like to know I called the police! They'll be here in about one minute, so I'd run if I were you! If you leave now we'll tell them a dog knocked the trash bot over, but if you stay, assault on Servicers, plus wrecking a public robot, plus harassing that Cousin, plus trying to force a sensayer to break vows, that's going to be one fat old fine!"

"Shit, they're right!" The skies were suddenly the enemy as the little mob searched for the falcon-streaks of cop cars.

"Book it!"

"You got lucky this time, Servicer shitsacks!"

"Bring the Cousin!"

"Leave the Cousin, they'll track them."

"Take a picture, we can find them later."

The troop stunned Carlyle with a camera flash, then bolted.

Watching the troublemakers run, leaving their fingerprints on the robot and their signatures stamped on the pavement by their Humanist boots, not a few of the Servicers laughed at the amateurs.

"Hey, sensayer," the Servicer leader called up, "you'd better be more careful what you say about Mycroft Canner or you're going to have mobs after you too!"

Carlyle leaned over the bridge's rail, gasping as he saw the Servicers clustered barely ten paces outside the plastic flaps of Bridger's cave. "What are you doing down there? That's a private yard!" Actually, it wasn't, but one tended to forget that the ever-empty public garden of the flower trench did not belong to its young master and his toys.

"We're here on a job. Come on down, I'll show you."

"Shouldn't I wait here for the police?"

All below laughed.

"The police aren't coming. That was what we in the business call a big fat lie. That makes us both liars, doesn't it?" The Servicer leader winked. "Everyone knows Mycroft only sees European Doria-Pamphili. Isn't that right, Cousin Foster?"

Carlyle tensed. "You know who I am?"

The Servicer grinned, like one who's just revealed a good poker hand. "It wasn't hard to guess. It's okay, people, that's the sensayer Mycroft said might come, the good one, not the evil one. Now let's get the picnic cleaned up and see what we've lost."

The other Servicers snapped to it, fifteen of them, their dappled uniforms making them look like boars around a watering hole as they bunched over their banquet.

"Then you do know Mycroft Canner!" Carlyle rushed down the stairway.

The Servicer leader met him at the bottom. "Of course. Who else do you think called us here, the Tooth Fairy?" A hat, that is how one could spot the leader, the only hat among the bunch, a cloth cap, black in this case, round with a small brim in the front and a central button. It is an unofficial uniform which sprang up somehow as those closest to me began to be regarded with some fraction of the reverence I receive from my peers; I do not have the right to discourage it.

Carlyle started with the obvious: "Where's Mycroft now?"

The Servicer Captain shrugged. "Stuck somewhere is what they said, but off the streets, safe. I'm supposed to tell you that a kid called Bridger has been moved to a safe house, but they're fine, and have all their important toys with them."

You wonder, reader, how I sent word if I am trapped without my tracker? She will not override Dominic's orders, but no nun can resist a sinner pleading on his knees for her to help him make a single call.

"What are you doing here?" Carlyle asked.

"Mycroft asked us to box this stuff up." The Captain pointed to a pile of crates, which the Servicers were loading into a car, like bees filling a comb. "It's an amazing collection."

Carlyle peered into a box, finding fifty plastic action figures packed with care within.

"This cave's all packed, but the other is taking longer." A slop-spattered elbow pointed up-trench, where a newly trampled road ran past Bridger's cave another fifty meters to a second entrance concealed within the walls.

"A second cave?" Carlyle repeated.

"There's a lot more packing left to do if you'd care to help. Mycroft also said to warn you that the evil sensayer Dominic is planning to kidnap and rape you, so you should stick with us to stay safe."

Carlyle chewed on that one for a moment. "Can you take me to Bridger?"

The Captain smiled. "Sorry, Cousin. Safe houses are only safe if you don't leave a trail to them."

"Please, it's important!"

"No can do. You hungry? There's plenty to go around."

There was indeed, for their efforts had not been in vain: the picnic survived, burgers and hot dogs, cookies and pies, chips and salads, jellybeans irregular like pebbles, chocolate truffles round as if hand-rolled, mad layered cakes four and five tiers tall, and fruits of every color heaped in mounds as if by a miserly monkey. Drinks stood ready too, bottle upon bottle of the rarest juices and colored sodas, all dutifully labeled, and not a few of them misspelled.

The Servicer Captain laughed as Carlyle gaped. "Look at that fruit, almost too beautiful to be real, isn't it?

Carlyle laughed to himself, a silent, breathy laugh. "Yes, perfect. The perfect power to feed the Servicers."

"What?"

Carlyle waved the 'what' away. "I thought you were only allowed to accept food for work."

"We are working. Mycroft knows we'd work for them for nothing, but they always leave a spread. So, how'd you get lucky enough to have our Mycroft looking after you, too?"

Carlyle took an unhappy breath. "Do you really all know Mycroft Canner? All the Servicers know?"

The Captain's eyes, better than most at reading men, grew narrow. "Off the record?"

"Off the record," Carlyle confirmed.

"If you've met Mycroft then you know it doesn't take a genius to realize there's something special under there. No one knew what at first, but with time we figured it out. There are signs."

"Yes. Yes, it would have to come out sometime."

"Not every one of us has actually met Mycroft," the Servicer Captain continued. "Everyone knows, though. It's amazing how many people can keep a secret when they know the whole world will turn into an angry mob if it gets out. You know one died this morning."

"One what?"

"A Servicer the mob mistook for Mycroft. I'm sure there'd have been more deaths but we've practiced for this, moving in groups, handling crowds. The administration didn't think to plan for our protection if word got out, but Mycroft did."

"I'm sorry." You will not blame Carlyle for having a one-track mind. "Look, I can't explain why, but I really, really need to see Bridger. There's never been anything so important."

The Captain's smile beamed condescension. "Is the world going to end in the next couple hours if you don't?"

"It might."

"I'm sorry," she answered, "but I genuinely don't know where Bridger is, just that it's a safe house. I'd help you if I could. Look, nobody can trap Mycroft for long. Stick with us and we'll get a visit, or another message, soon I'll bet, and then you can ask Mycroft to take you to Bridger. Meanwhile, relax and have a . . ." The Captain frowned, lifting a green striped ball from the picnic blankets. "Do you know what kind of fruit this is? We've been trying to guess at some of them for an hour. The inside has pink and orange blotches and tastes like raspberry, but none of us has ever seen one before."

Carlyle stared at the fantasy which Bridger calls a 'razzalope.' "I don't know. It . . ." His eye caught on another Servicer passing by with a crate of time-darkened Barbies. "Are these boxes all toys?"

"Yeah, the second cave's full of them. Want to see the collection before we box the rest? It's an amazing sight."

Snatching a 'strawberanna' en route, the Captain led Carlyle toward the second cave.

"Where are you taking it all?" Carlyle asked as more crates trudged past. "To the safe house? Won't that leave much more of a trail than just taking me?"

"It's going to Sniper's Doll Museum."

Carlyle's breath caught. "Sniper's?"

"Mycroft arranged it. Leave it to Mycroft to know everyone who's anyone."

The Cousin frowned. "I thought they only had Sniper Dolls at the Sniper Doll Museum."

"Until now they did. Apparently Mycroft convinced Sniper to make a new wing for this, a special exhibit on the pathos of the discarded toy. It should be really something."

It was already 'really something' even arrayed in the semi-dark of Bridger's second cave. The toys stood in phalanxes, row upon ten rows upon a hundred rows. As a library overstocked with relics crams shelves together to the maximum, hardly leaving room for scrunched shoulders to pass, so Bridger had crammed this cave, ten times the size of the other, with shelves, and then crammed every shelf with toys. It was a labor of love: children set with mommies and daddies, colts with mares, warriors with rivals, villains with heroes ready to stop them if they stirred, all with accessories, not the ones they came with but the sorts of things they would want to have on hand if wakened. They were lovingly posed: teachers at plastic blackboards, families at dinner tables, whole bash'es fishing together, making breakfast, dancing, moments in which one would not mind being trapped forever. Those with missing limbs were bandaged and placed in doctors' office play-sets, though the mobs of wounded outnumbered the doll-faced nurses like war victims. There were toy soldiers too, hundreds, who could not set down their plastic arms, but were posed as if in training, shooting targets, ducking obstacle courses, no combat, no casualties, the Green team carefully segregated from enemy Yellow. Can you picture Bridger, reader, picking these orphans from the garbage one by one? Can you see him scrubbing the centuries' muck from painted faces and calling each one 'friend'? It was the Major who volunteered to teach him that you can't save everyone. "Take your time," was how he started. "Your powers prove you're fated to be one of the special ones. Maybe someday, gods willing, you'll find a way to bring them all to life, and overthrow death's tyranny forever, but not today. Today we're scouts, learning about this world, and making plans. You don't bring in the army until you have the tents and grain to house them too."

"I've seen this before," Carlyle whispered. The Message doesn't have to be a burning bush, reader. From the Maker of planets, atoms, and electrons, the Message can be a thought.

"You have?" The Servicer Captain scanned the plastic hordes.

"Not this exactly, but I've had this feeling before, looking at something just like this. It was recent . . . What was it?" Carlyle chewed his thumbnail, struggling, atoms bouncing in their scripted paths. "Where did these come from?"

"The trash, apparently. There's a trash mine here. They're Twentieth to Twenty-Second Century mostly, all carefully cleaned up and fixed. It's going to be a really moving display, the idea of this many things that people used to love, abandoned."

Carlyle wandered through the shelves, not studying individual objects but vistas, the long stretch of close-crammed clutter that had been so much more than clutter to someone once. The atom strikes. "Jehovah . . ."

The Captain was not close enough to hear. "What?"

"Avignon. The icons collected at their house, that's where I've seen this! It's the same! Discarded things that people used to love, all crowded together by someone who can't stand to see them rot. An icon collection—a giant No-No Box." Carlyle rushed from row to row, unpacking his thoughts less to his companion than to the toys themselves, or to himself. "Why didn't I see it before? Mycroft wouldn't divide their time between the two of them unless they were equally important. And Bridger being what Bridger is, the other must also be . . . not toys necessarily but, like Bridger, they must have . . . That's why the Emperor would pick them, out of all the children in the world, and that's why Heloïse would talk like they're a god. If people raised at Madame's found something like Bridger they'd worship it."

The Servicer rushed to catch Carlyle among the cramped aisles. "Sorry, what? I can't hear you when you're rushing around like this."

Carlyle's eyes came into focus on the Servicer at last. "I'm sorry, you're totally the wrong person for me to discuss this with."

A frown of sympathy. "Anything I can do to help?"

"Short of taking me to Bridger, no," Carlyle answered. "I can call a car myself."

"Whoa, slow down." The Captain caught Carlyle by the shoulder as he started to bolt. "A car? Sorry, I can't let you go."

"What? Why not?"

"I told you, that evil sensayer Dominic is after you. I'm under orders to keep you here with us until the threat blows over."

"Under orders?"

"It's just an expression," the Captain claimed, though her dark eyes said different. "You're in real danger. Whatever you're doing, it can wait."

"That's my decision," Carlyle countered, "not yours."

"For the last time, this is serious." The Captain seized Carlyle by the coils of his scarf, dragging him back toward the picnic. "You're being offered food and hospitality by people for whom a little food is a big deal. Now sit down!"

Carlyle found himself shoved into a group gathered within the bridge's shadow, where a pair of Servicers had stripped the trash-smeared shirts from their backs to dance. It was beautiful, not one of society's formulaic, social dances, but the primitive enjoyment of the body, reaching, kicking, leaping, ducking, close as daredevils, always a hair's breadth from scraping one another's cheeks, or sharing sweat. It wasn't until one, thrusting with knife-straight fingers, scored a touch upon the other that Carlyle realized they were sparring.

The sensayer's voice grew cold. "Servicers aren't allowed to practice combat sports."

The Servicer Captain stared. "You say that with the public finding out that Mycroft Canner is a Servicer? That's reason enough to study self-defense if we didn't have others!"

A long frown. "I should go."

"No." Strong hands seized the scarf which looped around Carlyle like a harness. "I said, I'm under orders. You're staying here, safe."

"I have someone indescribably, incomparably important to find."

"You're staying here."

"Against my will?" Even as kind a soul as Carlyle can become nasty when the friendly face before him is less real than his mission. "I could message the Servicer Program about your little combat practice, have your paroles revoked. I will if you keep getting in my way. No, better yet, I know who to message."

"Stop!" The Captain seized Carlyle's arms with practiced speed, but tracker messages are fast as twitching. "What have you done?"

"Nothing that will hurt you. I just accepted an invitation I was offered to meet someone called Heloïse in Paris in an hour. It's an hour from here, so if I don't leave immediately, a lot of important people will start asking why."

I will not subject you, gentle reader, to the full breadth of this Servicer's knowledge of profanity. "Mycroft didn't warn me you were too stupid to live. You do realize I meant 'kidnap and rape' literally, right? We're talking about Dominic Seneschal."

"I know the kinds of threats that Mycroft makes. I've been to Paris, I know more than you."

The Servicer Captain frowned. "I also know the kinds of threats that Mycroft makes, and I've known Mycroft years longer than you have. This was a real threat."

Hush fell as the two competed, stare for stare. They both think they know me. They both think they know me so well.

"It's on again!" A young Servicer broke the silence. "Channel 1113."

As when a cloud consumes the sun and makes an afternoon's bright colors dim at once, so the Servicer Captain grew instantly cold. "Last chance, sensayer. I know Mycroft. I know the threat is real. I want to help you. But I won't let you endanger all the others if this person in Paris really will get us in trouble if you don't go now. Decide. Cancel the signal or go."

Carlyle smelled a rat. "What's on again? 1113, that's a tracker channel?"

"Crap is what's on, crap only we care about. Now, choose: safety or Paris?"

It was no choice, reader, not for a sensayer. Not now that the thought had come: that there are Two.

But Carlyle did make another choice, in the car en route to Paris, those sixty minutes. He tuned his tracker in to Channel 1113. It turned out to be a minor news station broadcasting from a square in Ankara, where Tully stood again upon his soapbox: "What do you think caused the great wars of the past?" he ranted, this time to a larger sliver of the listening world. "Economic instability? We have that, the economic giants, Masons, Mitsubishi, desperate to tear one another down. Was it prejudice? One group hating another? Walk down a street and hear the way angry people use 'Mason,' 'Cousin,' 'Utopian,' as if they were insults. If we magically plucked a war expert from the past and showed them the present, they'd say in an instant that we're on the verge of war. The only reason our current experts haven't said it is that we don't have any. We believe so blindly that war's impossible that we hardly study it anymore. You think the Hives are too friendly, too closely allied, too civilized to make war? The nation-states thought the same thing about each other in 1914, right before the First World War broke out. All it takes is one spark. That time it was the assassination of an Emperor's nephew. What will it be this time?"

※※※※※※※※※※※※※※※※

Martin Guildbreaker's Last Interlude: "The Utopians Aren't Dirty like the Rest of Us"

NOTE OF MARTIN GUILDBREAKER, 03/27/2454: CAESAR, DO not read this. Nor you, *Domine*, not yet. All that I have and all that I am are open before the pair of you, always, but these are the raw notes of something not yet quite transparent. They would hurt you. They would hurt you, Caesar, by making you unable to continue as you have. You could not trust, could not endure, but at the same time you could not act, not on the little that is here. I would not see you so paralyzed. As soon as there are answers, enough for your awakened rage to know its foe, I will tell you. Until then, mighty Caesar, I trust you to trust me. As for you, *Domine*, read not this transcript yet. For you the price is grief. I would not have you suffer until I can, at least, bring with that suffering the consolation of understanding.

* * *

08:38 UT, 03/27/2454, Universal Free Alliance Police Headquarters, Romanova.

Commissioner General Ektor Carlyle Papadelias: "Well, well, if it isn't Martin Guildbreaker! What brings you to my office at this hour of the night? Or is it not night anymore? Nine-thirty A.M.! Where does the time go?"

Guildbreaker: "I want an unbiased second opinion."

Papadelias: "Don't set those down here, this is my Mycroft Canner desk, you don't want to get your files mixed up in these. Use that desk, my Everything Else desk. Don't mind the mess. This is about *Black Sakura*, I assume?"

Guildbreaker: "I want an unbiased second opinion."

Papadelias: "About time. I've been telling you from the start this wasn't a matter to be handled without me. Now, I know better than anyone how tangled poly-Hive law can get, and I agree sometimes the world is better off when you and your team lubricate these things, but I have seventy years' experience at this and you have six, so when I send you a message that I need to see you about something ASAP, it shouldn't take you four days to turn up here."

Guildbreaker: "I want an unbiased second opinion."

Papadelias: "Quite a mountain of files you've got here: flight plans, autopsy reports, sensayer session schedules, old *Sniper* magazines . . . What's brewing? Something big, I could've told you that four days ago."

Guildbreaker: "I want an unbiased second opinion."

Papadelias: "What's happened?"

Guildbreaker: "I want an unbiased second opinion."

Papadelias: "Understood. Shannon, cancel whatever I have scheduled in the next five hours, and make sure nobody not nobody comes in here unless the Emperor's on fire."

Guildbreaker: "Thank you, Commissioner. I'll lock the door."

Papadelias: "I'm going to shuffle these files so I read them in a random order without influence from how you arranged them."

Guildbreaker: "I organized them alphabetically by the ninth word in each document."

Papadelias: "Random enough. I'll ask you yes/no or fact questions from time to time as I read, but no opinion questions, sound good?"

Guildbreaker: "Yes. I'm recording this conversation for the record. I'll have it reviewed by an independent party to verify that I didn't suggest any conclusions to you."

Eight minutes of reading in silence.

Papadelias: "So, one engineer's report says the damage Aki Sugiyama's fiancé's 'suicide kit' did to the car shouldn't have been enough to make it crash, but the other two didn't find anything suspicious."

Guildbreaker: "I've ordered another three engineers to review the wreck. I expect their reports by the end of today."

Papadelias: "The engineer who was suspicious was the same one who said the flight plan was fishy?"

Guildbreaker: "Yes. There are 162 standard flight paths from the origin to the destination city, of which only two guarantee that the car would not hit any habitations if it crashed. It was on one of those two. The likelihood of that is one point two percent, and the passenger could not control which flight path the car took."

Papadelias: "This is sketchy. I see the hints, but this is nowhere near enough to make an accusation of complicity, not in court. Not when we have this call between Aki Sugiyama and O'Beirne in which O'Beirne explicitly states suicidal intent."

Ten minutes of reading in silence.

Papadelias: "Esmerald Revere's notes on Cato Weeksbooth classify these 'episodes' into two types."

Guildbreaker: "In Type A Cato demands an emergency sensayer session and appears in a state of extreme distress. In Type B Cato doesn't see Revere, but puts in twice the normal number of hours at the museum that week, and museum colleagues report Cato skipping meals and displaying other signs of agitation."

Papadelias: "Twenty-seven out of forty-seven car crashes in the past five years were immediately preceded by one of these episodes. That's roughly half of all crashes."

Guildbreaker: "I'm still working on the preceding five years, but I've had to get the crash reports through back channels, since the standard channel is to call Ockham Saneer."

Papadelias: "One episode preceded Revere's death, and got worse right before the O'Beirne crash."

Guildbreaker: "Yes."

Papadelias: "Before, not after."

Guildbreaker: "Yes."

Two minutes of reading in silence.

Papadelias: "This says Cato has eight to eleven episodes per year, and half of them don't precede car crashes."

Guildbreaker: "Yes, almost exactly half."

Papadelias: "But the other half do."

Guildbreaker: "Very precisely half."

Twenty-one minutes of reading in silence.

Papadelias: "This is sketchy."

Guildbreaker: "What?"

Papadelias: "The death of Yangtze Dekker in a car crash 11/22/2453 resulted in their widow appealing to their brother on the news, which probably ended the Six Lakes Hostage Crisis. The death of retired *Romanov* editor Anlevine Gorz-Marmalade in a car crash 08/08/2452 drastically weakened the Nurturist faction in the European elections. The death of Madden Manila in a car crash 05/15/2451 made Mycroft Gao drop out of the anti-Mitsubishi-land-grab movement. The death of Kirkegard Ranker may have passed the Reservation Welfare Act. The death of Jay Daiko may have saved Rongcorp & Subsidiaries. The death of Herrera Lee may have eased the Greenpeace Mitsubishi factionalism. But none of this is direct influence, these are all friends, cousins, ex-roommates, sometimes with four or five degrees of rather sketchy separation from the effect they're supposed to have had."

Guildbreaker: "Yes."

Papadelias: "Connections no one would spot unless they were already looking for something suspicious, just like with Sugiyama's grandba'kid's fiancé."

Guildbreaker: "Exactly."

Papadelias: "How many of these did you find? These politically consequential crashes."

Guildbreaker: "Thirty-four so far, roughly five per year or fifty percent of all car crashes over the last seven years."

Papadelias: "Thirty-four? Was whoever did this analysis told which crashes were preceded by Cato's episodes?"

Guildbreaker: "No."

Papadelias: "Yet it seems every single politically influential death was preceded by an episode."

Guildbreaker: "So it seems."

Papadelias: "And the crashes which were not preceded by episodes seem to have had no meaningful political consequences."

Guildbreaker: "So it seems."

Papadelias: "Thirty-five deaths over seven years. The rafting accident that killed their ba'pas was five years ago, right?"

Guildbreaker: "Correct."

Papadelias: "So this has to have started before that."

Guildbreaker: "At least two years before."

Four minutes of reading in silence.

Papadelias: "Hmm . . . You intend these as control groups?"

Guildbreaker: "Which?"

Papadelias: "Proportion of lethal food poisoning victims whose deaths had a detectible political impact, two point two percent; proportion of bee-sting deaths with a political impact, two point five percent; proportion of deaths from elevators breaking, two point three percent . . ."

Guildbreaker: "Yes, control groups. I had my analyst do precisely the same analysis of these groups that they did on the car crash deaths, since it's possible that, with five degrees of separation, anyone's death can have a traceable political impact. Two percent can, it seems, but two percent is not fifty percent."

Papadelias: "No. No, it's not."

Eighteen minutes of reading in silence.

Papadelias: "Where did you get this data?"

Guildbreaker: "Which?"

Papadelias: "Cato's episode in January did not precede a crash, but preceded the suicide of Tipper Casterman, which pulled Haleakala Banks out of the Nurturist movement. Cato's episode in November preceded the alcohol poisoning death of Carlyle Gali, which stopped their uncle's string of inflammatory speeches against President Ganymede. Cato's episode in August preceded an unforeseen reaction to new medication which killed the infamous blackmailer Colorado Dix."

Guildbreaker: "Three weeks before that episode, an experiment Cato conducted in the Junior Scientist Squad lab in Chicago suggested the possibility of that very medication causing such a fatal reaction when combined with another rare drug, but Cato tried to destroy the data. I stole the files."

Papadelias: "You just confessed to a crime."

Guildbreaker: "I know."

Papadelias: "These deaths, these people who didn't die in crashes, they have no connection of any kind to the Saneer-Weeksbooth bash', to *Black Sakura*, to anything. What did you do, analyze every single person who died the day after one of Cato's episodes to see if any had a political impact?"

Guildbreaker: "The two days after, yes."

Papadelias: "How? There must have been thousands."

Guildbreaker: "Tens of thousands. At first I asked the Romanovan Censor if they could do some calculations for me, but they were too busy. Their deputy Jung Su-Hyeon Ancelet Kosala was also too busy, and Toshi Mitsubishi is biased, so I asked Mycroft Canner."

Papadelias: "Naturally."

Guildbreaker: "Mycroft was also too busy, so I asked Jung Su-Hyeon to recommend someone else who could do calculations on this scale. They said I should hire a Cartesian set-set."

Papadelias: "Cartesian specifically?"

Guildbreaker: "Cartesian specifically. They're capable of following dynamic charts with up to forty-five variables at once, so they can do the work of ten Censors, at least as far as reading data goes."

Papadelias: "That's the same kind of set-set Eureka Weeksbooth and Sidney Koons are, right?"

Guildbreaker: "Yes. I hired one as the Censor recommended, and that set-set is also how I found the political connections of the car crash victims. The connections are so indirect that, on my own I would only have spotted a handful of them, but the set-set found them in a flash. All they needed was a computer system with software for tracking the relationships between all people in the world. Five such computers exist to my knowledge: the computers in the Romanovan Censor's office, the Tracker System, the Transit Computers in the Saneer-Weeksbooth bash', the identical computers at the Salekhard backup site, and the Utopian Transit System computers, which are what I used for the purpose."

Two minutes of reading in silence.

Papadelias: "From this report, the victims tend to be, how should one put this . . ."

Guildbreaker: "Unpromising individuals."

Papadelias: "I was going to say 'losers,' but that'll do. People with few friends, low-impact hobbies, and jobs which don't generate much that's used by anyone else—no artists, researchers, teachers, great industrialists, corporate leaders, athletes, or anything."

Guildbreaker: "Yes."

Papadelias: "And all the victims are either Masons, Cousins, Brillists, or Hiveless. No Humanists, no Mitsubishi, no Europeans, and, of course, no Utopians, since the Utopians have their separate transit system."

Guildbreaker: "Humanists, Mitsubishi, and Europeans have died in crashes on occasion, but Cato did not have episodes before those crashes, and less than two point five percent of their deaths were influential, just as in the case of beestings or elevator crashes. And they die in crashes substantially less often than Masons, Cousins, or Brillists."

Papadelias: "How did no one notice that before?"

Guildbreaker: "Perhaps because there are many more Masons and Cousins anyway. Or perhaps because the entire press and media of the whole world is united in a conspiracy to conceal this. Or something in between."

Papadelias: "Heh. And one of them has the gall to go by 'Sniper.'"

Guildbreaker: "You see it, don't you?"

Papadelias: "It's too much. I expected a small conspiracy, a couple murders, not dozens over years, thirty-five using the cars themselves, as many by other means, but Cato knew . . . No wonder the others wouldn't let Cato quit and become a Utopian."

Guildbreaker: "Yes. Yes, that was what led me to this, actually."

Papadelias: "Oh?"

Guildbreaker: "Cato said, quote: 'The Utopians aren't dirty like the rest of us.' From the point of view of someone who runs the cars, the thing which most distinguishes Utopians from everyone else is that they have their own separate system. Utopians can't be killed in crashes, and you won't find any Utopian names in the lists of people killed by other means either."

Papadelias: "Of course not. Anything that kills a Utopian they investigate until they solve it. If I were an assassin I'd never touch them."

Guildbreaker: "Exactly. Utopians don't profit from the system and they aren't targeted by it. They're untouched, 'clean' from Cato's perspective, while the rest of the world . . ."

Papadelias: "While the rest of the world has been held together by shoestrings and assassination for the past seven years."

Guildbreaker: "For the record, Commissioner General, would you please explain out loud the conclusion that you've come to, so a third party can compare it to my independently derived conclusion which I recorded just before I came?"

Papadelias: "Relax, Guildbreaker. I know you're a Mason, but there are limits to how methodical you have to be."

Guildbreaker: "For the record."

Papadelias: "Fine. Since coming of age, the current generation of Saneer-Weeksbooth bash has been carrying out a series of systematic assassinations. The two Cartesian set-sets, Eureka Weeksbooth and Sidney Koons, can use the Transit System computers to figure out how to influence events by identifying low-profile people to assassinate, whose deaths won't seem suspicious but will have the desired impact. This bash', or someone controlling it, has been using these assassinations to manipulate world politics for at least seven years. They've conspicuously avoided killing any Humanists, Mitsubishi, or Europeans, either because those Hives are backing them, or just because the bash' are Humanists, they have old ties with the Mitsubishi manifest in the ancestry of Sniper, Cato, and Eureka, and . . . no, I have no theory about Europe at the moment. The assassins know they can't kill too many people in crashes or the sudden increase will look suspicious, so members of the bash' had to develop other ways to kill, culminating in the unfortunate Cato Weeksbooth, who's been using their scientific expertise for murder, and feels so guilty about it that they come close to attempting suicide every time. Twelve times a year for seven years makes at least eighty murders, is that about right?"

Guildbreaker: "My set-set is still looking at earlier years."

Papadelias: "It's hard not to see it when you look. All it took was someone to point us at the Saneer-Weeksbooth bash' and connect it with Sugiyama through *Black Sakura.* Someone wants this exposed."

Guildbreaker: "Yes, that's very worrying. I still have no clue who, or why. Do you?"

Papadelias: "Only hunches. It's best not to share hunches."

Guildbreaker: "May I ask a couple more details?"

Papadelias: "Fire away."

Guildbreaker: "How do you account for the suicide deaths? The recording of the phone call to Aki Sugiyama proves O'Beirne was talking about wanting to kill themself, whether or not that was what actually made the car crash, and the autopsy of Esmerald Revere left no doubt that that was suicide. If you review the list of supposed victims, more than thirty percent of those who didn't die in crashes are suicides."

Papadelias: "Suicide is the most common cause of death. Any smart killer tries to make their murders look like suicides."

Guildbreaker: "Would you guess this conspiracy involves every member of the Saneer-Weeksbooth bash' or just some of them?"

Papadelias: "No telling yet, but my gut says all. They must know Cato is the weak link; if they've involved Cato they'll have involved everyone. Plus, every member of that bash' is insane to some degree. Being a mass murderer will do that to you. So will murdering your own ba'pas when they find out."

Guildbreaker: "Then you agree the rafting accident was no accident?"

Papadelias: "I investigated that myself when it happened. There was no evidence of foul play, but it always smelled fishy to me. Now we know why. This system couldn't work if the parents were against it, if nothing else the older set-sets would have figured it out sooner or later."

Guildbreaker: "Do you think the bash' calls the hits themselves, or are they working for someone?"

Papadelias: "It would be wonderful, wouldn't it, if they were calling the hits themselves? Then we could jail them and have an end of it. But Ganymede sure did look worried talking to Sniper at the party. And it's been people at the top, not in the bash', above the bash', working so hard to keep me off the case. Hive leaders involved in eighty assassinations over seven years will make Mycroft's rampage look like a slow news day."

Guildbreaker: "Do you think Mycroft knew about this? They spend time with the Saneer-Weeksbooth bash'. A lot of time. Mycroft doesn't have spare time to spend."

Papadelias: "Maybe we shouldn't have switched desks after all."

Guildbreaker: "Mycroft's murders were thirteen years ago. We don't know yet if this goes back that far, but the kids would have been awfully young. But the Mardi murders were the most politically influential deaths in centuries."

Papadelias: "No, I don't . . . Mycroft was the mind behind . . . maybe. But the Mardis' deaths were too early, and too conspicuous to fit the profile. And they didn't exactly benefit the Humanists, or any Hive."

Guildbreaker: "Not all the deaths benefited Humanists. There are deaths here which benefited Masons, Cousins, or Gordian, many with more general benefits, to end a crisis, calm things down, anti-Mitsubishi land riots, Nurturists, all our hot spots."

Papadelias: "Yes. That sounds like something a lone bash' might plot. Especially if the set-sets can see these things coming. Though possibly your definition of benefit is too strict. All Hives benefit when the world is stable and the economy is strong. Given how incestuous politics is today, a death that helps the Masons short-term may be a long-term good for everyone. Ganymede recognizes that, Andō recognizes that, MASON recognizes that."

Guildbreaker: "Yes. Commissioner General, I've been thinking . . . in a larger sense, this . . . assassination system . . . it's arguably a good thing for the world. The vaguer economic influences aside, some of these murders provably saved hundreds of lives, thousands in some cases. Cumulatively many thousands. Thousands at the cost of dozens. We're not talking about a secret underbelly of mass murder here, we're talking about a secret underbelly of killing one to save ten thousand."

Papadelias: "Mm. Nurturism and the Mitsubishi land grab are the most volatile issues in our world right now, and a good third of these hits seem to have been designed to calm those down. If they hadn't, I wonder what those set-sets see in their numbers. What would've happened?"

ADDENDUM of Martin Guildbreaker, 05/21/2454: I feel compelled to edit myself here. It is strange rereading this history as an editor, with the fuller context adding layers to the facts. But nothing has changed more than this moment. I gave a different answer then, which I pass over here, a useless, reasonable, Mycroft might say rose-tinted answer. But now, as I reread, I hear a different answer, not in my voice, in Tully Mardi's, prefaced by Mycroft's desperate, silent plea: "Don't say it! Saladin, don't let them say it!"

War.

Papadelias: "You thought hard, didn't you, before bringing this to me?"

Guildbreaker: "Yes, it was hard. But I don't have the right to make this judgment call alone. My mandate is to smooth over minor transgressions whose exposure would do more harm than good, but 'minor transgressions' is generally restricted to crimes which have not resulted in a death. This has resulted in at least eighty, even if it's saved many thousands at the same time."

Papadelias: "I almost hope we won't be able to find enough evidence. Because if we make this public we're going to be the ones who started the fire."

Guildbreaker: "Then you agree we don't have enough evidence yet?"

Papadelias: "Not nearly enough. This is circumstantial, statistics, probabilities. You can see it, I can see it, but no panel would convict with just this, not with charges on this scale. Eighty murders. If we're going to nail the assassins we're either going to need a confession, or to catch them red-handed."

Guildbreaker: "That's another reason I came to you. Working together we should have a better shot."

Papadelias: "Has anyone besides us seen the evidence you just showed me?"

Guildbreaker: "Only my hired set-set, though they've been carefully isolated, and they don't know why we are researching this. They don't know know the cars were more important than the beestings."

Papadelias: "No one else? Not Mycroft Canner?"

Guildbreaker: "No, Mycroft has been busy with the Seven-Ten list. Dominic Seneschal is currently pursuing the investigation independently; I don't know whether or not they have discovered what I have."

Papadelias: "Anyone else?"

Guildbreaker: "I have no reason to believe that the *Porphyrogene* cannot read my mind."

Papadelias: "I get the feeling it was hard for you to put that so bluntly. I'll return the favor and not ask."

Guildbreaker: "Thank you."

Papadelias: "Guildbreaker, is there any chance J.E.D.D. Mason is in on this? They have their fingers deep in every pie. I've met them often enough to know they're incomprehensible to us mere mortals, but if anyone could tell it would be you."

Guildbreaker: "It's absolutely impossible for *Dominus* to be involved."

Papadelias: "How can you be sure?"

Guildbreaker: "The *Porphyrogene* is incapable of willing or permitting death. I can't explain precisely why, but you know how, before vat-meat, strict Buddhists didn't eat meat because you never know if any given chicken might be a reincarnation of your dead grandparent? This is infinitely stronger than that, literally infinitely. Why do you think Mycroft Canner can't kill anymore?"

Papadelias: "Can't and won't are very different things, Mason."

Guildbreaker: "I know. I said 'can't' and I meant it."

Papadelias: "Well, then, whatever impossible thing your J.E.D.D. Mason did to Mycroft Canner, let's hope they can do it to ten billion more people before this news breaks. Eighty-five murders, it'll be worse than the Set-Set Riots."

Guildbreaker: "No, not ten billion people. Seven. Seven is enough."

HERE ENDS
Too Like the Lightning,
THE FIRST HALF OF
Mycroft Canner's History.

CONTINUED IN
THE SECOND HALF,
Seven Surrenders.

AUTHOR'S *Note* AND *Acknowledgments*

ADA PALMER

I wanted it so much. So much sometimes it felt like I couldn't breathe. Sometimes I would cry, not because I was sad, but because it hurt, physical pain from the intensity of wanting something so much. I'm a good student of philosophy, I know my Stoics, Cynics, their advice, that, when a desire is so intense it hurts you, the healthy path is to detach, unwant it, let it go. The healthy thing for the self. But there are a lot of reasons one can want to be an author: acclaim, wealth, self-respect, finding a community, the finite immortality of name in print, so many more. But I wanted it to add my voice to the Great Conversation, to reply to Diderot, Voltaire, Osamu Tezuka, and Alfred Bester, so people would read my books and think new things, and make new things from those thoughts, my little contribution to the path which flows from Gilgamesh and Homer to the stars. And that isn't just for me. It's for you. Which means it was the right choice to hang on to the desire, even when it hurt so much. And it was worth it. But it took a lot of friends to help me through. It took the teachers who oversaw the long apprenticeship that is learning to write: Martin Beadle, Katherine Haas, Peter Markus, Olive Moochler, Mary Shoemaker, Hal Holiday, Gabriel Asfar, James Hankins, and Alan Charles Kors. It took advisors who lent their expertise for my world-building: Irina Greenman, Weiyi Guo, Sumana Harihareswara, Yoon Ha Lee, Mary Anne Mohanraj, Johanna Ransmeier, and Sabrina Vourvoulias. It took friends who read the manuscript and told me that it really was good enough, when I needed so badly to hear that: John Burgess, Anneke Cassista, Valerie Cooke, Gina Dunn, Greer Gilman, Matt Granoff, Betsy Isaacson, Walter Isaacson, Ashleigh LaPorta, Michael Mellas, Lindsey Nilsen, Brent O'Connell, Priscilla Painton, Luke Somers, Warren Tusk, Milton Weatherhead, Alexa Weingarden, and Ruth Wejksnora. It took the friends who helped me launch this firstborn into the world at last: Lila Garrott, Teresa Nielsen Hayden, and Jo Walton. It took Lauren Schiller, who, for sixteen years and counting, has listened to me blither incoherent shards of plot when I can't stand to be the only person in the world who knows. It took Jonathan Sneed, who is taking us to Mars now, stepping-stone by stepping-stone, and Carl Engle-Laird, who changed what friendship means for me, and is a real Utopian. It took my parents, the potent booster rocket of their untiring support. It took my mother Laura Higgins Palmer's creativity and industry, my father Doug Palmer's deep love of the fruits of imagination that I love. It took my agent, Amy Boggs, and my editor, Patrick Nielsen Hayden, who were excited to find a work about utopia, progress, about the future's growing pains, but not the cataclysm of dystopia that has so dominated recent conversations. It took Tor, and all the people there who have dedicated their lives to helping the conversation continue: Miriam Weinberg, Irene Gallo, Diana Griffin, my excellent cover artist Victor Mosquera, my indulgent and meticulous copy editor Liana Krissoff, and the brilliant book designer Heather Saunders, who turned my request for period typography into pure text art. But, above all, it took the communities whose firebrand discourses of hope and future-building make me so excited to offer more fuel for their flames: the small communities of my science fiction and fantasy clubs, Double Star at Bryn Mawr, HRSFA at Harvard, the whole little intellectual utopia of Simon's Rock College; and, beyond them, it took the vast, diasporic community of readers who see us among the stars. I received my hard-fought "Yes" at the 2013 San Antonio Worldcon, and I remember staggering back to our Cushing Library booth in the Dealer's Room so overwhelmed that I could barely choke out the syllables to explain to my colleague Todd Samuelson why I was sobbing. And the pain ended. But the intensity didn't. It transformed into something different, an acceleration instead of an exhaustion, just as overwhelming but so positive: it became gratitude. Because I wanted it so much, and I got it. So my work has just begun. I look forward to the next part of the Conversation—the part we have together. Thank you.

Turn the page for a sneak peek at
book II of the Terra Ignota quartet

SEVEN SURRENDERS

Available February 2017

Chapter the FIRST

Nihil Obstet

Nihil Obstat—'Nothing prevents it'—was the old license-by-fiat which kings and inquisitors pronounced in stifled ages when no printing press could give its inky kiss to paper until Tyrant Church and Tyrant State had loosed censorship's universal gag. But 'nihil obstet' is something else when He appends it to our permissions page, Good Jehovah Mason. 'Obstet' is a prayer, one He made over and over to the many authorities who guard humanity: His Imperial father, the Cousin Chair, the King of Spain, the Sensayers' Conclave, the far-seeing Censor, Brill's wise Institute: 'Let nothing prevent it.' They feared as much for Him as for themselves, tried to sow doubt in Him, asked Him by His many names: Are You sure You want to do this, J.E.D.D. Mason? Tribune? *Porphyrogene?* Prince? Tenth Director? Tai-Kun? Xiao Hei Wang? Jed? Jagmohan? Micromegas? Jehovah Epicurus Donatien D'Arouet Mason? Are You sure You want this snarling, wounded Earth to learn so much of You? But Madame D'Arouet, who raised Ἄναξ Jehovah in that strange bash'-out-of-time she cultured in the gold-drenched heart of Paris, also taught Him numbers: one and many, less and more. So, the same grim calculus that compelled Cicero and Seneca to give their lives for bleeding Rome compels Jehovah now to end the desperation-pain of the ten billion who cry for answers, even at the cost of worse pain to those dearest to Him, and Himself. For your sake, reader, He prayed, to one, to many. And for His sake I pray too, to That One Power—absent from our permissions page—Which could still stop us, as It stopped firebrand Apollo. The many mouths of Providence have swallowed up a thousand histories, and could swallow one more. So I pray: Let nothing obstruct this book and the Good it aims at. If there is benevolence in You, strange Creator, *nihil obstet.*

Sniper's Chapter

RESTRICTION: THIS SECTION MUST BE EXCISED BEFORE THIS DOCUMENT MAY BE PUBLISHED OR DISTRIBUTED. PRIVATE ACCESS MAY BE GRANTED BY JUDICIAL ORDER.

RESTRICTION ORDERED BY: The Conclave of Sensayers of the Universal Free Alliance.
REASON: Libelous attribution of criminal acts to a licensed sensayer.

RESTRICTION ORDERED BY: Cousins' Legal Commission.
REASON: Potential harm to the public peace, potential harm to minors herein discussed.

RESTRICTION ORDERED BY: Ordo Quiritum Imperatorisque Masonicorum.
REASON: Instigation of violence against a *Familiaris Regni*.

RESTRICTION ORDERED BY: Universal Free Alliance Commissioner General Ektor Carlyle Papadelias.
REASON: Strong evidence that substantial parts of this document are an alteration or forgery with destructive intent.

DURATION OF RESTRICTION: Five years, renewable pending review.

* * *

Howdy, fans and foes! This is your very own Sniper. First, let me assure you that I'm alive and well. The fugitive lifestyle suits me fine, my wounds are healed, I have plenty of allies, and I will kill Jehovah Mason for you, that I swear, today, tomorrow, a year from now, however long it takes. They can't guard the little prince forever. Tyrants and assassins have a great symbiosis. Assassins are always evil and despised (even when our effects are good we're still a bad means to a good end) until tyrants crop up. Then suddenly assassins are heroes, lifelines; suddenly we alone have the power to save the world without a revolution and the destruction revolutions bring. You admit you need us. But, between tyrants, you forget that assassins will only be here, ready, when you want us if we've been here, ready, the whole time. You feel dirty keeping such a weapon in the house, but somebody has to keep one or it won't be there when the bad wolf comes to huff and puff. My office is no less a pillar of this age than Censor or Anonymous. I serve with no less pride.

Second, I should say I'm only writing this one chapter, and Mycroft will take over again when I've had my say. Mycroft went to great lengths to contact me so I could describe this event, which did come next in sequence. I agreed to relate it only on condition that they promise not to touch a word of what I wrote. It's a privilege I intend to abuse to the utmost, and I'll have my say about Jehovah Mason before I'm done. But I'll start first with the part that will make your usual narrator squirm the most: correcting their willful omission and giving you a proper physical description of Mycroft Canner.

Mycroft is average height, shorter because they stoop, and swimming in their oversized uniform, like a statue wrapped in sacking, waiting to be restored. Their hair is curly in that classical Greek way, off-black, closer to a grayish tint than brown, and overgrown around the sides and forehead, as if they imagine so marvelous a creature could hide itself beneath a few stray locks. Modern science has kept their face as fresh at thirty-one as it was at seventeen, when all it took was a glance from Mycroft Canner to make the strongest shudder, but now those devil eyes lock tamely on the floor. They're brown eyes if you get a look at them, bright brown and antique feeling, like the brown tint which makes old wine richer than new. There's a scarring on their upper lip where violence has split it once too often, which gives a sense of hidden fangs. But the real prize comes when you strip away their uniform and bare the skin beneath, a tapestry of scars, all shapes, all vintages: the crumpled edges of old cuts and bites, the roughness of burns, strap-sores around the wrists and ankles, the ley lines of surgery, bullet holes round like little kisses, all layered on top of one another like a graffiti wall which tempts you to add your own mark. There's a story behind every scar, and I've spent many lucky hours tracing that skin and asking about each; Mycroft answers about one-third of the time.

The Mycroft you remember from the news was lean, all muscle like a starving scavenger. That hasn't changed. The wildest stray goes soft after a year of warm laps and petting, but not Mycroft. I don't believe Mycroft starves themself only as self-punishment. It could be that they don't want to taint such a body with whatever unhealthy slop Servicers' patrons tend to offer, but I suspect it's just that our predator finds common food hard to choke down after what they've tasted. Their famous hat (and even I was surprised to learn it came from Dominic Seneschal) is round, brown, something like a newsboy cap, though more patches than cloth at this point, with only the remnants of what might have been a brim. Mycroft lied to you, you know. They said there was no Beggar King to command the Servicers, but the sight of that hat makes the others snap to attention as surely as a crown. It's not for the crimes that the other Servicers idolize Mycroft, it's what Mycroft's done since. Even in Hell they're stunned to find an angel among them, willing to be as much a guardian as a fallen angel can.

Today's Mycroft genuinely is as obsequious in person as they are in print, a self-styled slave in this world which has none. But if you sit with them awhile, and talk, and coax, the formality fades, the hunch which hides the still-strong shoulders loosens, the hands begin to splay like claws, and eventually the beast I call True Mycroft pokes its nose above the surface. It's not a prisoner in there, not fighting to break free, just resting inside Slave Mycroft like a ship in harbor, saving itself for something. Slave Mycroft has only one expression: apology. As for True Mycroft, their expressions are unreadable, or rather you're wrong if you try to read them, like when the shape of a dog's face makes it seem to smile or frown where really you're just projecting human expressions onto an inhuman thing.

Like most of us, I first laid eyes on Mycroft Canner on the news just after the capture, as the police wheeled them past row on row of emergency forces. Mycroft was so serene then, basking in the procession as if that transparent coffin-cage was a triumphal chariot. We'd already heard Mycroft's reasons for the Mardi killings from the recorded speeches they left beside the later bodies. This was the supreme act of violence of this century, done not by a government, not a Church, not a tribe, not an army, but by an individual. Ever since villagers first wielded sharpened sticks in their chief's name the State had held a monopoly on supreme violence, but the Hive system ended that. Mycroft called their killings a demonstration of a liberty our era had not realized we possessed, proof of history's progress if seventeen deaths were enough to shock the world; historically, seventeen deaths is a good day. Philosophers had long speculated about Savage Man, whether the conscience is innate or implanted by society, and whether the human mind is actually capable of willing evil for the sake of evil—even the most heinous killers still tend to imagine some goal (revenge, profit, personal pleasure, some mad command). It's an important question, fundamental really—can we choose actions that purely make the world worse without any perverse perceived benefit?—but we couldn't discover whether the true Human Beast could exist back when the Beast was like a craftsman in an age of mass production, negligible beside the infinitely greater evils: Democide and War. There before the cameras Mycroft preached that, in these days of peace when we choose our Hive and values for ourselves, human individuals finally have the chance to be the worst thing in the world, and the right to be proud of our choice if we are not. That was the first time I fell in love with anyone outside my bash'.

It was a month after the arrest that Eureka told me Mycroft Canner wasn't executed after all. We had to make them ours, that was clear. My crush aside, I always say a killer can smell a killer, and with yours truly on the news every five minutes, Mycroft had surely scented me by now. Eureka tracked Mycroft down among the Servicers, and Ockham paid the visit. It took moments for each to recognize what other was. Laconic Ockham delivered simply, "Come," which Mycroft matched with an instant, "Yes, Məəəer Saneer," in Mycroft's signature vague diction which lets you think they're saying 'Member' but underneath it's really 'Master' leaking out. Lesley and I had spent weeks concocting blackmail enough to collar the beast (and keep them silent, which was Ockham's concern), and were a little pissed to find our schemes superfluous. We'd sent the trapper after a wolf and caught a fawning puppy; there was no choice but to adopt it. It was supposed to be my puppy, but Thisbe set their sights on it, and when Thisbe stirs even O.S. trembles. I still got Mycroft as a playmate, storyteller, sparring partner, but only Thisbe got them at night, and (as I've learned now) never touched them. Just as well; as one learns from the obituaries of the wealthy perverts Mycroft used to prostitute themself to, raising money to help other Servicers, if you sleep with Mycroft Canner you don't live long (and thanks to reading the first half of this history, I now know to call that phenomenon Saladin).

Enough authorial abuse for now. My kidnapping on March twenty-seventh, that's what I'm supposed to talk about. It happened at six A.M. by my schedule. I'd just endured a nasty (but deserved) chewing out from my fencing coach (obnoxious but worth putting up with, since it's so hard to find a coach who won't fall in love with me). I'd removed my tracker for a shower when an odorless and fast-acting drug knocked me cold.

It's hard to say when I awoke, since the world I woke to was so like a dream. I couldn't see; I couldn't move; I couldn't speak. I wasn't bound or gagged. It was my hands, my arms, my legs, they all lay limp, and when I tried to call for help, not only would the sound not rise but even my lips refused to form the words. I could feel, and recognized at once that I was lying in the molded contours of a Lifedoll box; I know the shape, since fans often ask me to have myself delivered in the packaging so they can have the pleasure of unwrapping me. My first thought was that I might be one of my dolls come to life (no, at the time I did not know about Bridger's power to bring toys to life, it's just that my profession made me think hard about these things), but my tongue could move, enough to keep me from choking, and I found the notch on the inside of my top left molar which no doll has, which I had etched there for just such eventualities (I told you, I thought hard about these things). Clearly, then, I was no doll. I was breathing. I could swallow (with difficulty), could blink and move my eyes (though the packaging strap across my eyes was as solid as a blindfold), and I could control my bladder and anus enough to keep from soiling the box. A few other muscles did tense slightly as I strained—my jaw, some spots on my belly, one spot in my neck—so I set to exercising them, to see if I could get my blood pumping a bit and so flush chemicals from my system faster, if chemicals were the cause. With concentration I detected spots of soreness scattered around my body which I guessed were remnants of however this paralysis had been achieved. Fear? I didn't feel much fear. I thought about trying to induce panic to get my heart rate up, but better to keep myself sharp, and ready.

The first words I heard were muffled, both by the box and by a voice distorter, which left the syllables gritty and robotic. « Now, let's see this surprise that was worth dragging me out here. » I do not speak French, but I hear it often, and Spanish gives me enough of a start to piece the simple stuff together.

« It might have been dangerous bringing it to Your Holiness's office. I tried to decorate this place to make you feel at home. »

« It's perfect. All my favorite posters, and the rug's so cushy. »

« I am a professional. »

« Mmm. That you are. »

The two paused and, from the sound of it, made out. There were two voices, both veiled by distorters. I'm not going to use names. The police promised (in writing) not to use this testimony as evidence against anyone, but the police aren't so good with that sort of promise. You know which sensayer was promised Sniper in return for handing over the Cousin Carlyle

Foster to a certain Blacklaw. If I omit the names then I maintain reasonable doubt.

« Is this the surprise I hope it is? » Hands made the packaging flex.

« If you've guessed, it isn't a surprise. »

I felt clean air on my chest as the box opened. « Oh! Gorgeous . . . » Hands explored my chest. « It's real? The real Sniper? »

« I pay my debts, Your Holiness. » Another hand guided the first to test my pulse.

« The real Sniper. That's really the real Sniper? »

« I'll give my oath on it, if you doubt. »

« Did you get them to consent? »

« Of course not. I knew you'd want to do that part yourself. »

« Mmm. How did you snatch them? Did you take the Canner Device for a spin? »

« And draw a swarm of Moonmen down upon my head? No, no. Stealth and patience, Your Holiness, stealth and patience. »

Hands lifted my arm, the touch delicate but not gentle. « They're limp. Are they unconscious? »

« That would be no fun. It's conscious, just frozen like a doll. It can hear us, and when you unwrap the eyes it'll be able to see, so make sure your mask stays in place. »

Hands played with my fingers, bending them to test resistance. « How did you do this? »

« The paralysis? A very delicate application of this and that. It's not my invention; Madame's had this sort of special request before. It's not permanent, it needs to be refreshed every few hours, but I can arrange another round if need be. »

« Oh, you've outdone yourself! You can have Carlyle! You can have any pawn you want! »

The other laughed. « You deserved a prize today. That imaginary friend you identified from the boy's drawings was just what I needed, trick worked like a charm. »

« That child you asked advice about, you broke them successfully? »

« Am breaking. No need to rush. I've three of his little friends hostage, and you wouldn't believe what treasures are already flocking to the bait. »

« Little friends? I hope you're not breaking any Black Laws, harming minors? »

« Nothing of the sort. Besides, I'll hardly need such bait once I have little Carlyle to finish things for me. »

« And God? The common God, I mean, are you making progress? You dropped such taunting hints. »

Another hush for kisses.

« God's almost mine. »

« How long? »

A chuckle. « Patience is a virtue, Your Holiness. Think of it as a balance for today's delicious vice. Your doll awaits. »

"Mmm." Practiced hands gripped me under the arms and eased my torso forward until I flopped into an embrace. Some long hair caught in my lips as my face fell against bare skin, and I felt breasts against my chest. "Oops! Careful!" They switched to English to address me, laughing as they adjusted my head so my cheek could rest on their shoulder. "What a fragile thing you are, Sniper, and so light! I always imagined the real thing would be heavier than the dolls."

« Careful you don't strain its neck. Actually, better put this neck brace on it. I didn't want the brace to spoil the effect when you opened the box, but there's real danger of straining something, like with babies. »

"Well, we can't have that, can we, Sniper? Can't have you getting hurt. Come here." My New Owner (what else can a doll call the one to whom it's given?) held my head still for the Gift-giver to strap the brace in place. That helped, kept my head centered as my Owner tipped me forward into a cuddle. It was an intense embrace, no awkwardness, no holding back, the kind of hug two people can only achieve after long intimacy, but anyone can give in an instant to a stuffed bear. Amazing. "There, is that better? Now let's get you out of your box and settled somewhere comfortable."

« Let me help. » I felt the second person's hands now, midsized enough to belong to either sex, but fierce as clamps. « On three, ready? One, two, three! »

The two of them carried me a short way, then laid me on soft carpet with my head and shoulders propped against a cushion.

"There." My Owner laid my hands neatly at my sides. "Much better. Now, let's get this packaging off so we can see your pretty eyes."

They picked at the packing strip which protects the doll eyes during shipping, splitting the seal with fingernails which (almost) succeeded in not scratching my skin. Even common lamplight seared after such darkness, and I closed my eyes at once, flinching as much as I had power to flinch.

"Oh!" my Owner cried. "Did the bright light hurt you? Here." They leaned close enough to veil me with shadow, and restored complete darkness to my left eye with a soft kiss on the eyelid. "Let me make it better."

The kiss moved, one eye, then the other, then down my cheek. "There, that's better. Now open your eyes. It's okay."

Squinting at first, I saw a clean white half mask covering the upper half of a light face, with a wash of black hair behind it, leaking over a bare body which was probably not as beautiful as I remember, but I'm about as objective here as Mycroft is about Thisbe. The room behind my Owner was a collage of me: posters, portraits, some quite rare, all different costumes, naughty, nice, formal, skimpy, all five sports, all seven Hives, and dominated by the 2442 limited-edition of me slumped shirtless in a chair with puppet joints drawn on my skin and the strings of a marionette holding me half-upright. I've always liked people who like that one.

"There. Welcome home, Sniper."

As they kissed my lips which could not kiss back, I felt, at last, my long-sought, threat-free love. In my years as a professional living doll I can't count how many times I've been brought home by a fan who'd dreamed of a night with the original, but the consummation often fails to meet their expectations. Those who want a doll as a lover tend to be timid, shy of being touched, more comfortable with plastic and make-believe. I've made myself as benign as possible: hairless, childlike, not strongly gendered either way, and I always let myself be dressed, be fed, be led, but I still touch back, kiss back by reflex, have the potential to be active. That potential spoils the illusion, like when you know a ba'sib is in earshot in the next room, and the fact distracts you even if they do nothing. As long as I could act, Owners weren't as safe with me as with my dolls. Bondage doesn't solve this, makes it worse, actually, since the bonds are just reminders of the power they're restraining. Here, though, with my power not constrained but gone, my Owner was as comfortable as when you sit naked in an empty house, or sing in the bathroom, so I tasted at last that easy affection which only dolls and dildos had enjoyed before. I could feel how much it was changing me even as it happened, the granting of such a visceral wish rewiring things inside my mind, not just the conscious iceburg tip but down into those black depths that even Brillists barely understand. At the time, Thisbe and Eureka hadn't told the rest of the bash' about their "black hole" in Paris or what lurks in it, so I had no way to recognize that this was trickle-down of the same threat. My Owner didn't study with Madame D'Arouet, but absorbed through the growling Gift-giver the same techniques, as through some dark umbilical: sniff out the forbidden appetites that people don't admit they have, and make them so real that afterward the normal world feels dull as black and white. Mycroft showed you how Chair Kosala and the Anonymous can't kindle the fire anymore without their 'he's and 'she's and lace and waistcoats. Mycroft was right to use the word 'addiction.'

"And now for the real mystery." My Owner's hands traced a slow path down my sides toward the second packing strip which protected my most private parts. They glanced over their shoulder at the Gift-giver. « You've been waiting for this, haven't you? »

« Actually, I already saw. » The Gift-giver stood behind my Owner, also masked, and with a black cloak which hid everything but a spot of shadowed throat. « Apologies for not waiting for Your Holiness, but I had to towel it off and get it boxed up. It was quite suspenseful, the rumors being so contradictory. »

« I know. » My Owner eased my thighs apart. "You're a naughty thing, Sniper, spreading confusing rumors to keep us guessing." I couldn't look down, but saw a subtle smile as their fingers cracked the seal. (I thought hard about whether to reveal this here, but it's time. I remain infinitely grateful to everyone who helped me keep the secret this long: the Celebrity Youth Act, my coaches, doctors, teammates, journalists, my many fans who knew, and many more who burned to know but respected my request so much you even rioted outside *The Scoop* that time they threatened an exposé. But it's time to free you all from that silence, that mystery, to let you see completely what I was, now that my doll days are over.) "A boy," my Owner announced. "Not surprising. No, wait." They leaned closer, their long hair tickling my thighs, which could not twitch. "Both! Oh, excellent." They lifted my penis gingerly and reached past to feel the vaginal folds behind. "You sweet thing, you didn't want to disappoint fans who got used to either model. How thoughtful!" They spread me further, the room's air cold against the wetness of my labia. "It's a beautiful job, seamless!" They turned again to the Gift-giver. « Which sex were they originally, do you know? »

The Gift-giver leaned forward. « I couldn't tell. Everything down there looks genuine. I could take some hair to the lab. »

« No need. This is how Sniper should be, now that I think about it. » My Owner withdrew their hands from my penis carefully, as if handling a baby bird. « Oh! It twitched. » They chuckled their delight. « Can they perform? »

« Of course. The paralysis is very selective. It'll take some massage, but you can get it up if you want. »

« Mmm. Not much massage from the look of it. Somebody's enjoying themself. » My Owner ran a finger up my cheek. "Aren't you?"

Knowing no answer would come, my Owner tasted my lips again and eased me forward, their affection washing over me like a good movie, which takes you to all the peaks of passion without you having to lift a finger. They were used to my body, knew just how my shoulders swing, and at what height to hook my chin over their shoulder.

« How long can I keep them? »

It was a burning question for me, too.

The Gift-giver shrugged. « That's up to Your Holiness. If you want to keep it permanently I can bring what you'll need, but it'll be difficult keeping its Olympic physique from deteriorating in captivity, and there'll be quite the manhunt. I recommend catch-and-release: you enjoy yourself, then have me return Sniper to the wild and take it again when next you're in the mood. »

« Would that work? »

« Certainly. I estimate another two hours until the rest of the bash' realizes Sniper's missing, but they'll hunt in secret for at least a day before letting the news get beyond His Grace the Duke. So long as we get Sniper back this evening there won't be any larger fuss. We can erase its memory as extra security if you like, but I'm sure it won't breathe a word of this to anyone. » They switched to growling English. "If I can do this much to it when I'm calm, it can imagine what I'd do if I were angry."

My Owner hugged me closer. "There's no need for threats. My Sniper won't want to spoil this, not when I'm done. I know what Sniper wants. I've known for ages what my Sniper really wants."

You probably imagine I thought something defiant and heroic here. Some addictions only need one dose.

« Of course, Your Holiness. I apologize for insulting your abilities. »

« Mmm. I'll have you do some penance for that later. »

« As you wish, Your Holiness. »

My Owner stroked my hair, flicking stray black strands out of my eyes. "Sniper's turn first, though."

The computer distortion made the Gift-giver's chuckle sound like a computer's dying scream. « Maybe you should keep it permanently. There's enough nastiness around its bash', it might be safer here with you. »

« I'll think about it. »

I thought about it too, realizing that all I could do was lie and wait for my Owner to make this decision which would literally determine my entire world, and have a big impact on everybody else's. Duty was enough to make me wish for freedom, but that was the only moment I can remember that I've ever wished the duty wasn't mine.

The Gift-giver turned to go. « I have work. I'll be back before the paralysis wears off. I brought some doll clothes for dress-up, they're in the chest
back there. »

« Thanks. »

« Give me a call if you see any twitching. Athletes often have a fast
metabolism, so there's a chance things will wear off faster than normal. »

« Right. »

The Gift-giver came within my line of sight as my Owner shifted me
onto their lap. I searched for hints of identity (skin color, weight) beneath
the cloak and beaked plaster-white mask, but this foe was too practiced.
« Enjoy. »

Enjoy my Owner did, every inch of me, but I'll skip the details. It was not
all sex. A lot of it was being held, that warm, trusting embrace. A lot of it was
talk. My Owner talked about what it's like being able to see people's hidden
obsessions, like having X-ray vision and spotting all the ailments doctors
haven't discovered yet. They talked about the nature of secrets, speculating
about why one feels the need to share secrets with someone, whether one
imagines something might happen if one says them aloud, like knocking on
wood, or whether it just feels more real when there's a witness. They talked
about the state of the world, about ideas of God which I won't repeat, and a
lot about gender. Gender they called a universal language which we're all supposed to pretend we can't read. Most just play blind or try (as we know we
ought) to eliminate the traces of it, and the ancient inequalities those traces
threaten to revive. But, they said, cunning folk can use that language to attack
targets with body rhetoric we can't acknowledge, let alone resist. My Owner
used a strongly gendered persona intentionally to make people uncomfortable, just as I used my neuter one to set people at ease. We were two house
cats who had both learned again the true purpose of claws and fangs; my
Owner had taken to hunting, while I had tried to have myself declawed. Now,
having read the first half of Mycroft's history, I know to blame Madame
D'Arouet for these ideas. Mostly, though, my Owner talked about power.

"I need a break from power, Sniper. It sometimes feels like I've been
playing the manipulation game forever, and once you're in you can't stop. I
enjoy it, I wouldn't give it up for anything, but my rival is also very good,
and I have to turn everyone around me into a pawn on my side to keep
them from becoming a pawn on theirs. I need a break, just once in a while,
like this. It's different with you. You can't try to use me, and I don't want
to use you even though I could. You're off-limits to my rival, so I can safely
make you off-limits to me, too. I can relax. There's no power with the two

of us like this, just fun. I'm sure you need a break too. It's a very hard game you play keeping Ganymede in power. It must be exhausting, all the training, and competitions, and stunts to keep voters from thinking about anyone but you and Ganymede. But there's no spotlight here. With me you can stop performing, and you don't need to worry about your obligations when there's absolutely nothing you can do about them. You can relax. Isn't that what you really want, Sniper? A life where you can finally relax?"

I could have tried to answer somehow, give a long blink, a distinct breath, but that would have spoiled it, undone these hours which truly were the pinnacle of my avocation. There's a word to chew on, 'avocation': a second great occupation that takes you away from your vocation, like a musician sidetracked by acting, a teacher by politics, Thisbe by making movies, or my ba'pa designing dolls, all important tasks but secondary still. I don't blame the parents who made me and Ockham rivals for O.S. (it made us stronger), but when Lesley entered the picture it was clear there would be a winner and a loser when we grew up, no ties. When the fuss over being a Lifedoll model made me a child star, I saw a second path before me, a surer shot than the fight for bash' leadership, which was always fifty-fifty. The rest agreed a celebrity in the house would be a good addition to our arsenal, so I worked like a maniac to secure my fame: studying for the press, keeping informed, full of jokes, always the most fun to interview, then finding a sport at which my small body (neither exceptionally strong nor fast) could excel, and working to remain competition-worthy through three Olympiads and counting. I loved my avocation, suffered for it, and I took very seriously the duty of belonging to everyone who loved me. But that still came second, and my bash' vocation first. I do apologize to all who were in love with what I was. I miss you too, and if you contact my underground and host me for a night I'll do my best to be your Sniper again, but that comes second. My Hive, all Hives, come first. I am a Humanist because I believe in heroes, that history is driven by those individuals with fire enough to change the world. If you aren't a Humanist it's because you think something different. That difference matters. I will not let Jehovah Mason undo the system which (as Mycroft sacrificed so much to prove) gives us the right at last to be proud of what we choose to be. The Hives must be defended. Never before has one tyrant been in a position to truly threaten the whole world, so never in history has my true vocation been so necessary. I will kill Jehovah Mason for you; please accept that as my apology.

I'm over my five-thousand-word limit already. What else should I cram in before I go? The Bridger parts are true. There's proof. Unlike Mycroft, I won't let you get away with pretending it's madness. Don't trust the gendered pronouns Mycroft gives people, they all come from Madame. The coup is happening, don't let anybody tell you different. As for the resistance, I'm not expecting most of you to volunteer to fight and die, but if you support my side, all it means is that you love your Hive, and that you'll cheer for us when the deed is done. The First World War was the moment humanity learned to count its casualties in millions, but as a Humanist I must ask, as my bash' founders asked: which changed the world more? The loss of millions or of that handful who would have been the next generation's heroes? Wilfred Owen left behind a tiny collection of poems, not enough to even make a book, but still the most upsetting things I've ever read; if Owen had lived they might have revolutionized literature, spurred presses and politics away from the guilt-laden bravado which would light war's fire again, or driven countless readers to suicide. Karl Schwarzschild corresponded with Einstein from the trenches and deduced the existence of black holes while rotting knee-deep in muck; if Schwarzschild had lived they might have accelerated physics by fifty years, enabled *Mukta* two generations earlier, or given the Nazis nukes. Owen and Schwarzschild; calculate carefully which firebrands to snuff and one death can redirect history better than any battle. That was the foundation of O.S.

—*Ojiro Cardigan Sniper, Thirteenth O.S., May 23rd, 2454*

* * *

END OF RESTRICTED SECTION. PUBLIC ACCOUNT RESUMES.